Elvi Rhodes was the eldest of five children brought up in the West Riding of Yorkshire in the depression between the wars. She won a scholarship to Bradford Grammar School and left to become the breadwinner of her family. A widow with two sons, she lives in Sussex. Her other novels include *Opal*, *Doctor Rose*, *Ruth Appleby*, *The Golden Girls*, *Madeleine*, *The House of Bonneau*, *Cara's Land*, *The Rainbow Through The Rain*, *The Bright One*, *The Mountain*, *Spring Music*, *Midsummer Meeting* and *The Birthday Party*. A collection of stories, *Summer Promise and other stories*, is also published by Corgi Books.

For more information on Elvi Rhodes and her books, contact her website on www.elvirhodes.com

She knew Hester was only trying to be kind – at least, she thought that's what it was. Every day Hester came to the little motherless household bringing scones, or a curd tart, or flowers from her gardens. But Ruth found herself wishing more and more that Hester would stay away.

And then the day came when her father said he had something to tell her. 'Hester and me's going to be wed, Ruth! You'll have a new mother!'

It was then Ruth knew she must go away. But she did not realise then how far she was to go and how much was going to happen to her.

RUTH APPLEBY – the sage of a Yorkshire girl in love and in war.

www.booksattransworld.co.uk

*Also by Elvi Rhodes*

OPAL
DOCTOR ROSE
CARA'S LAND
THE GOLDEN GIRLS
MADELEINE
THE HOUSE OF BONNEAU
SUMMER PROMISE AND OTHER STORIES
THE RAINBOW THROUGH THE RAIN
THE BRIGHT ONE
THE MOUNTAIN
SPRING MUSIC
PORTRAIT OF CHLOE
MIDSUMMER MEETING

*and published by Corgi Books*

Elvi Rhodes

# Ruth Appleby

**RUTH APPLEBY**
**A CORGI BOOK : 0 552 12803 1**

First publication in Great Britain

PRINTING HISTORY
Corgi edition published 1987

17 19 20 18



Set in 10/11pt Baskerville.

Corgi Books are published by Transworld Publishers, 61–63 Uxbridge Road, London W5 5SA, a division of The Random House Group Ltd, in Australia by Random House Australia (Pty) Ltd, 20 Alfred Street, Milsons Point, Sydney, NSW 2061, Australia, in New Zealand by Random House New Zealand Ltd, 18 Poland Road, Glenfield, Auckland 10, New Zealand and in South Africa by Random House (Pty) Ltd, Endulini, 5a Jubilee Road, Parktown 2193, South Africa.

Printed and bound in Great Britain by Cox & Wyman Ltd, Reading, Berkshire.

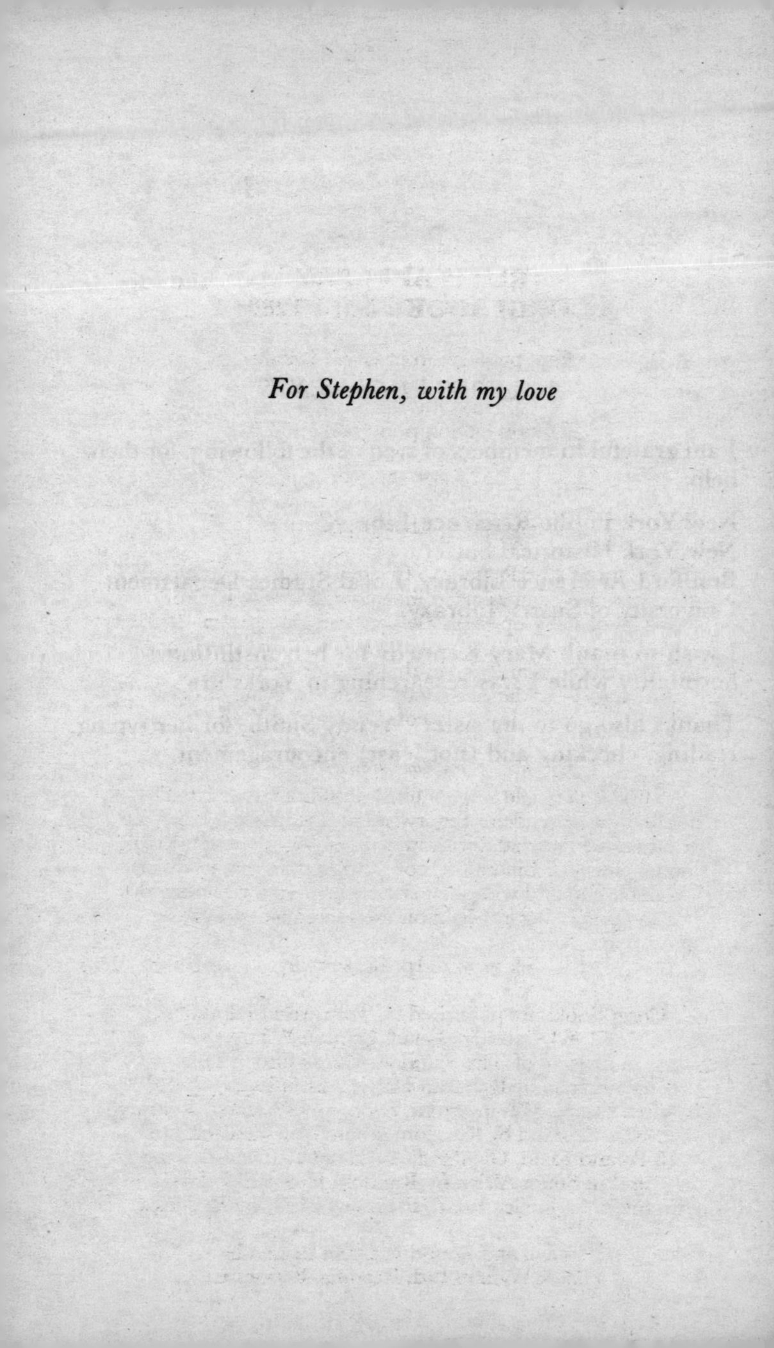

*For Stephen, with my love*

## *ACKNOWLEDGEMENTS*

I am grateful to members of staff of the following, for their help:

New York Public Reference Library
New York Historical Society
Bradford Reference Library, Local Studies Department
University of Sussex Library.

I wish to thank Mary Kennedy for her unstinting hospitality while I was researching in Yorkshire.

Thanks also go to my sister, Wendy Smith, for her typing, reading, checking and (not least) encouragement.

# *Part One*

# 1

The wind was bitter, penetrating the chinks between Ruth's cloak and bonnet like daggers of ice, teasing the thin covering of powdery snow which lay on the ground, venomously blowing at the backs of the small funeral party as they returned down the steep path to the village. Ruth's right hand, hidden beneath her cloak, was reasonably warm, but Maria grasped the other, and since neither child had mittens, the little warmth they had in their flesh was no match for the weather.

Ruth had not felt cold during the funeral service, but then she had not felt anything one was supposed to on such an occasion. Since the hour of her mother's death an impenetrable calm had lain on her. Everyone had taken it for courage, remarked how brave she was, and what a comfort to her poor father.

Though she had absorbed every detail of the funeral – the lowering of the coffin into the deep-dug hole, the sharp rattle of symbolically-scattered earth, the Reverend Broadhead's solemn voice, quite different from his everyday one – none of it seemed to relate to her. Nor at any point did she shed a single tear. Aunt Sarah Gaunt and Uncle Matthew, her cousin Ernest, the neighbours, had all wept to some degree. Even her father, whom she had never before seen weeping because it would have been unmanly, had not tried to hide the tears which ran down his white face.

Then, as if a signal had been given, all weeping stopped. There was a great blowing of noses, after which the grown-ups began to talk to each other as they followed Maria and herself down the hill.

'It'll snow again,' Mrs Johnson observed. 'You mark my words!' She said it with satisfaction, as if it would make a fitting end to the day.

Mrs Johnson lived next door to Ruth's family. In twenty-five years almost no funeral in the district had taken place without her. She enjoyed a good funeral and would sometimes journey as far afield as Otley, or even Bradford, to attend an extra special one. She dressed in black winter and summer because, she said, it so often came in handy.

'I wouldn't linger afore riding back to Burley Woodhead if I was you,' she advised Aunt Sarah Gaunt. 'Drifts as high as a house you can get on them moors! I heard tell of a man once – well, it were a month afore they found him. Stone dead of course. But they said being buried in the snow had preserved him quite remarkable!'

Her voice had risen to a cheerful note. 'Have you noticed,' she continued, 'that when it snows in February, it stays on the ground a long time? I've known it bide until Easter.'

'I can't say that I have.' Sarah Gaunt's usually soft voice was as sharp as the wind. 'And I don't think you need fret yourself on our account. We'll be setting off back soon after tea. There's no leaving livestock for long.'

Her voice softened again as she spoke to Ruth.

'You and Maria run ahead, love! Put the kettle on to boil and tell Grandfather to stir the fire. We shall be glad of a warm when we get in. Ernest, go with your cousins!'

Ernest, at sixteen years old, walked in a no-man's land between his parents and his young cousins. Once he would have raced us to the bottom of the hill, Ruth thought, but now he was too grown-up. But at twelve years old shouldn't she also be beyond such pursuits?

If you ran too fast down Church Hill it became difficult to stop at the bottom, where it joined the main street of the village. It was hard to judge the exact moment to brake, before you lost control and went flying into someone. But today there would be no question of her going her fastest, partly because of the solemnity of the occasion, partly because of the snow, but also because Maria still clung to her, and Maria had short, ten-year-old legs.

'I wish I could run down there myself,' Aunt Sarah said.

There was no chance of that. Aunt Sarah was small, and as fat as butter, so that she rocked from side to side as she walked. It had needed the help of her husband, Matthew, and her brother William to get her up the hill to the churchyard.

'Come on then, Maria,' Ruth said. 'Hold tight! I promise not to go too fast.'

She tried to concentrate on matching her steps to Maria's as they hurtled down the slope, and then it seemed, suddenly, that the rapid movement not only set the blood circulating around her body, but began to stir her emotions. She started to feel again – and was ashamed that her first feeling after all those days was one of relief at increasing the distance between herself and the churchyard. She had loved her mother dearly, had admired the elegance and prettiness which had never entirely left her, even in the last weeks of her long illness. But what had just happened up there in the churchyard was not to be thought of. Sooner or later she would have to go back there, to place fresh flowers on the grave; but not yet. She clutched Maria's hand more tightly as they sped towards the centre of Barnswick.

'Careful now, childer!' Aunt Sarah's voice floated down from somewhere behind them.

Barnswick was the last village before the moorland proper, clinging to the lee of the long hillside at whose foot, two miles to the south, the River Aire ran through a fertile stretch of valley before the land began to rise again towards Shipley. Thomson's woollen mill, where several of the men in Barnswick, including Ruth's father, earned their livings, was built on a spit of land which ran between the river and the Leeds and Liverpool Canal. Her father was the maintenance man. When anything went wrong with the spinning frames, the weaving looms, the carding or twisting machinery, he put them to rights, though this often meant working through the night, when the machines were idle. Ruth wondered whether he would have to go in tonight or whether the master might have allowed him time off.

At the bottom of the hill, as they turned right into the main street, Maria began to whimper. 'I'm cold,' she complained. 'I'd rather have stayed at home with Grandfather and Willie.'

'It wouldn't have been respectful, our Maria,' Ruth reproved her. 'Your own mother's funeral! Willie stayed at home because he's little, and Grandfather because of his chest.'

When they reached the house, Grandfather held open the door and the heat of the cottage rushed out to meet them.

'Come in quick!' he said. 'Tha looks perished!'

He bent down and took Maria into the circle of his arm, speaking in a gentle, low-pitched voice.

'Come to the fire, doy. Get thyself warm. Thee as well, Ruth love.'

With his one hand he took off Maria's cloak and bonnet, then he held the colder of her two hands in his warm one, squeezing it to bring back the life. He had lost an arm more than thirty years ago, on a night when he had marched with the handloom weavers to destroy the new power looms which they reckoned were robbing them of their jobs. Aunt Sarah had been a little girl then, and her brother William only three years old.

Ruth never tired of hearing her grandfather tell the story, especially the bit about how he had taken the Luddite oath, had been made a member of the secret society:

> 'I, Enoch Appleby . . . do solemnly swear that I will never reveal to any person or persons under the canopy of heaven the names of the persons who compose this secret committee . . . and I will use my best endeavours to punish by death any traitor . . . though he would fly to the verge of nature. . . .'

'That tale's got whiskers on it!' her father would say. 'The Luddites were wasting their time, Father. Anyway, machinery's here to stay.' Her father had an affinity with machinery.

It was the only subject on which the two men quarrelled. But what her grandfather seemed, to Ruth, to be most proud of was not how he had lost his arm, but that he had managed to do almost anything with his remaining one.

'So make the most of what you've got,' he always finished up. 'That's what counts!' Ruth reckoned he couldn't have thought that way when he was a young man, and a Luddite.

Willie, grizzling and whimpering, held out his arms to Ruth and she picked him up.

'What's the matter, then?' she asked. 'I wasn't away long, was I?'

He was three years old. There had been another child, who had died in infancy, between Maria and Willie. Because he seemed likely to be the last of the family, and his mother dreaded losing her only son, Willie had been coddled, kept little more than a baby. It was Ruth's ambition to turn her brother into a plump, rosy little boy, but her mother said it would never happen.

'He's a Manson,' she said. 'All the Mansons are fine-boned, delicately made. All blue-eyed and fair-haired, too.' Ruth's hair was dark and her eyes were the colour of amber.

'There are racehorses and carthorses,' Mrs Appleby had told her. 'The Mansons are racehorses.'

It was clear to Ruth – 'every inch an Appleby' – that she was a carthorse.

She had never seen a racehorse. It was not racing country until you got over towards York, or south to Doncaster, but after hearing her mother's remark Ruth had studied carthorses. Strong, sturdy creatures they were: a mite slow-moving, though one day it had pleased her to see a carthorse break into a gallop, so that everyone in the street had to move out of its way.

She held Willie on her left hip while she crumbled a slice of bread into a dish and poured warm, sweetened milk over it.

'Here's your pobbies, then!' she said. 'I daresay you're quite hungry.'

'Ruth feed me!' he demanded.

He refused to eat until she gave way and spooned the food into his mouth. She was still at it when the rest of the funeral party streamed into the house, bringing the wintry air in with them.

'My word, it's grand to be in the warm!' Aunt Sarah said. 'Now if you like, William, me and Ruth will make the tea. Maria can look after young Willie for once. Our Ruth's too attached to him for her own good!'

'It's only natural,' her brother said. 'She's had most to do with him, her mother being badly that long.'

'Ruth's still a child herself,' Aunt Sarah persisted. 'Twelve years old, and for the past two years she's practically been the woman of the house.'

'I can't help that.' William reddened, put out of humour.

'Well we'll say no more about it now,' his sister soothed him. 'It's been a bad day for all of us, especially for thee.'

'The worst of my life,' he said. 'She was everything to me, Jane was. Allus too good for me, I knew that from the start. But I never regretted marrying her and I don't think she did either.' He bent his head, buried his face in his hands.

'There lad, don't take on!' Sarah said.

To be fair, she thought, Jane had not been a bad wife and mother, though she'd always felt herself a cut above the Applebys. If William hadn't left his job in the mill that summer they were on short time, to work on the canal boats, he wouldn't have stopped off at Skipton when the fair was on. He wouldn't have met Jane Manson playing truant from her fine home. He'd have married a village lass – strong and healthy, someone his own class. Well, no use crying over spilt milk and speak no ill of the dead! Jane had made her brother happy, choose how!

It was a pity, though, that Jane's family had never come to terms with the Applebys. They had not attended their daughter's wedding and Jane had never heard from them since.

'Did you write and tell the Mansons – about Jane's death?' she asked William.

'As well as I was able,' he replied. 'I'm not much of a writer. They didn't reply.'

The little room was packed now, with those who had attended the funeral and, Ruth noted, with others who had popped in for the funeral tea. Aunt Sarah had taken the responsibility for the meal, carrying most of the foodstuffs over from Burley Woodhead in pannier baskets.

'I've never seen such a spread,' Ruth said. 'Not even at Christmas!'

There were slices of boiled ham, cold roast pork, salt beef, pickles, beetroot in vinegar, two plates of bread and dripping, currant teacakes, apply pasty. On the sideboard, waiting to be moved on to the table when there was room, was a spice cake, saved from Christmas, together with a lump of cheese. As well as tea to drink there was home-made ginger wine, or peppermint cordial for those still feeling the cold. Ruth had not eaten since breakfast and could hardly bear to wait for the start.

She stood at the corner of the table, next to Aunt Sarah, helping her to hand out the cups of tea. Uncle Matthew took Maria on his knee and several neighbours clucked around Willie, offering him titbits from their own plates. Cousin Ernest sat halfway down the table, already heaping his plate with the fruits of his mother's cooking.

'Now think on, everybody,' Aunt Sarah said. 'Make a good tea!'

'I must say, you've put on a lovely table,' Mrs Johnson observed.

'She should know,' Aunt Sarah muttered – but Ruth could tell she was pleased. It was a point of honour that the funeral tea should be a good one; a sort of last tribute.

Ruth, sitting at the table now, glanced around her. Everyone was concerned with the meal, helping themselves to food and plying their neighbours with it. It seemed to her that no-one remembered what it was about, the reason why they were there. Even her father, so recently overcome by sorrow, was now obviously enjoying his victuals.

She was suddenly sickened, unable to swallow another

bite. And then she – who had remained dry-eyed when everyone else had wept – felt a pricking and a smarting in her eyes. She stared down at the white tablecloth which a neighbour had lent, seeing its woven pattern of roses and lilies through a haze. She wanted to run out of the house, but she was so jammed in by bodies that it was impossible to escape. She clenched her hands under the valance of the tablecloth and willed herself not to cry.

When she had control of herself again she looked up, and saw her grandfather watching her. He was not eating. His plate was empty. Although he had lived with them since his second wife had died twelve years ago, and though her mother had been reasonably kind to him, it had never seemed to Ruth that the two of them had much in common. So is he thinking about my mother, she wondered, or about someone else, long since gone?

Ruth had been named for her grandfather's first wife, his greatest love, which was perhaps why he seemed to have a special feeling for his elder granddaughter. Ruth had never known a time when he wasn't there, and although she knew it was wrong, that one must love one's parents next best to God, in her heart she confessed that she loved her grandfather more than anyone in the world – except perhaps Willie. She hoped he would never die, but next birthday he would be sixty, which was a great age.

She clasped her hands even more tightly under the table, and silently prayed. 'Dear God, take my mother to be with Jesus, and don't let Grandfather die! Amen.'

Aunt Sarah's voice broke in.

'You've hardly eaten a thing, our Ruth! Here, try this bit of pasty. You must keep up your strength, love.'

She was right. Also, it was a sin to waste good food and now that she had prayed Ruth felt hungrier than ever. She bit into the pasty. It was bursting with juicy apples, tangy with cloves, the delicate flakes of pastry escaping to fall on her plate.

When the meal was over the women cleared away and the table – trestles and boards borrowed for the occasion – was taken down. The room was by now stiflingly hot, but people still drew their chairs into a big semi-circle around the fire.

'Maria, love, come and sit on my lap,' Grandfather offered. He was sitting in his Windsor armchair with the sheepskin over the back to make it more comfortable.

Maria pouted. 'I don't want to. I want Ernest to take me to see the horses.'

'They're tethered on the edge of the moor, love,' Aunt Sarah pointed out. 'It's right cold out there, and a wind with it.'

'I don't care,' Maria said. 'Please, Ernest! Please!'

Ernest looked to his Uncle William for guidance, but William turned to his sister.

'What dost think, Sarah?'

Sarah had long ago realised that her brother didn't like making decisions, large or small. It was as if he had used up his lifetime's initiative in that one defiant act of marrying Jane Manson against everyone's wishes.

'I don't think she should stay out long,' Ruth put in. 'The night air makes her cough.'

William nodded in agreement.

'All right then, Ernest,' Aunt Sarah said. 'Off you go, but be back in twenty minutes.'

Everyone else settled down. Their tongues loosened by warmth and food, they began to reminisce about Jane Manson.

'I'll never forget clapping eyes on her when William first brought her back to Barnswick,' a neighbour said. 'She wore a white cotton dress, patterned wi' blue flowers, and the hem all embroidered. She had a fine wool shawl around her shoulders and hair the colour of gold corn peeping from under her bonnet. Pretty as a picture, she were!'

'And always kept her house and childer nice,' another neighbour added.

In fact, Ruth thought, her mother had never been close to any of the neighbours and they had considered her stand-offish. But all that seemed to be forgotten now, and only tributes were being paid. Then, as she listened, the conversation turned to other funerals they had attended, though Ruth noticed that the subject seemed not to depress anyone in the slightest.

'There's this much about a funeral,' Mrs Johnson said. 'You do know where your loved ones are. Safe in the arms of Jesus. With a wedding, now, you can never tell what's in store.'

When births, marriages and deaths had been exhausted the talk turned to general matters, to which Ruth only half listened: the sugar tax, the high cost of flour, the weather prospects for the rest of the winter. They touched upon the vicar, who was not unpopular, and his wife, who was; and on their daughter, Miss Caroline Broadhead. Ruth was pleased that everyone spoke well of Miss Caroline since she was the person she most admired. She was not many years older than Ruth herself. Ruth wanted to be as like her as possible, and especially to speak in her refined manner.

Although her own mother had been educated, and had taught her children to read, it was Miss Caroline who had lent Ruth books from her own shelves. She had introduced her to the poetry of Wordsworth, Thomas Campbell, Keats; to Sir Walter Scott's novels and – a special favourite of Ruth's – to the essays of Charles Lamb. Also she sometimes handed down clothes. She had given Ruth the dress she was now wearing. It had been a rich, deep blue then, but had had to be dyed black for mourning.

'What about somebody doing a turn?' Mrs Johnson suggested presently. 'Providing it were nothing comic it'd be showing no disrespect. Mrs Appleby liked a nice song or two.'

'How about Enoch giving us a recitation?' someone said.

'Please, Grandfather!' Ruth begged. 'Do "Ye Mariners of England".'

With a show of diffidence, he allowed himself to be persuaded. 'All right, lass. I'll do it for thee,' he said.

Ernest and Maria had returned, their faces rosy from the exercise in the cold air. Ruth would have liked to have gone with Ernest. She was tremendously fond of him and thought that one day, if he should ask her, she might marry him. But when her grandfather started to recite one of his favourite poems, all other thoughts left her. It was a poem she had learnt in the small classes Miss Caroline held at the vicarage for some of the village children, and she had taught it to her grandfather.

'Where Blake and mighty Nelson fell
Your manly hearts shall glow
As ye sweep through the deep
While the stormy winds do blow.'

Her grandfather's voice trembled with passion. Ruth shivered, and was glad of the warmth of the house.

Everyone applauded, and when an encore was called for he obliged at once with the poem which was his own favourite. Though by nature the most peaceable of men, he now took up a belligerent stance, his right foot forward, his clenched fist thrust out and a fierce expression on his face.

'How canst thou break my head,
Since my head is made of iron,
My body made of steel,
My hands and feet of knuckle bone?
I'll challenge thee to deal!'

On the last word he lunged forward as if he was about to plunge a sword into the heart of his enemy.

Then someone said, 'Now you, William. Give us a song, William!'

William Appleby gave them 'When Love with unconfined Wings' and 'Drink to me Only'. His rich, untrained baritone filled the small room. It seemed to Ruth that he did not really see the company who sat so silently around him; he was singing for his dead wife.

When the applause had died down someone called out ' "Home Sweet Home", William! Sing us "Home Sweet Home"!' It was still all the rage.

Ruth caught her father's eye and knew that he could not bear it. Of all the songs her mother knew, 'Home Sweet Home' was the one she had sung most beautifully. Sometimes the two of them, husband and wife, had sung it as a duet. She looked towards her Aunt Sarah and shook her head.

'It's getting late,' Aunt Sarah said quickly. 'We shall have to be going. Matthew, Ernest, bring the horses down and saddle them up. I'll be packing our things.'

Willie had fallen asleep on a neighbour's lap and Maria, sitting close to her father, stared into the fire with heavy eyes.

'We'll be off then,' Mrs Johnson said.

Even so, she managed to be the last to leave. She patted Ruth on the head as she went. 'It's grand to see thee looking after the little 'uns' she told her. 'Tha's a good lass, Ruth. And now thou'll have to be a sister and mother both.'

'I'm going to undress Willie down here in the warm,' Ruth said when Mrs Johnson had gone. 'Then I'll carry him up. Maria, fetch your nightshift and you can get undressed by the fire as well, just this once.'

The big bed in which her mother and father slept - in accordance with local custom, which said that a woman must keep an eye on her family until the end, it had been set in the living-room during the last few months - was now back upstairs again. From tonight Grandfather would once again sleep on the sofa downstairs. On this cold night Ruth envied him. It was so warm and cosy here, in contrast to the bitter chill which she knew awaited her in the bedroom where she slept with Maria and Willie.

They were not a family given to outward expressions of affection - Ruth scarcely remembered her mother kissing her and the most her father did was to chuck her under the chin in passing - but when she stood before him to say goodnight he put up a hand and stroked her hair.

'Be as good as thy mother were, love,' he said. 'Thou'll not go far wrong!'

Her grandfather, though he had no words, drew Ruth into the circle of his arm and kissed her.

Long after Aunt Sarah and her family had ridden away over the moors, and the house was quiet, Ruth lay in bed, her arms around Willie, Maria curled up against her back for warmth. She thought about the long day which had now ended; about her mother and the months of her illness; about the funeral. She thought about the churchyard, imagining its cold brightness under the moon. And she recalled Mrs Johnson's parting words, 'And now thou'll have to be sister and mother both.'

She drew her brother and sister closer, so that all three of them were entwined in one form. They would stay together forever. Nothing should ever separate them, and she would look after them all. And then at last the tears began to race down her cheeks, falling on Willie's hair.

# 2

'I'm glad thou's going to stay the night with thy Aunt Sarah,' Enoch Appleby said. 'There and back over the moor in one day is too much for a little lass.'

Ruth was packing food for the journey: two thick slices of bread spread with lard, sprinkled with salt, then wrapped in a clean piece of muslin which she knotted inside a kerchief so that it would swing from her wrist and leave her hands free. In her pocket she had a small white turnip – a 'neddy' – to gnaw on when she felt hungry, which was most of the time.

'I'm not a little lass,' she objected. 'I'm almost as tall as you, Grandfather.'

'That's true,' he admitted. 'I don't know where you get it from. None of the Applebys has height and your mother were a little bit of a thing. You've grown too fast these last two years. You're nobbut skin and bone!'

That wasn't surprising, Ruth thought. She was always on the go. Flesh had no time to settle on her, except that her dresses were getting too tight across the chest.

Sometimes her grandfather tried to trap her into taking time off by asking her to read to him; but there was no time to read during the day and when evening came all she wanted was to sleep. Occasionally her grandfather won. She left whatever she was doing and read aloud to him, which was a great joy to both of them. He had never learned to read.

'You don't eat enough,' he grumbled. 'Of course it's right that your father gets the best, because he's the wage-earner – but you need nourishment as much as Maria and

Willie, and bread dipped in gravy's not enough. Don't think I haven't seen you! You'll outgrow your strength and be poorly and then where will we all be?'

He often went on like this, but only, she knew, because he cared about her.

She hadn't wanted to go to Aunt Sarah's, and certainly not to stay the night. Cousin Ernest had brought the invitation when he'd ridden over a fortnight earlier for Barnswick Feast, and Ruth had refused it at once; but that night after she'd gone to bed, when Father returned from the Shoulder of Mutton, Grandfather got on to him about it. Neither of them seemed to realise that every word they said downstairs could be heard through the wide cracks in the floorboards. Usually she was too tired to listen, but on hearing her own name she had perked up her ears.

'The lass needs a change,' Grandfather said. 'She's done nowt since Jane died but slave after the rest of us.'

'I can't help that, can I?' her father replied. 'I have to go out and earn a living. Only relaxation I get is my sup of ale in the Shoulder. Dost want me to give that up to help in the house?'

She knew by the tone of her father's voice that there would be the hurt look in his eyes, a pushing out of his underlip, exactly as Willie did when *he* was upset. She wanted to tell him that it didn't matter. She didn't mind a bit.

'All I'm saying,' Grandfather persisted, 'is that our Ruth would be better for a change and I think you ought to tell her she must go. And there's other things. Women's stuff. Things her mother would have told her. Who's going to talk to her about that? Art thou?'

'I can't,' William said. 'I can't be mother as well as father. I'm not cut out for it. Couldn't one of the neighbours? Couldn't Hester?'

'Hester? You must be daft, lad!'

Ruth stuffed her fingers in her ears when they mentioned Hester. She wanted nothing to do with Hester. Then she took them out again because she didn't want to miss anything – but the conversation was over. Next morning when she got up to make his breakfast and pack his dinner for him to take to work, her father said, 'I want you to visit your Aunt Sarah, Ruth. She'll be disappointed else.'

So there she was a week later, setting off.

'I've left you all the food you'll need,' she said to her grandfather.

He held up his hand to silence her.

'I don't want to hear another word, Ruth! Dost think we're gormless enough to starve werselves? Now get off wi' thee. It's best to walk afore the sun's too strong.'

'All right,' Ruth replied. 'The children should sleep another hour yet. Remind them I'll be back tomorrow.'

'Happen they'll be glad to get rid of thee for a bit!' He smiled, and she knew he was teasing her, but she didn't like it. Her family's dependence on her – Father's and Grandfather's as well as the children's – was the source of her strength. It was what she lived for. Their need both kept her going and rewarded her. She did not find it a fit subject for jest.

As she walked away up the moor road her grandfather stood at the door watching. When she reached the bend in the road which would take her out of sight she stopped and turned around. He was still there. Her impulse was to turn back, to run to him as fast as she could. She wanted him never to be out of her sight. In the whole of her life she had never before left him for more than an hour or two. How could she be sure that he would be there when she returned? Anything could happen.

She stood there irresolutely, reluctant to go on, unsure of her welcome if she went back. And then her grandfather waved, and motioned with his arm that she was to get going. The habit of obedience was strong in her. She waved back and began to stride over the moor.

It was going to be another warm day. Although where she walked was clear and sparkling in the early morning sun, in the distance the moors and sky merged into a heat haze, mauve-tinged by the heather which stretched to the horizon.

In August there were fewer flowers than earlier in the year: buttercups, clumps of burdock, daisies beginning to open in the sun, a patch of stonecrop growing on a rock. Also the bilberries were ready for gathering. But always at this time of the year the heather outdid everything else. Insignificant in its single flower-heads, the sheer mass of blossom covered the ground like a huge purple shawl, carelessly flung to bunch over the hillocks on the moor.

It was six miles, mostly uphill, from Barnswick to her uncle's farm, and the going was rough and uneven. Even so, she reckoned she'd be there long before dinnertime. She could dawdle as much as she liked. She was already hungry and she brought the turnip out of her pocket and bit into its hard white flesh. She would walk another mile or two before stopping to eat her bread. But not too far, because she had the pain again in the lower part of her back. Perhaps she had strained herself at the washtub? If it didn't go away she would get some liniment from Mrs Gomersall, who had herbs and ointments to cure everything.

At the summit of the moor she picked a handful of bilberries. There were larger outcroppings of rock here, big enough to throw pools of shade in the strong sunlight. She chose such a spot and sat down. When she had eaten the bread, followed by the bilberries whose rich, purple juice stained her fingers, she lay down and pressed her back against the ground for comfort which, in spite of the nagging pain, she eventually found.

It was glorious here on top of the moor, sun-warmed, but tempered by the breeze which never quite left the high places, though today it was no more than a slight disturbance of the air. The only sounds were the steady hum of the bees in the heather, and a skylark ascending in the distance.

It was good to be alone for once, though she was ashamed of her pleasure in not having the children with her. Alone, one could be anybody, go anywhere, think without interruption. It was a luxury she seldom enjoyed. But after a while her thoughts turned back home again and she decided that as soon as Willie was old enough to manage the walk, she would persuade her father to take the children to Aunt Sarah's. Aunt Sarah *was* his sister and he didn't see her often. In spite of enjoying solitude when it was offered, Ruth thought she would hate a life in which she could not see her brother and sister, her father and grandfather, every day. But not Hester. Never Hester.

And then she was furious that the woman had entered her mind. She had firmly decided not to think of Hester.

Hester was always around; in and out of the house, bringing a few scones she had baked, or a fresh curd tart. She knew exactly what everyone liked most, so that Maria was usually the recipient of a piece of pretty material, or a ribbon, and for Ruth she brought flowers from her garden. Except that it might be unlucky, and also because she liked them, Ruth would have have been pleased to see the flowers fade and die at once. Perversely, one lot always seemed to last until the next arrived so that Hester was, so to speak, ever present.

'She's only trying to be kind,' Grandfather said. 'You're a sensible lass. You must understand that.'

It would not have mattered as much had not her father so plainly liked Hester. Although he was often tired and irritable, when Hester entered the house everything was different. He would look up and smile, make a place for her to sit down, even let her tease him, and laugh about it.

'She's good for thy father,' Grandfather said. 'She cheers him up and that's what he needs. He has a lot on his plate, your dad has.'

'I don't see why his children can't cheer him up,' Ruth grumbled. 'He knows we'd do anything for him.'

'Of course you would,' Grandfather said patiently. 'But it's not the same, lass. Surely thou can see that?'

For her father's sake she tried to, but it wasn't easy. And what she also resented was that her brother and sister seemed to have gone over to the enemy. Maria spent much of her time with Hester and whenever Willie was missing he could be found in her cottage, a few doors away.

Hester had been away in service until a few months ago,

when she returned to Barnswick because her mistress died. Having always been gifted with her needle she decided to try her hand as a seamstress, making clothes for the better-off families in and around Barnswick. It was going well. She had lots of orders, and therefore to Maria's delight there were always spare pieces of material to pass on. Some of them were only big enough to dress a doll; others were of a size to fashion a neckerchief, or even a shawl. Recently she had also made a feather cushion for Grandfather's chair.

'It's very kind of you, Hester,' Grandfather said. 'It's a real bit of comfort to my back, just where I need it.'

And added to everything else was Willie's growing pleasure in Hester; Willie whom Ruth had brought up almost from the beginning. It had always been *her* knee he climbed on, she who must sit next to him at the table, put him to bed, dress him. No-one but Ruth could comfort him if he was hurt.

That was how it *had* been; but sometimes, now, when Hester was in the house of an evening, laughing and talking, seemingly without a care in the world, Willie would scramble on to her lap. Hester would stroke his hair, or gently tickle the back of his neck with her long, supple fingers. Once Ruth had caught her father smiling at the picture they presented. She had rushed out of the house and run up to the moor in a fury.

This morning, lying on the grass on top of the moor, Ruth prayed once more, as she now did nightly, not that any actual harm would come to Hester – she was too scared to do that – but that she would go back into service and be quite happy, in some place a long way from Barnswick. Ruth did not begrudge her any amount of happiness as long as she took it elsewhere. After that, they could all settle down to their lives again.

As always, she felt better when she had prayed. In spite of countless previous requests to the Almighty which had not been answered to her liking, she made each one with the confidence that this time it would work. God *must* see that it was the best way. She closed her eyes to rest, though it was important that she shouldn't fall asleep in case she dozed too long and arrived late at Aunt Sarah's.

She was dreaming about a dog, hearing its deep bark in the distance, and then there was a warm, wet tongue on her ankles and it was no longer a dream but her cousin's collie bitch, Rowan. Ruth sat up quickly and the dog jumped on to her lap. So Ernest must be somewhere near, since Rowan followed him everywhere. Then she saw him riding towards her, his horse breasting the hill at a slow trot.

'I was fast asleep,' Ruth called out. 'Rowan found me!'

Her cousin was so handsome. His eyes were darker than her own and in the sunlight his brown hair was tinged with copper. She noticed the immense strength of his shoulders and neck and, because his shirt was unbuttoned almost to the waist, she saw the mat of dark hair on his chest. When he held out his hand and took Ruth's, briefly, she felt a warm wave of pleasure.

'Ma thought you might be a bit tired,' he said. 'Would you like to ride Polly?'

'Yes please.'

She had thought that he would remount, then swing her up into the saddle beside him, and that they would ride the rest of the journey together, so she was disappointed when he lifted her into the saddle and, taking the rein, began to lead the mare. Still, it was good to be riding. She was so very tired, in spite of her rest. She leaned forward, laying her head against the mare's sturdy neck, and by the time the farmhouse came in sight she was almost asleep again. Not so Polly. On seeing her homestead the horse broke at once into a gentle trot which thoroughly wakened Ruth. Ernest laughed, running beside them to keep his hold on the rein.

'She allus does that! Steady as a rock until she smells her stable and then as frisky as a two-year-old.'

Aunt Sarah came out into the yard as they arrived, wiping her hands down her white apron, her round pink face creased in a smile.

'Why, bairn!' she said. 'You look that hot! Come on inside where it's a bit cooler.'

Ruth followed her aunt into the kitchen while Ernest took the mare to the stable. In spite of the heat from the great iron range which almost covered one wall of the room, the stone-flagged floor and thick walls kept the house cool. The air was rich with the smells of food, from the newly-baked bread cooling on a side table and from the black iron pot which steamed and hissed over the fire. The larded bread and bilberries seemed now in the distant past and Ruth's stomach contracted with the sharpness of her appetite.

'We're having summat special today,' Aunt Sarah said. 'Seeing as it's a special occasion.'

'A special occasion?'

'Well it's not every day you're here, love. You're right welcome – and to prove it your Uncle Matthew has killed a chicken. Well, to be honest, a boiling fowl. But with a few carrots and onions and a bit o' this and that, you'll see how tasty it'll be. A bit hot maybe for this weather, but your uncle always likes a hot meal when he comes in at dinnertime.'

While she talked she put knives and forks on the table, filled a dish with salt from the large wooden box on the mantelpiece, put plates to warm on the trivet.

'Can I help?' Ruth asked.

'Nay,' Aunt Sarah said. 'You're not doing a hand's turn while you're here. It's only four-and-twenty hours when all's said and done, so make the most of it. You can start by sitting in your uncle's armchair until he comes in.'

Ruth felt herself enveloped in a blanket of loving care. For the few minutes while she sat there, waiting for the meal, listening to her aunt's chatter, she was aware of happiness so tangible that she might have caught hold of it, plucked it out of the air. And the feeling did not lessen when her uncle, followed by Ernest, came into the house and they all took their places at the table.

'My word, lass, you've grown fast since I last saw thee!' Uncle Matthew said. 'Hasn't she shot up, Sarah?'

His wife nodded agreement. 'But she could do wi' a bit of fattening up, I reckon.' She filled Ruth's plate, heaping it with pieces of succulent chicken and with vegetables swimming in gravy.

Uncle Matthew bowed his head. 'Bless, O Lord, this food to our use and ourselves to Thy service. Amen,' he said briskly. 'Now make a good meal, our Ruth.'

'Do that,' Aunt Sarah encouraged. 'There's more i' the pot - and a curd tart to follow.'

After dinner the men went out again, Uncle Matthew to attend to the sheep towards the top of the moor and Ernest to repair the roof of the byre.

'Allus something to do,' Aunt Sarah said. 'Though there's little enough return for it. The ground won't grow crops, except what'll barely feed the animals. And the house and barns are just about falling down. I don't know what our Ernest'll do when he comes to get wed. This place won't support another family.'

Ruth looked at her aunt in surprise. Because they were a self-sufficient family, not relying on an employer for their living, it had never occurred to her that times might be hard for them. 'But I thought . . .' she began.

'We get by,' Aunt Sarah said. 'We grow our own food, make a bit now and then from the sheep. I take my eggs and butter to market. But there's nowt to spare. I'm not grumbling mind! Your Uncle Matthew's the best in the world, and Ernest is a good lad.'

'Is Ernest going to get wed then?' Ruth asked. She was conscious of a deep feeling of disappointment inside her.

Aunt Sarah laughed.

'That's for sure! He's a right one for the lasses, our Ernest is! Though whether he's got his eye on anyone special or not I don't rightly know. In my opinion he has a dozen on a string, down there in Ilkley!'

Ruth was thankful that there was no-one special, but if all the girls were after him she doubted if he'd stay single long enough for her to grow up and marry him. In any case she could only do it if it would work out for Willie and Maria, Father and Grandfather. So if in the meantime Ernest *did* marry someone else, she would devote herself entirely to her ready-made family. The virtuous thought gave her a melancholy content.

'Speaking of . . .' Aunt Sarah began – then broke off and began poking the fire.

'Yes?'

'Nowt. I've forgotten what I were going to say. Deng this fire! It won't draw!'

Ruth could see nothing wrong with the fire.

'And you say your father's well?' Aunt Sarah asked.

'Well enough. Tired, sometimes. But well.'

'It must be a hard life for him,' Aunt Sarah said. 'Not having a wife. Oh, don't get me wrong, love! I know you take good care of 'em all. You're a little champion. But your father's still young. And I daresay it's hard work for thee an' all.'

'No it's not!' Ruth said quickly. 'It's not at all. I can manage perfectly well. Has anyone said I can't?'

Ernest had been over to Barnswick. What stories, she wondered, had he carried back?

'Of course not, love! There now, don't take on! You do very well, considering. Everyone says so.'

Gradually she coaxed Ruth out of her sudden dark mood, and after that the day passed pleasantly enough. Ruth savoured the small happenings: seeing the three horses and the pig, walking up the moor to meet Uncle Matthew, looking around the house. In the little-used parlour she studied the sampler which, framed in oak, hung over the mantelpiece. It had been worked by her grandmother, Ruth Appleby, when she was eight years old.

'Jesus permit Thy sacred name to stand
As the first effort of an infant hand
And while her fingers o'er the canvas move
Incline her tender heart to seek Thy love.'

'What was Grandma Appleby like?' she asked her aunt.

'Nay lass,' Sarah answered. 'It's a long time ago. She smelled nice – and if you hurt yourself, if you fell or got a cut or anything, you'd run to her for comfort. I remember that.'

When bedtime came Aunt Sarah said, 'Our Ernest is

letting you sleep in his room for tonight. He'll sleep on the sofa downstairs.' She lit a candle and preceded Ruth up to the bedroom.

'I've forgotten to bring a nightshift,' Ruth confessed.

'Then you shall have one of mine. I've got one put by.'

Ruth fervently hoped that it was not the new one she knew her aunt had prudently laid aside, together with a pair of white stockings, to be buried in. 'Everything proper and to hand when the time comes' Ruth had heard her say. She was relieved when her aunt returned with an old, much-mended, but beautifully-laundered nightshift. It was white cotton, tucked down the front, and big enough to fit her three times over. They both shrieked with laughter when she put it on.

There was still some daylight left when Aunt Sarah went back downstairs. Ruth gazed out of the window, down the moor towards Ilkley and the river valley. There were too many trees for her to see the river, but she remembered it well. One day her father had taken herself and Maria along its bank, as far as Bolton Abbey. Ruth thought about that day as she climbed into the soft feather bed. A whole bed to herself! She seemed to sink down, down, down into its softness, while at the same time floating on the lightest of clouds.

When she awakened next morning the room was golden with sunlight and she knew she must have slept late. Simultaneously with her waking she was aware of a feeling of malaise; of not being herself and of never having felt quite like this before. And then, before she had time to sort out her feelings, came the sensation of wetness between her legs. Puzzled and apprehensive she was still not quite awake – she threw back the bedclothes. Her screams at the sight of the vivid stains on the sheet, and the blood still wet on her nightgown, brought her aunt running into the bedroom, breathless and white, her hand on her heart.

'What is it? What is it, child?'

'I'm bleeding! I'm bleeding to death! Aunt Sarah, I'm bleeding to death. Look!'

Ruth did not dare to move, her eyes fixed on the bright red

patch. When Aunt Sarah's eyes followed Ruth's the colour came back into her face. She sat on the bed and took her niece's hand, cold and trembling, into her own.

'What is it? What's the matter with me?' Ruth cried. 'Am I going to die?'

Aunt Sarah drew her close, holding Ruth's shaking body against her own.

'Of course not, you daft ha'porth!' she said. 'It's just your poorly time come, that's all!'

'Poorly time?' Ruth pulled herself away and looked sharply at her aunt. So she *was* ill!

'Unwell. It's called being unwell. It means you're almost a woman, my lamb. It happens to us all. Some say it's the curse of being a woman. The best thing is to be born a man, but since we can't pick and choose we have to get used to it. I'd have thought you'd have started a year ago, being as you're fourteen. I took it for granted. Did nobody tell you then?'

'Tell me what?' Ruth said. 'I don't know what you're talking about.'

'Well never mind now. It's all right and no cause for alarm. We'll get you cleaned up and change the sheet and then I'll get you a bit of breakfast. You shall have your breakfast in bed for once. A good thing your Uncle Matthew and Ernest went out this hour past. Now you stay where you are and I'll fetch you a cloth and show you how to fix it. There's nowt to worry about, love, so cheer up! After breakfast we'll have a little talk.'

When everything had been done and Ruth had finished her breakfast – it was surprising how heartily she could still eat – Aunt Sarah sat on the chair by the bedside.

'Well now, love, I don't believe in keeping lasses in ignorance. It can lead to trouble. So first of all, do you know where babies come from?'

'Oh yes,' Ruth assured her. 'They're inside the mother's body. I know all that. That's why she swells up in front. I can't quite see how they get out, though.'

'How do you think?' Aunt Sarah prompted.

Ruth hesitated. 'Well as far as I can see, that's what the belly button's for. Somehow . . . .' Her thoughts on this were vague. 'Somehow I suppose it bursts open like a flower and the baby comes out.'

'And do you know how the baby gets in?' Aunt Sarah asked.

'Oh yes!' Ruth said. She was on firm ground now. 'It gets in when two people kiss on the mouth. Only they have to be married. It doesn't work if you're not married.'

Later, Sarah Appleby told her husband that she didn't know what had impressed her most: Ruth's complete confidence in what she believed or her almost total ignorance of the truth.

'Well, perhaps I'd better put you right on one or two things,' she said.

What she told Ruth then cast a large, cold cloud over the remaining hours of her niece's stay at the farm, and remained with her for a long time afterwards. She was disgusted and felt dirty by what was happening to her own body, but that was nothing compared to the horror she felt about the rest. It couldn't be true! It mustn't be true because if it were it meant that her own mother, her father, her grandfather, Aunt Sarah. . . . It was unthinkable.

When Uncle Matthew came in to his dinner Ruth looked at him with new eyes, and she had no wish to look at Ernest at all. She realised that he had never done this thing, perhaps never would, but he knew. The only consolation she could find in the whole business was that as they had all had their children a long time ago it no longer went on. There would be no point in it. She took what comfort she could from that.

She's taken it very well, Aunt Sarah thought, observing Ruth's expressionless face. She's taken it in her stride.

After dinner it was time for Ruth to return to Barnswick. She refused Ernest's offer to mount her on Polly for part of the journey. She felt he had only to look at her to be aware of her condition, and for the first time in her life she was embarrassed to be with him.

'Thank you, I'd rather walk,' she said.

Physically she felt fit and well again and the pain in her back had gone. It seemed as though being unwell, horrible though it was, had somehow made her feel better.

It was the same route she took back to Barnswick. She saw and heard the birds again – this time there was a snipe, perched quietly on a rock, and curlews overhead. Once again she was dazzled by the heather. But everything was different now. The previous day seemed years away.

When she reached home everyone was in the house, including Hester. William welcomed his daughter with a beaming smile.

'Have you had a nice time, then, our Ruth?' he asked.

Suddenly Ruth felt, much though she loved her aunt and uncle, and her cousin, how good it was to be home with her own family again. She hoped that Hester would leave soon so that she could tell the others about her visit (though there were some things she would never speak of), but Hester made no move to go.

'Well, William,' Hester said after a while. 'Aren't you going to tell her then?'

Ruth knew, even before her father reached out and took Hester's hand in his, that something terrible was about to happen. She knew it by the way they smiled at each other, shutting out everyone else. Her father had never smiled at his children in that way.

'I've got something to tell thee, Ruth love,' he said. He spoke quietly but he couldn't keep the joy out of his voice. 'Hester and me's going to be wed! I'm to have a wife again and you'll have a new mother, Ruth!'

It took a second for the words to sink in – a second of horror and disbelief – and then Ruth flew at him, her arms flailing as she tried to separate, physically, her father and Hester.

'You can't!' she shouted. 'You can't, you can't! We don't want her. She's not our mother and we don't want her here. Everything was all right until *she* came. Send her away, Father! Please send her away!'

She beat her clenched fists against his chest. He caught

her wrists in his strong hands and forced her to be still, but his strength was powerless against the spate of words which came from her, and the sparking hatred in her eyes.

'Send her away! She spoils everything! We don't want her!'

He held on to Ruth, saying nothing while she raged. Hester stood beside him, her face a mask of calm certainty, seemingly unmoved by Ruth's anger against her. Maria stood apart, watching, but Willie ran to Hester and clung to her skirt. At the sight of the fear in her brother's face, Ruth's anger turned to weeping.

'Please, Father! I'll be good. I'll do everything properly. I'll do everything as good as *she* can. There's nothing *she* can do that I can't!'

As she said the words she remembered the shameful thing Aunt Sarah had told her only a few hours ago. The thought isolated itself in her mind, grew and grew until there was room for nothing else. She sprang out of her father's arms and looked at him in horror.

'Not you!' she cried. 'Not you!'

As Ruth turned and ran out of the room, Hester put her hand on William's arm.

'Don't fret, love. She'll get used to it. She'll have to.' Her touch and her voice were as firm as rocks. If William had thought of running after his daughter, he changed his mind.

It was Enoch Appleby who went, making his slow, painful way through the village and up the moor road. He knew where he would find Ruth. She lay face down in the heather, her head on her arm, her body shaking with sobs. With difficulty he lowered himself on the ground beside her, saying nothing, but touching her gently on the shoulder to let her know he was there. When she had finished crying he spoke quietly.

'It's what's best for thy father, Ruth love. You must think on that. She'll make him a good wife, and I daresay she'll be good to thee if only thou'll let her.'

Ruth turned over, sat up, glared at her grandfather with accusing eyes.

'I don't want her to be good to me!'

'Thy father needs a partner,' he said. 'When you're a

grown woman you'll understand. One day it will happen to thee.'

'Never!' Ruth cried. 'Never, never, never!' She saw that he was puzzled by her vehemence but she was too ashamed to tell him what she knew.

'Never's a long time, lass,' he replied.

They sat there in silence until, in the end, he said, 'We must go back, love. We can't spend the rest of our lives sitting on the moor. For a start, I'm not all that comfortable!'

Ruth sprang to her feet. How thoughtless she was to have this old man sitting on the rough, tussocky moorland, walking all this way to find her, and now he would have to walk back again.

'I'm sorry, Grandfather. I didn't think.'

She put out her hand and helped him to his feet. His face was pale, and lined with fatigue. She offered him her arm and together they walked back down the moorland track to the village.

# 3

William and Hester planned to marry at Michaelmas.

'There's nothing to be gained from waiting,' William said. 'We're not children and we both know what we want. Besides, what's the point of paying two rents? The sooner we're wed, the sooner Hester can move in here.'

Hester was already in the house most of the time. It seemed to Ruth that she had all but taken over. In her firm and quite pleasant manner she involved them all in her plans, whether they liked it or not. Maria revelled in it, Grandfather was quietly neutral. Ruth hated every proposal, every idea, every fancy which flowed from Hester's busy mind. She was pleased, therefore, when her father protested, though too mildly for her liking.

'I don't go for all this fuss and palaver, Hester love,' he said. 'Dressmaking, cleaning, scrubbing, baking. What *I'd* like is for us to walk up to the church the first Saturday afternoon I can get off work, and have the vicar marry us without any fuss or bother.' He sighed. 'I suppose it's too much to hope for?'

Hester's laughter pealed out. 'It certainly is, my lad! It's all very well for you. You've been through it afore. It's my first time – nay, I hope it'll be my only time – and I intend to make the most of it.'

Making the most of it included fashioning completely new outfits not only for herself but for each of her stepchildren-to-be, as well as a new shirt for the prospective bridegroom.

'But there's no need for you to worry, Will lad,' she told

him. 'All you have to do is be there on the day, spruced up and willing. Me and the children'll see to everything else.'

She talks as though she owns us, Ruth thought. Well, she doesn't own me and never will. But she had realised since that first evening that she was powerless to prevent her father going through with this marriage. All she could do now was to try to act as though Hester did not exist, was not always bursting into the house with measuring tapes, scissors, pins, lengths of cotton. Maria was ecstatic at this state of affairs but Ruth refused to show any pleasure at the sight of the pretty purple and white sprigged cotton which was to be made up into her new dress.

'Hester means well,' Grandfather said. 'And you'll look real bonny in yon frock.'

Everyone, it seemed, was on Hester's side.

One morning when Hester, her mouth full of pins, was kneeling at Ruth's feet, adjusting the hem of the new dress, Miss Caroline called. In her usual manner she tapped lightly on the door and walked straight into the living-room. At the sight of Ruth she stopped short, standing in admiration in front of Hester's handiwork.

'Why, it's beautiful!' she cried. 'Ruth, you're going to look lovely! You are a very talented seamstress, Miss Brown. And I may have a special need for your talents myself.' But when Hester looked to her for an explanation she quickly changed the subject.

'What I really came for,' she said, 'was to bring Ruth this volume of poetry by Mr Alfred Tennyson. It came in a parcel of new books from Leeds. The vicar is no longer certain about Mr Tennyson's beliefs, but since he has not forbidden me I think that in the meantime to read his poems can do us no harm.'

'Why, miss, that's very kind of you,' Hester said.

'Thank you Miss Caroline, only I don't get much time to read,' Ruth broke in. It seemed as if from now on even Miss Caroline was to be shared with Hester.

'Nonsense!' Hester said briskly. 'Of course you've got time. Now that I'm here to help. Why, when your father and I are wed I really don't know what you'll find to do with yourself all day long.' She turned to Miss Caroline. 'I can see we shall have to find her some occupation,' she said pleasantly. 'Satan finds mischief for idle hands. Isn't that so, miss?'

'So they say,' Miss Caroline answered. 'But Ruth's never had time to prove it. Ruth, can you spare a few minutes to walk a little way with me? I'd like to talk to you about my classes. You haven't been for some time.'

'Of course she can go with you,' Hester said quickly. 'It'll do her good to be out on such a lovely day. Only give me a minute while I slip this over her head.'

Ruth was furious at Hester's granting of permission for her to leave the house. How dare she? But for her curiosity as to Miss Caroline's purpose she would have refused to go. She was sure it had nothing to do with the classes. She had not had time to attend those since her mother's death and Miss Caroline had long ago ceased to mention them.

'Shall we stroll a little way up Moorside?' Miss Caroline said as they left the house. 'I have something to tell you, Ruth.'

'As you please, miss.' She couldn't imagine what it could be and was suddenly afraid. Was there to be more trouble?

'Is there something wrong?' she asked.

'Nothing wrong, Ruth. Quite the reverse.' Miss Caroline hesitated a little, then said:

'I am to be married, Ruth. The Reverend Charles Longhill has asked my father for my hand, and my father has consented. The two of them are old friends.' She spoke quietly and firmly, in a well-modulated voice which it had always been Ruth's desire to emulate.

'Oh Miss Caroline!'

She was too taken aback to hide her dismay. A friend of the vicar's. Why, he must be quite old. The vicar was over forty, Ruth felt sure. To her mind a Prince of the Blood was not too good for Miss Caroline. Or an officer in the army, or a famous poet. . . . But an elderly clergyman . . .!

Miss Caroline interrupted her thoughts.

'I am very happy about it. The Reverend Longhill is a good, kind man. He will be a considerate husband. He has a living at Singleton, in Nordale.'

'But that means that you'll be leaving Barnswick!' Ruth cried. This was without doubt the worst summer of her life. Everything was going wrong.

'Naturally,' Miss Caroline replied. 'In fact we are to be married soon after your father and Miss Brown. Which brings me to my real purpose. I shall need a housemaid, Ruth. Mr Longhill has an old housekeeper, a Mrs Peterson, who has been in his family since before he was born, but the new vicarage is large and one person will not be enough to look after it. He has been kind enough to agree that I may ask you, though he himself has never met you, whether you would like to come to work for us. Would you like that, Ruth?'

'Oh Miss Caroline, you know I would! To be with you, that is. But I couldn't. I couldn't leave the children, nor my father and grandfather.' Ruth was a little surprised that Miss Caroline hadn't seen this for herself.

They had reached the top of the hill where the road petered out into the moorland track. Although it was still forenoon the day was hot.

'Let us sit down for a minute,' Miss Caroline said. 'I think the grass is dry here.'

When they were both seated she leaned across and touched Ruth's hand; almost as if they were friends, Ruth thought.

'Ruth,' Miss Caroline began, 'sooner or later you will have to leave your family. When your father has a new wife it will be natural for her to take over as mistress of the house. Wouldn't you rather go with me than go into service elsewhere? Or go to work in the mill?'

Ruth drew sharply away from her. What had she done that all these terrible things were happening to her? God must be punishing her for something.

'My father said he'd never let any of us go into the mill,' she replied. 'Even with the new laws he says the hours are too long and the work too hard. He's seen too much of it.'

'I'm sure he wouldn't want you to,' Miss Caroline said gently. 'But I think you'll find you have to do something, Ruth. So why not help to look after Mr Longhill and myself?'

Like a flash of lightning it came to Ruth that there was more to this than had so far been said. 'Does my father know you were going to speak to me?' she asked suspiciously.

'Well, yes.' Miss Caroline looked confused. 'Naturally the vicar spoke to him first. It was only right.'

'And Hester Brown?'

'Neither my father nor I have discussed the matter with Miss Brown,' Miss Caroline replied.

But no doubt my father will have, Ruth thought bitterly. It will all have been settled between them, behind my back, without any thought of what will please me! She could have borne it better if only her father had talked to her himself. It seemed that she was to have no choice at all. She felt sick at heart, and helpless.

'Very well, Miss Caroline,' she said curtly. 'I'll come with you. I can't pretend I want to leave home, but I'll try to serve you well.'

Ruth rose to her feet and began to march back down the road on her own, but Miss Caroline ran and caught up with her.

'I'm so pleased, Ruth,' she said. 'And now we shall have to move quickly. There's so little time. Tomorrow I intend to ask Miss Brown if she will make my wedding dress. And then there'll be all your new things: dresses, caps, aprons. We shall all be very occupied.'

It was the opinion of everyone who saw her on her wedding day that Hester made a beautiful bride. Her gown of pale blue figured sateen – it was before the day of white dresses for weddings – with the close-fitting bodice coming to a point over the gathered skirt, set off her rounded figure and rosy complexion. Fine piping in a leaf pattern, and a row of small double bows down the centre seam of the bodice relieved the simplicity of the line, and matching bows trimmed her brocade shoes.

There were women watching the wedding who criticised Hester. Ruth heard them, and she thought Hester did too.

'She's setting herself up too high, that one!'

'You're right at that! What call has a working man's wife to be dressed so fine?'

If Hester had heard, it seemed not to upset her. Nothing could cloud this day for her. Ruth tried to rejoice at the sight of her father's obvious happiness – and she intended to give no-one the chance to think that she was unhappy. No-one should suspect her true feelings.

Except, she thought, her grandfather. It had never been easy to hide anything from him. He was not able to climb the hill to the church but afterwards, at the meal, his eyes met Ruth's and she saw sadness and understanding in them, as she had on that other occasion, after her mother's funeral. Once or twice during the last few weeks she had sensed that he wanted to talk to her about her father and Hester, but she had evaded him. Nor would she discuss her forthcoming departure. Though it drew nearer all the time, and Miss Caroline was in a flurry of preparation in which she tried to involve Ruth, it still seemed unthinkable that it would actually happen.

Aunt Sarah and her family were at the wedding, Uncle Matthew downcast with worry over the potato blight, which had done so much damage in the previous year.

'I pray it don't come here again,' he said. 'I don't know how we'd manage two years running. But they say it's back in the south, and as far north as Lincolnshire.'

'Cheer up, Matthew,' William encouraged him. 'It may never happen. Anyway I thought it were a good harvest this year, barring potatoes?'

'Happen for some,' Matthew sighed. 'Them as can grow corn on their land's doing all right. That's not me.'

'Well, we must count our blessings,' Aunt Sarah said cheerfully.

There were several quips about Ernest being the next one

to be wed and Ruth wondered if by this time there *was* someone special. Since she herself no longer wished ever to marry there was now no question of Ernest waiting for her. But she hoped he would stay as he was a little while longer. Once people married everything changed.

Aunt Sarah was pleased that her niece was taking a place with Miss Caroline.

'It will be the making of you, lass,' she said. 'Mind you keep your eyes and ears open and learn all you can. You're a bright lass, our Ruth. You'll not be in service all your life, you mark my words!'

Then what was to happen to her, Ruth wondered? All she had ever wanted from life was to be happy with her family, and now she was to be banished. There was no other word for it.

That night her father and stepmother made love in the next bedroom with no inhibitions at all. Ruth pushed her fingers in her ears and buried her head under the bedclothes, trying to shut out the murmurings, the sharp cries, and most of all the insistent, rhythmic sound. It was worse, far worse, than she had imagined. Through the night it beat in her head like a drum.

Miss Caroline's wedding to the Reverend Charles Longhill took place two weeks after Hester's and William's. The bride looked pretty enough in the dress Hester had made for her, but she was an altogether quieter, less exuberant one; with her pale skin and light brown hair in every way less vibrantly colourful than Hester.

The very next day Ruth left Barnswick with the bride and groom, in the carriage they had hired for the occasion, to start her new life with them in Nordale. Parting from the children and Grandfather was almost more than she could bear. She prayed that she would not break down.

'Look after thysen, little love,' Grandfather said. 'Be a good girl and try not to fret.'

'I don't want to go,' Ruth muttered desperately. 'I don't want to leave you, Grandfather.'

He held her close, and though she had been determined not to cry, her tears flowed, soaking the rough cloth of his jacket. When she raised her head and looked at him there were tears in his eyes also.

'There now,' he said. 'Don't take on so!'

'I'll write to you,' Ruth promised. 'Maria can read out my letters.'

For the first few miles Ruth saw nothing of the countryside through which they passed. All she could visualise was the cottage in Barnswick where she had lived all her life up to now. Nordale was about thirty miles distant but to Ruth it might as well have been on the other side of the world.

From time to time Mrs Longhill - which from now on, Ruth told herself, she must remember to call her - pointed out features of interest.

'The railway is making good progress,' she said. 'It is almost finished to Keighley and soon after that we shall have it as far as Skipton. It will be a great convenience to us all.'

In the end, for the sake of politeness, Ruth raised her head and tried to show an interest. They were passing through Skipton now, the carriage rattling and bumping over the cobbles in a most uncomfortable manner.

'See!' Mrs Longhill said. 'There is Skipton Castle of which we once spoke.'

Of more interest to Ruth was that this was the town where her father and mother had first met, at the fair in this wide street, which appeared just as her mother had so often described it. It was lined with stalls today, and the space left in the centre was crammed with carts and animals and crowded with people so that it was difficult for the carriage to get through.

She wondered if her mother's family still lived in these parts. It was strange to have grandparents, aunts, uncles, cousins, whom she had never seen. Perhaps one day one of them would discover her in Nordale and claim her to live with them.

After Skipton the road climbed towards Grassington and from there ran all the way with the river in view. They passed through an old, grey village which Mr Longhill said was Kettlewell, and shortly afterwards came to Buckden. There they turned off the road and crossed a packhorse bridge into Nordale itself. The way was hardly more than a track and they were bounced about in the carriage until Ruth felt quite sick.

The hills were higher and closer in here. Isolated houses and an occasional small farm, on the eastern slopes at the far side of the fast-flowing river, were reached by narrow bridges. Sheep strayed on to the track so that more than once Ruth was sure they must meet with an accident.

'We are almost there, my love,' Mr Longhill said to his bride. He didn't smile much, let alone laugh, but he was unfailingly courteous towards her. He did not speak to Ruth.

The church and vicarage at Singleton stood side by side across the river, reached by a hump-backed bridge. The house, the church, the bridge, and the dry-stone walls which ran so straightly up the steep fellsides, were all built of the same pale grey limestone, though now its colour was warmed by the late afternoon sun. As they crossed the bridge and drew up in front of the house Ruth observed a small, elderly woman standing by the gate.

'Ah! Here is Mrs Peterson, come to greet us!' Mr Longhill said.

The woman welcomed Mr Longhill with respectful enthusiasm, gave his wife a smile and a polite bob. They followed her into the house, and in the wide, stone-flagged entrance hall she turned to Ruth.

'Bide here while I take the master and mistress to their room,' she said.

Without a glance at Ruth, Mrs Longhill took her husband's arm and ascended the stairs with him, led by Mrs Peterson. Now I am really alone, Ruth thought, watching them go. How shall I bear it?

She wondered if she might sit down. She felt sick and shaken from what had been the longest journey of her life. But better not. When she saw Mrs Peterson coming down the stairs again she stood stiffly to attention, not sure what was expected of her.

'Now there's no need to look scared,' Mrs Peterson said. 'No-one's going to eat you! Come with me.'

Ruth followed Mrs Peterson through a door at the back of the hall, into a kitchen so spacious that she thought it would contain the whole of the cottage in Barnswick. A black iron range covered most of one wall and there was a large square table in the centre of the room.

'Take off your cloak and hang it on the hook there for the time being,' Mrs Peterson said. 'When I've given the master and mistress a cup of tea we'll have one ourselves, and then I'll show you where you're to sleep. After that you can help me to make the supper. Ruth, isn't it?'

'Ruth Appleby, if you please, madam.'

'Well, Ruth,' Mrs Peterson said. 'I expect you to work hard, do as you're told, and no back answers. And I daresay we'll get along as well as may be.'

Mrs Peterson was really old, Ruth thought. Small, round-shouldered, with wispy hair drawn back under her white cap. Her voice was as thin as her body but her tone, though sharpish, wasn't unkind. Ruth felt that, like her master, she was not going to smile much. But best wait and see. If this was to be her life from now on she'd have to learn to live agreeably with the old woman. And what was there to smile about, anyway?

'I don't come from these parts,' Mrs Peterson remarked. 'As I daresay you can tell. Nor the vicar neither. It's a far cry from Sussex.' Ruth had the feeling that both of them had come, like missionaries, to convert the heathen – whom Mrs Peterson, at any rate, had expected to be covered in woad and living in caves.

The kitchen tea was strong, and accompanied by oatmeal parkin so good that Ruth reckoned Mrs Peterson had learned about it from the natives. The old woman, observing Ruth's hunger, offered her a second piece.

'You look as though you could do with feeding up a bit,' she observed. 'Well, you'll find the vicar's quite generous with food, as he is with everything. Plain fare, but plenty of it. Now when you've finished that we'll clear away and I'll show you where you're to sleep.'

She conducted Ruth to a small, square room in the attic. It was pleasant enough, with a dormer window which looked down the dale, towards Buckden. In the other direction, rising behind the vicarage, there was a cleft in the hillside from which a stream, quickening to a miniature waterfall over an outcrop of rock, ran down and along the edge of the vicarage land. It would be agreeable to fall asleep to the sound of running water.

The room was furnished with a narrow bed, a chest of drawers with a small mirror on top, a wash-basin and a ewer on a stand, and a chair. On the floor there was a pricked rag rug, and under the bed a plain white chamber-pot. There was half a candle in the candlestick on a small table against the wall.

'You can put your bits and pieces on the table,' Mrs Peterson said. 'Likewise on the top of the chest. Be economical with the candles. They cost sixpence a pound. Now you're to keep your room tidy, a place for everything and everything in its place. The bed to be made before breakfast every morning and the room thoroughly turned out once a week.'

'Yes Mrs Peterson.'

'Then I'll leave you to unpack your box. Don't be long, and come down to the kitchen as soon as you've finished. There's plenty to do.'

When Mrs Peterson had left, Ruth put her clothes in the chest: another new grey dress besides the one she was wearing; aprons, caps, chemises, petticoats, drawers. Her father and Hester had seen to it that she was adequately supplied, more then ever before in her life. At the back of a drawer she put the 'poorly cloths' Aunt Sarah had given her. Somehow she would have to summon up the courage to speak to Mrs Peterson about the arrangements for such things – laundering and so on.

Already she sensed that things would no longer be the

same between Miss Caroline and herself. Even on the journey she had noticed a difference. Miss Caroline – no, Mrs Longhill – was polite enough but now she was the mistress and Ruth was the servant. She had thought of Miss Caroline as being part of home, but now she felt that her mistress had left Barnswick well and truly behind, in thought as well as in fact. It was natural that she should turn to her new husband, but need she turn away from me, Ruth thought.

On the table she placed her bible, and the prayer book she had been given at her confirmation. Also a small white jug she had won at Barnswick fair, and, last of all, a sprig of late heather. Only a few hours ago she had walked up to the moor to pick it, but already that seemed another world. She was no longer a part of it, but neither could she envisage a new life here. She did not belong anywhere.

She was standing there, plucking up her courage to return to the kitchen, when Mrs Peterson came in. She did not knock. Ruth faced the fact that as a servant she had no right to privacy.

'I've got a minute or two to spare,' Mrs Peterson said. 'The vicar is showing Mrs Longhill the garden, so I'll take you over the house. No time like the present, and that way you'll be ready all the sooner to start your duties.'

'This is the parlour,' she said. 'We clean this room every morning before breakfast: the grate to be blackleaded – see you get a good shine – the fire to be laid and lit. The marble fireplace we clean with soda, pumice stone and chalk. Shake the rugs outside; sweep the carpets. We save all the tealeaves and sprinkle them on the carpet before it's swept. It slakes the dust and brings up the colours lovely.'

Ruth soon gave up trying to remember the list of jobs which Mrs Peterson rattled off in every room in the house. She just hoped that she would learn as she went along.

Next morning, after a night in which she slept better than she expected to, Mrs Peterson gave her a box full of cleaning materials and filled her arms with sweeping brushes and dusters. Ruth discovered that 'we' meant 'you'. Almost all the tasks which the housekeeper had reeled off were to be Ruth's.

'I do the cooking,' Mrs Peterson said.

By the end of a week Ruth could complete the parlour in the time allocated by Mrs Peterson.

'But my hands are sore from the soda and pumice stone,' she complained.

'They'll soon harden,' Mrs Peterson assured her. 'Try rubbing a bit of fat into them.'

After breakfast, for which she was always ravenously hungry, Ruth started on the rest. The master bedroom first: slops to empty, chamber-pots (delicately flower-patterned for the best bedroom) to clean; the enormous bed with two mattresses, one of them feather, to shake and make; ewers and basins to wash out, mirrors to polish. And so it went on, in every room in the house, day in day out, the daily jobs only varied by the weekly ones.

Ruth was glad when some of her duties - cleaning silver for instance - kept her in the kitchen, because then Mrs Peterson would chat to her and she felt less lonely. True, the talk was usually about her master, the Reverend Charles Longhill, second only to God in her eyes.

'I've known him since he was born,' she frequently said. 'I was a young housemaid then, in his parents' home.'

In her eyes he was the embodiment of all virtues, though it must, Ruth thought, be knowledge gained from the past since now he did not speak at all to his domestic staff. He never set foot in the kitchen and if Ruth unavoidably met him while carrying out her duties in another part of the house he went past her with downcast eyes. She supposed his mind was full of deep thoughts about the following Sunday's sermon.

But when he climbed into the pulpit on a Sunday to speak to his small flock, he was a changed man: full of fire and passion and promises of the wrath of God towards miserable sinners. At least this was always the content of his sermons at evensong. Mrs Peterson and Ruth were not free to attend morning service but they were obliged to appear at evensong.

'He doesn't stint his sermon at evensong,' Mrs Peterson

said. 'It's just as long, and some say even more fiery. It's greatly to his credit. There are some reverend gentlemen who wouldn't take the trouble for their evening congregations.'

She was able to count most things to his credit. Ruth thought he probably reckoned his humbler parishioners were more prone to sin and in greater danger of hellfire.

She saw little now of Mrs Longhill. She came into the kitchen occasionally, but mostly Mrs Peterson went into the parlour to receive her orders. One link, however, remained between Ruth and her mistress. From time to time Mrs Longhill lent her books. One day Mrs Peterson conveyed a message to Ruth.

'The mistress says to tell you the vicar has kindly agreed that you can go into his library any Tuesday afternoon, when he's out visiting the sick, and choose yourself a book. You're to make sure it's something suitable and write down what you've taken. I don't know what you want with all this reading, I'm sure. But that's the vicar for you – kindness itself!'

From then on Ruth never failed to take advantage of that privilege.

Then one morning, early in December, Mrs Longhill came into the kitchen herself and spoke directly to Ruth.

'I am to visit Barnswick!' she announced. 'The vicar has kindly agreed that I may go and see my family before Christmas, though of course I shall return well before the festive season begins. It is a busy time for the vicar and we must all be here to sustain him.'

'Of course I shall visit your family, Ruth,' she continued. 'You can count upon that. I shall tell them how you are progressing and enquire after them so that I can bring you news. And if you have any messages, or perhaps Christmas gifts, I shall be glad to deliver them for you.'

How possibly to provide gifts became Ruth's total preoccupation over the next few days. She had no money – not yet having been paid any part of the six pounds a year which was to be her wages. And even if the vicar had thought to advance her something, there was no shop nearer than Grassington, more than ten miles away. And yet, send something she must, now that the idea had been put into her head.

'Why not write a little poem for everyone in the family?' Mrs Peterson suggested. 'You're fond of poetry and you do a nice, neat script.'

'I haven't got any suitable paper,' Ruth pointed out.

'Well now,' Mrs Peterson said. 'I daresay the vicar would have some nice white paper if I was to ask him. He could deduct the cost from your wages.'

So it was decided. Ruth knew scores of poems; it was simply a question of choosing the right ones. Grandfather's was the most difficult. It would have been easy to send him a sea poem, but she sought for something which would express her feelings about being parted from him. And then at last she found it, in a book she borrowed from the vicar's library. The poem was entitled 'Present in Absence'.

'Absence, hear thou my protestation
        Against the strength
        Distance and length;
Do what thou canst for alteration;
For hearts of truest mettle
Absence doth join, and Time doth settle.'

She decorated each poem with a border of pen and ink drawings and felt reasonably pleased with the results. Choosing the poems had brought her a little bit nearer to their recipients. So as not to seem rude she had even included one for Hester. When she handed the gifts to Mrs Longhill on the evening before she left, Ruth plied her with messages and questions for her family until Mrs Longhill held up her hands in protest and cried out for Ruth to stop.

'No more, I beg of you, Ruth! I shall never remember the half of it!'

Mrs Longhill was away for five days, during which the vicar spent most of his time in his study, presumably composing more fiery sermons for the approaching season of peace and goodwill.

'Ruth, I've decided to teach you a bit more cooking,' Mrs Peterson said on the second day. 'I know you've looked after your family, but I must say, your knowledge seems a bit limited.'

It would be, Ruth thought. It had been a question of filling everyone at the least possible cost. Anyhow, how many ways could you cook potatoes? How many changes could you ring on a scrag end of mutton? At least it would be more interesting than the hated housework; but Ruth had no illusions as to why Mrs Peterson's not inconsiderable skill was to be passed on to her. It was in order that the task might become hers. Each day Ruth spent with Mrs Peterson confirmed the fact that the housekeeper, though admittedly old and tired, was lazy. Yet she did not want the standards of housekeeping to slip and she saw in Ruth a means of keeping them up with the least trouble to herself.

So while Ruth's head was full of thoughts about what Mrs Longhill might be doing in Barnswick, who seeing, she learnt to roast a joint of beef so that the blood followed the knife when it was carved; to steam an egg custard which would neither curdle nor separate; to make a white sauce without lumps; to bake a tin of parkin which would not sink as it cooled. She enjoyed making the parkin most of all because of the rich, spicy scent which filled the kitchen.

The tuition was not one-sided. Mrs Peterson could not turn out a good Yorkshire pudding to accompany the beef, hers being solid and heavy. Ruth explained that to make the pudding as light as thistledown one must sit at the open door, preferably in a good draught, and beat the air into it.

'Though they do say,' she added pertly, 'that you can't hope to do it really well unless you're Yorkshire born!'

'Right, my girl!' Mrs Peterson replied, sharp as a needle. 'I believe you. From now on, *you* make the Yorkshire!'

She was pleased with Ruth's progress overall. 'You can help me with the Christmas cooking,' she promised graciously.

She crossed the kitchen and gazed anxiously out of the window.

'There's snow on the way,' she observed. 'And when snow comes here, it comes with a vengeance. We could be cut off from civilisation with the poor mistress marooned the Lord knows where!'

But the snow did not come. Nothing happened to prevent Mrs Longhill's safe return and she was back in Singleton four days before Christmas. When she entered the house she went straight upstairs to rest, not even pausing in the hall to take off her cloak.

'She's uncommonly fatigued from the journey,' Mrs Peterson reported to Ruth later.

'When do you think she'll be rested?' Ruth asked anxiously. 'I'm dying to hear about everyone. I can't bear to wait!'

'Keep busy,' Mrs Peterson counselled. 'That's the way to make the time pass. I should know!' She was rocking in her chair in front of the huge kitchen fire.

It was the following day before Mrs Longhill came downstairs and then she came at once into the kitchen.

'I'm sorry, Ruth,' she said. 'I didn't want to keep you waiting, but I was quite unusually upset by the journey and the vicar insisted I should rest quietly. Now let me give you all the news! Where shall I begin?'

'Well then . . . Maria has grown out of all knowledge and your stepmother is having to let down all her dresses. She is going to be as tall as you. And since she is now thirteen years old there is some talk of her going into service if a suitable place can be found. But it must not be too far from home, so that they can keep an eye on her, see that she is all right.'

Who is keeping an eye on me, Ruth wondered? I'm a long way from home. She presumed they were relying on God and Mrs Longhill, but to her mind they were both too remote.

'Willie is as sweet as ever,' Mrs Longhill continued. 'He liked his poem and he sends you his love.'

As clearly as if he were there Ruth could feel Willie's presence, his arms around her neck. She looked down at the floor to hide the tears which pricked at her eyes, and the squares and diamonds of the rug on which she was standing blurred into each other.

'And Grandfather?' she asked, looking up again.

The slightest of frowns creased Mrs Longhill's high forehead and was gone again.

'Your grandfather has not been too well, I think. But we must remember that he is old . . . .'

'But he's better now?' Ruth interrupted. 'He is better now, isn't he?'

'Yes. Yes, he's better now. And will perhaps continue so if the weather is reasonable this winter. And your father and stepmother are well and happy, and I have a very special piece of news for you. The other children don't know yet, but I was bidden to tell you. Hester is to have a baby in the summer! At the end of June it will be. A new brother or sister for you. Isn't that splendid!'

Without waiting for Ruth's reaction to the news Mrs Longhill continued.

'And now, best of all I daresay! I have promised your family that they shall have you home for a short visit after Christmas. The vicar has agreed to that, though you have been with us only a short while. You are to have three whole days off to make the visit. Is that not most generous of him?'

'It certainly is,' Mrs Peterson broke in. 'And just like him, I must say!'

Beyond a muttered 'thank you' Ruth could say nothing. The shock of Hester's news – though now it had come she recognised its inevitability – was submerged in her joy at the prospect of going home. She could find no words. In her head she made a calculation of the time which must elapse between now and then. Perhaps no more than a month. Four weeks. Twenty-eight days. How many hours?

'We shall fix the exact date when Christmas is over,' Mrs Longhill was saying. 'The vicar will arrange with Dick Parker to take you on his cart when he goes to Skipton. I am sure Dick will be pleased to oblige. From there you can get the coach . . . .'

Dick Parker and his cart, or shanks's pony – Ruth didn't

care how she got there. Her fatigue was completely gone and she felt capable of walking the whole thirty miles to Barnswick, starting at that moment.

'But you must put it out of your mind for the time being,' Mrs Longhill said. 'There will be a great deal to be done here at Christmas and we must all pull our weight.'

'That's what I always say, ma'am,' Mrs Peterson agreed. 'Many hands make light work, eh Ruth?'

She really believes that, Ruth thought. She really does believe it. But it didn't matter. She felt as if she herself had the strength of ten.

# 4

On New Year's Day the snow began to fall: silently, in thick, heavy flakes which blotted out the fells, levelled the river meadows to the height of the road and hid from view every house and barn in the long sweep of the dale. And while the snow was still falling a strong wind swept down from the north, so that wherever the snow met an obstacle it piled into a drift. By the time it ceased, two days later, it was impossible to tell where the road ran, and the river was a black line, bordered only by a few white-shrouded trees along its banks. The bridge at Singleton was blocked to the height of the parapet. Day and night the temperature stayed below freezing point so that the snow remained hard-packed and icy. The sexton dug a path from the vicarage to the church and that, for almost two weeks, was the only exit from the house.

'It's a sight worse for the farmers,' Mrs Peterson said. 'Most of their sheep are buried under that lot!'

'They'll starve to death, the poor things,' Ruth sighed. She could hardly bear to think of it.

'It's not starvation they die of,' Mrs Peterson said. 'They suffocate because they pack together under the snowdrifts. As it happens, they'd have been better left on the high ground instead of being brought down for the winter. There's fewer drifts on the fells. I tell you, my girl, there'll be a deal of hardship in this dale before the winter ends!'

When the day came that Ruth should have ridden on Dick Parker's cart to Skipton, she looked out of the window and saw no break in the snow. A few birds - sparrows, a rook, a robin and a tiny wren – miraculously alive in spite of the weather, perhaps because they roosted around the chimney pots, fed greedily on the crumbs she had thrown out for them, and flew away again.

Miserable, she turned away from the window and spoke to Mrs Peterson.

'I wish I could fly!'

'It's the only way out of the dale,' Mrs Peterson agreed.

The snow stayed on the ground, now diminishing a little, now building up again as more fell, until the middle of February. It was impossible for any wheeled vehicles to move and not easy for horses. Sleds, hastily improvised, or borrowed from children, became the most useful form of transport. Ruth felt as much a prisoner as if she had been cast behind iron bars. And like a prisoner she thought all the time of home and loved ones. Would the snow never go?

Then, on a day in February, a thaw wind blew from the west and the air turned mild. The snow melted and ran from the meadows and fells into the river, turning it into a slate-blue torrent. And Mrs Peterson, venturing out too soon, took a chill which rapidly turned to bronchitis.

'She must on no account leave her bed,' the doctor said. 'At her age it could have grave consequences.'

So Ruth had the whole of the housework as well as the care of an invalid. And as if that was not enough, on the day after the doctor's visit Mrs Longhill announced that she was pregnant.

'No matter how I entreat him,' she said happily, 'my dear husband will not allow me to lift a finger! But I know how efficiently you cope with everything, Ruth. I am sure we shall manage!'

In fact, Mrs Longhill was not at all well, and if Ruth had had any feelings left over from her deep fatigue and her bitter disappointment at missing her visit home, she would have sympathised with her, done what she could to relieve her mistress's sickness, which seemed to go on all the time. She did, however, find sympathy for Mrs Peterson. Though the long wait before Ruth could see her own family was almost unbearable, Mrs Peterson's case was worse. Her only relative was a sister in Sussex. 'But we're too old, and it's too far to travel,' Mrs Peterson said. 'We shan't meet again in this world.'

Easter came and went before the housekeeper was considered fit enough to be left. Mrs Longhill also improved as the weeks went by, so by mid-May it was decided that Ruth could at last make her visit home.

'It's to be extended to a week,' Mrs Peterson told her. 'And it's to count as your summer holiday. It's wondrous generous of the vicar to allow you a whole week's holiday and nothing deducted from your wages. Especially with the cost of things. Everything going up! Common flour three shillings a stone, if you please!' She all but choked with indignation, and started a fit of coughing.

'Bring me back a bottle of that Barton's cough syrup,' she said. 'I daresay you'll get it in Skipton. Don't get out of the coach in Keighley There's fever there, they say.'

So on the morning of a day late in spring Ruth sat up on the front of the cart with Dick Parker Dick worked for Farmer Trench, a mile down the dale from Singleton, and lived in Buckden. Occasionally the farmer lent him to the vicar to do odd jobs in the house and garden. It was because he had an errand to do for Farmer Trench in Skipton that today had been chosen for the journey.

'They do say as the railway'll be running from Skipton, come September,' Dick said. 'It'll go all the way to Leeds. If you'd waited until September you could have gone on one of them new trains!'

He had a true dalesman's voice: slow, and quieter than a townsman's because he never had to shout to make himself heard.

'I couldn't wait another minute,' Ruth said. 'I'd walk it first! You don't know what it's like. I don't suppose you've ever worked away from home?'

'I've lived and worked in Buckden all my life,' he admitted. 'And my family before me. The furthest I've been is Skipton.'

Nevertheless, he was not dull, Ruth thought. And he was good to look at with his long legs, broad shoulders, tanned skin. She liked Dick Parker. He was the kind of young man she would have chosen for the elder brother she so often wished she had.

The horse walked slowly along the unmade road, which now looked as though it had never known snow. Those ewes which had survived the winter had been brought together for lambing and the few, flat meadows along the bottom of the valley were crowded with them, and with their bleating, fast-growing offspring. All the trees were now in leaf, except the oaks, still black silhouettes against the sky.

'That means a wet summer,' Dick said. 'The oaks being late.'

Ruth didn't care about the rest of the year. Let it do its worst! Today was glorious and she was on her way home.

'Would you like me to bring you back next Saturday, meet you here in Skipton?' Dick asked. 'I daresay Mr Trench'll let me have the cart. Any road, how'll you get back else?'

'I don't know,' Ruth said. 'I'll find a way.' She didn't want to think about her return.

'Well then, I'll be looking out for you,' Dick promised.

The house door was open and when Ruth walked in from the brightness of the street her first thought was how small and dark the room looked after the spaciousness of the vicarage. It seemed, perhaps because of the addition of Hester's bits and pieces, not a great deal bigger than her attic bedroom there. Her second impression was that Hester, eight months pregnant, filled the room – not just with her physical size but with her exuberance. Her skin glowed like a polished apple, her clear eyes shone; her heavy breasts and voluptuously-rounded abdomen made neater figures seem niggardly by comparison. Ruth was so taken aback by her stepmother's appearance – quite different from that of Mrs Longhill, though there was barely a month's difference in their pregnancies – that for a moment, staring at Hester, she saw nothing else.

'Hello, Ruth love!' her grandfather exclaimed. 'Come on, give us a kiss. Thou's a sight for sore eyes!'

Ruth turned to him at once, and was shocked to see with what difficulty he rose from his chair to greet her. And he was so thin. When he embraced her she felt the sharpness of his bones and the slightness of his body against hers.

'Oh Grandfather, it's grand to see you! It's been such a long time,' she said. 'Did you receive all my letters?'

'I did that, lass,' he answered. 'Maria read them to me, I think she got fed up wi' me wanting to hear 'em over and over again.'

'I should think he knows 'em by heart,' Hester said. 'Though I'm surprised you found time to write so much. I never did when I was in service. But then I suppose things are different with Miss Caroline.'

'I usually write last thing at night,' Ruth told her. Wearied to death, tired to the bone, she could have added.

Then Willie, hearing her voice, came running in from the yard. She'd been disappointed that he wasn't at the door to greet her, but that was forgotten as she lifted him up and held him close. He submitted to her kisses, but soon wriggled uncomfortably, and she put him down and held him at arm's length.

'You've grown,' she said. 'My word, how you've grown! And put on weight!' He had never looked so healthy.

'Good food and plenty of it,' Hester put in. 'He never goes short. I see to that, don't I, my lamb?'

Willie smiled at her. 'Yes, Mam,' he said.

So Hester was his mam now? Well, it was to be expected. He was only a little boy and he needed a mother. Ruth determined to be glad for his sake. And what about Maria? Was she Hester's girl now?

'Where *is* Maria?' she asked. 'I thought she'd be here.'

'I sent her to the butcher's for a bit of suet,' Hester said. 'I promised your dad a meat-and-tattie pie wi' a suet crust when he comes in from work. I daresay you won't say no to a plate of pie, will you? Or has fancy cooking spoiled your appetite for plain fare?'

'We don't have fancy food,' Ruth said. 'The vicar wouldn't allow it. But Mrs Peterson's teaching me to cook a few different things.'

Hester laughed. She had a loud laugh; not raucous, but ringing with enjoyment, filling the room.

'Well I never!' she cried. 'Did you hear that, Grandfather? Our Ruth's learning to cook!'

Ruth's first thought when Maria returned from the butcher's was to wonder how it was that in eight months everyone could have changed so much. Grandfather older, and so frail; Willie plump and taller; Maria - well, Maria was prettier than ever. Her breasts were beginning to develop, her waist was already fining down. The new cotton gown she wore, skilfully tucked and darted by Hester, emphasised the changing and delicate contours of her figure. She looked older than her fourteen years and was pleased when Ruth said so.

'Do I look different, then?' Ruth asked, curious.

Maria, head on one side, studied her sister carefully. 'You speak different, but I can't rightly say how.'

'She's more of a woman, that's what it is,' Hester said. 'Ruth's fifteen. Some girls get married at sixteen.'

'Not our Ruth,' Grandfather broke in sharply. 'There's plenty of time for that.'

'And who'd be good enough for thy Ruth, eh Grandfather?'

Though she smiled, Hester's tone was a bit too sharp for teasing. She turned the pastry she was mixing on to the baking board, rolled it into shape and draped it over the heaped-up meat and potatoes in the big oval dish.

'Perhaps she's already got her eye on someone! Is that it, Ruth?' she said.

Maria's face lit up. 'Oh Ruth, you haven't!'

'Of course I haven't!' Ruth was annoyed to feel her cheeks reddening, as if she was, in fact, guilty.

When her father came home from work Hester was just in front of Ruth to receive his embrace - which was no doubt right and proper, though not usual in Barnswick where couples, once married, no longer demonstrated their affection in public. But when it came to Ruth's own turn she had nothing to complain of in the warmth of her father's welcome. He held her tightly in his arms and she knew that he had missed her and was glad to see her again.

The pie was delicious. Mrs Peterson never made suet pastry and Ruth had almost forgotten how tasty it could be. Thick and succulent; crisp and golden on top, soft inside, absorbing the rich gravy. If this was a sample of Hester's cooking, no wonder the children thrived. Willie finished a large serving of pie, scraping his plate of every last morsel. Grandfather, however, ate little, not even finishing the small helping he had accepted.

'Come on Dad, eat up! You don't eat enough to keep a sparrow alive!' Ruth was sure her father meant the words kindly, but he spoke as if her grandfather was not a grown man but a child who had to be cajoled into doing what was good for him.

'He doesn't get any exercise, that's what it is,' Hester said brightly. 'How can he work up an appetite sitting in his chair all day? He should try to get out a bit, get some fresh air.'

'I daresay you're right, love,' William agreed. 'But it's not easy for him.'

They were talking *about* her grandfather, not *to* him, discussing him as if he were not there. But if it upset him he gave no sign. He sat and waited for the others to finish so that he could move back to the comparative ease of his armchair. Ruth noted the hollows beneath his cheekbones and the way the flesh sank in under his sharp jaw. His eyes seemed not to be focusing on anything and she felt that he had cut himself off, was no longer hearing what was being said.

'I'll side the table and wash up,' she offered.

'No need for that, Ruth,' Hester said quickly. 'After all, you're a visitor now.'

She did not mean it the wrong way, Ruth told herself. Surely she meant to be kind?

'Shall I put Willie to bed then?' Ruth asked later on.

'No need for that either,' Hester said. 'He's a big boy now. He puts himself to bed.' She turned to Willie. 'You go on up, my lamb. Mam'll come and tuck you in in a minute or two.'

For the rest of the evening they talked about small things. Hester was interested in Mrs Longhill's pregnancy and surprised that the other woman should be so sickly. 'It's nature, when all's said and done,' she remarked. 'A woman should be at her best.'

She smiled at her husband, brimful of confidence in her own state. He reached out and took her hand. 'You certainly are, lass,' he said proudly. 'Don't you think she looks bonny with it, Ruth?'

Ruth could not deny it.

Her father was a changed man, too; happier, less nervous, as if responsibilities had been lifted from him instead of added in the shape of a wife, and a child to come. Their pleasure in each other, his and Hester's, was so overt that to be for long in the same room with them seemed an intrusion.

'I think I'll go to bed,' Ruth said. 'I'm a bit tired.' Maria had been gone an hour, protesting at having to go before her sister. Hester, who was skilfully turning the collar of a shirt, stopped in the act of threading her needle.

'Yes . . . well . . .' she began.

Why was her stepmother suddenly nervous, Ruth wondered? She seemed to be searching for words, looking towards her husband for help.

'Hester thought it'd be more comfortable for you to sleep at Mrs Johnson's. She has a spare bed. There's not much room here, as you know. So we arranged. . . .'

The words rushed out of William as if he had learnt his part and now wished to be delivered of it as quickly as possible. 'She's looking forward to having you,' he concluded.

But there was the same room in the house as there had always been, Ruth thought. Until eighteen months ago she had slept all her life with her brother and sister, with the rest of the family secure under the same roof. All one family.

'As your dad says, we thought it'd be more comfortable for you.' Hester was her normal self again, brisk and cheerful, 'More what you're used to now,' she added.

Grandfather took Ruth's hand in his – she was standing beside his chair.

'Give me a goodnight kiss, love. Sleep well. And come round early in the morning. I'll be waiting to see thee.' He spoke calmly, as if for Ruth to sleep with a neighbour instead of in her own bed was entirely normal, though the grip of his hand on hers told her that he understood. She took her cue from him. In any case, it had all been decided. She kissed her grandfather and her father, bade Hester a civil goodnight, and went next door to Mrs Johnson's.

Mrs Johnson took Ruth upstairs to the immaculate little bedroom which had been cleaned within an inch of its life for her arrival.

'I've turned down the bed,' she said. 'Goodnight and God bless, then.'

When she had gone downstairs again Ruth undressed and got into bed. On the other side of the bedroom wall, only inches away, was the room which had always been hers. If she were to tap on the wall Maria or Willie might hear her and stir in their sleep. Yet now it seemed like another country, from which she had been exiled. She pressed her face into the pillow, wetting Mrs Johnson's best linen pillowcase with the tears she could no longer hold back. Finally, she fell asleep with her arms outstretched over the empty half of the wide bed.

By nine o'clock next morning the warmth of the sun was already drawing the scent from the gillyflowers at the front of her father's cottage. Not without difficulty, Ruth persuaded her grandfather to allow her to carry his chair to a warm spot just outside the door. She fetched the rug which he used on his sofa bed at night and wrapped it around his legs, tucking it in firmly at the sides so that he should not feel the vestige of a draught.

'Not that there is any draught today,' she observed. 'I've seldom known it so still.'

She sat down on the doorstep beside him. The step had been swilled clean earlier that morning by an unwilling Maria, and edged around with white scouring stone to give it an artistic finish.

'That's right,' Hester called out. 'You two sit there and have a nice talk! I'll get on wi' the work!'

The words, though pleasantly uttered, pricked like a fine-pointed needle. Ruth rose to her feet again.

'I'll gladly help you,' she offered. 'Perhaps you're the one who ought to be resting. Tell me what I can do.'

'Nothing at all,' Hester said firmly. 'I can manage quite well. You're all right where you are, both on you.'

Outside my living-room, did she mean? Out from under my feet?

'Sit down, Ruth love,' Grandfather said quietly. 'Leave her be. Hester is never happier than when she's turning the house inside out. One of these days she'll take a duster to me. No, we'll bide here while we get the chance.'

'You should get Hester to bring you outside more often,' Ruth said. 'In summer, I mean. Folk would pass the time of day with you. You'd feel less lonely.'

'Who said owt about being lonely?' he asked.

Was it better to acknowledge pain, or ignore it, pretend it didn't exist, Ruth asked herself. And should she respect his feelings by keeping quiet, or force him into talking about them? Her instinct was that since they saw each other so seldom, it was better to speak out.

'It stands to reason,' she said.

'There are plenty as wouldn't agree with you,' he replied. 'A man wi' a son, two grandchildren living in the same house, a daughter-in-law who looks well after his creature comforts. There's many a one would count that as riches.'

Thus he denied the loneliness which, every time she looked at him, Ruth saw in his face. She recognised it because she so often experienced the same thing. The number of people around you didn't matter, and in the last twenty-four hours she had also discovered that blood relationships might not be enough. It was whether you belonged in the spirit.

'But you haven't said that *you* do,' she persisted. 'Count it riches, I mean.'

He didn't answer at once. After a while he said, 'I've had my share of riches, love. Two wives I've been happy with. Five children, though three of them were taken early. When I was young, a cause I believed in. The trouble is, they all come together, not spread out evenly through life. Yes love, I've had my riches. Seen 'em come and go like a gambler's fortune. And you're still my treasure, Ruth.'

She wished with all her heart that she could pick him up and carry him away to some place where the two of them could live for the rest of his life. She ached with love for him, and sorrow that she could do nothing. If she were married and had a home of her own. . . . But she was not yet sixteen, and in any case she didn't want to get married. But one day, perhaps, for his sake. . . .

'If ever I do have my own home,' she said, 'you shall come and live with me. We'll have a garden and I'll build you a summerhouse where you can sit every day.' They smiled at each other, pretending it would all happen.

'Are you going to see thy Aunt Sarah?' her grandfather asked presently. 'She'd be pleased at that.'

'Yes. I thought I'd ask Maria to walk over with me. We'd set off early and go for the day.'

'Well, while you're at it,' Grandfather said, 'you could happen put some sense into Maria's head. It's stuffed full o' rubbish!'

'Rubbish?'

'She wants to go into service. Well there's nowt wrong wi' that and she can't stay at home forever. . . .'

'Then what do you mean?'

'She wants to go off to Leeds or Bradford. Wants to see life, as she puts it. But when all's said and done, she's a village lass. I worry about what could happen to her in a place like that.'

Ruth thought he was right to worry. Neither he nor she had ever been to Bradford (though it was considerably nearer than Singleton) but they had heard plenty of stories about it. It could be a dangerous place. What did the Methodist hymn say?

'On Bradford likewise look Thee down
Where Satan keeps his seat.
Come by Thy power, Lord, him dethrone
For Thou art very great.'

As for Leeds, that was infinitely worse. Leeds was Babylon.

Maria was more than willing to accompany Ruth to Aunt Sarah's, if only because it would free her from the household tasks which Hester insisted she carry out.

'She says that if I want to go into service, then I must know how things are done,' she grumbled. 'That way I'll rise sooner, she says.'

'Don't you want to rise?' Ruth asked her. They were walking across the moor.

'Of course I do. But not the way Hester means. She's talking about me being a parlourmaid, or even a cook. But I haven't the slightest intention of being a servant for one second longer than need be.' Her voice was rich with scorn. 'I'm agreeing in the first place because I want to get away from Barnswick. On the other hand. . . .' A thought suddenly struck her. '. . . I might consider being a lady's maid. A lady's maid goes everywhere, meets all kinds of people.'

'You might just meet other lady's maids,' Ruth pointed out. 'But if that's what you fancy why don't you ask Hester to teach you to sew?'

'I haven't told Hester. I've only just thought of it. Promise you won't tell!'

Ruth promised. She found Maria's aspirations amusing, but not serious.

'What would you really like to do most of all? If you could choose, I mean?' she asked.

'But I *shall* choose,' Maria said firmly. 'Perhaps not right away. But in the end I shall do exactly what pleases me.'

'But what *will* you choose,' Ruth persisted.

Maria thought for no longer than a second.

'I . . . shall . . . choose . . . I shall choose to be an actress!'

'An actress? But you can't! You don't know anything about it!' Ruth cried. 'No-one in our family has ever been an actress.'

'Then I'll be first,' Maria replied pertly. 'I'm pretty enough. You can't say I'm not pretty enough.'

No-one could say that. With her fair hair curling to her shoulders, her wide-set blue eyes and tilted nose, the rose-petal skin and the fine-boned figure that their mother had bequeathed her, Maria was undeniably pretty; and would one day be beautiful.

'And I daresay I can sing well enough,' she continued. 'If I get a job in Bradford I shall use part of my wages to take singing lessons.'

'Sing? You don't mean you'd appear on the music hall? You can't possibly mean that?'

'I might,' Maria said. 'What's wrong with the music hall?'

In spite of her mature appearance Maria was only thirteen, Ruth reminded herself. Her young sister couldn't be expected to know these things. And then she realised that neither did she. What exactly *was* wrong with the music hall as a profession she really didn't know; only that it was not a career to be followed by any decent woman.

But Maria prattled like the child she was, Ruth thought. There was no need to worry. On the other hand, in the near future she would be leaving home, possibly facing the temptations of Bradford.

'I shan't stay in Bradford or Leeds,' Maria continued, as if reading her sister's thoughts. 'I want to go everywhere. London – Paris – even America! Wouldn't you like to see the whole world, Ruth? Wouldn't you like to go to America?'

'Not a bit,' Ruth said firmly. 'I never even wanted to leave Barnswick.'

She looked around at the rough moorland, noticed a grouse rising from the heather, heard the plaintive 'pee-wit, pee-wit' of a lapwing, looked up at the sky with its white fluffy clouds propelled by the breeze which had sprung up again. She would never want to be far away from this. It must surely be the most beautiful place on earth – and it was her life's blood. But in her heart she already knew that the cottage in Barnswick was no longer her home.

The wind veered to the north and she shivered. 'Let's walk faster,' she said to Maria.

There had not been time to let Aunt Sarah know they were coming and when they presented themselves at the farmhouse Ruth had the feeling, just for a moment, that they were not welcome. When she opened the door to them her aunt's usually placid countenance was set in an anxious frown. For a second she stared at them without recognition, but then her face changed, breaking into a smile, and she greeted them with her usual warmth.

'Why Ruth! Maria! Come in, loves. This is a right surprise! Why didn't you let me know you were coming? I knew you were to be home on a visit, Ruth, and I hoped you might come. But you could have put a letter in the penny post.'

'I'm sorry, Aunt Sarah,' Ruth said. 'We didn't decide until yesterday. We thought we'd come while the weather was fine. Have we come at a bad time?'

'Why no, love. You're both as welcome as the spring.' Nevertheless Ruth noticed the hesitation in her aunt's voice, felt that her words were forced.

From the porch a door opened into the kitchen, which had been built with small windows to keep out the worst of the moorland weather, and was therefore dark. They were well into the room before Ruth noticed the girl standing at the sink. What struck her first was the brightness of her red, riotously curly hair. Until Aunt Sarah spoke the girl continued with her work at the sink – she was peeling potatoes – without looking up.

'This is Charlotte,' Aunt Sarah said. 'Charlotte Smith.

These are my brother William's girls, Ruth and Maria.'

When the girl turned her head to acknowledge them, Ruth noticed her green eyes and the freckles on her milk-white skin. Maria stared openly and Ruth prodded her sister between the shoulders to remind her of her manners. All the same, she herself was equally curious. Aunt Sarah offered no explanation as to why Charlotte was there. There were no neighbours near to the farm and it was unthinkable that Aunt Sarah had hired help in the house. They were too poor for that.

'I'll pour you both some milk and butter a teacake,' Aunt Sarah said. 'Then Maria can go and look at the new calf while you and me, Ruth, go into the parlour and you can give me all your news.'

That was odd for a start. The parlour was used only on the rarest occasions. Now Aunt Sarah rushed them through their milk and teacake and all but pushed Maria in the direction of the byre before ushering Ruth into the parlour. There they sat facing each other, in armchairs shrouded in covers, and on her aunt's face was the anxious look Ruth had seen on their arrival. She's changed too, Ruth thought. While her father had shed years over the last few months, his sister had begun to look old.

Aunt Sarah took a deep breath and leaned forward to speak.

'I thought it best Maria should be out of the way while I told you. She's nobbut little. When you get back home you can ask your father to say what he thinks is fit for her. But you're older, and sensible. . . .' She hesitated.

'What is it, Aunt Sarah?' Suddenly Ruth felt a dreadful weight of anxiety. 'What's wrong? You're not poorly, are you? Uncle Matthew's not poorly?'

'Poorly? Why should we be poorly?'

'You don't look well,' Ruth said.

Aunt Sarah nodded. 'That's worry,' she replied sharply. 'Nowt but worry. That's what children bring – not that you ever have, nor ever will, I hope. . . .'

Ruth waited for the unusual outburst to finish.

'That girl in the kitchen,' Aunt Sarah said at last.

'Charlotte? She's very pretty, isn't she. What's she here for?'

'Oh aye, she's pretty enough,' Aunt Sarah nodded. 'I daresay that's the top and bottom of it. As to why she's here – that's the whole point. She's here because Ernest is going to wed her. That's why she's here.'

Her voice trembled with anger. Ruth couldn't understand why. It had seemed to her that everyone (except herself) liked the thought of marriage.

'But Aunt Sarah, aren't you pleased?'

'Not in the circumstances. Our Ernest's gone and got the girl into trouble. Got her in the family way, the silly young fool. She's barely seventeen and she's got neither father nor mother. Her employer has turned her out, lock, stock and barrel, though the child's not due until November. So she has nowhere else to go. In any case, our Ernest'll have to wed her.'

Ruth felt cold and a bit sick. Her father and Hester, Miss Caroline and the vicar – and him a man of God, too. But they were all married. If you were married and you wanted children, then you had to do it. But not Cousin Ernest and the red-haired girl in the kitchen.

'Of course it's not the first time in the world and it won't be the last,' Aunt Sarah was saying. 'You think nowt about it in someone else's family but in your own it's different. At least wi' us. We're good Methodists. How shall we hold up our heads in chapel? Worst of all, how are we going to manage? This place doesn't bring in enough to feed an extra cat. There's no goodness in the land, you see, love. And it'll not stop at one bairn. Starting at seventeen she could have a dozen!'

'Is she nice, Charlotte? Do you like her?' It was all Ruth could think of to say.

'Oh she's pleasant enough. But as feckless as a new-born lamb!'

And frightened of Aunt Sarah, Ruth reckoned. She had not seen her aunt in this mood before and she was thankful not to be the cause of it.

'Though I blame Ernest as much as her,' Aunt Sarah conceded. 'It takes two to make a babby. Any road, love, there it is. I had to tell you afore Uncle Matthew and Ernest came in for their dinner. We'll not speak of it then.'

She rose, and led Ruth out of the parlour. 'I don't know what's to become of us, I'm sure,' she sighed.

It was indicative of her state of mind that she asked nothing about Ruth's affairs, or the welfare of the rest of the family. Ruth didn't look forward to meeting Ernest at dinnertime. She almost wished she and Maria had not come.

In fact, everything passed off reasonably well. Maria, Ruth learned afterwards, knew all about the affair almost as soon as she did. After viewing the new calf with some speed, she returned to the house where a few well-aimed questions soon had the story out of Charlotte.

'She's very pretty,' Maria said when they were walking home. 'I wish I had red hair. It's very striking. Dost think it would suit me better than my own, our Ruth? But of course I wouldn't like to have freckles.'

The news about Ernest caused scarcely a ripple at home, though Grandfather seemed more concerned than the others. Ruth was sure that none of them were aware of the poverty of the small farm. They saw Aunt Sarah and her family mostly on special occasions - weddings, Christmas, funerals - when everyday standards of living were put aside. But today, for instance, when her aunt had not expected visitors, the dinner had been meagre: thin soup and dry bread which had to be stretched to the limit to feed two extra mouths.

The rest of Ruth's stay in Barnswick passed uneventfully and all too quickly. Hester, though always with a smile, continued to treat her as a visitor, refusing all offers of help. When the time came for Ruth to leave she realised that however often in the future she returned to this house, she would not be coming home.

'When shall I see thee again, love?' her grandfather asked on the morning of her last day.

'I don't know,' Ruth confessed. 'It won't be this year. Perhaps not until the spring of next year.'

It seemed an eternity away. She had a cold feeling in her heart about what the intervening months might bring.

'But you think on what I said,' she reminded him. 'When I have my own home you shall come and live with me!'

But although she left Barnswick with a heavy heart, when she stepped down from the coach in Skipton and saw Dick Parker waiting there her spirits lightened. She had not given him a thought while she was in Barnswick but now, as she saw him walk towards her, she felt a surprising pleasure.

'Thou's in good time,' he said. 'I've not been waiting long.'

He didn't actually say he was pleased to see her but it was all there in his smile and in the warmth of his voice. Ruth had a new feeling of belonging, of arriving somewhere where she was no longer a stranger, but had a friend. He led her to where he had left the horse and cart, and helped her to climb up.

In one short week away from it she had forgotten how beautiful Wharfedale was; how splendid the fells were, today emerald green in the sunshine; how the river sparkled along the valley. When they left Buckden behind and turned into Nordale, Ruth wondered if one day she might perhaps learn to think of this place as home.

# 5

On a day early in July, looking out of the window, Ruth saw the postman wobbling along the road on his 'dandy horse'. He wobbled because the machine, with its large, narrow-rimmed wheels, was not suited to the rough surface, but since the Post Office had issued the contraption to its employees in rural areas he felt obliged to use it. Ruth had little hope that he was bringing anything for her since she seldom heard from her family, but after he had ridden away again Mrs Longhill summoned her to the morning-room and handed over a letter.

'Thank you kindly, ma'am' Ruth said. 'It's Maria's writing.'

'Well, aren't you going to open it?' Mrs Longhill asked pleasantly.

Ruth wanted to take the letter to her own room, to read it in private, but she knew that it was expected that she would peruse it in front of her mistress and always be ready, should the lady hold out a hand for it, to pass it over so that her mistress might see it for herself. Mrs Longhill, to do her justice, had never made this request, but it was the notion that she had the right which irritated Ruth. She resented the fact that every corner of her life must be open to her employers, though probably they saw it as responsibility for her welfare. Ruth saw it as an intrusion.

She opened the letter and began to read, though not aloud. When Mrs Longhill queried her with a look she said, 'Maria writes that my stepmother had her baby on the thirtieth of June. A bonny girl, weighing eight pounds at birth, and she is to be called "Pansy".'

Ruth paused, not wishing to divulge the contents of the rest of the letter, however trivial they might turn out to be. Fortunately Mrs Longhill was so diverted by the news of the birth, which served to turn her thoughts at once to her own state, that she forgot to be interested in anything else.

'I think perhaps I should have a cup of chocolate,' she mused. 'You know the vicar insists I keep up my strength.'

'I'll make it right away, ma'am,' Ruth said – and made her escape.

It was not permissible to go to her own room at that time of day, but luckily Mrs Peterson was not in the kitchen so Ruth sat down at once to read the rest of her letter. The mistress's chocolate could wait.

> '. . . and she is to be called "Pansy". Do you not think that an elegant name? Maria is so plain. Grandfather's chest is improved but the best news is that I have secured a position in the Manningham district of Bradford, which is a very nice district. My master is a wool merchant. Mam is making me new dresses, one for best as well as for work. I daresay Bradford is a very smart place. . . .'

So Maria had got her way. Well, Ruth didn't envy her. She had no desire for town life. If she no longer belonged at home with her family, then the vicarage was as good a place as any. She didn't want to be a servant all her life, but for the moment nothing else was possible. She looked forward to Mrs Longhill's baby and hoped that when it was born she might have a share, however small, in looking after it. As for Hester's child, she gave it no thought at all. It had no connection with her.

A few days before the vicarage baby was due Miss Prendergast, the monthly nurse, moved in.

'She'll keep us going all right,' Mrs Peterson said gloomily. 'I can tell that by the look of her. It'll be fetch this, fetch that, as if we were all slaves!'

She was proved right. When the time came, a hot night in August, Nurse Prendergast had both Mrs Peterson and Ruth hard at it, filling cans with hot water, supplying fresh bed linen, bowls of soup, infusions of the herbal tea which Nurse had brought with her and insisted her patient drank. At the end of it all, so far into the night that it was hardly worth going to bed, Mrs Longhill gave birth to a son. He was a tiny scrap, so frail that his father baptised him within the hour, giving him the names 'Benjamin Charles'. Because of her privileged position Mrs Peterson was called to be present at the baptism.

'He's weakly, that's a fact,' she told Ruth when she returned to the kitchen. 'But he's the spitten image of the vicar when he was born – and look at the master now. You wouldn't think he'd been a delicate baby, now would you?'

Ruth thought it inconceivable that the vicar had ever been a baby at all. As he was now – middle-aged, remote – she thought he must always have been.

In the end Mrs Peterson's optimism was justified. Though Nurse Prendergast was retained for a further six weeks, since Mrs Longhill herself made only a slow recovery, by the time she departed the baby appeared to be on the mend. But it was Mrs Longhill's own delicate state which gave Ruth an even better chance than she had hoped for. One day Mrs Longhill summoned her to the bedroom.

'The vicar,' she announced, sitting up in bed, eating her breakfast, 'will not hear of me caring for little Benjamin entirely by myself. He has ruled that I must have help. And knowing your fondness for children, we have decided that *you* shall be the one to assist me. Therefore I shall engage Dick Parker's young sister, Florrie, to help Mrs Peterson with some of the household tasks, so that you may devote as much of your time as possible to our child's welfare. Moreover – and I think you will be agreeably surprised by this – you are to be paid an extra pound a year in acknowledgement of your greater responsibilities. Now what do you say to that, Ruth?'

'I'm delighted, ma'am,' Ruth replied truthfully.

'But I must warn you,' Mrs Longhill went on, 'Florrie Parker is inexperienced. Also she will not be living in, so there will still be plenty for you to do in the house.'

Ruth was not daunted. She went about her new duties with a good will. When she watched the tiny baby in his cradle, observed the milky paleness of his skin, the transparency of his eyelids on the too-rare occasions when his dark-blue eyes were closed in sleep, and heard his cry, more feeble than a new-born lamb and as plaintive as a curlew, she felt a resurgence of spirit, called forth by a new challenge.

At the time she took over her nursery duties she had been in Nordale just over a year. Deliberately, since her visit home, she had tried to push Barnswick out of her thoughts, quickly absorbing herself in some task whenever a sharp memory of the cottage or the moors or the churchyard threatened her peace of mind. It was less easy to stifle her thoughts of Willie and her grandfather. The passage of time, as little Benjamin settled to his mother's milk, began to thrive and to take notice of his surroundings and to smile when she approached him, did nothing to subdue her longing for them.

Ruth's only news of Barnswick came by way of Maria's letters from Bradford. Her sister's employer generously gave her a day off from time to time for the purpose of visiting her family. Maria had taken to Bradford like a duck to water. Her letters were full of what the fashionable ladies of that city were wearing, of how she had re-trimmed her Sunday bonnet, of where she had been and was about to go. She seemed to be much in the company of a fellow servant named Daisy.

> 'Imagine,' she wrote. 'Daisy and I are to see *Vitorine the Orphan of Paris* at the Theatre Royal. It is for the first time in Bradford and will cost us sixpence each in the gallery. I am consumed with excitement at the prospect!'

But somewhere in the letter she would say 'Grandfather is well', 'Father is grown stouter' or 'Willie has got over his chill'. Ruth wrote regularly to her grandfather and could only hope that Hester read out her letters to him.

'I would have liked to have allowed you to visit your family this Christmas,' Mrs Longhill said to Ruth one day in December. 'But in the circumstances I am afraid there can be no question of it. Little Benjamin still needs great care, and naturally the vicar and I will be busy with all the hospitality which the season brings.'

'By which she means,' Mrs Peterson said later, 'that she and the vicar are to give a small musical party here.'

'When?' Ruth asked. 'Who will be invited?' She liked the sound of it. It would be extra hard work, but a bit of excitement to compensate.

'At the end of December. They're to invite suitable people from Nordale as well as from Buckden and Kettlewell, perhaps even Grassington. But Florrie can give you a hand. She can stay the night then and share your room.'

In the intervals between looking after Benjamin, Ruth helped Mrs Peterson to prepare the food: ham patties, mincemeat pies, spice cake, creamy Wensleydale cheese, as well as several fancy sweetmeats. She had found an unexpected enjoyment in cooking and was glad of the chance to do something different. It was even more interesting when, on the night itself, she was allowed to hand around the food in the interval between the musical items.

'I didn't know the vicar played the violin,' she remarked to Mrs Peterson.

'Always has, from a small child,' Mrs Peterson said proudly. 'He could have been a professional if the Lord hadn't called him otherwise. He'd have rivalled Paganini, I don't doubt!'

'She must be deaf as a post,' Florrie commented when the housekeeper was out of earshot. 'It sounded like our two cats fighting!'

Ruth giggled. 'I agree. But you'd better not let her hear you.'

Later, when the party was over and Ruth and Florrie were getting ready for bed, Florrie said, 'Mam says I can ask you to our house on New Year's Day. If the mistress'll let you have time off, that is. And I don't see why not. You've worked your fingers to the bone this last week or two.'

When asked, the following morning, Mrs Longhill acquiesced. 'You may have the half-day off for the New Year. If the weather holds good you may stay out until half-past nine o'clock. But if there is any sign of snow you are to return at once, no matter how early the hour. We could not do with you being snowed up to Buckden.'

'My word, but you're a lucky girl,' Mrs Peterson said when Ruth returned to the kitchen. 'It just shows what a truly Christian gentleman the vicar is.'

Ruth hoped that the night would remain fine so that she needn't leave the party early. She didn't in the least mind the three-mile walk from Buckden. If the clouds kept off there would be a moon, and in any case she would carry her lantern.

'You'll not need to worry,' Florrie told her as they made the beds together. 'Our Dick'll walk thee home, see if he don't.'

It was as well Mrs Peterson was not present to hear that, Ruth thought – not so much the words as the giggles and winks with which Florrie accompanied them. Being short of sixteen, though she knew she looked at least two years older, Ruth was not allowed followers. Not that she thought of Dick Parker as a follower. He was Florrie's brother and, she was happy to acknowledge, her friend. All the same she wondered whether Mrs Peterson had not marked his regularity, since the summer, at Sunday evensong – after which it was natural that he should sometimes speak to her in the churchyard. (Florrie did not come to work on Sundays.) But if she did notice, Ruth thought, she would almost certainly attribute Dick's improved attendance to the drawing power of the vicar's sermons. And his frequent presence in the vicarage kitchen on weekdays was put down to his fondness for his sister. Whenever his work allowed it he called at the end of the day to take Florrie home.

'He's a brother in a thousand, that one!' Mrs Peterson said with approval. Florrie pulled a face at Ruth behind the old woman's back.

So on New Year's Day, as soon as the midday meal had

been cleared, the two girls left the vicarage and walked down the dale. Ruth was surprised to see Dick waiting for them by the packhorse bridge.

'I thought you'd still be at work,' she said.

Dick smiled. 'It's a slack time. Mr Trench reckoned I could finish a bit early. Come lambing time he knows I'll have to make up for it. We'll be on the go day and night then. Lambs is mostly born at night.'

'You should have seen me and Ruth rush out of the house the minute we'd finished,' Florrie said. 'We were frightened Mrs Peterson would give us something else to do.'

'Have we come too soon?' Ruth asked. 'If so, I could give your mother a hand.'

'There's no need,' Dick replied. 'The kitchen's threng wi' women - and Florrie's just on her way there, aren't you, Florrie? You're a guest, Ruth. But you and me could climb the Pike if you've a mind to.'

Ruth looked across to the high fell which dominated the village beneath. The winter's afternoon already had an end-of-day feeling to it: a sharp nip in the air, a dulling of light which drew the green out of the fells and left them grey-black and menacing. She shivered, and pulled her cloak more closely around her.

'I don't fancy it,' she said. 'Besides, it'll be dark soon. I wouldn't like to be up there in the dark. We could lose our way.'

'Not me! I know it like the back of my hand, like I know every inch of this dale.' Dick failed to hide his disappointment at Ruth's refusal to climb the Pike.

'I'd like to another time,' she assured him. 'I really would. But not now. I'm perished.'

While Florrie ran ahead, Ruth walked with Dick to his parents' cottage, which was hidden away behind the inn, almost at the foot of the Pike. As they entered, Mrs Parker looked up from her task of laying the table. Dick clearly got his good looks from his mother. They both had the same warm smile, the same blue eyes which, without guile, seemed to be seeing more and further than could other people.

'Come and sit by the fire,' Mrs Parker invited. 'Tea won't be long.'

Thus Ruth was made welcome, but without fuss, as if it was natural and right that she should be there.

'I wanted us to climb the Pike,' Dick said. 'But Ruth wasn't having any.'

'I should think not, you daft ha'porth,' Mrs Parker replied briskly. 'She's got more sense.'

At the tea-table Ruth was seated next to Dick, and plied from all sides with delicious food. When the meal was over, and cleared away, Mr Parker took a concertina down from a shelf.

'Come on then,' he said. 'Let's have a bit of a sing-song.'

Dick looked at Ruth as if seeking her approval.

'That would be nice,' Ruth said.

They all joined in. Christmas carols first of all, and then the old songs everyone knew. In singing, Dick lost his self-consciousness. His pleasant baritone voice reminded Ruth of her father's and when, by request towards the end of the evening, he sang 'Drink to me only with thine eyes' the Parkers' living-room was for a moment blotted out and Ruth was back in Barnswick, on that evening almost three years ago now, after her mother's funeral. Looking back, though the facts were against it, she remembered that as a happy evening, a time when she had belonged.

And then the applause broke in on her thoughts. She raised her head and saw that Dick was looking at her intently. She felt confused, and was glad when Mrs Parker's firm, kind voice brought everything back to normal.

'Now Ruth, how about a bit of spice cake and a glass of ginger wine?' she was saying.

'I'm sorry,' Ruth shook her head. 'I really couldn't take another thing. Besides, I must be going. Mrs Longhill said nine-thirty sharp. But I've had a lovely time and I thank you kindly.'

'Well if you must go, you must,' Mrs Parker said. 'Our Dick'll walk you back.'

They walked mostly in silence. Dick seemed tongue-tied,

but Ruth was not sorry for that. She was too tired for conversation. She had risen at five that morning to get through her work by dinnertime.

The air was frosty now, the sky clear and star filled. The ewes, having been brought down from the high pastures, huddled together on the lower ground. Twice she heard a fox bark on the fells, and all the time, as they walked, the sound of the fast-flowing river accompanied them.

'I've never been out in the dale as late as this,' Ruth said. 'I like it.'

'It's grand,' Dick agreed. 'It's grand any time, summer or winter, day or night. All the same, I'm getting out.' Ruth stopped dead, turning to face him.

'Getting out? What do you mean? Why?'

She knew at once that she didn't want him to leave. Apart from Florrie, he was her only friend in the dale. She could no longer think of Mrs Longhill in that light.

'There's nothing doing here,' Dick said. 'A man can't make a good living in Nordale. He'll be a farmhand all his life, not able to support a wife and family in any sort of style.'

Ruth began to walk on again. 'Are you thinking of getting married, then?' she asked. She knew he was two-and-twenty but Florrie had said he was not the marrying kind, that he'd never looked twice at any girl in the dale.

He was a long time in answering. 'Not yet awhile,' he said at last. 'But one day I shall. And when the time comes I want to have something to offer.'

'But where will you go?' Ruth asked.

'Over to Wensleydale. Farming's better there. More varied. A man could likely get a job there, perhaps with a cottage; perhaps in time have his own bit of land. That's what I want, my own bit of land.'

'That's what my Uncle Matthew's got,' Ruth said. 'He doesn't actually own it. He pays rent. But he says he can't make a decent living off it.'

'He would in Wensleydale,' Dick spoke confidently. 'The land's in good heart over there.'

They had reached Singleton bridge. Dick put out his hand and touched her on the shoulder.

'Wait a bit here,' he said.

'I can't. I have to be in.' She could see the lamps lit in the vicarage and knew that they would be sitting up for her.

'Only a minute,' Dick persisted. 'It wants five minutes to half-past. I want to ask thee something.'

His hand still rested on her shoulder. Although his voice was as soft and quiet as ever, there was a note in it which excited her, so that she was tempted to stay.

'What is it then?' she asked.

'Will thee go out with me on thy next afternoon off? It'll be all above board. I'll ask leave of the vicar.'

'He'd never give it,' Ruth said.

'Well in that case we'd go without asking,' Dick declared boldly. 'I don't mean you no harm, Ruth. I'd like to show you Wensleydale. We'd walk up to the top of Nordale and over Fleet Moss. From there you can see where Wensleydale lies. You'd like that, wouldn't you?'

'I'll have to think about it,' Ruth said. 'I'll have to see.' It was suddenly impossible to commit herself to anything at all.

Without another word she left him and ran across the bridge towards the house. Before taking the path which led around to the kitchen door she turned, and saw Dick still standing on the bridge, watching her. He raised a hand and waved.

Mrs Peterson was sitting in the kitchen, her face flushed from the fire. 'In the nick of time, my girl,' she said. 'I'll be off to bed, then. You'd best get on and lay the breakfast table.'

Ruth took off her cloak. Since she would be up before anyone else in the morning, could she not risk leaving the table until then? But better not, in case she overslept. She was so tired.

Ten minutes later, already in her nightgown, she opened up her bedroom shutters and looked out, as she did every night before getting into bed. The night was bright enough for her to see the fells, and the outline of the trees by the river. Dick would be well down the dale by now. A fox barked again, the sound carrying in the clear air, and she wondered if Dick heard it too.

A new year, she thought. She always believed that each new year must be better than the last and that anything - by which she meant anything good - could happen. But now she felt in her bones that 1848 must be the best yet.

In its early stages the year looked like being a replica of the previous one. On the third of January the snow came; not with the fury of the previous winter, not drifting overmuch, but thick, and freezing hard where it fell, so that once again everything was at a standstill. For several days Florrie was marooned in Buckden and Dick had no excuse for visiting.

With Florrie's tasks now added to her own, Ruth had no time to think of anything except the job in hand. Only in bed at night, in the minute or two before sleep claimed her, did she sometimes think of the evening at the Parkers' house, the walk back through the dale, and Dick's request to take her out on her afternoon off. Well, the way things were going, goodness knew when that would be!

Then no sooner did the snow melt into the ground, swelling the river, than Mrs Peterson continued the year's repetitive pattern by succumbing once more to bronchitis. But like the snow, it came in a milder form than before.

'She says she was ever so poorly last winter,' Florrie remarked.

'So she was. Too poorly to be cantankerous. Now she's everlastingly wanting something. I'm sick of making beef tea and egg custards,' Ruth grumbled.

'She's always on at me to shake up her pillows,' Florrie said. 'I never get them right. Still, she's old - and tired.'

'I'm tired,' Ruth sighed. She was stirrring a nasty concoction of arrowroot in a pan over the fire and if she wasn't careful it was going to burn again. 'I wish just for once I could be ill. Nothing painful. Just so's I'd have to stay in bed. I wouldn't want waiting on hand and foot, neither. Just left to sleep and sleep!'

'It's wicked to wish to be poorly,' Florrie warned. 'You could be struck down.'

But she was not. Ruth's good health persisted through everything.

It was well into March, with Ruth's sixteenth birthday come and gone without recognition from anyone, before Mrs Peterson was up and about again. Ruth had had no time off at all, so she chose a moment when Mrs Peterson seemed in a good mood before she made her request.

'Do you reckon Mrs Longhill might allow me two or three days off so I could visit Barnswick?' she asked. 'I'm worried about my grandfather. He never does too well in the winter.'

'We don't, not at his age and mine,' Mrs Peterson agreed. 'I'll speak to the mistress in the morning.'

Ruth knew as soon as Mrs Peterson came back into the kitchen the next morning that it was no good. Yet at the same time there was an air of excitement about the housekeeper, a new gleam in her eye.

'The answer's "No", Ruth. And for why? Because – would you credit it – there's another one on the way! So what with little Benjie only seven months old – and now he'll have to be weaned – you can't be spared at all!'

'But it's not fair!' Ruth cried. 'It's not fair!'

Mrs Peterson held up a hand to silence her.

'Whoever said life was fair, my girl? However, the mistress has kindly said that you may have next Sunday afternoon off, from two o'clock on. Always providing, that is, that Florrie will come in and look after Benjie.'

Florrie was willing. When Dick called for her that afternoon she told him 'Ruth's having next Sunday afternoon off.'

'In that case,' Dick said quickly, 'we can have that walk you promised me, Ruth.'

They were out in the yard, feeding the hens, so he was able to speak freely.

'I didn't promise,' Ruth replied sulkily. She was sorely

disappointed by Mrs Longhill's refusal to let her go to Barnswick, and nothing else had the slightest appeal. But Dick stood before her, big and solid, cap in hand, barring her way and demanding an answer.

'I told thee I wasn't afraid to ask the vicar. It shall be all open and above board.'

'No,' Ruth said quickly. 'No, I don't want you to do that. All right then, I'll go with you, Dick, and thank you for asking me. But no-one is to know except Florrie here.'

'Not tell Mrs Peterson?' Florrie looked shocked. 'You can't mean not tell Mrs Peterson?'

'I can and I do. It's only to be between the three of us, otherwise I won't go.'

She couldn't explain, even to herself, why it must be so. It was unlikely that the vicar would refuse since he had a high opinion of Dick. The truth was, she supposed, that she wanted one small corner of her life to be her own, her actions neither permitted nor forbidden.

'If that's how you want it,' Dick said.

'It is. We'll arrange a meeting place. Not too close.'

After a week of rain Sunday was mercifully fine, though there was a sneaky wind blowing and the sunshine was fitful, now illuminating the green dale, now withdrawing petulantly behind banked-up clouds. At five minutes past two o'clock Ruth crossed the bridge and took the path northwards. Had the vicar, exhausted from his sermon and the heavy luncheon which followed it, not been having a well-earned nap in his study, had not Mrs Longhill been well into her afternoon rest in bed, they might from their side of the house have seen Dick Parker take the same path fifteen minutes earlier. He was waiting, as arranged, where the next narrow bridge spanned the river. He doffed his cap as Ruth approached.

'Good afternoon,' he said formally. 'I'm glad thou could come.'

They wasted no time, but began to walk. From that point the dale narrowed, steeper on both sides and rising in front of them as they walked towards its head. There were fewer trees here, and no livestock save for a few sheep grazing on the fellside. The river cut deep into the ground, rushing over rocks and boulders, as if impatient to get away from its source. It was too early in the year and too cold for flowers but Ruth found a patch of surprisingly late snowdrops.

'If you look carefully where it's sunny you might find celandines,' Dick said. 'It's not too soon.'

They passed through two hamlets with strange-sounding names. 'They do say the Norsemen were in this dale a long time ago,' Dick explained. 'I daresay it's not changed much since then.'

When they had left the last hamlet behind, the way was steeper than ever; now dipping, now climbing, but always rising. January's snow still lay in the folds of the hills. They had turned east and were now nearing the summit. It seemed to Ruth that they were on the very top of the world, as she envisaged it from the globe in the vicar's study.

'The last lap,' Dick said, raising his voice against the wind. 'Now close thy eyes,' he commanded. 'I want to lead thee up this last bit. Don't open them until I say so!'

Breathless, Ruth nodded agreement. Dick took her arm, holding her in a firm grip as he guided her over the remaining yards of rough ground to the top of the hill.

'Now,' he said.

She opened her eyes. A long way below – she felt as if she was standing on the edge of a precipice – Ruth saw a wide land stretching to hills on the far horizon. There were broad, green meadows, with sheep and cattle grazing; ploughed fields, farms, grey stone villages. Everything was brilliant in a new burst of sunshine.

'That's it!' Dick told her. 'That's Wensleydale!'

There was an immense pride in his voice, as if he had created the scene himself.

'You make it seem like the promised land,' Ruth said.

She was smiling, but he was suddenly serious.

'It *is* my promised land. A man could make his way there. Dost think it could be thy promised land, Ruth? I'd be good to thee, work for thee, look after thee always.'

I should have expected this, Ruth thought. But she hadn't. She remained silent, not knowing how to answer.

'I'm sorry,' Dick said. 'I've put it badly. I've thought and thought how to say it. I even consulted a book about it. "Nature is the best tutor" it said - so I spoke what was in my heart. I'm sorry if it's not come out right, Ruth.'

He stood there stiffly, twisting his cap in his strong hands, his eyes looking anxiously into hers. He would be kind and faithful. She would have a place of her own to do with as she liked. They could have Grandfather to live with them - she was sure Dick would agree.

She looked down again at the spreading dale. *Was* it her promised land? It was hard to know. She felt herself rootless, with no idea of where she ought to be. She had hardly begun to live and there was nothing to tell her which way her life should go.

'I don't know what to say,' she confessed. 'You shouldn't have asked me. We only came out for a walk.'

Dick took both her hands in his. His grip was firm and strong. She liked the feel of it.

'Leave it be then,' he said gently. 'I didn't mean to rush thee. But now you know how I feel, Ruth - what I have in my mind. I shan't change - though happen you will - and in my favour.'

'I don't know,' Ruth said. 'I'm confused. Promise not to speak of it again and then we can go on being friends.'

'I can't promise, Ruth,' he shook his head. 'It's asking too much. But I'll try to be patient.'

On the way back they separated at the bridge where they had met. Ruth ran ahead, reaching the church in the nick of time for evensong. The fact that it was her half-day off did not exempt her from church attendance. She slipped into the pew beside Mrs Peterson as the vicar was beseeching as many as were here present - which was not many - to accompany him to the throne of the Heavenly Grace.

'Almighty and most merciful Father,' she confessed

breathlessly, 'we have erred and strayed from Thy ways like lost sheep. . . .'

From that weekend the weather remained good, sun and rain appearing at the right times and in the right quantities.

'The lambing's gone well this year,' Mrs Peterson remarked. 'Yonder low meadows are thick with ewes and lambs. It reminds me of home.'

'The lambs must be nigh on ready for market,' Ruth said. 'And the hay's doing well. If the weather holds there might be a second crop, come September.' She now knew enough of farming matters to realise what a difference that would make to next winter's feed.

Dick came less often now to the vicarage, being fully occupied on Trench's farm. Since the day when they had walked over Fleet Moss Ruth had thought often of his proposal, though he had not mentioned it again. There were times when, at everyone's beck and call, Benjamin crying, Mrs Longhill demanding this and that, Mrs Peterson nagging for more help with the cooking, its acceptance offered her an escape which it seemed madness not to take. At other times, when the demands were not so great or she had more strength to meet them, she experienced a freedom of spirit which refused to be tied down to anything.

She had met Dick secretly once or twice since that Sunday and, ostensibly at Florrie's invitation, she had visited his home in Buckden. She liked Dick. She wanted to love him. But more and more often there was that inner voice which told her that Dick Parker was not the one, insisting that in some other place her fate was waiting for her. But what other place? What other person? She couldn't imagine that. On the face of it her life seemed bounded by Nordale.

She had still not been given time off to visit Barnswick and she determined to ask Mrs Longhill once again, this time face to face. But once again – though pleasantly – the request was refused.

'You must see that with the baby due in October, and with my health as delicate as it is,' Mrs Longhill said, 'the vicar would not hear of such a thing. I would not like him to know that you had even considered it. I need you here to look after Benjamin. You can imagine, can you not, how he would miss his Ruth?'

She could. She knew that Benjie's love for her was almost as great as hers for him. He was her anchor in this house. She had transferred to him the affection she had once had for his mother and he was also, she supposed, the recipient of the love she would have liked to have showered upon Willie.

'It's just that my grandfather is old . . .' Ruth tried to explain.

'I realise that,' Mrs Longhill interrupted. 'I often worry about my own dear father. The vicar and I are not unmindful of the circumstances and, in fact, we had thought that after the baby is born, and before the montly nurse leaves, we might be able to allow you a visit home. You see how we have your welfare at heart!'

That would mean October. Hester's second child was due in November – so Maria had written. Ruth felt she was destined to visit Barnswick just before the birth of Hester's babies. She had not yet seen the first one, who was now a year old.

In mid-September the grass stood high again in the river meadow. Another week's sun and it would be ready to harvest. Ruth had a mind, if she could get any time at all, to help in the hayfields. Perhaps Mrs Longhill might let her take Benjamin and he could sit on the edge of the field with some of the village children. He would enjoy that. For now, she had spread a rug on the lawn and he was amusing himself crawling to the edge of it and being scooped up and brought back again.

As she sat there she saw the postman riding towards the vicarage. Perhaps there would be a letter from Maria? She was pleased, therefore, when a few minutes later she was summoned to the parlour. She picked up Benjamin and carried him with her. Mrs Peterson was with the mistress and she took the child from Ruth and went out with him.

'I have news for you,' Mrs Longhill said. She was looking pale this morning. Ruth held out her hand for the letter.

'The letter is for me,' Mrs Longhill spoke quietly. 'It is from my father. I am sorry, Ruth, but the news is bad. . . .'

'Grandfather!' Ruth cried.

In that second all that she had promised him – a place in her own home, comfort, security, happiness – and would now never fulfil, rushed into her mind.

'Not your grandfather, Ruth,' Mrs Longhill said. 'Your father, I am afraid. There was a fire at the mill. He did not get out in time. And now your stepmother is in danger of losing her child. You are to return home at once. My father says you are greatly needed. The vicar will make arrangements for your travel.'

She had more to say, but Ruth did not hear it. For the first time in her life she had fainted.

# 6

It was a pity, Ruth thought, that her very first journey on the railway – though the line had been open from Skipton for a year now – should be on such a sad errand. She sat in the corner of the carriage, trying to focus on the passing scene, but over the green valley of the River Aire images of her father were superimposed: her father in all his moods; laughing, sad, angry, tired – all the ways she had ever known him. Each image of him remained until the fierce red and orange flames licked around it, consumed it; and then the next one arose out of the ashes.

She was dimly aware of her fellow passengers: a pompous man with a plump little wife; a young woman with a child. She heard their giggles, their cries of excitement and apprehension as the train gathered speed. Snatches of conversation came through to her.

'We're doing all of twenty miles an hour! Could be more!'

'Isn't that rather dangerous, Henry?'

'It's progress, my dear. Progress!'

'Well I think they ought to have windows in the second-class carriages. I'm covered in smuts!' That was the young lady.

Afterwards, whenever Ruth recalled that journey, she heard their voices clearly. To her the speed only meant that she would reach home more quickly. In spite of her fear of what lay ahead, she longed to be with her loved ones.

The train slowed down and stopped. The husband consulted his watch.

'Shipley!' he said. 'Dead on time!'

Ruth climbed down to the platform, left the station, and set off to walk the three miles to Barnswick. She reached the river, low after the dry summer, and crossed by the stepping stones. On the far bank the long climb over the rough road began. Cows grazed along the verge and an occasional cart passed, its ironclad wheels sending up dust. She walked quickly, sometimes breaking into a run, desperate to reach home.

When she came to the cottage the street door was open. She stopped, drew a deep breath, felt her heart thumping with apprehension. When she went in from the bright sunshine the house seemed darker than ever and at first she thought there must be no-one at home. Then she saw her grandfather, slumped in his chair, almost lost in the gloom. She thought he was sleeping and she stood for a moment quietly, so as not to waken him. Stepping closer she saw that his eyes were open, but unfocused, staring at nothing. He had neither seen nor heard her.

She was deeply shocked by his appearance. He looked so old, so small and thin. His clothes hung on him, and his hair – of which he had always been so proud – was matted and untidy. Ruth felt a sudden urge to pick him up and hold him to her like a child. She wanted to comfort him as he had so often comforted her.

'Grandfather, it's me,' she whispered. 'Ruth!'

Recognition dawned slowly in his eyes, as if he was being dragged back from some far place which he has unwilling to leave. And then suddenly he recognised her, and held out his arms, and they were locked in a fierce embrace.

'It's good to see you, Grandfather.'

'And thee, lass. Thou's like a light i' the darkness!'

When he let her go he said: 'All the same, Ruth love, I wish it were thy father thou were embracing instead of me. The Lord knows I could have been spared better nor him. Why should I live, and him not?'

'Where is Father now?' Ruth asked.

'He's upstairs in the children's bedroom. You can't see him, love. You wouldn't want to. He were . . . he were so badly burned that they fastened up the coffin as soon as they put him in.'

Consumed in the red and yellow flames, Ruth thought. But not, at least in this world, to rise out of the ashes. Was it possible that in another world he would? She found it hard to believe.

'Did you see him, Grandfather?' she asked.

'Aye. He were my son, weren't he?'

'How did it happen?'

He hesitated. 'Nobody knows how the fire started. But wool's greasy stuff. Once it takes hold there's no stopping it. You could see the flames and smell the smoke all the way from Barnswick. Your dad were working on his own, you see, making repairs to the looms at night so as not to hold up the day shift. They got there as quickly as they could, but it were too late. When they found him he was near the entrance, as if he was trying to make his way out. But a beam collapsed in front of him. . . .'

He was interrupted by a moan from the room overhead.

'Hester!' Ruth exclaimed. Since coming into the house she had not given her stepmother a thought.

Enoch shook his head.

'Poor lass! She's likely i' labour and she's middling bad. The baby weren't due until November.'

'I'll go to her,' Ruth said. 'Has the doctor been?'

'He came this morning. There's nowt to be done. We must bide our time, that's all. Mrs Thornton's looking after her. She's slipped home for a minute, but she'll be back.'

Mrs Thornton was Barnswick's unofficial midwife. She had brought Willie, Maria and Ruth into the world.

At the top of the narrow stairs Ruth paused for a moment outside the room where once she used to sleep, and where her father now lay in his coffin. Then she lifted the door latch and went in, and stood there beside the shiny wooden box. It looked too small to contain him.

Her father had enjoyed life so much. More than anyone she had ever met, he knew the value of everyday pleasures: his family, his friends, his singing, his tankard at the Shoulder of Mutton, even his work. It was impossible to think of him as dead. She looked at the metal plate on the coffin. 'William Appleby. 1809 to 1848.' Thirty-nine years old.

And then there was a sharp cry from the next room and Ruth ran at once to Hester.

She had never been able to feel any friendship for her stepmother, though she was aware that for the short time she had been married to him, Hester had made William happier than most men. And she had been good to Maria and Willie. Yet everything Hester has done, Ruth thought, from her arrival on the scene in that first year of Father's loneliness, has served to change *my* life. She could not accept the fact that it was her mother's death, not Hester's coming, which had wrought the change.

But when she went into the bedroom, saw Hester gripped by pain, her usual ruddy skin a dreadful grey, her thick dark hair dank with sweat, Ruth was, for the first time, stirred by pity. She leaned over the bed and took her stepmother's hand, cold and clammy, in her warm one.

'I'm sorry to see you like this,' she said. 'What can I do for you? Could you take a cup of tea? Perhaps with a teaspoon of brandy in it? I could run across to the Shoulder for some.'

'Nowt,' Hester whispered. 'I don't want owt. When's the doctor coming again?'

'I don't know,' Ruth said. 'Would you like me to fetch him?'

But Hester had closed her eyes, was no longer listening. Ruth had never seen anyone look so desperately ill. Her breathing was quick and shallow and there was a dark area of skin around her dry lips. Should she call the doctor again, Ruth wondered? Or fetch Mrs Thornton? *She* would know what to do. Hester seemed now to have fallen asleep, or into unconsciousness – Ruth wished she knew which. She tiptoed out of the bedroom and went downstairs, and was relieved to see Mrs Thornton coming into the house.

'Hester's very ill, isn't she?' Ruth asked.

Mrs Thornton shook her head sadly.

'She's bad, and that's a fact. If it has to be a choice we must hope we lose the bairn. Better that than the mother. *If* we have a choice.'

'But perhaps neither?' Ruth pleaded. If Hester were to die she felt it would be a judgement on herself. 'I'm sure you'll save them both, you and the doctor between you!'

'We'll have to see,' Mrs Thornton's tone of voice offered no encouragement.

When the midwife had gone upstairs Ruth made a pot of tea. Tea was expensive, and from now on would be even more of a luxury in this house, with no man's wage coming in, but at the moment they needed it. She took a cup to Mrs Thornton, and an extra one in case Hester could be persuaded to take a sip, and then she sat down beside her grandfather and they drank in silence. There was nothing else to be done. Everything in the house was spotless. Neither Ruth nor her grandfather wanted to eat. All that was left was to wait.

'Where's our Willie?' Ruth asked presently.

'He's at Mrs Mercer's wi' little Pansy. She took 'em both right away and they're to stay wi' her. Folks have been very kind. Your father were well thought of, Ruth.'

'Perhaps I'll go down and see them,' Ruth said. 'There's not much I can do here. Shall you be all right?'

'Of course I shall,' Enoch replied. 'Willie'll be pleased to see thee.'

There were two children sitting on Mrs Mercer's doorstep and inside the house, which smelled of urine and dirt, were another half-dozen or so. The youngest was in Mrs Mercer's arms, suckling noisily at her large, blue-veined breast. The fruitful Mrs Mercer was one of Mrs Thornton's most regular clients. A smile of welcome widened her face when she saw Ruth in the doorway.

'Eeh, come in love!' she cried. 'Willie, look who's here!'

Willie dropped a wooden animal with which he was playing and ran to meet Ruth. She lifted him into her arms and held him close, feeling the warmth of his body.

'My word, but you're a big lad,' she said. 'Nearly too heavy for me to hold now!'

'Have you brought me a present?' he demanded.

'No. But I'll buy you one in Barnswick,' she promised.

Ruth wondered if her little brother comprehended their father's death, and for the first time she asked herself what was to happen to him if Hester did not survive. In all except blood Hester was now his real mother. Who would care for him – and for her grandfather? He wriggled in her arms and she put him down, and looked around for Pansy.

There was no need to ask which of the several children she was. The small girl, tottering unsteadily from chair to chair around the room, was so like her father that Ruth almost cried out at the sight of her. It was not only her colouring and features which so favoured him, but the whole, happy character which shone out of her bright eyes and creased her round face into a smile.

'Yes,' Mrs Mercer said. 'Thy dad'll never be dead while this one lives! And she's a grand little lass, never a minute's trouble.'

As if she knew they were talking about her, the child smiled directly at Ruth then dropped on all fours and crawled rapidly towards her. Ruth picked her up and held her. It was impossible not to be taken by her.

'There, Pansy love,' Mrs Mercer said. 'Ruth's your big sister!'

'She's not,' Willie protested. 'She's *my* sister!'

After a while Ruth left them, promising Willie that on the next day she would take him to the shop, where he could choose a present for himself.

'I'd offer to stop and help you to put the children to bed,' she told Mrs Mercer, 'but I think I should get back to Hester.'

'Think nowt about it, Ruth love,' Mrs Mercer said. 'I'll have 'em all i' bed in no time!'

So she would, Ruth thought. Probably unwashed and sticky, but curling up like puppies, gaining warmth and comfort from each other.

When she returned to the house, Maria had arrived.

'Mr Singer sent me all the way from Bradford in his

carriage,' she said. 'He wouldn't hear of me coming by train in case I might have to walk from Shipley. He is the most considerate of men.'

Maria was smartly dressed, already in black, which suited her fairness. She was so confident in her bearing that Ruth found it difficult to think of her as younger than herself. She had a worldliness which Ruth feared she herself would never possess. Not even her sorrow at her father's death – and that was genuine enough – could quite subdue Maria's spirit. She brought a liveliness into the sad house which, momentarily at least, cheered even their grandfather.

Somehow the evening passed. There was no change in Hester's condition. The doctor called again and was no more optimistic. At a little before eleven o'clock Mrs Thornton came downstairs.

'There's nowt you two can do here,' she said. 'Best be getting to bed and let Mrs Johnson do likewise.' They were to sleep in the neighbour's spare room. 'If so be as I need either on thee, I'll knock on the wall.'

Ruth felt it a comfort to have Maria near. Sharing a bed was like returning, for a brief spell, to happier times. When they snuffed the candle they lay in the dark, talking; keeping their voices low so as not to disturb Mrs Johnson, whose snores came to them loud and rhythmic from the next room.

'I shall *never* have a baby!' Maria declared. 'Never ever. It's so *unrefined*!'

'You'll change your mind,' Ruth said.

'I shan't. You'll see I shan't. Not ever.'

Next morning, the day of their father's funeral, both girls slept late.

'I'm sorry, Mrs Johnson. You should have wakened us,' Ruth said.

'No use in waking to sorrow afore need be,' Mrs Johnson replied. 'And don't think you're going without breakfast because you're not. You'll need all your strength today. I always make a point of eating well afore a funeral.'

Nevertheless, Ruth slipped home before breakfast to see what had happened in the night.

'Nothing,' Mrs Thornton said. 'But it's my opinion the baby's bound to come today – though what the outcome will be God alone knows – and he's keeping his own counsel!'

Grandfather looked tired and ill. Ruth felt sure that while she and Maria had slept so soundly, he had lain awake.

'Sarah'll be here afore long,' he said.

'Is Ernest bringing Charlotte and the baby?' Ruth asked.

'I don't know,' Grandfather replied. 'I hope so. He's my first great-grandchild, you know – and I haven't seen him yet. He's named after me.'

The thought seemed to enliven him, so Ruth was pleased, when Cousin Ernest arrived with his parents, to see Charlotte and the baby with them.

Enoch held out his arms to the child and Charlotte, though seeming reluctant, handed him over.

'Why, he's the very image of William as a baby!' Enoch exclaimed.

In fact, little Enoch was the double of Charlotte, with her green eyes and abundant red hair, but Ruth was glad that no-one contradicted her grandfather.

William Appleby was buried in the same grave as his first wife, where Hester would also lie when her time came; and who knew how soon that might be? Ruth's grief was harsher by far than at her mother's death, now almost four years ago. Perhaps it was because then there had been a purposeful future for her. She had been needed. Now only Grandfather needed her, and there was nothing she could do for him.

With Hester so ill there was no question of a meal after the funeral and only Aunt Sarah and her family returned to the house with Maria and Ruth.

The house was bustling with activity, Mrs Thornton and the doctor both in attendance, Enoch pent-up by his physical helplessness; for in the short time they had been away Hester had given birth to a daughter. It transpired later that the child must have given its first cry at the precise moment of William Appleby's interment.

'The Lord gives and the Lord takes away,' Uncle Matthew said.

Ruth gave him a sharp look.

'Then the Lord doesn't show much sense in who he chooses!' she cried angrily. 'A new baby can't replace my father!'

There was a shocked silence at her outburst. It was broken by the doctor, speaking in a normal voice, though he looked at Ruth with some concern.

'The baby's well. Small, but strong. I think she'll do. As for Mrs Appleby, well, we shall have to see. She's lost a lot of blood. But with careful nursing. . . .'

'Which I'll see she gets,' Mrs Thornton promised. 'No need to fret about that, Doctor.'

'Let her sleep as much as she can,' the doctor said. 'Sleep is Nature's healer.'

'We'll make a bit of a meal afore we ride back.' Aunt Sarah stood up. 'You can help me, Ruth love.'

'I'll help,' Charlotte offered.

'No need,' Aunt Sarah replied. 'You look after the bairn.'

It was not the words, but her brusque manner which brought a flush to Charlotte's cheeks. Ruth, calmer now, wondered just how bad things were between the two women.

'Why don't you and Maria take little Enoch a walk up the moor road?' she suggested. 'Give him some fresh air.'

When they were gone, Ruth turned to helping her aunt. 'He's a lovely baby, little Enoch,' she said.

'Oh, he's that all right,' her aunt agreed. 'And the double of our Ernest when he were little.'

Ruth opened her mouth to protest, but thought better of it. She was always saying the wrong thing. But for sheer blind prejudice she found that hard to beat. She still had to learn that all relatives claim the young of the family as favouring their own side, unless there are blatant faults, in which case they can readily be attributed to the other side.

'He's got a bit of a paddy, though! He gets that from his

mother,' Aunt Sarah said. 'Anyway, he'll soon be off walking, I shouldn't wonder, though he is only ten months old.'

But once they had stopped talking about her grandson, Sarah Appleby lapsed into silence; an uncomfortable silence, nothing companionable in it; nothing to do with shared grief. In the end Ruth spoke out.

'Is anything wrong, Aunt Sarah? Are you not well?'

'I'm well enough. Tired. And not getting any younger. And William's death has hit hard. . . .' She hesitated.

'What else?'

'Well . . . the farm's not doing much. We've had losses with the sheep we can't afford and nothing seems to come out of the ground. And now there's five mouths to feed and five bodies to clothe. It won't run to it. That's the top and bottom of it. It won't run to it!'

'Will Ernest and Charlotte ever have their own home?' Ruth asked.

Her aunt sighed. 'I don't see any chance of it. Our Ernest can't get another job. Farming's all he knows and there aren't many jobs going. He talks of emigrating. Talks about it all the time.'

'Emigrating? He can't be serious!'

It sounded totally unlike Ernest. He had always seemed rooted in the moorland farm. Was it Charlotte's idea, then? Was this the root of the trouble?

'Oh he's serious all right! Everlastingly reading pamphlets and suchlike. He even went to a meeting.'

It all sounded impossible.

'Would . . . would you and Uncle Matthew go with them?' Ruth forced herself to ask the question. If the answer was to be 'yes', how could she bear it? Not her beloved aunt, who was more to her, much more, than a mother?

'No, we're too old for that. Too set in our ways. I doubt if your Uncle Matthew could stand the crossing. Ten weeks in a ship! No, if they go, they go alone.'

And take your heart with them, Ruth thought. But even the sight of her aunt's bleak face could not keep back the relief which flooded through her own heart. If it came to pass, she vowed, she would do everything she could to comfort her aunt and uncle. She would try to be a true daughter to them.

'Any road,' Aunt Sarah said briskly, changing the subject. 'The food's ready. As soon as the others come back we'd best set to and eat. We have to get back. And I heard Maria say she was going back to Bradford today. What about thee?'

'Tomorrow morning, if all goes well. But what if Hester. . . .'

'Hester'll be all right,' Aunt Sarah said. 'When I went up to see her she was sleeping peaceful. Mrs Thornton'll see to Hester until she's on her feet again.'

'And after that?'

'Who knows? She's not the first to be left, nor she won't be the last, poor soul. If her needle doesn't keep her then Parish Relief'll have to.'

'And Grandfather?' Ruth asked.

'He'll have to go on Parish Relief, I'm sorry to say. I can't do owt for him, much as I'd like to. Nor can you.'

Perhaps I could send him part of my wages, Ruth thought, but they were meagre to begin with, and would what she could contribute be as much as Parish Relief, or would he be better off with that? It would all have to be sorted out.

During the meal Ernest started to talk about emigration. He was bursting with enthusiasm; it was clearly his hobby-horse.

'But how would you afford it?' Ruth asked. 'And what would you do in America?'

'I'd farm.' He was all eagerness, his voice strong, his eyes shining. 'In America there's land for the asking. Good land, i' good heart. A man can live well, providing he works hard. As for how I'd afford it, I'd join an emigrants' society. They help you to get there, make a start.'

'How?' Her uncle and aunt were silent – Ruth supposed they had heard it all before – but she was curious. She had never seen Ernest so eager about anything. Charlotte's face also was lit with enthusiasm but she left the talking to Ernest.

'You pay a shilling a week – that's for an average family of five. When there's enough money in the kitty they draw lots for the next families to sail. Everyone goes on paying until all the families in the society are out there. It might take five or six years for some but the lucky ones will go nearer the beginning.'

'It includes a plot for a house, and some land,' Charlotte broke in, unable to contain herself. 'Everyone helps everyone else to begin with, and then you get your own land to cultivate.'

Ernest turned to his grandfather.

'What do you think of it, Grandfather?' he enquired.

'You're asking an old man,' Grandfather said. 'It's a young man's dream. If I were a young man now . . . but the young must make their own dreams come true.'

Aunt Sarah turned on him sharply. 'Father! Don't encourage him. He's daft enough as it is!'

'And don't thee *discourage* him, lass,' Grandfather replied. 'It's his life. Let him be his own master. In the end you'll not keep anybody by holding them back. Not that you could hold him back if he had a mind to go.'

'It's nonsense, that's what it is!' Aunt Sarah was shouting now and Uncle Matthew took hold of her arm to restrain her.

'Remember the lass upstairs,' he said. 'We don't want to waken her.'

'Supposing he fails!' Aunt Sarah cried. 'What then, in a strange land?'

'Well,' Grandfather smiled, 'I do believe as how ships cross the sea i' both directions. He could come home again.'

'But we wouldn't fail, Ma,' Ernest said. 'We're young and strong. Things would be better for us in America. Why, I daresay in no time at all I could be sending a bit of money home to you!'

'I don't want your money!' Aunt Sarah said fiercely.

'*I* would like to go to America,' Maria remarked suddenly. 'Perhaps I could go with you?'

Everyone except Aunt Sarah laughed at that, more than

the remark merited, so as to break the tension.

'Well, we'd best be getting home to Burley Woodhead afore making plans for travelling farther,' Uncle Matthew said.

'And now I suppose I must return to Bradford,' Maria sighed, when the others had left. She assumed the languid voice of a woman to whom travel was so commonplace as to be boring.

'Promise me you'll visit Barnswick whenever you can!' Ruth pleaded. 'You know I can't. And promise you'll write to me more often.'

'Of course I will,' Maria said.

But Ruth was not sure that her sister would keep either of those promises.

Afterwards, when she thought about it, it seemed to Ruth that they had all talked only about the future. There had been nothing of her father and their past lives with him; no memories, as there had been at her mother's funeral. It was as if the sudden horror, and the manner of his death, had sealed their lips.

When Ruth left next morning it seemed certain that, in Mrs Thornton's capable hands, Hester would recover. The baby, who was to be called 'Rose' because it had been her father's favourite flower, had begun to take nourishment and would almost certainly thrive. Willie, playing with the wooden cart Ruth had bought him, scarcely noticed her going, but bidding farewell to her grandfather was anguish to both of them. Parting from him had always been the worst moment of leaving Barnswick, even when her father had been alive to care for him. Now it was hardly to be endured. For his sake she tried to hide her feelings, but it was impossible.

'I can't bear it,' she cried. 'Why did it have to happen? What harm did Father do to anyone? Why did God take my mother? Why couldn't we all be happy together, like other families?'

'Questions!' Enoch said. 'Them's questions only the Almighty can answer.'

Although he was gently chiding, Ruth saw the tears in his own eyes.

'Then why doesn't he?' she demanded. 'I've been good. I've told the truth. I've said my prayers. And you've been the best man in the world. Why does God punish us?'

'Remember the scriptures, Ruth,' he said. 'Blessed are they that mourn, for they shall be comforted. The Lord chasteneth whom he loveth.'

'Then he must love us very much,' she cried bitterly. 'I must say, it doesn't feel like it!'

His goodness and simple faith was more than she could bear. She knelt beside him, burying her head in his lap, sobbing. She felt as if her heart would break into pieces. He let her cry, saying nothing except to repeat her name as he bent over her, but she felt his tears fall on her neck.

Presently she rose to her feet. The time had come.

'I'll write often,' she told him. 'Hester can read my letters to you. Perhaps she'll even write a reply.'

'I wish I'd learned to read and write,' he said. 'It would have changed my life.'

'I've missed thee, Ruth,' Dick Parker said when he met her at the railway station.

'I've only been away three days.'

'I know,' he said. 'It seems longer.'

It did to Ruth, too. She felt herself a different person now, years older. It seemed to her that every time she went to Barnswick life deteriorated a little more.

She sat up on the front of the cart with Dick, the old horse slowly pulling them up the lower part of the dale between Skipton and Grassington, and tears of sorrow, self-pity and a desolate loneliness ran down her face. With part of her she tried not to let Dick see that she was crying, but with another part, which was stronger, she wanted him to know her misery. And hearing her sob, he did so. He drove the horse on to a grass verge and tied it fast to a gate.

'He needs a rest after the hill,' he said. 'Let's leave him be while you and me sit in the field.'

The hay had been cut, perhaps earlier the same day. It was dry and sun-warmed and smelled fragrantly of the various grasses of which it was composed. Dick gathered armfuls of it near to the edge of the field and piled it against the shelter of the limestone wall, and they sat down in the sun. He took her hand.

'I'm not much wi' words,' he said. 'But I'm sorry, Ruth. I wish I could comfort thee.'

His words, and his gentle touch, were all she needed to set the tears flowing again. After the leave-taking from her grandfather she had thought there were no tears left in her, but now her whole body shook with sobs again, all the misery in her pouring out. She felt Dick's arm around her, and then when he drew her towards him she buried her face against his shoulder.

When she had calmed down a little he put a finger under her chin, and raised her head and kissed her; gently at first, his lips brushing her tears; then fiercely, his mouth open, his tongue parting her lips. Then they were lying on the ground and the masculine scent of his body was stronger than the smell of hay in her nostrils, and his hands were undoing her bodice and exploring her breasts. He bent his head and took her nipple gently in his teeth. She felt a spasm of pain and delight, a totally new and wonderful experience.

She arched her body against his. She was magically alive with longing, searching, and she did not know what for. But when he lifted her skirts and came between her legs she knew that she had found it. And when it was over, when she had been seared by the sharp but welcome pain, and baptised in his fountain, she knew at once that here in her own body was the answer to loneliness. She knew that she had discovered a solace which would never fail her. She could scarcely recognise, so different was it from her sparse explanation, that this was what Aunt Sarah had talked to her about. In connection with her aunt, of course – and even more with the Reverend Charles Longhill – it was still ridiculous, if not impossible.

They lay still for a little while, not speaking, their fingers lightly touching.

'I'm sorry, Ruth,' Dick said at last.

'Don't be,' Ruth replied. 'I'm not.'

'But if owt should happen. . . .'

'Happen?'

'You know. You *do* know, don't you?'

She supposed she did, but her mind was still full of the ecstasy of those moments. Remorse might come – if nothing worse – but she was not ready for it yet.

After a few minutes Dick said: 'I've got something to tell thee, Ruth.'

'What is it?' She was sleepy now. She pulled handfuls of hay into a pillow beneath her head, and closed her eyes.

'I've got a job in Wensleydale, starting October. Only a farmhand to begin with, like now. And I'll have to live in the farmhouse for a bit. But I'll do better soon enough. Happen by this time next year there'll be a cottage for me.'

'But you'll be leaving Wharfedale!' Ruth cried, wide awake now. She felt that she had only just found him, could not bear to let him go.

'I'll see thee as often as I can. We can meet on Fleet Moss. Thou'll not forget me, Ruth?'

'No,' she promised. 'I'll never forget you.'

'And you know I want us to marry. I'll not press for an answer now, it'd not be fair. But I reckon we're suited, you and me. Promise me you'll think on it.'

'I promise.'

Then she lay down again and pulled him on top of her, and he began to kiss her again. The sun dipped in the sky so that the stone wall cast a long shadow, cooling the stubble. The forgotten horse whinnied close by. With the setting sun the evening insects whirred and whined and jumped into activity.

'We'd best be going,' Dick said presently.

# 7

From the very first moment of her return to the vicarage Ruth was caught up in a whirlwind of work. When she walked in at the back door Mrs Peterson said: 'You're back then. Well, put on your apron. You're just in time to make a bit of pastry against tomorrow.'

Ruth supposed it was Mrs Peterson's way of taking her mind off the sad events of last week. But she would be surprised, Ruth thought – astounded, horrified – if she knew what other thoughts raced in her young servant's mind, if she could catch a glimpse of the vivid memories of what had happened with Dick Parker. Ruth went about her tasks in a dream, but her preoccupied state was naturally attributed to grief.

'Only two weeks now to the mistress's confinement,' Mrs Peterson reminded her. 'Tomorrow we start to clean through the house, top to bottom. So it's up with the lark, my girl!' She spoke as if Ruth had been away on holiday and must therefore have abounding strength and energy.

'Florrie will be worse than useless,' Mrs Peterson continued. 'She's given her notice to leave, taken a living-in job in Skipton. She's no longer interested in what's to be done here.'

That turned out to be true. Florrie played around, taking twice as long to complete every task. She was full of talk about her new post. 'It'll be a sight more lively than here,' she said. 'There's plenty going on i' Skipton.'

'There's enough going on here right now,' Ruth told her sharply. 'I'd be glad of a bit of help if you'd condescend to give it.'

Florrie looked at Ruth in surprise. 'Hark at you! You have come back in a funny mood. What's got into you?'

'Oh nothing much,' Ruth retorted. 'Only that my father's dead, my stepmother's ill, and I'm worried sick about my grandfather! Nothing at all, really!'

She could hardly tell Florrie that, most of all, her mind was on Dick. He had already gone to his new job in Wensleydale, with a promise to return on his first free Sunday.

Ruth's conscience was troubled over Dick: not because of what they had done together – that had been wonderful and whenever she thought about it her body ached, her breasts tingled with longing to experience it again – but because she now knew, had known it from the day after he had brought her home, that he was not the man she wanted to marry. It was strange that a sexual union which left nothing to be desired should so clarify the state of her mind.

And still, and yet, she might marry him. She had not totally dismissed the idea. Married to Dick, she would be able to give her grandfather a home, would be free to renew that wonderful sexual experience as often as she wished, and, of course, to have children. Unlike Maria, Ruth had no limit in her mind as to the number of children she would eventually bear.

It shocked her that she could make such a cool analysis of the situation. That alone told her that she was far from being in love with Dick. But she would be fair. When the time came for decisions she would not deceive him. If she agreed to marry him she would offer him what she could – affection, duty, loyalty – and he could decide whether it was enough.

'Hard work drives trouble away,' Mrs Peterson said, hearing Ruth's exchange with Florrie. She had a fund of such sayings, but this time she was proved maddeningly right.

By the time the monthly nurse was installed once again, and Mrs Longhill was delivered of her second child – a daughter, to be named Prudence – Ruth had almost ceased to think or dream about anything. Getting through the day, with her bed at the end of it the only goal, absorbed all her energies.

A day or two after the baby's birth, with Mrs Longhill lying-in and the nurse making more work than the rest of the household put together, Florrie left.

'We've no sign of anyone to take her place,' Mrs Peterson said. 'She chose to go at a very inconvenient time, I must say.'

They were to have a full-time, living-in servant, who would share Ruth's bedroom, a prospect which did not please her.

'It seems there are no servants to be had in the country,' Mrs Peterson grumbled. 'I can't understand it. And the vicar such a considerate man to work for.'

Fortunately the new baby thrived. She took the breast well and slept at night without the drops of laudanum with which the nurse had dosed the infant Benjamin when he could not sleep. Benjamin, who had been walking for a month, found himself less welcome in his mother's room and followed Ruth around the house like a pet lamb. She loved him more than ever.

Ruth herself thrived too. In spite of all the hard work she began to put on a little weight. 'You're getting quite mature in the figure,' Mrs Peterson remarked. 'Your bust is filling out nicely!'

If it occurred to Ruth – and how could it possibly occur to Mrs Peterson – that there might be a good reason for this, she dismissed it from her mind at once. It was true that she had missed a period, but that could mean anything or nothing. She was never very regular. She was not sick in the mornings and when occasionally nausea swept over her it was easily put down to fatigue, or to something she had eaten. Her mind refused to believe that anything could happen the first time one had intercourse.

'Well,' Mrs Peterson said, coming into the kitchen one morning a few days after the monthly nurse had left, 'you'll be pleased to hear that the mistress has found a new servant at last. But she has no experience so I don't know how she'll make out.'

Ellen Hardcastle turned out to be a fourteen-year-old wisp of a girl with mousy hair and pale blue eyes. She came from 'over the hill', from the higher part of Littondale, and she was as silent as her native dale. She missed her family badly. Getting ready for bed the first night she said, 'I'm glad I'm sharing your room, Ruth. I've never slept on my own afore.'

Ruth hadn't the heart to tell her that she wasn't welcome in it. In fact she was as quiet as a mouse and Ruth hardly knew she was there. Later on she had good reason to be thankful that she was.

With two babies in the house Ruth had thought, as Christmas approached, that there would not be much entertaining. She was wrong. Early in December Mrs Longhill actually came into the kitchen to discuss with Mrs Peterson the refreshments for a party she and the vicar intended to give.

'We must remember our position in society,' she said firmly. 'The fact that we have now been blessed with two little ones must not blind us to our obligations, nor cause us to lower our standards.'

She spoke, Ruth thought, as if she were the mistress of a large establishment in London instead of a country vicar's wife in a remote Yorkshire dale. But marriage had completely changed Miss Caroline. There was nothing left of the friendship they had known in Barnswick. They were simply mistress and servant now.

'What she means,' Ruth said pertly when Mrs Longhill had left the kitchen, 'is that her servants must keep up the standards!' She looked at the three of them: an old woman, herself not yet seventeen, and a raw child of fourteen.

'Now then, miss!' Mrs Peterson reprimanded. 'Remember your place!'

But throughout December it was they who slaved away – or at least Ruth and Ellen did. Apart from being disinclined for work, Mrs Peterson was showing her age more than ever and was not capable of sustained effort.

'I'm handing the puddings over to you this Christmas, Ruth,' she said. 'By rights they should have been made on Stir-up Sunday, only I was too busy. Perhaps we should say the collect anyway?'

So Ruth made the rich mixture and in turn the three of them stirred it, reciting meanwhile the collect for the Sunday before Advent. 'Stir up we beseech Thee, O Lord, the wills of Thy faithful people; that they, plenteously bringing forth the fruits of good works, may of Thee be plenteously rewarded.' Ruth added her own silent prayer that the puddings would be eatable.

Since her father's death she had written regularly to her grandfather, but there had been no word in reply from Hester. She had also written to Maria, reminding her of her promise, begging for news, but when Maria at last replied the news was all of herself, nothing of Barnswick.

> 'To my infinite regret,' she wrote, in the flowery style she now affected, 'I have been quite unable to visit my childhood home. There are so many diversions here that the time flies by on wings. I have recently been to a performance of Mr Handel's *Messiah* and, would you believe it, the Second West Yorkshire Yeomanry is to hold a Regimental Ball in the New Year, in the Exchange Buildings!'

On and on she went, never telling Ruth what she wanted to know. Her only real news at this time came from Mrs Longhill. 'My father tells me in his latest letter that Hester and the baby are doing well,' she informed Ruth.

'And Grandfather?'

'He does not mention your grandfather.'

Afterwards, Ruth could not remember that she had done anything unusual on the twenty-third of December. She and Ellen between them had turned out the dining-room, giving it extra spit and polish because of Christmas. When they went to bed that night Ellen, as usual, was asleep within minutes but Ruth, though deadly tired, was curiously wakeful; not quite feeling herself but not able to put a finger on what was wrong.

She fell asleep at last, but in no time at all the pain in her back wakened her again; insistent, demanding. Even before she had come to, it rapidly circled her belly with a sharpness which made her cry out – and waken Ellen.

'What's the matter?' Ellen sat up in bed, rubbing her eyes with her knuckles like a sleepy child.

'I don't know,' Ruth said. 'Something I ate. The meat pie, I daresay.'

'Will I get you anything?' Ellen asked drowsily.

'No. Go back to sleep.'

The pain had left as suddenly as it had come, except for a small reminder in her back. But before Ruth could settle down to sleep again it returned, only this time much sharper, as if it would split her body in two. Against her will, she cried out with the agony of it.

'I must fetch Mrs Peterson,' Ellen said. 'I must fetch her at once!'

Ruth made no protest. She was afraid of this savage pain, which was unlike anything she had ever known.

Mrs Peterson came, and gave her a concoction.

'Ground ginger in hot water,' she told Ruth. 'Nothing to beat it for shifting the wind!'

But nothing eased the pain. It engulfed her in successive waves, each one stronger than the last, and then it was one long pain, tearing at her guts. When she sat on the chamber-pot to try to relieve it, the blood came.

'Fetch Mrs Longhill!'

Ruth heard Mrs Peterson's voice from a long way off. The pain demanded her total concentration now.

'I shall die!' she gasped. 'I'm going to die!'

'I think we must send for Dr Baxter,' Mrs Longhill said hurriedly. 'I will waken the vicar.'

Neither Mrs Longhill nor Mrs Peterson understood what was wrong with Ruth and it was not until half-past five next morning, when the doctor at last arrived, that a name was put to it. He had been urgently summoned by the sexton, whom the vicar had sent off on horseback, and he was annoyed at being dragged from his bed in Kettlewell, so early on Christmas Eve; especially as by the time he arrived it was all over. By then, drenched in sweat, and exhausted, all Ruth wanted was to sleep.

The doctor was brusque in his analysis.

'A miscarriage. There's nothing I can do. One way or another she brought it on herself. I daresay she's been drinking some concoction of raspberry leaves and penny-royal. It's what these servant girls do to bring it on.'

Mrs Longhill looked from Ruth to the doctor, her eyes wide with horror, her face drained of colour. She swayed on her feet and the doctor put out a hand to steady her.

'Dear lady, don't distress yourself so! She's not the first servant to get herself into trouble and she won't be the last. I sometimes think they get too much free time!'

'A miscarriage? Are you *certain*, Doctor?'

'Of course I am, Mrs Longhill. You didn't know the girl was pregnant?'

'Never,' she whispered. 'Never!'

He crossed to the basin. Mrs Peterson poured water from the ewer and he washed his hands.

'Well, there it is. I suppose it's as well she lost it. There are enough bastards in the world.'

Bitter anger gave Ruth the strength to speak.

'I suppose because I'm a servant, I suppose because I'm not married, me and my baby don't count for anything? Well he does to me, and I'll thank you not to call him a bastard!' Her voice sounded strange to her; weak and croaking, but at the same time filled with a passion she had not known she felt. She hated this man.

'That will do, Ruth!' Mrs Longhill said sharply. 'I will not countenance you being rude to Dr Baxter.'

The week which followed was amongst the most lonely of Ruth's life. Hardly anyone came near her and she was not told what was to happen. With the vicar's views on hellfire she was sure she would not go unpunished, that he would feel obliged to deputise for God. Though it was clear that Mrs Longhill could hardly bear to talk to her, her mistress felt it her duty to ask certain questions.

'Who is the father?' she demanded.

Ruth said nothing. She had not decided whether or not to tell Dick, but if he were to be told it would be by her, not by the Longhills.

'How *could* it happen?' Mrs Longhill cried. 'How could it happen *here*? I have cared for you as if you were my own family!'

'It didn't happen here.'

'Ah! So it was while you were in Barnswick?' Mrs Longhill clutched at the idea. 'And your father newly in his grave . . . perhaps not even in his grave!'

It was clear to Ruth that she had plumbed the depths of depravity. It had not seemed like that at the time. But if Mrs Longhill felt better that her servant had fallen from grace in distant Barnswick, then let her think it. It would keep Dick out of the picture.

During the whole of Christmas Day Ruth lay on her back in bed. In the morning she heard people coming to church, and she wondered about Dick. He would have Christmas Day off and he would surely call at the vicarage on some pretext or other. What would they tell him?

After morning service, when the last of the footsteps, and voices exchanging greetings, had died away, she heard the vicar ride off, the clip-clop of the horse's hooves as clear as a bell on the cold air. He would be taking Christmas communion to the sick. She should have known better than to think he would bring it to her, miserable sinner that she was.

For her Christmas dinner Ellen brought her a bowl of oatmeal gruel. She never did discover how the puddings turned out.

'There were a young man at the door after church,' Ellen said. 'He brought Christmas greetings from himself and his sister, who used to work here. He was ever so sorry not to see you but he wished you a merry Christmas.'

'What did Mrs Peterson tell him was the matter with me?' Ruth asked.

'She said you had a chill on the kidneys and you'd be in bed for a few days yet. He said he had to go back to work tomorrow. I can't stop,' she added nervously. 'Mrs Peterson says I mustn't talk to thee.'

Mrs Peterson came in to see Ruth just the once.

'How could you do this to the vicar?' she demanded. 'And at a season like this, too, with all his extra services and obligations!'

Ruth was tempted to tell her that at the time she had not had the vicar in mind, but since Mrs Peterson had not come to bring her any comfort, she simply turned her face to the wall. The housekeeper left the room, muttering about ingratitude.

On the thirtieth of December the doctor called again and pronounced Ruth fit to get up. Though she felt weak, it was good to be dressed again. She was ready to go downstairs to the kitchen when Ellen came into the room.

'Mrs Peterson says you're to stay in your room until you're sent for,' she said nervously.

'Why?' Ruth asked.

'I don't know, Ruth. It's what I've been told to say.'

As Ellen scurried out of the room like a frightened mouse, Ruth sat down again. She had a strange, dull feeling in the pit of her stomach. What was happening now?

She did not have long to wait. Fifteen minutes later Ellen returned, looking more scared than ever.

'You're to go at once to the vicar's study,' she announced. 'Oh Ruth, throw yourself on his mercy! He *must* forgive you!'

'I don't need the vicar's forgiveness,' Ruth said coldly. 'He's not God, even if he thinks he is.'

'Oh Ruth, please don't talk that way!' Ellen implored, her eyes filling with tears.

When Ruth entered the study the vicar was sitting at his desk; a large mahogany desk with a green leather top, which Ruth polished with loving care every Wednesday. It was the piece she liked best in the whole house. He did not raise his head as she came into the room, and not once in the short interview which followed did he look at her. Instead he fixed his eyes on his hands, which were clasped together on the desk, studying them as if the words he must say were written on his bony fingers. He unclasped them just long enough to push a small packet across the desk towards Ruth.

'Here are your wages in full,' he said. 'At my wife's generous insistence I have not deducted one penny for the week you have spent in bed under our roof, being nursed back to health by the kindness of your mistress's heart.'

Ruth took a step forward and picked up the packet. Her instinct, almost irresistible, was to throw it at him, but she was fast learning that there were impulses which a person in her position could not afford to follow.

'I need hardly tell you,' he continued in his dry voice, 'what a blow you dealt to she who cared so much for your welfare. You have wantonly and cruelly deceived her. You will now pack your belongings and be ready to leave the house within the half-hour.'

His voice was smooth, cold; nothing of hellfire in it. Ruth thought she would have preferred it if he had shouted at her.

'You mean I'm dismissed?' she asked stupidly.

'Naturally! You do not suppose that I could continue to employ you in a house where I have the welfare and character of two innocent children in my charge? Even Mrs Longhill, generous though she is, would not agree to that. Nor can you hope for a reference. What could I say of you?'

'You could say that I had worked my fingers to the bone for you!' Ruth cried out. 'That I have cared for your son and loved him as if he were my own.'

'I will thank you not to speak of my son,' he said evenly. 'And now – and again because of my wife's insistence, because of her concern for your health – I have hired a conveyance to take you to the railway station at Skipton.'

'Then may I bid farewell to Mrs Longhill?' Ruth asked.

'No,' he replied. 'She realises that such a move would be too upsetting for her. You will go to your room now, and when you have packed you will wait there until the conveyance arrives.'

When he had finished speaking he sat there silently, his head bowed, waiting for her to leave.

She could not move. The shock of his words had so drained what little strength she had that for a moment she was powerless to take even one step.

'That is all,' the vicar said.

And then a swift, burning anger, such as she had never known in all her life, welled up inside her, rose like bile in her throat. It came to her aid, bringing her all the strength she needed. She took one step forward and picked up the paperweight from the vicar's desk – a large pebble upon which Mrs Longhill had painted wild flowers as a birthday present for her husband. She raised her arm and flung it hard at him, not caring where it hit him, wanting only to hurt him as the whole world had hurt her; wanting to see his cold, impassive face break with ordinary human emotion.

He had no time to move. Her action was so swift that he was hardly aware of it until the stone struck him full in the face. Blood poured from his nose, splashing in large crimson blots on the sheaf of white paper in front of him. But Ruth did not care. She did not care if he bled to death in front of her. She was too angry to be frightened.

'But that isn't all I have to say!' she screamed. 'You are a devil! You aren't a man, you're a devil! You have no love, no charity, no compassion in you. I hope God punishes you as you've punished me!'

In the middle of her outbursts, she noticed that the paperweight had fallen on to the desk, badly marking the surface. For a split second she felt sorry about that.

Then she tore from the room. She was dimly aware of Mrs Longhill running in but she brushed past her and flew upstairs to her bedroom. Anger gave her the strength to pack her few belongings and by the time Ellen – red-eyed and in tears – came to say that the conveyance was at the door, there was no sign left that Ruth had ever inhabited the room.

For the last few minutes before Ellen appeared, Ruth stood by the window, looking down the dale. Her passion had cooled now. She felt weak, and without hope. But not repentant, not one bit repentant.

It was a sunless day, the clouds low, obscuring the tops of the hills and threatening rain. The dale had weather to match every mood, Ruth thought. In the two years or more that she had been in Nordale she had almost come to think of it as home. Now it was unlikely that she would ever see it again.

For most of the journey to Barnswick Ruth deliberately tried to think of nothing, to let her mind go blank. But thoughts pushed their way in. What should she do? Where could she go? Would Dick, even if she wished it, still want to marry her? And what about Grandfather?

Need she tell Grandfather the truth – it would break his heart. Could she not say that it had been her own choice to leave the Longhills, that they were not suited to one another? But sooner or later Mrs Longhill must write to her father and he would feel obliged to speak to Ruth's family. Ruth thought he might be kinder than his son-in-law, but it was not something he would take lightly. Perhaps Mrs Longhill had already written during the days Ruth had been confined to bed. Since the railways had come the post travelled more quickly, and it was possible that her grandfather already knew everything. And Hester of course. At this very moment they might be expecting her arrival.

When Ruth went into the house Hester was sitting on an upright chair by the table, peeling potatoes. Pansy was playing on the rug in front of a small fire and Willie sat surrounded by his toy animals. The baby slept peacefully in its cradle. Ruth saw at once that her grandfather was not in the room, but she took it for granted that by some miracle he had improved enough to get upstairs and was resting in bed. It was a stupid thought, but no other explanation occurred to her. Hester looked startled by Ruth's appearance, and jumped to her feet.

'What are you doing here? What do you want?' she demanded.

Ruth stared at her. It was reasonable that Hester should be surprised, but her attitude was definitely hostile.

'I came home . . . for a visit,' she temporised. 'Is Grandfather asleep? Can I waken him?'

Hester stared at her without speaking.

'What is it?' Ruth asked quickly. 'There's something wrong, isn't there? Is he ill?'

'He's gone,' Hester said. 'Where did you think he was? Hiding under the table?'

'Gone!' Ruth shrieked the word at her. The baby wakened and started to cry. 'Gone! Why didn't you let me know he was ill? Why didn't you send for me?'

She was beside herself, shouting at the top of her voice for the second time that day. Willie screamed.

'I said he's gone,' Hester shouted back. 'I didn't say he was dead, did I? Stop yelling at me, miss!'

Ruth felt dizzy with relief. She was still weak from her miscarriage and the journey had been trying. She must try not to take things the wrong way.

'I'm sorry. You startled me. I misunderstood.'

He had gone to Aunt Sarah's, of course. They had fetched him for Christmas and he was staying on for the New Year. Ruth heartily wished that he could stay there for good.

'You mean he's gone to Aunt Sarah's?' she said more calmly. 'I wish I'd known. I'd have gone straight there.' She was too tired now to walk over the moor but she would set off first thing in the morning. She knew she wasn't welcome in Hester's house but Mrs Johnson would give her a bed for the night.

'He's not at thy Aunt Sarah's neither,' Hester replied.

Fear gripped Ruth again.

'Then where is he? What are you keeping from me?'

'He's gone to Dudley House,' Hester said reluctantly.

Everything that the day had contained came together in Ruth's head. She thought, for a moment, that she must go mad. Then she skirted the table, gripped her stepmother by the shoulders, and began to shake her as if she was no more than a rag doll.

'Dudley House!' she shrieked. 'You sent my grandfather to Dudley House? How dare you do such a thing?'

Dudley House was the workhouse. It was reputedly neither fit for man nor beast; 'reputedly' because few people who went in there ever came out to tell the tale. The dread of one day being an inmate darkened the life of every poor person for miles around.

She continued to shake her stepmother, screaming in her rage. Shock alone, since the older woman was physically far more powerful, rendered Hester helpless in the girl's grip. She could do nothing except cry out.

'Stop, Ruth!' Willie cried. 'Go away! Stop hurting my mam!'

It was Willie's words which brought Ruth to her senses. She let go of Hester and Willie ran to his stepmother, flinging his arms around her. Once out of Ruth's grasp, Hester recovered quickly.

'I dare all right,' she retorted, her voice shaking with anger. 'Because there's nowt here to *keep* him on. If it weren't for the bit I earn I daresay me and my bairns would be in Dudley House an' all. *And* your Willie. It's my toil as keeps us, and it won't stretch to your grandfather.'

'Why couldn't he go on Parish Relief?' Ruth demanded.

'Because he's got nowt to begin with. If you have a little bit, then they make it up wi' Parish Relief. If you have nowt - then it's the workhouse. It's as simple as that.'

'Why didn't you tell me?' Ruth persisted.

'Could you have given him a home?'

'I could have sent him some of my wages.'

'Well you didn't, did you?' Hester replied. 'I don't recall that you sent owt. Anyway, it weren't only money. He needed a lot doing for him. Sitting there, day in, day out, hardly able to get off his backside. I've got plenty on wi'out him. Three children and no husband.'

'Why didn't you tell Aunt Sarah?' Ruth asked. 'Surely she'd have had him?'

'Thy Aunt Sarah's badly,' Hester said. 'They didn't come over at Christmas because she's i' bed wi' bronchitis. No use to bother her. No, Dudley House is the proper place for such as your grandfather. They get fed and looked after, don't they? What more do you want?'

'Fed and looked after?' Ruth cried. 'Are you mad? Up at half-past five every morning, winter and summer. Chopping wood, sawing logs, binding firewood. As for food – do you call a bowl of thin pea soup food? Do you? But he shan't stay! Make no mistake about it, he shan't stay!'

On the very next day she would get her grandfather out of Dudley House. Of that she was certain. What they would do, how they would manage, she had no idea. She had the few pounds from her wages (and thank heaven she had not thrown it back in the vicar's face). That would keep them, perhaps, in some cheap lodging-house until she could decide what was to be done. She was young and strong. There must be something.

'When did he go?' she asked Hester.

'Day after Christmas they took him. He's been there five days now. I daresay he'll have settled down, gotten used to it.'

'He doesn't have to settle down,' Ruth said. 'I shall have him out tomorrow.' With that she turned and went out.

Mrs Johnson was as kind as ever and willingly agreed to give her a bed for the night.

'I saw him go,' she said. 'It were a cold day. He looked perished. But you mustn't be too hard on Hester. She's had a bad time and no mistake.' But Ruth was in no mood to make allowances for Hester.

It was surprising, she thought, that Mrs Johnson didn't ask her what she was doing in Barnswick. Ruth had decided to say she'd been unwell, and had been given a few days off to recover her strength. Indeed, except that she was deadly tired, she had herself almost forgotten the reason for her homecoming in the more important matter of her grandfather's plight.

Ruth left Barnswick next morning. Dudley House was just

outside the village of the same name and the easiest way to get there was to walk. She was feeling better after a night's rest – surprisingly, she had slept well.

'Make a good breakfast,' Mrs Johnson advised. 'And I've packed you a currant teacake for a "biting on", though you should be at Dudley afore dinnertime.'

Ruth planned to find somewhere in Dudley where she and her grandfather might stay for the night. With a place to take him to, she thought, the Workhouse Master would be more likely to let her grandfather go with her. If the workhouse was as overcrowded as everyone said, then surely they'd be only too pleased to get one inmate off their hands?

In the village she stopped at the blacksmith's.

'I'm looking for lodgings for me and my grandfather,' she said. 'Somewhere homely, and not too expensive.'

The blacksmith straightened up and looked at her. He saw a tall thin girl, with dark hair escaping from under her bonnet. Large amber-brown eyes, filled with anxiety, met his. She was about the same age as his own daughter but she looked as if she had the troubles of the world on her.

'I reckon Mrs Taylor will look after thee,' he told Ruth. 'She sometimes takes lodgers.'

Ruth took to Mrs Taylor the moment that lady opened the door. She had the same kindly look as Aunt Sarah. Moreover, she had a room to let on the ground floor, with two beds.

'A shilling a night, to include supper and breakfast,' the landlady said.

Ruth paid in advance for the first night. She thought it a mite expensive, but it looked a respectable place, and Mrs Taylor had been sympathetic about Grandfather.

'I could tell you a few tales about yon place,' she remarked, jerking her head in the direction of Dudley House. 'Tales as would make your hair stand on end!' Ruth hoped she wouldn't, at least until she had Grandfather safely out of it.

'I've some stew and dumplings only needs warming up,' Mrs Taylor said. 'You look as if a good meal wouldn't come amiss.'

When she had eaten, Ruth set off for Dudley House. It was about a mile from the village, set back from the road, with tall iron gates, securely locked, at the entrance, and a few yards inside them a lodge. The big house was visible at the top of the drive. It was several storeys high, with many small windows, some of which were barred. Ruth rang the bell at the gate and a man came out of the lodge to attend to her.

'My grandfather's in here,' she said. 'I want to speak to the Master about him.'

'Oh you do, do you?' he replied, not unkindly. 'Then you'd best come in. I don't know as the Master'll see thee. He's a very busy man. First off, what's your grandfather's name?'

'Enoch Appleby. He came here five days ago, just after Christmas. I've come to get him out.'

From the look he gave her she thought that mustn't happen often.

'I've got lodgings,' she went on. 'He's to live with me. So could I please see the Master and arrange it as quickly as possible?'

The man continued to look at her strangely, and then at last he said, 'It'll not do you any good, love.'

'You can't tell,' Ruth replied. 'If I could just see the Master I could explain to him. It was a mistake, sending my grandfather here!'

'What I mean, love,' the man said slowly, 'is that it won't do you any good, nor your grandfather neither. You see, lass, he died the day afore yesterday.'

She stared at him. It couldn't possibly be true. Not her grandfather; not when she had come to fetch him; not at last when he was going to live with her and everything was going to be all right. Why was this man lying to her?

'You must have made a mistake. Perhaps you've got the name wrong?' Her voice was sharp, pleading with him. He *had* to be wrong, otherwise she couldn't bear it.

The man consulted a list pinned to the wall, then turned back to her, shaking his head.

'I'm sorry, miss. There's no mistake. A letter was sent to his next-of-kin, Mrs Sarah Gaunt. I thought you'd likely come from her, to collect his bits and pieces. Not that there's much. Are you Mrs Gaunt's daughter?'

So it was true. It was all true. Grandfather, how could you? How could you leave me when you knew I'd come for you? She thought she was crying the words aloud, but all that came back to her was her voice – flat, low, saying, 'She's my aunt. I'm Ruth Appleby.'

'Ah! Then there's a letter for you,' the man said. 'It's with his things.'

'My grandfather couldn't write,' Ruth answered mechanically.

'Happen not. He'd have got someone else to write it for him. Any road, here it is, plain as a pikestaff, Miss Ruth Appleby. Now will you take the rest of his things, or will Mrs Gaunt be coming?'

'I'll take them,' Ruth said.

He handed her a small bundle. 'We like you to open it on the spot, just in case there's a query.'

It contained a bible, a penknife with a horn handle, a clay pipe, and the verse which she had written out for him two Christmases ago: 'For hearts of truest mettle, Absence doth join and time doth settle.' At the end of a lifetime this was the sum total of her grandfather's worldly possessions.

'Will you open the letter now?' the man asked.

'No. Later. Can I see my grandfather?'

'Nay lass, you're too late,' he said gently. 'He were buried yesterday, on the Parish. We had the usual instructions that in the event of his death he should be buried here, and in those cases we don't wait. We haven't the room, you see.'

Those would have been Hester's instructions, Ruth thought. A pauper's grave.

'I can show you the place,' the man offered. 'If we don't take too long. Just wait while I lock up here.'

He took her to a graveyard high on the slope behind the house. 'It's consecrated,' he said. 'You don't need to worry about that.'

Ruth surveyed the freshly-turned earth and looked around for a flower she could place on the grave, but it was the last day of December and there was nothing in bloom. Everything was dead, dead, dead. She wished she was too. If her grandfather's grave had been open she would have thrown herself in. She could think of nothing to live for.

When she got back to the lodgings she sat down in her room and opened the letter.

'My Dearest Ruth (she read)
I want you to have my bible and the
penknife is for Ernest. Don't fret
for me lass. I've had a long life
and many blessings and you've been
one of the best. Be a good girl.
Your loving Grandfather
Enoch Appleby'

It was more than she could bear. She heard her grandfather's voice in the words. She saw him on the morning they had sat in the sun outside the cottage door. She smelt the sweet scent of the gillyflowers.

She flung herself on the bed in a paroxysm of weeping, wailing like an animal in pain – until Mrs Taylor came running, and took her in her arms.

'At least,' Ruth sobbed, held against Mrs Taylor's plump form, 'at least he never knew the worst about me!'

'The worst?' Mrs Taylor said comfortably. 'A young innocent like you? What is there to know?'

Where can I go now? Ruth asked herself. Who would have her? The only hope was Aunt Sarah. It was too late today. Her aunt's house was all of seven miles away and darkness fell early at this time of the year.

'Dry your eyes, love, and I'll get you a bite to eat. No use mourning on an empty stomach. Then I'll put a warming-pan in your bed and you can get an early night.'

She slept hardly at all. There was too much to think about, both past and future. She couldn't expect to stay long with Aunt Sarah; where would she get a job? With the prospect of supporting her grandfather she had somehow been full of confidence about the future. Now it had all left her.

All through the night she thought about the problem. When morning came, bitterly cold and still dark, she had made up her mind. She knew what she must do.

# 8

'Happy New Year, love!' Mrs Taylor said, reminding Ruth, as she left Dudley that morning, what day it was. 'Happen you'll have better luck in 1849,' she added. 'There's nowt like a new beginning.'

But you can't wipe out the past as if it didn't exist, Ruth thought. Walking away from Dudley – with the feeling that once again she was deserting her grandfather – she thought back to the moment on last New Year's Day when she had looked down Nordale from her bedroom window, all eagerness for what 1848 would bring. Well, now she was glad to be rid of it.

When she reached Aunt Sarah's Ernest opened the door. 'My word, this is a surprise and no mistake!' he exclaimed. 'Come in, our Ruth. Happy New Year!'

She followed him into the kitchen.

'Look what the wind's blown in, Charlotte!' he said.

Charlotte came forward to greet Ruth, little Enoch at fourteen months tottering unsteadily behind her.

'You look frozen,' she said pleasantly. 'Come over to the fire and get warm.'

Ruth stretched out her hands to the red glow, wondering if she would ever again be warm all through her. There was no sign of Aunt Sarah.

'Ma's in bed, poorly,' Ernest told her. 'She were taken bad afore Christmas and she's slow to mend. But the sight of you will do her good.'

'The letter hasn't arrived then?' Ruth asked.

'You mean you wrote to tell us you were coming?' Ernest

said. 'Nay, we've heard nowt.'

'So you don't know Grandfather's dead?' She made no attempt to break it gently; her mood was not tactful. 'You none of you know how he died in the workhouse and was buried in a pauper's grave?'

Ernest stared at her in astonishment, Charlotte standing silently behind him.

'You didn't know that while you were having a good Christmas, Hester was making arrangements to send him away?' Ruth accused him, her voice sharp and cutting.

Ernest's face flamed. He stepped forward and took hold of Ruth's wrists, as if he would forcibly stop her. 'Now hold on, Ruth! Hold on! No, we didn't know any of that. Did you?'

'No,' Ruth admitted. 'How could I?'

'And how could we, do you suppose? Do you think we'd have let it happen if we'd known? I wrote to Hester just afore Christmas, explaining about Ma being badly. She didn't write back.'

'She wouldn't, would she?' Ruth said bitterly.

'Poor old Grandad!' Ernest said. 'Poor old gaffer! I'm real sorry, Ruth love. Had you best be the one to break it to Ma? She'll be very upset.'

Ruth went upstairs. Frost, like thickly appliquéd lace medallions, patterned the bedroom window, and water in a cup by the bedside had formed a solid block of ice. She was thankful that she still wore her cloak.

Propped up in bed to ease her breathing, her nightcap pulled down over her ears, Aunt Sarah seemed to have shrunk inside the shawls which had been heaped upon her against the chill of the room. Ruth supposed that there wasn't enough coal for her to have a fire in the grate, but this was no way to cure a bad chest.

Ruth stood in the doorway of the room for a few seconds, looking at her aunt who was drifting on the edge of sleep. Presently, Sarah opened her eyes and saw her visitor. A wide smile of welcome broke over her face as she brought her niece into focus. Seeing Aunt Sarah so unusually ill and helpless, Ruth was filled with grief for her sake at the news she had brought.

'Why, Ruth love, I thought I were dreaming! Whatever are you doing here? But whatever it is, it's welcome. You'll do me more good nor a bucket o' medicine. Come here and give us a kiss!'

Ruth kissed her aunt and then, clasping her hands tightly in her own, she said what she had to say as gently as possible.

'Nay lass!' Sarah said. 'Nay lass, it's a bad do!' She searched around for further words to express her grief, but could find none, and kept repeating herself. 'Nay, but it's a bad do!' Tears ran down both their faces, and though neither could shoulder the other's pain, they were glad of each other's company in their sorrow.

'You know I'd never have let it happen like that,' Aunt Sarah said presently. 'Not i' a thousand years. Not my own father! He were a good father, Ruth. Always had time for us when we were little. Always listened. I wouldn't have let it happen.'

'I know,' Ruth assured her. But it *had* happened.

She wondered again what her grandfather's thoughts and feelings had been in those few days at Dudley House. Was it because he had no hope that he had lasted so short a time? Or was it just possible that right to the end he had believed that she would find out, and come to him? She prayed that it was so, but she would never know.

She was aware what her aunt's next question must be.

'And I suppose you've come home for a day or two's holiday? Well, that was Providence all right! When must you go back?'

So Ruth told her the truth, but not quite the whole truth since she kept Dick's name out of it. That was wiser than she knew since it deflected her aunt from the shock of the announcement and gave her something to pursue.

'But Ruth, the man should marry you! Surely he'd marry you if he knew?'

'He wanted to marry me before any of this happened,'

Ruth said. 'I daresay he still does. But Aunt Sarah, I don't want to marry him. If I was still having the baby I daresay I'd consider it, but losing it made it quite clear to me that I didn't want what he offered.'

She thought about Dick, standing there on Fleet Moss, offering her his promised land. But it was not for her.

'But you *liked* him?' Aunt Sarah pleaded. 'You must have liked him?'

'Of course,' Ruth said. 'I still do.'

'There's many a good marriage founded on liking,' her aunt told her. 'It's stuff as lasts. And he'd have made you a home.'

'I know,' Ruth replied. 'That would have been my main reason for marrying him. I don't love him, Aunt Sarah.'

'But Ruth love,' Sarah said gently - and she had not uttered a word of reproach - 'you *need* a home! What are you going to do? How will you get another job? You know I'd have you here, love, but it's not possible. Whatever shall you do?'

Ruth took a deep breath and summoned all her courage to put into words what she had decided after her sleepless night at Mrs Taylor's.

'I'm going to America!' she announced. 'No, don't say anything yet, Aunt Sarah! Just listen. I've thought it all out.'

'It's our Ernest put you up to this,' Sarah interrupted. 'He's the one who's been at you!'

'No he hasn't, Aunt Sarah. It's not even been mentioned between us. I don't know for sure that Ernest *is* going to to emigrate.'

'Oh, he's going to do that all right,' Sarah said angrily. 'He's already joined the emigration society. He's up the earholes i' pamphlets and instructions and information. He thinks I don't know, but I do. All he's waiting for is his number to come up. And now he's persuaded you!'

'He hasn't!' Ruth protested. 'I may have got the idea from him in the first place, but that's all. I'd decided to go whether he did so or not. If he'll have me with him and

Charlotte, then so much the better for me.'

'You'd never have done this if your grandfather had been alive!' Aunt Sarah cried.

'Happen not,' Ruth agreed. 'But he's not. And Willie doesn't need me. There's no place for me here. You as good as said it yourself.'

'But you'll marry, Ruth. There'll be someone come along. . . .'

'And rescue me? I don't want that. I don't want marriage as a lifeline. I want *what* I want, *when* I want it. I want to be me, Ruth Appleby. I want to belong to *me*. Not to anyone else.'

'Rubbish!' Sarah's tone was scathing. 'You're talking daft. You're still only a bairn, Ruth love. If you go to America you'll still have to depend on someone for a living.'

'But I'll earn it,' Ruth said. 'From now on I want to make my own way in the world, be independent.'

'Now you sound just like our Ernest. But it's not the same for a woman, it can't be.'

'Perhaps it is in America. Who knows? And I'm not afraid.' But of course she was. Deep inside she was terrified.

'Now I think you ought to get some sleep, Aunt Sarah,' Ruth said. She started to tuck the bedclothes more closely around her aunt, but Sarah pushed her away.

'Sleep?' she cried. 'With all you've just said on my mind? Are you daft or summat? I'm getting up and coming downstairs. If there's any plotting and planning going on I want to be there. I'm not lying i' bed while you tell me what bit you want me to know!'

By this time she was out of bed and Charlotte was running upstairs to see what the commotion was about.

'You can get me my clothes,' Aunt Sarah ordered her. 'I'm getting dressed. Ruth'll give me a hand. You tell Ernest to see there's a good fire for me to come down to.'

It seemed as though anger had given her the strength that rest in bed had failed to produce. Or perhaps, Ruth thought, it's the challenge of the situation. After all, she's an Appleby!

'Now we'll say nothing to the others about your little affair,' Sarah cautioned when Charlotte had left the room. 'Except that later I shall have to tell your Uncle Matthew. Him and me have never kept things from each other. But he's fond of you. He'll not be one to judge harshly.'

'Thank you, Aunt Sarah,' Ruth said. 'And I do understand how you feel about the rest, about the emigration. I really do.'

Sarah stopped in the act of fastening her stays around her vast body. In the ice-cold room the sweat of weakness beaded her forehead and her upper lip.

'Oh you do, do you?' she said. 'You understand, do you? You know what it's like to bear a child and bring him up – and see him leave you and go to the other side of the world, knowing you'll not see him again? You know what it's like to part wi' your grandchild, to know there'll be others you'll not set eyes on? You understand how it feels when you can't read a letter, nor write one in reply? You understand all that, do you? Well, you're a clever young woman, Ruth Appleby!'

Her words went in like a knife. Ruth could find no answer. When her aunt was dressed she walked slowly down the narrow staircase in front of her in case, in her weak state, she should stumble.

From New Year's Day onwards, the whole of 1849, the last year she expected to spend in England, was to Ruth simply a period of temporising; of waiting, though seldom patiently, for the only event which had come to mean anything. It was not a time of inaction, for there was plenty to be done. If Ernest was keen, Ruth was ten times keener. While he and Charlotte went steadily ahead making their preparations, Ruth rushed at hers as if the summons to depart might arrive the very next day.

In theory that was possible. She had quickly joined the emigration society of which her cousins were already members, and it had been agreed that she should count as part of their family. Each month lots were drawn for the names of the next families to leave, and the fortunate ones were given only a short time to make their final preparations.

Charlotte was busy with preparations of another kind. She had confided to Ruth that she was pregnant again.

'Only don't tell Ma,' she begged. 'She'll be that angry wi' me. Anyway, she'll know soon enough.'

Poor Charlotte, Ruth thought, to be married, yet not able to take pleasure in her pregnancy – though she perhaps misjudged her mother-in-law a little.

'When is it due?' Ruth asked.

'The middle of June.'

Ruth caught her breath. It was when she would have had her child.

When he knew of his wife's pregnancy Ernest requested that none of their names should go into the ballot until after the baby's birth.

'I don't want you confined on board ship, love,' he said. 'Let alone on that trek across America!'

Although they would land in New York, they were to go immediately from there to Wisconsin where the English, including several families from the West Riding of Yorkshire, had begun to settle.

'Happen you'll change your minds when the babby comes,' Aunt Sarah remarked when she heard. 'Who in their right senses would want to take a babby in arms on a journey like that?'

'It's no use, Ma,' Ernest said gently. 'My mind's made up and you'll not change it. I've begged you and Father to come with us. There's older folk than you have taken the step and I reckon it'd be a better life for both of you. I don't believe it's Father as won't go. It's you is the obstinate one!'

Once, when they were alone together, Ruth asked her aunt, 'Why won't you come? What's the reason?'

'It's not that I'm afraid of living in a strange place, Ruth. I could do that – aye and work hard an' all. But. . . .' She faltered. 'But I'm afraid of dying there – and that's the truth. When you get older (she was not yet fifty) you begin to think about death. It's frightening. But to be where you've always been makes it easier. And I've lived hereabouts since I were born. I wouldn't want to die in a strange land.'

'But you'd have your family around you,' Ruth pointed out. 'When the time comes that will make up for everything.'

'My roots are here,' Sarah said quietly. 'They go deep. If you were a gardener, love, you'd know as there are some things you can't transplant. Disturb their roots and they wither. I'm like that, Ruth.'

She and Uncle Matthew had agreed, in spite of her strong disapproval of Ruth's plans for the future, that she should live with them until the time came to leave. Ruth slept on a sofa downstairs. She didn't mind. In any case, nothing was for long. She was grateful not only to be with her aunt and uncle in that last year, but to be near Ernest and Charlotte so that they could discuss, usually when the older couple had gone to bed, the life which lay so tantalisingly before them. Ernest regularly had advice from the emigrants' society and this he would read out aloud.

'Take a good supply of flour and biscuits. Take a good book or two. Keep yourself clean from head to foot and provide yourself with opening medicine in case of need. Be ready to work hard in your new country. . . .'

He broke off. 'I'm ready to do that,' he said. 'I'll work all hours God sends.'

'So will we all,' Ruth agreed. 'Go on reading.'

He found the place again, following the text with his forefinger. 'Prepare for difficult times, and ask for God's blessing on your venture.'

'There's a long list of equipment here,' Ruth pointed out. 'Look! A strong iron pan for cooking our food on board. No end of clothing. . . .'

'It'll take us all our time to afford that lot,' Ernest said doubtfully.

'But it just goes to show,' Ruth said, 'that they were right when they said emigrants shouldn't wait to leave until they were too far gone in poverty, but should go while they still have enough to provision themselves.'

'It's sound enough advice for those that can afford to follow it,' Charlotte remarked.

Ruth had been fortunate enough to find a job in Ilkley. The landlord of the inn which Ernest visited when his mother and his wife became too much for him knew of a coffee-house in the town which needed a kitchenmaid, and because he put in a good word for her, Ruth was given the job without references. She was paid four shillings a week and given her midday meal. She thought it was good pay, but well earned.

Every week she was able to give Aunt Sarah something for her keep and she had a little left over to save. She managed to persuade Ernest to take a proportion of this to augment his savings. It was hard for him to scrape together more than a few coppers at a time.

'I don't like taking your money, Ruth,' he protested. 'It's not right.'

'But it is,' Ruth argued. 'You must know that the companionship of you and Charlotte in a strange land will be beyond price to me.'

She should have realised, there and then, by the glance Charlotte gave her husband and the way in which he refused to meet it, that her plan to accompany them was a bone of contention. But she pretended to herself that she had not seen it, or that she had misinterpreted it.

She hated her work in the coffee-house, standing all day long at the sink in the ill-ventilated pantry. She was glad when her work was done and she could walk back to the farm, filling her lungs with the keen moorland air.

She cherished those walks. Every tuft of grass, flower, bird, was precious to her and she wanted to store them in her memory, against the day when they would no longer be hers. As the long, cold winter merged into spring she wondered if America, or any place on earth, could be as beautiful as her native moors.

She wrote to Dick, not mentioning her miscarriage, telling him of her plans. 'I know I could have made you happy, Ruth,' he replied. 'And if ever you want me, you know where I am.' She wished with all her heart she could have found contentment with him.

Throughout that spring they saw nothing of Maria, and only the occasional letter came. She clearly had no time for Burley Woodhead when there was so much going on in Bradford.

'She's gotten too grand for us,' Aunt Sarah said.

'I don't think so,' Ruth replied doubtfully. 'But you know how she always likes to be in the centre of things.'

Then at the beginning of summer Maria wrote to say that she was coming to spend a few days with them. But a day or two before she was due, Ernest returned from Ilkley with unwelcome news.

'There's cholera in Leeds and in Bradford,' he said. 'It looks as if it's bad, an' all.'

'Ruth, you must write at once to Maria,' Aunt Sarah urged. 'Tell her she mustn't come yet. We have to think of little Enoch.'

'And of Charlotte,' Ernest pointed out. 'She's not strong at the moment. She's fit to catch whatever's going.'

So Ruth wrote at once, asking Maria to postpone her visit and bidding her take care of herself. She gave her letter to the postman with a heavy heart, wondering if she would ever see her sister again.

Charlotte's daughter was born on the first of June, a week or two earlier than expected.

'She's to be named "Jane" after Charlotte's mother,' Ernest said. 'I could wish she was stronger, and Charlotte happier.'

Aunt Sarah shook her head. 'I'd be glad to hear the little mite cry more. It's not natural for a babby to be so quiet.'

Eventually, both mother and baby gained strength, and Ruth saw relief replace worry in Ernest's face as his daughter began to thrive, and his wife to smile at him.

On a day in autumn Ruth told her aunt, 'They say the cholera's on the wane now. It would be safe for Maria to come. I do so long to see her, Aunt Sarah!'

'Then invite her, love. You've been right patient,' Aunt Sarah said.

Maria replied that she was to be allowed to come for two days in the week following her letter.

'I shall ask for two days holiday myself, then,' Ruth said. 'And if the old skinflint won't give it to me I shall take it just the same. He can do what he likes about that!'

She was on her way to Ilkley, to meet Maria, when she saw the postman climbing the hill.

'There's a letter for your Ernest,' he told her. 'I reckon it's from them emigration people.' He usually guessed at the contents of letters, and stood around waiting for his guesses to be confirmed.

Ruth's heart began to thump so loudly that she thought he must hear it. 'I'll turn back and take it myself,' she said, trying to sound calm.

They were all in the kitchen where she had left them a few minutes earlier. Aunt Sarah was at the table, kneading the bread dough; Ernest and Uncle Matthew, back from the top field, were taking a late breakfast. Charlotte sat feeding her baby while Enoch played on the hearthrug.

Ruth handed the letter to Ernest. It seemed to her that they must all know what it contained. Ernest opened it in silence, his hands trembling. Aunt Sarah stopped kneading. Uncle Matthew cupped his hand around the mug of tea he was holding. For a single moment, Charlotte stopped suckling the child. The only sound in the kitchen, while they watched Ernest reading the letter, was from Enoch, happily singing a nursery rhyme.

'We've drawn lucky!' Ernest said quietly. 'We sail out of Liverpool next March the eighth on the *Flamingo*, bound for New York.'

Sarah's hands, imprisoned in the bread dough, could not wipe away the tears which ran down her face. They dropped in the earthenware bowl, and were absorbed, so that when, later, Ruth helped to eat that morning's baking, she imagined she could taste the bitterness of the tears. Her uncle gazed at the tea in his mug as if the hot liquid might be the

Atlantic Ocean itself. Charlotte said nothing, but her face lit up with pleasure and she bent her head over the baby so as not to show it.

'March the eighth,' Ruth said, breaking the long silence. 'My eighteenth birthday. Perhaps that's a good omen?'

It was a cruel, tactless thing to say and she could have bitten out her tongue the second the words were spoken, but the excitement bubbling inside her was too much to contain.

'I'm sorry, Aunt Sarah!' she cried.

But Ernest was by his mother's side, his arm around her shoulders. Without speaking, she elbowed him out of the way and continued with her baking, thumping and banging the dough into shape, all the time her tears falling silently. Ruth went out of the house and ran down the steep moorland path all the way to Ilkley. She must not be late for Maria.

The next day Ruth persuaded Maria, not without difficulty, to walk over to Barnswick with her.

'I don't see why we should!' Maria protested. 'I've little enough time as it is.'

'I want to see Willie,' Ruth said. 'I want us all three to be together. It might be for the last time.'

She had to make sure that Willie was happy, and thriving. Having been all this time contented about his welfare, now that her leaving was fixed and certain, she had begun to have misgivings. Supposing Hester should turn against him?

'Of course she won't,' Maria said. 'You know she'd never do that.'

'All the same, promise me that you'll visit him often when I've left – make sure that all goes well with him.'

'I promise.'

'Swear it on our mother's memory,' Ruth insisted.

'I swear it.'

'And you'll write often and tell me about him?'

'Yes. Oh do stop it, Ruth!'

So they walked across the moor. The heather had faded from its summer brilliance, emerging a deeper, softer purple from the counterpane of autumn mist which covered the ground.

Although Ruth now knew that she would be on the moor throughout the coming winter, and perhaps if she was lucky see the first, early signs of spring, she knew she was now taking her farewell of its chief beauty. She would not see the heather again. Much as she had wanted her sister's company, she almost wished Maria was not there. She wanted to fling herself to the ground, to lie there with her body pressed against the purple glory. For the rest of the journey Maria prattled on about Bradford, but Ruth did not hear a word.

When Ruth saw Willie she realised that she need not have worried about him. He had grown another inch or two but he was still plump and rosy, with a solid contented look about him. He greeted his sisters with a mild show of affection but it was obvious that his home was here with Hester, and that he was happy in it.

Hester, except that she was a little thinner, seemed no different. Ruth doubted that anything would dim her stepmother's exuberance for long. No reference at all was made to Enoch Appleby, though Ernest had written to Hester with the news. But Hester made them reasonably welcome.

'I daresay you'd like something to eat,' she said.

'I'm ravenous!' Maria admitted.

'And you, Ruth?'

'I'm not hungry,' Ruth replied quickly. 'Thank you all the same.'

Hester shrugged. 'Suit yourself. Then I'll boil you a fresh egg, Maria.'

She knows, Ruth thought, that I could never take another bite from her. But she had not come to quarrel with Hester, she had come to see Willie.

She must get it over with quickly, and leave. Every minute she was in the house where she had spent most of her life, crowded as it was with memories of her parents and her grandfather, made it more difficult to bear up. If she was not to break down completely, and in front of Hester, she must say goodbye to Willie, and go. She bent down and took him in her arms. He pulled away, startled by the vehemence of her embrace.

'It will be a long time before I see you again, Willie,' she said. 'Be a good boy, won't you? Always say your prayers, and ask God to bless your Ruth.'

Then she ran out of the house, bumping into Tom Firth, the landlord of the Shoulder of Mutton, as he came in.

'Why, it's Ruth!' he exclaimed.

She ran past him without speaking. He turned and watched her, puzzled. He had known Ruth since she was born. Her father had been his best friend. Why would she do that? He shrugged, and went in to see Hester.

Ruth had called to see Mrs Johnson, looked in on one or two of the other neighbours, and was halfway up the hill to the churchyard before Maria caught up with her.

'We had a lovely tea,' Maria said. 'I had two eggs and some seed cake. Why didn't you stay?'

'What a question!' Ruth exclaimed. 'You know I wouldn't take anything from that woman, and I don't know how you can, Maria.'

'I can easily. Hester was pleased to see me, to give me a meal. But then you were never fair to Hester, were you? Right from the beginning you were against her.'

'You liked her because she was always giving you things,' Ruth accused her sister. 'Making you pretty clothes.'

'I liked her because she was amiable and good-tempered. I like pleasant people. They're more fun.'

'Your feelings don't go very deep,' Ruth said angrily. 'If they did you'd hate her for what she did to Grandfather.'

'And yours go too deep,' Maria answered. 'You take a pride in feeling everything deeply. I think that's rather boring. I *did* love Grandfather, and I'm sorry he died, but I'm not going to hate Hester to please you.'

Ruth closed her lips firmly. She would simply not say another word on the subject. She didn't want to quarrel with Maria, today of all days, when they had so little time left together.

She went into the churchyard and found their parents' grave. There was no headstone, but it was neatly tended and there were fresh flowers in a stone jar. Had Hester placed them there? Was it true, what Maria said, that she had never been fair to Hester? She pushed the thought away.

For a few minutes she knelt by the grave, and was presently joined by Maria. Then without speaking she stood up and walked away, down the hill, back towards the moor. Maria caught up with her as they reached the end of the village.

'Why do you want to go to America if it makes you so unhappy?' Maria asked.

'Who says I'm unhappy?'

'Anybody can see that. You're a streak of misery.'

'It's just that I don't like leaving places – or people,' Ruth said. 'That's all. But I still want to go. It's my best chance. Wouldn't you like to go, Maria? Wouldn't you like to come with us?'

Maria pulled a face. 'Not me! Not into the wilderness – tilling the ground, milking the cows. At the mercy of wild animals and insects and snakes and goodness knows what horrors! No thank you. Give me the city! Now if you were settling in New York. . . .'

'We shall be in New York less than a day,' Ruth said. 'But I'm sure Wisconsin's not as bad as you make it sound.'

'I daresay it's worse!' Maria replied.

'Oh Maria, I shall miss you so much!' Ruth cried, thrusting her arm through her sister's as they walked.

Christmas came and went and Ruth was glad to see the back of it. There was neither joy nor peace in the house and she found herself wishing the time away until it should be March. She could not bear her aunt's desperate face, nor her uncle's increasing silence.

By the beginning of February they had collected together most of their provisions. Tea, oatmeal, sugar; a precious jar of goose fat for rubbing into the children's chests should they take bronchitis on the journey. They took senna pods and a small bottle of brandy against bowels under- or over-active; a bottle of Dr Barton's cough mixture and, of course, their bibles and prayer books. From her savings Ruth had bought new boots, stockings, a warm flannel petticoat and a gown made of Yorkshire wool.

'Though it's nowhere near as much as they recommend,' she said.

'And we have even less,' Charlotte replied.

'Which is a blessing in disguise,' Ernest broke in. 'Because how are we going to carry it all, with two bairns besides? Don't forget, either on thee, that every ounce has to be carried in bundles on our backs!'

'How *are* we to get to Liverpool?' Ruth asked, not for the first time. It was their constant anxiety.

'If the worst comes to the worst we shall have to take the train to Manchester. If we gave ourselves time we could walk from there to Liverpool. I'm loth to spend money on railway tickets,' Ernest said. 'We'll need every penny we have when we get to America.'

'I suppose you'd like us to walk all the way to Liverpool?' Charlotte put in crossly.

'If it weren't for the children, I would,' Ernest admitted. 'If it were summer I'd do it even wi' the children. We could push a handcart. Plenty of folk as good as us have done it.'

'Well *I'm* not going to,' Charlotte declared. 'And that's flat!'

'Don't carry on so,' Ernest replied patiently. 'I've said it's the wrong time of the year for that. No, unless I can come up wi' something soon, it'll have to be the train.'

As late as the end of February it looked as though this was what they would have to do, and then one evening Ernest returned from a visit to Ilkley flushed with excitement. When he entered the kitchen, bringing a great gust of cold air with him, he was all smiles. He pulled Charlotte into his arms in an embrace so fierce that she drew back, staring at him.

'Nay, I'm not drunk!' he assured her. 'I've only had my usual pint. But I've got good news, lass!'

Aunt Sarah did not so much as lift her head from the rug she was making, but Ruth watched the way the rug hook stabbed the canvas with increased speed and vigour, as if she wanted to hurt it, and Ruth knew that her aunt was as tense as she was herself.

'I met up wi' Alfred Carter,' Ernest said. 'You remember Alfred? Well, he's working on the canal now, going 'twixt Bingley and Liverpool, carrying cloth. One thing led to another and he says if we're so inclined, and we don't mind a bit of inconvenience, he'll take us all on the barge to Liverpool – and nothing to pay! We'd only have to walk as far as Bingley. It's a rare chance.'

Aunt Sarah's rug needle dropped from her fingers and clattered on the stone floor.

'Rare chance!' she flared. 'Hast lost thy reason, Ernest Appleby? Hast taken leave of what little sense thou were born with? Two little bairns – one of 'em nobbut a babby – five days and five nights on a canal barge at this time o' year?'

'Don't fly off the handle, Ma,' Ernest said. 'I don't doubt but what Alfred'll rig up a bit of shelter. And we'll wrap up warm. Anyway, it's the best bet so far.'

'Best bet!' Aunt Sarah stormed. 'You must be mad!'

'Leave him be, Sarah,' Uncle Matthew said gently. 'He's old enough to know what he's doing.'

Ernest turned to Charlotte and Ruth.

'Well, what dost think? Will it do?'

'It will for me,' Ruth said.

'And me,' Charlotte agreed. 'As long as we take proper care of the children.'

'We must be prepared to put up wi' a bit of discomfort,' Ernest said. 'But don't worry, the good times will come later.'

Aunt Sarah was right in saying that it would take five days to reach Liverpool, since the barge could go no faster than the horse which pulled it. Then, fearful of things going wrong – their greatest dread was that they would be late and that the ship would sail without them – they decided to allow an extra twenty-four hours.

On that last night they finished packing their bundles, tied them securely and left them in the kitchen ready for the morning. After that there was a good meal of mutton stew and Aunt Sarah's feather-light dumplings (none of which anyone could eat) and they went to bed early. For Ruth it was impossible to sit there in the kitchen, seeing Aunt Sarah's stricken face, in a silence which was more deafening than words. Ruth thought her aunt would have sat up all night to prolong the time with them, but her uncle – who had tried bravely all day to behave as though nothing untoward was happening – put his arms around his wife's shoulders and led her away to bed. She went as if to her execution.

Ruth did not sleep much, and when Ernest came downstairs next morning she was already up and doing.

'Half-past five,' he said softly.

Ruth opened the door and went outside. There were stars in the clear, dark sky, and a white frost over the moor. It would have been easier to set off in the daylight but it wasn't possible. They had a long walk over the moor to Bingley and Alfred Carter couldn't afford to wait for them if they were late.

When she went back into the house her aunt was busy with the last meal she would prepare for her family. They forced themselves to eat the porridge, the eggs fresh from the nest, for they had a long day before them. The last hour on the farm was an eternity. It seemed to Ruth, what her aunt had long suspected, that to part with loved ones while they are still living, with never a hope of seeing them again, was worse than losing them by death. For a moment, just before they left the house, as she and her aunt clung tightly to each other, the silent tears coursing down their faces, Ruth hated America and wished that it had never been discovered.

But once they had left the house, and were at last too far away to hear her aunt's and uncle's farewells, or to see them as they stood outside in the yard, silhouetted against the lighted kitchen, excitement began to creep into Ruth and her spirits began to lift.

They met up with Alfred Carter sooner than expected. He

was waiting for them with his barge by the first footbridge over the canal as they came down from the moor. It was almost daylight now, still cold and frosty. The horse blew great jets of steam from its nostrils as it stood on the towpath, patiently waiting for them to board.

There was a minute cabin on the barge, no more than a place for the bargee to take shelter.

'For you ladies and the children,' Alfred Carter said. 'It will keep the worst of the weather off.'

'If it's all the same to you,' Ruth said, 'I'd like to stay outside for a bit. At any rate until we've gone through the locks. Perhaps Enoch would like to watch with me?'

She had seen locks working before, but never these famous 'five-rise' ones, the longest 'staircase' on the canal. She stood on the deck while the water rushed in through the sides of the great oaken gates, lifting the barge higher and higher until they were level with the water in the next basin. Then the gates opened and they went through. It was an experience to be repeated many times as the canal climbed to the top of the Pennines.

'If you think that's exciting,' Alfred Carter laughed, 'just you wait until you go through the tunnel!'

By regular standards, Ruth supposed, the canal journey was uneventful. At night she and Charlotte crowded into the cabin with the children and they kept each other warm. The men sheltered under a tarpaulin slung across the corner of the barge. To relieve the tedium of the days they sang, or told stories to Enoch. Sometimes Alfred allowed Ruth to leave the barge and walk beside the horse on the towpath, to stretch her legs.

And then at last they came to the tunnel. At the entrance a small boy and a youth were waiting.

'Lead yer hoss ower the top, mister!' the boy shouted.

'Gi' yer a hand wi' the legging!' the youth offered.

Alfred Carter accepted both offers. Had she known what was in store, Ruth thought afterwards, she would have begged to walk over the top with the horse.

'Now,' Alfred said. 'You'll not like this next bit. This

tunnel's a mile long, and it's dark and wet. You two ladies would be best off in the cabin wi' the children.'

Ruth had heard about 'legging'. She knew all about it in theory and tried to explain it to Enoch.

'You lie on your side on the edge of the barge, raise your legs until your feet touch the wall, and then make a walking movement. You have to push hard against the wall to drive the barge forward.'

'He's too young to understand,' Charlotte protested. 'Are you coming into the cabin or not?'

'Not,' Ruth replied. She had a better idea. She turned to Alfred Carter.

'I'm the same height as the youth you've hired,' she said. 'Seeing there are three of you, it would make sense if I made a fourth and helped to leg.'

Alfred looked at her in astonishment.

'You can't leg,' he told her. 'It's not a job for a woman.'

'Canal women do it,' Ruth said.

'It's not very. . . .' He sought for the right word. '. . . seemly!'

He meant that her skirts would have to be tucked up around her waist.

'As it will be dark, that won't matter,' Ruth said.

Reluctantly, he agreed, and Ernest and Ruth took one side while Alfred Carter and the youth took the other.

'We must all keep in time,' Alfred instructed them. 'I'll call out the rhythm.'

Ruth tucked up her skirts and clenched her teeth, and as Alfred called out the beat she pushed hard against the slippery wall, and was relieved and delighted to feel the barge moving.

She hated every minute of the tunnel: the thick, inky darkness, the icy water which dripped from the limestone roof; the dank, sour smell and the lack of air. When the first shaft of light showed at the end of the tunnel it was like waking from a nightmare.

'That's it, then!' Alfred Carter said briskly. 'It's all downhill from now on. We shall soon be in Liverpool!'

# 9

The *Flamingo* was a three-masted ship, what Ernest described as 'square-rigged'. Though when they set eyes on her, her sails were furled, to Ruth she looked magnificent. Except in pictures, she had never seen a ship.

'It's such a beautiful name,' she said ecstatically. 'It sounds so romantic. She'll be like a great bird, skimming over the water.'

'I don't care if she's called the *Quacking Duck* just as long as she's steady,' Charlotte replied.

The dockside was the busiest place Ruth had ever seen in her life. Between passengers waiting to board, porters, sailors, orange-sellers, touts, piled-up cargo, there was scarcely room to move. All around them people sat on their boxes and held on to precious bundles, patiently waiting for whatever might happen next. Some were eating, and Ruth guessed that they had broken into the food supplies they had brought for the voyage. A few lay on the ground in exhausted or inebriated sleep, oblivious to children and dogs who clambered over them, or to the kicks from porters who found them in the way.

'Why can't we go on board?' Charlotte asked. 'Do we have to stand here all day?'

Jane was crying; a fretful whimper, as if she was struggling to fall asleep and could not.

'Here, let me take her,' Ruth said.

Somewhat reluctantly, Charlotte handed over her daughter – and looked displeased when the baby fell asleep almost at once in Ruth's arms. Ruth could never understand

Charlotte's unwillingness to let her help with the baby. It seemed as though she liked to keep those she loved to herself, as if by sharing, some part of them would be lost to her forever.

'I'll try to find out what's happening,' Ernest said. 'Don't any of you move an inch from here and don't take your eyes off those bundles. I don't doubt this place is full of rogues.'

He sounded irritable, which was unlike him. He had been brusque and taciturn all morning, giving short, sharp answers to Charlotte's questions. Ruth could almost have believed that he wanted to turn around and go back home. All her apprehensions were swallowed up in excitement, but then she did not have the responsibility of a wife and family. But when Ernest returned he sounded a little more hopeful.

'They'll still loading cargo,' he told them. 'After that we can go aboard. But first we have to go to the doctor's shop to get our health certificates. That's it yonder.' He pointed to a hut in front of which a line of people was already forming. 'We'd best get over there,' he said. 'It might be a long business.'

Apart from waiting in the queue it was the shortest business Ruth had ever encountered. The doctor sat at the open window of the hut, from which position, without ever moving, he examined the passengers. He scarcely glanced at her. His eyes were fixed on the forms which he was signing and stamping as fast as he could go.

'Do you feel well?' he asked.

'Never better.'

'Tongue,' he snapped.

She put out her tongue but he did not examine it. He was already handing her the piece of paper which certified that she was in good health and not suffering from any infectious disease. His examination of her cousins was every bit as cursory.

By the time they had their health certificates the cargo, mostly cotton cloth from Manchester, had been stowed.

'Emigrants are the chief cargo on this ship. I only

hope. . . .' Ernest's words were drowned in the call which went up from the ship, and the outburst of cheering from the *Flamingo's* passengers.

'All aboard, Ernest! Did you hear? Oh Ernest, Charlotte, it's happening at last!' Ruth jumped up and down, waving her handkerchief in the air. 'It's the moment we've been waiting for!'

There was no time for her cousins to answer. Still cheering, the passengers had started a mad rush towards the gangway, shoving and pushing at anything and anybody in the way.

'Give passage to the women and children!' someone shouted. 'Make way there!'

Whoever he was, his words floated away unheeded. It was every man for himself and no concessions given. It was lucky for the Appleby family, Ruth thought, that they had Ernest, carrying Enoch on his back, to batter his way through. Enoch began to cry. He did not like the noise, and all these people pushing him.

'It's all right, lad,' Ernest said. 'Stick tight hold, that's all.' He turned his head to check on the others. 'Keep together!' he cried. 'Whatever happens, keep together. And hold on to the bundles!'

'Easier said than done!' Ruth yelled. 'People get in the way. I can't keep up with you!'

Though she had fallen a little behind she managed to keep her cousins in sight. Then suddenly there was a strong wave of pressure from behind, as if all the world was at her back. She felt certain that she must fall on her face and be trampled underfoot. She was more frightened than she had ever been in her life, but fright gave her strength. She raised her arms, still managing to cling to her bundle, and lashed out. She was fighting for air and space – and then she lost her balance. Miraculously, she did not fall down. The crowd was so thick that she was carried along with it. But she was losing sight of her family.

'Help! Ernest, help!' She yelled at the top of her lungs, calling again and again until at last he heard her terrified screams. With difficulty, he made his way towards her, Charlotte clinging to him for dear life.

But at last they reached the top of the crowded gangway. Sailors waiting there hauled them roughly on to the ship, not caring how they landed. In front of Ruth an old woman, not moving quickly enough to please them, was thrown so heavily that she landed on her back on the deck and was too winded to rise.

'Mind what you're doing!' Ruth shouted angrily to the sailor. His reply was to give her a sharp pull forward and then a shove in the back, which knocked her to her knees.

'You treat cargo better!' she yelled furiously.

He spat in her direction. 'Cargo's valuable!' he sneered.

'For heaven's sake,' Ernest begged, 'don't waste time arguing, Ruth. We must get to our bunks or they'll be taken!'

'How can they be taken?' Ruth said. 'We have them booked and paid for. A bunk for each of us and one for the children to share.'

It was their first lesson of many, that what was promised and paid for bore little relation to what would be received. Ruth was horrified when they went below and she saw their sleeping space.

'It can't be true!' she cried. 'One bunk six feet long and six feet wide for all of us? And one filthy, straw-filled mattress? I don't believe it!'

A sailor nearby – he was pushing people into the hold as if he was packing meat – called out to her.

'You a single lady?'

'I am. Travelling with my family.'

'As well for you then. We usually puts the single ladies in to share bunks. With the men if they're lucky!' He leered at her and she wanted to strike him.

'Don't make a scene, Ruth,' Ernest pleaded. 'It'll not do any good. We must make the best of it.'

'Very well, Ernest.' He was right, and she determined not to let the sleeping arrangements upset her. In any case, she would spend most of her time on deck. She was not to know that, once at sea, they would only be allowed on deck at certain times, like dogs let out to exercise.

'Never mind,' she said, surveying the cramped space between the tiers of bunks, wondering if there was room to sit upright. 'Never mind, it's not forever! And at least we've been lucky enough to get a bottom bunk.'

Charlotte was sitting dejectedly on the edge of the bunk, her face chalk white, her eyes closed.

'I feel seasick already!' she moaned.

'Charlotte, you can't!' Ruth said briskly. 'We're still in the harbour. Come up on deck with me. You'll feel better for some fresh air.'

'I'd sooner lie down,' Charlotte muttered.

'I'll stay with her. You take Enoch,' Ernest said.

From the deck, Ruth looked out at Liverpool. It was the first city she had ever seen. She had set foot in Skipton and passed through Keighley, but these were small country towns. Only in books had she seen buildings as magnificent as those which rose up before her, and she had never, anywhere, seen so many people. The river, so wide that she would have mistaken it for the sea, was full of craft of all sizes, though most of them lay at anchor.

'I wonder why that is?' she said to Enoch.

An answer came unexpectedly from a middle-aged man leaning on the rail nearby. At least she thought him middle-aged, but his voice wasn't and when she looked at him again she saw that under his haggard features and emaciated frame he was still young, perhaps in his late twenties. He spoke with a strong Irish accent, soon to be a familiar sound on board since most of the emigrants were Irish – and most of them as scrawny and hollow-cheeked as he was.

'It's the wind which is contrary,' the man told her. 'Until it changes the ship will not sail.'

'Oh but the *Flamingo* sails on tomorrow morning's tide,' Ruth informed him confidently.

'Only if the wind allows,' he said, smiling at her ignorance. 'The power is truly in the wind.'

Ruth thanked him for his information and a few minutes

later he raised his hat and walked away. Enoch grew restless, so they walked around the deck until he decided that he had had enough and that only his mother would do.

Ruth did not enjoy her first night on board. Modesty forbade her to undress properly and get into her nightshift in front of so many people, though it was so hot below decks that she felt obliged to take off her top skirt and her blouse. Also, she was acutely embarrassed at having to share her cousin's bed, especially as they would be squeezed so closely together in the small space.

'How shall we arrange ourselves?' she asked.

'The baby by the wall. Ernest next to her,' Charlotte said. 'Then me, then Enoch – and you on the outside.'

'And what if the baby wants feeding?' Ernest asked.

'Then you can hand her over to me.'

It was impossible to stretch out, let alone toss and turn, as in her restlessness Ruth wanted to. She lay rigid, not allowing herself to move in case she should disturb the others. She was aware, though no-one spoke, that for much of the time Ernest and Charlotte were also awake. At one time she felt Charlotte turn towards her husband, and knew that they were in each other's arms.

There was plenty of sleep going on around her. The snoring rose and fell like an ill-tuned orchestra, interrupted by the curses of those who, like herself, could not sleep. The stuffiness in the hold was made worse by the acrid smell of unwashed bodies. Not far from her a man retched violently – thought whether from sickness, since they were scarcely moving, or from drunkenness, she did not know. Several babies cried, though Jane slept well. Ruth told herself that once they were at sea things would be better. Then towards morning, she fell asleep.

When she wakened Ernest was already up and dressed.

'A happy birthday to you!' he said.

She was eighteen years old.

'The wind has changed,' he told her. 'It's blowing from the east now. They say that if it keeps up we shall sail on time.'

'And once we're at sea the food will be given out,' Ruth said. 'We haven't much left – and very little water.'

'Well then, if we want to say goodbye to the old country, we should go up on deck,' Ernest suggested.

Charlotte shook her head. 'I'd sooner stay where I am. Anyway, someone has to look after our belongings else they might get pinched. It'll be dog eats dog on this voyage!' In any case, she had no ties in England, no-one it grieved her to leave. And no matter what Ruth said, she *did* feel sick. She would like to go to sleep now and not wake up until they set foot in America.

Nothing Ruth had ever imagined prepared her for the magnificence of that day's scene on the Mersey, though she saw most of it through a mist of tears. All the ships, large and small, which had been held up for days past, had now unfurled their sails and were putting to sea. As the *Flamingo* herself cast off and manoeuvred into position to sail down the broad river, a wild cheer went up from the emigrants on deck. She reckoned there must have been as many as four hundred of them.

But she could not cheer. Instead of Liverpool, with its splendid buildings and famous docks, she saw, first Nordale, with the long sweep of the fells, and the river running through the valley, then her own moorland, clothed in purple heather. She saw it all as plainly as if it had been magically transported from Yorkshire and spread out on the quayside, the moors stretching away in the distance until they met the skyline.

And then she saw the faces of her aunt and uncle, her father and her grandfather, Maria and Willie – everyone she had loved and still loved and must leave behind. And Dick's face was amongst them.

There were not many signs of sadness on deck. A few old people watched with impassive faces, as though they no longer felt anything, but most of the people were in high spirits, talking and laughing. As the *Flamingo* moved down the river the wind began to fill the sails. A man struck up a tune on a concertina and those near him began to dance.

Ernest put out a hand and touched Ruth's arm.

'Don't fret, love! The best is yet to come,' he said. But there were tears in his eyes too.

In the weeks and days which followed Ruth clung to those words of Ernest's. And most of the passengers, she thought, must have relied on similar thoughts to see them through. By 'passengers' she meant those who travelled steerage. It was said that the few cabin passengers on board sailed under very different conditions.

'I doubt *they* are overcrowded,' Ernest remarked. 'Or short of food and water.'

'And I doubt *they* get such rough treatment from the crew,' Ruth said angrily. 'They wouldn't dare treat cabin passengers the way we're treated!'

She wondered if the cabin passengers caught the illnesses – especially dysentery – which were rife in the steerage. There was supposed to be a ship's doctor aboard but no-one below decks had set eyes on him.

They had been afloat only a few hours when a seaman shouted down the hatch.

'Everybody muster on deck for the roll call! Quick about it, I ain't got all day!'

There were cries of protest, for though the sea was not yet rough, many people were already sick, and unwilling to stir.

'Those as don't muster for the roll call don't get no rations,' the seaman shouted. 'No roll call, no food – nor water neither!'

'Food is the last thing I'm interested in,' Charlotte said. 'I'd rather just stay here.'

'You can't do that, love,' Ernest argued. 'It's not just food, it's water as well. We can't afford to miss the water ration.'

Reluctantly she dragged herself out of the bunk and, with Ruth carrying the baby and Ernest holding on to Enoch, they went on deck. After the roll call the third mate, with two helpers, doled out the rations.

'You're getting oatmeal, bread, potatoes, tea, ship's

biscuits and a piece of fat bacon,' he shouted. 'Three days' supply. You're a lucky lot and no mistake!'

It sounded well enough until they saw the size of the rations.

'My youngest could manage that lot and he's only two!' a man complained. 'It's no good to a grown man!' He was ignored.

'Drinking water every day,' the third mate shouted. 'No expense spared!'

'What about water for cooking and washing?' a woman asked.

'There's plenty of sea water,' he answered. 'Ready salted, too.'

'Where's the fresh meat we were promised?' a man standing near to Ruth called out. 'The prospectus says fresh meat.'

The third mate glared at him.

'Them that are lucky'll get fresh meat later on,' he retorted. 'Them that makes trouble'll get none.'

Then Ruth saw that he deliberately gave the man who had asked the question only half the bacon ration he was entitled to. 'That's what happens to them as asks awkward questions,' he said grimly.

In this instance it mattered little. There were enough passengers ready to believe that they would never wish to eat again, let alone eat fat bacon.

'Take mine, lad!'

'And mine!'

'And mine!'

Far more than the man had been denied was pressed upon him.

'Good luck to you for speaking up!' someone cried.

'You'll be sorry for that, all of you,' the seaman said. 'When you get really hungry you'll be sorry you gave so much as a mouthful away.'

No-one believed him. He was trying to frighten them. After all, they had paid for their rations; they were entitled to them.

Then, with food to be cooked, the rush for the stoves began. There were four stoves situated amidships; great monsters which spat out showers of sparks.

'They terrify me!' Ruth said. 'Why, the sparks alone could set the whole ship alight. And how are we to get near? There must be more than fifty passengers to each stove.'

'Follow me!' Ernest was determined. 'I'll make a way through.'

Ruth had volunteered to cook the first meal. She made a little oatmeal porridge for Enoch, and for the three adults she cooked bacon and potatoes, in the iron pan they had brought from home, and used some of the water ration to make tea.

'The bacon's none too fresh,' she said. 'But I'm hungry.'

'So am I,' Ernest admitted.

The two of them ate well, but Charlotte could not face the meal.

'I'll just have a bit of bread and a mug of tea,' she said.

Ernest looked at her anxiously.

'You'll have to do better than that, love. Remember you've got the baby to feed. You can't do wi' your milk drying up for want of nourishment.'

'I can't help it,' she replied. 'I can't eat.'

Ruth could hardly blame her. With the lack of air, the smells, the unrestrained vomiting of a woman in the top bunk (why had she ever thought they were lucky to get a bottom bunk?) it took real hunger and a strong stomach to face food.

By the third day they were out into the Atlantic. It was then that the wind changed round to the north-west and the first, and worst, of the storms hit the *Flamingo*. The sea roared like a pride of hungry lions, thudding against the side of the ship like a thousand battering-rams, so that it seemed that at any moment it must break through and drown them all. Ruth tried not to show her terror when the timbers creaked and moaned like tormented spirits and she could hear the waves breaking on the deck above them. But as well as being frightened, she was angry. She could not bear the thought that after all they had gone through, all they had sacrificed to get so far, it should end like this. Would they ever see America, or would they all end up at the bottom of the sea, food for the fishes? She had not known that weather like this existed.

On the second day of the storm a seaman bellowed down the hatch.

'No rations until the storm's over!'

'What about the water?' someone called.

'No water neither. Not until the storm bates!'

His words were lost in the frightened screams of the women, the crying of terrified children, the loud cursing and swearing – and sometimes praying – of the men.

Ruth wanted, physically, to hit back at the storm, which went on and on, which was striking at *her*. At her worst, on the third night, faint from lack of food, her throat parched with thirst, she had a crazy idea that the storm was singling her out for punishment, was expending its venom to get at her. She hated it. She hated it as if it was a personal devil. She was no longer aware of the people around her, only of herself and the storm. At the height of her anger, unable to stop herself, she beat a loud tattoo with her clenched fists on the wooden edge of the bunk.

'Stop it, damn you! Stop it!'

Her cries and thumps awakened both children, and when they started to cry, Charlotte screamed at her.

'What do you think you're doing?'

'I'm sorry! It's the storm. It's driving me mad!'

'We all have to bear the storm,' Charlotte cried. 'Why is it any worse for you? Why do you allus have to be so special?'

Ernest tried to calm down both women.

'Hush now. We must try to sleep if we can.'

Ruth came quickly to her senses. But there was no stopping Charlotte and Ruth realised, as the words poured out of her, that she was releasing the pent-up feelings of many months.

'I won't hush!' she shouted, turning on Ernest. 'Tell her

to hush! Why is she allus right and me allus wrong? Ruth this, Ruth that, Ruth says, Ruth thinks. You should have married her. You should have kept her i' the family. The rotten, stinking, Appleby family! You got her into our bed, so why not? Perhaps you'd like her to change places wi' me, so as you can give her a cuddle in the night?'

Ernest clapped a hand over her mouth. 'Stop it!' he commanded. 'You're talking nonsense.'

Ruth struggled out of the bunk and, wrapping herself in her shawl, she lay on the floor. She was already dressed, they all were, in preparation for the shipwreck which they felt sure must come. For the moment she was so shocked by Charlotte's naked, sexual jealousy that she forgot to be frightened by the storm. From now on, though she knew of nowhere else where she could sleep, she resolved never to share her cousin's berth again. And as far as possible she would keep her distance from Ernest. She was unaware of any undue familiarity between herself and her cousin; they seemed as they had always seemed since childhood. But she would take no chances.

But what of the future, she thought, lying there on the floor? It was clear that she wasn't wanted by Charlotte, and if Ernest did want her with them, then that would only make matters worse. She felt totally and truly alone. And when the woman in the top bunk threw up again and the sour vomit splashed down on her and soaked her skirt, it was the last straw. She buried her face in her hands and burst into bitter tears.

She had to get out. No matter how bad the storm was she had to go on deck, where at least the air was clean. But because of the storm the hatches had been battened down and no matter how hard she searched she could not find a way out of the hold. But she did find an unoccupied corner of the floor, away from everyone she knew. There she stayed until morning.

Soon after dawn the storm suddenly abated. Ruth was there waiting when the hatches were raised and she escaped at once and went up on deck. Although, officially, steerage passengers were only allowed there at certain times, no-one took any notice if a few people walked the deck. Curiously, there were very few who availed themselves of this privilege.

The stench which rose from below, to where Ruth stood at the top of the hatchway, was worse than anything she could ever have imagined. Dysentery among the passengers continued and during the storm almost everyone had been sick, so that with the lack of sanitation the steerage was truly awash. And then the smell did something that the worst fury of the storm had failed to do. Ruth felt her stomach heave, and rushed to the side of the ship, where she was violently sick over the rail.

When it was over she raised her head and breathed in deeply. The air up here was clean and fresh. The wind had, by comparison, almost dropped, and the March sun made a path of gold across the water. Had it not been for splintered wood and debris lying on deck, and a ripped sail or two, the storm might have seemed no more than a bad dream.

She was standing by the ship's rail, thinking about Charlotte's outburst, worrying about what she should do, when she heard a woman speaking to her.

'I asked, are you all right?' the woman said.

She was standing by a part of the deck which jutted out above the place where Ruth stood, by which Ruth knew that the woman was a cabin passenger. No-one from the steerage was allowed up there.

'All right?'

'Yes. How have you weathered the storm? Was it awful down there?'

'It was,' Ruth said. 'It was terrible. But I'm all right – which is more than can be said for some.'

'I wanted to come down. Before the storm, I mean, to see if there was anything I could do. Neither the captain nor my husband would let me. They said it wasn't fit.'

'It isn't,' Ruth agreed. 'There are four hundred people down there. It isn't fit for them.'

The woman flushed, though Ruth hadn't meant to rebuke her.

'I've seen you on deck with your husband and little boy,' she said. 'Are they well?'

'Quite well, thank you – though he's my cousin, not my husband, and the child is his. His wife suffers badly from seasickness and keeps mostly to her berth.'

'Poor soul,' the woman said. Then: 'I have a little girl on board. I must go to her now. Perhaps I shall see you again – and please tell me if there is anything I can do.'

After that, since she now spent as much time as possible on deck keeping out of the way of her cousins, with whom she felt a constraint, Ruth saw the woman for several days in a row. Once or twice Ruth took Enoch with her and on one occasion the woman on the upper deck was accompanied by a little girl.

'This is my daughter, Anna,' she said.

The child was about five years old, fair-haired, immaculately dressed, and seemingly friendly.

'Would you like a sweetmeat, little boy?' she called out to Enoch – and threw one down to him.

'How are things going,' the woman asked.

'Badly. Our rations have been cut again,' Ruth said. 'We're receiving no fresh meat at all, and not enough water. Also, there's a great deal of sickness for which we need medicines. I know the ship is supposed to carry a doctor, but he doesn't come near us. I dare say he's afraid to, for fear of catching something!'

'What can I do?' the woman asked.

'Well for a start, madam, you could tell the captain. I feel sure he must already know, since it's his ship, but it might be good for him to realise that persons of influence, like yourself, who might report him, also knew. He won't care about any of us, of course.'

For two days after their conversation Ruth did not see the woman, and then on the third day a man leaned over from the upper deck and called out to her.

'Are you the young woman my wife, Mrs Carson, knows?' he asked. 'You answer her description.'

'I expect so,' Ruth answered. 'I don't know the lady's

name and I haven't seen her these last two days. I hope she's well.'

'She is not well,' he said. 'She has a chill and is confined to bed. So is our daughter. I have been sent to ask you whether, if I can arrange it with the captain, you would consent to look after them. My wife is travelling without a maid or nurse and I am of little use in a sickroom.'

'I would be pleased to help if I could,' Ruth replied.

'Then come back to this same place in an hour's time, when I shall have spoken with the captain.'

Ruth hurried back to the berth, gave Ernest and Charlotte the news, and began to make herself as tidy as she could.

'It might be interesting,' she said. 'At any rate it will help to pass the time.' And it will get me out of your way, she thought.

'Who knows,' Ernest said, 'perhaps they'll have a bit of food to spare. If you could get something to tempt Charlotte. . . .'

'I'll try my best,' Ruth promised.

Charlotte had her mind on other things.

'There's a baby four berths along, ill with a high fever. Enoch was playing with the other children in the family only yesterday. What if it's something bad? What if it spreads? What if Enoch and the baby take it?' Her voice was hoarse with anxiety.

'Don't fret, love. I daresay it's no more than a chill. They'll be all right.' Ernest tried to comfort his wife, but Ruth saw the anxiety in his eyes.

She went back on deck at the appointed time and within a minute the man appeared.

'Would you come up here?' he called out. 'I'll take you to my wife's cabin.'

Their quarters turned out to be a small suite, with two sleeping cabins and a minute dining-room. Mrs Carson, lying in a bunk with a blanket thrown over her, was clearly relieved to see Ruth.

'Anna and I are much better,' she said. 'Especially Anna.

But I have told her all the stories and rhymes I know and she is getting bored. Also, I should dearly love to rest. Could you come for a few hours each day, do you think?'

For the next few days Ruth spent most of her waking hours with Anna, reading to her from the small collection of books Mrs Carson had brought on board, playing games, making up stories. From the first she took her meals with Anna. Food was plentiful and there was as much water to drink as she wanted. At the end of the first day Ruth presented herself to Mrs Carson.

'If you please, ma'am. . .?'

'What is it, Ruth? Is Anna misbehaving?'

'Not at all, ma'am. We get on well together. It's just. . . .' She hesitated.

'Well?'

'Well ma'am, there's some scraps of food left over and . . . it's bold of me to say so . . . but if it was going to be wasted I know my cousins would feel the benefit. They've cut our rations again. But only if it was going begging of course!'

'Why, Ruth, of course you may take it!' Mrs Carson exclaimed. 'You may take whatever is left over at the end of each day. I am quite distressed to think of your family going hungry!'

So for three days Ruth took food, and sometimes water, to her cousins, and since the food was of a better variety, Charlotte was tempted into eating.

'And you will have my rations, since I don't need them,' Ruth told Ernest.

He shook his head. 'They've stopped your rations. They reckon you're not due, since you're eating with your employers.'

On the fourth morning of their arrangement Ruth presented herself to Mrs Carson as usual - but to a troubled-looking lady.

'I'm afraid our little arrangement must come to an end, Ruth,' she said at once.

Ruth could hardly believe it. 'But why, ma'am? Have I not given satisfaction?'

'Most certainly you have,' Mrs Carson answered. 'I am more than pleased with you. But the captain has informed me that there is a case of smallpox in the steerage. A baby, poor little mite. It would not be safe to have you going to and fro between the steerage and our quarters. You do see that, don't you?'

Ruth felt sick at heart. It was bad enough having to sleep in the steerage – lying on the floor wherever she could find a place, where cockroaches and rats could run over her while she slept. To go back to spending her days there was unendurable. There must be some way out of it!

'Would it be possible . . .' she began.

'Yes?'

'I mean, if I didn't go back to steerage? If I never went back until the end of the voyage, could I stay with Miss Anna? Look after her all the time? And you too! There are lots of things I could do for you, ma'am. I'm good with my needle.' Heaven help her if that lie were put to the test! 'I wouldn't want payment, and I'd sleep on the floor – anywhere!'

Mrs Carson looked at her husband.

'I'm fit and well,' Ruth told them eagerly. 'The doctor could examine me if you wished.'

'You do realise,' Mrs Carson said, 'that you would not be able to see your cousins at all until we reached New York? Not even if they were ill. *Especially* not if they were ill.'

'I don't think they'd miss me,' Ruth confessed. 'In fact the arrangement might be a relief to them – except for the extra food.' Which would in any case, cease, she thought, if she could no longer work for the Carsons.

'Well, if you're quite sure,' Mrs Carson said. 'But I should not want you to go back there at all, not until we are ready to disembark. And from this very moment. I should require you to send a note to your cousins by one of the crew. He could bring back those of your possessions you will need for the rest of the voyage.'

Charlotte, Ruth thought as she penned the note, would be delighted. And though Ernest might not be so pleased, it would make matters easier for him. Enoch would miss her most, and she him.

So she joined the Carson household and settled with them. The days passed happily enough but at night, in the tiny cabin she shared with Anna, she sometimes lay awake and thought of her cousins, down below in that hell-hole. And she knew that if she had been made welcome from the start, she would still want to be with them, in spite of this comparative luxury. If she could have been part of a warm, loving family, it was what she would have liked most of all. But she was not wanted and knew she never would be. It had been a mistake ever to force herself upon them.

'Mr Carson's father has a prosperous cotton business in Manchester,' Mrs Carson said one day in her friendly manner. 'My husband is going to New York to make new contacts. I know *I* shall enjoy our time there. They say there is most interesting society, with lots of concerts and plays and cultural pursuits. And of course there is a great deal of money to be made.'

Ruth drew a deep breath, summoned all her courage, and blurted out the question which had been churning in her mind day and night for some time.

'Could I go to New York with you, ma'am? Could I work for you? I would do any job you wished, and to the very best of my ability, if only you'd give me the chance.'

She felt herself growing hot at her own temerity, but Mrs Carson showed very little surprise.

'I've been expecting you to ask me that question,' she admitted. 'But surely you wish to go to Wisconsin with your cousins? And would it not be much wiser, for your sake, to do so?'

Ruth told her something of the situation between herself and her cousins.

'But Mr Carson and I are only in New York for a year,' Mrs Carson pointed out. 'What would you do at the end of that time?'

'Something will turn up,' Ruth said with confidence. 'And if it doesn't, I promise I will join my cousins. Things might be better between us after an absence. You will not need to have me on your conscience.'

'I must confess,' Mrs Carson smiled, 'that I would like to keep you with us. I have said as much to Mr Carson. If you were not to accompany us I would have to find someone in New York. It would be pleasant to have an English girl and Anna is already fond of you.'

'And I of her,' Ruth said.

So it was arranged.

At breakfast on the day before they were due to arrive in New York Mrs Carson said, 'I think you could go below and see your cousins today. The doctor tells me that the danger of smallpox is now past.'

More than one person had died, and been buried at sea, but it was the funeral of the baby who was berthed near to her cousins which affected Ruth most. Not only was it the first death, but it could easily have been little Enoch, or Jane.

The ship's carpenter had sewn the tiny body into canvas, weighting it at the feet with coal, so that it would sink rapidly. Everyone on board who was free to do so had attended the funeral, Ruth standing with the Carsons on the upper deck. A porthole was opened amidships and on a plank lay the small body. The captain read the funeral service and the first mate raised the plank and tipped the small bundle into the water. It floated for a second and then sank. Ruth thought she would never forget the bereaved mother's demented scream.

'Tell your cousins what you have decided,' Mrs Carson said. 'See if they approve.'

When Ruth went down to the lower deck it was a hive of activity, with the strangest thing she had so far seen taking place. Men, women, and all except the smallest children, were on their hands and knees, busily washing every inch of the deck, supervised by the third mate and half a dozen rough-looking sailors, who kept them at it every second. She found Ernest and Charlotte on their knees with the rest, with Enoch, as far as a three-year-old could, keeping an eye on the baby nearby.

'What in the world is happening?' Ruth enquired.

'You may well ask,' Ernest replied bitterly.

'Of course you wouldn't know, would you,' Charlotte said with asperity. 'Now that you're a cabin passenger.'

'What is it?' Ruth persisted.

'The steerage passengers have been ordered to scrub every bit of the deck so that it's clean for the quarantine inspection,' Ernest explained. 'There's been more water used on this floor than we've had to wash ourselves and our clothes in since we left Liverpool!'

'I'm sorry,' Ruth said. 'That's terrible. And I would willingly get down and help you, but Mrs Carson is waiting for me.'

'We don't need your help,' Charlotte retorted quickly.

Ernest sat back on his heels. 'Anyhow, we're about finished,' he said more reasonably.

Charlotte stood up, drying her hands on her skirt. Ruth was dismayed to see how thin she had grown. Both she and Ernest had lost weight during the voyage, but Charlotte could ill spare it.

Ruth told them her news.

'You've done mighty well for yourself, I must say!' Charlotte remarked.

'But you don't want me with you, Charlotte! You never did. Admit it!'

Charlotte refused to answer, but Ruth knew she was right. Ernest was torn two ways.

'I daresay thou'll be all right. I wouldn't let you do it else. But we shall miss thee, Ruth; Charlotte, as well as me and the children. So promise thou'll come to us when the year is up. Promise!'

Ruth's eyes met his. If you only knew how much I long to come with you now, she thought. But there was nothing to be said.

'I promise I'll consider it,' she told him. 'And remember, I shall send my share of the Emigrant Society's dues every quarter out of my wages. You must let me do that or I can't think of rejoining you.'

When Ruth wakened on the morning of May the tenth

her first thought was that this, God willing, was the day they would sail into New York harbour. She wakened Anna and dressed her and the two of them went on deck.

The lower deck, shining clean now, was thronged with steerage passengers. They had somehow spruced themselves up, dressed in whatever was their best, collected their belongings together, and now waited to go forward into their new lives. The man with the concertina, whom Ruth had noticed on the day they sailed from Liverpool, struck up a tune; only this time it was not a dance, but a hymn of thanksgiving and praise, in which everyone joined.

'All people that on earth do dwell,
Sing to the Lord with cheerful voice. . . .'

The sound grew and swelled, as the singers somehow found new strength to praise their God, until the ship was filled with their harmonies. Ruth, looking down from the upper deck, her hand clasped around Anna's, lifted her clear soprano voice with the rest, though it was difficult to sing because of the tight aching in her throat and the tears which pricked at her eyes.

She caught sight of Ernest and Charlotte in the crowd, and at the same time they saw her. When they waved to her, and held up little Enoch to see her better, she could no longer keep back the blinding tears. She saw the scene in front of her through a mist.

The ship was sailing into the harbour now. It looked quite different from Liverpool, and not only because the sun was shining. There were scores of boats and ships of every kind, with a forest of masts and rigging outlined against the clear blue sky. A cacophony of ships' sirens filled the air. The sun shone over everything, sparkling on the water, and what with that and her own tears it seemed to Ruth that the sea was scattered with diamonds. In spite of her grief at being parted from her cousins, she could not help but feel excited. There was something in the air, an energy, a vibrancy, which she had never experienced before. It filled her, lifted her spirits, and she remembered Ernest's words, and said them out loud to the little girl beside her.

'The best is yet to be, Anna! The best is yet to be!'

Her words were carried away on the breeze, to join the tumult of sounds. She felt sure and confident that they were true.

Mr and Mrs Carson joined them.

'I am afraid we shall not see your cousins when we disembark, Ruth,' Mrs Carson said. 'The steerage passengers must go through quarantine, which I'm afraid will delay them considerably. For cabin passengers, of course, it is not necessary.'

# *Part Two*

# 10

'So now that we have been here almost three months,' Mrs Carson said, 'what do you think of New York, Ruth?'

She was not really looking for an answer. She was concentrating on her appearance, adding the finishing touches before setting out on yet another shopping expedition. The Carsons had quickly made friends. They were a pleasant, handsome couple and New York had welcomed them, showering them with invitations. Naturally, all this activity made it necessary for Mrs Carson to renew her whole wardrobe. Everything she had brought from Manchester now seemed so provincial. New York was so chic, so fashionable.

'What do I think of it?' Ruth smiled, 'Why, ma'am, I think it's wonderful! Incredible! It's so exciting.'

She had felt the excitement in the air the minute she had stepped off the boat. Her whole body tingled with it. She just knew, she knew with absolute certainty, that in this vast, noisy, busy city, *something* would happen to her, and it was bound to be something good. Life, from now on, was going to be quite different from anything she had ever known. Adventure awaited her around every corner.

'And so big, so busy. Five hundred thousand people, Professor Woodburn says there are. Sometimes I think they're all on Broadway at the same time!'

She adored Broadway. The shops – so many, such variety! A person with money could buy just about anything. And the hotels! Splendid buildings with grand entrances and such smart people going in and out that it was a pleasure just to stand and watch them. She had dared to step inside Mr Brady's photographic establishment to view the wonderful daguerreotypes and portraits he had taken. The very best people went to him and it was her intention, once she had saved the necessary two dollars, to do likewise. She told herself she wanted to have her photograph taken so that she could send it to Aunt Sarah, but really it was for herself. She was curious to know how she looked to other people.

'I could never tire of New York, ma'am,' she said. 'Not in a lifetime!'

'Good!' Mrs Carson replied absently. Would her bonnet take more ribbon, or perhaps a flower or two, to give her height? 'And now I absolutely must fly! So much to be done! Everything must be ready for an early start tomorrow. See that your own things and Anna's are packed, Ruth.'

They had been invited to spend a week or two at the country house of Mr Josiah Barnet, a banker on Wall Street, whom Mr Carson had met in the course of business. Mr Barnet was rich. His wife, it was said, was even more so, and well-connected. They were lucky, Mrs Carson declared, to have received such an invitation. There was no knowing who they might meet there.

'I'm afraid it's very hot again,' she said. 'Perhaps you should not take Anna out today. But use your own judgement.' Ruth was a sensible girl. She could safely leave Anna in her care.

When Mrs Carson had left, Ruth suggested, 'I think you ought to have a little nap, Anna. After that we'll go out, if it's not too hot.'

'Can we go to Wagner's ice-cream parlour?' Anna asked.

'We'll see. For now you must lie down on the bed and go to sleep.'

Anna was asleep in ten minutes. Ruth sat down and took a letter from her pocket. Before they had parted on the *Flamingo* she had given Ernest the name of the boarding-house where the Carsons had made arrangements to stay, and he had promised to write to her the minute he and Charlotte arrived at their destination. A dozen times since then Ruth had visited the post office in Nassau Street, but no letter came. Sometimes she wondered whether her cousins were still alive. They could have been attacked by Indians; they could have run out of food and water and suffered a terrible death by starvation. Or perhaps they were still wandering in that long stretch of country which lay between New York and the State of Wisconsin?

'You are letting your imagination run away with you,' Mrs Carson had said. And yesterday she had been proved right. When Ruth called yet again at the post office a letter was waiting for her. Now, while Anna slept, she read it for the tenth time.

> 'We are fit and well,' (Ernest wrote). 'Little Jane thrives, as do we all. Charlotte did not enjoy the journey up the Hudson River and through the Canal, nor the horse-drawn wagon which followed. She is with child and the bumping added to her sickness.
>
> Everything is different from Ilkley though we have met up with a family from Leeds, which makes it more like home.'

When she first read the letter, standing out there in the heat of Nassau Street, Ruth was overcome by a pang of homesickness so severe that it felt like a pain burning inside her. It was strange that, truly enamoured of New York as she was, she could still feel like this – choked with a desire to hear the broad vowels of her native Yorkshire. There was a score of different accents and tongues around her as she stood there, but not the one she wanted.

Today she felt better. So Charlotte was to have another baby? Somehow in the confines of that tossing, stinking ship her cousins had managed to make love, perhaps even when she was lying with them. No wonder Charlotte hated her.

There had been no mention in Ernest's letter of Aunt Sarah. Ruth had written to her four times and lived in the hope that her aunt would get the minister to reply. She had also written to Willie and Maria, even to Mrs Johnson. Though she was not really homesick, penning the letters somehow kept her close.

Anna stirred in her sleep, opened her eyes slowly.

'Are we going out now?' she asked.

'Not yet. It's still very hot.'

'Tell me about where we're going tomorrow then,' Anna demanded.

'I've told you a dozen times. To the country. We're going to a big house called Millfield. I daresay there'll be a shady wood, and trees and rocks to climb. And other children to play with. Mr and Mrs Barnet have three children.'

'Is it a long way?'

'Twenty-three miles. And now I must finish packing.'

Not that her packing would take long. She had few clothes, and fewer still suitable for the hot weather. How she would have managed had not Mrs Carson handed down two dresses, both of fine cotton, Ruth didn't know. They were invaluable.

When she had packed she washed Anna's hands and her own in a basin of cool water, put on their bonnets, and took Anna's hand to descend the stairs. As they reached the hall Professor Woodburn came in from the street. His face was flushed and damp and he mopped his forehead with a large handkerchief. The professor was Mrs Gutermann's most prestigious boarder, and her favourite. She cosseted him, served his favourite dishes, bullied him into changing his clothes when he came in drenched from one of New York's torrential showers.

It had surprised Ruth that the Carsons should choose to live in a boarding-house, until she discovered that in New York it was quite the thing – always supposing that the establishment was high-class and in a good locality. Spring Street, just off Broadway, was fashionable, and no-one could describe Mrs Gutermann's as other than high-class. Ruth had heard her boasting to the Carsons.

'I take mostly professional people,' she'd said in her strong voice with its pronounced German accent. 'Professor Woodburn; Mr Gossop from the New York Society Library, Miss Fontwell who has a position in the New York Historical Society, and so on. All my boarders are ladies and gentlemen.' She did not mention Mr Pierce. He was a manager in Brooke Brothers, Men's Outfitters – and being in trade was only admissible by the skin of his teeth and because, Mrs Gutermann being a widow, she could look to him to undertake certain practical tasks, to make himself useful. Anyway, he *was* a manager. Had he been an ordinary shop assistant it would not have done at all.

'Good afternoon, Miss Appleby, Anna,' the professor said. 'How cool you both look!'

'We're not really,' Ruth replied. 'We're going out in search of fresh air, if there's any to be had. We shall go to your Washington Square. It's not too far and there'll be shade from the trees.'

She called it *his* Washington Square because he was professor of English in the university there. According to Mr Carson, the professor had taken his degree at Oxford, but he had been in America for several years now.

'There *is* a little shade in the square,' he agreed. 'Though it is not cool anywhere. Perhaps one day when you are in that direction you will allow me to show you my department in the university.'

'That would be most pleasant,' Ruth said.

The professor seemed not to realise that she was a servant, perhaps because she was so much with the Carsons as to seem almost a member of the family. But when she got to know him better she was to realise that he treated all women, servants or otherwise, as if they were ladies.

When they stepped into the street the damp warmth hit her in the face and the heat of the pavements struck through the thin soles of her shoes so that every step of the way was like treading on hot cinders. She could never, in her wildest dreams, have imagined the summer weather of New York City. In the early mornings the heat came in through her open bedroom window and when, later, she went out to take the air, there *was* no air, only a dense, clinging humidity.

She walked slowly, Anna's damp hand in hers, keeping to what shade there was from the buildings. Sweat beaded her face and soaked her body in the most unladylike way. In spite of having sponged herself down in cold water to close the pores, and liberally applied powdered chalk to absorb the perspiration, she could feel the rivulets of sweat running down her back and the insides of her thighs.

'If we walk up Broadway we'll pass Wagner's,' Anna said. 'I want some ice-cream.'

'Then want must be your master,' Ruth snapped. 'We'll just stop talking about it *if* you please!'

She was ashamed of her sharpness, but the heat seemed to penetrate her brain, taking over her senses so that she was no longer in control. She felt like slapping Anna.

In spite of what Professor Woodburn had said, it *was* a little cooler in Washington Square, especially as they were lucky enough to find a vacant seat under a tree. Ruth had discovered Washington Square on her second day in New York. Its air of peacefulness was in such contrast to Broadway, and to the harbour and waterfront on the day they had landed. She loved these contrasts which the city afforded. Whatever one's mood, it seemed, there was a place to match it.

'I'm bored,' Anna said. 'Can't we play a game?'

'It's far too hot to run about,' Ruth told her. 'You may pick daisies and I'll show you how to make a daisy chain.'

While Anna picked flowers, Ruth observed every detail of the dress and deportment of the people in the square, for she hoped one day to emulate them. She did not dislike her present job, but she had no intention of doing such work forever. She meant to get on in the world. She had no idea at the moment what she would (or could) do, but she knew that something good was bound to happen. She could feel it in her bones. And hopefully it would happen before too long. She couldn't wait until she was old. How terrible to be thirty and not to have realised one's ambitions!

But today the square was unusually quiet. Anyone who could do so had already left the city for the comparative cool of the country. She would be glad when they themselves followed suit.

'We must return home,' she told Anna when they had

made the daisy chain and hung it around the little girl's neck. 'But since you've been so good, you shall have your ice-cream!'

Broadway was as crowded as ever. Clearly there were many people who couldn't afford to escape the heat of the city. Two horse-drawn buses careered down the middle of the road, the drivers racing against each other, scattering everything in their way, including the piles of rubbish which lay stinking in the heat. But it was cooler in Wagner's and the ice-cream was deliciously cold to the tongue and delicately flavoured with just enough vanilla. Ruth had never tasted ice-cream before coming to America and now, like Anna, she could have eaten it all day long. The two of them scraped their dishes clean.

When they emerged it was hotter than ever.

'It feels like a storm,' Ruth said. 'We'd better hurry.'

Mrs Carson was already back. She lay on the chaise longue, fanning herself.

'I'm quite exhausted!' she exclaimed. 'All the shopping one has to do! But one must be suitably dressed for a country visit and I had absolutely nothing fit to wear. Anna, my pet, I have collected your new dress and in a moment you shall try it on.'

'Does it rustle?' Anna asked.

'Rustle?'

'I want a dress which rustles when I walk. Like yours, Mama.'

Mrs Carson smiled fondly at her daughter. She found it difficult to refuse her anything.

'Well, since it is of the finest Swiss cotton I'm afraid it won't, my pet. But when you go to dancing school in the Fall you shall have a taffeta dress and you will rustle like a lady in a ballgown. How will that do?'

'And new slippers with bows?' Anna said quickly. She was adept at recognising and seizing the favourable moment.

'New slippers with bows,' Mrs Carson promised. 'And now, Ruth, will you ring for some tea? Mr Carson took me to Astor House for luncheon and it was all quite elegant, but the food was so rich it has left me thirsty.'

Everything was elegant: food, clothes, buildings, speech. It was the fashionable word.

Mrs Carson fanned herself, sighing with exhaustion.

'It is *so* hot! Thank goodness it will be quite different in the country. We shall be able to breathe there.'

Ruth was not sure what difference twenty-three miles would make to the climate, but at least there would be no hard pavements or buildings to reflect the heat. There would be grass underfoot, perhaps a lake. And on the moor at home, she thought suddenly, there will be a breeze, and the heather will be in bloom.

'Mama, I want to try on my new dress,' Anna said.

'Very well, my dear. Ruth shall unpack it and put it on you. Goodness knows what we shall do if it needs any alterations, since we have discovered that Ruth is *not* a needlewoman, and I have far too much to do before we leave.'

Soon after they had arrived in New York Anna had torn a dress and Mrs Carson had handed it to Ruth to repair. She had been horrified at the botch Ruth made of it and Ruth had begun to wish that she had taken a few of Hester's proffered lessons. She could do with being able to sew for her own sake. She had saved enough to buy a length of material in the market, but by the time she had enough money from her wages to pay a dressmaker, the summer would be over.

Fortunately, Anna's dress fitted perfectly. Mrs Carson smiled.

'Spared again, Ruth!'

It was mid-morning when they left the city and the heat was already building up again.

'Last night's storm has done little to clear the atmosphere,' Mr Carson said. 'But I have ordered the carriage hood down so we shall benefit from the movement of air.'

'Then we must take our parasols,' Mrs Carson decided.

Ruth wore the pale lavender cotton dress which Mrs

Carson had given her. It fitted closely, since Mrs Carson was thinner than her servant, and flatter-chested. She had pinned a bunch of violets on her bonnet and put new, light grey ribbons on it. She was aware of Mr Carson looking at her, and when he handed her into the carriage to sit beside Ruth she felt quite the lady. Or almost. Elegant kid gloves like the ones Mrs Carson wore would have improved her image, but she possessed none. So far, gloves had been something to keep out the raw cold of the Yorkshire winter. Now she would have liked them to have covered the warmth of the hand which Mr Carson took lightly in his.

For his part he noticed, not the dress but the slender-waisted, full-breasted figure it adorned; the pretty face and the abundant dark hair which the bonnet framed; the large amber eyes which met his as he helped her in. He felt the warmth of the hand, which was not soft to the touch like his wife's, but firm. He was not sure whether the pulse which beat in their joined hands was hers or his.

They were quickly in the country. Above Twenty-third Street the buildings began to thin out. A few well-to-do people, preferring a quiet existence, had built houses north of there, but once they had passed those and were driving along the Bloomingdale road, there were only isolated farmhouses and cottages. As they drove north the landscape became more rugged, with hills, and great outcrops of rock which reminded Ruth of home, though the Manhattan hills were gentler, with nothing of the size of steepness or the Yorkshire fells.

'Thank goodness there are some trees,' Mr Carson remarked. 'The shade is so welcome. Anna, close your mouth or it will be filled with dust from the road!'

At Manhattanville they stopped to water the horses and to refresh themselves with a drink of lemonade from an inn. The lemonade, cold as ice, in a deep earthenware jug with slices of lemon floating on top, was delicious.

'And now we must be on our way again,' Mr Carson said.

Millfield was the largest house Ruth had ever seen. A

long drive curved towards a three-storeyed, white building, with steps leading up to its porticoed door and on either side of the doorway a wide, pillared verandah. A coal-black manservant came out to the carriage and showed them into the house. He was magnificently tall, broad, and handsome, and Anna stared at him so hard that she tripped, and fell up the steps. She was not yet used to seeing black-skinned people. This man was even more splendid than Sammy, the page-boy at Gutermann's, though he lacked Sammy's braided uniform and turban. He seemed kind, too, putting out a hand to set her on her feet again.

Mrs Barnet, accompanied by a boy of about Anna's age, was in the spacious hall to greet them.

'Did you have a tolerable journey? Was it very hot? How nice to meet you all!'

Mrs Barnet carried too much flesh on her small frame, so that her figure appeared several years older than her face. Her gown looked expensive, Ruth thought, but it would have suited her mistress better than it did its owner. Also it was too elaborately trimmed for the country. She had pretty fair hair which escaped from its disciplined coiffure in tendrils around her long face.

'Mr Barnet has an errand on the estate,' the lady continued. 'And George and Daisy are out riding. Children are so energetic, are they not? I expect your little Anna is the same! And here is Edward, who has so been looking forward to a new playmate!'

She gave the boy a push and he and Anna faced each other, glowering. Ruth felt sure that but for the presence of their parents they would have stuck out their tongues.

'We had a pleasant journey, thank you,' Mrs Carson said. 'Anna, say hello to Edward.'

Ruth was glad for her mistress's sake that Mrs Barnet seemed so friendly. Mrs Carson had been a little apprehensive about their visit. Mr Barnet was no more than a business acquaintance, but with true American hospitality he had taken pity on the young English couple who had no means of escaping from the city.

'Now Reuben will show you to your rooms,' Mrs Barnet announced.

Ruth longed to go with Anna to their room. She wanted to wash her face and hands in cold water, if possible to lie down for five minutes. She felt quite sick and dizzy from the long drive over the bumpy road.

'I have put your daughter in a cot in your room,' Mrs Barnet continued. 'We have a very full house, but in any case I'm sure you'll want her with you. Then Reuben will take your maid to the servants' quarters.'

So the fluttering Mrs Barnet knows where *I* belong, Ruth thought.

She waited alone in the great pillared hall until Reuben returned. From the slight smile he gave her she judged him friendly, but dignified; conscious of his positon in the household.

'Please come with me,' he said.

At the back of the hall a flight of stairs led down to the servants' kitchen. That, too, was on a larger scale than anything she had ever known. She remembered how huge she had thought the Longhills' kitchen on her arrival in Nordale, and reckoned that it would have fitted into a corner of this one. There were at least eight people in it, most of them busy. Only two men and a woman, who sat at a centre table, were not at work, though the woman had a piece of sewing in her hands. The men looked up as Reuben led Ruth towards them.

Ruth knew at once that she had seen one of the men before. While he regarded her with evident interest, she searched her mind. Had she passed him on the street – on Broadway perhaps? But why should she have remembered him? He had a pale face, deep blue eyes, hair darker and straighter than hers, and a mouth which curved and turned up at the corners in an almost feminine way. A pleasant enough appearance, but in no way memorable.

'Come and sit yourself down,' he invited.

The moment she heard his soft Irish voice, Ruth remembered. He was the man on the *Flamingo*, the one who had explained to her why so many ships lay at anchor. And the reason why she had been so slow to recognise him was that on the ship he had looked so much older. Now the years had fallen away from him. His face had filled out, the slight hollows beneath his cheekbones owing nothing to hunger and serving only to accentuate his agreeable features; the slight tilt of his nose, the long, Irish upper lip, the blueness of his eyes. Ruth now put him at no more than five-and-twenty.

'Sit ye down,' he repeated. He poured a drink and pushed it towards her. It was pale green, with a delicious new taste which turned out to be that of limes.

'Ye looked startled when ye saw me,' the man said.

'Not startled,' Ruth contradicted. 'Puzzled. I knew I'd seen you before and I couldn't think where.'

'I doubt that,' he replied. 'I've not been in the country long. And you could say I get about a lot without meeting anybody. I'm coachman to Mr Barnet. Mostly in New York City, up here only for the summer. Besides, I couldn't have forgotten you!' He raised his glass to her. 'Sean O'Farrell, at your service!'

'Ruth Appleby. But you *have* forgotten me, Mr O'Farrell. We met on the *Flamingo*.'

He looked surprised, studying her face intently until she felt embarrassed. Had she also changed in a few short months?

'Of course!' he exclaimed at last. 'You're the lady with the little boy!'

'My cousin's child. They went on to Wisconsin.'

'I kept a lookout for you on the ship. You seemed to vanish.'

'Well, here I am now,' Ruth said.

'And very welcome. But I'm forgetting my manners, so I am. Introductions! Now this elegant young lady . . .' he indicated the woman '. . . is Miss Polly Beard.'

Miss Beard, for whom Ruth thought 'drab' would have been a better description, inclined her head.

'And this gentleman is Mr Herbert Fraser. Their master and mistress are visiting here.'

Mr Fraser gave Ruth a strong handshake, his round, apple-cheeked face creasing in a smile. Then as she was about to explain her own presence there, the outer door of the kitchen opened and a man entered.

He was tall: elegantly dressed for riding in well-cut white breeches and a black jacket which fitted to perfection over his broad shoulders and deep chest. He was dark-skinned, as if there might be Mediterranean blood in him. In fact, Ruth thought, his features were very like those of a man in the reproduction of an Italian painting which had hung in the Longhills' drawing room. He had a straight but prominent nose, a well-shaped generous mouth, dark eyebrows which almost, but not quite, met over the bridge of his nose. But most noticeable of all – it was something apart from his physical appearance – he had a presence which immediately dominated his surroundings. It would be easy to forget everyone else when he was there.

The Irishman sprang to his feet.

'See to Prince,' the newcomer said. His voice was deep and strong, matching his appearance. 'I shall want the carriage in an hour's time, O'Farrell.'

Ruth could not take her eyes off him. Then, as he seemed about to leave, he shifted his gaze from Sean O'Farrell and caught her staring. He stared back and, blushing with confusion, she rose to her feet and gave him a little bob.

'I don't know you, do I?' he asked. 'Are you new here?'

'I'm Ruth Appleby,' she replied. 'I belong to Mr Carson.'

Mr Barnet – it was clearly he – continued to look at her, and while he did so she could not look away.

'Do you, by Jove!' he said.

Then he turned, and left the room.

# 11

Ruth found herself obliged to share a bedroom with Polly Beard. Miss Beard – to her face only Sean O'Farrell dared use her first name, bringing a blush to her cheeks whenever he did so – was lady's maid to Mrs Harvey Telscombe. 'Servant' seemed too coarse a word for such a refined creature and indeed she made it plain that she did not usually inhabit a servants' hall.

'Naturally I have my own little room,' she assured Ruth. 'Which Mrs Telscombe has furnished especially for me. She is a woman of refined taste and comes from one of our oldest families. I daresay *you* are not used to servants' halls either.'

Since sharing a room with her was clearly going to be more bearable if Miss Beard could suppose Ruth to be a cut above the other servants, Ruth humoured her.

'No. I've never been used to that. I share Anna's room and live close to the family.'

Miss Beard nodded with satisfaction at her reflection in the spotted mirror, before which she was brushing her sparse, dun-coloured hair. Then she put down the hairbrush and inspected her countenance. Ruth wondered if she was gazing at the dark whiskers which sprouted on her chin and made her so appropriately, though unfortunately, named.

'Of course we shall not be staying here long,' Miss Beard said. 'Were it not that Mr Telscombe had business to discuss with Mr Barnet I doubt we should be here at all. We are not really on visiting terms. Indeed, we are on our way to the Astors.'

Even Ruth, ignorant as she was of New York society, knew about the Astors. Who didn't? Now she pleased Miss Beard by opening her eyes wide and looking suitably impressed.

'Tell me, Miss Beard, is it true that Mr Astor's income is two million dollars a year, four dollars a minute? I can't believe it!'

'Oh, I'm sure it will be true,' Miss Beard said nonchalantly. 'Not that my mistress talks much about *money*. I know in New York it is wealth that counts, but I am pleased to say that it is not so everywhere. In Virginia it is family which matters, and the Telscombes are a very old family. At home there we move in the highest circles.'

'As the Carsons do in England,' Ruth replied impulsively. She doubted if it was anywhere near the truth, but clearly it made Miss Beard happy. Ruth resisted a fleeting temptation to bring in Queen Victoria and the Royal family, deciding that her almost total ignorance would quickly let her down.

'The Barnets are *nouveau riche*,' Miss Beard confided. 'Their wealth has secured them a place in New York society – and one must admit that Mr Barnet is a very presentable man, though somewhat offhand. But it is different in Virginia.' When she spoke of Virginia it was in reverent tones, as if it was the last stage on the journey to heaven.

'Is Mr Barnet well liked?' Ruth asked lightly.

'Well enough,' Miss Beard conceded. 'My mistress likes him, but then all the ladies do. And his wife is pleasant. But his children are odious, as you will find out.'

Ruth soon came to share Miss Beard's opinion of the Barnet children, especially of Edward, but Anna was attracted to him and within twenty-four hours was his willing slave. She followed him everywhere, allowing him to bully and browbeat her for all he was worth just as long as he didn't banish her. Sometimes it was Ruth's job to look after them both, though not often, since Edward had his own governess, Miss Fitch, who was omnipresent and jealously guarded her position. Ruth hated the way Anna let herself be dominated by this selfish boy.

'You should stand up for yourself, Anna,' she told her. 'Never give in to a bully.'

He had taken all Anna's coloured chalks, so that she was reduced to standing and watching while he drew the pictures.

'I *want* Edward to have my chalks,' Anna said flatly. 'I *like* watching him draw. He does it better than I do.'

Since Ruth was required to be less and less with the children she found herself with too much time on her hands, and since she was unused to idleness she found the vacant hours trying. Mrs Carson noticed Ruth's listlessness and rightly interpreted its cause.

'You could help *me* more,' she suggested. 'You could help me dress my hair, manicure my nails. Most of the ladies here have their own maids.'

So it was arranged. Ruth never felt that she was good at it, but it made a change, and she enjoyed listening to her mistress's accounts of her days. She thought too that Mrs Carson liked having her there. She was still a little unsure of herself in American society.

'I hope *you* are enjoying yourself, Ruth,' Mrs Carson said one evening.

In fact, Ruth heartily wished herself back in New York. She was bored at Millfield.

'Yes, thank you, ma'am,' she replied dutifully. 'Though I haven't always enough to do. It would be pleasant if . . .' She hesitated.

'Yes?'

'Well, perhaps you might allow me to go for a walk from time to time, instead of waiting around in the servants' hall. But only when you weren't likely to need me, of course.'

'Very well, Ruth,' Mrs Carson agreed. 'But see to it that you don't go too far, and try always to be in the house when you think you might be needed.'

Not all Ruth's time with the other servants was disagreeable, but she quickly found that Millfield's own staff had little time for the servants of visitors, especially anyone they thought might consider themselves superior. In this, in spite of her repeated offers to help Mrs Cranbrook, the cook, she found herself classed with Polly Beard and Herbert Fraser. She sensed, too, that her English accent kept her a little apart, made her sound uppish.

She doubted that in ordinary circumstances Herbert Fraser and Polly Beard got on well together. He had a valet's professional mistrust of all lady's maids. Ruth thought he was also disappointed that his opposite number wasn't young and attractive. But in the face of the enemy they presented a united front.

Sean O'Farrell was no-one's enemy. He was friendly to everyone.

'They're all all right really,' he told Ruth. She had been irritated by the cook's refusal of her offer to make a simple white sauce, though Mrs Cranbrook was up to her eyes in work.

'Remember,' he went on, 'we're all the same kind. We should band together.'

'What do you mean?' Ruth asked.

'That's our strength,' he said. 'Sticking together.'

Though she had certainly never thought herself superior to her fellow servants, Ruth had no wish to be too close. She knew already that to think like a servant was the surest way to remain one – something she was determined not to do.

Sean was always busy. Members of the house-party were constantly taking trips; calling on neighbours, going on picnics, inspecting local beauty spots. He was forever in demand, in spite of which he remained affable and good-tempered. Ruth was in the servants' hall one day when he returned from yet another picnic.

'Did you have a good time?' she asked him.

''Twas not bad. The sun would have shone brighter if yourself had been there. Why were you not with the children? The little devils could have done with a firm hand!'

'Mrs Carson said there wasn't room in the carriages. Miss Fitch went instead.'

'Nonsense!' he said. 'I'd have been delighted for you to

have been squeezed in next to me. And the less room the better!'

His blue eyes invited her to imagine what it would be like (which she did, and found the thought quite pleasing).

'It's a good thing I don't take you seriously,' she told him. 'I might be annoyed.'

'Oh, but I am serious,' he assured her. 'And it's a stupid woman who'd be annoyed by a compliment. You're not stupid, Ruth.'

She had sensed from the beginning that his compliments to her were of a different kind from those he bestowed so liberally upon every female in sight, but she couldn't tell him that, while in her heart she liked them, she might be annoyed by his assumption that they were always acceptable.

'Yorkshiremen don't go in for paying compliments,' she said. 'They think it's a bit soft. So their womenfolk don't always know how to accept them.'

'Which is a pity,' Sean stated. 'Compliments oil the wheels of life. Even a bit of flattery doesn't go amiss.'

She knew that Sean found her attractive. She would have liked to have made the truth plain – that the feeling, though not one to be taken too seriously, was mutual. But that was too big a step for convention to allow. Convention demanded that a woman must skirt around the truth, fobbing off a man while leading him on. To be too direct was to be unfeminine.

'Perhaps when I get a minute to meself we can have a picnic of our own,' he suggested. 'There's one or two places I'd like to show ye.'

'Oh I couldn't,' Ruth said quickly. 'Not just the two of us!'

'Well then, if you don't think that's proper, we can take Herbert and Miss Beard,' he conceded. 'It won't be half the fun, but I daresay we'll manage.'

'That would be all right,' Ruth said. 'And now, if you'll excuse me, I must go to my mistress.'

Mrs Carson proved to have no need of her. 'Not for at

least an hour,' she said. Anna was immersed in a game with Edward under the watchful eye of Miss Fitch, who gave Ruth no welcome: so she decided to go for a walk.

She knew better than to walk around the front of the house. Servants, except when summoned, must never be visible. It would not do for some occupant of the house to look out of the window and actually see one walking across the lawn.

She took a path across the land at the side of the house and found that it led to a small wood which girdled the top of the hill on which the house was built. Having walked through the wood, she emerged on to a small, high plateau, from which a wide sweep of the countryside below was visible. One could sit here and admire the view, she thought; or lie almost hidden by the tall golden grasses which, perhaps because the place was not easy of access, had been left to grow to their full height and now filled the air with their mingled scents.

Ruth chose a place and sat down. There had been a shower earlier in the day, and although the hot sun had dried the ground again, a sharper-than-usual smell of earth and growing things still lingered. She lay back on the ground and inhaled deeply. When she closed her eyes, the sun warm on her face, she recognised the perfume of the grasses as ones she had encountered before. And then she remembered Dick; the journey back from Skipton, and her first and only taste of lovemaking, there in the field.

It was almost two years since then, but the scents in her nostrils were so evocative that every detail of that occasion came sharply into her mind. She could remember the feel of Dick's hands on her body, his voice in her ear. She did not think at all of the consequences, only of the act itself. And remembering it – it seemed more as if she relived it – her whole body ached, tensed, fidgeted. She held her arms across her aching breasts so tightly that her fingers dug into her flesh, but whether in an effort to contain herself or as a substitute for someone else's embrace, she didn't know. Nor did she know whose embrace she was seeking. It didn't matter.

She was not sure how long she had been there, or how long she might have remained, had she not been disturbed. It was the thud of a horse's hooves, very near, almost on her, which jerked her back to reality. She jumped to her feet, screaming in terror, certain that she was about to be trampled on.

At the sound of her scream the horse stopped short, reared, whinnied loudly in distress and fright at the figure which appeared suddenly, noisily, from the long grass just beyond its forelegs. While the rider tried to hold on, to calm the horse and to prevent himself being thrown, Ruth ran as fast as she could towards the wood.

'STOP!'

It was a voice not to be disobeyed: authoritative, commanding. She stopped at once.

'Come here!'

Reluctantly she turned around – and saw that the rider was Mr Barnet; also that he was exceedingly angry, his eyebrows meeting in a fierce scowl, his dark eyes blazing.

'Come here at once, I say!'

The horse was a big one, a grey of about seventeen hands. Though it was quieter now, Ruth walked forward with trepidation, stopping a few yards short of it. Horse and rider towered above her.

'Don't you ever do that again! *Never, ever*, do you hear?' There was an ice-cold anger in Joss Barnet's voice which lashed Ruth as if he had used the whip in his hand.

'Are you aware that you could have caused an accident – a serious accident? This is a most valuable horse!'

Ruth's fury suddenly equalled his.

'I'm aware that *he* could have harmed *me*!' she retorted. 'I move quickly so that I shouldn't be trampled to death. Am I supposed to lie down and be killed, then, so that your horse shan't be frightened?'

The words rushed out. She didn't care what she said, or that he was who he was. But when she came to the end of them, and stood there trembling, she realised that if he remembered her he would certainly report her to Mr Carson. Such insolence – that was what it would be called – could cost her her job. There was nothing else for it, she would have to apologise.

But why should she? He had not shown the slightest concern for her. She might be hurt, but *he* didn't care. He hadn't so much as asked. She looked up at him, well aware that her rebellious thoughts must show in her expression. To her surprise, the anger left his face. There was a twist to his mouth which, though not going so far as to be a smile, showed some amusement.

'I know who you are,' he said. His voice was still stern. 'You are the young lady who belongs to Mr Carson.'

Ruth's faint hope that he would not remember her died. But she was emphatically *not* sorry for anything she'd said, and she decided that nothing in the world would make her say she was.

'I wouldn't have frightened your horse deliberately,' she replied.

'I should hope not. That would be both stupid and dangerous. At any rate you seem to have come to no harm.'

'I didn't know I shouldn't come here. It's the first time I've done so.'

'Who said you shouldn't come?' he asked.

'Servants are not to go where their masters frequent.' She was aware there was nothing of the servant in her voice.

Now he did smile, and it changed him completely, lifting the lines of his face so that he appeared hardly older than herself, though she knew from Miss Beard that he was almost thirty.

'I can't see that stopping you,' he said. 'You are a pert young woman. However, you may come here whenever you wish. It is not a place I usually frequent.'

'Thank you, sir.'

He continued to look at her and she could not take her eyes off him.

'But if I chose to do so, what then, Miss Ruth Appleby?'

She was astonished, and secretly pleased, that he had remembered her name.

'Since you have given your permission, sir,' she said slowly, 'why then, I would come here just the same.'

He nodded, then turned and rode away at a canter.

Ruth dawdled back through the wood, reluctant to return. The moment she set foot in the house, Cook called out to her.

'You'll be for it, my girl! Your mistress has been ringing for you this past fifteen minutes!'

'Where on earth have you been?' Mrs Carson asked crossly when Ruth appeared.

'I'm sorry, ma'am. I was out walking and forgot the time.'

'Well if you're going to be absent when I need you, you must cease taking walks!'

Ruth thought Mrs Carson had been put out by something other than her small misdemeanour. At a guess, she had had a tiff with Mr Carson. But it behoved her to tread warily if she didn't wish to find her new-found freedom curtailed – and that was the last thing she wanted.

'I'm really very sorry, ma'am,' she repeated. 'I promise you it won't happen again.'

'Well, see that it doesn't,' Mrs Carson replied. 'It pleases me to give you privileges, but I don't care to see them abused. Now, what shall I wear this evening? I think the grey silk might be suitable.'

When Ruth had brushed and pinned up her mistress's red-brown hair, which always shone as though newly burnished, she thought how lovely Mrs Carson looked. She had a skin of a creamy paleness which Ruth envied. Her own rosy cheeks were so countrified. And now that Mrs Carson's awkward mood had passed, her brown eyes were clear and soft again.

'Yes,' Mrs Carson said, looking in the mirror. 'I think that will do nicely.'

'You look beautiful, ma'am,' Ruth told her.

'You mustn't flatter me, Ruth,' Mrs Carson said pleasantly. 'Flattery is bad for us.'

'It's not flattery, ma'am,' Ruth replied. 'And compliments, so I've been told, oil the wheels of life.'

Mrs Carson gave Ruth a questioning look.

'Well, I daresay that's true – if the compliment is

genuinely meant. And now I have some news for you. On Saturday evening there is to be a special party here: an orchestra, dancing, and several important guests. I must certainly look my very best *then*! I think the affair will call for my new yellow satin.'

'You will outshine everyone, ma'am,' Ruth said.

Mrs Carson pulled a face. 'That's enough, Ruth. Now please go and see to Anna. The strange child has chosen to sleep in Edward's room tonight; but I am sure she will want to see you and perhaps you can give Miss Fitch a hand.'

At suppertime in the servants' hall all the talk was of the coming party.

'We had one once before,' a housemaid said. 'You never saw anything like it! Coloured lanterns hanging from the trees; a quartet of musicians playing from a boat on the lake, as well as a band for dancing . . .'

'Drink flowing like a river in spate,' Reuben put in.

'And tables laden with food,' Mrs Cranbrook added. 'Where I'm supposed to find the time to prepare everything I don't know! We can't call on Delmonico's out here in the country, not like the city. Well, I suppose it will all fall on me. I'll be at it every minute the Lord sends!'

'I'll help,' Ruth offered. 'I can make pastry. And jellies. Lots of dishes. I'd like to help.'

'We'll have to see,' Mrs Cranbrook replied doubtfully.

'I heard there were to be fireworks,' Sean said. 'It'll be a grand affair and no mistake.'

Ruth turned to Miss Beard. 'What do you suppose Mrs Telscombe will wear?'

Miss Beard conveyed superiority, disdain, and several closely-allied feelings, in a single sniff. At the same time as her nose wrinkled, the corners of her mouth turned down and her eyelids drooped. She really had no need of speech. It was all there in her face. Nevertheless she condescended to reply.

'I'm afraid we shall not be present. We leave here on Friday. I believe I told you that we are to move on to the Astors?'

'What a pity you will miss the party,' Ruth said.

'One grows weary of parties,' Miss Beard replied languidly. 'And fireworks are a little vulgar, don't you think?'

Ruth had seen fireworks only once; at Barnswick's own celebrations to mark the wedding of Queen Victoria and Prince Albert. She had been six years old then and she had thought the fireworks the most beautiful sight in the world. She had never forgotten them.

Sean caught Ruth's eye and winked at her. 'Well then, Miss Polly, if I'm to have the pleasure of your company on an outing it will have to be soon. And isn't it the luck of the devil that the master don't require me tomorrow afternoon? Now if you two charming ladies, and Herbert here, can persuade your betters to free you from the chains for an hour or two, we're as good as on our way!'

So it was arranged. Ruth looked forward to it and she thought that, secretly, Miss Beard did also. When Ruth went into the attic that night she caught Miss Beard standing in front of the mirror, holding a navy muslin dress with a cream lace collar against herself. Flustered by Ruth's appearance, she tried to hide the dress, but she was too late.

'It really becomes you,' Ruth said. 'Shall you wear it for the picnic?'

'I doubt it,' Miss Beard replied. 'A lady never dresses too finely for the occasion.'

Ruth awakened early next morning. While Miss Beard slept on she rose quietly, dressed, and went out. There was no-one about as she left the house and walked towards the wood. This hour, before the heat began to build up, was the best time of day to be out of doors, and since her mistress would be asleep for some time yet she was free to go as she pleased. There was an unusual excitement in her this morning, though even to herself she did not admit the reason.

In the deep shade of the trees - great oaks, spreading beeches, sycamores, which had been there longer than Millfield House - the air was almost too cool, and underfoot there was a damp, springing feeling to the ground. But where the wood ended she stepped into another world. The ground which nurtured the long golden grass was hard and dry. Already, so early in the morning, the sun shone brightly.

She walked forward to the edge of the plateau. From where she stood the downward slope and the valley below were clearly visible. The countryside here was so different from her native dales and moors. It was richer, yet less splendid. More fertile, so that man would be able to tame it as he had never, in thousands of years, been able to tame her wild moors.

Would Mr Barnet ride this way, or would he still be in bed? She knew in her heart that that was why she was here. The thought had been inside her ever since he had spoken, though she had continually pushed it away. But now, since no-one else inhabited this early world of hers, she would allow it to remain.

But was her imagination too hard to work? Had she read something into his words which was not really there? Had her feelings and longings as she had lain in the grass, remembering Dick and their lovemaking, her body crying out for a repetition of the act, forged a false link in her mind? She thought not. She remembered the way Joss Barnet had looked at her. She knew she was not mistaken about that.

She continued to stand at the edge of the plateau. No horse and rider should take her by surprise today, nor easily overlook her. Her sharp eyes scanned the countryside below and, in spite of the sun, she felt a shiver, though not unpleasant, of apprehension.

She did not have long to wait. Within a few minutes she saw him riding towards her up the hill, his horse's harness glinting in the sun. When she was quite sure he must have seen her she sat down.

He breasted the hill, riding straight for her, coming so close on the great horse that Ruth had to steel herself not to move from the spot. She looked up at him and he acknowledged her presence by a brief glance, but without slackening speed he rode past her, towards the wood. Ruth could hardly believe it. She had been so sure of his intentions.

And then she realised that the hoofbeats of his horse had come to an abrupt stop. She turned her head, saw him tether his horse at the edge of the wood, watched him as he walked towards her. She noticed his long, powerful legs, the immaculate cut of his close-fitting breeches, his purposeful stride.

As he drew near she made a half-hearted move to rise. She did not count this as a master and servant situation, yet she didn't dare to presume too far. She looked to him for a lead and he gave it to her.

'Stay where you are,' he said. 'You look comfortable there.'

He stared down at her, studying her in every detail with no pretence that he was doing otherwise.

He saw a young woman, slight of figure, with narrow, sloping shoulders and a waist his two hands could easily have spanned, yet full-bosomed, the outline of her breasts, the small mounds of her nipples, thrusting against the sprigged cotton dress which was slightly too tight for her. The neckline was low and the upper part of her breasts swelled against it, dividing to reveal the shadowy cleft between them. Her neck rose in a long, rounded column to a face which, though not classically beautiful - the nose was too tilted, the mouth too wide - was heart-stopping in its freshness, its air of innocence combined with its look of deep, untapped feminine knowledge. Was she aware of the effect her large, amber-coloured eyes, her curving red lips, might have on a man? He couldn't tell. There was something about her which baffled and intrigued him.

'The grass is warm already,' Ruth said.

His face broke into a smile. She knew what she was about all right. 'You tempt me to try it,' he replied and dropped down beside her.

'I'm sorry,' she floundered. 'I didn't mean. . . .'

'Don't be coy,' he said. 'It doesn't suit you.'

His voice was sharp, yet as intimate as if he had known her for a long time. There was to be no paddling around in the shallow waters for *this* man, Ruth thought. And with the thought came a tiny prick of fear.

'I'm not being coy,' she protested. 'I was trying to be polite. I'm not very good at polite conversation.'

He didn't answer. For several seconds they just sat there. Ruth wished he would say something – anything. She found the silence unbearable. In the end she said the very last thing she intended.

'I must go!'

'Why?' he asked.

'Mrs Carson might need me.'

'Your mistress will be asleep, as you well know.'

Then he leaned towards her and took both her hands in his and began to study them as if they were entirely new creations, the like of which he had never seen before. He contemplated the palms as if he might be seeing past and future in them, and then he turned her hands over and examined the backs. Though tremors ran through her body at his touch, she wanted to draw away. She had always hated her hands. She was ashamed that they were large, and neither smooth nor white, but hard to the touch, and calloused, with the knuckles already swollen. Servant's hands, which nothing could disguise. She would have preferred him to concentrate on her face, which was more presentable.

'And supposing *I* need you?' he asked. 'Supposing I say I want to look at you, to hear you talk in your funny English voice? What if I tell you you've not been out of my mind since last evening?'

'Why, I'd not believe you,' Ruth said. 'And you shouldn't talk to me so. It's not fitting.'

He threw back his head and laughed loudly. 'Don't tell me you worry about what's fitting! I don't believe *that*!' His eyes, which were darker than Ruth remembered, almost black, sparkled with amusement.

'You have a low opinion of me,' she said, 'that you think I don't care what's right.'

'I didn't say that. I said you wouldn't worry about what was fitting. A question only of manners.'

She flared at him. He was trying to put her in the wrong again. 'So now you're saying I'm ill-mannered?'

'Ah! I've made you angry,' he said. 'Good! You're exciting when you're angry. I thought so yesterday evening.'

'Well, are you saying I'm ill-mannered?' Ruth persisted.

'I'm saying that I think you don't care about the stupidities of convention. That you're honest with yourself and don't dissemble. Otherwise you wouldn't be here. You knew I'd come, didn't you?'

'I thought you might,' she admitted reluctantly. How could he make her confess such a thing? It was brazen of her.

'You *hoped* I might. You wanted me to. If not, you could easily have avoided this place.'

She could think of nothing to say.

'Let's be honest with each other,' he said. 'Let's have no more talk of what's fitting. And now I think you *must* go. I don't want you to be in trouble with your mistress.' It was agony to him to dismiss her. She had aroused him so much that he wanted to take her here and now, on the ground. But there was something about her which forbade the crudity.

Ruth jumped to her feet, bitterly disappointed that he dismissed her so suddenly, but determined not to show it. He stood up and walked beside her to the edge of the wood where his horse was tethered. Then, before mounting, he took her chin between his finger and thumb and tilted her face towards his, kissing her lightly on the cheek.

'Where is your room?' he asked. 'Where in the house do you sleep?'

'I shared a room with Mrs Telscombe's maid.' She was trembling now from head to foot.

He nodded, and started to ride away. When he was almost out of sight she called after him.

'They leave tomorrow!'

He didn't look back. There was no telling whether he had heard.

Back at the house the kitchen was a buzz of activity. Cook

was making fresh cornbread rolls for breakfast and lesser mortals were hard at it with brooms and mops. Ruth walked through the kitchen and ascended the back stairs, looking neither to right nor left, afraid that her face might give her away. She wanted, desperately, to be alone. She wanted to think about what had happened, what might happen. But solitude was impossible.

Miss Beard was there, easing the tightly-knotted rag curlers out of her hair. Ruth took off her dress, hastily moving a stem of grass which fell to the floor, poured water from the ewer into the basin, and set about washing herself. She splashed herself liberally, trying to reduce the flush which she could still feel on her cheeks.

'Well,' Miss Beard said, 'we have a fine day for it! Just as long as the heat doesn't build up into a storm.'

'A fine day?'

'For the outing! Mrs Telscombe has kindly said that I may be free from two o'clock until six. I hope your mistress will accord you the same privilege.'

Ruth had totally forgotten the outing and her immediate feeling was that she didn't want to go. She wished to be quiet. She felt, deep inside her, that there would be decisions to make. Or should she simply let things take their course, give herself up to the almost overwhelming attraction Joss Barnet had for her? But to do that was in itself to make a decision. It was clear that he was attracted to her. She was sure he would seek her out again.

The thought of Mrs Barnet entered her head only fleetingly, to be as quickly dismissed. It was inconceivable that she could take from Mrs Barnet anything that was rightly hers, nor did Ruth flatter herself that Joss Barnet's interest in her was anything but transient. It was too much to expect, not the way of the world.

So Sean O'Farrell and his pleasantries would not be to her taste today. He was perceptive. He would sense that she was not herself. And she knew that this outing had been contrived by him so that he could make progress with her. She *did* like him. She liked him very much. Had Joss Barnet not joined her this morning she might have felt quite differently about the plan.

All these thoughts raced through Ruth's head while Miss Beard continued to babble. She heard the lady's voice but she had no idea what she was saying until a sharpness in Miss Beard's tone signified that she was repeating the same remark.

'I'm sorry?' Ruth queried.

'Perhaps you should take some soap and water to your ears,' Miss Beard said acidly. 'I said, what shall you wear?'

'I'm sorry. As a matter of fact . . .' Ruth hesitated.

'. . . I'm not sure that I can go.'

'Not go? *Not go*? Why ever not?'

'I . . . I don't feel well. I think perhaps I have a chill.'

'But if you don't go then I can't go!' Miss Beard cried. 'Could you not take a powder? Or perhaps you will feel better by two o'clock?'

Ruth had never seen anyone look so disappointed. The older woman's face puckered and for a moment Ruth thought she might cry – which was unthinkable in Miss Beard. It dawned upon Ruth with some surprise that the outing was to be a great treat for Miss Beard, and that in spite of all her high-faluting talk, not many of those came her way. Ruth knew she could no more disappoint her than she could snatch a toy from a baby.

'Well, I daresay you're right,' she agreed.

'I'll ask Cook to give you some cinnamon water,' Miss Beard declared. 'That should do the trick!'

'Thank you,' Ruth said. 'I'm sure it will.'

Since she hated cinnamon water next only to cod-liver oil it would be a suitable penance for having given Miss Beard a nasty moment.

# 12

When Ruth and Miss Beard arrived at the rear door of the house, the carriage was already waiting.

Ruth thought how smart Sean looked. He had discarded his uniform and wore his best suit, a light pearly grey, with a brightly-coloured necktie, and a rose in his buttonhole. His grey hat, which he swept off with a flourish as the ladies approached, was set at a jaunty angle. Mr Fraser was, as usual, dark-suited, but as a concession to the occasion he also sported a rose in his lapel. Miss Beard, in the navy muslin with the cream lace collar which yesterday she had affected to consider too fine for the event, carried a cream parasol. Ruth wore Mrs Carson's lavender cast-off with her one and only bonnet, and was therefore all the more pleased by Sean's appreciative look as his glance took in her appearance from top to toe.

''Tis a beautiful sight the pair of ye are!' he said. Ruth knew, as his eyes met hers, that the words were meant for her.

For all the world as if she and Miss Beard were ladies of quality, he ceremoniously handed them into the carriage, the two of them to sit together in the back, while Herbert Fraser sat beside Sean in the front. Ruth guessed that the seating arrangements were for the benefit of whoever might be watching their departure, and that they would not prevail.

'Where are we bound for?' she asked.

Not that she cared. She was here in the flesh to oblige Miss Beard, but her mind was filled to the brim with Joss

Barnet. Even Sean's obvious appreciation of her had served mainly to boost her confidence as to how she would look in that other man's eyes, if by some absolute miracle they should meet him for a moment as they were driving through the grounds of Millfield House. All she really wanted, if she could not be in *his* presence, was to be left alone so that she could recall and relive in her mind every moment of that morning's encounter, and dream about what the future might hold for her. He had said she didn't care about the stupidities of convention. Was he right?

Sean gathered up the reins and drove off at a smart pace.

'Just you wait and see!' he said.

It took Ruth a second or two to realise that he was replying to her question, not to the thoughts which whirled around in her head.

''Twill be a pleasant surprise, I promise you,' he declared.

'I'm sure it will,' Ruth agreed. 'I like the countryside around here - what I've seen of it. Don't you, Miss Beard?'

'It's quite pleasant,' her companion conceded. 'Though after Virginia . . . Now if you were to take a drive around Williamsburg. . . .'

'I hope I may, one day,' Ruth said.

There was silence for a while. When she was not holding forth on the almighty Telscombes, or the glories of Virginia, Miss Beard had little to say; and Ruth was in no mood to talk.

In fact, she noticed little of the countryside through which they passed. The harvest had been gathered and she was vaguely conscious of the glint of the sun on the gold and brown stubble. Where, in one place the track was lined with trees which stood between the carriage and the sun, she became gratefully aware of the cool shade cast by their dense foliage. On her lips she tasted the dust raised by the horses' hooves and the wheels of the carriage. But these small experiences had the remoteness of a dream. Real life was going on inside her.

She felt - it was much more than a memory - Joss

Barnet's strong hand holding hers, his lips on her cheek. She raised a hand to touch the place, as if by such an action she might capture the feeling forever.

But with Sean O'Farrell around, the silence and tranquillity could not last. Ruth had no idea how long they had been driving when Sean turned the horses off the road on to a narrow side track. It was the sharp turn, together with the speed of his driving, which flung Miss Beard over on to Ruth, and her sharp squeal as it happened which brought Ruth back to reality.

'I beg your pardon, ladies! The going's rough just here.' From the wide grin on Sean's face as he turned around to look at them, Ruth suspected that he had swerved on purpose.

'Are ye all right, Miss Polly?' he asked with concern.

'I'm quite all right, Mr O'Farrell,' she replied.

'I'm driving down towards the river,' he said. 'I thought perhaps you'd like to stop within sight of it.'

The ground sloped away now, and when, after a downhill mile, Sean stopped the carriage, there before them was the Hudson River. It was broader than Ruth, used to the fast-flowing rivers of Yorkshire, had expected, and was busy with craft plying in both directions.

'Spread the rug on the ground, Herbert,' Sean ordered. 'We'll have it right there.'

He indicated a patch of ground near some willows. There was dappled shade for those who preferred it or, by moving just a little, the afternoon sun for those who could stand the heat.

'Now, Miss Polly,' Sean said. 'What's your pleasure?'

'Oh, I think I must choose the shade,' Miss Beard replied. 'Too much sun spoils the complexion.'

'And that's a risk you mustn't run,' Sean said gravely.

Miss Polly took his words as a compliment and treated him to a coy smile of invitation, meant to suggest that he should sit beside her; but Sean had already marked Herbert Fraser for that position of honour, stopping just short of pushing him to the ground.

'Herbert's the same,' he smiled. 'Can't stand the sun on account of his delicate skin!'

He winked at Ruth as he indicated the place where she might sit and then, having settled them all to his liking, he fetched the food from the carriage.

'I'm pleased to say Cook relented,' he told them, spreading it out before them. Ruth thought it more likely that his silver tongue had got around her. As well as the cake – light, fluffy stuff with frosty icing and no body to it, Ruth privately thought – there were freshly baked rolls, split and filled with ox-tongue. Then, when the blackcurrant cordial was poured, Herbert Fraser brought a flask out of his pocket and proceeded to add a generous measure to the glasses. Miss Beard at once cried out in horror.

'Oh, no, Mr Fraser! I'm strictly teetotal, as you know!'

'Oh come on,' he entreated. 'A little drop of rum never did anyone any harm!'

'Oh I shouldn't. I really shouldn't!' Miss Beard protested.

'Why not try it just this once,' Herbert said persuasively. 'A special occasion. It could do you all the good in the world.'

Ruth had the feeling that he was desperately trying to inject a bit of life into the party and she felt guilty that she, for one, had so far been very dull company.

'Well, I really don't know,' Miss Beard fluttered. 'What do you advise, Mr O'Farrell?'

'Well, now,' Sean said. 'We all know there's no more sorry sight in the world than a lady who's had a drop too much, but a spoonful or so can be highly medicinal. Just the thing for keeping off the heat.'

'I thought rum kept out the cold,' Miss Beard said doubtfully.

'So it does, ma'am. So it does! The cold in the winter and the heat in the summer,' Sean assured her. 'The two extremes, so to speak.'

'Well, if you think. . . .'

Herbert Fraser poured the spirit into her glass.

'It really is quite pleasant,' she said. 'As a medicine, that is.'

The two men took liberal helpings but Ruth put her hand over the top of her glass when the flask came in her direction. Once, she being childishly curious, her father had given her a sip of the tot of rum he had bought to ease her grandfather's chest. She had hated the taste of it and spat it out immediately.

Not so Miss Beard. She sipped at her cordial with evident pleasure, and when Herbert Fraser offered her another nip she accepted without hesitation.

'That's right, Miss Beard,' he said. 'There's nothing that one dose will do for you that two won't do better!' He poured himself another to keep her company.

'Why I do believe you're right, Mr Fraser!' Miss Beard agreed happily.

Ruth supposed it was Miss Beard's lack of acquaintance with alcohol which accounted for its rapid, and in her case beneficial, effect. She was now all amiability – a quality none of them had looked to discover in her.

'The spirit to give you spirit!' Herbert chuckled. 'Hey! Get that? The spirit to give you spirit, I said!'

'*Very* witty, Mr Fraser,' Miss Beard said. '*Very*, very clever. I don't know when I've heard anything quite so clever! The spirit to give you spirit! Oh dear me, that *is* good, Herbert!'

She giggled and then began to laugh. The laughter pealed from her until the happy tears rolled down her thin face.

'Oh Herbert you are a caution, really you are!' She whooped with laughter, so infectious that the others had to join in.

'The spirit to give you . . . spirit,' Miss Beard gasped. 'Oh dear me!'

'I didn't know you had it in you, Herbert me boy,' Sean said. 'Did you, Ruth?'

'No,' Ruth admitted. She was not quite sure what all of them – she along with the rest – were laughing about; but there they were, rolling about with mirth, and Herbert

Fraser looking as pleased as Punch. It was the most successful moment of his life.

Gradually, when they were exhausted, the laughter died. Miss Beard gave a final small giggle.

'Oh dear me! I'm quite worn out with it all! I think if you'll excuse me I'll just take a little nap. Just a little one, that is, if you'll kindly excuse me!'

'Forty winks,' Herbert said. 'A good idea, Polly. I'll do the same meself.'

A few minutes earlier Ruth would have welcomed the idea of everyone going off to sleep (not that Sean showed any sign of doing so) as an opportunity for her to indulge in her own thoughts, but the fits of uninhibited laughter had restored her to something nearer to normality, and at last she was present with her companions in mind as well as in the flesh. Not that she could entirely stop thinking about Joss Barnet. Whatever happened, whatever was done or said, he was there in the corner of her mind.

In no time at all Miss Beard was fast asleep. She lay on her back, her usually sallow face rosy, her mouth open and emitting regular snores which, though reasonably genteel, would have horrified her if she had heard them. Herbert Fraser's snores were another matter: a robust, masculine, uninhibited production. Moreover, they did not time themselves well with Miss Beard's. Sean looked at Ruth and they started to laugh again, but since neither of them wished to waken the sleepers they stifled their mirth.

'Let's walk down to the river,' Sean whispered.

Ruth nodded her agreement and he put out his hand and pulled her to her feet.

There was no path, and the ground was too stony to be described as a meadow. Outcroppings of dark rock, large and small and sometimes steep, interrupted the coarse, sunbrowned grass.

'Take my arm,' Sean offered.

'Thank you, but there's no need,' Ruth said. 'Where I come from it's tougher country than this.'

'And where I come from,' he told her, 'it's soft and

beautiful. Greener than anything you've ever known, with gentle hills and blue lakes. And the people happy. Or they were until the potato failed; turned black and rotten and stinking with corruption, so that they killed the pigs and the people got fever. When the potato fails, everything goes. There's neither food nor work. Then it's hell, though the country is still like heaven itself.'

Ruth had never heard him speak with any seriousness before, had hardly seen him without a smile on his face. Now there was longing and bitterness in his voice and she caught a glimpse of the man she had met on the boat.

'Is that why you left Ireland?' she asked. 'Because of the famine?'

'I could have stayed,' he said. 'I might have lived. Some did – though my family's not among them.'

'Your family?'

'My mother and father. My wife's parents. The famine killed them. Do you know what one of your English dukes said? He said we should learn to live on curry powder, mixed with water! The Indians existed on it, he reckoned.'

He had almost forgotten the faces of his parents. Though both in their early forties when they died, he had thought of them as old. His in-laws he had never liked.

'And my wife and baby,' he added. 'We'd been evicted when we couldn't pay the rent because the potatoes failed. Oh, we weren't the only ones. It took the police and the soldiers to turn some of us out. After that we lived in a "scalp".'

'A scalp?'

'A dug-out ditch, roofed over with wood and grass. Our baby was born there. He was our first. He lived a week. Eileen couldn't nourish him. When he died in her arms in the scalp, she hadn't the heart or the strength to survive.'

'I'm sorry,' Ruth murmured.

'Well, God rest their souls,' Sean said. 'The pair o' them.'

His wife he would never forget. Dark, thin, too pale. A gentle girl with a face as pretty as this one beside him. But with less spirit, he reckoned.

They walked for a few minutes in silence. Ruth could find

no comfort to offer him. His words were all it needed to remind her of home, and while he, presumably, thought of his beautiful green homeland and his dead wife and baby, her thoughts turned to her loved ones. Aunt Sarah and Uncle Matt; her father, Willie, Maria. She could not bear to think of her grandfather.

And then suddenly Sean's mood changed. He smiled again, and when he spoke his voice was lighter.

' 'Tis not the day to be thinking of the past,' he said. 'Also we've walked far enough. We'll sit down right here and watch the boats on the river.'

They chose a flat rock, but it was so hot from the sun that the heat burned through Ruth's clothes and she had to move to the slightly cooler grass.

'No, it's the future that counts now,' Sean said. 'So what's the future to be, eh?'

'I think whatever we make it,' Ruth replied.

'You think it's as simple as that?'

'I think the intention is simple,' she told him. 'Perhaps carrying it out won't be.'

'So what's your intention?' he asked.

'I don't know,' Ruth admitted. 'Though I do, in a way. I know I'm not going to be a servant all my life. I'm going to be free.'

'Free, is it? And what will you do with your freedom?'

'That I don't know,' Ruth confessed. 'But I want to make something of myself – I didn't always think so. All I wanted once was to stay where I was. Maria was the one with ambition.'

'Maria?'

'My sister. She's a servant in Bradford. You'd like Maria. I miss her so much and she hardly ever writes to me.'

The memory of Maria came sharp and clear; pale gold hair curling around her pert, pretty face. She would likely never see her sister again, so that in her mind she would always be as she had been on that last walk over the moor to Barnswick. But why did she not write?

'We're most of us slaves,' Sean said. 'Even those of us who think we're free are slaves to something. Even if it's only our own ambition.'

'But if we're free we have the choice,' Ruth objected.

'Do we?' he said. 'Are we not driven every bit as much as a master drives his servants?' He smiled at her. 'Anyway, 'twould not suit you, being a fine lady.'

So! This morning she had been told that she was ill-mannered; now it seemed she was not fit to be a lady!

'I suppose you think I'm not good enough? Well let me tell you . . .'

'I said no such thing,' Sean interrupted. 'You could hold your own with the best. I said 'twould not suit you, and I meant it as a compliment. You're not the one for dressing up, visiting, gossiping, idling your time away.'

'Is that all ladies do, then?'

'Most of 'em,' Sean said. 'I've seen plenty in the last few months.'

'Well, that's not what I want,' Ruth admitted. 'What I want is to be in charge of myself, to decide what I will or will not do.'

'I wish ye all ye wish yourself,' Sean said. 'But there we go, getting solemn again. We're supposed to be having a good time today!'

'I *am* having a good time,' Ruth assured him.

Against all her expectations, she was enjoying herself. In spite of her unwillingness to join the outing, and the remote mood she had been in for most of the day, in the last few minutes she had begun to feel herself a real person. She was also discovering that there was more to Sean O'Farrell than the frivolous charm which he presented to the world.

'How wide the river is here,' she said. 'And to think I might have sailed up it had I not chosen to be independent. I was to go with my cousins to Wisconsin, you know.'

'Did they make the journey safely?' Sean asked.

'Yes,' she replied. 'I had a letter.'

He stretched out an arm and pointed to a steam vessel going north. The deck was crowded and several passengers leaning against the rail waved a greeting. Ruth and Sean waved back.

'Good luck to ye all!' Sean called out at the top of his lungs. 'They'll need it,' he told Ruth. 'It's certain sure that there are poor devils on that boat who've been cheated and don't yet know it. When they get to Albany they'll find the tickets they paid over the odds for won't take them any further. It'll take all that some of 'em have left to buy a ticket up the Canal. So your cousins were lucky.'

'Ernest has his head screwed on the right way,' Ruth said. 'You don't take in a Yorkshireman that easily.'

Sean laughed. 'Now it's different with the Irish. They're easily taken in, on account of they're so tremendously honest themselves!'

'And modest with it!' Ruth said. 'But what about your future? You haven't said yet.'

'I don't know,' he answered. 'I'm still thankful to be alive and eating three meals a day. But I'd like to see my own kind better off than they are.'

'You mean the Irish?'

'I've left Ireland behind,' he said. 'America is for me. I mean my own class. The working-class. The world's servants. I'd like to see them better treated. So should you. They're your class too, Ruth.'

'They're not!' she flared. 'Oh, it's not that I think myself better, not a bit. But I will *not* be tied down. I shall always be myself, choose how. No-one's going to stop me.'

'Whoa!' Sean held up his arms in a pretence of fending her off. 'No-one's trying to.'

'I'm sorry,' Ruth said. 'I get carried away.'

'A passionate Englishwoman,' he remarked. 'It's a contradiction in terms.'

'I'm a Yorkshirewoman,' Ruth said. 'We might take a bit of rousing, but when we believe in something we don't mind saying so. Still, like you I've left all that behind. America's my country now.' She spoke firmly, but deep inside her she was less sure.

'Shouldn't we go?' she asked. 'We must be back by six

o'clock. Mrs Telscombe requires Miss Beard no later and I daresay Mrs Carson will require my services too, even if Anna doesn't.'

Sean threw back his head and laughed loudly.

'Have I said something amusing?' Ruth asked. 'If so, pray enlighten me.'

He jumped to his feet and pulled her up after him. His eyes, meeting hers, were intensely blue and lively and she noticed the fine laughter lines on his face. It was strange that a man who had known so much sorrow could radiate so much life. He was a good person to be with, even if he did laugh at her.

'You're a real contradiction,' he said. 'One minute you disown the servant class, the next you're worrying about being a minute late for your duties! My dear little Ruth Appleby, you've got the conscience of a servant – and no bad thing either!'

'Sean O'Farrell,' she shouted furiously, 'I have *not*! While I have to do the job I'll do it properly. But I'll not do it forever, and it shall never own me. I'll show you! One of these days I'll make you eat your words!'

He backed away from her in mock fear, but he was still laughing at her and though she meant every word, she couldn't continue to be angry with him.

'I'll race you to the top of the hill,' he said.

He easily outpaced her. She struggled up the last few yards and arrived at his side breathless.

When they reached the others Herbert Fraser, his homely face creased with impatience, was standing by the horses, but Miss Beard was still asleep and wakened only at their approach. She blinked, yawned, sat up: dazed, not quite sure where she was.

'Dear me,' she said. 'Did I fall asleep for a minute? How very ill-mannered of me!'

''Tis nothing,' Sean assured her. 'The heat of the day, no less. But now I'm afraid we have to return to Millfield.'

By some manoeuvre which was so swift that Ruth did not observe it, she found herself sitting up in front beside Sean, while Miss Beard and Herbert Fraser kept each other company in the back of the carriage.

'It was good of your Mr Barnet to lend us the carriage,' Ruth said when they were driving along.

It gave her infinite pleasure simply to utter Joss Barnet's name. She wondered if she would be fortunate enough to see him when they returned to Millfield. There was no reason why she should. She had no excuse for going into his part of the house and she had not seen him near the servants' quarters since that first afternoon. She pinned all her hopes on the following morning when, she had already determined, she would go to the plateau again. So, she was sure, would he.

'He's not a bad master,' Sean acknowledged. 'Not that he'd have lent the carriage – or freed me – unless it was entirely convenient to him. Self first every time.'

'You make a harsh judgement,' Ruth said.

'Not harsh. True. Besides, if he hadn't been selfish, hard, ambitious, he wouldn't be where he is.'

'Is he very wealthy then?' Ruth asked. Not that she cared.

'Rolling! And getting richer all the time, they say. A finger in every pie. His main business is in banking, but now he's expanded into ships.'

'Ships?'

'The new Barnet line. Mostly carrying cotton from the South for transhipment to Liverpool – which is where your Mr Carson comes into the picture. Also, he's started building ships on the East River. He goes after what he wants and gets it.'

'And Mrs Barnet?' Ruth asked. 'What about her? Is she . . . are they . . .?' Though she preferred not to think about Mrs Barnet she could not prevent herself asking the questions.

Sean laughed. 'She certainly knows how to spend his money! Clothes from Paris, entertaining, travel. A beautiful house in St John's Park and now she wants to move to one of the new ones in Gramercy Park. Thinks it's more genteel.

'I suppose she loves her children,' Sean continued. 'But give me warmth in a woman.'

'She doesn't have it?'

He shrugged. 'There's no love lost. Perhaps beacause he plays the field. Or perhaps that's *why* he goes after the women. Who knows where anything starts?'

'Women?' She didn't want to know. She wanted to close her ears to it. So why did she ask?

'Oh, he's a ladies man all right! And from what I've seen the ladies seem glad of it. Don't tell me he hasn't made a set at your pretty mistress!'

It was unthinkable. Mrs Carson was devoted to her husband. And yet at Millfield she had been more than ever concerned about her appearance, wanting to be well-dressed and attractive at all times. And I have helped her to be so, Ruth thought, jealousy surging through her. But it couldn't be true, it just couldn't.

She didn't want to hear any more. Of course she did not believe a word Sean O'Farrell was saying. It was nothing more than servants' gossip. Even so, she would rather it remained unspoken. And even supposing - just supposing - that any of it was true; well, it would be quite different in her own case. After all, a man could change, couldn't he?

'Perhaps we shouldn't talk like this,' she said primly. 'After all, he *is* your employer.'

Sean took his eyes off the road long enough to turn and give her an astonished look.

'You beat the band! Since when have servants not discussed their employers? It goes with the job. Anybody knows that - including them!'

'Then perhaps I'm not your typical servant after all,' Ruth said triumphantly.

For once, when they got back, Anna needed her. 'Will you bathe her and put her to bed before attending to me,' Mrs Carson said.

Anna was full of prattle about where she had been and what she had done.

'Miss Fitch took Edward and me for a walk and we gathered stones and pebbles. Then Edward's papa took us on the lake in a rowing-boat.'

'Edward's papa?' Ruth, soaping Anna's small body, tried to keep her voice steady.

'Yes. I splashed my hands in the water but he wasn't a bit cross.'

'Did Miss Fitch go with you in the boat?' Ruth asked.

'Yes. But she didn't row. Mr Barnet rowed the boat and he let Edward and me have a turn with one oar. I like Mr Barnet. Do you like Mr Barnet, Ruth?'

'Yes.'

'I don't like Miss Fitch,' Anna went on.

'Now you mustn't say things like that,' Ruth admonished her. 'Miss Fitch is . . . kind.'

And lucky, she thought. Perhaps if she herself had been more insistent on spending time with Anna . . .? But then she would have had no time for taking walks.

She heard Anna's prayers, tucked her into bed and kissed her goodnight before going to Mrs Carson. Her mistress was already dressed for dinner.

'If you would just pin up my hair,' she said. 'You are getting so good at it. Did you enjoy your afternoon?' she added as Ruth brushed her hair.

'It was most pleasant, thank you, ma'am,' Ruth replied.

'Sean O'Farrell is a personable young man,' Mrs Carson observed. 'Do you not think so?'

'Why yes,' Ruth agreed. 'He's very nice.'

'You could go farther and fare worse than O'Farrell.'

Ruth's eyes met Mrs Carson's in the mirror. There was no mistaking her mistress's meaning. But how very far she is from the truth, Ruth thought.

'I have not thought of Mr O'Farrell in those terms,' she replied. 'Nor, I am sure, has he of me.'

'Perhaps you should,' Mrs Carson said frankly. 'I should like to see you settled before Mr Carson and I return to England. I know it will not be for some months yet, but time passes quickly. I say this because I have the feeling that you no longer wish to join your cousins in Wisconsin. Am I right?'

'Yes, ma'am. You are quite right,' Ruth admitted. 'There is no place for me there.'

'I should have thought . . . with the new baby . . .' Mrs Carson began.

'No, ma'am,' Ruth interrupted. 'I shan't go to Wisconsin.'

'Then perhaps you should take what I have just been saying even more seriously. As for your point that Mr O'Farrell does not see you in that light, that is surely up to you?'

'You mean . . . I could make myself attractive enough to him?' Ruth was fairly sure she could, but she had another question in mind of greater importance.

'Of course you could,' Mrs Carson assured her. 'And you would make him a good wife.'

'Excuse me, ma'am,' Ruth said, 'but is it your opinion that a woman can attract any man if she has a mind to?'

Mrs Carson did not reply at once and Ruth wondered if she had gone too far and annoyed her mistress. Mrs Carson was peering closely at her own image in the mirror. She smoothed the dark wings of her eyebrows, pinched her cheeks to make the colour come. Then she studied her maid's reflection in the glass.

How the girl had changed since their first meeting on the ship! She had been a little waif then, in her Yorkshire homespun. Though come to think of it, she had known how to ask for what she wanted. But now she had an air of confidence, a bloom on her skin, a light in her eyes. The New World certainly agreed with her. Yet even now I know little about her, Mrs Carson thought. She keeps herself to herself. All things considered, she would be better married.

She turned around and faced Ruth directly.

'Not any man. Not any woman. But I'm sure you'd have no difficulty, Ruth.' The dry note in her voice did not escape Ruth.

When Ruth climbed into her bed that night Miss Beard was packing for her next day's departure and she was far more talkative than usual, regaling Ruth with the names and pedigrees of notables with whom she might be privileged to breathe the same air. She longed for the silly woman to stop prattling and to blow out the candle. She wanted to lie there in the dark, alone with the thoughts she had had to suppress for so much of the day. Alas for the weakness of the flesh! Within two minutes Ruth was fast asleep and Miss Beard still in full spate.

But next morning Ruth awakened early and, leaving Miss Beard to her gentle dreams, dressed quickly and hurried out of the house. It was another golden day. She still retained her English habit of noting each day's weather, always expecting changes, marvelling at the hot sunny days which followed one after the other, almost with monotony.

When she reached the plateau she remained standing, watching for Joss Barnet, waiting for the moment when she would see him riding towards her. There was no longer any need for her to be 'discovered'. Her sole purpose in being there was to meet him and she was content that he should know it.

He was late this morning. Or was she earlier than she thought? Had she misjudged the time? No matter. She was happy to wait for him, certain that soon she would see him riding towards her. Then as the minutes passed and there was no sign of him, she considered that perhaps he had overslept. It could happen. Or had his horse gone lame, cast a shoe? She sat down and prepared to wait as long as was necessary. She knew that in the end he would come.

After a few more minutes she became restless, and stood up again, her eyes searching the slope of the hillside and the valley below, trying to determine whether some small movement down there was a man on horseback or merely a trick of her imagination. Should she set off down the hill to meet him? But perhaps he would come by another route and then she would miss him.

At the end of what she reckoned must be an hour, she faced the fact that he was not coming. She dropped to the ground again and lay down, burying her face in the sweet-smelling grass. She had been mistaken ever to think that he would come. She had let her overwhelming desire feed her imagination; had read something into his words, his looks, his actions, which had not been there at all. Her face burned with the shame of it. Such was the feeling Joss Barnet had aroused in her, that not for one moment did it occur to her to blame him for anything. It was all her fault.

Sick at heart, she wept. Then she dried her eyes on the hem of her petticoat and went slowly back to the house.

'So you've decided to put in an appearance?' Cook said. 'I do seem to recall something about you offering to help me with the party preparations. But of course if you've changed your mind. . . .'

'I haven't,' Ruth snapped. 'I'm ready to start now. I don't want any breakfast.'

'Hoity-toity! What's the matter with everyone this morning?' Cook demanded. 'There's Sean O'Farrell and the master left in a hurry this hour past for New York City, both without a bite inside them – and now you.'

'Gone to New York?'

'That's what I said.'

With Mrs Cranbrook's words Ruth's appetite immediately returned. So he had not failed her after all! How could she have thought that he would? Something unforeseen and urgent had happened, since Sean had obviously known of it yesterday afternoon, and there had been no opportunity for him to inform her. Relief surged through her like a physical infusion of new blood.

'I've changed my mind,' she said. 'I would like some breakfast. Suddenly I'm hungry. When will they be back?'

'Sean? How should I know? I don't understand business. What I *do* understand is that if the master's not home for the party tomorrow, the mistress won't be pleased – and that's putting it mildly. Don't you dawdle over your breakfast then, not if you intend to make yourself useful. There's plenty to be done.'

Ruth worked all that day as though she had the strength of ten. They prepared chicken pies, the pastry as light as Ruth's heart, turtle soup, a haunch of venison, jellies, blancmanges, syllabubs, trifles, and a host of other dishes, with still more to be done on the day of the party itself. Mrs Cranbrook unbent so far as to show approval.

'You've done very well,' she conceded.

Mrs Carson, knowing how much was involved, had excused Ruth from all other duties until Anna's bedtime hour. And now it approached. She took off the voluminous apron Cook had lent her and went in search of her charge.

Anna was in tears.

'We're going home,' she sobbed. 'I don't want to go back to Mrs Gutermann's. I want to stay with Edward. I want to live with him for ever and ever!'

Ruth could think of few worse fates, but her stomach lurched at the thought of leaving Millfield.

'How do you know we're leaving?' she asked. 'Who told you?'

'Miss Fitch,' Anna wailed. 'I don't like Miss Fitch. I hate her! I daresay *she* wants me to go!'

'Perhaps she's mistaken,' Ruth said, though she doubted if Miss Fitch was ever wrong. 'We'll ask your mama the moment she comes in.'

'I'm afraid it's true,' Mrs Carson told them. 'Of course we were only invited for ten days or so.'

Ruth had lost count of time. To her, the long summer days had stretched ahead, world without end.

'We are going to leave on Sunday,' Mrs Carson went on. 'Not too early in the day, since I daresay we shall all be tired after tomorrow's party.'

'Anna tells me she never wants to leave Edward,' Ruth said after the child had gone to sleep.

Mrs Carson smiled indulgently.

'Dearest Anna! She's a little young for a holiday infatuation, but we all have them sooner or later. Thank goodness they never last! And the more intense they are, the shorter the duration, so Anna should soon be over it.'

'Will Mr Barnet be back for the party?' Ruth asked.

'I expect you mean will O'Farrell be back,' Mrs Carson said. 'And the answer is, I don't know. Mrs Barnet tells me that she expects her husband when she sees him. It's a fact that American men seem to put business before everything. Thank goodness Englishmen are not like that!'

Next morning Ruth was down in the kitchen early, eagerly hoping to find Sean there. He could well have returned late at night and she not heard him, though she had stayed awake for a long time, listening for the sound of the horses, the carriage wheels on the drive.

There was no sign of Sean but Mrs Cranbrook was already at work.

'I hope you're ready to help me,' she said. 'Everybody is busy with this and that – as if food wasn't the most important thing!'

'I'll help, Mrs Cranbrook,' Ruth agreed. 'They're not back then?' She tried to sound nonchalant.

'Not back? Oh, you mean O'Farrell and the master? Not that I know of. There's no telling when *they'll* return. Sometimes they're gone for three or four days at a time.'

'But surely . . . with the party?'

Mrs Cranbrook shrugged. 'He's a law unto himself, the master. Not for the likes of you and me to question why.'

The heart had gone out of the day. Ruth fetched and carried and stirred and whipped, praying every moment that Joss Barnet would return before they left Millfield next day. But when the day had dragged to evening – in spite of all there was to do the time now passed slowly – and still there was no sign of the two men, she began to lose hope.

In the evening, bone-tired, she left the kitchen and went to put a reluctant Anna to bed. Then she turned to helping Mrs Carson. She brushed her mistress's hair and piled it on top of her head in a cluster of curls, carefully and meticulously arranged to look quite casual. It was a style Ruth had devised herself and Mrs Carson was delighted with the result.

'It looks so different,' she said. 'You really are quite clever at this, Ruth. And now for my dress.'

She looked beautiful in the yellow satin, the low-cut bodice tight against her slight figure, the skirt billowing out. But

Ruth had no heart either to appreciate or to envy her mistress. Her spirits were at their lowest ebb.

Mrs Carson gave her maid a sharp, compassionate look. She thought she knew the cause of this mood and in a way she was glad to see it. At least it showed that the girl's mind was working in the right direction.

'Don't worry, Ruth,' she said kindly. 'I daresay O'Farrell will be back tomorrow before we leave. And if not, there is always New York when the Barnets return in the fall. And now I shan't need you again this evening, so apart from looking in on Anna from time to time, you may do just as you please.'

Had she not been so downhearted Ruth would have enjoyed herself. But she had given up all hope of Joss Barnet returning that evening and nothing else in the world mattered.

The party scene was pretty enough. Coloured lanterns hung in the trees which fringed the lawn and bordered the lake beyond. Torchlights, flaring against the night sky and reflected in the water, had been set up wherever it was suitable. Already the orchestra had begun to play and the elegantly dressed to appear.

Ruth had no heart for it. She climbed the stairs to her room, then undressed and went to bed, wetting the pillow with her tears which, held back all day, now flowed unchecked. Her only comfort was not to have Miss Beard in her room, to be able to suffer in solitude. Though she thought sleep would never come, eventually it did. She fell asleep to the sound of music drifting upwards from the drawing-room.

When she wakened it was still dark, the orchestra still playing, though it was not that which had aroused her. Penetrating her sleep she had heard the faint click of the door latch, and then the familiar squeak of the hinge as the door to her room slowly opened. She raised herself on one elbow, blinking her eyes, trying to see in the darkness. But enough light came from the landing on to which the door opened to silhouette the man standing there. It was Joss Barnet.

Shock made her cry out, and he closed the door and moved

towards her in quick strides, putting his hand across her mouth to stop her scream. Then he sat on her bed and, without a word from either of them, she went willingly into his arms and was held close in his embrace. She felt his heart beating strong and fast against hers. They stayed like that for a long moment and then he said, 'Light the candle.'

'I can't,' she whispered. 'Someone will see the light under the door.'

'No matter if they do,' he said. 'They will not think of me here. Only my coachman knows I am home. I have not yet joined the party.'

'You came to me first?' She could hardly believe it.

He would not tell her, this funny bewitching little English girl, that he had come to her first because he could not keep away from her. She had been on his mind since the morning he had seen her from his horse; frightened yet defiant, sparking with anger. Almost, but not quite, she had come between him and the work he had had to do in New York City. The moment the work was done he had ordered his coachman to drive him back to Millfield as fast as the horses would go.

'Light the candle,' he repeated.

Ruth's fingers trembled as she obeyed him. Then she lay back on her pillow and they looked at each other as if it was for the first time. He traced the contours of her face with gentle fingers, outlining the curve of her mouth, stroking her temples. Without any hurry, in spite of the impatience which had brought him here, he caressed the length of her neck and the slope of her shoulders.

From out of nowhere, Ruth remembered Dick Parker: but not, this time, the pleasure of her union with him, only the pain it had brought her on the Christmas Eve following.

And now although her whole body cried out for fulfilment and she longed for Joss Barnet to complete what he had surely come to do, she knew that she must not let it happen. She turned her face away from him, pushed his hand from her.

'No!' she cried. 'You must not!'

He gave not the slightest sign of having heard her, continuing to stroke her neck, and now inserting his fingers under the neckline of her nightshift. She tried again to push him away.

'Please! Please don't!' she cried.

It was surprise which made him stop for a second. He smiled at her, an unexpectedly tender smile.

'I won't hurt you,' he said. 'Don't be afraid.'

'I'm not afraid of being hurt.'

'Then what . . .?'

'I'm afraid of afterwards,' she said hesitantly. 'If I were to have a child. It would be the end of the world for me.'

'But you won't,' he assured her. 'I'll see to that. I'm not totally callous.'

'You promise?'

'I promise.'

She lay quiescent and felt his strong fingers, quicker now, move to unfasten the buttons of her shift one by one. And when he had undone her gown, and had difficulty in lifting it over her head, she raised herself from the pillow and helped him to take it off. Then he pulled down the sheet, which was all the bedclothes she had needed on that warm night, and she lay naked before him.

She observed him without shame as he looked at every part of her. Her pleasure was in him, and in his delight of her. When, at last, he stripped off his clothes and came into her, it was as if this was the moment to which all her life had been leading.

He was a skilful lover: tender and gentle in the beginning, then powerful, persistent, rough almost – until, his passion rising in harmony with hers, the climax came like the bursting of a thousand stars, like the beginning and ending of the world.

Afterwards they lay quietly side by side, not speaking, until he said, 'I must go.'

'Not yet,' she begged. 'You can't leave me yet.'

She turned over and lay on top of him, trying to pin him down with her own slight weight, and he began to fondle her and she him, and almost at once they were making love again.

'You are a sorceress,' he told her when it was all over. 'An enchantress. Women as tempting as you should be kept out of the sight of mortal men.'

'You're not a mortal man,' Ruth said. 'You're a god!'

He laughed out loud.

'Hush!' she cautioned. 'Someone will hear you.'

'I'm a real man all right,' he said. 'As I've just proved to you. And would again if time allowed.'

Then he stood up and quickly began to dress.

'I must go and do my duty as a host for what's left of the night.'

'Don't leave me,' she begged. 'Please stay!'

He looked at her in surprise, spoke brusquely.

'But of course I must go. There's no question.'

Long afterwards Ruth realised that this was the moment when she had learned that she could never come first with him. However much he might desire her, she would have no more than the allotted space in his life.

'When am I going to see you again?' she asked.

That, also, was the wrong thing to say.

'I can't make plans,' he said sharply.

'But we leave tomorrow!' she exclaimed.

That took him by surprise. 'The deuce you do! Well I shall see to that. My wife will extend the invitation to the Carsons. I take it they're not promised elsewhere?'

'Oh no,' Ruth said. 'We're going back to New York City.'

He finished dressing, then came and held her by the shoulders, kissing her lightly on the mouth. As he was leaving he turned around and threw a small box on to the bed.

'From the city,' he said. 'You see that I had you in my mind!'

He was out of the room before she could open the box, a dark blue leather affair, lined with white velvet, against which lay a fine gold chain with a small oval locket set around the edge with seed pearls. She gasped in amazement. It was without doubt the most beautiful thing she had ever owned, or ever would. Such delicacy, such refinement! Her fingers trembling with excitement, she fastened it around her neck. It should remain there for ever. She would never take it off.

# 13

'Well, it was a splendid party,' Mrs Carson remarked.

Ruth had just finished dressing Anna and had sent her off to nursery breakfast.

'So they were saying in the kitchen, ma'am. I'm glad you enjoyed it.'

She felt full of charity towards the whole world this morning. Beneath her dress the chain and locket lay warm against her skin. Her hands strayed towards her neck in a desire to touch it, to reassure herself that everything she remembered of last night was true.

'And what did *you* do?' Mrs Carson asked in a kindly manner.

'Me? Oh, I went to bed early. I was tired,' Ruth said.

'Very sensible.' The girl had probably been moping for that good-looking coachman. Mrs Carson raised a hand to her mouth and stifled a yawn. 'I'm sure before the day is out I shall almost wish I had done the same thing!' It was not true. In her yellow satin she had been the belle of the ball, the recipient of a score of compliments, and she had enjoyed every minute of it. 'But since you have been in the kitchen this morning you will know that your friend O'Farrell is back?'

'He wasn't there,' Ruth said truthfully. She had been glad about that, not wanting to meet him; not wishing to talk to anyone just yet.

'Ah well! It was exceedingly late when Mr Barnet joined us last night. This morning, really. Mrs Barnet had quite given up hope. In fact it was so late that the party was dying, but our host's appearance gave it new life. He was full of high spirits. One would never have thought, to see him join the dancing, that he had only that moment arrived back from the city. So perhaps he had taken pity on O'Farrell and said that he may have a later start this morning.'

'Perhaps so,' Ruth agreed. 'Did you dance with Mr Barnet, ma'am?'

'Why yes, as a matter of fact I did! He is an exceedingly good dancer too.'

What would it be like to dance with him, Ruth wondered? To wear a satin gown, low at the neck, as full as could be in the skirt so that it would swirl in the waltz. It would be the palest green, the green of young beech buds, and trimmed with silver. She would wear no jewellery except the locket he had given her - and perhaps one diamond star in her beautifully coiffed hair. He would hold her lightly in his arms, gazing only at her as they twirled around and around. Eventually everyone in the ballroom would stop dancing to watch the entrancing spectacle they made.

Mrs Carson's voice interrupted Ruth's dream.

'But all good things come to an end, and we are to leave immediately after luncheon. Mr Carson has ordered a carriage to be here for us at two o'clock. So while I am at breakfast, Ruth, will you please get on with the packing?'

'But . . .' Ruth stopped herself. It was not possible to tell her mistress that she knew better, that they were to stay on. So in the meantime she must make some pretence of obeying instructions. She had no fear that Mr Carson, at any rate, would not be delighted to stay longer at Millfield if Mr Barnet wished it. He clearly set great store by his host. And naturally Mrs Carson would do whatever her husband thought best. Ruth derived a certain satisfaction from the knowledge that it was she, a servant, who was changing the course of events for her betters.

All she wanted in the whole world was that she should be wherever Joss Barnet was. Millfield, New York City, Timbuctoo - it was of no consequence so long as they were both in the same place, so long as she could see him and be with him whenever possible. She blessed Providence that had taken Miss Beard away and left her in sole possession of the attic.

When Mrs Carson left the room Ruth began, in a desultory fashion, to fold her mistress's gowns as if for packing. Though the trunk had not yet been brought up – and would not be, she thought with pleasure – she must appear to co-operate. It was essential that she should do all she could to stay in Mrs Carson's good books and so ensure that she had as much free time as possible. Perhaps, Ruth considered, if she thought that I wanted to spend it with O'Farrell. . . .

When Mrs Carson returned from breakfast Ruth waited for the order to replace the gowns in the closet. It did not come.

Instead Mrs Carson said, 'Please hurry with the packing, Ruth. And find out why the trunk is not here. It would be most ill-mannered not to be ready to leave at the appointed time.'

Something had gone wrong. And she could not ask what.

'I trust that Mrs Barnet is fully recovered from the party?' she floundered.

Mrs Carson stared at her. It had hitherto seemed to her that Naomi Barnet found little favour with her maid, so why so solicitous? What a strange girl she was sometimes.

'It seems so,' she replied. 'Indeed, our hostess said how much she would have liked us to have stayed on a few more days, but other guests are expected tomorrow and the house will be quite full. Now *please* hurry, Ruth. You don't seem to have accomplished much so far.'

Ruth turned away, hiding her face in the closet under the pretence of unhooking another gown. It was unbearable. How could she conceal her miserable feelings? She must speak with Sean O'Farrell at once. He was her only hope of finding out where Joss Barnet was, and that she *had* to know. She could not possibly leave Millfield without speaking to him.

'I'll go down and see about the trunk immediately,' she said.

There was compassion in the look Mrs Carson gave Ruth as she ran out of the room. Poor child, she was almost in tears. There was no doubt that she had rushed off to see O'Farrell and it was clear that she thought more of him than she admitted. I must somehow see to it that they meet in New York, she decided.

Sean was in the kitchen, dressed in his livery and obviously about to leave. He seemed as eager to see Ruth as she was to find him.

'Thank goodness ye've come,' he said. 'I thought I must leave without so much as a farewell. I'm off this instant. The master has to go over to Westchester about a horse and we shan't be back until late afternoon. But I wanted to tell ye, I shall somehow see ye in New York. Depend upon it!'

He gave her hand a vigorous shake, and was gone. Ruth stood there unbelieving. It couldn't happen like this. It just couldn't. There must be something she could do.

She ran out after him, around to the front of the house where she was not supposed to go. She saw Joss Barnet climbing into the carriage. She stood there, hidden in the shadow of a tall pillar, and watched him being driven away; and it was as if everything that mattered in her life was leaving her. How could he do this? How could he leave her without a word? When the carriage was out of sight she went slowly back into the house.

'He'd be a good catch for any woman, that Sean O'Farrell,' Mrs Cranbrook declared.

The rest of the morning was horrible. She went about the job of packing in a mute, trance-like state.

'Try not to worry, Ruth,' Mrs Carson said. 'I'm sure you'll see him in New York.'

Would she? Sean, yes. He had said so. But would she see Joss Barnet again? Yet he had clearly not intended so swift an end to what was between them. Her hand went towards the locket which was hidden under her gown. As her fingers traced its shape she was temporarily comforted.

'I daresay you're right, ma'am,' she replied.

'And now you must try to be more cheerful,' Mrs Carson

said briskly. 'It is quite bad enough having Anna in the mood she is in!'

Anna was red-eyed and pale, and had refused breakfast. In spite of her own opinion of the horrible Edward, Ruth sympathised with her.

On the stroke of two the carriage was at the door. At five minutes past the hour Mrs Barton was bidding her guests a cordial farewell.

'It has been such a pleasure having you here,' she gushed. 'I am so sorry that you have to go.'

She's not sorry at all, Ruth thought. Nor is my mistress sorry to be leaving. Apart from Anna, I am the only one who really cares, and my heart is breaking. She was pleased that no-one thought to look at her. She knew she could not keep her feelings out of her face.

'We must all meet in the city in the fall,' Mrs Barnet was saying.

'My wife and I look forward to it,' Mr Carson replied politely.

When would that be, Ruth wondered? And what chance was there that she would see Joss Barnet then?

Mr Carson gave the signal to the coachman and they left. Ruth was glad that she sat with her back to the driver. It meant that she could see Millfield, with all that it meant to her, until the very last moment when the curve of the drive took it out of their sight. When they had arrived at Millfield – was it only ten days ago? It seemed another lifetime – she had been awed and impressed by its splendour, though not noticeably moved. Now she felt that she was leaving her heart behind in this beautiful white edifice. But not in its stately rooms or in its great kitchen. It was the small attic room which she would never forget.

They made a silent journey. It seemed no-one was in the mood for conversation. By late afternoon they had left the Bloomingdale Road and entered Broadway, and at the sight of it everyone's spirits seemed suddenly raised.

'It seems so familiar now,' Mrs Carson observed. 'Almost like coming home!'

It was true, Ruth thought. Although she had been here no more than a few months, and although everything was so different from her beloved Yorkshire, at this moment she had the feeling of belonging. There was some sort of solace for her in coming back to Broadway; as if the surging crowds, the hundreds of pedestrians who milled about on the sidewalk, calling out to each other, crossing the street under the very feet of the horses, were, in spite of their various nationalities, all akin to her.

The road was, as usual, choc-a-bloc with horse omnibuses, hackney coaches, carriages, carts, animals and people. The numbers who had fled the city for the summer seemed not to have thinned the crowds at all. And it was hot; incredibly hot and humid. Already she was sweating again.

They skirted Union Square, drove down past Grace church, and as they passed Wagner's Anna's face brightened at the thought of ice-creams to come. With difficulty, the driver manoeuvred the horses to make the turn from Broadway into Spring Street.

'It seems to me to be particularly crowded here,' Mr Carson said. 'What can be happening?'

'Perhaps a street performer,' his wife suggested. 'You know how a good one always draws the crowd.'

'Oh, I hope it's the magician,' Anna cried. 'Or the man with the puppets! Have you seen the man with the puppets, Mama?'

'I have, my dear. He's very clever.'

They were into Spring Street now. Mr Carson craned his neck, trying to see over the crowd. 'I am afraid it is nothing so pleasant,' he said quickly. 'There is an ambulance. What is more, it is drawn up outside Gutermann's.'

Mrs Carson clutched at his arm.

'Oh my dear, whatever can have happened? George, you must make your way through and see what is wrong. I shall stay here with Anna and Ruth in case it is something very unpleasant – or even infectious. And for your sake and ours, my love, I beg you not to go too near!'

They watched with trepidation while Mr Carson elbowed his way through the crowd. An ambulance never failed to draw onlookers.

'Perhaps someone has met with an accident,' Ruth said. 'Oh dear, I do hope it is not Professor Woodburn! It cannot be Mr Pierce or any of the other men. They would not be home at this time of day.'

'Now, Ruth,' Mrs Carson said. 'It is quite likely that it is no-one from Gutermann's, but a street accident. Someone crossing the road in the way of the horses.'

Then, just for an instant, the crowd moved a little to one side and the two women saw, quite clearly, men bearing a stretcher descending the steps of Mrs Gutermann's house.

'Oh dear! Can you tell who it is?'

'No, ma'am,' Ruth replied. 'We're too far away. In any case, whoever it is is covered by a blanket. And lying very still.'

'I fear the worst!' Mrs Carson exclaimed. 'Oh how I wish Mr Carson would return! What are we to do?'

When Mr Carson, who had had a word with the ambulance men and had spoken to a man in a top hat who looked as if he might be a doctor, came back to the carriage a minute or two later, his face was grave.

'The cholera!' Mrs Carson cried. 'I can tell by your face, George, that it is the cholera!' She flung her arms around her daughter and held her close. 'We must protect Anna at all costs!'

'Calm yourself, Elizabeth,' Mr Carson said. 'It is not the cholera, or indeed anything infectious. Nevertheless the news is grave. It is Mrs Gutermann, and she has had a seizure. They are taking her to the City hospital, but from my short conversation with the doctor it seems that the outlook is not good.'

He addressed the Coachman. 'As soon as the ambulance leaves, drive forward to the house.'

Mrs Gutermann lay quietly in her hospital bed for a week, between life and death, and then gave in to death. Little was know about her. It seemed that she had no connections at all in

New York. Mr Gutermann was long since dead and they had no children. Over the years her boarders, though she was never close to any of them, had taken the place of family and friends. It was they, and her servants, Mrs Cruse and May, who visited her during those last days. By nothing more than coincidence – they were taking their turn with the rest – Mr and Mrs Carson were with her at the end.

'But it would not have mattered,' Mrs Carson said. 'It would not have mattered if no-one had been there. She was not conscious.'

'You must not say that, Elizabeth my dear,' Mr Carson chided her gently. 'We can never know what comfort our presence can give, even to one who no longer seems to be with us.'

Mrs Gutermann had not moved or spoken since the moment of her stroke, which had occurred in the very room where Mrs Carson now sat on the sofa, wiping away her tears as she described the death-bed scene. Mrs Gutermann, so May said, had been inspecting the room to see that everything was in order for the Carsons' return.

'How dreadful to die like that, in a foreign country,' Mrs Carson sighed. 'So far from home!'

'But, my love, New York *was* her home,' Mr Carson said. 'She had lived here many years.'

'No, George,' his wife contradicted. 'She was German. Heidelberg was her home. That much we do know.'

It was plain to Mrs Carson that America would always be a foreign country; a place where those born in other lands might sojourn while pleasure and duty claimed them, but must leave in the end. It was a place to live, not to die in. She and Aunt Sarah would have understood each other completely, Ruth thought. Her eyes misted at the thought of Aunt Sarah. She missed her so much. She longed to see her and hear her, to be folded in her warm embrace.

Professor Woodburn, having been longer in the house than any other boarder, was expected to know most about Mrs Gutermann, and he was with the Carsons at this moment, the three of them discussing what was to be done.

'She never spoke to me of relatives and I do not recall that she received mail from Germany,' he told them. 'I think it is likely that she has cut all ties with her homeland.'

'Nevertheless we must find out what we can,' Mr Carson said. 'There is the question of the house – though I daresay it is rented – and all its contents, as well as any personal possessions she may have left. Perhaps it would be a good idea, Professor, if you and your wife were to look through Mrs Gutermann's belongings in the hope of coming across some information, and I will find a lawyer who will deal with the case. I daresay my friend, Mr Joss Barnet, will recommend one. All the same, I'm afraid it will take some time to settle the affair.'

'Very well,' Professor Woodburn nodded. 'And I think, if you agree, that we should foregather with Mrs Gutermann's regular boarders and put them in the picture as to what is happening.'

So after the funeral all who had attended gathered in the Carsons' sitting-room. Ruth was pressed into serving each one of them with a glass of Madeira which Mr Carson had provided at his own expense.

'Well now . . .' Mr Carson began.

'One does not wish to speak out of turn,' Mr Gossop interrupted in a rush, 'but it is important that we know what is to befall us.' He had a high, nervous voice at the best of times and now it positively trembled. Incongruously, since he was tall and thin, with a drooping ginger moustache, he reminded Ruth of a new lamb. She had seen such a one on her uncle's farm, bleating piteously because it had lost its mother.

In fact, she thought, standing by the sideboard, ostensibly to serve further refreshment but also because no-one had noticed and dismissed her, most of the assembled company had the air of lost sheep, waiting to be rounded up and safely penned, with Mr Carson and Professor Woodburn playing the parts of sheepdog and shepherd. All the same, she was sorry for them. Perhaps they had been genuinely fond of Mrs Gutermann. In any case they had suffered a serious interruption, with which they seemed ill equipped to deal, to their well-ordered, comfortable lives.

'Of course,' Mr Carson said. 'For all our sakes we must straighten things out as soon as possible. That is what we are here to discuss.'

'If I can be of any *practical* help,' Mr Pierce offered eagerly, 'I shall be delighted. I am pleased to say that I was sometimes able to be of service to the late Mrs Gutermann – God rest her soul.'

Mr Pierce, Ruth sensed, was the least sure of all the boarders of his position. He must therefore be the most anxious that there should be as few changes as possible.

'If we *must* find somewhere else it would be as well to do it soon,' Miss Fontwell said. She had been sitting in the corner with closed eyes, and Ruth thought she had dropped off to sleep, but her voice was brisk and businesslike. 'Boarding-houses fill up quickly in the fall.'

Professor Woodburn turned to Mr Carson.

'What Miss Fontwell says is quite true. It is the way things work in New York. It is customary for those who wish to make a change to do so at the end of the summer vacation. And then, of course, there are always new arrivals in the city in the fall. Although vacancies naturally occur during the change-over, the best places fill quickly.'

'But we don't want to leave,' Mr Pierce put in plaintively. 'I think I speak for all of us here.'

'Naturally,' Miss Fontwell said. 'I was merely trying to be *sensible*.'

Ruth wondered how well they all got on together. Like most families they probably had their differences. But by the nodding of heads and murmurs of assent it seemed that on this occasion they were all in agreement.

'Well then,' Mr Carson said, 'we must see if somehow we can keep going. Perhaps for a few days we should try to continue exactly as we are. And if any one of you has a suggestion to make, perhaps you would bring it to myself or to Professor Woodburn?'

'Gladly,' Mr Gossop bleated. 'It's good of you to take the responsibility.'

Thus the Carsons and the professor were appointed (or, with the way of the English in a foreign country, had appointed themselves) to deal with the situation.

During Mrs Gutermann's stay in hospital, and for a few days before the funeral, Mrs Cruse had been dealing indifferently with the cooking while May did most of the housework. It was this arrangement that Mr Carson suggested should continue for a little while longer.

Mrs Cruse was quite unequal to the task. She had never classed herself as a cook. At the lowest possible rate of pay she had taken only the simplest steps in cooking, and then only under her employer's strict supervision. Mrs Gutermann, though as a matter of prestige she had never let it be known, was the expert. Without her Mrs Cruse was lost.

At the end of a week of inedible meals Mr Carson, in the dining-room, pushed his plate away from him.

'Is something wrong, dearest?' his wife asked.

'You know very well what is wrong,' he answered. 'It's no use. I cannot eat it. The meat is always either half raw or burnt. The gravy is watery, the vegetables tasteless. As for the puddings . . . I am sick to death of lumpy semolina!'

'I must say I am thankful that in this heat I have very little appetite,' Mrs Carson confessed.

'Then you are fortunate,' her husband snapped. 'But I have not lost my appetite for decent food, nor, I suspect, have most of my fellow guests!' He had raised his voice and now turned around in his chair. None of the boarders were eating. 'You see!' he said. 'They have all given up!'

'I must admit,' Mr Gossop said, 'that I have seldom enjoyed my food less than in the last few days.'

'We used to have such *good* meals,' Mr Pierce sighed. 'Do you remember Mrs Gutermann's custards?'

'Well, for my part,' Miss Fontwell declared, 'I do not feel that I am getting value for money.'

'You see, Elizabeth,' Mr Carson said when they were

back in their own sitting-room, 'we all long for a decent meal! You really must speak to Mrs Cruse.'

'But she is not my responsibility,' Mrs Carson complained. 'I am a boarder here like everyone else.'

'We have undertaken to see this matter through, and we must all pull our weight,' Mr Carson said firmly. 'Surely you do not expect me to concern myself with the domestic staff? My task, undertaken voluntarily, is to see to the legal and financial aspects of this sad affair.'

'I'm sorry, George,' Mrs Carson apologised. 'I will speak to her, though I don't know what difference it will make. It's clear to me that the poor woman is not capable.'

'I just can't do it, ma'am,' Mrs Cruse said tearfully when Mrs Carson spoke to her next morning. 'It's not what I was engaged for and if Mrs Gutermann could speak she would tell you. It's not that I won't, but it's not in me – let alone that I have a queasy stomach which won't take more than a cup of arrowroot or a bit of steamed fish.'

Which explains a good deal about our menus over the last few days, Mrs Carson thought.

'So I'd be grateful, ma'am, if you'd see your way to engaging a new cook as soon as possible. Much as I'd like to help out, this I can't do.'

Mrs Carson sighed. 'Very well, Mrs Cruse. I'll see what I can do.'

'And then there's all the work of the house,' Mrs Cruse continued. 'Which May can't keep up with, no matter how!'

That was self-evident. Dust was accumulating in corners, clean towels were no longer in plentiful supply; and Mrs Gutermann would have been horrified to see the state of her brass door knocker, which she had always caused to be cleaned every day.

'But how am I to find a cook at such short notice? And at this time of the year?' Mrs Carson demanded of her husband when he came home that evening. 'I am at my wits' end. I pin my hopes on Mr Barnet being able to advise me. You did say that they were returning sooner than expected?'

'Yes. In order to attend Miss Jenny Lind's concert at Castle Garden,' he confirmed.

'Oh how wonderful! I do wish we could go,' Mrs Carson said.

'Well, I do not!' He was emphatic. 'I am sick to death of Miss Jenny Lind. No-one speaks of anything else. Broadway is blocked with sightseers each time she moves out of her hotel, with the result that the traffic comes to a standstill and no-one can go about their business. As for the newspapers!' He snatched the copy of the *New York Times* from the table. 'There you are! "Movements of the Swedish Nightingale". A whole column devoted to her doings. Barnum must be making a fortune out of her. He's no fool!'

'They say he had to raise a large sum of money to persuade her to come,' Mrs Carson remarked.

'They also say – I have it on good authority – that Joss Barnet helped him considerably.'

'In which case they could surely obtain tickets for us!' Mrs Carson said brightly. 'Oh, do try, George. I do so want to see her. And if she is what brings the Barnets back to New York, then even you must allow she has her uses!' She smiled up at him, laid her small white hand on his. I'll lay ten to one she manages to go, Ruth thought.

She was doing a jigsaw puzzle with Anna in a corner of the room and had heard every word of the conversation with mounting delight. She would willingly have pinned a medal on Miss Jenny Lind. But from the first mention of the Barnets' return she kept her face hidden in case her feelings should show.

In spite of the happenings at Gutermann's, the thought of Joss Barnet was with her all the time. Sometimes, of necessity, he was pushed to the back of her mind, but more often he was at the centre of her thoughts. She had fervently hoped that he would pay another visit to the city, even though his family was at Millfield, but if he had done so she had heard nothing of it. She felt sure that if there had been such a visit Sean would have sought her out.

Next morning, as if her thoughts had caused him to

materialise, there was a knock on the door and May came in to deliver a message.

'If you please ma'am, there's a Mr Sean O'Farrell at the door would like to have a word with Miss Appleby, if that's convenient.'

Mrs Carson turned swiftly, smiling at Ruth.

'Why, of course it is! Ruth, put on your bonnet and you may take an hour off to walk with O'Farrell – that is if he wishes you to. But no longer, mind!' She was all amiability. She delighted in a proper romance, especially if she could play handmaid to Cupid.

'He's ever so handsome,' May said enviously as Ruth followed her to the kitchen. 'You are lucky!'

But there was no greeting from Sean. His expression was grim, his blue eyes cold and hard.

'Where can we talk?' he asked shortly.

'We can go for a walk if you wish. Mrs Carson has given me an hour off duty.' She could not make out what was the matter with him.

He rushed out of the house, hardly waiting to see if she followed him. She had to run along Spring Street to keep up with his stride.

'What's wrong, Sean?' she asked. 'Why are you behaving like this?'

He made no reply, simply walked on, not slackening his pace. She wanted, above all, to ask him if everything was well with his master, but somehow she dared not. In silence they kept on walking until they reached Washington Square.

'Please stop, Sean!' Ruth begged. 'I have no breath left. And I want to know what is the matter.'

'Very well,' he said. '*This* is!'

He took a letter from his pocket and handed it to her. 'I would prefer not to deliver it,' he told her brusquely. 'But I have no option.'

She knew at once that it was from Joss Barnet. Her hand shook as she took the letter. When she made a move to put it in her pocket – much as she longed to know the contents she did not wish to open it in front of Sean – he stopped her with a word.

'No! Ye have to read it. I've been ordered to take back an answer. Yes or no. And if it's what I think it is and ye've the sense ye were born with, the answer will be "no".'

'I must sit down,' Ruth said. Her legs were trembling. She sat on the nearest bench and Sean continued to stand, glaring down at her. She had not thought he could look so stern.

She tore open the note. 'Washington Square, this day at three o'clock. Yes or no by my coachman.'

That was all. No tenderness. No hint that he had missed her, longed to see her. No signature even. Yet it was all she needed, and every word was poetry. She read it again, and then read it for the third time. She had almost forgotten that Sean O'Farrell was there.

'Well,' he barked.

'Tell your master "yes" '.

He lost his temper then.

'You're a little fool! You're wrong in the head!' he shouted without restraint. Two women walking by stopped to listen, but he took no notice of them.

'How do you know?' Ruth said. 'You can't have read the note.'

'I don't need to,' he stormed. 'I can guess. And let me tell ye, it's not the first one I've delivered and will doubtless not be the last! Don't fool yourself you're the only one!'

'Stop it!' Ruth cried. 'I don't want to know that.'

'Then ye should,' he said angrily. 'Have ye no self-respect whatsoever? Do ye want to be just like the rest? There's a name for them, if ye want to know!'

'I'll thank you to stop insulting me, Sean O'Farrell!' Ruth yelled. The two women were listening with avid interest but she didn't care. 'I know what I'm doing, and so does your master. It has nothing to do with you.'

She could not expect, nor did she, that Joss Barnet had never looked at another woman. But that was in the past.

'Oh, *he* knows what he's doing all right!' Sean sneered. 'He's a past master at it. Trust him.'

'I do,' Ruth said. 'And how can you, his coachman, know anything about Mr Barnet's feelings? Or mine either for that matter? And what is it to do with you anyway?'

'I know him *because* I'm his servant,' Sean retorted. 'And don't you forget that in spite of your high-falutin' ideas, that's what *you* are. A servant. That's how my employer sees you.'

'He does not! How dare you. . . .'

He shouted her down. 'And it's my business because I care what happens to you. Someone has to stop you making a fool of yourself. I respect you. He doesn't.'

'Oh yes he does!'

For a few seconds neither of them spoke. Ruth was angry beyond words. Who did he think he was, this Sean O'Farrell? Then he came and sat beside her and took her hand, and though she tried to pull it away, he would not let her go. When he spoke his voice was gentler.

'Don't have anything to do with him, Ruth,' he pleaded. 'I'm not saying he's the worst man in the world. He's decent enough in some ways. But he'll do you no good. Please let me tell him "no".'

She shook her head. She could not even consider it. Sean O'Farrell did not know what his master had already done for her. He had raised her to pinnacles of feeling which she had not known existed. She could hardly wait for it to happen again. Let the future take care of itself.

Thinking about the ecstasy in store for her, her anger against Sean melted.

'I'm truly grateful for your concern, Sean,' she said. 'I take it as a compliment. But it's misplaced. And the answer is still "yes" - and that's final. I shan't change my mind, no matter what you say. I'm just sorry you had to know.'

'Don't let that worry ye,' Sean replied bitterly. 'What servants know doesn't count, because, you see, they don't really exist. Their opinions don't matter and they have no feelings. One day ye'll discover that.'

'Sean, I don't want to quarrel with you,' Ruth said. 'I hate to hear you so bitter and I hope I'll prove you wrong.

And now I must go. Mrs Carson said not more than an hour.'

He stood up, looked down at her, his usually cheerful face puzzled and worried.

'It seems I can't make ye see sense any more,' he said. 'So will you at least remember this much. If ye need a friend, ye know where to find me. And no questions asked.'

'I'll remember,' Ruth promised. But she knew he was worrying about nothing.

Ruth had wondered how she would leave the house that afternoon without Anna. In the end it proved easier than she had expected.

'Oh dear!' Mrs Carson said. 'There is still household shopping to be done and Mrs Cruse and May are up to their eyes in chores.'

'I'd be glad to do it, ma'am,' Ruth offered quickly. 'I'll go on my own so as to be quicker, and I'll take Anna out later, if you agree.'

'I would appreciate that, Ruth,' Mrs Carson said gratefully.

She was in Washington Square far too early, but when, within a minute of the hour striking, she saw Joss Barnet walking towards her, so great was her relief that she started to run to him. He frowned, and raised a hand to signal her to slow down – which she did at once, walking forward with as much decorum as she could muster. How splendid he looked with his broad shoulders, long legs, strong handsome face tanned by the sun. How proud she was to be meeting him!

'We must be swift,' he said at once. 'This place is too public.' No word that he had longed to see her, no expression of pleasure at the sight of her.

'I've missed you,' she faltered.

'But you knew I would come? You surely did not doubt it?' he asked.

'Did you miss me?'

'Of course I did. Why else would I be here?' He spoke

more gently, smiling at her so that she was reassured.

'Can we not sit down for a minute?' Ruth asked. 'No-one knows us.'

'No-one knows *you*,' he corrected her. 'But perhaps for a minute only.'

They sat on the same seat that she and Sean had occupied that morning, though she had no thought in her head of the Irishman now. To her disappointment, Joss Barnet did not sit close to her, and when she stretched out her hand towards his he touched her fingers only briefly, and then withdrew his hand. But his eyes met and held hers, and in them she recognised, beyond all doubt, the same intensity of longing that she knew in herself. It was all she needed.

'I have arranged a place where we can meet privately,' he said. 'A place where we can be alone. There is a house in Broome Street, at the corner of Mercer Street.'

'When?' Ruth asked eagerly. 'Oh, please let it be soon!'

He smiled at her eagerness – 'Tomorrow morning, at eleven. Is that soon enough?'

'I'll be there!'

She did not know how she would get away, but she knew that nothing would stop her.

'Good!' he said. Then he left her. At the corner of the square, before the turning took him out of her sight, he turned and raised his hat and she waved her hand in reply. The whole meeting had taken no more than ten minutes. Ruth walked through to Broadway, did her shopping, and went back to Spring Street without a care in the world.

Mr Carson had returned from the city and he and his wife were once more discussing the domestic situation. It was the main topic of conversation these days.

'If the worst comes to the worst, my dear,' Mr Carson said, '*we* can move elsewhere. None of this is strictly our responsibility. And yet I am sure it is not one you would wish me to evade?'

'Of course not, George,' Mrs Carson agreed. 'We could not possibly desert – for that is what it would be – at a time like this. But what *are* we to do? I am no nearer to finding a cook and *I* cannot be expected to do it!'

Ruth took a deep breath.

'But I can, ma'am,' she said.

The Carsons turned to her in astonishment, as much from hearing her interrupt them as from the words she had uttered. Though in the unusual position of spending time in their company, she was still a servant – the more so since they had visited Millfield, which, Ruth privately thought, had gone to Mrs Carson's head a little. It was therefore assumed that she did not have ears, and had a tongue which functioned only at the proper time, and certainly not when her betters were speaking. But in this case, when what she had said had sunk in, her temerity was immediately overlooked.

'*What* did you say?' Mrs Carson asked.

'I can cook. I learned to cook in Yorkshire.'

She had made the offer on a sudden impulse born, somehow, of her new state of elation. She felt full of confidence; nothing was beyond her. The notion that the possible new arrangement – since she would have to leave the house every day to do the marketing – would make it easier for her to see Joss Barnet whenever he wished it, only came consciously into her mind after she had spoken.

'Perhaps I can't cook as well as Mrs Gutermann,' she said. 'And certainly not the same dishes. But I can serve reasonable meals. That is, if you can spare me. I realise that it would leave me less time to spend with Anna, and it would not be suitable for her to be too much in the kitchen.'

'Why, I don't know what to say!' Mrs Carson looked both relieved and bewildered. 'I had not even considered such a possibility. But since you yourself suggest it. . . .' She warmed to the idea. It was at least a temporary solution. She had no knowledge of Ruth's capabilities but it seemed unlikely that her cooking could be worse than Mrs Cruse's.

'If you are sure you can manage,' Mr Carson said doubtfully. She was so young. It was quite a responsibility. 'Perhaps we should consult Professor Woodburn? I believe he is in the house now.'

'I am sure you *could* do it, Miss Appleby,' Professor Woodburn declared when the idea was put to him. 'But I am not so sure that we should impose on you.'

'It would be no imposition, I assure you,' Ruth said.

'And it would not be forever,' Mrs Carson put in eagerly. 'Only until we can sort things out.'

'Very well then,' the professor agreed. 'We will give it a trial. But remember, if you feel at any time that it is too much, you must not be afraid to say so.'

Within the half-hour Ruth was in the kitchen.

'You're as welcome as the flowers in spring,' Mrs Cruse said.

Within the next hour she was in the market, buying food for that evening's meal. She scrapped Mrs Cruse's menu of steamed flounder and rice pudding and gave the boarders succulent roast rib of beef and featherlight Yorkshire pudding, followed by a deep-dish apple pie. The meal was later than usual, but there were no complaints. On the contrary.

'Everybody sent you compliments,' May told her when she came back into the kitchen with the empty dishes. 'What's more, there's not a scrap left on the plates!'

It could be, Ruth thought, because it was the first square meal the boarders had had in a fortnight – but she hoped not.

Later, when everything had been cleared away, when Mrs Cruse had gone home to her family and May to bed in the attic, Ruth sat at the kitchen table to work out the week's menus. It was something Mrs Peterson had taught her to do. Then from the menus she made a list of replenishments she would need for the larder, which was woefully understocked. The exercise gave her a sense of satisfaction and purpose. It occurred to her that she had not felt like this since she had set foot in New York.

But when, a little later, she turned out the lamp and crept into her bed in Anna's room, it was not of grocery lists or meals or menus that she thought. Her mind was totally on Joss Barnet, and tomorrow's meeting. She closed her eyes and willed herself to fall asleep quickly, so that morning would come all the sooner.

# 14

Ruth's first thought on waking, as it had been her last before she fell asleep, was that today she was to see Joss Barnet. Only a few hours from now and they would be together. But how would she live through those hours?

Her second thought, which caused her to leap out of bed, was that she was responsible for cooking breakfast for sixteen people, and it must be served on the stroke of eight.

Anna was still asleep, her fair hair spread over the pillow, the new rag doll which her father had given her as a consolation prize for the loss of Edward, still clutched in her arms. She was a peaceful sleeper.

Mrs Carson had agreed that while Ruth was helping out in the kitchen, she herself would look after her daughter as much as she could, but Ruth knew that she would still be expected to do many things for Anna and this morning she did not have the time.

She poured cold water into the basin and washed quickly, then ran downstairs. May was already in the kitchen, the stove lit, the kettle on the boil. Sammy had arrived and was on the back porch, cleaning shoes.

'I know a tray goes up to Mr and Mrs Carson,' Ruth said. 'Does anyone else have early tea or coffee?'

'No, thank goodness,' May replied. 'Not unless they're poorly. Mrs Gutermann would always send a cup to anyone she knew wasn't up to the mark. She was kind that way.'

'Then I hope everyone's fit and well this morning,' Ruth said. 'I'm late. What time does Mrs Cruse arrive?'

Mrs Cruse opened the door as Ruth was speaking. With a

smile and a nod she hung her cape and bonnet on a hook, enveloped herself in a large white apron, and set to work, fetching the mutton chops from the larder, arranging them in the tin for the oven. She turned her head aside as she handled the raw meat and Ruth, noticing the pallor of her face, guessed she was feeling squeamish again.

'It's all right, Mrs Cruse,' she said. 'I'll deal with those if you like. I want to trim off some fat before I put them to cook.'

'Trim the fat off?' Mrs Cruse queried. 'You'll find it very expensive if you waste the fat.'

'I won't waste it, I promise you. I'll use it some other way,' Ruth assured her. 'Are you not well this morning?'

'Not at my best,' Mrs Cruse confessed. 'And my little Alfred - he's the youngest - ain't well neither. I've left him with Myrtle - she's the next eldest - so I hope he'll be all right. But if you're sure you can manage the breakfasts, I'll be glad to make a start on the parlour. It needs a good turnout.'

There was so much for Ruth to do in the next hour that she had to concentrate hard on her duties. She tried not to think of Joss Barnet, and what the day was to bring. She was glad when the first meal of the day was satisfactorily over and those boarders who had to earn their livings had gone off to do so. Leaving May to dry the dishes, she sought out Mrs Carson.

'I should go out to do the marketing,' Ruth said. 'I thought I would go to the Fulton Street market. Mrs Cruse says it's a good place.'

'Take me, Ruth!' Anna cried. 'Take me! I want to go!'

Mrs Carson looked undecided.

'I don't think that would be a good idea, ma'am,' Ruth said quickly. 'It's quite a way. And I understand it's a rough area, and very crowded. I shouldn't like Anna to pick up any infection.'

'You are quite right, Ruth,' Mrs Carson agreed. 'Anna must stay with me. Perhaps you will find time to take her for a walk this afternoon?'

'Most certainly,' Ruth said. She would have promised the moon and the stars to get away.

'Will you take Sammy with you to carry the basket?' Mrs Carson asked.

'Not today,' Ruth replied firmly. 'Sammy has a lot to catch up with here. I daresay I can manage on my own for once.'

'Very well. And you will perhaps not have to do this work a great deal longer. Professor Woodburn has found the address of a person in Heidelberg who might turn out to know something of Mrs Gutermann. He will write to her at once. She may not be a relative, but perhaps she will give us some useful information.'

Broome Street is only a block away from Spring Street. Ruth found the house easily enough, but at first she was too nervous to present herself. She walked along the street another two blocks, trying to gather courage. Then she walked back again, climbed the short flight of steps to the front door, and resolutely rang the bell.

Kate Garner, opening the door, saw a tall, slender girl with a fringe of dark silky hair under the brim of her bonnet, and large golden-brown eyes, wide with apprehension. She was clutching a large lidded shopping basket, holding on to it tightly, as if for protection. A strange accoutrement for such an occasion, Mrs Garner thought. But she was a good looker all right!

'Come in,' she said. 'Your friend is already here.' She never referred to her gentlemen by name. They often gave her false ones anyway, though she was seldom deceived. 'Up the stairs and the first door on the left.'

How kind the woman was, Ruth thought, to let Joss Barnet bring her here.

She's as innocent as a babe unborn, Mrs Garner thought. She doesn't know what it's all about. She shrugged her shoulders and went back to her own quarters. After all, she had her living to earn.

Ruth went upstairs and tapped nervously on the door.

'Enter!'

She sighed with relief as she heard Joss Barnet's unmistakable deep voice. She opened the door and, seeing him standing there, ran into his arms without even stopping to put down her basket. He disengaged himself and took it from her, setting it aside.

'I observe that this accompanies you everywhere,' he said, smiling at her. 'But you won't need it for a while! Now take off your cloak and bonnet.'

While fumbling with the ribbons and clasps, her fingers trembling so that she was clumsy, Ruth glanced around and felt slightly shocked. It was a smallish room, dominated by an outsize bed with a rich crimson brocade coverlet and heaped-up pillows. The fact that the bed was turned down shocked her still more. Even to her inexperienced eye the purpose of the room was quite clear. Though comfortably, even richly furnished, it bore none of the signs of permanent occupation: no trinkets, books, photographs, odds and ends on the dressing-table; everything exceedingly tidy. There were two elegant armchairs, a painted washstand with a ewer and basin, and fresh towels on the rail; and, incongruously, on a small table close to the bed, a tray set with cups and saucers of fine English bone china. Joss Barnet saw her looking at them.

'Mrs Garner does everything well,' he said. 'At exactly the right moment she'll appear with a pot of coffee. You'll see!' He broke off suddenly. Now why had he said that? What an inconsiderate fool he was! It was not part of his plan ever to hurt this girl. This girl was different.

He was too late. So he has been here before, Ruth thought. Well it would be naive of her to suppose otherwise. But it was in the past, and, she told herself, the past didn't concern her.

He saw the disappointment in her face, held out his hands and drew her into his arms. 'Dearest Ruth,' he whispered, 'nothing matters now except you and me!'

It was true. How could she think otherwise? And then he lifted her up and carried her to the bed, and she lay there quietly while he took off her garments one by one and threw them to the floor.

In what followed, all the doubts, disappointments,

apprehensions she had had, all the longings of the past weeks, were wiped out; consumed by his passion, and by hers which answered his with equal ardour. If she had ever thought that nothing could surpass what they had in the stuffy little attic at Millfield, then she was wrong. They both proved that.

When they were, for the moment, indescribably and wonderfully fulfilled, lying back on the pillows, there was a knock on the door and Mrs Garner called out.

'Coffee is ready if you are!'

'Bring it in,' Joss ordered.

She entered, coffee-pot in hand, smiling face. Ruth was discomfited, and pulled the sheet up to her chin to hide her nakedness. She was acutely aware of the heap of clothes on the floor and especially of her shabby, patched underwear lying on top of the heap. But Joss and Mrs Garner seemed to take everything as a matter of course. Mrs Garner poured the coffee, added liberal helpings of sugar, and handed it to them.

'That'll put new life into you,' she said.

'She embarrasses me,' Ruth complained when Mrs Garner had left the room.

Joss laughed, sipped his coffee.

'Mrs Garner's all right. A great sense of romance, coupled with a practical turn for making money. A formidable combination!'

'Is that what you like in a woman?' Ruth asked.

'I like *you*,' he said gently. 'Never mind about the rest. I like you exactly as you are.' Why did women always ask about other women?

'Ignorant, shabby, naive, without talent!'

'Oh come now! Unspoilt, funny, exceedingly pretty, and with a very special talent of knowing how to please a man!'

She received his assessment as the highest praise, proud and grateful that she had pleased him.

'But I am sure your wife has all these qualities, and more beside,' she said. 'Has she not?'

She could have cut her tongue out at the root! The

moment the words were out, dropping like lead weights on to a sheet of glass, she knew she had made a colossal mistake. It did not need the sudden stiffening of his body to tell her that.

How could she have been so stupid? How could she have said it? And yet she knew that, though the question had been asked carelessly, the longing to know, to match herself against this other woman, was deep inside her, and had been for some time. Does he love her as he loves me? Surely not as he loves *me*? Did they still . . .? Were they . . .? Could his wife ever have loved him as I, Ruth Appleby, do now? The desire to know, to be privy to all that he was or ever had been, however much the disclosures might hurt, gnawed at her like an ulcer. But she should not have asked. She should never have asked.

The silence between them seemed to go on forever. He made no reproach, and his drawing away from her was almost imperceptible. But his body no longer touched hers at any point and she felt cold in the warm bed. Then, in a swift movement, he flung back the bedclothes, inadvertently jogging her arm so that she spilled coffee on the clean white sheet. He leapt out of bed and began to put on his clothes.

'I'm sorry!' Ruth exclaimed. 'The coffee. . . .'

'Get dressed,' he said quictly. 'Never mind the coffee.'

'I didn't intend to say. . . .'

'Get dressed,' he repeated.

The ice in his voice was worse than anger. She could have borne it if he had stormed at her, let her explain. She felt as though he had gone a thousand miles away from her.

'I'm truly sorry,' she said.

'Then get dressed at once!' It was a sharp command.

She got out of bed, quickly reaching for her shift and pulling it over her nakedness, which now ashamed her. Then in the same moment she realised that he was treating her like a servant and, worse still, that by her prompt obedience to his barked commands, she was acting like one.

She could not and would not accept this. He had not hired

her. In what was between them, in what they had just shared, she counted herself his equal. And for her own self-respect she could not allow herself to be treated otherwise. She climbed back into bed again and leaned against the pillows. He looked at her in surprise.

'I told you to get dressed!'

'I will dress in my own time,' Ruth replied. 'Not when you order me to!' All her courage went into the words, and though she tried to speak calmly, they rushed out in a voice which sounded nothing like her own.

Joss Barnet stopped in the act of fastening his shirt buttons. He stared at her in disbelief and she glared back at him. She was thankful that he could not know how much she trembled underneath the sheet. While she glared at him he began to grin, and then he laughed out loud.

'By God! If it weren't that my carriage will already be at the door, and I have an appointment in the city, I'd be back in there with you! Then I'd show you who was boss!'

All his good humour had returned. She was forgiven. Indeed, he spoke with the kind of indulgent pride he might show towards a precocious child. It is not in him to treat me as an equal, Ruth thought. But he must. She would have nothing else.

'Come along now,' he said. 'No more games! Out of bed and dress yourself.'

'I will do so the moment you have left,' Ruth answered, not moving an inch. 'You needn't think I shall stay. And I shall apologise to Mrs Garner for the coffee stain.'

He glowered at her. 'No need,' he said shortly. 'She's paid to deal with dirty linen.'

In any case, Ruth thought, she could not possibly walk out of the front door while Sean O'Farrell waited there with the carriage. It was bad enough that he had to know: to show herself would be brazen. Her face reddened at the thought of it.

Joss Barnet pulled on his gloves and picked up his hat. 'Very well then,' he said stiffly. 'If you choose to behave like the child you are, I shall take my leave of you. Good day!'

He was gone. What had she done now? It was the end. He would never want to see her again, ever! All her anger melted away. She leapt out of bed and ran to the door after him. It was too late. As she opened the door and called out his name, oblivious of the fact that she was not dressed, she heard him taking his leave of Mrs Garner, and then the door banged and he was gone. She ran to the window and watched his carriage as it disappeared in the direction of Broadway.

All she wanted in the world was to see him again. Her discomfiture at the clandestine nature of their meeting, her distaste for the businesslike arrangements, faded away before the irresistible attraction he had for her. How could she pretend to care about equality? He could call any tune he liked and she would dance. Willingly. Only let this not be the end. Let him not ignore her. That she could not bear.

She dressed quickly, and left. Mrs Garner did not trouble to see her out.

'Your friend Mr O'Farrell hasn't called again,' May remarked one morning. 'He's such a handsome man. Aren't you going to see him again?'

'I don't know,' Ruth said shortly.

She wanted to see him. It would embarrass her, but he was her only link with Joss Barnet, of whom she had heard nothing since the morning in Broome Street. She had tried to drive him out of her thoughts by plunging herself into work, of which there was more than enough.

Each day brought new experiences, and she discovered that there was more to running a boarding-house than she had thought.

'But I'm not really running the house,' she remonstrated one morning when Mrs Cruse asked her a question about chair covers in the parlour. 'I'm no more than a temporary cook!'

'Well, we have to look to someone for orders,' Mrs Cruse said. 'Mrs Gutermann used to tell us what to do and we did it. I'm not the one to be running to Mrs Carson, even if she was willing, and you're better than me and May at deciding things. We look to you.'

'That's right,' May agreed.

Ruth took her orders from Mrs Carson. Each week she submitted the menus to her mistress for her approval, and tried to consult her about the running of the house. But Mrs Carson was not interested in that. With some reluctance, she took on the job of domestic expenses.

'I will pay the bills as they come in, Ruth,' she said. 'And I will give you a housekeeping allowance to take care of the marketing. You must keep a strict account of what you spend and we will go over the figures once a week.'

She sighed. 'This is not something I enjoy doing,' she admitted. 'I had hoped to escape it during my stay in New York. But no household runs efficiently unless accounts are kept, as I am sure you know from having kept house for your father.'

'I never did,' Ruth said. 'Keep accounts, I mean. My father gave me his wages and I bought what I could. When the money ran out before next pay day, as it always did – well, we managed as best we could.'

'I see,' Mrs Carson said. 'Well, *we* must keep accounts. The money is not yours or mine. And in doing so I expect you will learn something about the management of money which will serve you well when you have a home of your own.'

Which would be never, Ruth reckoned. She would never marry now.

'I'll be careful with the marketing,' she promised. 'Though I'm not used to it and I daresay I'll make mistakes.'

'At first perhaps,' Mrs Carson agreed. 'But you'll get used to it.'

Ruth did make mistakes, not only in what she bought, but in her timing. By trial and error she discovered that to obtain produce at its best she must be at the market early in the day, well before she cooked the breakfast – and this meant rising earlier than any servant girl. But also she found that the chefs from the best hotels, where quality was of prime importance, shopped at this time. They could have the pick of everything and could afford to pay for it, so that the price was high for her too. If she went to the market later in the day everything was cheaper, though not so fresh.

Had she been able to combine her marketing with meeting Joss Barnet, all other considerations would have been swept aside. What *he* wanted would have decided the time. As it was, with no word from him, each day she debated whether quality, freshness or price was the most important for her menus – so that sometimes she walked to the market when the dark sky was only just streaked with daylight, and at other times she did not go until late afternoon.

'It's not fit for you to be going down Fulton Street in the dark,' Mrs Cruse protested. 'You should take Sammy with you.'

'That's not possible,' Ruth pointed out. 'He doesn't sleep in the house and I can't expect him to leave his home any earlier than he already does, simply to escort me. He has to walk over from the East Side. In any case, I'm not the least bit nervous or afraid. Everyone is most civil to me.'

'Well, it's not suitable,' Mrs Cruse grumbled.

'I'm happy to take Sammy with me when I go later in the day,' Ruth said. In fact she did that as much to give him a change of scene as because she needed his help with the baskets. He was a thin, eager child; much too small for his ten years.

'Sammy needs feeding up,' she told Mrs Cruse.

'I push as much food into him as I can,' Mrs Cruse said. 'But if I turn my back for a minute, he stuffs what I give him into his pockets to take home to his family. His father's out of work.'

'I know,' Ruth said. He was one of the many hundreds of unemployed in New York.

Ruth enjoyed the new routine. She was never bored. If only she could have heard from Joss Barnet, or have set eyes on him, life would have been tolerably good. As it was, when she went to bed, dog-tired, at the end of each day, she fell asleep thinking of him.

One day when Mrs Carson had finished going through the accounts she said, 'You are very good at your job, Ruth. So from today and until we are able to make more permanent arrangements, I am giving you a free hand to run things as you wish. Moreover, we shall pay you ten pounds a year more for your added responsibility. Of course I am here to advise you should you need me, and I shall still inspect your accounts. So what do you say to that, eh?'

'Thank you for your confidence, ma'am,' Ruth replied. 'I'll do my best to please.' Since she was more or less doing the job already, she was delighted to be given a free hand and ten pounds a year in addition. 'There's just one thing though . . .'

'Yes?'

'I would like you to speak to Mrs Cruse and May and Sammy, if you please. Explain to them. We all get on well together and I don't expect any difficulty, but if you were to inform them that I'm in charge, then I can tell them how I want things done.'

'Very well,' Mrs Carson said. 'I'll do that at once. There's no time like the present.' She was delighted that the girl had taken the responsibility.

They went out to the kitchen together. When Mrs Carson had spoken – and left – Ruth had her own say.

'I require everything to be well done,' she told them. 'My standards are every bit as high as Mrs Gutermann's. But I shall work alongside you, and as hard as you do. And I shall try to make things better for you. In the first place I shall see to it that you have some regular time off.'

Never, she vowed, would she submit anyone who worked for her to the kind of regime she had endured at the Longhills.

'We shall keep the house clean and tidy and do everything we can for the comfort of the boarders. They come first. And from now on May will help me in the kitchen since I believe you, Mrs Cruse, prefer housework to cooking?'

'Oh I do,' Mrs Cruse agreed. 'I'll be thankful to be out of that!'

'As for Sammy,' Ruth said, 'Sammy's duties wil be much as before – except that he need no longer wear those ridiculous clothes.'

Mrs Gutermann had dressed him – it was the fashionable thing to do in high-class boarding-houses – in a white, long-trousered suit of vaguely Indian design, and on his head a white turban with a huge red glass brooch in front. It sat oddly on his purely African visage.

When Ruth spoke, Sammy's small body drooped. He raised large, anxious eyes to hers.

'What is it, Sammy?' she asked. 'Have I forgotten something?'

He gazed at her mutely. May prodded him in the back but he would not speak.

'It's the uniform,' May said. 'It's what you said about his uniform.'

'What about it?' Ruth asked. 'Speak up for yourself, Sammy. I won't bite you!'

'I like it, missa,' he said nervously. 'Please missa, I'd like to wear it all the time.'

'You *like* wearing the uniform? The turban and everything?'

'I like the turban best, missa. I'd like to wear it all the time.'

Of course he would. How stupid she was not to realise that. His uniform was all that gave him significance. Clearly, he would feel diminished without it.

'Well, if that's how you feel, of course you may wear it. But not quite all the time. Only when you're on duty in the house. It wouldn't do for the yard work; cleaning shoes, chopping wood.'

His round black face shone with happiness, white teeth gleaming in a broad smile.

How easy to please him, Ruth thought. How little he asked. She must see to it that when there were any leftovers available, he had a share to take home to his family, as Mrs Cruse already did to hers.

With her new responsibilities Ruth had less and less time for Anna, though sometimes she found an hour in which to take her for a walk. Anna spent much of her time in the kitchen, sitting on a high stool, rolling pastry, chattering with Ruth or May, or Sammy.

'I *must* engage someone to look after Anna,' Mrs Carson said one day, coming into the kitchen in search of her daughter. 'It is not good for her to be so much indoors.'

'I *like* the kitchen,' Anna said. 'Besides, Ruth is going to show me how to make peppermint candy.'

But Ruth knew what Mrs Carson meant. It was not suitable for her daughter to spend so much time in the company of servants.

'I have some very special news,' Mrs Carson went on. 'What do you think? Mr Barnet has secured seats for Mr Carson and myself to attend Miss Jenny Lind's concert at Castle Gardens! I am so excited. Even Mr Carson is pleased at the thought!'

Ruth's heart thumped at the mention of Joss Barnet's name.

'Shall Mr and Mrs Barnet accompany you?' she asked.

'Oh yes! We shall be a party of eight, and we have been invited to take supper with them. That is another thing I came to tell you. We shall not be in to supper on Thursday.'

'I want to go!' Anna cried. 'I want to see Jenny Lind! I want to see Edward!'

'We shall not be seeing Edward, my darling,' Mrs Carson said. 'And there it is impossible for you to come with us.'

Ruth thought quickly.

'If you please, ma'am . . .' she ventured.

'Yes, Ruth?'

'I was wondering if *we* might go. Just to see Miss Lind's arrival, I mean. And after we've served supper, of course. It would be a great treat for us – Mrs Cruse, May and myself. And if you'd permit it, Anna could come too.'

'I want to go! I want to go! I want to see Jenny Lind!' Anna persisted.

'It's an historic occasion,' Ruth said. 'Something to remember. Some say she's the greatest singer in the world.'

Mrs Carson hesitated. 'There will be crowds. There always are.'

'We'd take the greatest care, ma'am,' Ruth assured her.

Mrs Carson gave in. 'Very well then – and always providing Mr Carson gives his consent. And now, Anna, you must come with me.'

I shall see him, Ruth thought. I shall see him. She had no doubt of it.

'They say Barnum pays Jenny Lind a thousand dollars every concert,' Mrs Cruse said. 'And allows her a maid and a man-servant and a carriage at her disposal!'

'They say a man found one of her gloves, and now he's charging people to kiss it. Ten cents to kiss the outside, twenty-five to kiss the inside!' May said. 'My, but I'm looking forward to seeing her – and all the fine people arriving for the concert.'

All I want is to see *him*, Ruth thought. If they could squeeze their way to the front of the crowd by the entrance – and she was determined that they should – then he might even catch sight of her. If only they could set eyes on each other again she felt that all would be well.

For the rest of that Tuesday, in the kitchen, all the talk was of Jenny Lind, and of the treat they were to have on the Thursday, waiting for her arrival at Castle Gardens. On Wednesday morning, when breakfast was over, May and Mrs Cruse started on the house so that when they came to leave it for an hour or two everything would be in apple-pie order, no cause for complaint. Ruth rearranged her menus to make a meal quick to serve and eat. The dirty dishes could wait until she and May returned.

Mr Carson had turned up trumps and decreed, because they were taking his dear little Anna, that they should have a carriage all the way there.

'He has ordered it to be at the door the minute supper is over,' Mrs Carson said. 'Moreover, for the return journey – for it will be well past Anna's bedtime – he has said that you may hire a hackney coach for which he will pay. Can you do that, Ruth?'

Ruth took her meaning. Servant girls did not hire hackney coaches. They were for ladies and gentlemen, businessmen, New York's better-off citizens. But she had already decided that tomorrow she would not be a servant. She would be a lady. Mrs Carson had recently given her another cast-off dress, this time in a deep, rich blue, with yards of material in the skirt - and tonight she planned to re-trim her bonnet. If she caught sight of Joss Barnet, and he of her - which was the whole point of the exercise - he would see a lady standing there.

But none of it was to happen. On Thursday morning news came which threatened to take Ruth away from Joss Barnet forever.

She was about to leave the house. There was a shop in Canal Street where she knew she could buy the herbs she needed for that evening's supper dish. In the act of tying her bonnet strings she was summoned to the Carsons' room. Mr Carson was still there, which was strange, since he usually left the house immediately after breakfast. Mrs Carson sat in an armchair with her husband hovering protectively close. Her eyes were red-rimmed and she clutched a crumpled handkerchief.

'Something is wrong?' Ruth said quickly. 'There is bad news?' She felt immediately sick with fear.

Mrs Carson nodded. In the short pause before Mr Carson replied Ruth pictured Joss Barnet thrown from his horse; injured, dying. Then in quick succession she thought of Aunt Sarah dead, Ernest and all his family swept away in a hurricane, Maria or Willie mortally ill. Why Mrs Carson should weep at any of these calamities she did not stop to consider.

'We have to return to England,' Mr Carson was saying. 'My father has died suddenly and I am needed at once. We shall not come back to New York. There is the business to think of, and my mother to comfort.'

Ruth's mind spun. 'We' clearly included her. She was

immediately torn by violent and conflicting emotions. She would see her beloved Yorkshire again. She would be reunited with her darling Aunt Sarah, Uncle Matt, Willie, Maria. Then, following close behind, the sure and certain knowledge that she could not leave New York. She could not leave the city where Joss Barnet lived, where she knew she would one day see him again.

'I'm sorry,' she said. 'When must you go, sir?'

She deliberately said 'you', not including herself, but was there any way she could be forced to return with them?

'As soon as possible,' Mr Carson answered. 'I am very much needed. We shall travel in one of the new American steamships and be back in England again quite quickly. And of course we will pay your fare and you will have a job with us in Manchester. You need have no worries.'

'I . . . I can't go back, sir!' Ruth said quickly. 'I can't go back to England!'

Mrs Carson raised her head. 'Can't go back? What do you mean, Ruth?'

'I'm sorry, ma'am. You've been most kind to me, you and Mr Carson, and I shall never forget it, not as long as I live. But I don't want to go back to England now.'

'Then you must join your cousins in Wisconsin,' Mr Carson said. 'You must write to them at once, today, so that your letter arrives ahead of you. I will do all I can to arrange your transport, but I must warn you that it is a long and arduous journey.'

'I'm sorry, sir. I haven't made myself plain. I don't want to go to Wisconsin either. I feel the same way about that as I did before. I want to stay here in New York.'

It was as if she had said she wanted to live on the moon.

'Live in New York, on your own?' Mrs Carson cried. 'Why, that's impossible! What would you *do*?'

'We could not allow it,' Mr Carson said firmly. 'As your employers we naturally feel responsible for you. As my wife so rightly asks, what would you do?'

Ruth felt herself being caught, imprisoned. She could not allow it. She had to break free.

'Couldn't I do exactly as I'm doing now? If he would agree, I could be responsible to Professor Woodburn, at least until something is settled. The house is not to be closed, is it, sir?'

She had mentioned Professor Woodburn's name without much thought, but she could not have done better.

'I suppose it isn't – not yet at any rate,' Mr Carson agreed. 'With our own distressing news we have hardly had time to think of matters here.' He sighed. 'I daresay Professor Woodburn will see to things until we hear from Heidelberg and the lawyer can settle everything. After that, who knows? You could easily find yourself without a home or a job!'

'But it is bound to be some months yet,' Ruth said. 'I'm sure when the time comes, especially with the experience I've gained here, I shall find a suitable post.'

She turned to Mrs Carson. 'You've said yourself, ma'am, that I run things well. I'm sure I could be of service to Professor Woodburn and the other boarders. I'd do my very best, ma'am.'

'Well, that is a consideration,' Mrs Carson replied. 'Though I would much rather you came with us, Ruth.'

'I'm sorry, ma'am,' Ruth said.

Mrs Carson took in the firm set of Ruth's mouth, met the steady look in her eyes. She understood the girl's feelings. She did not want to leave New York with all its excitements. Manchester would be dull by comparison, and having her mother-in-law to live with them would not be to her liking. As one woman to another she almost envied Ruth. She turned to her husband, gave him a questioning look.

'I shall speak to the professor today, then,' he said. 'I have a great many matters to see to and I would like this one settled.' He turned and spoke to his wife. 'I think I might also consult Mr Barnet. Perhaps he will be good enough to take my place in this matter, vis-à-vis Professor Woodburn. He knows New York and his advice would be invaluable.'

'Do that, dearest,' Mrs Carson said. 'Thank you, Ruth. That is all for the present.'

Ruth hesitated. 'There's just one more thing. . . .'

'Yes?'

'Miss Jenny Lind. . . .'

Mrs Carson looked more shocked than at any time since Ruth had entered the room. 'Jenny Lind is *quite* out of the question,' she said. 'We are in mourning! I am sure none of us would wish to go now.'

'I can't go to Castle Garden's,' Ruth told May and Mrs Cruse. 'Nor Anna. But that needn't prevent you going, though you'll have to walk, or get the omnibus.'

She didn't really care about Jenny Lind. She had not been going with the hope of catching sight of the singer. But never mind, Joss Barnet was to be reminded of her existence by Mr Carson himself. Surely he would wish her to remain in New York – or had he truly grown tired of her and would be glad to see her go? She wished with all her heart that she could see him and speak to him, put her case to him, before Mr Carson did so. But it was impossible. She had no way at all of making contact with him.

# 15

Two days later, in the middle of the afternoon, Sean O'Farrell burst into the kitchen where Ruth, Mrs Cruse and May were at work. He confronted Ruth, his eyes sharp with anxiety, a small tic pulsing in his temple.

'I've got to talk to ye! On a private matter. So stop what ye're doing!'

She was standing by the table, beating the eggs for a cake. The whisk dropped from her fingers and clattered to the floor. He had a message from Joss! She was sure of it. Sean O'Farrell would no longer visit her unless he had been commanded.

'It's urgent and important,' Sean said curtly. 'Where can we go?'

Bending down to pick up the whisk, she hid her face from the interested gaze of Mrs Cruse and May, and spoke calmly, giving no hint of the tumult inside her.

'I can't think what all the mystery is about,' she lied. 'I suppose we could use Mrs Gutermann's sitting-room – though as you can see, I'm busy.'

May had come to a standstill in her eagerness to miss nothing, gazing at Sean with admiring eyes. She believes he has come to make a romantic declaration, Ruth thought. But as far as Sean was concerned, that could not have been further from the truth.

Mrs Gutermann's room had not been occupied since her death. It was a large square room at the back of the house, darker than it need have been because of the heavy furniture and hangings. Ruth had thought that if she got her way with

Mr Carson it might be reasonable for her to occupy this room herself, in which case she would make great changes. But Mr Carson had said nothing in the last two days. She had no idea where she stood.

Sean followed her in and closed the door behind him.

'Well?' She could no longer keep the eagerness out of her voice.

'Ye can't leave!' he burst out. 'I won't let ye and I've come to put a stop to it!'

'Leave?' What did he know about her leaving? Where was the message she was waiting to hear?

'I said leave. Didn't I hear the two of them discussing the matter in the carriage as we drove here? The master and your Mr Carson.'

'You mean . . . you mean Mr Barnet is in this house? Now?' She could hardly believe that some deep empathy had not told her so the moment he had set foot within.

'I do mean that. So listen to me before they get at you. Which will be any minute now. Don't let them ship ye back to England, Ruth, nor yet to Wisconsin. I don't want ye to go!'

A stab of fear pricked at her. But of course he must be mistaken.

'You've got it wrong,' she said.

He shook his head. 'Didn't I tell ye, I heard 'em! Ruth, listen to me, will ye. I know as things stand this minute I've got nothing to offer ye except friendship. But it won't always be so.'

'I could never take anything but friendship,' Ruth interrupted. 'Even if you could give it. I'm surprised and grateful that you offer even that. You must know, none better. . . .'

'There's little I don't know about himself. More than you ever will. And I know ye think ye're in love with him, but 'tis not really so. 'Twill pass.'

How little this man knows me, Ruth thought. Or else he is deceiving himself. How little he understood the depth and intensity of her feeling for Joss Barnet.

'And if it doesn't pass?'

'But it will,' he said confidently. 'Don't let them send ye

away, Ruth! Don't let them force ye into something ye don't want to do!'

Before she had time to answer there was a knock at the door. It was May.

'I'm sorry to interrupt. You're to go to Mr Carson at once, Ruth.'

Ruth was conscious of Sean's eyes on her as she hastily checked her appearance in Mrs Gutermann's looking-glass. She wished, how she wished, that she didn't have to appear before Joss Barnet in an apron, that her face was not pink and shining from the heat of the kitchen and that her hair was tidier. What would he think of her, seeing her like this? She pushed the stray wisps of hair under her cap and set that straight on her head. It was the most she could do.

'I shall wait right here until you come back,' Sean said.

Professor Woodburn was with Joss Barnet and the Carsons. When Ruth entered the room he rose to his feet though Mr Carson did not do so. Joss Barnet was standing over by the window and Ruth's glance went straight to him, looking for recognition in his eyes. There was none. But how silly of me, she chided herself. It was neither the time nor the place. He would find other means.

'You know why we have sent for you?' Mr Carson was saying. 'We have given a great deal of thought to the matter of what shall become of you now that my wife and I are obliged to return to England. There are several points to consider and we want to be sure that we are doing the best for all concerned. . . .' On and on he went, not coming to the point.

'It is Mr Barnet's opinion that you would do better to return to England with us, rather than risk the hazards and temptations of a long journey to Wisconsin. . . .'

Ruth did not hear the rest of his sentence. It wasn't true! How could he? How could Joss be so cruel? Surely he knows how I long to stay, and why? She looked across at him, willing him to return her look, but he was gazing out of the window at something happening in the street below. How could he be so unfeeling?

Mr Carson was droning on. Professor Woodburn interrupted him. 'Perhaps we should tell Miss Appleby what we have actually decided. I'm sure she is most anxious to know.'

I don't care, Ruth thought miserably. If I'm not to stay here, what does it matter where I go?

'I was coming to it,' Mr Carson said. 'Well, Ruth, Professor Woodburn thinks you will do well here, and it was he who persuaded us in the end. So you are to stay. We have agreed that your proposal to run the boarding-house, temporarily, was a reasonable one in the circumstances, and that it may be implemented.'

Ruth's head swam. For a moment she thought she would faint – but from relief and pleasure that she was not to be banished after all. Gone, immediately, was the idea that Joss Barnet had not wanted her to stay. She was sure that he had simply felt obliged to put forward all points of view – perhaps so as not to sound too eager. But of course he had agreed in the end. It was unthinkable that he should not have, she looked towards him again and this time his eyes met hers; but there was nothing in his look to show the feelings that she knew he must have. There was nothing of the gladness which filled her own heart.

I should not have agreed to her staying, Joss Barnet thought, seeing her radiant face. I have been weak. I should have stuck to my guns, not listened to a university professor who knows nothing of the real world and suspects even less. I know why she wants to stay. And when the end comes, as it must, I'm going to bring her unhappiness. That troubled him more than he would have believed possible. But she stirred his heart and his senses, this little, proud-as-a-princess, exciting servant girl, who sat there in her cap and apron, a smile of pure pleasure on her lovely face. It was a face which haunted him when he was away from her. But he was a fool, and she should have been sent packing for her own good.

'The arrangement is therefore as follows,' Mr Carson said. 'Professor Woodburn has offered to stand *in loco parentis* as you might say, until you come of age, or until you take another job where your employer will be responsible for you.'

'Or until you marry!' Mrs Carson interposed. It was the first time she had spoken.

'Quite so,' Mr Carson continued. 'Mr Barnet will pursue all enquiries into the matter of Mrs Gutermann's heirs and the settlement of her estate – which seems to amount to the contents of this house. During this time you will run the house. If all is going well when Mr Barnet locates the heir – who is most likely to be in Germany – he will consider whether or not he himself might offer to buy the business as an investment. Where you will fit in then will be up to Mr Barnet and Professor Woodburn. Nothing definite can be promised, but I am sure we can confidently leave the matter in their hands. Is that all quite clear?'

'Oh yes, sir!' Ruth said. 'Thank you, sir!' Joss really did want her to stay on or he would not have gone to such lengths.

'And you are quite satisfied with the arrangements? You realise you take some risk? And that you may still change your mind and return with us to England in a few days time?'

'I thank you most kindly, sir,' Ruth replied. 'I thank you all. If you please, I would like to stay here.'

Professor Woodburn smiled at her. He hoped he had done the right thing in persuading the others. Though he liked most women and respected them all, there was something special about Ruth Appleby. Though she was independent and capable, she brought out all his protective instincts. He determined that he would do everything he could for her.

'Then that will be all,' Mr Carson stated.

Joss Barnet had not spoken, nor did he now. But it didn't matter, Ruth thought. Everything was going to be all right.

'Mr O'Farrell's still waiting for you,' May said when Ruth went back to the kitchen.

Ruth had forgotten about Sean. When she went in to him

she still felt as if she was treading on thick white clouds.

'Well?'

'I'm to stay,' Ruth told him happily. 'For the time being at any rate, I'm to run Gutermann's.'

'I'm glad,' Sean said. 'Let's hope it keeps ye too busy to have your mind on other things.' And then his face darkened and his tone changed. 'And now, as I'm no more than a paid servant and I can't afford to lose me job, I'll deliver the message I was sent to deliver. He says eleven o'clock tomorrow morning, and ye'll know where. Ruth, I beg of ye not to go . . .!'

Ruth was glad when May interrupted them once again.

'Mr Barnet's ready to leave.'

'Did you really want me to go back to England?' Ruth asked Joss Barnet next morning. They had made love and it had been perfect. Joss had been tender, more gentle than on previous occasions. It seemed to Ruth that their relationship had deepened.

'For your sake, yes I did,' he answered.

It would be better, he thought, if he could tell the brutal lie, say once and for all that he wanted her out of his life, hurt her now to save worse hurt later. But he could not do it. He was disturbed at his lack of willpower. It had never been like this before. Nor, in his heart, did he want to be bound more closely to her. His way ahead was straight, clear, continuing successful. It was not on the cards that anyone, even this desirable woman, should change his direction.

He raised himself on one elbow and looked at her. Her dark hair was spread against the pillow; her amber eyes were shining with fulfilment. He had never seen eyes of such a colour. Her skin glowed with health; pink on her cheeks, deeper rose on her curving lips, dazzling white on her firm, full breasts. She was totally beautiful, and did not yet know it. And when they had made love her beauty was always intensified as if she had been visited by something beyond the bounds of reality.

He kissed the shaded hollow at the base of her neck and

the dark cleft where her breasts divided.

'But for my sake you know I don't,' he murmured. 'Nevertheless you should go. You know the circumstances. You know you can never be more than the smallest part of my life, Ruth.'

At barely twenty, he had married the only child of the rich Septimus Grayson. It was Naomi's wealth and his own great flair for investment (together with a large slice of luck – he was known on Wall Street as Lucky Barnet) which had made him, by now, almost as rich as her father. Joss Barnet soon recognised – perhaps he had always known – that he had been bought by Grayson for his daughter simply because she wanted him. He had come more expensive than sable coats, strings of ponies, a sailing ship, a country mansion – but Septimus Grayson could deny his daughter nothing. More than once since then Joss would have liked to have used his money to buy himself out of what had long been a loveless marriage, but Naomi was not to be bought. She enjoyed her position as the wife of one of New York's richest, most handsome men. And since the physical side of marriage had quickly lost interest for her, she was never tempted to stray.

If her husband did so, no matter, as long as he was discreet. It lessened his demands on her, saved her trouble. But she would never let him go. New York society demanded respectability, even from its richest women. Joss Barnet went along with that.

And there were the children. They held him by a silken thread of love which was far stronger than the steel chains which fettered him to his wife.

'That smallest part of your life happens to be the largest part of mine,' Ruth said. 'I'll never leave you as long as you want me. But if ever I think you don't, I shall go out of your life at once.'

At the end of the week the Carsons sailed on the steam packet for Liverpool. Ruth and Anna were in tears at the parting.

'I don't want to go!' Anna wailed. 'I don't want to leave Ruth!'

Mrs Carson took her daughter in her arms, trying to soothe her. 'Of course you don't, my darling. And see how sad Ruth is to part from you! But you will soon be seeing Grandmother Carson again. You'll like that.'

'Shan't!' Anna cried. 'I don't like Grandmother Carson.'

Nor do I, Mrs Carson thought. And I don't want to leave New York. Her father-in-law could not have chosen a more inconvenient time to die.

Ten days after the Carsons had left, Ruth faced the fact that she was pregnant.

It's too early to be sure, she told herself, lying awake in the middle of the night. I'm not more than a fortnight overdue. But she *was* sure. Ever since that fateful miscarriage, which she thought she had at last put out of her mind, her body had settled into its regular rhythms which none of the many changes and upsets she had encountered had disturbed by so much as a day. Until now.

There was, too, an unfamiliar feeling, a tingling in her breasts; and once, on the day on which her period should have started, there had been this strange, gripping spasm, not exactly a pain, but equally powerful, in the lower part of her body; as if her womb was fighting to retain its new burden.

But it was none of these physical symptoms which convinced her that she was pregnant. She just *knew* that it was so. She knew that she carried another life in her.

She did not want it. She was dismayed, outraged, horrified. Nothing, not even the fact that it was Joss Barnet's child, could make this baby welcome. Though she desired Joss above everything in the world, the desire did not include having his child.

So what would happen to her? When the worst came to the worst, as it inevitably must, she would somehow look after the baby – but who would look after her? Lying there in the night, she was desperately afraid.

Grey daylight filtered through the curtains, picking out the brass handles on the chest of drawers, creeping towards Mrs Gutermann's wide bed. She had moved into this room the day after the Carsons had left, so that their rooms could be made ready for the new boarders. She got out of bed and drew back the curtain. The sky was lightening rapidly now, but the new day brought no solution. She washed and dressed and went to the kitchen.

'My word, you're early,' May said. 'I'm not long down meself. But there'll be a cup of coffee any minute.'

'It will be welcome,' Ruth replied. She felt shivery and a little sick. 'Then I'll get the workmen's omnibus and go down to the harbour for the fish. It's always freshest there.'

'Why not wait here until Sammy arrives and take him with you?' May suggested. 'He won't be long.'

'No,' Ruth said. 'Sammy has plenty to do. I'll be fine on my own.'

'You look a bit peaky to me,' May remarked. 'Are you not well?'

'I'm perfectly all right!' Ruth snapped out the words and was instantly sorry when she saw May's affronted expression. 'I'm sorry, May! It's just that I didn't sleep well.'

Could May possibly guess? But of course not; nothing could show yet. But eventually it must, and Mrs Cruse, with her wide experience of pregnancies (she had six children), would not continue to be deceived. Ruth wondered just how long she could keep it from her.

She put on her cloak and bonnet and picked up the basket. 'Tell Mrs Cruse I won't be long. I'll take the omnibus in both directions.'

By the time she had turned from Spring Street into Broadway the sun was fully up and there were people on the street. She doubted if Broadway was ever empty of people, even in the middle of the night. When the omnibus came it was crowded with men going to work; nevertheless the driver stopped for her, as was always the case with a woman. Women of any and every class were treated with respect in New York, at least in public.

'Move up there! Let the lady sit down!' a man called out when Ruth climbed into the bus. It was impossible to move any closer but a passenger stood up at once and offered her his seat.

'Thank you,' Ruth said. 'You're very kind.'

The waterfront was busy, as always. From the number of anxious-faced, bundle-carrying folk who stood around looking lost and bewildered, Ruth surmised that a shipload of immigrants had recently landed. A young woman, fatigue in every line of her face, leaned against the harbour wall, a small child clinging to her hand. She caught Ruth's eye and Ruth stopped and spoke to her.

'Good morning. A fine day! Have you just landed?'

The woman smiled, and shook her head, not comprehending. Then she spoke in what Ruth took to be German. All they could do was smile at each other. As Ruth was about to move on a young man came up. The woman spoke rapidly to him and indicated Ruth.

'My wife is sorry that she has no English and could not understand you,' he said.

'I only said "Good morning" and asked if she had just landed,' Ruth explained. 'Nothing more.'

'We have. And in the last hour I have managed to find a room for the night. Tomorrow we move on. We are going to Kansas. My wife *erwartet ein Kind.*' He could not find the word and gently touched his wife's abdomen.

Pregnant. But she has you, Ruth thought in a sudden rush of envy. You seem a kind man. You will look after her when the time comes.

'Good luck then,' she said.

She walked a little further, and then stopped to lean against the harbour wall herself. She looked towards the ships lying at anchor in the harbour. Might one of them be going back to England on the next tide? Should she ever have come to this country? Would it have been better to have stayed in Yorkshire and faced life there? She couldn't conceive what would happen to her in New York, now. Would Joss Barnet want anything more to do with her, once he had learned of her condition? What would he say?

Gone, also, was all hope of being allowed to run the boarding-house. Gutermann's was solidly built on respectability. Mrs Gutermann had selected her boarders, and they had chosen her, with mutual confidence that they would never let each other down. Because of their regard for Professor Woodburn and the Carsons (and perhaps because she could cook) Ruth's twin disabilities of youth and spinsterhood had been kindly overlooked. But an illegitimate child? Never!

She dragged herself away from the harbour wall and walked on to the place where the fishermen had spread out the night's catch. She surveyed the wet, shining fish, their myriad colours glinting in the sun; studied the varieties carefully, as if the choice she was about to make was the most important thing in her life. It was a relief to change the direction of her thoughts, if only to fish. In the end she chose flounder.

'Everything's on,' Mrs Cruse said when Ruth walked in. 'May said you didn't seem well so I thought I'd make a start.'

'I'm quite well now,' Ruth assured her. 'It's a lovely morning and the fresh air has quite restored me.'

'Well that's all right then,' Mrs Cruse said. 'We can't do with you being poorly, can we?'

'No,' Ruth agreed. 'There's far too much to do – and I must get on with it.'

All day she concentrated hard on her cooking, choosing dishes which demanded her attention. Everything must be as perfect as she could make it and she tried to think of something to please everyone. She made a delicious fennel sauce to go with the fish, and cooked a variety of fresh vegetables to perfection; baked apple turnovers with the lightest of puff pastry. Mr Gossop would appreciate those.

Since she had been in charge Ruth had reinstated Mrs Gutermann's procedure of going into the parlour, precisely thirty minutes after the evening meal had ended, and serving tea to those of the boarders who had gathered there. On these occasions she wore neither cap nor apron and appeared among them almost (though never quite) as an equal. Mrs Gutermann *had* been their equal for these few minutes each day, but then she had had maturity on her side.

On the evening of this day Ruth, unusually, produced a brandy sponge cake – something Mrs Peterson had taught her to make when the Longhills entertained. The boarders were delighted and fell upon it as if they had not just finished a substantial meal.

'Why, this is wonderful!' Mr Pierce said. 'Are you perhaps celebrating something special of which we are unaware? Could it by any chance be your birthday?'

'No, sir. That is in March,' Ruth replied.

By which time, she thought, she would not be here. She would not be pouring tea for this group of people of whom, in such a short time, she had grown so fond. She felt she had an affinity with her boarders, perhaps because they, too, were people with no real place of their own.

'Well, whatever the reason, we are the lucky beneficiaries,' Mr Gossop smiled.

She could not tell them that she had chosen the most difficult dishes she knew so that all her attention would be needed and she would not be able to think of other things. Also, in her heart, it seemed to her that she was pleading with them not to think too harshly of her when the time came. She was offering up a sacrifice.

It was already arranged that she should see Joss Barnet next morning at the house in Broome Street. She would have to tell him about the baby. If there was to be any help for her anywhere it must come from him, though nothing he could do could make things right.

She arrived in Broome Street before Joss. In the bedroom, without even taking off her bonnet, she sat on the edge of her chair, waiting for him. When he did not come she moved to the window and looked down the street from behind the lace curtains. A few minutes later, though it seemed like an hour, she saw his carriage draw up outside the door. When he alighted her heart raced, as it always did at the sight of him, though this time apprehension was mixed with the pleasure. As Joss crossed the sidewalk to the door, Sean O'Farrell drove the carriage away. Poor Sean! She was glad that he had not actually seen her arrive. She heard Joss's rapid step on the stairs and then he bounded into the room. So big he was! So vigorous, so full of life. She experienced a quick and unusual feeling of resentment at his exuberance.

'What are you doing standing there?' he asked, smiling at her. 'Why aren't you in bed? There's no time to waste today. I have to be back in the city within the hour.'

He was already unbuttoning his jacket, but Ruth remained where she was, not moving. Why? he wondered. She had always been as eager as he, and she was not coy. Nor was she a moody girl. He frowned, puzzled.

'Then if you have so little time, perhaps you could spend it listening to me,' Ruth said. Fear made her speak sharply.

'*Listening* to you? What do you mean?' He had taken off his jacket and was removing his boots. 'What in the world are you talking about, Ruth? Get into bed, there's my good girl!'

'I'm talking about the fact that I'm going to have a child!'

She felt as if the words hung in the air like so many balloons; as if they no longer belonged to her and all this was happening to somebody else. Even the voice which uttered the words was nothing like her own.

'What did you say?' He was staring at her.

'I said I'm going to have a child.'

He looked at her long and hard, as if he was trying to weigh up what she had said; almost as if he didn't believe her. But why should he think she would lie?

'Rubbish!' he said at last. 'You can't be! I made sure . . .'

'Not sure enough, then. It isn't rubbish. It's true.' She felt angry that he doubted her, even for a second.

'Have you seen a doctor? What did he say?'

'I don't need a doctor to tell me about my own body. I just

know, beyond all doubt, that I'm having a baby.' Her voice trembled. She was near to tears. He heard her fear and opened his arms to her. She rushed into them and when he held her close she knew that somehow everything would be all right.

He felt her trembling against him. 'Don't worry,' he said. 'If you're right. . . .'

'I *know* I'm right!'

'Very well then. You needn't worry any more, Ruth. I'll take care of everything.'

He sounded so confident, so kind. She was reassured. By some miracle. . . . But what miracle?

'You make it sound simple,' she said.

'It is. Don't worry.'

'But how can I not worry?' Ruth asked. 'Gutermann's? The boarders? What will *they* say?'

'The boarders? What have they got to do with it? They won't know. A day's indisposition and you'll be back to normal.'

'A day's indisposition?' Ruth queried. 'I don't understand. I told you I was having a child.'

He held her at arm's length, looked into her face, saw her confusion. It was true, she really didn't know what he was talking about! Even women of his wife's class knew about these things, so why would not a servant girl? But he was sure she was not feigning ignorance. He felt a sudden great compassion for her as her frightened eyes looked into his. He must go gently.

'I mean,' he said quietly, 'that I will send you to someone . . . I know of a good woman . . . and by whatever means she considers suitable, she will rid your womb of the child. She is very kind. She will not hurt you. And afterwards you will no longer be burdened.' And it must never happen again, he resolved.

'Do you understand me?' he asked.

She looked at him stupidly.

'God in heaven, girl! Did your mother teach you nothing?' He could not contain himself.

In the back recesses of her mind Ruth heard a group of women gossiping. They were talking about fat old Mrs Beswick who lived in one of the squalid cottages behind the Shoulder of Mutton. With a child's unerring instinct she knew that something of interest was being discussed and she kept quiet, pretending not to listen.

'She's right handy wi' a darning needle, even if she never sews a stitch!' one of them said. 'Aye, an' a mucky one at that!'

'It did for Gladys Greenleaf, God rest her soul!' another one put in.

Seeing Ruth look up, they changed the subject, with a remark about little pigs having big ears. She had not understood their conversation until this moment, here in Broome Street, New York. Now she knew what they had been talking about, and what Joss Barnet meant.

Her reaction was immediate, compounded of the memory of horrible Mrs Beswick, of dead Gladys Greenleaf, and of her own miscarriage. She did not consciously think of any of these reasons. Her decision was instinctive, and all the stronger for that.

'No! I won't do that!' she cried. 'You can't make me!'

Joss took her hand in his, led her to the bed where they sat together on the edge.

'Now come along, Ruth. Don't be foolish!' He was patient but firm, smoothing back a tendril of her hair which had fallen across her face. 'It will be all over in no time at all, and in a day or two you'll be as good as new. You don't suppose I'd let you come to any harm, do you?'

'I don't suppose you would,' Ruth conceded. 'You'd just get rid of my baby – *your* baby. Is that all there is to it?' It occurred to her then, she wondered why it had not done so earlier, that it was not the first time he had made such arrangements. He knew exactly what to do, where to go. The knowledge added to the weight on her heart.

'Well, I'm not going to do it,' she said. 'I'm going to keep my child.'

He drew away from her, began to dress again. So there

was to be no lovemaking today, Ruth thought. Well, that suited her. She could not have gone through with it. And yet, if he were to take her in his arms now, kiss her, touch her. . . . But he walked away from her.

'How can you possibly keep the child?' he challenged her. 'How can you possibly provide for it, bring it up here in New York?'

'I don't know,' Ruth said. 'But it's your child as well as mine.'

'Of course it is. I acknowledge that – though you know as well as I do that I could not do so publicly. And you won't find me ungenerous, Ruth. If you insist against all common sense and reason on having this child, then I'll send you into the country until it's over. But be sensible, Ruth. Even if I provide for you, how will you make out afterwards? Money won't solve all your problems. What can you do with a bastard child? And what will the world do *to* a bastard child? Make no mistake about it, that's what the child will be, and the world won't be kind to it!'

She caught her breath sharply at the sound of the word. Unknowingly, he had used the one word which could wound her most, and yet at the same time stiffen her resolve. It was the word which had been used on that Christmas Eve in Nordale. She heard the doctor's cold sneering voice. 'There are enough bastards in the world.' And now it was happening to her again.

'You speak as if my feelings were of no account,' she said angrily. 'As if my baby was worthless – so much rubbish to be thrown away!' She had not accepted those values on the first occasion, nor would she now.

'So what do you intend to do?' Joss Barnet pressed her. She was being a fool to herself and to the child, but how could he make her see that?

'I don't know.' She had no idea what to do next. The future was menacing and she was desperately afraid. 'But I know this much. Nothing and no-one is going to separate me from my child!'

Until a short time ago she had not wanted the child. Now,

suddenly, she did. She was ready to give it all the love in the world. Moreover, she determined that from the moment the baby was born she would be taught to value herself. Already she thought of the baby as a girl, a girl who was going to have everything she had not.

Joss Barnet donned his jacket, drew on his gloves, adjusted the angle of his hat in the looking-glass. Then he turned to Ruth and took both her hands in his. He was frowning, but his eyes were kind, his voice gentle.

'I can see you won't listen to reason, now,' he said. 'I'm trying to understand, though everything I advocate is for your own sake, Ruth. Perhaps when you have had a little more time to think you'll see things differently. But you must not leave it too long.'

Ruth let go his hands, turned away from him.

'I don't need any more time. I've given you my answer, and all the time in the world won't change it.'

'Very well,' he said. 'I shall come to see you at Gutermann's in a day or two. If you persist in your foolish ideas there are bound to be business matters to discuss.'

He left the room. Ruth heard him running down the stairs, and then the slamming of the door as he left the house, not even waiting to see Mrs Garner. That lady will be surprised by the shortness of our meeting, Ruth thought. Or was she used to affairs ending and new ones beginning? Would it only be a matter of time before Joss Barnet was here again? But it would not be with her.

She left the house and walked towards Broadway. In the glass of a shop window she saw her image reflected and noted how calm she looked. But it was not so surprising. She was numbed by all that had happened; her feelings were paralysed. All she knew was a deadness of the spirit which even pain could not penetrate.

# 16

When Ruth opened her eyes next morning the same heaviness was on her, though for a few seconds she did not remember why. Then it came back to her. It had not, after all, been some nightmare which would go away when the day came. The miracle was that she had slept at all, after hours of tossing and turning, worrying and wondering. But she had at last fallen asleep because in the end she had made up her mind what she would do the next day. She had always, from childhood, had this way of making decisions, large or small, as she lay in bed at night. Small ones were sometimes changed next day; big ones seldom. She knew that she would go through with last night's resolution.

She got out of bed – and at once dashed to the basin and was sick; but when it was over she felt steadier. She dressed slowly, then looked at herself critically in the mirror. Would Mrs Cruse and May notice her pallor, and the dark smudges under her eyes? If so, she must say once again that she had slept badly. If she could keep the truth from them a little longer, then neither they nor the boarders need ever know that she had been pregnant.

It was fortunate that the heat from the stove as she cooked breakfast brought up her colour, though it was difficult to deal with the nausea which attacked her again as the rich smell arose from the ham she was frying. Ruth gripped the pan handle, and by willpower and good luck managed not to succumb. When the last of the food had gone to the dining-room she thankfully moved away from the stove and poured herself a cup of weak, milkless tea.

'I might be a little longer with the marketing today,' she said. 'As I didn't go out before breakfast there'll be extra to do. Remind May that all the bed linen must be changed this morning and the laundry made up.'

'I'll give her a hand,' Mrs Cruse replied.

Ruth left the house, as usual carrying her basket. Joss Barnet was right when he said it accompanied her everywhere, and on this occasion she would have been glad to have left it behind. How was it going to look, turning up at his place of business carrying a basket? Though she was neatly and tidily dressed, she would hardly appear as a bank customer.

As she left the house she ran into Miss Fontwell, who worked at odd hours in the Historical Society, sometimes staying until late in the evening, sometimes not starting until mid-morning.

'A pleasant day,' Miss Fontwell said. 'But then the fall is always the nicest time in New York, don't you think?'

'I haven't experienced it yet,' Ruth pointed out.

'Of course not! How silly of me. But it seems as if you have always been with us!'

'Thank you.' How kind they all were. How she would hate doing anything at all to upset them.

At the end of Spring Street the two women turned in different directions. Ruth had decided to walk to Wall Street rather than take the omnibus. She pushed ahead through the crowds, unusually, for her, seeing nothing. Everything which mattered in the world now was going on inside her own head. As she walked she silently rehearsed the words she would say when she saw Joss Barnet. She prayed that she would not falter, or break down in the speaking.

At Trinity Church she turned left into Wall Street. She did not know the exact whereabouts of Joss Barnet's bank, only that, like most of the city's banks, it was located here. Which side of the street should she try first? She decided on the south side, with its more imposing buildings.

She was not in a state of mind to be impressed by any of

them. As for the scores of men milling about, dodging between the traffic, crowding the sidewalk, and occasionally bumping into her – they were simply a sea of dark suits and featureless faces under wide-brimmed top hats as she searched for Joss Barnet's bank. She passed new Merchants' Exchange, the pride of Wall Street with its wide steps and pillared entrance, with scarcely a glance. When she reached the Bank of America, followed by the Bank of New York, she began to take more notice. Surely he must now be somewhere near? And then, when she thought she must stop a passer-by and enquire, she found the place.

It was an elegant building, even more imposing than the Bank of the Manhattan Company next door. On the wall at the side of the ornate marble doorway a modest brass plate said 'Barnet's Bank'.

She took a deep breath, gripped the handle of the hated basket even more tightly, and walked through the doorway. It was twice her height, and if it had been built to enhance the importace of the bank in contrast to all who entered it, did its job well. Just inside, a doorman dressed in dark green livery with brass buttons barred her way. He had no need to speak. He simply stood in front of her, looking down. Surely he was the tallest, broadest man in New York.

Ruth took a deep breath.

'I would like to see Mr Joss Barnet, please.'

The doorman raised bushy eyebrows. 'You would, would you? Well, I'm afraid that's highly unlikely.'

'I wish to see him,' she repeated.

'If wishes were horses . . .' he began.

'I know. Beggars would ride. Now would you be so kind as to have someone inform Mr Barnet that I am here, and would like to see him. My name is Miss Appleby.' She was amazed at her own temerity, but it was probably the only way to deal with this man. She had to get past him.

'Do you happen to have an appointment?' She flinched at the sarcasm in his voice.

'I do not. But I'm sure Mr Barnet will see me when he knows I'm here.'

'He sees no-one without an appointment. What's more, I daresay he's in a meeting.'

It was Ruth's good fortune that at the moment of this impasse, someone else entered the building. While the doorman's attention strayed to the newcomer she dodged past him, crossed the entrance hall and seated herself on one of the elegant crimson upholstered chairs. Seconds later the doorman returned, now towering above her as she sat. Oh yes, she was afraid of him, afraid of his power, but she had no intention of showing it.

'You can't sit there!' he said brusquely.

'I *am* sitting here,' Ruth said. 'I shall continue to sit here until someone informs Mr Barnet of my presence. And when I *do* see Mr Barnet you may be sure that he will not be pleased at the way you have treated me. Perhaps he does not know that this is how his clients are received!'

Without knowing it, she had hit the mark. He looked at her, at the head held high, at the bright, angry eyes in the pale face, and wondered. She didn't look like a client; she was too young, too shabby, not at all the sort of person who would use this bank. Bu you couldn't always tell. To his great relief he saw Mr Barnet's private secretary descending the stairs at the back of the hall.

'Well, miss,' he said to Ruth, 'don't take my word for it. Here's someone who will confirm what I've said.'

'This young person,' he announced as the secretary approached, 'wishes to see Mr Barnet. She doesn't have an appointment and I've told her it's impossible.'

'All I have asked,' Ruth said quietly, 'is that someone should tell Mr Barnet that I'm here and would like to see him. Let *him* decide whether he will see me or not. But I am sure he will.'

She was no longer as sure as she sounded, but she *must* see him, she *must*. If she didn't do so now she was not sure that her resolve would last. Oh, why was everything against her, even these two stupid men? Tears of anger and frustration filled her eyes as she faced the secretary. It was all he needed. A woman's tears were something he could not stand.

'What did you say your business was?' he enquired.

'I didn't,' Ruth replied. 'I'll tell that to Mr Barnet.'

He gave her a long look, bit his lip in indecision, then said, 'Very well, miss. I'll tell Mr Barnet you're here. But don't be surprised if he can't see you. He's a very busy man.' It went against his better judgement. He could get a ticking-off for this.

'My name is Miss Appleby,' Ruth told him.

He was away five minutes, during which time Ruth continued to perch on the edge of the chair and the doorman, with a sour look, went back to his duties. She studied the intricate pattern of the black and white marble floor, lifted her eyes to the slender, white marble columns which rose through two storeys to an elaborate ceiling and felt herself totally insignificant. How had she dared to come here? When she saw the secretary coming back down the stairs she rose to her feet. Please God, she prayed, please God let Joss see me! And please God give me strength to say it. Let me not change my mind!

'Kindly come with me,' the secretary said.

He had not missed the swift look of surprise on his boss's face when he gave the girl's name. He wondered what it was about. Women, other than his wife, and she seldom, did not visit Barnet in his office. And this young woman, clutching her basket, was, in spite of her confidence and a certain air of breeding in the way she held her head, chin up and defiant, not of his class.

Ruth followed the secretary across the hall and up the curved staircase. The grandeur of the place was like that of Millfield and for a moment brought back to her, with a sweet poignancy, all that happened there. Well, she would never see Millfield again, that was for sure. But her thoughts came swiftly back to the present when, on the first wide landing, the secretary halted at a heavy mahogany door, and knocked.

'Come in!'

The sound of Joss Barnet's deep voice gave Ruth momentary strength, but when she saw him at his desk, saw the coldness in his face, it left her again. As she approached him across the expanse of exquisite carpet she began to tremble. She wanted to turn and run, to change her mind about everything. How could she bear to go through with it? But now she was standing in front of his desk, rooted to the spot.

Joss Barnet addressed the secretary. 'That will be all, Crompton.' When the secretary had closed the door behind him he spoke to Ruth.

'You had no right to come here! How dare you come to my place of business!' He spoke quietly, but his voice was as cold as a winter's day, his face a mask of anger.

Oh God, let him at least be kind, Ruth prayed. I can't bear it if he's not!

'I told you I would come to the house. You should have waited for me. I don't conduct my personal affairs in my office.'

Suddenly, the chilly harshness of his tone struck an entirely different chord in her. How dare he speak to her so! How dare he! It was *his* child she was carrying. She would not be treated as if she was the sinner and he the sinned against; a nobody, to be dealt with where and when he chose.

'And I do not conduct mine in *my* place of work! It is even more difficult for me!' Sharp anger raised her voice and she knew from the expression on his face that he was afraid she would be heard beyond the room. Well, let her be! Let that smooth-faced secretary and that bullying doorman come right in and hear it all!

'I came to you because I've reached a decision,' she said. 'It's important to me, though I daresay it will mean little to you.' No-one would know what anguish the decision had caused her, nor how she had longed for someone to be by her side, to give her counsel, to assure her that she was doing the right thing. 'I wasn't prepared to wait until it suited you to call on me. I have to do it quickly.'

Anger made her nauseous again. She held tightly to her basket while the room spun round. Joss Barnet saw her sway a little, saw the colour drain from her face.

'Sit down, Ruth.' He spoke more gently. 'Here, let me pour you a drink of water.'

Her teeth chattered against the glass. The gentle concern in his voice melted her anger as swiftly as sun on snow.

'I understand,' Joss said. 'We'll say no more about that. I'm glad you've come to your senses, Ruth. It's the right thing. I will make the arrangements for you to see the woman I have in mind, and I will let you know the time and place. She will tell you what you need to do afterwards. And don't worry, nothing will go wrong, I promise you!'

He could not understand why she was staring at him with such a look of astonishment.

'You don't need to worry,' he repeated.

It was several seconds, during which she continued to look at him in surprise and disbelief, before she spoke.

'You think I want to get rid of my baby, don't you? You think that's why I'm here? You're quite wrong! I told you before that I could never do that. I meant every word. Didn't you believe me?'

'I did believe you. I thought you had now changed your mind, come to a more sensible conclusion.' Then why *was* she here? If nothing was changed, why couldn't she have waited to see him?

'Sense has nothing to do with it,' Ruth replied. 'Feeling is what I'm talking about.' But how could he understand? He knew nothing of her miscarriage and of the harsh things that had been said to her then, and that nothing could ever make her part with this child. She was full of a strange, yet deep, conviction that the child in her body needed her, wanted to be born; that she owed it to the one who had not been. It was the one thing in the world of which she now felt completely sure.

'In that case I don't understand why you're here,' Joss said. 'What other decision could be urgent?'

'I want to go home.'

'Home?'

'Back to England. To Yorkshire. I want to go back to my Aunt Sarah. That's where my baby will have the best chance, the most love. With my own people.'

She wanted, desperately, to do everything now that was best for the baby. Never mind herself. It was as if she needed to seek its forgiveness, to make some tremendous sacrifice to expiate the sin she had committed in conceiving the child. And in her heart she knew that to leave New York, this city which in a few short months had seeped into her bones and which, most important of all, held this man who faced her across the desk – for she would always love him – was the biggest sacrifice she could make. Without a doubt it would be best for the child. Her little daughter would grow up in an atmosphere of loving security which she, on her own, could never give her in New York.

'Are you absolutely sure?' Joss asked slowly. It was a not unreasonable solution, but it was the last thing he had expected of her. Did she mean it or was she acting on impulse? Women were emotional creatures, never more so than when they were pregnant. He wanted what was best for her – within the limits beyond which he could not go. He cared for her more than he had ever intended, or ever thought possible.

Ruth took a deep breath, braced herself. It was her last chance. After this there was no changing her mind.

'Quite sure! So because I have no money of my own I am obliged to ask you if you will please buy me a passage to Liverpool, and give me enough money to get from there to my aunt's home in Yorkshire.'

She had said it. The worst was over. She felt empty and hollow. Every minute from now on she must cling hard to the thought of the baby, and to the joy of seeing Aunt Sarah and Uncle Matthew again. And her beloved moors, though winter would be on its way by the time she reached them. She would never know what a New York winter was like.

'If that is what you want, Ruth, then there is no trouble in arranging it,' Joss Barnet said slowly. 'I will see to it that you have a cabin on a steamship, so that you can travel in comfort. Also, you must allow me to give you some money to ensure the baby a good start in life.'

'I don't want money from you,' Ruth replied. 'Only enough to get me home.'

'There's little enough I can do,' Joss said. 'Even though I'd like to do more. At least allow me to do something for the child.'

'Very well,' Ruth agreed. 'I will take a hundred dollars – no more – and that only because my aunt is poor and I shan't be able to earn money for a while.'

She stood up. She had to go. She had to get away from this man because she longed to touch him, longed for him to leave his desk and take her in his arms, telling her that everything would be all right and that he could never let her go. She was afraid that if he so much as touched her hand in parting she would break down and all her resolve would melt away.

He rose from his chair and started to follow her to the door.

'No! Don't see me out!'

'Very well then. I will bring to Gutermann's everything you need for the journey in a day or two. Ruth . . . I shall. . . .'

She was out of the door, running down the stairs, before he finished the sentence . . . 'I shall miss you.'

More than she would ever know, he would miss her. He turned back to his desk and saw that she had left her basket behind. He picked it up, held it for a moment, then put it in a cupboard, locking the door on it.

When Ruth reached Spring Street May handed her a letter. 'All the way from England!' she said. Ruth recognised Maria's writing and tore open the letter, eager for news. Before long now she would see Maria, whom until today she had sadly never expected to see again. She noted with surprise that the letter had been sent from an address in Glasgow, also that it had been a long time on the way. She read it quickly.

'It is not without sorrow that I have parted from the Sugdens,' her sister wrote. 'I had the great good fortune to be offered a post with a theatrical touring company, playing at the Theatre Royal in Bradford. Who knows where it may all lead? As you see we are presently in Scotland, but we do not stay more than one week in any place. Well, as you know, I always wanted to travel. . . .'

There was no word of Willie, or Aunt Sarah and Uncle Matthew. But never mind, I shall see them all for myself before long, Ruth thought; although it might now be some time before she set eyes on Maria.

She refolded the letter and put it on the mantelpiece, to be read again at leisure.

'It's from my sister,' she said. 'She has joined a theatrical company and is touring the country.'

'An actress!' May cried. 'Fancy having an actress for a sister!'

'I'm not so sure that she *is*,' Ruth said. 'I think it far more likely that she is an assistant to the Property master or some such dogsbody.'

May looked disappointed. 'Why do you say that?'

'Because I know my sister. She doesn't mention any part she's played and if there'd been one she would certainly have said so. But she told me when we were children that one day she'd be an actress, so I daresay she will be in the end.'

'Is she pretty?' May enquired.

'Very pretty. She's nothing like me. She has fair, curly hair, delicate features and a rose-petal skin. And she's small and dainty.'

Privately, May thought Ruth was pretty – but she wasn't a person to whom you could say such a thing. Though she was considerate, and good to work for, in some way she kept herself to herself more than May would have wished.

Ruth, going about her work in the house, recalled the last time she had been with her sister, when they had walked over to Barnswick to see Willie. She remembered the peaty moorland underfoot, the grouse rising from the heather, the plaintive 'pee-wit, pee-wit' of a lapwing, the sky with its fluffy white clouds propelled by the ubiquitous breeze. It was the kind of dear remembrance she must cling to as she implemented her plan to leave New York.

Very soon now she must tell the boarders she was leaving. Thank God, because she had moved quickly, there was no need for them to know that she was pregnant. She would not be the first immigrant to return because of homesickness; there was always a steady stream of them. And the fact that the Carsons had gone and left her behind would add credibility to her actions. But there was no need to mention anything quite yet. She could wait a day or two, until Joss Barnet confirmed that he had booked her passage. The truth was that she hardly knew how to face them.

For the rest of that day she made herself think of the good things about returning to England, the chief of which was that she would be with Aunt Sarah again. She acknowledged that ever since she had landed in New York she had longed to see her aunt, to hear her homely voice. Well, it wouldn't be long now. The steamships were much faster, and bound to be more comfortable than the *Flamingo*; and she would be a cabin passenger in her own right this time. Once with Aunt Sarah, everything to do with the baby would fall into place.

It was with great delight, and some envy, that next morning May handed Ruth yet another letter. How wonderful it must be to receive letters. She had never had one in all her life.

'From my cousin in Wisconsin this time,' Ruth said, recognising the writing. 'I wonder what news he has?' And what he would think when she wrote back and told him that she was returning to Yorkshire.

As she read the letter the world went dark. She felt as if she was drowning, the great waves closing in over her head, the sea trapping her in its depths. It couldn't be true! Fate couldn't do this to her! What had she ever done to deserve it?

'Are you all right, Miss Ruth?' May asked anxiously.

Ruth slumped in the nearest chair. Then she read the letter again.

'. . . in case you have not been informed I have to break the sad news that my mother died in her sleep on the 14 August. I am pleased to say she had not suffered. I know how you will grieve, Ruth. You thought a lot of my mother, and she of you. . . .'

She could not read any further because she could no longer see the words on the page.

Not Aunt Sarah! Not now, when she wanted her, needed her more than ever before! Aunt Sarah would never let her down. She couldn't. Not Aunt Sarah!

Except for her grandfather, Aunt Sarah had shown her more affection than she had ever known. Ruth had a hundred memories of her but what she recalled now, what she remembered so vividly, was that final parting on the bitter February morning: the moment when, walking across the moorland track with her bundle over her shoulder, she had turned for a last look and had seen her aunt silhouetted against the lighted rectangle of the open door. Her arm was still raised, waving to the family who for her had already been swallowed up in the darkness. Ernest was wrong to say his mother had not suffered, Ruth thought. It was likely she had done so up to the moment of her death. But at least she had had one wish: she had lived and died, and been buried, in the place she loved most.

May's voice aroused Ruth. 'I'll make you a cup of tea.'

'Put a drop of brandy in it,' Mrs Cruse advised. 'And then she should go and have a lie-down.'

Ruth picked up the letter which had fallen to the floor and read the rest of it.

'. . . My father has decided to cast his lot with us. He arrives on the steamship *City of Manchester* which docks first in Philadelphia and then New York about the last week in October. I have decided to come to New York to fetch my father, but in case I am not there in time, will you meet him from the boat. . . .'

At three o'clock on the afternoon of that same day Sean O'Farrell called. He looked tense and worried, Ruth thought, fidgeting with his hat as he held it in his hands. Surely Joss Barnet could not have confided in his coachmen that she was leaving? Not that it mattered now. There was nothing left of her plans.

'I'm not needed this afternoon,' Sean said. 'Can you come out with me for a while?'

'I'm sorry,' Ruth replied. 'I'm too busy.' It was not true, but she felt so unutterably tired, so totally depressed.

'She's had a bit of bad news,' Mrs Cruse said.

Sean looked at Ruth.

'My aunt has died.'

'I'm sorry, I know you thought a lot of her.'

He didn't know anything. How could *anyone* know what her aunt's death had done to her?

'You don't look up to much,' Sean said. 'If you won't come out with me, surely you can take a few minutes to sit in your own room?'

'Of course she can!' Mrs Cruse broke in. 'She's been peaky for a day or two now. And all this on top of it, it's a blow. Works her fingers to the bone and what thanks will she get, I ask you? Go on, Miss Ruth. May shall bring you and Mr O'Farrell a tray of tea.'

Ruth had no energy left to argue. Sean followed her into Mrs Gutermann's sitting-room, which would now never be hers. They sat at opposite sides of the stove, drinking the tea which May brought alomost at once, neither of them speaking.

It was this unusual behaviour on Sean's part – he was not one to keep silent for long – which roused Ruth from her apathy.

'Is there something wrong?' she asked. *He* could not be grieving for her aunt.

'Yes.'

'What is it?' She didn't really want to hear, but he was a friend, even if he did disapprove of her ways. Perhaps to hear his problems might lighten her own for a minute or two.

'I'm here to tell ye that I can no longer go on with things as they are.'

She was jerked out of her self-regard by his voice, which shook and broke with emotion. She had never heard Sean so wretched. It was far more disturbing than his anger.

'I can't stay in his employ,' he said savagely. 'Not while you and he carry on. I care too much. That house in Broome Street . . . don't you realise what sort of house it is? Me driving him there, knowing. . . .' He faltered. For once in his life he could find no words. He buried his head in his hands.

Ruth was filled with compunction; not sorry for what she had done, but that it had hurt him so.

'I tried to come and go without you seeing me,' she said. 'At least I recognised how you felt.'

He had raised his head. 'What difference do you think *that* made?' he asked harshly. 'I knew, didn't I?'

She saw the torment in his eyes. Well, at least Sean could now be put out of his misery.

'You shan't have that again,' she said. 'I shan't be going there.'

'You mean ?' He looked at her in disbelief.

'I mean precisely what I said. I shan't be going to Broome Street again. Or anywhere like it. It's over, that's all!' But in her heart how could it ever be over?

It was enough for Sean. He immediately read into Ruth's terse words all that he wanted to believe. He jumped to his feet, took Ruth's hands in his and gripped them until it hurt her. He was all urgency.

'Ruth, will you marry me? Say you'll marry me! I'll do anything for you, Ruth. I'll work my fingers to the bone. I swear I'll make you happy!'

She stared at him in amazement. How could he ask such a thing?

'Give me a chance. . . .'

She had to cut him short.

'I'm pregnant!'

'Say you will, Ruth!' It was as if he had not heard her.

'Listen to me! Stop talking and listen! *I'm with child*!' She shouted at him because she had suddenly come to life, and she could not bear the agony of it. 'Do you not hear me?' she cried. 'I'm with child! I'm going to have a baby! A bastard, they'll call it. A little bastard! I was going to my Aunt Sarah, who loves me and would have loved this child for my sake. And now she's died. She's dead, dead, dead! I can't go anywhere. Where can I go? So leave me alone. I can't bear any more. For God's sake *GO*!'

All the pent-up feelings of the last twenty-four hours rose up in her like a tide of vomit and poured out without volition. She slid to the floor and buried her face in the seat of the chair, sobbing as she had not done since her grandfather's death. Everything which had ever brought grief to her now returned and all her past sorrows heaped themselves on top of her present burden. She thought of her dead parents, her grandfather, Nordale and what had happened there, Aunt Sarah, her coming child – all in one great explosion of wretchedness.

Above everything else she longed for her aunt. She wanted to be close to her, to be comforted by the sound of her voice and the touch of her hand. Now no longer in control she heard herself crying out in anguish. 'Aunt Sarah! Aunt Sarah! Why did you have to die? Why did you leave me?'

And with the thought of Aunt Sarah she wanted her home. She wanted, far more than she had when she had made the decision to return, to see Barnswick, the steep green hills, the rock from which bright waterfalls gushed, the sound of running water. She wanted to run back to where she belonged.

She was not sure how much of this she cried out aloud in her grief. Sean was kneeling beside her. He lifted her up and held her against him, speaking gently, trying to comfort her. His comfort had nothing of sexuality in it, as Dick Parker's had had on that other occasion. It was like that of a grown man for an unhappy child. He was her father and her grandfather, and she was a small child.

In the end she was too exhausted to cry any longer and Sean lifted her up and helped her back into the armchair.

He looked at her for a long time, as if he wanted to say something and couldn't.

'Then all the more reason,' he said in the end, 'why you should marry me. All the more need for me to look after you.' He spoke quietly, steadily. She couldn't believe what he was saying.

'But it's Joss Barnet's child!' she said. 'You know that!'

'I know.' She would never realise the pain her few words had caused him. But while she knelt there, crying, he had searched into his own feelings and he knew that he would manage. With Ruth as his wife he would manage anything.

'And I mean to keep it,' Ruth went on. 'Though for its own sake, not because it's his.'

'It's your child as well,' Sean said. 'If we marry it will belong to both of us.'

'You mean you don't mind fathering another man's child?' She could have bitten out her tongue at the carelessness of her words.

His eyes blazed.

'Of course I mind!' he snapped. 'Do ye think I'm not human? But I love ye and want to marry ye, child or no child.'

'But you know, Sean, that I don't love you, not in the way I ought if I were to marry you. I like and respect you,' Ruth said. 'I wouldn't want to lose your friendship. But you would always know that I married you for the sake of the child.'

'I know all that,' Sean replied. 'I'm not a fool. But respect and friendship are good foundations, and feelings can change. I'm willing to take the gamble.'

She could not believe that her feelings for Joss Barnet would ever change. Even though there was now an unbridgeable distance between them, he was still unbearably attractive to her. She did not even blame him about the child because she was sure he had not intended it so. The difference between them lay in their sense of values. They saw life through different eyes.

'But how could you find it in your heart never to hold all

this against the child?' Ruth asked. 'If things went wrong, wouldn't you blame her?'

'The child would be yours and mine,' Sean answered. 'It would have to be so from the start. Insofar as it lies in us, and by the grace of God, we'd need to wipe all other thought from our minds – yours as well as mine.'

'It would be the only way,' Ruth said.

'And we would have other children,' Sean continued. 'It would be wrong to make any difference between them.'

Ruth looked at him long and steadily. He was a good man. What had she done to deserve him?

'So will ye consider marrying me, Ruth?' he asked.

'Yes,' Ruth said slowly. 'Yes, I'll consider it. I'll give you my answer tomorrow. And Sean. . . .'

'Yes?'

'You do me a great honour. More than I deserve. Whatever my answer, I shan't forget what you've done. And now there's a lot to think about.'

'And no time to waste,' Sean reminded her gently.

'I know.'

'There is something else,' he went on. 'You must realise that I can't stay with Barnet. I must find another job and it won't be easy. You know how much prejudice there is against the Irish!'

Ruth knew. The Irish and the Germans were far and away the most numerous of immigrants into New York: it seemed that every ship which docked in the harbour brought one race or the other. But while the Germans were accepted, and forged ahead in spite of the language difficulties, the Irish were heartily disliked and their religious influence feared by the native New Yorkers. They found it difficult to get either houses or employment. Several times Ruth had seen advertisements for jobs which said 'No Irish need apply'.

'And there's no way,' Sean said, 'that I can pretend I'm not as Irish as the pigs o' Dublin!'

Ruth smiled. 'No, that's something you can't disguise.'

'But I don't fear for the future,' he declared. 'And nor need you if we're together.'

That evening Ruth went to bed as soon as she had served the boarders with their evening tea. She desperately wanted sleep and oblivion but she knew she would not get it until she had sorted out her mind. She would try, she resolved, to decide everything without emotion – yet it was the deepest emotion, that which determined her to have her child and keep it, which governed everything else. In the end all other considerations were subject to it.

She *did* consider Sean. She considered him carefully. He already knew how little she would be bringing to the marriage. At least she had been honest with him, so that later on he would not feel let down. Just now she set great store by not letting anyone down.

Even if she married Sean, the future would not be rosy. He was unlikely ever to get a good job. They would go through life poor, and although she was not afraid of that for herself, it was a far cry from the plans and dreams of a future in Gutermann's which had swirled and whirled in her head until she had discovered her pregnancy.

Could she be a good wife to Sean, she asked herself as she tossed and turned? Could she renounce her thoughts about Joss Barnet? Would she ever forget the sight of him riding up the hill at Millfield, on his great grey horse, a giant of a man! How would she forget his passion and her desire when they had been together? Could an act of the will accomplish all this? But there was no question of keeping both men in her life. If Joss was to remain, Sean could not enter.

It was, in the end, the child who must not suffer, no matter who else did. This was what mattered most now. She turned on her side, her hands curved across her abdomen as if to shield and comfort the baby in her – and slept.

# 17

Ruth slept later than usual next morning, and would have been later still had not May, out of the kindness of her heart, brought her a cup of tea.

'Should I draw back the curtains?' May asked.

'Yes please.'

It was a bright October day. Even the dark colours of Mrs Gutermann's room could not absorb and deaden all the light which flooded into it. A few trees were visible from the window and Ruth marvelled, as she had each day that fall, at the brilliance and clarity of the leaves: scarlet, yellow, orange; great splashes of vibrant colour. There was a sumach tree in the yard, its elegant 'fingered' leaves crimson and vermilion as the sun shone through them. It was as if the foliage was not dying, but had taken on a splendid new life.

'I'll be down in a minute or two, May,' Ruth said.

Breadfast had hardly been cleared away before Sean arrived, having, he explained, just delivered his master to Wall Street. Ruth pushed from her mind the remembrance of her own visit there yesterday.

'I must be back within the hour,' Sean said. 'Mrs Barnet requires me to drive her to Stewart's emporium.'

Ruth took him at once into Mrs Gutermann's sitting-room. He refused to be seated and they stood, both of them rigid, in the centre of the room.

'Have you my answer, Ruth?' He held his arms straight by his side, his hands clenched, like a man in the dock awaiting sentence.

'Yes.'

Ruth was no less nervous. In spite of all her thinking late into the night, had she made the right decision? But she was not going to change her mind now.

'Then?'

'I'm deeply touched by your offer, Sean. It's more than any woman could have hoped for. . . .'

He broke in roughly. 'Never mind all that! Do ye accept it? For God's sake Ruth, do ye accept it?'

'Yes,' she whispered. It was done, sealed.

If she had brought him all the wealth of New York Sean could not have been more delighted. Yet what she had brought him, Ruth thought, was a reason for losing his job, a marriage short on love, and another man's child. She was ashamed not only of the paltriness of her offering, but of the reluctance with which she was making it. His evident pleasure humiliated her all the more and she couldn't stop the tears which ran down her face.

He took her in his arms and wiped her cheeks, then he kissed her gently, as if she was a fragile piece of porcelain which might break under his touch. This was not the bold, lively Sean she knew. She hoped he would not increase her debt to him by being too kind. And yet she craved kindness.

'I'll be good to ye, Ruth.' He was holding her at arm's length now, searching her face as if he was seeing her for the first time. 'Never fear!'

'I know you will. I don't fear.'

'Then. . . . and I'll ask this once, and not again . . . can ye not bring me any love?'

She wished with all her heart that she could give him the answer he wanted to hear.

'You know I can't,' she said. 'Not as you mean it. But I will do everything I can to be a good wife. And there'll be no other man than you. That I promise. Also . . .' she hesitated.

'Well?'

'You need have no fear, Sean, that I shall fail in my wifely duties. I shall share your bed and shall be yours whenever you want me.' She blushed at her own frankness.

'But unwillingly?'

'No, Sean. You shan't find any difference in me from a woman in love with you.'

'Love can grow from affection.' Sean clutched at hope. 'Perhaps it will be so with you, Ruth.'

'Perhaps.' But she did not think it likely.

'And now, Sean, I have something else to say. I've thought of something which might work well for both of us.' The idea had emerged in the night, thrown up from her spinning-top mind.

'First of all we must consult Professor Woodburn about our marriage. He has put himself in the place of a parent to me and I wouldn't care to arrange anything of importance without him. I value his friendship and desire his blessing.'

'I agree with all that. But why. . . .'

'Wait! I haven't finished. I intend to ask him if, after we are married, I may continue in my present job, at least until the fate of the boarding-house is settled. You would come here to live with me. I am sure it will be the best solution for everyone and I cannot imagine that he will refuse me.'

'But how, if you are pregnant . . .?'

'No-one except you and I will know about that in the beginning. It grieves me to deceive the professor, above all people, but it's for the best. My condition will make itself known soon enough, but that will be after our marriage. We can say we want to be married quickly because my uncle and cousin will be here and I want someone of my own at the wedding. At least my plan will give us breathing space.'

Sean turned away, walked towards the window; stood there looking out, every line of his body rigid and unyielding.

'Well?' Ruth asked. 'What do you think?'

He turned round.

'I don't like it. Oh, I agree it would be better not to tell anyone about the child until after we're married. But if we live here, if you stay in your present job, we'll be beholden to Barnet. That I won't have! You can't ask that of me, Ruth!'

'I don't,' Ruth said. 'You're wrong. There's no obligation

to Mr Barnet. I work for the professor. Mr Barnet is simply trying to trace Mrs Gutermann's heir, as a favour to Mr Carson. Nothing more than that.'

'And when the heir is found?' Sean asked. 'What then?'

'Why then if Mr Barnet decides to take a financial interest in the business, that will be another matter.'

'It most certainly will!' Sean said briskly.

'We'll face that if and when it happens. I won't go against your feelings, Sean. And there is one other matter of importance.'

'What?'

'You mustn't give your notice to Mr Barnet until after we've settled our marriage plans with the professor.'

Sean broke in angrily. 'Not give in my notice? But I can't possibly stay with him. You can't expect it!'

'You *must*, Sean. Professor Woodburn will see it as his bounden duty to consult Mr Barnet as to your suitability as a husband. If Mr Barnet is obliged to say that you will soon be out of a job, the professor won't view you with favour.'

'And who is Barnet to give *me* a character?' Sean demanded.

'Your employer. Who else can give you one! Whether you like it or not, what he says matters.'

'It's not the way I wanted it,' Sean protested. 'Why can't we simply get married and find a room somewhere?'

'Because we have to think of the future,' Ruth said. She felt impatient with his obstinacy, but he looked so miserable that she tried not to show it. 'You said yourself that you might not get a job quickly.'

He sighed. 'Very well then. We'll do as you say. But the moment it's all arranged, Barnet has my notice.'

'Of course! And there's nothing in the meantime to prevent you looking around for another job.'

'You may be sure I'll do that,' Sean promised.

'And if Professor Woodburn agrees that we may stay on here for a while, at least we'll have a roof over our heads.'

But it was far more than a sheltering roof, Ruth thought. It was a life only just begun, which she did not want to leave.

She was confident that she could cope with the work, even during her pregnancy. Beyond that she couldn't see, except that she planned to make herself indispensable to Gutermann's as long as it existed.

'But the moment Barnet becomes financially involved . . .' Sean warned her.

'*If* he does.'

'. . . we get out. We will never be indebted to him. His life mustn't touch ours at any point. I shan't mention him again, Ruth – you needn't fear that – but this much has to be said and understood: it will be for us as if he never existed.'

I can't do it! I can't! The words cried out in Ruth's heart. She would turn her back on her decisions, let her life take its course. How could she possibly endure a future never to be touched by Joss Barnet? Then she turned her mind to her baby and her baby's future, as from now on she always must, and kept silent.

'Then we'll go to Professor Woodburn today,' Sean said. 'I'll come back when I can. Perhaps around six o'clock.'

'That should suit,' Ruth agreed. 'He'll be back from the university then. He seldom goes out after that.'

To Professor Woodburn they appeared, later that day, as lovers impatient to be wed. Ruth hated deceiving this good man, but it was necessary. There *was* no deception on Sean's part. He was what he appeared to be, a man in love and eager to marry. Ruth thought it was Sean's demeanour which overcame the professor's surprise and hesitation.

'I love Ruth with all my heart,' the Irishman declared. 'I shall do everything to make her happy.'

Professor Woodburn turned to Ruth.

'And you, my dear?'

'I want to marry Sean as much as he wants to marry me,' she replied.

'But you have not known each other long,' the professor demurred.

'We met on the boat coming over,' Ruth said quickly.

'Ah! I was not aware of that. Well, though I have never attained it myself, I believe that to be happily married is a great blessing. Naturally I must consult with Mr Barnet before I give my final agreement. Not to Ruth's remaining in her post here – I can see no objection to that, and Mrs Gutermann's rooms will suit the two of you – but to your suitability, Mr O'Farrell, as a husband for Ruth. I must have Mr Barnet's opinion on that.'

Ruth laid a firm hand on Sean's arm. Though she had warned him to expect it, this remark might be more than he could stomach.

'I think you will find no obstacle there, Professor,' she said. 'I believe that Mr Barnet thinks highly of Sean.'

Professor Woodburn smiled at her. Such a kind smile he had, as if everything he looked on pleased him.

'Well, I am sure you will be proved right,' he answered. 'And I shall seek his opinion as quickly as possible. I can see that neither of you wishes to be kept waiting.'

'I would like to have my uncle and cousin at the wedding,' Ruth said. 'And they cannot be in New York any more than a day or two at the most.'

'Well, I must thank you for continuing the enquires with regard to Mrs Gutermann,' Professor Woodburn was saying to Joss Barnet. The latter had ostensibly called upon the professor to report progress, though in his pocket he carried the steamer ticket for Ruth. 'These matters move slowly, especially when another country is involved,' the professor went on. 'And now there is something quite different about which I must consult you. It concerns Miss Appleby.'

Joss Barnet looked up quickly. So she had already told the professor of her intended return? And since he was smiling it seemed that he approved of the idea.

'She wishes to marry your coachman, O'Farrell,' the professor said.

'Marry O'Farrell?' He was genuinely surprised. Where did O'Farrell come into it? Were they, then, to return to England together? He had not suspected that there was anything at all between them. But not knowing how much Ruth had told the professor, he said no more.

'They came to see me yesterday. They would like to marry soon because Miss Appleby's uncle and cousin are to be in New York for a short time. Her aunt has died, and the husband is to live with his son in Wisconsin. I see no objection to the marriage myself, but I do not know O'Farrell and I must have your opinion as to his suitability as a husband for Miss Appleby. I hold her in high regard and would wish things to go well for her.'

'Of course,' Barnet said. So that was it. Her aunt had died. In his heart he was glad she would not be going back to England, though there was nothing more to come of their affair. But to marry O'Farrell? That was another matter. Were they all to go to Wisconsin, then?

'After they are married she would like to stay in her post here,' the professor continued, answering Barnet's unspoken question. 'There would be room for O'Farrell whenever his duties allowed it – if that was convenient to you. It would be good for Gutermann's to have Miss Appleby here, but we must consider what is best for her.'

Joss hesitated for a moment, then said, 'There is nothing against O'Farrell except that sometimes I have known him to drink too much. But that would perhaps change when he was a married man. He is the best coachman I have ever had.'

'She won't be needing him to drive a coach,' the professor replied dryly. 'How do you think he would rate as a husband?'

'I daresay he would make a good husband.'

But not good enough for Ruth. He was not the man for Ruth. Joss recognised with surprise that the emotion which briefly shot through him at the thought was jealousy.

'I should like to have a word with Miss Appleby,' he said. 'Perhaps one or two questions. . . .'

When Ruth went in to see Joss Barnet – he was using the Carsons' former sitting-room – he was seated at the table.

'Please sit down,' he said.

'I should prefer to stand, thank you.' She wanted to get it over with quickly. It was almost more than she could bear.

'I'm sorry to hear about your aunt. That is why you have changed your plans?'

She nodded her head.

'I've brought your steamship ticket with me. And the money. Might you not find friends, or other relatives, in England?'

'I've decided to stay here,' Ruth said. 'Since you've spoken with Professor Woodburn you know the reason why.'

'He tells me you wish to marry O'Farrell. Are you sure about that?'

'Quite sure!'

'There is one other alternative. I would willingly send you into the country, make you an allowance. Or better still pay for you to go to Wisconsin.'

'I wish to marry Sean O'Farrell,' Ruth replied.

He could not make her out. She showed no emotion at all. And why did he himself not feel relieved at the idea?

'Does he know everything?' With the fingers of his left hand he drummed a sharp, staccato beat on the table. Ruth had never before seen a sign of nervousness in him.

'That is my business and his,' she said quietly.

'But as you said yesterday, the child is mine.'

'And as I have discovered, you would like me to get rid of it. You cannot suddenly place a value on the child.' The words came bitterly from her lips, but inside she still wanted him to take her in his arms, to tell her that everything would be all right. Angry with herself, she pushed the thought away.

'Since you ask, he does know. I am not so dishonest as to deceive him in that.'

Though she could well have done so, she thought suddenly. And would it not have been better for everyone, including Sean? Perhaps her honesty had been nothing more than self-indulgence.

'I have told Professor Woodburn that I have nothing against O'Farrell,' Joss said. 'But I am telling you, Ruth, that he is not the man for you – nor are you the woman for him.'

His voice was softer now, and because of that she could no longer look at him. She fixed her eyes on an oil lamp on the table, staring at it as if she had never seen such an object before, opening her eyes wide to prevent the tears. She wanted him to dismiss her, to get it over with; but she knew that when he did so and she left the room, it would be the end between them.

'Then there is nothing more to be said. Except that I did not intend it to be like this, Ruth. And if there is anything I can do – perhaps when Mrs Gutermann's estate is settled – then I shall be only too pleased to do it.'

She looked directly at him, her eyes meeting his.

'I doubt that my husband would agree!'

She left the room.

Mrs Cruse and May were highly approving of Ruth's engagement to Sean. 'He's a lovely man, I must say,' Mrs Cruse remarked. 'He reminds me a bit of the late Mr Cruse when he was young.'

'I think he's ever so handsome,' May said dreamily. 'Did he sweep you off your feet?'

'Something like that,' Ruth replied.

At Professor Woodburn's suggestion she took Sean into the parlour with her that evening when she went to serve the tea, so as to introduce him to the boarders. When everyone was present the professor clapped his hands and called for silence.

'Ladies and gentlemen,' he said. 'Please allow me to introduce the young man who stands at this moment by Miss Appleby's side. He is Mr Sean O'Farrell. And I wish you to meet him – indeed I commend him to you – because he has asked our Miss Ruth Appleby to marry him and she has made him the happiest of men by her acceptance!'

The professor turned a beaming smile on both of them. Sean's answering smile was equally wide but, though Ruth smiled with her mouth, he saw the sadness in her eyes and knew a moment of fear for both of them. But the moment was quickly over, swallowed up in the congratulations and good wishes which came from all sides.

'Moreover,' Professor Woodburn called out above the chatter, 'Miss Appleby has consented to keep on with her job here, to stay and look after us, at least for the time being!'

'Then we forgive you!' Mr Pierce said to Sean. 'Just as long as you do not take Miss Appleby away from us. Or, rather, you may take her for a very little while, providing you return her as Mrs Sean O'Farrell!'

Mrs O'Farrell! It was the first time Ruth had thought about changing her name – but then she had few of the thoughts of a bride-to-be. She felt sad at the prospect of losing her own name before she had made it count for anything. Who, now, would ever hear of Ruth Appleby?

Since both Uncle Matthew and Cousin Ernest were due in New York at the end of October, Ruth and Sean decided to marry early in November, before the start of Advent

'I should like, if you are agreeable, to be married in Grace church,' Ruth said. 'It isn't far away and it's where I attended with the Carsons. Though in a way it's a strange choice for a couple as modest as us, since anyone who is anyone in New York gets married in Grace church. Since society is moving north all the time it has quite taken over from Trinity.'

Her only fear, as they walked up Broadway to Tenth Street next morning to make the arrangements, was that the vicar might not consent to marry them there.

'How can he refuse, for heaven's sake?' Sean asked.

'I daresay you're right,' Ruth agreed. 'And you are quite sure you don't mind – I mean being married in my church?' She had discovered only the previous evening, though she should have guessed it, that Sean was a Catholic, though he had not practised his faith since leaving Ireland.

'I've told ye,' he said. 'It doesn't matter to me any more. I'm happy to do whatever you want. I don't care if we're married in Barnum's museum, as long as it's legal and it pleases you.'

'But you don't mean the ceremony will mean nothing to you?'

'The promises will. They couldn't mean more if I was to give them before the Holy Father himself. But not the place.'

'Well, you'd better not let Dr Taylor hear you say that,' Ruth warned him.

It was strange that she, so much less 'good' than Sean, would not have felt properly married unless in her own church. Perhaps just because she *was* a sinner she felt the need.

The Reverend Dr Taylor welcomed them, and made no objections. 'I have seen you here before, with the English lady and gentleman,' he told Ruth. 'Though not for the last few weeks.' They would have to be married early in the morning of the day they had chosen, he said, because a fashionable wedding was to follow later on.

'Early morning will suit us very well,' Ruth said.

Though she knew she should, she could not bring herself to tell him about the baby. Sean kept silent.

One evening during the week before the wedding Sean rushed into the house in Spring Street, looking more than ever pleased and excited.

'What do you think? I've found a new job!'

He picked up Ruth and whirled her around until she begged for mercy, May meanwhile looking on and screaming with delight.

'Put me down,' Ruth cried. 'Tell me what – and where?' With the situation as bad as it was in New York – large numbers of men out of work, and the hostile attitudes towards the Irish – his news seemed miraculous.

'With William Tweed in his brush-making factory in Pearl Street,' Sean said. 'I start the Monday after I leave Barnet, so I won't have a day without a job.' He had given in his notice to Joss Barnet the day after their wedding plans had been agreed. 'Moreover, Mr Tweed's going to give me a day off for the wedding!'

'Which is more than *I* can spare,' Ruth reminded him. 'But brush-making? Do you know anything about it?'

'Not a thing,' Sean confessed cheerfully. 'I've never known anything except horses. But I'll soon learn. The important thing is that I've got a job. All thanks to William Tweed, who isn't prejudiced against the Irish.'

'They say that's because he wants their votes,' Ruth said. 'A lot of people don't trust Tweed.'

'Well, he can have my vote and welcome,' Sean replied. 'I reckon it's a fair exchange for a job.'

It was during the same week that Professor Woodburn asked Ruth to spare him a minute.

'I wish to discuss a matter of some importance,' he began. 'It concerns a new boarder.'

'I'm well aware that we need one,' Ruth said. 'It doesn't make sense to leave the Carsons' rooms unoccupied. How did Mrs Gutermann find new boarders? Did she advertise? I know the *New York Herald* is full of such advertisements.'

'Never,' the professor said. 'When she had a vacancy, which was seldom, it was always filled by recommendation. She never had to wait long. Which brings me to the point. . . .'

'I'm sorry.'

'We have a new member of faculty in the university, a Mr Francis Priestley who joined us this term to lecture in Natural Sciences. His home is in Williamsburg, Virginia. He is not properly settled in New York – his present lodgings are not to his liking – and I thought he might well fit into the Carsons' rooms.'

'Then he is a family man?'

'Oh no! He is not married. I think he would not require all three rooms, but possibly a bedroom and a sitting-room. He is, I think, reasonably well-to-do, and since he is engaged in writing a book I think he would appreciate the privacy of a sitting-room.'

'Which would leave only one room empty,' Ruth said.

'I suggest that that can wait until after your wedding,' Professor Woodburn replied. 'But I think if Mr Priestley is to come to us he would like to move in quickly.'

'I can have the rooms ready within the hour,' Ruth said.

The professor laughed. 'Well, not quite so quickly! But what do you say if I bring him around tomorrow to see the place?'

'Splendid. And if he is satisfied he can move in at once.'

Mr Priestley would be company for the professor, she thought. Though the latter was liked and respected by all the boarders he had few close friends. She looked forward to meeting Mr Priestley.

Ruth supposed she had thought he might be a little like Professor Woodburn: perhaps smaller, with greyer hair and rounder shoulders, and with spectacles. She had never met a scientist before. So when the professor introduced Mr Priestley the next afternoon her mouth fell open and she stared. And when her hand was taken in a strong grip she could think of nothing to say. Mr Priestley was more than six feet tall and correspondingly broad, though not plump. When he removed his hat he revealed a deep forehead from which his red-brown hair receded the very smallest amount. As he shook hands he looked her straight in the face from clear, grey eyes. He was utterly unlike anything she had imagined.

He inspected the rooms – they were exactly over Mrs Gutermann's and looked out on to the trees which Ruth thought of as hers – and was satisfied.

'They are exactly what I wanted. Could I possibly move in tomorrow?' he asked. 'If it is agreeable to you I would like to breakfast each day in my room and take the rest of my meals in the dining-room.'

'That will be quite agreeable,' Ruth assured him.

'Do not seat him at my table,' Professor Woodburn said to her later that evening. 'He is a charmig fellow and I have nothing in the world against him, but you must know how I value my privacy, and my little table tucked away in the corner. Besides, he would find me dull company.'

'Then where do you suggest I put him?' Ruth asked.

'Why not with Mr Pierce?'

'Mr Pierce?' It was a combination she would never have considered.

'Yes. Mr Priestley is somewhat shy. Mr Pierce will bring him out.'

'Well, if you think so,' Ruth said doubtfully. She decided she would make it no more than a temporary arrangement.

'I shall be rearranging the dining-room shortly, Mr Priestley,' she told him the day after his arrival. 'Then you may have your own table if you wish.'

'There is no hurry, Miss Appleby,' he said. 'Of course, I must not continue to impose upon Mr Pierce, but for the present he is telling me a great deal about New York which is useful for me to know.'

'And one thing you need to know is that there's no point in getting used to calling this little lady Miss Appleby, since by this time next week she'll be Mrs O'Farrell!' Mr Pierce said jovially.

'I must go down to South Street tomorrow, to the shipping offices,' Ruth said to Sean. 'I must find out when the *City of Manchester* is due to dock. It would be terrible if Uncle Matthew found no-one there to greet him.'

The next day was fine and crisp, with a coolness in the air which suited her, and the trees in their full glory. Any day the leaves would start to fall. Broadway was as familiar to her now as the village street had been in Barnswick. It was *her* street. She was now no more in awe of entering Stewart's emporium to match a reel of thread than she had been of going into Mrs Green's small dark village store for a ha'porth of liquorice humbugs.

She had no difficulty in finding out about the *City of Manchester*.

'If she reaches Philadelphia as planned,' the clerk said, 'then she'll arrive in New York in the last week in October. More specific I can't be. She's one of the most reliable of ships, but who can ever say what the Atlantic has in store?'

'Who indeed?' Ruth agreed.

'But if you will be so good as to enquire again in two or three days' time I shall be able to tell you precisely when you may expect to meet your uncle.'

'I'll do that,' Ruth said.

'I'm so excited I can hardly bear to wait,' she told Sean a few days later. 'The ship is already in Philadelphia and will dock in New York for certain on Monday.'

'Four days before the wedding,' Sean replied.

His words pricked at the small doubt which, whenever the wedding was mentioned, arose in Ruth's mind, and was promptly pushed away again. She had made the right decision, she was following the right course. Anything else was just nerves. She tried hard to match the enthusiasm in Sean's voice.

'Yes. I'm glad he'll be here to give me away. You'll like my Uncle Matthew, Sean. He's a quiet man. I think he always lived a little in my aunt's shadow, though he was never weak or subservient. He had to work all hours to make a living from that stony hill farm. I hope he'll have it easier with Ernest.'

Sean looked doubtful. 'It'll be no picnic. Ernest will barely have cleared the land yet. There'll be plenty to do.'

'Well, at least he'll be with his own family,' Ruth said.

She was looking forward quite desperately to see her uncle again. As well as his presence, he would bring her something of Yorkshire: his voice, his dry, no-nonsense turn of phrase. And there would be first-hand news of Willie and perhaps something of Maria – though surely he would never know where Maria was?

Then at last the day came.

'Take a bite to eat with you,' Mrs Cruse advised. 'You might have to hang around for hours. You'll get hungry and weary.'

Mrs Cruse did not know how true that was, Ruth thought. She had stopped being sick, but now she was hungry all the time, ravenously so. She packed several slices of bread, a wedge of mutton pie, a piece of ginger cake, fruit. Mrs Cruse looked on in astonishment.

'You should have enough there for a siege!' she remarked.

In South Street Ruth went into the shipping office to make last-minute enquiries of the clerk.

'The *City of Manchester* is already anchored,' he said. 'Step outside with me and I will show you.'

'When will the passengers disembark?' Ruth asked.

'They might be an hour or two. But you'll see the boats coming ashore.'

Sitting on a low wall, she waited for what seemed an eternity. She ate all the food she had brought, and half an hour later could have managed more. All the time she strained her eyes towards the ship, but the harbour was full of craft and it was difficult to make out what was happening. Then she saw the boats alongside the ship, but they seemed not to be loading. Was something wrong? Was there sickness? Could she – the thought struck her with horror – could she be in quarantine? But of course not or the clerk would have told her, and she would be flying the quarantine flag.

And then at long last the boats began to leave the ship and draw towards the shore. The sea, flat as a plate, reflected the blue October sky. Ruth hurried across to the landing stage, every moment recalling vividly how it had felt when she had landed with the Carsons. Less than six months ago, yet it seemed half a lifetime.

Her uncle was not in the first boat. When the second one drew near Ruth screwed up her eyes against the brightness of the water and the sky, and searched for him; but there were too many people in the way. The boat came in and tied up by the landing stage and Matthew Gaunt was already stepping off when Ruth saw him. He looked tired, dazed, shabby; so much older than she had remembered him. And seeing her uncle she longed, desperately, unbearably, for her Aunt Sarah.

'Uncle!' she shrieked at the top of her lungs. 'Uncle Matthew! Over here!'

He heard her familiar voice ringing out above the babble,

looked around and found her. Pushing through the crowd, they reached each other and she was in his arms.

'Oh Uncle, it's so good to see you!'

She had eyes for no-one else. It was not until she heard her name called by another voice that she turned her head sharply. For a moment she had thought . . . but it was not possible. . . .

It *was* possible! It was true! A few yards behind Uncle Matthew, smiling and waving as she moved through the crowd towards Ruth, was Maria!

# 18

'I just wish you did not have to go,' Charlotte said. 'I'm willing to welcome your father here, but I wish you didn't have to go to New York to fetch him.'

'I know you do,' Ernest agreed. 'But I've already told you, I'm not letting him make the journey on his own. He's not a young man, and until now he's never travelled more than a few miles away from home in all his life. You remember how *we* felt on the journey?'

Indeed she did. She wouldn't easily forget it. The queuing to see the quarantine officer on the *Flamingo*, then being rowed ashore in the little boat, so many of them crowded in that she felt sure the bottom must give way and they'd all be drowned right there in the harbour. Then the busy steamer up the Hudson River, all of them herded like cattle; another steamship from Buffalo across Lake Erie, and she feeling sick all the time, and that last, terrible ride in the coach over the rough plank road west of Milwaukee. They had to stay two night in Milwaukee, waiting for the stage coach which would take them west, and all their money would run to was a fifth-rate inn where, once the candle was blown out, she had lain awake listening to the rats scampering under the floorboards.

She had thought the plank roads, which had settled unevenly into the soil, were uncomfortable, but they were nothing compared to the deeply-rutted dirt roads to which they eventually gave way. By the time the stage reached Mazomanie, in Dane County, it was evening. She was bruised black and blue and as sick as a dog. She had never been so thankful in her life as when, as she hesitated before stepping down from the coach, a smiling woman at once relieved her of the baby and took Enoch by the hand, while the woman's husband took Ernest's bundles from him.

'I shan't ever forget the Atkinsons,' Charlotte said. 'They were the best sight I'd seen since leaving Burley Woodhead!'

Someone, it transpired, met the stage every week, just in case there was another family on it. The British Emigration Society had chosen Mazomanie as a place where their members might make a reasonable living, and surprisingly efficient arrangements had been made to help each family of newcomers settle in.

'Not that everyone in Dane County is English,' Mr Atkinson told them. 'There's a German family or two, and a few Norwegians. But most of the Germans stay around Milwaukee and the Norwegians go further north on the lake shore. I daresay people settle where it most reminds them of home, and where there's others who speak the same tongue. Still, we all get on well together.'

'You'll stay with us, love, and be welcome, until you've built your own house,' Mrs Atkinson said. Her warm Yorkshire voice (it seemed they came from Leeds) was like music in Charlotte's ears, but being overtired, she was confused by the words; apprehensive.

'*Built* our house?' she queried.

'That's right, love. We all have to build our houses. But there's plenty of timber for the felling, and your husband will find he'll get lots of help. We all help each other. It's the only way to survive.'

'We'll be fine, just fine!' Ernest said quickly. He sounded eager and excited, as if he was ready to chop down a tree at that very moment.

Mr Atkinson laughed. 'You'll need a day or two's rest, that's for sure. And tomorrow I'll take you to look at the land that's been allocated to you. I'm sure you'll find it to your liking.'

They were in the Atkinsons' home now, a one-storey log

cabin with a large living-room and four bedrooms leading off it, one of which they had made over to the Gaunts for as long as they needed it. Later, Charlotte found that the Atkinsons' house was a cut above the rest. Many had only the one big room, in which everything took place. Now both families – the Atkinsons had four children aged two to ten, and two grandmothers – sat around the long table, being served with slices of succulent mutton, potatoes and turnips, to be followed by apple pie. Charlotte, who had thought she would never want to eat again, suddenly found herself ravenously hungry.

'So what is our land like?' Ernest asked eagerly. 'Where is it?'

'It's about three miles from here,' Charlie Atkinson said. 'It's got all you need for your first holding. Some woodland to provide timber for a house; some open prairie you can plough up, and a bit of lowland where it's just marshy enough so that the hay won't ever run out. You've got a bonus in that your woodland is to the north, so it will break the winter winds. Don't forget that Wisconsin goes right up to the Canadian border. It can be pretty chilly in winter.'

'It all sounds grand,' Earnest enthused.

'And there's plenty of land around it when you want to buy more, which I daresay you will later on. You can buy land as cheap as a dollar twenty-five an acre, though this might cost you two dollars. It's decent land.'

'I can't wait to see it,' Ernest said. He turned impulsively to Charlotte, sitting next to him, and took her hand in his. Her face, as she answered his smile with her own, showed the first genuine happiness he had seen in her for months. Charlie and Meg Atkinson nodded to each other.

'There's plenty to be done,' Charlie told them. 'Trees to fell – they're mostly oaks around here – and the prairie land to break.'

Ernest laughed. 'Right now I feel equal to anything!'

In fact, when the Atkinsons took them the next day to inspect the land, they were astonished to see that an acre or two had been broken and planted, the new crops already growing.

'We put in corn for you. It's what grows best here and you can use it for most things. And oats for the livestock. You'll be wanting to buy a couple of horses, a cow or two, some pigs,' Charlie said. 'And over here near to where I reckoned you might want to build the house, we planted a few vegetables.'

'It's wonderful!' Charlotte cried. 'What can we ever do to repay you?'

'That's all right, love,' Meg smiled. 'When you've got yourselves dug in you'll find time to help new settlers in exactly the same way. All those of us who have enough room take it in turn to put up the newcomers when their houses are being built. You could easily have been with any one of half a dozen families.'

'We were lucky it was you,' Charlotte said shyly. 'I'm sure of that.'

'So am I,' Ernest agreed.

'You'll owe the seed merchant for the seed,' Charlie said. 'All in good time. And if you're a bit short when it comes to buying livestock you can borrow from the Association, against your first harvest. Of course it means paying interest.'

It seemed unbelievable to Charlotte, looking back, that it was no more than five months since she and Ernest had stood there, gazing at the rough land which was somehow to be their home. So much had happened in such a short time.

Early in the following week half a dozen men had ridden or driven from the surrounding areas, bringing tools, and had helped Ernest to clear the ground for the house, cut and fashion the logs from the tallest, straightest oaks. One neighbour supplied a yoke of oxen to help pull the logs to the building plot. When the logs had been shaped and notched, the house-raising began, and with it the house-raising party. Men and women and children appeared from all over Dane County, the men helping to raise the house, the women serving meals from the supplies they had brought with them. Corn bread, cakes, pies, coffee, and the luscious maple syrup which was there for the taking from sugar maples which grew so abundantly all around.

Everyone was so good-tempered. It seemed to Charlotte that even the children didn't quarrel or get in the way. And in the evening, when it was no longer light enough to work, they had gathered around a fire built from the off-cuts of logs, and there had been singing. German, and occasionally Norwegian, songs had been interspersed among the ones the English had brought from home. Voices in harmony had risen into the calm, dark night until in the end, the youngest children being already asleep, it was time to ride home under the starry sky.

The Gaunt family had gone back with the Atkinsons to sleep, but only a little longer now and they would be in their own house.

'I feel as if our new home has been truly blessed today,' Charlotte said. 'Everything was wonderful.'

After they had moved into their own cabin, a more modest affair than the Atkinsons', with only two bedrooms, Ernest borrowed money to buy two horses – which was necessary if they were to get about at all – a house cow, two pigs and some chickens.

'It's all we can afford to begin with,' he said. 'I can borrow a yoke of oxen to plough up the ground for planting.'

Feeding the pigs and the chickens, milking the cow, were Charlotte's responsibilities. Ernest was at work on the land every daylight hour through that first summer. She was not used to it – until she had married Ernest she had not been near a farm and all the time she had lived with her in-laws at Burley Woodhead she had taken as little part as possible in the outside work. There had been no need of her. Her mother and father-in-law and Ernest had done it all between them.

At first she had been afraid of milking the cow – afraid that it might kick, that a blow might land on her stomach, harm the baby growing inside her. Ernest laughed at her fears. 'Nonsense! Bella's as gentle as they come. And she likes being milked, or she will if you handle her properly. I'll show you how.'

By now, milking Bella morning and evening was the chore

Charlotte liked best. Making the butter and cheese from the surplus milk was hard work, but as she leaned against the warm animal, deftly directing the stream of rich frothy milk into the pail, Charlotte felt relaxed and tranquil; free, for a moment, of the fatigue which was with her these days from morning until night.

'I wish I had more time to help you,' Ernest said anxiously. 'But you know how much there is to do on the land. I can't neglect that or eventually we'll go short of food.'

'I know,' Charlotte replied. 'I'm not complaining. I'll feel stronger when the baby's born, I daresay.'

There was the winter wheat to sow. In August there was the hay harvest from the lower land, and after that the corn harvest. One or two farmers in Dane County had a McCormick reaper which they'd let out for hire, but this year Ernest had no money, or goods or services to offer in exchange, and he didn't want to go into more debt. He would have to harvest by hand. Charlotte was in no condition to help him – swinging the sickle would be beyond her – and most of the other farmers and their families were busy with their own crops.

'It's lucky in a way that we don't have much acreage to harvest this year,' he said. He was sitting at the table, the day's work finished, hungrily devouring the corned beef and cabbage which Charlotte had put before him.

'Next year by hook or by crook we'll have to hire the McCormick.'

The harvest, in fact, had been disappointing, but not only for him. After a poor summer it had been the same all over Wisconsin. Everyone said it was unusual and he hoped they were speaking the truth.

Later, there was the wood supply to get for the winter; trees to fell, logs to split, kindling to chop. The big stove in the centre of the cabin devoured wood at an alarming rate and they'd been warned that the winter might be a long one.

'The first frosts come in November,' Charlie Atkinson told them. 'After that it's snow and frost, snow and frost, for a long time.' Then he'd seen the worried look on Ernest's face. 'Don't worry,' he said. 'We'll all help with the food situation. It'll be your first winter. You haven't had the chance to stock up. Only see to it that you have enough fuel.'

It was the Atkinsons who, a few days later, brought Ernest the letter. They had been in town, at the general store and post office, where the letter had been lying for a day or two.

'Arnold – that's the postmaster – isn't supposed to let us have it as it's addressed to you,' Meg said. 'But he's easy-going and he knew we were riding over.'

'Thank you,' Ernest took the envelope. 'A letter from England. If you don't mind I'll open it.' He did not recognise the writing, which was quickly explained when he began to read by the fact that it had been written by the minister on Matthew Gaunt's instructions. He was aware of the silence around him as he read, everyone waiting for any snippet of news from home, and of the anxious look on Charlotte's face.

'It's from my father,' he said quietly. 'Bad news. My mother's died in her sleep. A sudden heart attack they think.' But her real death, he thought, with a pang which reached to *his* heart, had taken place on that March morning when he had walked away.

He saw, but could not understand, the scarlet flush which immediately suffused Charlotte's face and spread down her neck. He was not to know and she would never tell him, that for a few seconds when he had been silently reading the letter, she had feared that it might contain the news that both his parents had changed their minds and were coming out to join them; and that she had been swiftly and deeply upset at the thought. With Earnest's words she felt unaccountably guilty, as though something was her fault. Her flush was one of shame.

'My father's coming to join me,' Ernest continued. Sorrow at the news of his mother and delight at the thought of seeing his father mingled on his face. Charlotte put her hand on his arm.

'He'll be very welcome. And I'm truly sorry about your mother.'

'Perhaps we'd better go,' Meg suggested. 'Leave you be.'

'No, don't go,' Charlotte said. 'I'll make a pot of coffee.'

While Meg Atkinson kept an eye on Jane, who at sixteen months was running around getting into everything, Charlotte busied herself at the stove. In England they had never drunk coffee, but here everyone did. It was cheaper than tea. She didn't mind the fact that you had to roast your own beans and grind them up. She loved the smell of the roasting and had a small pride in her developing skill which told her when they were just right; dark enough, but not too bitter. As she made the coffee she thought about her in-laws.

'My father will go to see Ruth in New York. I'll have to fetch him from there,' Ernest said.

'But I'll be on my own!' Charlotte objected quickly. She knew at once that she would be terribly afraid. What if the Indians came? Though they had all been sent from Wisconsin to new reservations west of the Mississippi River, they still came back yearly to collect their compensation from the government. She had heard terrible tales of the Indians. And what about wolves? They said that sometimes if the weather was very cold the wolves would come down from Canada. Perhaps not as early as October, but you never knew. And she was seven months pregnant. Ernest seemed to forget that.

'You'll be all right,' Ernest assured her. 'I shan't be gone more than a week if the stage fits in. I'll be back well before the frost starts.'

'You'd be welcome to come and stay with us,' Meg said. 'Only I know you can't leave livestock to fend for themselves. But don't you worry. I'll pop over from time to time and see you're all right.' She turned to Ernest. 'Don't you fret. We'll look after her.'

'I'm more than grateful,' Ernest replied. Meg Atkinson was the most comforting woman in the world. Pretty, too, in spite of the fact that she was in her thirties, and had borne four children.

There's no point in me saying anything, Charlotte thought. But Meg won't be here at night when it's pitch black and you don't know what's out there on the prairie.

Two days later, when Ernest was ready to leave, Charlotte made her final protest. It was then that Ernest reminded her of the rigours of their own journey from New York. After that she let things be. It was the least she could do for her father-in-law, who had always been kind to her.

'Tell your father I look forward to seeing him,' she said. 'And don't forget what you're to bring back for Meg Atkinson!'

'I won't! It'll be the best tablet of scented soap I can find. Verbena for preference.'

'And the same for me, only lavender,' Charlotte said. It would be heavenly to wash with some real scented soap instead of the stuff all the women made themselves, which no matter what they did with it always managed to smell of animal fat. It would be a wonderful surprise for Meg, who had been so good to them.

'Look after yousolf,' Ernest told her. 'Keep the stove going. There's plenty of wood chopped and there's water for a day or two.'

Fetching the water was the only thing he worried about Charlotte having to do in his absence. The spring was at the bottom of a steep hill, and though he had fashioned a yoke which made it easier to balance two pails of water, it was hard going up the hill for his pregnant wife. He no longer let her do it when he was there, but there'd be no help for it when he was gone.

He kissed the baby and then Enoch. 'Look after your mother and be a good boy,' he said. 'I'll bring you back a present from New York.'

'Will you bring Auntie Ruth?' Enoch asked. 'I want Auntie Ruth.'

'Not this time,' Ernest replied. He would have liked to bring Ruth here, but it wouldn't do, even if she'd consent to come. It was a pity Charlotte didn't get on with Ruth.

When he set off Charlotte walked a little way down the

track with Ernest and the children. The track led eventually to the town, where he would pick up the stage.

'You've come far enough now,' Ernest said presently. 'Better turn back.' He took her in his arms and held her close. 'Back in a week,' he said. 'Take care!'

She watched him until he was out of sight, and then walked back with the children to the cabin. She had never felt so alone in all her life.

'I couldn't believe it!' Ruth said. 'I really couldn't believe it. I still can't!'

'Oh, you should have seen your face, Ruth!' Maria cried. 'I declare I never saw anyone so surprised. I thought you'd fall in the water from the shock!'

It was the late evening of the day they had landed. They were gathered together in Mrs Gutermann's sitting-room. By happy coincidence Ernest had arrived less than an hour ago. Her uncle's joy on seeing his son, Ruth thought, had been something special to behold. There were tears on his cheeks as they embraced, and Ernest's eyes were bright. Ruth thought her cousin looked healthier, stronger, but otherwise he was a man who would never change.

Ernest turned from his father to Ruth.

'You've grown up,' he said, frankly appraising her. 'In no more than a few months you've grown up. New York suits you, Ruth!'

'And Wisconsin suits you,' she replied. 'Not much doubt about that.'

'It does,' he admitted. 'It's a different life, and a better one. There's room for everyone, and if you're prepared to work hard and not ask too much, there's a living. I certainly don't regret the day.'

'And Charlotte and the children?'

'Thriving!' Ernest said happily. 'The new bairn is due at Christmas. It's a grand place for children.'

'Let me introduce Sean,' Ruth said. 'We're to be married next week. Sean's from Ireland.'

'As ye'll quickly recognise,' Sean smiled, holding out his hand.

'You'd both do well in Wisconsin, after you're married,' Ernest told them. 'I daresay it'd suit you down to the ground, Sean. Land is cheap and there's good horseflesh, which as an Irishman you'd appreciate.'

There was an instant, answering gleam in Sean's eyes.

And now that Ernest had been fed, everything had to be told again. But no-one minded that, Ruth least of all. Since the moment of their arrival, in the few intervals she had had from attending to her job, she had bombarded Maria and Uncle Matthew with questions. Now she could listen to everything again at leisure.

'Willie is well,' Uncle Matthew said. 'Growing like a young tree.'

'And Hester is to marry again – Tom Firth. What do you think of that?' Maria said.

'Tom Firth?' Ernest queried.

'Landlord of the Shoulder of Mutton. You can't have forgotten him, our Ernest. I reckon he's always had an eye for Hester,' Uncle Matthew declared. 'And he'll make a good husband and father.'

Ernest thought his father looked older, and thin. Then he remembered how thin they had all been when they'd landed from the *Flamingo*. No doubt a few weeks of decent food would put flesh on him. But would he be equal to the hard life of a settler? Well, they'd have to see.

'I'm right glad you came, Father,' he said.

Matthew Gaunt smiled, shook his head. 'I'd have been here afore if I could have persuaded your ma. But considering how suddenly she went in the end perhaps it was all for the best we didn't. God moves in a mysterious way.'

Supposing, Ruth thought in the small silence with followed her uncle's words, supposing Aunt Sarah had died on the voyage. She would have hated the thought of being buried at sea, in the cold grey Atlantic Ocean, even more than in a foreign soil. She had never been as far as the seaside, never wanted to.

Ernest turned to Maria.

'And what made you come, then? I never expected to see you here. I thought you were settled in Bradford.' In his heart he wonder what Charlotte would say when confronted by Maria. But they would have to manage. His little cousin must be made welcome. At the very least it would be another pair of hands.

'Oh no!' Maria said quickly. 'I entered the theatrical profession. I travelled in Scotland, you know. The Jamieson Players. You may have heard of them?'

Ernest shook his head.

'Which was why I didn't hear about dear Aunt Sarah right away. But when I did, the very moment, I left everything and went at once to poor Uncle Matthew.'

'You left your job?' Ernest said. 'That was good of you.'

A faint pink blush rose in Maria's cheeks.

'Well, not quite. I was resting. That's what we call it in the profession. The company had drifted apart.'

'You mean you were out of work?' Ernest teased.

'Resting!' Maria replied firmly. 'And of course something else would have turned up before too long, had I not decided that my duty was to accompany dear Uncle Matthew.'

'It was very noble of you,' Ernest said gravely.

Maria fidgeted. She never knew how to take Ernest. He had always treated her as if she was a child. But Uncle Matthew had been glad of her company and Ruth was delighted to see her.

'What parts did ye play then?' Sean asked. He liked this girl. She was pert and pretty and he thought she might be fun. Of course she did not have the deeper qualities of his Ruth and he doubted if she was anywhere near as clever. They were not at all like sisters, either to look at or, he guessed, in any other way. Ruth, at heart, was the giver. Her sister would take, but no doubt in an entertaining way so that people would be only too glad to give to her.

'As a matter of fact,' Maria said, 'I was never offered quite the part I wanted to play. One must be very careful, you understand, about the parts one accepts!'

'I understand completely,' Sean nodded.

He was awfully handsome, Maria thought. Fancy Ruth being engaged to be married after only a few short months. Ruth, who had always said she never wanted to marry. It must have been a whirlwind courtship. Well, she herself would not have been averse to being swept off her feet by this attractive Irishman!

Sean turned to Uncle Matthew.

'And what do you think of New York, sir?'

'Nay lad, I've hardly seen it. I've only just arrived, you might say. But it seems middling busy.'

His slow north-country voice was music to Ruth's ears. She would have like him to have gone on and on, but he did not have much to say. He had always been a quiet man and now, without Aunt Sarah to spark him off, he was more so than ever. But Maria had enough chatter for all of them.

'What do you think, Cousin Ernest?' she said. 'Ruth hired an open carriage from the quay. We drove all the way up Broadway! I must say, it's a hundred times busier, even, than Market Street in Bradford! And would you believe it? – would *anyone* believe it? We were held up – *all* the traffic at a complete standstill, because of a German band in the middle of the road! They simply refused to budge an inch until they'd played through their repertoire! I never before saw anything like it!'

'Well, I'm afraid you won't find anything like that in Dane County,' Ernest told her. 'When the fiddler comes, we have country dancing, and the women have quilting parties, and candle-dipping sessions – but no Germans bands in Dane County so far.'

'Dane County?' Maria queried.

'Where we live in Wisconsin.'

'It's a pity all three of you can't stay a bit longer in New York,' Sean remarked. 'We could have shown you around.'

'Oh but *I* can,' Maria said brightly. 'Naturally, I'm not going to Wisconsin!'

'Not going to Wisconsin?' Ruth hoped the dismay she felt

did not sound in her voice. And why should she be dismayed? Surely she was fond of her sister?

'Of course not,' Maria replied. 'Wisconsin wouldn't suit me in the least. Really, Ruth, can you see me at a quilting party – though I'm sure it's a very useful occupation? No, I shall stay in New York. Whatever made you think otherwise?'

'I took it for granted,' Ruth said. 'It's not easy in New York. Where would you live? How would you earn a living?'

Maria turned wide, reproachful eyes on her sister.

'Why, Ruth, I do believe you don't want me to stay! I was sure you'd be delighted.'

'Of course I'm pleased,' Ruth said hastily. 'It's just that. . . .'

'If you could let me stay here for a while,' Maria broke in. 'The teeniest little cupboard of a room would do for me. And I eat like a bird. Surely in a boarding-house of this size you have enough scraps left over to feed little me?'

Ruth felt Sean's glance on her. She knew what he was thinking. Why don't you want your sister to stay? The truth was she didn't know why. Just somewhere at the back of her mind the thought of Maria staying indefinitely in New York – which almost certainly meant staying in Gutermann's – made her uncomfortable.

But Maria's big blue eyes were swimming with tears and Sean's look was accusing. Accusing me, Ruth thought, not Maria. He was clearly taken with Maria.

'Well, yes, there is a room. It's a very small attic. And I suppose you could help in the house in return for your keep and perhaps some pocket money. But none of that is strictly mine to give you. I should have to ask permission for you to stay.'

'Oh, Ruth, I'll sleep anywhere! I'll do anything! I'll work my fingers to the bone for you!'

Maria clapped her hands, then dried her tears on the handkerchief which Sean promptly offered her. She was sure that in the end Ruth could not have refused her. 'Oh

Ruth, we'll be so happy together! And naturally I hope before long to find a niche in my own profession. I daresay there are any number of theatres in New York.'

And an even larger number of would-be-actresses, Ruth thought. But she did not say it out loud. What was the point?

'Well that's that, then,' Ernest said. 'And we can just manage to stay for the wedding but we must leave the day after, we can't afford to miss the stage.'

'I'm truly glad you'll both be at my wedding,' Ruth smiled.

'I've got summat for thee,' Uncle Matthew said. 'Your aunt allus said you should have it so I brought it wi' me.'

'What is it?' Ruth asked.

'Hold on a minute while I fetch it – only one of you'll have to show me where my room is, else I'll get lost in this great house.'

Sean went with him, and when they returned a few minutes later Uncle Matthew handed Ruth a parcel wrapped in canvas. She unwrapped it quickly and there, in her hands, she held the sampler which had always hung on her aunt's wall; the sampler worked by her grandmother, the first Ruth Appleby. She hardly knew what to say. Memories of her aunt, of the farmhouse, and then of her grandfather and her parents, engulfed her. She felt united with each and every one of them, as though nothing, neither time nor distance nor events, could ever separate them from her and from each other.

'It's the best present in the world, Uncle Matthew,' she said in the end. 'It will always be my most precious possession.'

'I'll fix it on the wall for ye,' Sean offered. 'Where do ye want it to hang?'

'By the side of the mantelpiece where I can see it every day,' Ruth said.

Ernest would be in New York by now, Charlotte thought. She was filling the water buckets at the spring. She had been as careful as she could about using water, so as not to have to fetch it often, had taken it from the rain barrel for washing the clothes and cleaning in the house; but the rain barrel water wasn't suitable for drinking or cooking, and this morning's porridge had taken the last drop of spring water. She debated whether she would fill, or only half fill, the buckets. But if she did the latter she would have to come again soon. She resolved to carry them as full as she could manage.

When she had filled them she adjusted the yoke on her shoulders to get the balance, then called to Enoch, who was playing at the narrow stream which ran from the spring.

'Come along Enoch. You're wet through again. You'll catch your death of cold one of these days.'

The hill was steep all the way back to the house, a distance of a third of a mile. Some settlers were lucky enough to have a spring right against the house, but with their parcel of land this had been impossible. She climbed with slow, steady steps, Enoch trailing a little way behind. She hoped that Jane, whom she had left asleep in the crib, wouldn't waken and cry before they got back to the house, or, worse still, climb out of the crib, which was really too small for her and would eventually be taken over by the new baby.

'Auntie Meg come today?' Enoch said.

'Not today,' Charlotte answered.

'Why not?'

'Because she came yesterday. Stop asking questions because I haven't the breath to answer.'

They were breasting the steepest part of the rise now. Charlotte dragged up each painful breath from what seemed like the bottom of her lungs. There was a burning sensation in her chest and throat. The yoke was uncomfortable on her shoulders – she had somehow not adjusted it properly – and the weight of the buckets tore at her body. How sickening it was that both she and Meg had forgotten the need for more water yesterday. Meg would easily and willingly have carried it. But now she would not be here for another two days. It was a stupid oversight and now she was paying for it.

Then, as she thought she couldn't possibly go another yard, she reached the top of the hill and had only the level strip of ground to cross to the house. She paused, and would have stopped to rest, except that she heard Jane crying. She set off again as quickly as she could. Her breathing was easier now, but the weight of the buckets was almost unbearable.

She had been in the house an hour, had given the children a meal and had something herself, when the pain started. She knew at once that the baby was coming. There was no mistaking this pain for any other. She was immediately terrified. What could she do? How would she manage? It would be days before Meg Atkinson came and long before then the baby would be here.

Quickly following the terror, and mingled with it, came her blinding anger at the whole Appleby family. 'What is my husband doing in New York – all of them cosy in New York – while I'm having his baby all on my own?' She cried the words aloud and Enoch came running towards her in fear at the rage in her voice.

I might die, she thought. But she must not die, because what would become of Enoch and Jane? But women did die in childbirth and there was no-one, no-one at all to help her. What would she do at the moment of birth?

When the first pangs subsided she tried to calm herself. She must think clearly now, before the pain came back. Meg Atkinson would not be coming, that was for sure. And it was equally sure that no-one else would pass this way. They were a mile off the track and more than three miles from the Atkinsons. She would either have to stay here and try to deliver the baby herself – could she do that? How would she deal with the cord? What if things went wrong, the baby came the wrong way? And what about the children? She must somehow get to the Atkinsons.

She would have to walk there. She could perhaps get herself on horseback, but there was no way she could do so with the children and they were too small to hold on of their own accord.

'What shall I do? Oh Enoch, what shall I do?' Her cry of anguish was caught up in the anguish of the returning labour pain. She gripped the edge of the table and bit her lip until she tasted the blood, in an effort not to cry out again and frighten the children. The pain was strong; she was sure that the baby would come quickly.

When it subsided she wiped the beads of sweat from her face and spoke as calmly as she could to Enoch.

'We're going to see Auntie Meg. We must set off at once. I shall push you and Jane in the little go-cart. You'll like that, won't you?'

She was not sure that she would have the strength to push the cart – a small affair which Ernest had made to take the children – but it was equally impossible for her to carry Jane so far. She would get the children ready, dressed in something warm, and put them in the cart, and then she would wait for the next pain. The moment it was over they would set off. Supposing the baby came while they were on the way? She was icy cold and shaking with terror at the thought.

She found the cart difficult to push. Her back ached to breaking point from the effort of bending to the low height of the cart. The small wheels got caught in the rutted track which the autumn rains had, in places, turned into a quagmire. Twice, along the track, the pains came again, with no more than a short interval between them now. They came with such ferocity that she sank to her knees in the mud, oblivious of the fact that her skirt was soaking. All she knew was that she wanted to go with the pain, to bear down hard to expel the child from her body – and that she must not do so: not here in the mud. She must hold on to it, fight this feeling which all but possessed her. The children watched with frightened eyes, Jane crying. When she was fit again to drag herself to her feet, Charlotte tried to comfort them.

'We shall soon be there! We shall soon be at Auntie Meg's!'

Was it true? She had lost count of time and distance. The only realities were the pain and the mud, and the ache in her breaking back from pushing the cart.

When she first saw the cloud of dust in the distance it did not register with her, and by the time it drew closer and resolved itself into a horse pulling a trap, with a woman driving, she was in the middle of a pain again; and this time she knew that it was final. There would be no holding back this time. She had run out of strength.

'Auntie Meg! It's Auntie Meg!'

Charlotte was only dimly aware of Enoch's voice calling, and of strong arms somehow helping her into the trap, where she lay on the floor. The pain was everything now. The rest of the world was dark; inky black and muddy. There was mud on her hands, her face, in her mouth. She knew that she must die because no-one could endure this and go on living. When the final tearing, rending, lacerating, rupturing pain came, isolating her from everything except itself, she screamed. The wind caught up the howl of mingled agony and triumph as the new life came, whipping it across the prairie.

# 19

The day of the wedding was one of those soft, mild days which sometimes visit New York even in November. Sitting up in bed, from where she could see out of the window, Ruth observed that a few brave leaves still clung to the trees. But the glory of the fall was over and it needed only a strong gust of wind to strip the branches entirely. She was glad that there were a few leaves left for her wedding day. She would like, she thought fancifully, to trim her bonnet with them.

There was a knock at the door and May came in, carrying a tray.

'Your breakfast, Miss Ruth. A lovely day. Happy the bride the sun shines on! And Mrs Cruse says you're to make a hearty breakfast.'

The last meal of the condemned, Ruth thought – then banished the thought at once. She must remember only the good which the day was to bring.

'And if you want anything else you have only to ask,' May said. 'If you'd like me to help you to dress. . . .'

'Thank you, but I shall manage nicely. It's enough that you and Mrs Cruse have seen to the breakfasts.' In fact, she wanted to be by herself for this last hour or two.

When May had gone Ruth got out of bed – she had no appetite for her breakfast – and took out her dress from Mrs Gutermann's immense wardrobe. She was to be married in a cream wool dress which Mrs Carson had passed on to her before leaving. It was finely tucked down the front of the bodice, the crinoline skirt falling in three deep frills, and trimmed with white and green braid. Sean had bought her a new bonnet for a wedding present, cream-coloured to match her dress, and this she had trimmed with small pink rosebuds and lilies of the valley.

Laying the dress on the bed, Ruth stood in front of the mirror and surveyed herself critically. Could anyone possibly tell? She thought not. Except that her breasts were fuller, there was no visible change in her shape. She placed her hands gently on her body where she believed the baby lay, as if to reassure it as well as herself that all was to be for the best.

Then she raised her eyes and looked at the gold chain with its locket which had hung around her throat, unseen beneath her clothes, since the night at Millfield when Joss Barnet had flung it on the bed. Every morning and night since then she had looked at it in the mirror, and now she must take it off and leave it off forever.

Her fingers were clumsy as she fumbled at the clasp, and at first she thought it would not come apart. When it did, she held it in her hand for a moment before dropping it into its box. She would never wear it again. Perhaps one day her daughter – *his* daughter. . . . But that was wrong and wicked thinking. As soon as ever she could she must dispose of the gift. She pushed the box to the back of a small drawer, and was locking the drawer when Maria burst into the room. Ruth withdrew the key and held it concealed in her hand. If Maria had seen her lock the drawer, nothing would stop her asking why.

Her sister was completely dressed and ready; looking adorable, Ruth thought, in an outfit of deep rose-pink which exactly matched the colour in her cheeks. Her blue eyes sparkled with excitement.

'Oh Ruth, you're not even dressed! How can you? And I know for a fact that Uncle Matt and Ernest are ready and Sean has already left for the church! If it were my wedding day I'd have been ready hours ago.'

'I shan't be long,' Ruth assured her. 'I have only to put on my dress and bonnet.'

Though in the mirror she could see no change in her

figure, the dress was a little tight. In another month it would not meet around the waist.

'Here, let me do your hair for you,' Maria offered. 'I'm much better at that than you are.'

She dressed Ruth's hair carefully, brushing it smoothly back from a centre parting into a chignon of curls at the back of her neck, which would peep out from underneath her bonnet. Then she set the bonnet gently on her sister's head.

Ruth tied the satin ribbons into a careful bow, and took a last look at Ruth Appleby, soon and forever to be Mrs Sean O'Farrell.

'You are too pale,' Maria criticised. 'Pinch your cheeks and bite your lips to make the colour come. Oh Ruth, I do envy you! Sean is so wonderfully handsome, and it's clear he simply adores you.'

'I am very fortunate,' Ruth agreed quietly. 'Are you sure Uncle Matthew and Ernest are ready?'

'Waiting in the hall by now, I should think. I saw them coming down the stairs. And Professor Woodburn and some of the others have left. You mustn't keep people waiting a minute longer, Ruth, even though it *is* the bride's privilege.'

When Uncle Matthew and Ernest saw Ruth their faces lit with approbation.

'You look a treat,' Ernest said.

Uncle Matthew touched her hand. 'Your Aunt Sarah would have been proud of you, love,' he told her quietly.

And Grandfather, Ruth thought suddenly? Would he?

'The carriage is already at the door,' Ernest said.

'Carriage?'

'Professor Woodburn ordered it. He said he wouldn't let the bride walk to church.'

'He's so good to me,' Ruth said. 'I shall never be able to repay him.'

She was about to say more when she was interrupted by a ring on the doorbell. When Ernest opened the door, Joss Barnet stood there on the step. He looked past Ernest, directly at Ruth, his eyes searching hers. An ice-cold wave of feeling swept her from top to toe and she thought she would faint. Then it seemed to her that the others must surely hear the beating of her heart as it thumped in her breast. Why did he have to come, today of all days? Didn't he know she couldn't bear it?

'I beg your pardon,' Joss Barnet said. 'I seem to have come at the wrong moment. I had hoped to see Professor Woodburn – a matter of business.'

'He has already gone to the church,' Ruth replied. Her lips were stiff so that she could hardly frame the words. 'Perhaps you had forgotten the date?'

'My sister is to be married in just a few minutes, from now,' Maria put in. 'There is our carriage waiting.'

Joss looked at Ruth. 'Your sister?'

'Allow me to introduce Miss Maria Appleby,' Ruth said. 'Also Mr Matthew Gaunt and Mr Ernest Gaunt, my uncle and cousin.'

Joss Barnet bowed formally to each of them, then turned to Ruth again.

'Perhaps I could leave a message with you for the professor – I will write it down if that is not asking too much.'

Ruth hesitated, then turned to her family. 'Will you wait for me in the carriage? I shall be no more than a minute, I promise. Mr Barnet, will you come in and write your note to the professor and I will see that he gets it.'

She preceded him into Professor Woodburn's room. 'Please write it as quickly as you can,' she said stiffly. 'I am already late.'

He closed the door behind him, then swung around and took her by both hands, holding her fast.

'Ruth, I don't want to see the professor; nor had I forgotten the date, as you well know. I came to say once more "Is this what you want?" It isn't too late to change, Ruth.'

'I can't. . . .'

'You can if you want to. I'll find somewhere for you. I'll see that you're looked after. Ruth, think again!'

She looked hard at him, as if one look might have to last her forever. She saw the pallor of his face and the pain in his eyes and knew that her marriage, so soon to be a reality, was driving a sword through him also. But he would get over it, she told herself, hardening her heart, not daring to do otherwise. As, she was determined, would she.

'I have no intention of changing my mind,' she said steadily. 'There is no more to be said. And now if you will permit me, I must go. I cannot keep my future husband waiting any longer.'

She brushed swiftly past him. He caught the frill of her crinoline in his hand but she jerked away, hurrying out of the house and down the steps to the waiting carriage.

'What handsome men you do know, to be sure,' Maria remarked. 'I hope we shall see him again.'

Ruth did not answer, scarcely heard. In a way, she was glad of the chatter which Maria kept up all the way to the church, since it covered her own silence.

'Just think,' Maria said. 'You, Ruth Appleby, all the way from silly little Barnswick, driving up Broadway, New York! In a carriage, going to be married to a handsome Irishman! And me, little Maria, sitting beside you! Who would have thought it? Oh Ruth, do you think the same thing will happen to me?'

'I shouldn't be surprised,' Ruth replied mechanically.

Ruth had forgotten, for the moment, that a society wedding was to follow hers, and when she walked up the aisle on her uncle's arm she was almost overwhelmed by the scent of the flowers - roses and lilies - with which the church had been decorated. It lent an extravagant touch to what was otherwise an austere wedding.

Sean was pale, and when he looked at her as she took her place beside him, she saw his anxiety. Her hands started to tremble and soon she was trembling from head to foot. She wanted to turn and run, away from Sean, away from the boarders who so sparsely occupied the front pews; out of the church and into the busy, everyday life of Broadway, where she could lose herself in the crowd. But the vicar had already started the prayers.

It was an awesome service. She meant every word of her

promises as she made them, but how would she carry them out? 'Till death us do part.' It was a lifetime away. She prayed with all her heart for strength to keep her vows, feeling that she was making them not only to her new husband, but to her child.

Before they left the church Dr Taylor wished them well. 'God bless you both,' he said. Then he stepped towards an urn crammed with cream-coloured roses, snapped one off and handed it to Ruth.

'Let us say from one bride to another. I am sure she who is to follow will not mind!'

Impulsively, Ruth pulled a spray of lilies of the valley from her bonnet. 'Then please give these to her, sir. We shall never meet, but I wish her luck and happiness!'

When they were back at the house those of the boarders who had not had to rush off to work gathered in the parlour. Ruth saw Miss Fontwell, emerged for the moment from the historical past and enjoying the present, Miss Potter, Mr Gossop, Mr Pierce, the professor, and several others, including, she was pleased to see, Mr Francis Priestley. Someone, Ruth had no idea who, had ordered an enormous cake from Delmonico's and the professor had provided Madeira wine.

Then Mr Pierce rapped loudly on the table and called for silence. When he had it, he cleared his throat and delivered himself of a short, carefully-rehearsed speech. Sean looked at Ruth with pride, agreeing with every complimentary word Mr Pierce said about her. It's all more than I deserve, Ruth thought, catching her husband's eye. She determined afresh, with everything in her, that she would make their marriage a success.

'And it is with great pleasure,' Mr Pierce concluded, 'that I and my fellow guests '(above all others he liked to think of himself as a guest rather than as a boarder)'. . . . desire that you both, Mr and Mrs Sean O'Farrell, will accept this small token of our good wishes!'

With which, from under its cover on a nearby table, he whipped out a water-colour painting in a gilt frame. It was a scene of the waterfront as painted from offshore. The harbour was full of ships and behind them, through the middle of Manhattan, ran the beginning of the wide street of Broadway. It was suddenly the most perfect present in the world. Ruth felt as if her boarders had given her New York.

She did her best to thank them, then said, 'And now I must change my clothes and get back to the kitchen, or there will be no meals today and you will all revise your opinions!'

Professor Woodburn put out a hand to stop her.

'No! It has been decided that you and your husband shall spend the rest of the day in whatever sort of pleasure you choose. May and Mrs Cruse, helped by your sister, will take over your duties here. So off you go, and we shall not expect to see you again today.'

'Let's take the omnibus to Battery Park,' Ruth said. It was New York's only park, at the southernmost tip of Manhattan, and a fashion parade for smart people. Today, in her wedding dress and new bonnet, Ruth felt the equal of any lady of quality, and luckily it was mild, so that she need not cover her dress with her old cloak.

'But I shall carry your cloak for you,' Sean insisted. 'Pride, and a little mild weather may keep you warm now, but later it will turn cold.'

A little after midday he said, 'I'm hungry. Shall we go into an eating house? And you shall choose anything you like from the list. No skimping today.'

They both decided on a dozen oysters, with steak-and-kidney pie to follow. 'That was my first taste of oysters,' Ruth remarked when she had tipped down the last one. 'I don't like the slippery way they slide down my throat.'

When Sean had finished his pie he mopped up the rich gravy with a piece of bread. 'That was good,' he said. 'And now, Mrs O'Farrell, what would ye like to do next?'

'Something which doesn't cost money! We've spent far more than we can afford.'

'You're wrong! Professor Woodburn gave me ten dollars

to spend on whatever took our fancy. Said it was a wedding present. So what shall we do?'

'Oh Sean, I've always wanted to go to Barnum's museum,' Ruth confessed. 'They say there's a live mermaid there!'

'No sooner said than done. It's only a few strides to Ann Street.'

They saw the mermaid, as well as Tom Thumb, a cherry-pink cat, and a host of other wonders with which Barnum regularly intrigued the citizens of New York. Ruth was thrilled by it all.

'And what I'd really like now is some ice-cream,' she declared when they emerged into an afternoon which was already turning cold.

'Here, you'd better put on your cloak,' Sean said. 'And you can't seriously mean you want ice-cream on a November afternoon?'

'Oh but I do! When I'm rich – which one day I mean to be . . .'

'When *we* are rich,' Sean interrupted.

'. . . I shall eat ice-cream every day of the year. A six-cent plate to myself, not shared with anyone.'

'Then you shall have one to yourself,' Sean said, laughing. 'After all, it is your wedding day!'

Ruth shivered, pulled her cloak around her. She no longer had any taste for ice-cream. Afterwards they walked slowly back up Broadway and turned into Spring Street, Sean hooking her hand through his arm in a proprietary manner.

'Let's go to Niblo's this evening,' he suggested. 'Round off the day. They say everyone should go there.'

'Then why don't we take Uncle Matthew, and Ernest and Maria,' Ruth said quickly.

Sean pulled a face. 'Why not just you and me?'

'But Uncle Matt and Ernest leave tomorrow. Surely we shouldn't begrudge them this pleasure? And can't you just imagine how Maria would enjoy it? Let's ask them the minute we get in.'

It was not what Sean had in mind. Ruth saw the

disappointment in his face when they found Ruth's relatives in Mrs Gutermann's sitting-room – which from now on would be the O'Farrells' sitting-room, she thought. He had waited all day for this moment alone with his new wife. But not yet, Ruth thought. Not yet.

Niblo's was only a block away, at Prince Street. Ruth had often heard music coming from the building and she knew that the Carsons had visited there. It was a place for all classes to enjoy a convivial evening with entertainment. Guiltily, in spite of her fatigued body and aching feet, Ruth hoped the evening would prove a long one.

The five of them sat at a large table which they shared with another party. When one of the strangers heard that they were a wedding party he insisted on buying drinks for all and toasting the bride and groom.

'And you'll be next, I shouldn't wonder,' he said to Maria, eyeing her with bold appreciation.

'Thank you, sir!' It could happen, she thought. She was seventeen, thirteen months younger than Ruth. She felt quite sure that New York was full of eligible men.

'This is a *wonderful* place,' Maria cried. 'Do look at the pretty garden out there, all lamplit and beautiful! Don't you think it's just wonderful, Uncle Matt?'

He smiled at her enthusiasm. That was Maria. Everything was either wonderful or horrible. No middle course. But she'd grow out of it. She was young. Come to think of it, though, she wasn't that much younger than Ruth. But Ruth always had an old head on her shoulders. Too much responsibility. Well, now she'd got someone to look after her. As for himself, he felt old, and out of his depth in this great place with it's high ceiling and the fancy carved frieze right around the wall. He had never seen anything like it. Of course everyone was very kind. Everyone seemed kind, and lively and enthusiastic, in New York. There was no wonder the girls liked it. But it wasn't his sort of life, all this rushing around. He'd be glad when he got into the country with Ernest. Got settled down, saw his grandchildren.

'What time do we leave tomorrow?' he asked his son.

'Straight after breakfast, Father. An early start.'

Ernest turned to Sean and Ruth. 'I wish you were coming with us, you two. You could set up there and have a good life.'

Sean's face lit with interest, as it did every time Wisconsin was mentioned. But he knew, or guessed, that Ruth didn't get on well with her cousin's wife. That was most likely the reason for her reluctance.

'Would you say we should settle in Dane County?' he asked. He was sure Ernest understood the purport of his questions.

'Not necessarily. Jefferson County is good. Fifty miles only from Milwaukee. We pass through on the way to Dane. The land is fertile there. They say you can get fourteen bushels of wheat to the acre, and sell it for cash. And there are bigger banks in Jefferson County – easier to borrow money to set up.'

Sean looked at Ruth with shining eyes. 'What do you say, Ruth? Doesn't it sound wonderful? Our own place!'

'And there are several British settlers in Jefferson,' Ernest added.

How could she get it into Sean's head, Ruth asked herself, that she would never leave New York? Nowhere in her life had she felt such a sense of belonging as in this great, bustling city. Every day, to walk in its streets breathed new life into her. She could not understand herself, but it was so – though at the same time she would never forget or cease to love her Yorkshire home.

In any case, and quite apart from her love for the city, she had her own plans for the future, though so far she had mentioned them to no-one. She would tell Sean when the time seemed appropriate.

She had decided that one day she would own Gutermann's; own it lock, stock and barrel. She had no idea how or when, but she was working on it and she knew, was convinced, without a doubt, that one day it would happen.

And deep inside her was that other reason why she could never leave New York. She might never see him again; she would never try to do so. She would be a good and loving wife to Sean – for the twentieth time that day she told herself so – but it must be here, in this city. She could not leave it.

'What about it, Ruth?' Sean repeated.

'You know my feelings, Sean,' she said quietly. 'But in any case it's too big a matter to decide over a glass of wine, late at night. Also, you know that I can't leave Gutermann's at the present time. I've given my word to stay until things are settled.'

'Very well then, for the present,' Sean acquiesced.

Ruth knew by his ready agreement that he would return to the subject. No doubt he thought she would change her mind when the baby was born. But she was grateful that he had decided to let it rest for now.

'What about poor little me?' Maria asked. 'I don't want to leave New York!'

They all laughed at her and the tension was broken.

'It's time we were off if we're to make an early start tomorrow,' Ernest said. 'And don't forget, either, we've got a newly-married couple here. *They* won't want to hang around all night, pleasant though it is!'

There was longing in Sean's eyes as he looked at Ruth. She was tired and wanted to leave, to return to the house, take off her shoes, unfasten her tight dress. But at the house the bedroom awaited her. Now that it was so near she wondered how she would bear it. No virgin bride, she thought, ever felt more reluctance: but hers was not for what she was to learn, but because of what she had already known.

'Well, perhaps one more glass of wine before we go,' she said brightly.

Sean looked surprised.

'Are ye certain? Ye're not used to it. It will surely go to your head.'

She could hardly tell him, hardly admit to herself, that that was what she hoped for.

All her reluctance, all her apprehension, proved unnecessary. Sean, though as passionate as any woman could have wished, was kind and thoughtful, and his demands that night were no more than she could fulfil, in spite of her fatigue. Indeed, once again the act itself brought her vitality, so that afterwards all her weariness was gone and she was no more than pleasantly tired and ready for sleep. On that, and all the nights which followed, she gave herself freely to Sean; never stinting, never holding back, no matter that his demands increased with familiarity.

And if sometimes at the height of their lovemaking she forgot whose arms she was in and whose body mingled with hers, Sean was none the wiser. It was not deliberate on her part. She tried to put all such thoughts from her but they attacked her when she was most vulnerable. And one could say, since these involuntary thoughts increased her passion and heightened her desire, that at such times she was a better wife to Sean. He certainly had no complaints. Indeed, since he confused sexual passion with love, he grew ever more hopeful. But Ruth knew that, try as she would, she was no nearer to loving him.

When Ernest and his father, after a wearying journey, at last reached Mazomanie, Charlie Atkinson was there to meet the stage.

'You're to come home with me,' he said.

'We can't,' Ernest told him. 'At least not for more than a minute or two. But if you could lend us horses – which I'd return tomorrow – it would be a great help. My father's very tired and it's a long way to walk. I want to get home as quickly as possible to Charlotte.'

Charlie Atkinson had taken the bundles and boxes and all the time Ernest was talking he was stowing them in the trap.

'We'll see,' he replied enigmatically. Ernest stared at him. He was so unlike his usual friendly self. The three men got into the trap, and with no further conversation except to discuss, briefly, the journey from New York, they made for the Atkinson home.

'Go straight in,' Charlie said when they got there. 'I'll see to the horses.'

When Ernest entered he saw the two younger Atkinson children playing on the floor with his own Enoch and Jane. Meg Atkinson left the pan she was stirring and rushed to meet him, taking his hands in hers.

'I don't understand,' Ernest said. He had a sick, hollow feeling inside him. Something was wrong. 'Why are the children here? Where is Charlotte?'

'Come with me,' Meg replied.

She led him to the best bedroom. Charlotte, pale as death, but with eyes shining like dark pools, lay back against her pillows; and by her side, in the bed, was the tiny baby.

'You've got another daughter,' Meg said. Then she went out and closed the door behind her. Charlotte held out her arms and Ernest went into them.

'Oh, Ernest, I'm so glad you're here! Ernest, it was terrible! I thought I'd never see you again. If it didn't been for Meg, driving over to see us because she realised she'd forgotten about the water, I think I never would have. Oh Ernest, please don't ever leave me again. Promise it will be the last time!'

He held her against him while she sobbed. 'I promise,' he said. 'I'll always be with you, Charlotte.'

He continued to hold her while she told him what had happened.

'I think we should call the baby Meg,' she ended.

'I agree,' Ernest said.

Within a few weeks of the wedding Ruth let it be known that she was with child, and that the baby was due early in the following August (thought she knew that it would make its surprise appearance in June). Fortunately the crinoline was the best possible garment for hiding her figure and it would be impossible, she reckoned, for anyone to determine her exact stage of pregnancy.

'You're just like me,' Mrs Cruse sympathised. 'Got caught quick! Nine months to the day I had my first, and if the typhoid hadn't taken Mr Cruse when it did I might have had a dozen now instead of only six!' It was clear that she considered the typhoid a blessing.

The boarders showed a fleeting interest. Such a condition was, after all, no more than the normal result of marriage. Only Professor Woodburn, considerate as ever, expressed the fear that Ruth might find the work of running the boarding-house too much for her.

'I'm sure I shan't,' Ruth said. 'I have Maria to help me now, as well as Mrs Cruse and May.'

Maria had made no real attempt to find a job, though she spoke vaguely of applying for a post in Stewart's emporium or, better still, of finding something in one of New York's theatres. But with Christmas not too far away there was plenty to do in the house, so that she more or less earned her keep. Best of all Maria liked shopping, and since Sean had cautioned Ruth in no uncertain terms about the folly of carrying heavy baskets, the two sisters often went together.

Sean was always on at Ruth to do less.

'A woman in your condition,' he warned. 'Up with the lark and on your feet most of the day. You should take more care or you'll risk losing the child.'

Ruth marvelled at his kindness. Most men in his position would have been relieved to have a wife miscarry another man's child. Not so Sean. It was as if he had totally convinced himself that the child would be the issue of both of them. He did everything he could to make things easier for Ruth, and issued stern instructions to Mrs Cruse.

'See to it that this obstinate wife of mine doesn't overdo things. She must rest every afternoon.'

'I'll see to it,' Mrs Cruse promised.

'My word,' she continued when Sean had left the kitchen, 'you can see Mr O'Farrell's cut out to be a father! Now Mr Cruse just left me to get on with it. But then he was never a strong man.'

Six days a week Sean worked hard for William Tweed in the factory, and in the evenings and on Sundays he did jobs in the house, or took Ruth for a walk around the streets. He was an ideal husband and Ruth was ashamed that, in spite of his worth, and of her admiration and respect for him, she could not love him as a wife should. If ever a man deserved to be loved, she thought, it was Sean O'Farrell. But love had nothing to do with deserving.

This, and the fact that it could not be long now before Mrs Gutermann's affairs were settled – and Ruth had no idea in what direction that would be – were the biggest clouds in her sky during the early months of her pregnancy. Of course there were days when she longed with all her heart for Joss Barnet. Even to have seen him walking by on the other side of the street, or riding in his carriage, would have eased her hunger. It never happened. And it was not for the want of trying that she failed to shut him out of her mind.

It seemed to Ruth that not since she was in Nordale, with the Longhills, had she worked as hard as on the run-up to her first Christmas in New York; though she had discovered not long after the Carsons' return to England, that the responsibility she had taken on brought tasks which as a maidservant she would never have thought of. Her eyes and her mind had to be everywhere. Even the weather, which in December had turned bitter, brought its problems. She came into the kitchen, chafing her ice-cold hands.

'Something will have to be done about Mr Gossop's room,' she said. 'It faces north and it's bitterly cold – and I've noticed he has a nasty cough. I must find a stove for him.'

'Give one of 'em a stove and they'll all want one,' Mrs Cruse warned.

'I daresay. Nevertheless. . . .' She turned to May. 'Did you remember the clean towels in Miss Fontwell's room?'

Could they *really* manage without Mrs Cruse on Christmas Day, Ruth asked herself? How would she share out the duties? Perhaps she had been rash in giving Mrs Cruse the day off, but it seemed to Ruth that Mrs Cruse's six children had first claim on their mother at Christmas.

Fortunately, in view of all that was to be done, she was as fit as a fiddle. Pregnancy suited her.

'You wait until you're eight months gone,' Mrs Cruse

said. 'That's the testing time. And you couldn't have a worse month than August, what with the heat and all. I know. My third was born in August. It was murder, I can tell you!'

Ruth recalled the heat of last summer, those days in New York before they had gone up to Millfield, before she had known that Joss Barnet existed. By August of next year her baby would be two months old. What would it be like, holding it in her arms? How long now before she felt it move in her body? The child she carried was never absent from her thoughts for long, though she tried not to refer to it in Sean's presence, letting him be the one to do so.

'I hope it's a girl,' he remarked one day. Perhaps, Ruth thought, he thinks a girl might favour me more than a boy could.

At a parlour tea a few days before Christmas she brought up the subject of what everyone had planned for the holiday. It seemed that most of her boarders would be staying put, partly because they had no choice, most of them having little or no contact with their families.

'My brother in Saskatoon writes regularly, as you know,' Mr Gossop said. 'But it is some years since I have seen him and it is a long way to travel.'

'I believe you have brothers in Buffalo,' Mr Pierce said to Miss Fontwell. 'That is not so far. Shall you be seeing them this year?'

'No.' Miss Fontwell spoke decisively. 'They are married and have families of their own. I shall be happy with a quiet Christmas here.'

'And I,' Miss Potter said. 'When term ends all I shall want to do is eat and sleep. Those children exhaust me. I have no energy left for anything else. I think I am not cut out to be a schoolteacher, certainly not for under-fives.'

'Then one wonders why you chose it,' Miss Fontwell remarked.

'It seemed the right thing to do at the time. My father left me a little money and it seemed a good investment, since I had to earn a living, to start a little school. I do not have much knowledge to teach older children, but really next year I think I shall take no child under seven.'

Most of the other boarders seemed to have reasons for remaining in New York. Neither Mr Pierce nor Professor Woodburn ever mentioned family. Captain Forsyth, recently retired from the Seventh Regiment, had acquaintances in New York where the regiment was stationed, but none of them had issued an invitation for Christmas-time.

'But pray tell us what your plans are, Mr Priestley,' Miss Potter asked.

In the few weeks that he had been with them Francis Priestley had become popular with the other boarders, especially with Miss Potter. Perhaps she sees an escape from those monstrous children, Ruth thought.

'I shall be going home to Williamsburg,' he said. 'My family always tries to be together for such occasions. My mother expects it – and of course it pleases us.'

On the morning of the day before Christmas Eve Maria had gone to Broadway, ostensibly to make some last-minute purchases but really to feast her eyes on the Christmas displays in the shops. Ruth was in her sitting-room, wrapping Christmas presents out of the sight of their recipients. When the knock sounded at the door and she called 'come in' she was surprised to see Francis Priestley enter.

'I came to tell you that I am just leaving,' he said. 'And to wish you the happiest of Christmases – though I am sure that for you it will be a busy one.'

'Thank you,' Ruth said. 'And may I wish you the same. In fact. . . .'

'Yes?'

'I wonder, Mr Priestley, if you are not in too great a hurry, whether you would perhaps join me in a glass of wine . . . to celebrate the season?'

Hearing herself she could scarcely believe that she, onetime (and not so long ago) servant, was saying these words to Mr Francis Priestley. How could she presume so? But it was to late to retract and he was showing no surprise.

'I would be glad to,' he replied.

She poured the wine, set ratafia biscuits on one of Mrs Gutermann's porcelain plates, and sat down opposite him. It was at this point she realised that she had nothing whatever to say! She looked at him blankly.

'I hope you will not work too hard over Christmas,' he said presently.

'Oh no, I shall not. My husband will see to that. And what shall you do in Williamsburg?'

'Not a great deal. Christmas Day is a family gathering – I have three sisters and several small nephews and nieces. And the following day I shall spend with my fiancée and her family.'

'Oh! I didn't know you were engaged to be married.' Nor, she felt sure, did Miss Potter, or her two youngest, prettiest and silliest boarders, the Miss Pearl and Ruby Trimhorn. Not to mention Maria.

'Yes,' he said. 'Though no date is yet fixed for the wedding since Helen – that is my fiancée's name – is not well. In the spring she is to take a cure in the Blue Ridge Mountains.'

'Then let us hope it will be a complete one,' Ruth replied.

She could just picture his fiancée: beautiful, fragile, rich – and beloved of Francis Priestley. Any woman (except, of course, one who was already married and bearing the child of a man she had adored, and still longed for) might envy her.

'Thank you,' he said. 'And now I must go. I shall be back early in the New Year. I have quite a lot of work to get through before my students arrive back for the new term.'

As he moved towards the door it opened, and Maria rushed in. The cold air had brought the colour into her cheeks and a sparkle to her eyes. In her dark red cloak, and a bonnet trimmed with red ribbon, she looked ravishing. Ruth was instantly aware of Mr Priestley's look of admiration for her sister.

'It's beginning to snow!' Maria cried. 'Isn't that exciting?'

'Mr Priestley might not think so, since he has to travel to Virginia,' Ruth told her.

Francis Priestley looked directly at Maria. 'I daresay you

would make most things seem exciting,' he said as he left.

'Oh Ruth , isn't he *so* good-looking!' Maria sighed.

'Very,' Ruth agreed. 'I imagine his fiancée thinks so too. He's engaged to be married.'

So for a short season the boarders became one family.

'It isn't all sweetness and light between them,' Ruth told Sean in the privacy of their bedroom. 'They have their differences. They might sometimes be too polite to express them but I can usually tell.'

'Such as what?' Sean asked.

'Well, Captain Forsyth thinks he's miles above Mr Pierce. Mr Pierce knows it, and it hurts him. Miss Potter is setting her cap at Mr Priestley – and what a shock she's in for. And then there is Miss Fontwell's little problem, which I've yet to solve.'

Miss Fontwell had sought out Ruth in private.

'I do not quite know how to put this,' she said. 'I am not one to complain, as you know, but I cannot stand it any longer. I refer to Mr Gossop.'

'Mr Gossop?' Ruth could not believe it. He was the quietest, mildest of all her boarders.

Miss Fontwell lowered her voice. 'Mr Gossop – *snores*! Loudly. And his room is next to mine. I would not for the world let him know it, and it is not his fault, though I do believe that if he were to try a small, hard object fixed to the back of his neck. . . . Indeed, he is a very pleasant gentleman, but I am a light sleeper. In short, Mrs O'Farrell, I would be more than grateful if you would move me to another room!'

'I'll do what I can,' Ruth promised. 'Perhaps I will move Mr Gossop. I am not sure that his room suits him.' But on whom could she inflict poor Mr Gossop and his snores? There was still one of the rooms which the Carsons had occupied, but it was a double, and as such she hoped eventually to rent it.

On the morning of Christmas Day, while most of her boarders were at church, Sean moved the tables together to make one large one, and all the boarders sat down together for Christmas dinner. After they had been served, Sean, Ruth and Maria ate in the kitchen with May. Sammy had preferred to take himself back to his family as soon as Ruth gave the word, carrying a large can of food she had put up for him, and with the few dollars his boarders had given him in tips tucked away in his pocket.

The three women had a small glass of sherry wine each and Sean had beer. In no time at all he was singing, all the old Irish songs. 'The Harp that Once' was followed by 'The Minstrel Boy', and by the time he reached 'The Last Rose of Summer' there were tears in his eyes and a sob in his resonant Irish tenor voice. May and Maria found it deeply touching and wept with enjoyment.

'It was lovely, Mr O'Farrell,' May said. 'Give us another!'

He refilled his tankard and drank deeply.

'Please, Sean!' Maria begged.

Ruth wished they would not encourage him. He had drunk too much and he was getting maudlin.

He looked fondly at Ruth. 'I've got one specially for you, my love. Specially for my dear wife. And we'll drink to that great Irish poet who wrote it. I speak of Thomas Moore, God bless him!' He spoke carefully, as if the words might trip him up. But when he started to sing it was different.

His voice soared, sweet as a bell, the words ringing out with emotion, and all the time he looked at Ruth with adoring eyes.

'Love thee, dearest, love thee?
Yes, by yonder star I swear. . . .
Love thee, dearest, love thee?
Yes, till death I'm thine!'

With the final couplet his voice rose in a crescendo, then faded to a whisper as he repeated the last line, not taking his eyes from her face. Ruth felt the tears sting in her own eyes, and when he put out his hand she clasped it to her own. If only . . . if only. . . . Her thoughts were in a tumult. In her head she repeated the words he had sung to her. But to whom was she saying them? With every bit of her she wanted them to be for Sean.

There was the deepest of sighs from May, but when she said, 'I daresay we could all do with a cup of cocoa after that,' the spell was broken. Sean had another beer and launched into another tune, this time a riotous drinking song.

'Going belling, dancing, drinking
Breaking wind or swearing, sinking.
Ever raking, never thinking
Lived the Rakes of Mallow.'

He jumped up from his chair and pulled Maria to her feet. Singing chorus after risqué chorus he jigged her around the kitchen until she was breathless and cried to him to stop.

He was still singing when he and Ruth went to bed, though by now the words were slurred.

'Do be quiet, Sean,' Ruth implored him. 'Everyone will hear!'

'What if they do? Isn't a man allowed to sing in his own home at Christmas-time?'

'You've had too much to drink,' Ruth said quietly. 'Go to bed.'

Contrary to all she had expected, he was asleep the moment his head touched the pillow. She tucked the blanket around his shoulders so that he would not get cold in the night, then she lay awake by his side, thinking over her first Christmas in New York. Next Christmas she would have her child. Where would they all be?

# 20

Early in the New Year came the opportunity to let the empty room. Mr Pierce came one evening to Ruth's sitting-room.

'Please sit down,' Ruth said.

'Mr O'Farrell is not with you?'

'No. He is not yet home from work.'

'Well, it was you I wanted to see, Mrs O'Farrell. I think I may have found you two suitable guests.'

'Two new guests?' Ruth said. 'That is interesting, Mr Pierce. Are they friends of yours?'

He hesitated. 'In a way. Yes, I think you could say that. I have met the gentleman through a business connection.'

'He works in Brooke Brothers?'

'No. At Stewart's. He is the buyer on fabrics – a very responsible post as I'm sure you'll appreciate. I have met his wife and she is most amenable. Indeed, Mr and Mrs Seaford are a delightful couple; charming, respectable. . . .'

'I'm sure!'

How could she tell this nice man – Mr Pierce was one of her favourite boarders – that however charming his friends, they might not be, well, *acceptable* at Gutermann's? For herself, she liked the sound of them, but with the rest of the boarders it could be a different tale. The trouble was that the Seafords were clearly in trade, not of the professional classes. Mr Pierce himself was the only person in a similar position ever to get into Gutermann's, and even after several years he was not totally accepted by everyone in the house.

Ruth had already summed up her boarders, though she

took them as they came. They were on the knife edge of not being rich enough, nor quite well-born enough, to feel totally secure. In New York, she had discovered, if you were a member of one of the old families then you could be forgiven a lack of money; if you were rich, then your antecedents could be overlooked. If you were *really* rich, then nothing could impede you, not even the way you had made your money. Mr Stewart himself, though in trade, would have been acceptable, but an employee, even if he *was* a buyer, was another matter. Most of her boarders, she thought, would want to keep their tight little world unsullied.

'They are English,' Mr Pierce continued eagerly. 'And therefore, I don't have to tell *you*, completely reliable. Anyway, tomorrow being Sunday, I have suggested they should call on you at three o'clock. I hope that will be convenient?'

'It is quite convenient to me,' Ruth replied. 'But you do realise, Mr Pierce, that it's not up to me who shall come as boarders here? I don't quite know who it *is* up to. Perhaps Professor Woodburn, or perhaps the boarders as a whole, including yourself. Anyway, I shall be pleased to meet your friends, and in the meantime I'll see what the professor has to say.'

'Either Mr Pierce is being quite naive,' Ruth said to Sean later that evening, 'or he knows exactly what he's doing – in which case he's not being fair.'

Sean made no reply. He was reading the newspaper, which at the end of the day came down from the parlour. Though he got on well enough with them when their paths crossed his, he was not vastly interested in the boarders. His kingdom, when he came home from work, was in the bedroom and sitting-room which he and Ruth inhabited, though the sitting-room was now shared with Maria. He didn't mind that too much. She was an amusing little thing, less serious than his Ruth; took it in good part however much he teased her.

'Did you hear me?' Ruth said.

'Yes.' He didn't lift his head from his reading. 'I don't

see what you're worried about. They want a room. There's a room vacant. I take it they're reasonable people and can pay. So what's the problem?'

'Sean, I've just explained!' Ruth cried. 'You can't have been listening! Mr Seaford is in trade. He works in a shop, even though it *is* Stewart's and he's a buyer.'

'I think Stewart's is the best emporium in New York,' Maria put in. 'I could spend all day there!'

'That's quite beside the point,' Ruth said. Really, her sister could be so exasperating. 'It's still trade. And this is a boarding-house for ladies and gentlemen, the professional classes. It always has been.'

'I thought there was no class distinction in America,' Sean remarked. 'I thought we were all equal.'

'You know perfectly well that's not true. I agree that it ought to be so, but it just isn't,' Ruth said.

'What about Mr Pierce then?' Sean queried. 'He's here.'

'Mr Pierce was Mrs Gutermann's business,' Ruth replied. 'You know, and so does he, that he's not quite like the rest.'

Sean grinned. 'I don't see any signs of horns and a tail!'

'Oh Sean, you are so maddening,' Ruth cried. 'You know perfectly well what I mean. Why are you trying to put me in the wrong?'

He put down the newspaper and raised his head. There was no smile on his face now and his eyes were hard.

'I know you are bending the knee,' he said. 'Kowtowing to what you think of as your betters. Setting yourself up as judge of who's worthy and who isn't.'

'I'm doing no such thing! I'm stating facts. Insofar as it has anything to do with me, I'm trying to think like a businesswoman.'

'I prefer you as a servant,' Sean said.

'You would!' She could have hit him. He was being as contrary as he knew how. 'You never want to rise in the world. Well, I do. I've told you before, I'm not going to be a servant all my life. I mean that. Anyway, I'm more than a little pleased that the decision about the Seafords isn't mine.'

'Then let's leave it,' Sean said. 'Put on your cloak and bonnet and we'll go to Niblo's. It's time you forgot about this place for an hour or two.'

Maria clapped her hands. 'Oh good! Can I come too? I'm sick of this silly quarrelling.'

'We are not quarrelling,' Ruth replied shortly. 'Anyway, I can't go to Niblo's. I have some jobs to do. And I'm really quite tired.'

'Oh, Ruth, no!' There was hideous disappointment in Maria's voice. 'Oh Ruth, we never go anywhere!' She turned to her brother-in-law. 'Say she must, Sean! Make her go. It will do her all the good in the world.'

He shrugged. 'You're her sister. Have you ever been able to make her do anything she didn't want to?'

'That's not true,' Ruth defended herself. 'I'm not obstinate and you know it. It's just that I really do have things to do. My job doesn't end at six o'clock in the evening.'

'Then leave your job,' Sean said. 'There's no need for it, not when I'm working. You're a married woman now. What's more, with a baby on the way. If I had my way you'd be taking it easier. . . .'

Ruth sighed. 'I honestly can't go with you this evening because I have the accounts to do. I can't leave them. But another evening I will, I promise you. Though it's not something we can do often. It *is* expensive,' she added.

'I'm earning,' Sean said. 'If I can't take my wife out with the money I earn, have a good time, what's the point of it?' He picked up the newspaper again, hid himself behind it and went on with his reading.

That was Sean, Ruth thought. Less than three months of marriage had brought out the differences, large and small, between them. She realised now – she was sure Sean did too – that at the time of their marriage they had hardly known each other. In the six months of their acquaintance they had, except for the picnic on the banks of the Hudson River, rarely spent more than a few minutes together, and she usually with her thoughts elsewhere. Thus their discoveries about each other had been made entirely within their marriage.

It was not all disappointment, far from it. Sean was the kind and caring man she had always taken him for. She knew that he loved her beyond her deserving and for that she would, perversely, always feel herself at a disadvantage, forever in his debt – though he would not see it like that. In sexual matters both of them were passionate and generous, their desires well-matched; and if the deepest feelings of Ruth's heart were not for her husband, it was not for want of trying. Nor would he ever know.

While Sean hid behind his paper and Maria sat sulking at the thought of the evening's entertainment of which she had been so cruelly robbed, Ruth got out the accounts ledger and set it on the table, pulling the lamp nearer so that she could see the columns of neat figures. She would always be grateful that Mrs Carson had taught her about household accounts. She now knew to the dollar just where she was, where they must pull in their horns, where she could allow a little extravagance, perhaps a special supper on a Saturday evening. It was all there in the neatly-written pages.

Sean lowered his paper again and looked at her, his usually good-tempered face strong with disapproval.

'Accounts! I do believe if the place was on fire that ledger would be the first thing ye'd save!'

She saw this boarding-house as her life, he thought. She was bound up in it. But it wouldn't last, couldn't when they had children. It would be a different life for them then and she would realise that. But at the moment the glamour of New York, and of this place with its well-bred boarders, had hold of her. Well, he'd go along with that for the time being. He knew how to be patient and it would be different in the end. Not even in his heart did he acknowledge any other hold which New York might have on her.

'You're wrong then,' Ruth replied.

'So what would you save?'

'My grandmother's sampler. Without hesitation.'

'Then I'm glad to hear it,' Sean said. 'Though I daresay you'd tuck the ledger under your other arm!'

It was in the area of money that one of their big differences lay. Not in the money itself, but in what it told of their attitudes to the present and to the future. To Sean, every day was a day to be lived there and then, a time to take whatever pleasures were available, and preferably in the company of like-minded friends, loved ones, acquaintances. And if such pleasures needed money, and there was money in his pocket, what else was it for?

Ruth lived for the future. Not just her own future, but that of anyone she loved, or who was dependent on her. And for her, now, the future was Gutermann's. However difficult the present was, the future was bright and satisfying; a time in which all of her dreams would come true – but only if she worked hard to make that happen.

But there were times, as now, when she felt a keen unhappiness at the distance her personality placed between herself and others. She *wanted* to be carefree and inconsequential, like her pretty sister; charming and outgoing like Sean, but nature had made her otherwise.

'Why don't *you* go to Niblo's for an hour?' she said. 'You and Maria? You know you'd enjoy it.'

Maria's face lit up and she clapped her hands again in excitement. How little it took to bring out the sunshine again for Maria, Ruth thought. She was like a child.

'Oh Sean, can we?' Maria pleaded.

She was sick of sitting here, doing nothing, listening to Ruth and Sean sniping at each other. She didn't want to sew or knit or crochet, or do any of the useful things she was supposed to do. And there wasn't a single exciting novel in the house, even if she had been inclined to read. A change was what she needed. Some gaiety, a few bright lights. Niblo's was the answer.

'Oh please say yes!' she entreated.

Sean put down the newspaper and looked at his sister-in-law. He was already smiling again.

'All right then, kitten. Just for an hour.' He turned to Ruth. 'Are ye sure ye won't come?'

'Not this time, really Sean. But I will next time, I promise.'

'Then we'll be back not a minute after ten,' he said.

'I must tidy my hair,' Maria fluttered. She was already halfway out of the room.

'And wrap up warmly,' Ruth called after her. 'It's a cold winter's night.'

At a quarter to ten Ruth put away her accounts. At least she would not be about them when Sean returned. At eleven o'clock there was no sign of her husband and her sister. But there is no need to worry, she thought. Niblo's is only around the corner. Doubtless they had fallen in with a jolly crowd and found it difficult to get away.

At half-past eleven she made herself a cup of cocoa, and at ten minutes to midnight she went to bed. She did not know what time it was when Sean climbed into her bed. She seemed to have lain awake forever, and then fallen into a sleep from which he now aroused her. She was aware first of the heavy fumes of beer and brandy, and then of his hands on her body, pulling her towards him. With a sharp movement she wrenched herself out of his grasp and turned to the wall.

'Oh, Ruth, mavourneen! Come on then!' He pleaded with her in thick tones, his hands all over her.

'Get away!' she said sharply. 'Keep off me! You're drunk again.' She edged herself to the farthest side of the bed.

'I am not drunk. I am no such thing. I had a little drink and now I want my little wife.' He enunciated each word slowly and carefully, in seeming good humour. And then his humour changed. 'And by God I'm going to have her!' he shouted.

With strong, grasping hands he turned her towards him, then pinned her on her back. 'By Jesus, I'll show ye what a wife's for!' he cried.

Long after it was over, when he, sated, snored in oblivion, and Ruth lay awake in the darkness, her bruised body ached and burned from his violence. She felt defiled, and in the end she got up and, while her husband slept soundly, washed herself from top to toe.

* * *

Sean, next morning, was all contrition, though Ruth doubted if he remembered the extent of his roughness and violence towards her.

'I had one too many,' he apologised. 'We fell in with a jolly crowd. It won't happen again.'

'Then let us forget it,' Ruth said. She was not sure that she could. Though the soreness of her body would heal, her memory might not be equally obliging. But the last thing she wanted was to recall the incident, or hear anything about it put into words.

Maria appeared, sleepy-eyed, at breakfast – but cheerful enough and making no reference whatever to the previous evening.

'Mr and Mrs Seaford are coming today,' Ruth said. 'I must see Professor Woodburn about it this morning.'

She presented herself to the professor soon after breakfast and put Mr Pierce's suggestion to him.

'I'm not at all sure why he asked me,' she confessed. 'It's not up to me to decide.'

'Nevertheless, what do you think?' the professor asked.

'Well, from Mr Pierce's description the Seafords sound pleasant enough. Also, everyone likes Mr Pierce – well, almost everyone,' she amended. 'And Stewart's is a very respectable store.'

The professor smiled. 'You put your case well.'

Perhaps because she had a slight feeling of guilt, Ruth thought, remembering Sean's reaction. At least if the Seafords were turned down it would not be her fault.

'Well,' the professor said, 'perhaps I should consult my fellow boarders – but not too closely. It is not entirely their concern, either. It is the concern of the owner of the business, and for the moment there *is* no owner. But have you given some thought as to whether the lady and gentleman concerned would themselves be happy here? It is one thing for *me* to say they may join us – and if they did I would welcome them – but I cannot answer for everyone else. However, I will take a consensus of opinions.'

'They are coming here at three o'clock,' Ruth reminded

him. 'May I know your views before then, and will you yourself be good enough to meet them?'

Towards the end of the morning the professor popped his head around the door of Ruth's sitting-room. 'I think if you take to the Seafords, you might gently encourage them,' he said. 'There were one or two objections – I shall not tell you from what quarter – but if the Seafords are reasonable people then I daresay it will be all right. In fact, it was the regard in which Mr Pierce is held which was in their favour.'

Ruth liked the look of Mr Seaford: of his wife she was less sure. He had a straight, military-type appearance, and in character seemed down-to-earth. Mrs Seaford had a discontented look on her plump face; a turned-down mouth, dullish slate-grey eyes. Her whole body seemed to sag, as if nothing pleased her, everything was too much trouble. She was also inclined to put on airs.

'Mr Seaford has a most responsible job in Stewart's,' she said. 'Mr Stewart thinks the world of him.'

'Mr Pierce tells us how happy he has been here for some years,' Mr Seaford broke in. 'It sounds just the place we are looking for and we shall think ourselves most fortunate if you can accommodate us.'

'Of course in England we had our own house. A delightful little place in Chester,' Mrs Seaford announced. 'I can't think why we ever left.'

'Mrs O'Farrell doesn't want to hear about our house in Chester, my dear,' her husband said firmly.

It was then that Ruth guessed why Mrs Seaford looked so unhappy. She was homesick. And because Ruth knew only too well how it felt (and still sometimes experienced it) she was sorry for her.

'Do *you* miss your home in England?' Mrs Seaford asked Ruth.

'I shall always miss it,' Ruth confessed. 'Though now I think of it a little less often. Perhaps because I have a job to do, and a husband. But I shall never forget my home.'

'Nor I,' Mrs Seaford said wistfully. 'And Mr Seaford will

not allow me to speak of it too often. He believes that to do so unsettles me.'

Ruth took them to meet Professor Woodburn. She never did get to know what transpired between them, but a little later May, when she came from serving tea in the boarders' parlour, spoke to her.

'When I went in the professor was introducing Mr and Mrs Seaford to the other guests. They seem ever such a nice couple; her so well-dressed and him so handsome!'

'Was Captain Forsyth there?' Ruth asked.

'No. He'd gone out earlier.'

So on the first of February Mr and Mrs Seaford moved into Gutermann's and as far as Ruth could see, things went smoothly. She purposely did not put them at a table too near to Mr Pierce in case it should look like segregation; nor did she ask for trouble by placing them in close proximity to Captain Forsyth.

One morning in the following week she was returning along Spring Street, having completed her shopping. It was a bitter day, the wind far colder than anything she had known in Yorkshire, the snow falling in thick, wet flakes, driving into her face so that she could hardly see where she was going.

Had her head not been lowered against the driving snow she would have noticed him sooner than she did, she could have reached him. As it was, she raised her head just in time to see Joss Barnet getting back into his carriage outside the door of Gutermann's.

Without a second's thought she shouted, cried out his name at the top of her voice.

'Mr Barnet! Mr Barnet!'

She ran forward, taking no heed of anyone in her path, almost knocking down a woman with a small child who got in her way.

'Mr Barnet! Joss! Please stop!'

But the whistling wind, and the rattle of the horse and carriage as it moved quickly away in the other direction, drowned her voice. When it was no longer any use, when the carriage had turned the corner out of sight, she stood still staring after it.

She had no idea how long she had been there when a man spoke to her.

'Are you all right, miss?'

'What? Oh yes! Yes thank you.'

'Then if I were you, miss, I'd get moving. That is if you don't want to turn into a snowman. Are you sure I can't help? Get you a hackney carriage?'

'Quite sure, thank you. I have only a few yards to go. But thank you for your concern.'

He was reluctant to leave her. She was as white as the snow which was settling on her cloak and bonnet and her eyes were anguished.

A few yards. By a few yards only she had missed him. It was not to be borne. She turned back to Gutermann's. On the doorstep her hands were too icy, she was too confused, to find her key. When she rang the bell Mrs Cruse came.

'God help us!' she cried. 'Where have you been? Get that wet cloak off at once, or you'll catch your death. And your hair thick with snow. You're just covered! Come into the kitchen straight away. There's some beef tea left will warm you up. You look terrible!'

'Has anyone called?' Ruth asked. Could she have been mistaken? It was a dark day and the snow was blinding. But she knew she was not.

'Yes. That Mr Barnet came, your sister said. He's not long left. And Professor Woodburn wanted to see you.'

'I'll go to him at once.'

Mr Cruse stood over her, arms akimbo. 'That you will not, if I may say so. You'll get warm and dry and something hot inside you before you step out of this kitchen!'

Ruth felt suddenly sick and dizzy. She sat down quickly on the nearest chair.

'There! What did I say? It's the cold, that's what it is. You shouldn't have gone out today, not in your condition. Here, drink this.' Mrs Cruse thrust the cup of beef tea into

Ruth's hands. Ruth curled her icy fingers around the mug and sipped the hot liquid.

'I know just how you feel,' Mrs Cruse sympathised. 'None better!'

Why did she have to miss him? After all this time – it was more than three months since she had set eyes on Joss Barnet, not since the morning of her wedding day – it could have done no harm for her to have spoken to him, as a friend or an acquaintance might. Nothing more. But the state she was in at the moment gave the lie to that. There had been a moment out there when, if she could have caught up with it, she would have thrown herself under the horse's hooves to attract Joss Barnet's attention.

And then she felt the child move. It was the faintest, most tentative flutter, yet she had not the slightest doubt about it. Without thinking, she cried out.

'She moved! Mrs Cruse, I felt my baby move!'

Mrs Cruse's smile was kind, but pitying; a professional to an amateur.

'Begging your pardon, ma'am, but you couldn't have. Not with you only three months gone. Not one of mine moved till five months – though mind you after that they kicked me around like I was a football. No, it's a bit of wind. That's what it is. The beef tea'll shift it presently.'

She's wrong, Ruth thought. I'm right and she's wrong. My baby did move. But she couldn't contradict Mrs Cruse. Though she longed to proclaim the event to the whole world, there was no-one she could tell. Not even Sean.

'I'd better go and see what Professor Woodburn wants,' she said. 'Thank you for the beef tea. I'm much warmer now.'

She took her damp cloak and bonnet into the sitting-room and found Maria there, darning stockings, her face pulled in a grimace of distaste for the job. When she set eyes on Ruth her expression changed, animation lighting up her eyes.

'Oh Ruth, that gorgeous man came! Mr Joss Barnet. I myself showed him in to the professor and he gave me the warmest smile. I do believe he was quite taken with me!'

Maria could usually believe that men were taken with her, Ruth thought. Usually she was right. Her pretty looks and happy manner seemed to have a universal appeal for the opposite sex.

Ruth stood by the stove, holding out her hands to its warmth, her back to Maria. 'Did he . . . did Mr Barnet ask to see me?' she enquired casually.

'Why no!' Maria sounded surprised. 'He simply asked for Professor Woodburn. But he remembered me, Ruth! "Miss Maria Appleby" he said – and bowed. Oh Ruth, he is so handsome. Do you not think so?'

'I daresay.' With the greatest struggle Ruth managed an offhand tone, showing nothing of the emotion which churned inside her. My baby . . . *our* baby . . . moved today, she wanted to cry out to him. Our baby is alive and moving inside me! He was the only person in the world to whom she could say it. But he had not even asked after her, had not said so much as 'How is your sister?' Maria must be mistaken.

'I'll go and see the professor now,' she said.

'Please sit down,' the professor smiled. 'You are looking a little pale this morning.'

'Thank you. I am really quite well,' Ruth assured him.

'Good! Well, Mr Josiah Barnet called. Indeed you have only just missed him. As I expect you can guess, his business was the matter of Mrs Gutermann's heir.'

Stupidly, she had not guessed. She had been so thrown off her balance by the brief glimpse of Joss and by the excitement about the baby that there had been room in her head for nothing more. Now, weakened as she was by too much emotion which she must not show, the professor's words hit her like a violent blow. In an instant, she could see nothing good ahead. This could be the end of all she had hoped for.

'She has been found?'

'Yes. She had moved to Cologne, which is why it has taken so long to trace her.'

Ruth was glad to be sitting down. Otherwise she thought

she must have collapsed, as now she felt her world doing around her. She had no doubt at all that the woman in Cologne would want to come to New York and take over Gutermann's. Nothing was more likely. And what will become of me, Ruth asked herself? There will be no place for me here. It was the pattern all over again; never a place which remained hers.

The professor's voice came to her from a long way off. 'You really do not look at all well, my dear Ruth. You must allow me to pour you a glass of Madeira.'

'I'm all right. Please tell me what is to happen.' There was a sharpness in her voice which the professor did not deserve, but she couldn't help it.

'If you are sure. . . . Well, it is the lady's wish that her aunt's effects should be sold, and the money from the sale transmitted to her in Germany. She wishes it to happen as quickly as possible since she has a particular use for the money. There is no question of her coming to New York, even for a visit. Did I tell you that she was a married lady with small children?'

Relief surged through Ruth. She felt the warmth come back into her cleeks. That was the first hurdle over. But if the woman wanted the money quickly. . . .

'How much will everything fetch?' she asked. 'I'm not prying. I have a reason for asking.'

Professor Woodburn shrugged. 'Who knows? Mr Barnet says, quite rightly, that we must have a proper valuation. His opinion is that the furniture will fetch about six hundred dollars. It would be considerably more, of course, if the beneficiary did not want the money so quickly. He also thinks that the goodwill must amount to little since, one could say, it was largely invested in Mrs Gutermann herself. I am not sure I agree with him about that, but he is a businessman and I am not.'

'It's impossible,' Ruth whispered. 'Six hundred dollars. It's quite impossible.'

With Sean working she had saved every penny of her wages since her marriage, and most of her salary before then. She had spent little on herself, had not even been to Matthew Brady to have her photograph taken. In all, she had fifty-two dollars, seventy-five cents. It had seemed a tidy sum – way beyond anything she had ever had in her life – until a moment ago. Now it seemed paltry. Six hundred dollars! She must have been mad to think she could ever do it.

'But my dear Ruth, I have not finished,' Professor Woodburn said. 'You must forgive me if I have taken a long time to come to the point – which is this. Mr Barnet has told me that he will buy everything – the rent and wages are already covered by the profits – and will instal you as manageress of Gutermann's.'

For a few seconds this news lifted her to the heights; then her elation rapidly turned to bitter disappointment.

'I'm sorry,' she said slowly. 'That can't be. I have never told you this before, but my husband and Mr Barnet do not get on. That is why Sean, of his own free will, left Mr Barnet's employment. They had a disagreement – it doesn't matter what about – and now Sean will not let me be beholden to Mr Barnet for so much as a penny.'

'But surely when you tell him. . . .'

'It's no use. His mind is made up.' She knew she would not even tell him of the offer. It would upset him dreadfully and he would almost certainly see it as something continuing between herself and Joss. No, she had made her promise to Sean and she would keep it.

'Then, my dear, what are you going to do? Indeed, one wonders what we shall all do if Gutermann's goes.'

Then for the second time that day Ruth felt the baby move, a small but distinct stirring. She thought afterwards that it was the baby's manifestation of its own life which gave her the courage to say what she did. She spoke for the child as well as for herself.

'Professor Woodburn. . . .' She didn't know how to go on.

'Yes?'

'Professor, I have saved a little. Fifty-two dollars and

seventy-five cents, but in a short time. If I could somehow borrow the money . . . pay it back a little at a time. You see it's my great ambition, my dearest wish, to own Gutermann's. I want to run it as my own business, not just to manage it. I'm quite sure I could make a success of it!'

'I'm sure you could. But. . . .'

'I would pay back every penny,' she said eagerly. 'And with interest; though of course it would take some time.'

'It is a question of whom . . .' he began.

She flushed scarlet. He thought she was asking *him* for a loan.

'What I have in mind is quite different,' she explained. 'I would not dream of asking *you*. I wondered if perhaps the boarders, between them, could lend me the money as an investment. I swear they would not lose by it in the end – and they could continue to live here.'

She was amazed at her own temerity. She was still a month from her nineteenth birthday. She knew next to nothing of business and finance. But at that moment, as she pleaded with the professor, she had all the confidence in the world. It was a confidence born of need and desperation. And she could see that her own conviction impressed Professor Woodburn.

'Well!' He was smiling at her. She looked so young, yet, in spite of that, so full of wisdom and determination as she sat there, her hands clenched by her sides. Always, she gave him the feeling that he wanted to do everything he could for her. He thought, as he often did, that she was exactly the kind of girl he would have wanted for a daughter if such happiness had been allowed him.

'Well, it is not the first time that you have put forward an unexpected idea. But I don't know. You have given me a great deal to think about and I do not have a ready answer.'

How would her husband take all this, he asked himself. That had to be settled. He had the feeling that she had made this proposition entirely of her own accord. He wondered, too, what O'Farrell's disagreement had been with Barnet.

'I will consider what you have said very carefully,' he

promised. 'In the meantime Mr Barnet has arranged for a valuer to call tomorrow afternoon and that will give us a definite figure to work on.'

'Is . . . Is Mr Barnet to bring the valuer?' Ruth asked. She could not bear it if he did – nor yet if he did not.

'No. I have no lectures tomorrow afternoon, so I have arranged to be here to receive him.'

After supper that evening, seizing a moment when Maria had gone to spend a little time with Mrs Seaford, for the two were unaccountably becoming friends, Ruth told Sean about her meeting with Professor Woodburn, though omitting the fact that Joss Barnet had offered his help. His first reaction, predictably, was against Joss Barnet's visit.

'I don't want him coming to the house,' he stormed. 'Do you hear me? I won't have him coming here!'

'You can't stop him,' Ruth replied equably. She must at all costs keep calm, hold her temper. 'It is not your house or mine to say who may come and who may go. In any case he came to see Professor Woodburn. I didn't set eyes on him.'

'Only because you weren't in,' Sean said quickly.

Ruth sighed. 'You still don't trust me, do you?' But remembering her feelings at the sight of Joss driving away, perhaps he was right not to.

'Anyway,' she went on, 'we're not discussing Mr Barnet. We're talking about Gutermann's.'

'It won't do,' Sean said firmly. 'You're biting off more than you can chew.'

'I'm not!' Ruth protested. 'I've thought about it carefully. I know it will work out.'

'Why can't we just find rooms where you and me can live with the baby?' Sean pleaded. 'I've got my job. I can support ye both. I don't even mind if we take Maria. Or better still, why don't we pack up and go to Wisconsin?' That was what he wanted. He hadn't liked New York from the first minute. He was a countryman, from the peaceful West of Ireland. The noise and clamour of New York, the rubbish piled in the streets, the ever-increasing traffic of Broadway which he had to traverse twice a day on his way to and from work, all seared into his brain. When he laid his head on his pillow at night the noises were still there in his head.

'We could have a good life in Wisconsin,' he said. 'Space and quiet. Room to bring up a family. You're from the country yourself, Ruth. How can you stand New York?'

She didn't know the answer to that. She just knew that when she trod its streets, breathed its (no doubt polluted) air, she came alive.

'Don't you understand, Sean? I can achieve something here – here in Gutermann's. It's something I want to do for myself; but not just for myself, for all of us.'

'You're a married woman. And soon we'll have a family. Not just one child. That's achievement enough for any woman.'

Why couldn't he understand that it wasn't enough for her? She wanted that, but she wanted more. She had to count for something in her own right.

'Well,' Sean said, 'we don't know that the professor will come up with anything. If he doesn't what then?'

They faced each other across the table, each searching into the other's face, each demanding of the other. If they couldn't stay here, Ruth thought, they would be condemned to some little hovel of a room on the Lower East Side. It would be all they could ever afford on what Tweed paid, and lucky to have a job at that. Or else. . . . But if she couldn't have what she had set her heart on, what did anything else matter?

'I'll make you a promise,' she said slowly. 'If Professor Woodburn doesn't come up with a scheme whereby we can stay right here, then we'll try our luck in Wisconsin. But if he does, promise you won't stop me from having to go. At least we can give it a try.'

There was no choice, Sean thought. There were those who would say that he should make her do what he wanted; that a wife was subject to her husband and must follow his lead. They didn't know his Ruth. And to be fair, it was her independent spirit which had been one of her attractions for him right from the first. He had never wanted a submissive wife. Well, he consoled himself, there was a good chance that Professor Woodburn would not raise the loan. Six hundred dollars was a lot of money. And in that case he knew Ruth would keep her side of the bargain. He had no doubt of that. Afterwards, he would do everything to make it up to her, give her a good life.

Two evenings later Professor Woodburn knocked on their sitting-room door.

'It's rather late, I know,' he said. 'But may I have a word? I shan't keep you long.'

'Will you have some coffee?' Ruth asked. She felt intensely nervous. There was no way of telling, from his manner, which way things were to go. 'Please sit down. You will find this chair the most comfortable.'

Sean was white-faced, rigid with tension, his jaw tightly clenched. For one of us things are about to go wrong, Ruth thought; for the other one, right. Yet they were a married couple. It shouldn't be like this.

'I have a plan to put before you,' Professor Woodburn said when she had seated himself. 'Here it is, and I'll waste no time. I have been able to raise a loan of five hundred and fifty dollars, which with the sum you have saved, Mrs O'Farrell. . . .'

As Ruth's spirits soared to the heights she saw the storm clouds gather in Sean's face, watched him open his mouth to speak.

'I am not at liberty to tell you how I have raised the loan,' the professor went on quickly. 'Except that it is not through Mr Barnet. He is not involved at any point.'

Sean gave Ruth an enquiring look.

'I have told Professor Woodburn that we have a private reason for not wanting to accept help from Mr Barnet,' Ruth said.

'You would pay back the loan at a reasonable rate of interest, by regular deductions which would initially be made from Mrs O'Farrell's wages,' the professor continued. 'It is interesting that Mr Barnet's estimate of six hundred dollars was a realistic one. It is exactly the sum the valuer quoted for a quick sale.'

'Mr Barnet is always realistic,' Sean said dryly.

But at this moment Sean's jibes had no effect at all on Ruth. She was elated. She felt the whole world transformed. She could see no flaw in the arrangement and no obstacle to its acceptance. Sean would not like it, but they had made their recent promises to each other in good faith, and had it gone the other way they both knew that she would have kept her word.

Sean struggled to hide his disappointment beneath his natural good manners towards the professor.

'Ye'll appreciate, professor, that it's a matter me and my wife will have to think about. . . .'

'But we've already . . .' Ruth chipped in.

'. . . Not that we haven't done so, but it'll need further discussion. Ye'll not expect an answer right away, I'm sure.'

'Of course not,' Professor Woodburn said courteously. 'It's an important step which you must both consider carefully. But please let me know as soon as you can.'

'In the meantime I can think of no adequate way to thank you and those good people who have done this,' Ruth said. 'Words are not enough.'

'Only one other person is concerned,' the professor replied. 'I am not at liberty to tell you who that is. But we all have every faith in you, should you choose to accept the offer.'

It was these words, the knowledge of the trust placed in her, which lifted Ruth's spirits even higher. She was sure, now, that she would never feel low again. The future stretched before her, full of promise. All she had to do was to persuade Sean into a like mind.

Since Maria came back into the room as the professor was leaving, neither Ruth nor Sean continued with the subject, but the moment she had left them again to go to bed, Sean took it up.

'I tell you I don't like it, Ruth! Can't you see that you'll be tying yourself hand and foot to Gutermann's? You'll be at everyone's beck and call. What about all that talk you once gave me about wanting to be free?'

'But I shall be free!' Ruth cried. 'Don't you see that? After a while Gutermann's will be mine – ours – to do with as we wish. If we don't want to keep it then, we can sell it at a profit.'

'Or a loss!'

Ruth struggled to keep her temper. Losing it now would achieve nothing.

'Why are you such a pessimist, Sean? Have you no faith in me?'

Suddenly he stood up, took his wife's hands in his and pulled her to her feet, holding her close against him.

'I do have faith in you, Ruth. I know what you can do. I know you can do anything. I just – don't want to lose you on the way.'

Then he held her at arm's length, looking into her eyes as if he was trying to read the future there.

'You won't,' Ruth replied. 'I promise you won't. Am I not married to you? We're bound together.'

'Then come to bed,' Sean said.

In the end it was all arranged, exactly as Professor Woodburn had suggested.

The months passed and summer came. The June night was warm, the temperature having dropped only a little from the hot day which had preceded it. Ruth no longer slept well now. Whichever way she lay in bed, the baby was too heavy for her and she could not get comfortable. And as Mrs Cruse had warned, the child kicked all the time, as if impatient to get out. So it was with relief that Ruth felt the first sharp pain and knew that her labour was starting.

'Here we go then, little one,' she said. 'Let's be good to each other.'

Presently, when the pains came with shorter intervals between them, she wakened Sean.

'It's time to fetch the midwife.'

He was out of bed in a flash, lighting the lamp, pulling on his trousers, pouring a little cold water from the ewer into the basin to sluice his face and waken himself thoroughly. He looked considerably strained and worried and Ruth recalled – with a flash of deep pity for his Irish wife – that this was not the first time he had been in this situation.

'Don't worry, Sean,' she said. 'Everything's going to be all right. I'm as strong as a horse. And mind you don't waken anyone as you leave the house.'

'I must go and wake Maria,' he protested. 'I can't leave you alone.'

'I'd rather be alone for a little while,' Ruth said. 'Maria will fuss so. I shall be all right until you get back.'

She had an overwhelming desire to be alone with her baby, at least for the present; only the two of them sharing the pain in the night. The strength of this desire overcame her fear, though soon the pains came with increasing force, so that at times she had to bite on the pillow to stop herself crying out. And as the time drew nearer she could not prevent herself, though she tried, thinking about the true father of her child. With all her heart, but against her will, she longed for him.

When Sean appeared in the room with the midwife Ruth was far gone in pain, and confused. She could not understand why Joss had sent his coachman instead of coming himself.

Her daughter was born as the first light of the summer's day came into the room, the sunlight throwing fingers of colour on to the wall.

'We shall call her Aurora,' Ruth said a little later, holding the small, dark-haired baby in her arms.

It was the seventh of June, 1851.

# *Part Three*

# 21

Maria looked at herself in the mirror for the tenth time that morning. There was no doubt at all that her face was really swollen on the left side. She looked awful, and could only hope that on her way to work she wouldn't meet a soul she knew. Not that she was likely to. After three years in New York, apart from the people in the house, she knew practically no one. Except of course, the staff in Stewart's emporium. But she would not see them on Broadway. It was already ten minutes after nine and they would be standing behind their counters, waiting for customers, which was where she ought to be. The only good thing about her swollen face was that it gave credence to the fact that she had been awake half the night with toothache, and had fallen asleep when it was time to get up.

'It's no use,' Ruth said. 'You will have to pluck up courage and go to the dentist. This is the third time you've had toothache in the last month. You have only to walk a few minutes down Broadway and I would go along with you. He'll have it out in a trice.'

Maria shuddered. 'Oh Ruth, I couldn't possibly. I just know I'd faint dead away!'

'Your face looks all funny, Aunt Maria,' Aurora said. She surveyed Maria with interest, her fine dark eyes, now opened wide in a fixed stare, seeming almost too large for her heart-shaped face. She was a beautiful child, there was no denying it, though whom she took after Maria found it impossible to say. She was neither like Ruth nor Sean. Also, beautiful or not, she was far too precocious for her three years.

'It's rude to make personal remarks,' Maria admonished her niece. The trouble was that the child had too much attention. Apart from the fact that Ruth and Sean clearly doted on her, and the women in the kitchen spoiled her, always giving titbits, she was also the pet of most of the boarders. What Aurora needed was brothers and sisters to take some of the limelight off her. One would have thought that by now she would have had them.

'Tell Aunt Maria you're sorry,' Ruth said.

'Aurora only said her face looked funny. It's *nice* funny.' She had this way of referring to herself by name, as if she was some sort of royal personage. Which she thinks she is, Maria reckoned. Also, she was far too articulate for her age; too clever and bright by half. Now she was poking her tongue into her cheek, trying to make it swell out, studying the effect in the mirror. But I do love her, Maria thought. I'm just crabby this morning because I've slept badly and my face hurts.

'You should be off,' Ruth told her sister. 'Won't you get into trouble for being late?'

'Not with Mr Horace Werner!' Maria said. 'The others might complain, but he won't, and he's the one who counts.' She started to smile at the thought, then winced at the pain it gave her to stretch her mouth. But the smile reached her eyes and Ruth answered it with her own.

'Poor Mr Werner! Sometimes I feel quite sorry for him, Maria.' She had met him once or twice, in Stewart's where he was a floorwalker. He was tall and thin, lugubrious-looking in his dark tails suit and high stiff collar. He had a sandy moustache which was too big for his narrow, pale face. But as befitted his job, he was the epitome of good manners, even obsequiousness towards the more important customers. It was expected of him.

'You needn't be,' Maria said. 'He's not sorry for himself. He thinks he's the cat's whiskers.'

'And I daresay you play up to him!' Ruth remarked.

Maria drew on her gloves, patted Aurora on the head – her mouth was far too painful to offer kisses – and departed.

Martin Wellbake was in the hall. He was the eight-year-old son of the two boarders who had taken Mr Gossop's old room. It had been overlarge for Mr Gossop but was cramped for the three Wellbakes, though they seemed not to mind. It was Maria's opinion that it was all they could afford. Mr Wellbake, a refined and educated man, had a post in the library, but probably he didn't earn much.

Martin Wellbake was a child who lurked.

'Are you waiting for someone, Martin?' Maria asked.

'Yes. Miss Potter and Mr Priestley.'

Of course. He was one of Miss Potter's pupils.

She had changed her rules and now took no child under seven years old, though it did not seem to make life any easier for her.

'I'm convinced that every seven-year old boy is under the direct influence of the devil!' she frequently said. 'And the girls are no better. Just more crafty!'

'Is it today Mr Priestley gives lessons?' Maria asked Martin. One morning a week Francis Priestley taught natural history in Miss Potter's school. Due entirely, Maria reckoned, to the kindness of his heart. Aurora preferred him above all the other boarders. Maria thought she showed good judgement.

It was clear that Miss Potter felt the same way, also that she took no notice of the fact that he was engaged to be married, except to be on hand to sympathise with him over his fiancée's protracted illness. Maria could see that. If there had been any chance at all, she herself would have been well to the front of the fray.

Miss Potter descended the stairs as Maria was speaking to Martin Wellbake. She was wearing another new outfit; a blue cotton dress trimmed with white, and a cream, face-framing bonnet. It was all so much more elegant than the plain black dress with its white collar that Maria was required to wear at Stewart's, and Maria could not deny that Miss Potter made a pretty picture as she paused on the stairs. She was pleased that Mr Priestley was not there to receive the full benefit.

'Priestley went back to get the ox's eye,' Martin said. 'He forgot it.'

'Ox's eye?' Maria queried.

'He's going to show the children how the eye works,' Miss Potter explained. She blanched at the prospect.

'He's going to cut it open,' Martin said with relish. 'I daresay it will bleed!'

'And I daresay you'll be disappointed if it doesn't!' Maria retorted.

She must go. She had no wish for Francis Priestley to see her in her plain black outfit, with a swollen face, especially when contrasted with Miss Potter's fresh appearance. But she was too late. He was already coming down the stairs. She quickly raised her hand and held it across the offending cheek, while trying to turn her face away from him, but it was no use.

'Why, Miss Maria, I do believe you have the toothache! I am so sorry. Please let me recommend my dentist to you. He is no more than ten minutes walk away from here. And he is very gentle.'

The sympathy in his voice soothed Maria's aching face as oil of cloves, or neat brandy held in the mouth, had failed to do. She wondered for a fleeting moment whether she should prevail upon him actually to escort her to his dentist, now? But though she had no objection to him seeing her terror – it would encourage his protective instinct – it would be another matter for him to see her gap-toothed, bleeding and spitting. Besides, she might well faint. It would not be proper unless Ruth were to be with her – in which case Francis Priestley would be superfluous. The thoughts chased each other through her head with the speed of light.

'Thank you,' she said through stiff lips. 'You are most kind. But at the moment I am overdue at Stewart's. In any case I'm sure it will all clear up quite quickly.'

'Very well then,' he replied. 'I hope it does. And since you are going in the direction of Broadway we may as well all walk along together.'

The pavements along Spring Street were too narrow for

more than two abreast. Adroitly, Maria manoeuvred herself into place beside Francis Priestley, leaving Miss Potter to be accompanied by Martin.

'I trust your fiancée's health is improving?' she ventured. Not for the first time, she wondered how he felt about being tied to a woman who had now been ill for more than three years. But if he truly loved her he would not think of it as a tie. Once, when helping Ruth with the housework, Maria had seen his fiancée's photograph in his room. She was quite beautiful, with a face of great sweetness; a calm, accepting face, with none of the fire which Maria sometimes thought she saw in his.

'Thank you for asking,' he said quietly. 'Her condition varies. Sometimes she is fit to go about a little, at other times she must spend quite long periods confined to her bed. We had hoped, by waiting until it was in its second season, that she might have been able to accompany my mother to New York to visit the World's Fair. But it seems that it will not be possible. My mother is to come alone.'

'Not with your father?'

'She is a widow,' he replied.

At Broadway Maria left the others – Miss Potter's school was in Great Jones Street. As they made their farewells and Miss Potter stepped back to walk with Francis Priestley, Maria turned to her.

'I'm sure you are in for a most interesting lesson,' she said sweetly. 'I myself have never assisted in the dissecting of an eye. I do so hope you will enjoy it!'

As she walked away down Broadway Maria mused upon whether Francis Priestley might actually prefer the kind of woman who turned pale at such an operation. He would perhaps consider it womanly. Supposing Miss Potter fainted, right there in his arms? And if she did, Maria thought crossly, she would not be bleeding at the mouth and minus a tooth! Had the action not been painful she would have gnashed her teeth.

She walked towards Stewart's reluctantly. The heat was already rising in the June day and she would be sticky before she reached the store. She didn't like her job there and was glad, really, that it was only temporary, just for a week or two because of sickness in the department. She disliked selling gloves to women who were so much more finely dressed than she – and only occasionally to a man who was buying a present for some lucky woman. But she had quickly grown tired of the domestic round at Gutermann's. It was hardly different from being a servant.

There had been a sharp discussion with Ruth when she had announced her intention of seeking a job.

'Mr Seaford thinks he might get me a temporary place on the glove counter at Stewart's,' she said. 'I shall be able to earn some money, be less dependent.'

'I'm sorry I can't pay you more. But at least you get your bed and board here,' Ruth pointed out.

'I know. I'm grateful. But I need new clothes. And I want to meet people. I'm never going to meet anyone here!' Ruth saved every penny she could, spending next to nothing on clothes, working all hours without complaint. 'I daresay it suits you, but it's not at all how I want to live,' Maria said. 'Anyway, you have Sean and Aurora.'

*She* had no-one.

'I'm twenty years old and still not married,' she cried desperately. 'The way I'm going I shall end up an old maid!'

Sometimes in moments of desperation, she thought there was nothing else for it but to marry Horace Werner. But he was thirty-five if a day, and a widower, which made him seen older still. And although he was kind, had a steady job, and clearly found her attractive, he was not at all what she had in mind as a husband. The truth was, as Ruth had pointed out to her more than once, that she set her sights too high. She didn't want to marry an ordinary man. The man she married must be handsome, well-to-do, but above all, different. Once she had thought that Sean was different – good-looking, debonair, though he *was* only a coachman. She had envied Ruth. But now even he had settled into a rut; not Ruth's, but one of his own making.

Broadway was more crowded than ever. If everyone stood still, she thought, you could walk on the tops of the heads of the people or of omnibuses, all the way from Spring Street to the Battery Park. And the dust was unbelievable, clouds of it getting into your eyes and mouth. She paused by a fruit shop, looking at the bananas and pomegranates and other exotic fruits she had never seen before coming to New York. She adored pomegranates, but the seeds got into her teeth, a painful thought at present. And then, inevitably, she came to Dr Levett's, the dentist's shop, with its gigantic models of artificial teeth in the window. It would be the bitter end if she was reduced to artificial teeth before she had found a husband; but even that thought did not give her the courage to enter. She hurried past.

It was an hour after her appointed time when Maria took her place behind the glove counter. The chief sales clerk, Miss Frisby, who had sold gloves in New York more years than she cared to remember, frowned heavily at the sight of Maria, but before she could remonstrate Mr Werner was seen making his way towards them. He seemed, as always, not to walk but to glide, as if on skates.

'I'm most terribly sorry, Mr Werner,' Maria said quickly. 'I'm afraid I have to tell the truth and say I overslept. I've been awake all night with the most terrible toothache!' She indicated her swollen face and lifted forlorn blue eyes to his.

'So I see,' he replied gently. Then, noting Miss Frisby's fierce expression, he became sterner. 'Well, see that it doesn't happen again. Perhaps in future you should arrange for a member of your household to awaken you should you oversleep.'

'Oh I will, Mr Werner! I will!' Maria assured him. His voice was stern but she saw the compassion in his eyes and knew that he was not the least bit cross with her; that in fact he would have liked to comfort her.

'I can recommend my own dentist if you feel you should have your tooth attended to, Miss Appleby,' he said. 'He is a most skilled practitioner.'

'Oh I couldn't!' Maria replied swiftly. 'I couldn't *dream* of taking more time off work. I'm sure it will be better soon.'

Miss Frisby sniffed as Mr Werner glided away from gloves, skirted trimmings, and was lost to sight in ribbons.

'All very well for *some* people,' she remarked frostily. 'I myself am a martyr to headaches, but do I ever take time off? Arrive late or leave early?'

'You do not,' Maria said agreeably. 'You are an example to us all!'

'Very well then, Miss Appleby.' Miss Frisby was mollified. 'But now that you are here you must try to make up for lost time. I want all the drawers thoroughly tidied, and the price tickets checked. After that you can bring some of the new lines down from the stockroom.'

'Yes Miss Frisby.' It was clear that she wasn't going to get a chance at selling this morning. As a matter of protocol, Miss Frisby was always first to serve, but if there were more customers than she could cope with, then Maria was given a chance. If there was anything at all she liked about this dreary job it was actually selling the gloves.

When she had first decided to find a job she had, naturally, wanted something in the theatre. 'After all,' she said to Ruth, 'it *is* my profession!' But in spite of the number of theatres in New York, she had been offered nothing, not even an assistant property mistress's job, or a prompter's. She would have swept the floors in the theatre rather than have sold the most elegant kid gloves in Stewart's.

But though no-one would give her a job there, she was able to visit the theatre quite often. Her wages were small but, in addition to material for clothes, they bought theatre tickets in the cheapest seats. Sometimes, though not often, she persuaded Ruth to accompany her; occasionally Sean. More than once, greatly daring, she had gone alone and nothing terrible had befallen her. But recently Mrs Seaford had taken to going with her and it was together they had seen Clive Masterson in *What Dreams Foretell*. That had been a wonderful experience and she hoped to see him again next week in *Man of My Heart*. The repertory company in which he was the juvenile lead was in New York for a season.

'I'm going for my lunch now,' Miss Frisby said presently. Stewart's, ahead of its time, had a canteen for its shop assistants. 'Stop what you're doing and get ready to attend to customers. I must say, you don't look very presentable with that face, but I do believe the swelling is going down a little. If you make any sales, see that you put them through my book.' Whether Miss Frisby was present or absent, the first sales always went through her book.

Maria stood there, waiting for customers. It was strictly forbidden to engage in anything else while thus occupied, and on no account could she talk to the junior, who was hidden away in the least conspicuous place in the department, let alone call out the time of day to Miss Wilding, who stood to attention behind the next counter, ready to sell trimmings. Not that Maria always obeyed the rules, especially in Miss Frisby's brief absences.

She longed to sit down. Last night's lack of sleep was catching up with her. But there was no chair, and if there had been one she would not have been allowed to use it. Gently, she prodded her tooth with her tongue. Without a doubt it was improving. She had been quite right not to go to the dentist. He could easily have made things worse.

When she first saw Clive Masterson walking towards her she didn't believe it. He must be a figment of her imagination because she had been thinking about him so much. But when he spoke, when she heard his rich, baritone voice, with its refined Virginian accent, utter the words 'I would like to look at some gloves, please,' she knew it was he. He was there, flesh and blood, in front of her.

'I beg your pardon . . .!' she stammered.

He smiled. He was used to the effect he had on women, and this one was exceptionally pretty, in spite of the fact that she had a swollen cheek and her large blue eyes were tired. She looked vulnerable; she appealed to him.

'I said I would like to see some gloves. White kid.'

She laid them out before him, every variety she could find. There was a wide choice and she hoped it would take him ages to make up his mind – but not so long that Miss Frisby would return and take the customer from her.

'These are pretty, with the mother-of-pearl buttons,' she suggested. 'Perhaps your wife might like these?'

She looked directly into his eyes, a deeper, darker blue than her own but equally thickly lashed.

'Alas, I am not married!' he said lightly, not taking his eyes from hers. 'The gloves are for my sister.'

It was true that he was not married. It was not true that they were for his sister, but then he did not suppose that this pretty little girl, with her unusual English accent, cared about that. They both knew why the question had been asked.

'I see. What size gloves does your sister take?' Maria asked. So he was not married!

He frowned. 'Now you have me. I'm not at all sure. Will you permit me to look at your hand, mademoiselle?'

Mademoiselle! How charming! She extended her hand to him and was mortified that it was not smaller, smoother, even cleaner, for she had been grubbing about in the stockroom.

He took the tips of her fingers in his and studied her hand with interest. No rings. No roughness, but the skin of her fingertips and palms was firm rather than soft. Hands which had known work, but which their owner was proud enough to care for. He liked that.

Maria felt herself blush as he held her hand. What if Miss Frisby came? But he was a customer and she was only doing his bidding.

'I take six and a half.' She aimed to pitch her voice low but it came out as an excited squeak.

'I think the lady for whom these gloves are intended has larger hands than yours,' he said. 'And if I may be so bold, not nearly as pretty.' Since the gloves were a present for his landlady, who was three times a grandmother, that was a fact. He was not sure if white kid was the thing for her, but she would be flattered to think that he had considered it so. If she never wore them she would keep them in a drawer and look at them from time to time.

'Then if you recommend them I will take these, only in a larger size,' he decided.

Maria wrapped them neatly, then fetched Miss Frisby's sale book and began to make out the bill. So soon over! Another minute and he would be gone. She must speak!

She stopped writing and looked up at him. Oh my, how handsome he was! Even more than on the stage, which as she well knew was not always the case. His hair was a dark burnished gold, his features like those of a Greek god, and his eyes twinkled as he smiled at her. He was not quite as tall as she had thought.

'If you please sir . . . that is to say. . . .'

'Yes?'

'Oh sir, you *are* Mr Clive Masterson, are you not? I couldn't be mistaken?'

'I am he,' he acknowledged. 'I am honoured that you recognise me.' He liked it, especially here in New York where he was not so well known as in Richmond, Virginia.

'Oh sir, I saw you at the theatre last week! In *What Dreams Foretell*. It was quite, quite wonderful!'

'Thank you,' he said graciously. 'You are very kind.' She was also dashed pretty, and more animated than anyone he had met for some time. The tired look had entirely gone from her eyes. As for her swollen cheek, why, he was quite taken with it!

'Is it possible . . .' she said breathlessly. 'Would you mind . . .? Could I ask you . . .?'

'You could ask me *anything!*' His tone was teasing. 'What do you want?'

'Would you give me your autograph? I should esteem it a great favour.'

He laughed. His laughter was just like music, Maria thought.

'Of course,' he said. 'What shall I write on?'

She tore a square from a sheet of wrapping paper. 'It's all I have,' she apologised. 'It doesn't seem quite fitting.'

'Nonsense!' He stood with his pen poised. 'May I know your name, mademoiselle?'

'Miss Appleby. Miss Maria Appleby.' Oh, how she hated her plain name.

He wrote with a flourish. 'To Miss Maria Appleby with sincerest wishes, Clive Masterson.'

'So you enjoyed *What Dreams Foretell?*' he asked, handing back the paper.

'Oh I did indeed,' Maria enthused. 'I hope next week to see *Man of My Heart*.' She blushed again as she said the words. She had not blushed so much in months.

'Then you must allow me to give you complimentary tickets,' he declared. He took them out of his pocket – he always had a couple to hand – and presented them with a flourish. 'I daresay there is some lucky young man who is all too ready to accompany you?'

'Not at all,' Maria said demurely. 'I shall attend with my married sister, or perhaps with a woman friend.'

He paid for the gloves and, with a deep bow, departed. When she had watched him across the length of the store, until he was out of sight, she looked down at the counter. He had left the gloves behind. At almost the same moment she heard Miss Frisby's footsteps. Quick as a flash she slipped the gloves into a drawer.

'Have you had many customers?' Miss Frisby asked.

'Only the one,' Maria replied nonchalantly.

In Mazomanie, a breeze lifted the washing which had already dried in the June sunshine. Two long lines of washing, stretching from the house to the post at the edge of the orchard Ernest and his father had planted three years ago – and back again. Charlotte came out of the house carrying the large oval laundry basket to gather it in before it became too dry, and therefore difficult to iron. There was always so much washing, every day the same. Eight of them now, counting Ernest's father. Since Meg, who had thrived as if being born in a trap by the roadside was the best possible start in life, there had been Kate and then Benjamin – her youngest and perhaps her dearest, because he would be the last. She knew that if no-one else did. At nine months she had reluctantly weaned him because she had come to the end of her strength and her milk had dried up.

She buried her nose in a sheet hanging on the line. It smelled delicious; of fresh air and grass and sunshine. Back in the house she folded the clean linen and put it aside for ironing. Then she set the table for the midday dinner, for which there was a stew on the stove. Summer or winter the men liked a hot dinner. They had always been used to it. For herself, she had no appetite these days, for stew or anything else, which was no doubt why was losing weight, her dresses hanging on her like sacks.

The two men came into the house looking pleased with themselves. 'That's half the bottom meadow cut,' Ernest said. 'Good stuff too. It's going to be a decent hay harvest.'

They sat at the table, the two men, Enoch, Jane and Meg. Kate sat in a high chair which her grandfather had made for her and Benjamin lay wide awake and gurgling in his crib. When she had served the others Charlotte put the milk to heat for Benjamin's bottle. Ernest looked up from his meal.

'What about you, Charlotte? You haven't set a place for yourself.'

'I'm not hungry.'

Ernest laid down his knife and fork. Suddenly the food choked him.

'You've got to eat, love. You must force yerself!'

'I couldn't face it,' Charlotte said. She had been nauseated serving the rich stew from the pan to the plates; the sight of it, the smell of it, was almost more than she could bear. 'Anyway, Benjamin's ready for his bottle.'

'You've got to eat,' Ernest repeated. 'How else will you get strong again? The baby can wait. He's quiet enough.'

If Ernest sounded angry Charlotte knew that it was because he was anxious. She tried not to let him see how bad she felt, seldom mentioned the dragging pains in her body and worst of all, the unutterable fatigue which was with her morning, noon and night. He had had enough on his plate in the last year, what with the farm, and building extra rooms on to the house for their growing family. And now that things were beginning to come together, now that they had adequate shelter and good food, and if they were careful enough money to clothe themselves simply, what did he want with an ailing wife to spoil it all? But eat to order she could not, and she could not down that stew.

'I'll have a bit later,' she promised.

'A piece of bread as like as not,' Ernest said. 'I know you.'

'Well, eat your stew,' Charlotte told him. 'It'll do no good for you not to eat either. And give Kate a hand.'

She tested the heat of the baby's milk on the back of her hand, then took him in her arms. The feel of his warm body against hers, the sound of his greedy rhythmical sucking, soothed her. She lowered her head and let fatigue sweep over her like a giant wave. She wanted to stay like this forever, never to have to move again, hardly to have to breathe.

Ernest finished his stew, pushed his plate away. He spooned up the last of Kate's meal and fed it to her, then fetched a flannel from the sink and washed her face.

'I'm going into town this afternoon,' he said.

At the sharp note in his voice Charlotte looked up.

'To town? Why? You're harvesting.'

'Dad can carry on with that. What doesn't get done today will have to wait. It'll come to no harm. The weather's settled here. It's not like England where you don't know if it's going to rain.'

'But why?' Charlotte persisted.

'I'm going to see Meg Atkinson about that girl to help you in the house. We've talked about it long enough, now I'm going to do it.'

Charlotte stared at him. 'We can't afford a girl in the house!'

'She'll not cost much. She'll have her home with us. We'll treat her right. She'll not want much more.'

I don't want to share my home with another woman, Charlotte thought rebelliously. It's mine. I want to keep it that way. Her father-in-law was different. He was helpful, unobtrusive, never interfered, even with the children. But an extra woman in the house would be another matter.

'I tell you I don't want anyone,' she said.

'She'd do as you said. She could do the washing, help you with the ironing. Whatever you wanted.'

Charlotte looked past Ernest to where the basket piled high with ironing awaited her. And tomorrow there would be more. And the day after, and the day after. Hours of standing on her feet with the pain eating at her.

'Very, well,' she agreed. 'But only a trial, mind.'

'There's Emily Watson,' Meg said. 'Her mother and father were taken within the week, with pneumonia. She's on her own and doesn't like it.'

'You think she'd come. You think she'd suit?' Ernest asked.

'I daresay she'd come. But only you and Charlotte can say if she'd suit. In my opinion she's a nice girl, but Charlotte. . . .' Meg hesitated.

'I know. She's a good wife and mother, Charlotte is. And she gets on well with Dad. But. . . .' He left the sentence unfinished. He remembered how, when Charlotte and Ruth had been together, sparks had sometimes flown.

'It's the way some women show their love, by feeling jealous,' Meg said.

'Yet I'd never be unfaithful to Charlotte,' Earnest replied. 'She must know that.'

Meg met the look in his eyes. '*I* know that. I always have. . . .'

Ernest sighed. 'Well, something's got to be done. She's not improving. The time's come when I've got to take things into my own hands. Charlotte's real ill, though she doesn't know it.'

Meg frowned. 'Are you sure she doesn't?'

'I can't be sure,' Ernest said. 'She admits to nothing more than being tired, and sometimes having a bit of pain – which she says is woman's stuff. We just don't talk about it.'

'You know what Dr Waterman told you,' Meg reminded him. 'About the specialist in New York.'

'I do, but Charlotte doesn't. He told me it was her only chance.' He had come from the doctor's house, a month ago, and poured his heart out to Meg. And had lived with the knowledge ever since, seeing confirmation of the doctor's verdict every time he looked at Charlotte.

'But I've made up my mind,' he said. 'If Emily Watson will come, and if I can leave her in charge for a week or so, then I'm taking Charlotte to New York. *Could* I leave her in charge, do you reckon?'

'She's only nineteen,' Meg pointed out. 'But I'd say she's capable. And fond of children. In any case I'd have the two youngest here. And I'd visit your place, see everything was all right.'

Ernest reached out and took her hand. 'Bless you, Meg! What would we do without you?' The colour came into her face and she turned away.

'The only problem is getting Charlotte to go,' Ernest went on. 'I thought perhaps I'd say we were going to visit the World's Fair, have a few days holiday, then spring the visit to the doctor on her when we were in New York. Will you do what you can to persuade her, Meg? She takes note of you.'

'I'll do everything I can,' Meg promised. 'And I think you're doing the right thing, Ernest. But first let Charlotte meet Emily Watson. What do you say if I bring her over tomorrow?'

'The sooner the better,' Ernest agreed.

The two women surveyed each other, green eyes warily meeting frank blue ones. Emily Watson sensed hostility as well as wariness in Mrs Gaunt's attitude, and wondered why. Well, she would have to see how it worked out. She wouldn't stay where she wasn't welcome. She'd liked Mr Gaunt at once, and Mrs Atkinson had said that Mrs Gaunt hadn't been well, so perhaps that was the reason. She had a lot on with five children under seven years old.

'Well then,' Charlotte said at last. 'Do you think you would come?'

'I'd like to,' Emily answered.

By the time she had been with them a week she was completely settled in. She was strong and cheerful, and took the hard work in her stride, including the dreaded washing and ironing. Enoch at six and a half and Janc, just gone five, together with four-year-old Meg were constantly in her shadow and were old enough to play the games she devised for them each day, leaving Charlotte to concentrate on the two little ones, especially the baby. Charlotte felt she could never have enough of her baby. She watched him all the time and frequently picked him up and held him close, rocking him to sleep in her arms. For this chance to spend time with Benjamin she would have tolerated Emily even if she had not, surprisingly, liked her.

She was in bed with Ernest, the two smallest children asleep in the same room, Enoch and his grandfather occupying the next room, and Emily sharing the small third room with Meg and Jane. The whole world, inside and outside the house, was stilled. Charlotte lay on her back in the wide bed, too tired to sleep – and knew, by his unnatural rigidity, that Ernest was lying awake in the darkness beside her. Presently he reached out and touched her hand.

'Are you awake, love?'

'I can't seem to get off,' she said.

'I was thinking . . . what about you and me taking a little holiday? You need one. It would buck you up.'

'I don't want a holiday,' Charlotte said. 'Where would we go?' She had no wish, nor had she the energy, to stir a step.

'Well . . . I thought we might go to the World's Fair in New York. . . .'

'New York!' She was incredulous. 'That awful journey!'

'It needn't be awful any more. We could go on the railroad this time. It's quick, and they say it's comfortable. We could stay with Ruth and Maria.' He sounded full of enthusiasm. In the dark she couldn't see the anxiety in his eyes.

'I couldn't leave the children,' Charlotte objected. 'Five children is too much for Emily to manage.'

'Meg would have the little ones. We'd only be gone for a week.' But she must never know that he had already discussed it with Meg.

'I don't want to go,' Charlotte said flatly.

What am I to do, he thought? She's *got* to go. There was a long silence between them before he decided what to say next.

'Charlotte?' There was no reply, but he knew by her stillness that she was not asleep.

'Charlotte, listen!'

'What is it? Go to sleep.' She didn't want to hear. The pain was beginning again. If she could fall asleep before it got worse . . . but she knew from experience that it would not be so, and the next best thing was to bear it alone; a fight between herself and the pain, which no-one else could enter.

'Charlotte, there's a doctor in New York . . . he might be able to help you. Charlotte, I want you well again, we all do.'

What would it be like to feel well again? Not since before Benjamin was born had she known a single day free from pain. But doctors couldn't work miracles. Only God could do that, and she had prayed to him night and morning without a sign that he had heard.

'Please, Charlotte! For my sake! And if not for mine, then for the sake of the children. For the baby.'

For Benjamin, she thought suddenly. She could do it for Benjamin. She could do anything for him, and he needed her.

'Very well, then,' she said quietly. 'But not more than a week. I can't leave the children more than a week.'

Ernest turned towards her and took her in his arms, kissed her gently, stroked her hair. She lay quiescent, her head on his breast. Making the decision, and the knowledge that what had been unmentionable between herself and

Ernest had now been spoken of, brought her a peace she had not known for a long time. Miraculously, by whoever's hand, she surmounted the pain and drifted into sleep.

A week later – Ernest said they must give Ruth time to receive the letter he had written – Charlie and Meg Atkinson came to take Charlotte and Ernest to the railroad station, and Kate and Benjamin to stay with them in Mazomanie.

Charlotte gave a last look around the living-room.

'I've been happy here,' she said to Ernest. 'It's been the happiest place of all for me.'

'You will be again,' he told her. 'Happy and well.'

She had kissed the three elder children, cautioned them to be good and to give no trouble to Emily and their grandfather; had given last-minute instructions to Emily and said her farewells to her father-in-law. There was nothing to do now except to leave, though her strongest temptation was *not* to do so, to give up the whole idea. Then Benjamin whimpered in her arms – she had refused to let anyone take hold of him for the journey to Mazomanie – and gave her strength. I'm doing it for you, my precious baby, she said – though not aloud.

At the railroad station it was almost more than she could bear to give him to Meg and it was Ernest who gently took him from her and handed him over. As the train drew away, Charlotte watched until the figures on the platform grew smaller and smaller and were finally lost in a cloud of dust.

In New York Ruth, waiting for Sean to come home, re-read Ernest's letter. He was less than specific about Charlotte, but for them to make the journey to New York, even with the excuse of the World's Fair, to which people were journeying from all over America, there must be something serious.

Well, in a few days her cousins would be here. She longed to see them again. And right now she had things to do. First of all she must see Professor Woodburn.

# 22

'Aurora wants a drink!' She tugged impatiently at her mother's skirt and Ruth picked up her daughter and held her on her lap.

'You shall have one in a minute.'

'And a cookie? Two cookies?'

'Very well, if you are good.'

She adored the child and could seldom resist her. She marvelled now, for the thousandth time, that anything so beautiful could belong to her. She doesn't look like me, Ruth thought, except perhaps in her mouth. In the small face Aurora's mouth was just too wide for beauty, yet somehow she gave beauty to it. For the rest, she was a copy in miniature of Joss Barnet: the same Italianate look, with his sculptured features, honey-toned skin, dark hair. But it was the eyes which were so particularly and disturbingly his, as much in expression as in colour, so that sometimes Ruth felt that it was Joss himself who gazed at her quizzically from beneath straight eyebrows.

And at Sean also. Not by a single word did Sean acknowledge the likeness, but Ruth knew that he recognised it. She had seen him turn away, unable to meet Aurora's bright eyes. He wanted to love her, he did love her, Ruth was sure of it, but there were times when it was all too much for him.

Matters were not made easier between herself and Sean by the fact that after three and a half years of married life she had failed to conceive. And now it seemed she might never do so, since for the past six months Sean had been unable to make love to her. It was not from the lack of desire. He came to her eagerly enough but, night after night, when their lovemaking went no further than the preliminaries, ending almost as soon as it was begun, they turned their backs on each other and slept, spiritually, if not physically, alone. Or too often did not sleep, but lay separately awake with jangled nerves, too aware of their own and each other's frustrations.

They never discussed the matter. Ruth wanted to, but Sean refused.

'At least tell me if something is troubling you,' she begged. 'I'm your wife. I want to help. For both our sakes.' He couldn't know, didn't wish to, she thought, what their lack of sexual intercourse did to her. As a woman she was not supposed to have these feelings, but she knew that her sexual needs and desires were as demanding as those of a man. There were nights when she was driven almost mad by the strength of her longing.

'Nothing is troubling me,' Sean said with sarcasm. 'Nothing except that I no longer seem to be a man!'

That was all he would say. The subject was closed.

So it seemed that Joss Barnet's child was to be her only one. In some ways she did not mind. It was not more children she craved but more loving. Aurora and the boarding-house occupied her waking hours well enough, and although in the first year of their marriage she had wanted to conceive for Sean's sake, increasingly now she thought it a blessing that she had not. Sean, though he loved children, would never make a responsible parent.

'Aurora wants a drink *now!*' her daughter said. Ruth put her down and rang for May.

'May, would you take Aurora for a few minutes? She may have a drink of milk and two cookies. But no more, mind!'

'Right you are,' May said. 'Come along, young miss. Let's see what May has for you in the kitchen.'

Aurora went happily enough. She was a sociable child and as long as someone danced attendance on her she didn't mind who it was.

Ruth put Ernest's letter on the side table for Sean to see when he came home from work that evening, though there was no telling what time that would be. It was not his Fire Department night, but he might still be late.

One evening, not long after he had started work, Sean said, 'Mr Tweed has persuaded me to volunteer for Fire Department duties. I'm to go in two nights a week.'

'Why should you do that?' Ruth asked. 'You work hard enough as it is – especially now that you've changed from the brush factory to his chair-making business. He gets enough out of you.'

'The New York Fire Department is manned by volunteers, so why shouldn't I be one?' Sean replied. 'Anyway, I shall enjoy it. Mr Tweed commands Engine Company Number Six – the best in the department. And "Americus" is far and away the best engine. Why, when they took it on tour – Baltimore, Washington, Philadelphia – hundreds of people turned out just to see it.'

'I know,' Ruth said. 'I read it in the newspaper.' She also knew that volunteers were needed. Some bit or other of New York seemed always to be on fire. She thought that perhaps Sean went into it for the glamour, enjoying wearing his uniform with its red shirt, boots, shining helmet. As it turned out, he was never more than one of the rank and file, doing the humblest jobs. And although the officers in the Fire Department were greatly admired when they turned out on their glistening machines, drawn by a team of mettlesome horses which careered swifter than the wind down Broadway, everything clearing a path before them, the men in ranks were often riff-raff, frequently drunk, or in trouble for brawling and looting. Ruth hated the idea of Sean mixing with them.

On the evenings when he was not on fire duty Sean usually went straight from work to Donnelly's ale-house, sometimes spending the whole evening there with his friends. The landlord and many of his customers were Irish, and in a city where the Irish were disliked they found solace in each other's company.

'I don't understand all this glory of Old Ireland stuff,' Ruth had said to Sean on the previous evening when he came home late and loquacious. 'Before we were married you told me you'd left Ireland behind. What had it ever done for you, you asked?'

'It gave me birth,' he replied solemnly. 'It gave me birth!'

She disliked him most when he was sentimentally drunk.

'And what about your precious Yorkshire?' he demanded. 'Have you grown too fine for it?'

'Of course not,' Ruth said. 'But I don't feel the need to celebrate it every evening.'

It was not the case that Sean came reeling home every evening; far from it. She knew by the smell of liquor on his breath that he always called at Donnelly's after work, but whether he had one drink and then came home to her, or whether he stayed for most of the evening, swilling liquor into his empty stomach, depended upon whom he met there. If his cronies were not to be seen he came home quickly. She thought that Sean did not particularly like drink, only what it did to him and the company it brought, so that when he did return home the worse for it she recognised her own guilt as well as his.

In Professor Woodburn's room Ruth came straight to the point. Any shilly-shallying and she was sure she would lose her courage.

'I know I haven't finished paying for Gutermann's,' she said nervously. 'But I *am* running it, even the financial side. Isn't that true?'

'Perfectly true,' Professor Woodburn agreed. 'So is there some problem?'

'And you think I'm quite capable?'

'Capable? Of course you are, my dear Ruth. Only think how you coped when our dear friend Mr Gossop died!'

Mr Gossop, alas, snored no more, unless in a better world. In 1852, while New York celebrated New Year's Day in its usual noisy fashion, he had quietly died. His cough of the previous winter had never quite left him, in spite of the fact that Ruth had moved him to a warmer bedroom and had regularly dosed him with a mixture of vinegar and treacle. He took to his bed shortly before the Christmas of 1851 and did not get up again.

Since his brother was snowbound in Saskatoon it had fallen to Ruth to arrange the funeral. 'Let me do it for you,' Professor Woodburn had said then. 'It is not woman's work.' She had read a criticism of Sean into his words, though he would never have voiced it.

'No,' she replied. 'Thank you all the same. Mr Gossop, alive, was my responsibility, though he was very little trouble. I would not wish to shirk that now.' Nor did she wish there to be any area of the business with which it could be said she couldn't cope.

'Very well,' Professor Woodburn had said. 'I expect it will be a small funeral.'

In fact, there were neither relatives nor friends present, only a colleague or two, and his fellow boarders. The three wreaths had been from them, and from Ruth and Sean and the domestic staff. It being the wrong time of the year for flowers, they were all of rather dark evergreens.

'Poor Mr Gossop!' Ruth said, remembering. Then she took a deep breath and brought herself back to the present.

'What I want,' she went on quickly, 'is your permission to change the name of Gutermann's to that of my own. Unless there is some legal reason against it. . . .'

'I am sure there is not. The place, in effect, is yours, and will be so entirely when you have paid off the loan.'

'Then would the person who made the loan object?' Ruth asked.

'Not at all,' the professor replied. 'I am sure of that.'

'Well then, I can't thank you enough,' Ruth said. 'And once again I'm grateful for your advice.'

He raised his hands in protest.

'Ruth, Ruth! When have I ever advised you about anything? You always come to me with clear ideas and your mind made up. All you want from me is approval.' The smile which accompanied his words took the edge off them.

'And will you once again thank whoever made the loan? It changed my life.' She was strongly of the opinion that it was the professor himself who had done so, though he would never admit it.

She determined to go that very day to visit the signwriter. The sooner she set the whole thing in motion, the better. But first she must speak with Mrs Cruse and May, tell them about her cousins' visit.

Leaving the professor's room she ran into Mrs Seaford. Mr and Mrs Seaford had dug themselves well into Gutermann's and were either accepted or tolerated by all except Captain Forsyth. He had never forgiven his fellow boarders for (as he muttered from time to time) lowering the standard. Ruth hoped that he might leave, but he was too comfortable. Besides, he liked something to grumble about.

But Mrs Seaford had made no real friend among the boarders so, having too little to do and a desperate need for company, she tried to make one of Ruth. Ruth didn't like this, but she tolerated it partly because she recognised Mrs Seaford's loneliness, partly for another reason.

The Seafords' room, and that of Francis Priestley, were immediately over those of Ruth and Sean. Sean, when aroused by drink, did not trouble to lower his voice and Ruth knew that Mrs Seaford was aware of what went on on these occasions. In any case she took the trouble, in the nicest possible way, to inform Ruth that she knew. This she did now.

'How are you this morning?' Ruth asked.

Mrs Seaford sighed. 'I don't sleep at all well these days. The slightest noise disturbs me. I am thinking of asking the doctor for a sleeping draught.'

It was said pleasantly, without rancour, so that Ruth felt immediately in the woman's debt. She knew she would have to pay the debt by accepting her next overture of friendship, perhaps by asking her in to tea when she knocked on the sitting-room door, or allowing her to tag along when she next went shopping, especially since Maria was not at the moment available. Ruth knew that, most of all, Mrs Seaford would have liked her to have confided in her, but there was no chance of that. The lady was also kindness itself to Aurora, making her the prettiest caps and dresses, seizing the slightest excuse to give her presents. Ruth did not welcome these attentions to her daughter, but recognised that they grew out of genuine affection, and for that she forgave Mrs Seaford much.

'I'm so sorry,' Ruth said sympathetically. 'Perhaps a glass of milk last thing, with a teaspoon of brandy . . .?' She hurried away. She had no wish to hear more.

Francis Priestley must also be aware of her quarrels with Sean, and sometimes Ruth felt ashamed to face him. But never, by a single word or look, did he betray his awareness.

She went into the kitchen.

'Aurora wants another cookie,' the child said.

'You've just had one. Two, I suspect. Isn't that right, May?'

'It is,' May confirmed. 'But no more, seeing as you said not to.'

'Aurora's *very* hungry!'

She had inherited her father's self-confidence. Ruth herself had a measure of self-confidence now, but she had had to work for it, gain it inch by slow inch. To Aurora it came as naturally as breathing. And mine is only in my ability to do my job, Ruth thought. Aurora's was complete. Please God nothing would ever destroy it.

'Very well then,' Ruth said. 'You may have one more small one.'

She informed Mrs Cruse and May of the contents of Ernest's letter.

'I shall see Dr Cooke today, to make an appointment for my cousin Charlotte,' she said.

'I'm sorry to hear the lady's poorly,' Mrs Cruse sighed. 'Perhaps the doctor will recommend Galvanism.'

'Galvanism? What's that?'

'I'm not quite sure,' Mrs Cruse admitted. 'But it's all the rage. You wear a pair of soles in your shoes, one copper, the other zinc. It makes some kind of current go through.'

'What does it cure?' Ruth asked dubiously.

'Practically everything,' Mrs Cruse replied.

'It sounds ever so dangerous to me,' May remarked. 'I wouldn't like currents going through my poor feet!'

'Well, at least your cousins will enjoy the World's Fair,' Mrs Cruse said. 'I daresay you'll go with them.'

'Oh yes,' Ruth agreed. 'I shall look forward to that.'

Now in its second season, the fair was still New York's most thrilling prospect. It seemed that everyone in the city, not to mention half of the rest of America, had visited or was about to visit the great iron and glass building which had been specially built between Fortieth and Forty-Second Street on Sixth Avenue.

'I heard Mr Priestley's mother is coming,' May said. 'Will she stay here, ma'am?'

'No, we haven't a suitable room.' Secretly Ruth was glad. She knew she would be afraid of the lady.

May sighed. 'A pity his fiancée isn't well enough to come.'

'Well,' Ruth said briskly, foreseeing a bout of gossiping which she did not wish to encourage. 'There are jobs to be done if we're not to be late with the luncheons.'

She always served a light repast to those of her boarders who were in the house in the middle of the day. Fortunately there were not many of them, and the food was of the simplest: a bowl of soup or some kind of egg dish. Having nothing else to do, Mrs Seaford was always present at this meal. Today she lingered at her table after the others had left the room and when Ruth went to clear away (she had promised May the afternoon off and Mrs Cruse was busy elsewhere in the house) Mrs Seaford spoke to her.

'I hope Mr O'Farrell is well today?'

'Quite well, thank you.' It's her way of informing me, Ruth thought, that she heard him come home last night. And how could she not, seeing that he had made enough noise to waken the dead in Grace churchyard! Thank goodness it had been an amiable noise: singing, joking, laughing.

'I'm sorry if we disturbed you last evening,' she said. 'Mr

O'Farrell was in such high spirits, so full of fun! The Irish in him, I daresay. I told him you would not be thankful to hear the ballads of old Ireland at midnight, and when I tell him that you *were* disturbed he will be most upset and will wish to apologise to you.'

'Oh please don't!' Mrs Seaford said quickly. 'It was nothing. In any case I had not fallen asleep.' But as Ruth moved away Mrs Seaford could not help adding, 'And I don't suppose anyone else heard.' Did she know it was Ruth's greatest dread, that the knowledge would spread to all her boarders? Not that *she* would spread it. Ruth did not suspect her of that.

Ruth supposed that she should be thankful that Sean, in drink, was usually jovially noisy. To be fair, it did not take a great deal of liquor to put him in this state. Only when he had drunk well over the odds did he become unpleasant (though it was all distasteful to her). Then he would be visited by a black mood as bitter as gall, and she would reap the consequences.

'I wondered,' Mrs Seaford went on, 'if you're busy this afternoon, might I take Aurora out for a walk?'

'I'm sure she'd enjoy that,' Ruth said. 'And as I can't take her on my errands, I'd be most grateful.'

After lunch Ruth left the house to visit a signwriter, a printer, and after that Dr Cooke.

'I want only a moderately-sized board,' she told the signwriter. 'It is to be affixed to the wall at the side of the door. The present one is larger than I like.'

'You'll need it large enough to take the words clearly,' he pointed out.

'I want only one word,' Ruth told him. 'Just "Appleby's" That's all.'

'We usually put "Boarding Establishment for Ladies and Gentlemen",' he demurred. 'How will they know what it is?'

'If they don't know, they'll ask. That's all I want. "Appleby's".'

From the signwriter she went to the printer and ordered

new billheads. He was even more reluctant to let her have just 'Appleby's, Spring Street' and suggested phrases like 'High-class Catering' and 'Home Comforts'.

' "Appleby's" is enough,' Ruth said firmly.

After that she visited Dr Cooke at his house in Gramercy Park, and with some difficulty made an appointment for Charlotte to see him.

'Your sister-in-law can count herself particularly fortunate that she has been given this appointment,' the receptionist said with some disaproval. 'Most patients have to wait three months to see Dr Cooke.'

When she came out of the doctor's house Ruth walked slowly along the road. To the best of her knowledge, Joss Barnet now lived in this newly-fashionable neighbourhood. As long ago as 1852 she had read in the social columns of the newspaper that he had moved here. And then, not many months afterwards, she had read the report of his divorce. It had given her a sick jolt when she saw it and she was glad to have been alone so that no-one could read the expression on her face. If only – if he had been divorced when they had first met . . .? But would it have made any difference? She liked to think that it would have, but in her heart she was far from sure. And in different circumstances she might never have met him at all.

Rumour said – rumour was rife in the gossip columns – that his wife had left him for another man, taking the children with her, but to Ruth, remembering Mrs Barnet, that seemed incredible. Who, having Joss Barnet, would look at anyone else?

She walked slowly, dawdled, staring up at the splendid houses, willing him to emerge through one of the dignified entrances, longing for the sight of him. But he did not do so. Perhaps he no longer lived there. She had heard and read nothing of him for almost two years now, and she had tried desperately hard in all that time not to think of him. But for a few minutes, today, walking where perhaps he might tread, she would indulge herself, allow her thoughts to go where they would.

She could not imagine that he had been married again or she would surely have read about it. But nor could she envisage him without the solace of female company. It was not in his character, of that she felt depressingly sure. Oh Joss, she thought, where are you? What are you doing?

Then she squared her shoulders, began to move briskly away from Gramercy Park, west towards Broadway and home. By the time she reached Spring Street, she promised herself firmly, she would stop thinking about Joss Barnet. But did he ever think of her?

When the kitchen door opened and Sean walked in, Ruth was still preparing the boarders' supper. She was pleased and surprised to see him so early. She hoped he was in a good mood. Apart from the news of her cousins' visit, she had her own bit of news to give him. He looked good-humoured enough, more than he had for some time. Aurora left the meal she was eating and rushed to greet him. He scooped her up in his arms and kissed her soundly.

'And what's my little girl been doing today?' he asked.

'Aurora went to see the fountains. Aurora had some candy.'

Sean looked at Ruth.

'Mrs Seaford took her to Union Square. Aurora, go back to the table and finish your supper.'

'Aurora doesn't want any more.'

'Nonsense,' Ruth said. 'You were eating well enough before Papa came in. Now be a good girl and clear your plate.'

'Naughty Papa!' Sean mocked. 'He interrupted your supper. Perhaps he should have waited outside in the yard until you'd finished!'

A sharp retort sprang to Ruth's lips, but she stifled it. How quickly he took offence. But this evening she had no wish to provoke him.

'Papa is teasing us again,' she said to Aurora.

When Ruth had finished the boarders' meal, so that it was all ready for May to carry in, she said, 'I'll put Aurora to bed, then serve the parlour tea. After that our own meal will be ready, we have some nice fish you'll enjoy.'

'Let me put Aurora to bed,' Sean suggested, following Ruth out of the kitchen.

Ruth hesitated. It was a task she enjoyed. She liked washing the child's silky little body, dusting her with the very finest powdered starch, dressing her in one of the pretty nightshifts Mrs Seaford had made; brushing her hair and tucking her into bed - and all the while listening to her prattle. And then the bedtime story. It was the hour of the day she enjoyed most with her daughter - she could not help but think of Aurora exclusively as hers though she tried hard not to show it. And Sean had certainly earned his rights.

'We'll do it together,' she said. 'In the meantime there's a letter for you to read, from Ernest. It's on the side table.'

When he had read it Sean commented, 'It doesn't sound too good.'

'No. I've made the appointment with Dr Cooke.' She would tell him later about the afternoon's other errands.

When Aurora was in bed - she always settled quickly - Ruth told May to take the tea into the parlour.

'I won't be long,' she said to Sean. 'We can talk about Ernest's and Charlotte's visit over supper - and there is something else I want to discuss with you. But won't you come and serve tea with me?'

'No thank you,' Sean replied. He was never comfortable in the boarders' parlour, though they were always polite to him - only because he was Ruth's husband, he reckoned. They seemed fond of her but he doubted if they'd give him the time of day otherwise. No malice on either side; he just wasn't their sort. A working man, and Irish at that! But there was a touch of bitterness in his self-mockery.

All the boarders were present for the evening tea. Some of them spoke of making up a party to go to Niblo's later in the evening.

'Mr Wellbake and I would adore to go,' Mrs Wellbake said to Ruth. 'If you'd be so kind as to keep an ear open for Martin.'

'Of course I will,' Ruth promised. She doubted whether Mr Wellbake would adore Niblo's, but his wife was a forceful woman.

Miss Potter looked expectantly at Francis Priestley. 'I'm sure you would enjoy to go,' she said.

'I would indeed,' he replied politely. 'But alas, I cannot. It is near the end of term and there are papers I must mark for my students.'

'If you would allow me, Miss Potter,' Mr Pierce broke in, 'I would count it as a privilege to escort you.'

It was not at all what Miss Potter had in mind, but she was too well-mannered to refuse. Besides, everyone (except Captain Forsyth) liked Mr Pierce.

Ruth returned to the sitting-room where she always ate in the evening with Sean and Maria. Her sister had arrived home from work, full of prattle about some man to whom she had sold a pair of gloves.

'Clive Masterson, no less!' Maria was still awestruck. 'And he gave me two tickets for the theatre for Monday evening. You will go with me, Ruth, won't you?'

'I don't think so,' Ruth said. 'Ernest and Charlotte arrive then. We must be here to greet them. Surely you will want to?'

'Oh Ruth!' Maria was agonised. 'I promise to spend lots of time with them while they're here. It's been confirmed that I'm to finish at Stewart's at the end of the week and I'll devote every single minute to them – except I *must* go to the theatre! I couldn't bear it otherwise. And seats in the stalls too!'

'Well, I'm sure Mrs Seaford will accompany you,' Ruth said, smiling indulgently at the sight of her sister's woeful face. 'By the way, some of the boarders are going to Niblo's this evening.'

Maria gasped with pleasure.

'Oh Ruth, do you think they'd let me go with them?'

'I'm sure they would – though I don't think the Seafords are going.' She would be glad for Maria to be out of the way so that she could talk to Sean in private.

When the supper had been cleared away and a bubbling Maria had left the house with the party of boarders, Ruth sat down opposite Sean.

'There is a matter about which I must speak to you,' she began nervously.

'Well since this is the third time ye've announced it, ye'd better speak out,' Sean said dryly. 'I can't think what it can be makes ye so solemn.'

She wasted no further time.

'You know that I've almost paid the loan for the contents of the house?'

Since taking over the finances of the house, to Professor Woodburn's obvious relief, she had been able to make economies here and there, and every penny of the money saved and profit earned had gone towards reducing the debt.

'I know,' Sean said. 'What about it?'

'And that when the last payment is made the business will be entirely mine?' She could say 'mine' because she had made the payments entirely from her own money. Not a penny of Sean's wages had contributed.

'Yes.'

'Well then . . . I want to change the name of the boarding-house from Gutermann's to my own name.'

'Is that all?' He simply could not understand what the fuss was about. It was unlike Ruth to be so nervous. 'There's nothing very terrible about that.'

'You do understand, don't you?' Ruth said slowly. 'I want to change the name from Gutermann's to Appleby's.'

She had thought for weeks about how she would make this announcement, how Sean would receive it. Now all the fears she had had were confirmed by the look on her husband's face. The colour had drained from him. His hands gripped the arms of the chair and the knuckles were as white as his face.

'Your name is O'Farrell. Ruth O'Farrell.' His voice was cold with anger.

'I know. I want to call the house Appleby's.'

'You are *not* Ruth Appleby. When you married me you took my name. Ruth O'Farrell's what you are, and always will be!'

'You don't understand, do you?' Ruth cried. 'You don't understand at all. All my life I've counted for nothing. Nobody thought Ruth Appleby was worth a damn. Well, now I want to show the world what Ruth Appleby has done! Is that so bad?'

'What Ruth *O'Farrell* has done,' Sean said stubbornly. 'I don't care a tinker's cuss if the place stays as Gutermann's, but if you want it in your own name, then your name is O'Farrell. That's what you will call it!'

'Why can't you understand?' Ruth pleaded. 'Why won't you just try to understand?'

Sean had risen and was pacing the room in angry strides. Now he stood still and turned around to face Ruth.

'Oh I understand all right! Don't kid yourself I don't understand. Ye don't want my name and ye never did. Now if my name had been Barnet. . . .'

'That's not fair!' Ruth protested. 'I was honest with you and I've kept my promise.'

Indeed she had not set eyes on Joss Barnet since the morning of her wedding day, though there had been times, especially in the beginning, when the longing for him had been so great that she felt she would have traded the rest of her life for one hour with him. But she had made no attempt to see him and she had tried hard to control her thoughts, to put him out of her mind – except for the short time in Gramercy Park this afternoon. She had hoped that Sean had put the whole affair behind him, though she could not know because it was never mentioned. But with Aurora looking as she did, perhaps that was too much to hope for.

'Oh, I know ye've given him up,' Sean said. 'There was no alternative because he gave *you* up!'

'He did not!' Ruth retorted hotly. 'It was my own decision, freely made.'

'It's my belief that he made no more arrangements to see ye once he knew ye were with child,' Sean said. 'But what would the story have been if he'd come after ye? Tell me that.'

'I've told you, I gave him up of my own free will,' Ruth insisted. She would never tell him that Joss had wanted her to get rid of the baby. For that Sean would hate him more than ever. 'But all this has nothing to do with the fact that I want to call this place Appleby's.'

'Why not call it Barnet's and be done with it?' Sean said. 'I don't doubt for a minute it was his money went into it.'

'That's a wicked lie!' Ruth stormed. She was shaking now with anger. 'Professor Woodburn has assured me most solemnly that Joss Barnet had no part in the loan.'

'And it suited you to believe him!'

'I believed him – I *do* believe him, because he's a man of honour. Professor Woodburn would not lie. You know that as well as I do, Sean O'Farrell!'

'Then whose money was it?' he asked sullenly. 'Answer me that.'

'I can't because I don't know. But since it's almost paid back, what does that matter now?'

He strode towards the door. In the doorway he turned around and shouted at her. 'You can call it O'Farrell's. You shall *not* call it Appleby's. I forbid you!' He went out of the house slamming all the doors behind him.

He had not returned when Ruth made herself ready for bed. She had no intention of waiting up for him because she did not intend to resume the argument. And she was quite clear what she was going to do. The house would be called Appleby's. If Sean had said his last word on the subject she would simply defy him.

But it was not quite so simple. She was well aware that it was a grave matter for a wife to disobey her husband. No-one would condone such a thing. Nature, it was generally agreed, had endowed the man with all the attributes necessary to conducting business affairs and making the decisions which went with them. The truly feminine woman could not possibly understand them. Unless, of course, she was widowed, like Mrs Gutermann – in which case

Providence might suddenly render her quite capable of conducting her own affairs. As far as Ruth could see, no-one subscribed more heavily to these benefits than women themselves. But not she!

Appleby's – she had secretly thought of it by that name for many months now – was as good as hers. In fact she would go to the signwriter and the printer again, urge them to complete the work quickly so that everything would be in place when her cousins arrived. And if Sean took down the nameplate, she would put it up again. If he tore up the new billheads, she would order more. She was utterly determined.

She wished Sean had not mentioned Joss Barnet. Memories of what they had been to each other crowded into her mind as she undressed for bed. She wished – however wicked it was, she could not help it now – that she was undressing for him. She felt sick with loneliness and longing.

Slipping off the last of her garments, she stood naked before the mirror. As if she was another person looking at her, she observed the slenderness of her waist and the voluptuous curve of her hips, the full firm breasts. Her skin was smooth and creamy-white, except for the deep rose of her nipples and the dark triangle of pubic hair. But who cared that her body was beautiful? What did any of it matter now?

She turned away from the mirror and covered her nakedness with her nightshift. Then on a sudden impulse she unlocked the drawer in which she had hidden the chain and locket, and took it out. She turned back to the mirror and, with trembling fingers, fastened the chain around her neck. The gold shone softly against her throat and the small pearls added their lustre to that of her skin.

She was still there, studying her reflection, when she saw the bedroom door open, and Sean was standing there, watching her.

He stood in complete silence, though she could tell from his flushed face and the brightness of his eyes that he was in drink. She remained rooted to the spot, as if she had been turned to stone – and then her hand flew to her neck in an abortive attempt to hide the locket.

Sean spoke. His voice was like a knife plunging into her.

'So ye put him out of your life, did ye?'

'I don't know what you mean . . .' she stammered. 'It . . . it belonged to my mother. . . .'

'Liar!'

'How dare you!'

'I collected it from the jeweller's for him, that day in New York. I knew then it was for you. So you were completely honest with me, were you?'

'Sean, I swear to you . . .! It's the first time. . . . It was too valuable. . . .'

Suddenly he raised his voice, shouted for the whole of New York to hear.

'Valuable! Valuable!'

Then he lunged towards her, took hold of her arms, his fingers digging into her flesh. The air around him was polluted with the stink of whisky. He pinned her arms behind her back and pushed her forward, forcing her to look at herself in the mirror.

'Whore's wages, that's what it is!' he thundered. 'Whore's wages, every golden link of it! Look at yourself. Look at a whore and a strumpet!'

She was suddenly terrified. Never before had she seen him in this violent mood. But she must not let him see that she was afraid. She must keep calm.

'Let go of me, Sean. You're hurting me.' She spoke quietly.

'Hurting you? You don't know the first thing about being hurt! But vengeance is God's and one day someone will hurt you as you've hurt me!' He twisted her arm so that she cried out with pain.

'I'd like to strangle you with it!' he yelled. 'Yes, strangle you! It's what you deserve. Why wait for God's vengeance anyway?'

'Sean, please! Please be quiet!' Ruth begged. 'Everyone will hear!'

'And what if they do? Do ye think I care about your damned boarders?'

She saw his face in the mirror; purple with rage, distorted. He looked crazy. She shivered with fear, and felt sick. She had to stop him, to calm him down. But how? He would not listen to her.

He was shouting at the top of his voice now, hurling abuse and insults of which 'whore', 'strumpet', 'adulteress' were the least vile. She knew that Mrs Seaford must be awake, hearing every word. Then his shouts wakened Aurora and she began to cry.

Ruth tried to free herself to go to the child, but Sean grabbed the chain around her neck and dragged her back. His eyes glittered with anger. Fear choked her. She had to get away. But when she tried again to escape him he held on to the chain, twisting it in his hand so that the metal cut into her flesh. She knew with a dreadful certainty, feeling the chain tighten still further, that in another moment she must lose her breath. She knew, too, that she must scream now, before it was too late.

She screamed and screamed; long piercing shrieks that she had not thought it possible to utter; screams which came from the depths of her body, screams of utter terror.

She did not know how long she screamed because in the end the world went black and the reflection in the mirror disappeared as she lost consciousness.

When she came to Francis Priestley was bending over her, his face full of anxiety.

'It's all right,' he said quietly. 'Everything's all right.'

'Aurora?' Surely Aurora had been crying, and was silent now?

'She's all right too.' It was Mrs Seaford speaking. Aurora was in her arms. 'If you don't mind I think I'd better take her up with me, just for tonight. She'll be more settled.'

A sound made Ruth turn her head. Sean was sitting on a chair in the corner of the room, his head in his hands as a sob escaped him.

# 23

Ruth knew as soon as she entered the kitchen that May had heard the previous night's happenings. She and Mrs Cruse were deep in conversation which ended in mid-sentence as Ruth walked in. On their faces she read a mixture of concern and curiosity. She decided to take the offensive.

'Good morning, ladies! May, I'm so sorry if I disturbed you last night. I had the most terrible nightmare and wakened screaming. Try as he would, poor Mr O'Farrell could do nothing to stop me.'

'Nasty things, nightmares,' Mrs Cruse said quickly. 'My second has 'em. Sometimes we can't do nothing with her. What was you dreaming about?'

'I'm not sure. You know how confusing dreams are. It was something about being attacked. Very frightening – but quite stupid of course. I just hope I didn't waken the whole household!' That was something she wanted to know about.

'You couldn't have,' May told her. 'Most of them was still at Niblo's.'

'Well, there you are,' Mrs Cruse said. 'Must have been something you ate. Pickles perhaps.'

Ruth was not sure that they believed her story. May must surely have heard Sean's ranting? But they pretended to believe, for which she was grateful. With any luck her boarders would do likewise.

'We haven't seen Mr O'Farrell this morning,' Mrs Cruse remarked.

'He went off to work early,' Ruth said lightly.

By the time Francis Priestley and Mrs Seaford had left last night, Sean was stone-cold sober and abjectly apologetic. Looking at him, cowering there in the corner of the room, Ruth no longer had any fear of him. He would not hurt her again. But she could not now bear him near her.

'Please, Ruth! Please forgive me,' he begged. 'You know I wouldn't harm ye! Not a hair of your head. 'Twas the drink in me.' He reached for her hand but she pulled away from him.

'I'm begging you, Ruth!' He could not bear her sudden coldness. It put a thousand miles between them. She had provoked him beyond his endurance but now he, not she, was paying the price. He felt unutterably lonely; bereft.

'Please, Ruth,' he entreated. 'Please forgive me!'

'I do,' she said quietly. 'And everything else can wait until tomorrow.' She had been unutterably weary, drained of strength.

'Then let me come to bed.'

'You can have the bed,' she said. 'I will sleep on the chair. Only be quiet and let us both get some rest.'

'I want to come on the bed with you.' He pleaded like a child. She shivered at the tone of his voice.

'No! I'm sleeping alone.' She was adamant.

So for the rest of the night Sean had sat in the armchair while Ruth lay awake in the bed. He was quickly asleep, with the heavy breathing of a man who has drunk too much, but the short June night was almost over before Ruth fell asleep. When she had awakened this morning, he was gone.

Looking in the mirror, shocked at the sight of her white face and dark-rimmed eyes, she saw that she was still wearing the chain. Also that there was a thin red line on the side of her neck where the gold had bitten into her. And on her arm there were purple bruises. Luckily, all the marks could be hidden.

She took off the chain, put it back in its box. Now she hated even to touch it, as if it had been defiled. Though she replaced the box in the drawer, she knew it could not remain there. She should never have kept it in the first place. Even while Sean was sobbing his apologies she realised the guilt for a marriage which did not work was hers as well as his. She also should be pleading forgiveness; but because the distance between them was her refuge, she could not utter the words.

Her guilt, she thought, was not so much in her affair with Joss Barnet, or in any other bone of contention, as in her lack of love for Sean. With a strong mutual love and trust they could have put Joss behind them. Given the unselfishness of real love they could have resolved the conflict of naming the boarding-house. But they did not have it, and they were both the weaker for its absence.

'I'm going to take a tray of tea to the Seafords,' Ruth said to Mrs Cruse. 'Mrs Seaford wasn't too well last evening. Then we'll do the breakfasts.'

She wanted to reclaim her daughter with the least possible fuss. Also, both Mrs Seaford and Francis Priestley had to be faced this morning. There was no pretending to them that she had been the victim of a nightmare.

Aurora was sitting up in the Seafords' wide bed, happily listening while Mrs Seaford recited nursery rhymes, neither of them seeming one whit worse for their disturbed night.

'Aurora likes the big bed,' she announced.

'I'm sure you do,' Ruth replied. 'But now you must come with Mama and allow Mrs Seaford to rest. Up you get!'

'She slept like a top,' Mrs Seaford said. 'I told her she'd had a bad dream and I'd taken her into my bed because Mama was busy.'

'I can't thank you enough . . .' Ruth began.

She didn't know how to continue. Mr Seaford was there, and in front of him she felt newly embarrassed, though she knew he was the kindest of men.

'What are friends for?' Mrs Seaford smiled.

Grateful though she was, Ruth did not want Mrs Seaford for a friend. In the present circumstances she did not want friends at all. She had no desire for sympathy; only to be alone, to work things out for herself without the world knowing.

'Aurora wants to stay with Auntie Seaford,' the child announced.

'Why not let her stay while you're busy?' Mrs Seaford suggested.

Ruth hesitated. She did not warm to the sight of her daughter in the other woman's bed, but perhaps it would be as well if Aurora did not come into the kitchen at present. She chattered like a little monkey.

'Well, perhaps for half an hour,' she agreed. 'And you are to be a good girl, Aurora.'

'My little daughter is a funny child,' Ruth remarked, back in the kitchen. 'Nothing would please her this morning except to go up to Mrs Seaford!'

'There's children for you,' Mrs Cruse said. 'And Mrs Seaford certainly has a way with her.'

Ruth dreaded seeing Francis Priestley, though she knew she must. It was possible that he had saved her life, though looking at the fine gold chain this morning she was not sure that it could have strangled her. Nor, in the cold light of day, did she know how far Sean might have gone in his rage; but she had been truly terrified at the time. She must thank Francis Priestley, and the sooner the better. After breakfast, before he had time to leave the house, she went upstairs and knocked on the door of his sitting-room.

He was at his desk when she entered. Springing to his feet, he motioned her to a chair, and sat down opposite to her.

'Mrs O'Farrell, are you all right?' he asked. 'I have been anxious about you, but I could not ask May at breakfast.'

'I am perfectly all right. I wish to thank you – which I do with all my heart.'

'I daresay the situation would have resolved itself without me,' he said. 'But when I heard. . . . I hope you will forgive me if I interfered.'

'Not forgive you. Thank you. My husband, as you saw, had had a little too much to drink. I'm afraid his friends lead him astray. But I am sure it will never happen again, and I am equally sure, now, that he would never have hurt me. I was foolish and over-emotional.'

She desperately needed to know how much he had heard – whether Sean's accusations, the terrible words he had used, had been audible in this room.

'You were wakened by my screams?' she asked. 'Or perhaps you were not yet asleep and heard my husband come in?'

He looked her straight in the face. 'I heard nothing until your screams wakened me,' he said.

She knew he was lying. She saw the compassion in his kind grey eyes and suddenly it was too much for her. She covered her face with her hands and the tears ran down between her fingers.

'I'm sorry,' she murmured. 'I would not have chosen to cry in front of you. Your kindness. . . .'

'Please don't be sorry, Mrs O'Farrell. It will do you good to cry.' She took the handkerchief he offered and dried her eyes.

'May and Mrs Cruse believe I had a nightmare,' she said. 'Or at least that is what they *pretend* to believe.'

'Tell yourself they do.'

'You think it is permissible not to face the truth?'

Without replying he rose from his chair, walked over to the sofa table, picked up a silver-framed miniature and brought it back to Ruth.

Ruth thought the woman might have been about thirty when the portrait was painted. She looked at a strong face: a long, straight nose, a wide brow from which dark hair sprang in a widow's peak, a mouth curving, yet resolute, and eyes which looked out from the portrait with some sadness. Except that the artist had painted her eyes in the purest cerulean blue, her son's were exactly like them.

'She was a handsome woman.' She couldn't think why he was showing her the portrait, unless to divert her.

'She still is,' he said. 'Though no longer young. But that is not why I drew her to your attention.'

'Then why . . .?'

He took the portrait from her, looked at it again, and set it back on the table before answering.

'I am the youngest of five,' he said. 'I have three sisters and there was an elder brother who died. I do not remember a time when my father did not drink to excess. I don't recall an evening when he was completely sober. My mother bore it by pretending that all was well. I daresay she sometimes pretended even to herself, as well as to her children and the rest of the world. I think perhaps it was only by refusing to face the truth that she held everything together.'

'And your father?'

'He died ten years ago.'

'Your mother sounds a remarkable woman,' Ruth said.

'She is a strong woman. You remind me a little of her. I think you are strong.'

His words, though meant to comfort, stirred the doubts which nagged at Ruth's mind. Was it her strength which was too much for Sean? Perhaps she had strength but lacked the wisdom to use it properly? Perhaps Francis Priestley's father had found his wife's strength too much to live up to? If I were a more pliant wife, Ruth asked herself, would Sean be a better husband?

'Thank you for telling me,' she said. 'And thank you again for your help. I wish I could repay you.'

'Then promise me one thing,' he asked. 'If ever you need help, or just a friend in whom to confide, promise you will come to me.'

'And put myself further in your debt,' Ruth smiled. 'Nevertheless I promise. And now I must get back to my duties.'

'I am sure my fellow guests will be sorry to hear of your nightmares,' he said as he held the door open for her. 'I think if Mrs Seaford were to make it known that you suffered so, you would be given a score of remedies!'

That evening Sean came straight home from work, not stopping for even a single drink at Donnelly's. He was quiet, not saying much, though not sulky. Except for one thing the events of the previous night might never have taken place. Neither Ruth nor he referred to them. But the one thing was crystal clear. He could not bear to have Aurora near him. Ruth watched as Aurora, coming into the room, went to him with arms outstretched and face lifted up for his greeting – and saw him turn away. It was done adroitly, so that to anyone other than herself it could have seemed accidental, but she knew it was not. She also knew, by the strain in his face, the pain in his eyes, that he did not wish to turn away from the child, but he could not help himself. There was something in him deeper and stronger than his conscious wish. Aurora looked surprised, but was quickly distracted by Ruth.

'Aurora, go into the kitchen and tell May that your papa is home and we would like some tea when it is convenient to her. You may stay there until it is ready and you may have a cookie.'

When Aurora had gone Ruth turned to Sean.

'I'm sorry,' he said quickly. 'I know it's not her fault. She's less to blame than any of us. But I can't stand it when she looks at me. I can't stand it any longer. Please don't blame me, Ruth. In time I'll get over it, I swear I will.'

'I'm not blaming you,' Ruth replied quietly. 'I know what you see when you look at Aurora. I've always known. And I've honoured you for the fact that you rose above it and gave her your love. So much love! Don't take it from her, Sean, I beg of you. Turn away from me if you must – but not from Aurora.'

'I don't want to,' he whispered. 'I can't help it. I will try, I promise.'

Ruth touched his hand. 'You have nothing to fear, Sean. I am your wife and I am faithful to you. Aurora is your daughter now as much as mine. I believe she loves you more than she does me.'

But when Aurora came back with May, and from then until she was tucked up for the night, Ruth could see that Sean avoided the child. He found a reason for not playing a game with her, took no part in putting her to bed, and made an excuse not to tell his customary bedtime story. Ruth watched them both with anxious eyes. It could not be long before Aurora, an intelligent three-year-old, realised that she had been cast aside by the person she loved most.

As soon as Aurora was in bed and before Maria had arrived home, Ruth fetched the chain and locket in its box from the bedroom. She put it on the table in front of Sean.

'It is foolish that this should come between us,' she said. 'It was the first time I have looked at it since before our marriage. It was a stupid impulse for which I am truly sorry.'

Sean pushed the box sharply away from him.

'No!' Ruth cried. 'You take it! Give it away; throw it in the river; do whatever you want with it!'

'You can send it back to where it came from,' Sean said truculently. 'I don't want to see it. You can't blame me for that.'

'I don't blame you,' Ruth replied. 'But if I do that, even without a message, he will know that it has come between us. Do you want him to know that? No, Sean, you shall be the one to get rid of it, by any means you choose. I daresay Mr Tweed has an orphanage he is interested in. Give it there and let them sell it.'

'Very well,' Sean agreed reluctantly.

'And now you and I will go back to where we were, as if last night had never happened.'

'I'd give anything if it hadn't,' Sean said eagerly. 'Anything. And I assure you, it'll never happen again.'

'I believe you,' Ruth replied. 'Also I share the blame. I know I'm not the best wife in the world.'

'But you are, you are!' Sean said impulsively. 'I daresay it's not your fault that you can't love me more.'

But I could act as though I loved him, Ruth chided herself. I could do loving things. She thought of Francis Priestley's mother, acting a part all those years.

'I do love you, Sean,' she told him quietly. She could say the words which comforted him with truth. In her own way, though it was not his, she did.

'If you like,' she said, 'after supper we will go to Niblo's together for a glass of wine.'

Her intentions were genuine but she could not help reflecting, as she left the house some time later on her husband's arm, that the sight of them in such amity might still the speculations of those of her boarders who did not quite believe in nightmares.

Two days later the new board went up by the side of the door. It was placed there in the morning and for the rest of the day Ruth found herself, on some pretext or other, frequently going out of the house in order to feast her eyes on it. When Sean came home from work he appeared with a face like thunder, but said nothing. His attitude to Aurora had not changed, though Ruth could see the effort he made, and he was not unkind to the child. But Aurora sensed that there was something wrong. From time to time she looked at him with a strange, lonely feeling inside her that she had never before known.

Halfway through supper Sean pushed his plate from him, rose from the table and put his jacket on to go out.

'Please Sean,' Ruth said quickly, 'remember that Ernest and Charlotte are arriving this evening and that you have promised to go to the railroad station to meet them.'

He left without answering her but to Ruth's great relief he reappeared in less than an hour. He could have been no further than a walk around the streets.

Ruth sometimes thought that part of Sean's trouble was that he had not adapted, as she had, to city life. At least with Joss Barnet he had the care of the horses, which he understood – but making chairs gave him little satisfaction.

Maria, meanwhile, was getting ready to go to the theatre. She had seemed totally in the clouds these last few days, Ruth thought. She doubted if her sister had even noticed the strain between herself and Sean, and Sean and Aurora, so taken up was she with some sort of interior life.

'How do I look?' Maria said, entering. 'Will I do?' Standing in the doorway she struck an attitude which would have done credit to a fashion drawing in a magazine. She wore her new blue dress, which she had finished only by sewing late into the previous night. Its wide hooped skirt emphasised, as it was intended to, her tiny waist, and the low-cut neck showed the curve of her breasts. Around her head she wore a confection of creamy net and chiffon – a bonnet would not be quite suitable for stalls at the theatre. She would have liked a jewel for her hair, but alas she had none.

'You look beautiful,' Ruth told her. 'Your dress is a triumph.'

Observing her sister, Ruth realised with something of a shock that she herself had not had a new dress for almost three years. In any case her last one had been dark and serviceable, suitable for her position in the boarding-house. Apart from the dresses which Mrs Carson had handed down to her, and these were now well worn and also out-of-date, she had nothing to wear for a special occasion – and in two days time she would be visiting the World's Fair.

No matter. Even if she could afford to spend the money on a dress, it was too late now. She resigned herself to apearing like a dark moth against the butterfly that was her sister. But she would be lost in the crowd. No-one would see her.

'Thank you,' Maria said. 'I do hope Mrs Seaford is ready, we don't want to be late.'

*Man of My Heart* was a delight! Maria sat enraptured, watching Clive Masterson stride across the stage, listening to his mellifluous voice. When he looked into the eyes of Clarissa, the heroine, it was as if he was looking into Maria's own eyes. When at the end of the first act he enfolded the leading lady in the most chaste, the most delicate of embraces, Maria closed her eyes and *was* Clarissa. She felt she must swoon with emotion, but when the storm of clapping began, marking the fall of the curtain for the first interval, she came to quickly. Opening her eyes, she seized Mrs Seaford by the arm and dragged her to her feet. Mrs Seaford was still clapping, dazed by the beauty of the performance so far.

'Quickly!' Maria said. 'We must move quickly!'

'Move? Whatever for? Maria, are you ill?' Surely she wasn't going to be tiresome enough to be taken ill in the middle of the play? But she did look unusually flushed and her eyes were too bright. 'Oh Maria, have you got a fever?' Mrs Seaford enquired.

'Of course not, silly! I am perfectly well. Oh Doris, just follow me quickly or we shall be too late!'

'Too late? What for?'

'We are going to see Clive Masterson – in his dressing-room.'

'Clive Masterson . . .?'

Maria did not stop to answer. It was all Mrs Seaford could do to keep up with her companion as she pushed past an attendant and went through an inconspicuous door, low down near the side of the stage.

They were in a passage which, with it grimy whitewashed walls and stone-flagged floor, was so totally different from the crimson plush and gilt trimmings of the front of the theatre that Mrs Seaford thought they must be in another building.

'Maria,' she wailed. 'Where are you taking us?'

'Don't worry,' Maria said loftily. 'Remember I am an actress by profession. I know my way backstage and one theatre is much like another. All narrow passages and stairways. Ah! Here we are!'

They had emerged into a small bare hall where an attendant sat. He jumped to his feet when he saw them.

'Here! Where've you sprung from? You're not supposed to come in that way!'

Maria smiled sweetly at him.

'Ah, but I am a member of the profession! We are here to see Mr Masterson. Will you kindly tell him that Miss Maria Appleby is waiting, with a friend, and that she has something to deliver to him?'

'Mr Masterson won't see you now. Not in the interval,' the man said.

'I think you'll find he will. I'm sure *you* could persuade him, if he needed persuasion, which he won't.' She spoke with more confidence than she felt. Could she be wrong? But she felt sure he had left the gloves behind deliberately, and he had certainly not been back for them. And he *had* given her the tickets. Tomorrow she was leaving Stewart's and she could not possibly take the gloves with her. If she did not accomplish it now she might never see Clive Masterson again, except across the footlights.

The thought was so terrible that her courage was at once renewed. Pressing a coin into the doorman's hand she gave him her most dazzling smile, standing close to him so that her perfume assailed his nostrils.

'Miss Maria Appleby,' she reminded him. 'Please hurry! The interval is only twenty minutes!'

'Very well then,' he agreed. 'Shall I say a fellow Thespian?'

'No!' Maria said quickly. 'Just my name and that I have something to deliver. He will understand.'

Within the shortest possible time they were being shown into Clive Masterson's dressing-room. Maria extended her gloved hand – one of the perquisites of working where she did was that she had been able to buy these beautiful white silk gloves, which were only the teeniest bit faulty, at a considerably reduced price. She had no need to feel ashamed of the hand over which Clive Masterson bent his lips in the most charming manner.

'Enchanté,' he murmured. 'How kind of you to seek me out – and how devastated I am that my humble dressing-room is not tidier to receive you and your friend.' He glanced enquiringly at Mrs Seaford.

'Allow me to present Mrs Doris Seaford,' Maria said. She had almost forgotten her chaperone's presence.

Mrs Seaford extended her hand like someone in a dream. She could hardly believe that any of this was happening.

'Pray do not apologise for the state of your dressing-room,' Maria said. 'It is exactly as it should be.' She averted her eyes from the messiness of the dressing-table and the heap of dirty clothes in a corner of the floor. Then she closed her eyes and breathed in deeply. 'Ah, the smell of greasepaint! How I love it!'

'You like the smell of greasepaint?'

'Indeed yes. But then I have been used to it. It is of all odours the most nostalgic.'

'Used to it? You can't mean . . . you're not telling me . . .?'

'Yes. I too have trodden the boards,' Maria said. 'With the Jamieson Players in Scotland. You may have heard of them?'

It would be truer to say that she had swept the boards with a long broom, helped to move the stage furniture, placed the properties so that they were to hand for the actors, packed and unpacked as they moved from town to town. But the details were hazy now. The way she remembered it she might well have been Clarissa in *Man of My Heart*.

'I am sure I must have. At present I cannot recall . . . but you make me wish that I had accepted one of the many offers I have had to tour Europe! We might have met earlier. But better late than never!' He gave full value to the words, said them as if they were newly-minted.

Maria blushed prettily. 'Well, here we are,' she said. 'I have brought the gloves you – inadvertently – left behind.'

'I hoped,' he said. 'I dared to hope . . .'

So I was right, Maria thought.

'I am to leave Stewart's tomorrow,' she told him. 'I went there only to oblige, of course. It is not my true bent, as I am sure you understand.'

'Of course,' he said. 'Then where . . .?'

'I live with my sister. She is the owner of a very high-class boarding establishment – Appleby's, in Spring Street.'

A bell rang. A boy knocked on the door and called out, 'Second act, Mr Masterson!'

'Alas!' Clive Masterson said ruefully, 'my muse calls me! But is it possible that I might have the pleasure of calling on you at your sister's establishment, my dear Miss Appleby?'

Maria feigned delighted astonishment. 'Why, I think so,' she replied, prettily confused. 'My sister would be pleased to meet you. But do not call on Tueday. We are to visit the World's Fair then.'

She held out her hand in farewell and then she was gone, dragging a still-dazed Mrs Seaford behind her. Afterwards Mrs Seaford realised that she had not said one single word in the presence of Clive Masterson.

Ruth was shocked by Charlotte's appearance. She had last seen her on the day they had disembarked from the *Flamingo*, now more than four years ago. She had been thin and pale then, after the terrible voyage, but that was nothing compared to her appearance now. It was not only that the flesh seemed to have melted off her, so that her bones were no more than covered, but the bones themselves appeared to have shrunk. She was smaller, slighter, than ever Ruth could have imagined. Her face, the skin tightly drawn over her cheekbones and jaw, was grey. The only colour left was in her hair – still vibrantly red and beautiful.

Fear struck into Ruth when she regarded her sister-in-law. She wondered if Ernest, used to seeing his wife every day, was quite aware of the devastating change.

'You must be tired after your long journey,' she sympathised.

'The train was reasonably comfortable,' Charlotte admitted. 'I slept some of the time. But yes, I would be glad to go to bed early. I'm always tired these days.'

She sounded gentler than Ruth remembered her, none of the waspishness there. As she showed Charlotte to the bedroom – she and Ernest were to have her room and Sean's while Ruth slept with Maria and Sean had a narrow bed in an attic – she felt a surge of affection for her sister-in-law. She wanted to cosset her, take some of the burden which she knew, by the look in her eyes, that her cousin was carrying.

Why had they not felt like this about each other before? What a pity that they had got across each other, quarrelled. And yet if we had not, Ruth thought suddenly, my life would have been totally different. I would have been living in Wisconsin. She knew for certain that in New York she was where she wanted to be. Apart from anyone else, or anything that had happened to her, she felt that she had been made for New York.

'I hope you have everything you want,' Ruth said. 'Tell me if you have not.' Impulsively, she folded her arms around Charlotte and kissed her on the cheek. How utterly thin and frail she was, almost weightless. But Charlotte did not draw away from her as she would once have done.

'Sleep well, Charlotte. And you must rest in the morning since you are going to see Dr Cooke in the afternoon. Also, if you feel that to visit the World's Fair on Tuesday is too much for you, why then, we won't go. No-one will mind in the least.'

'I'd like to go,' Charlotte said. 'And I know Ernest is looking forward to it. He wants to see the latest in farm machinery.'

'Tell me,' Ruth asked, 'are you happy in Wisconsin? I don't mean is Ernest happy – I mean are *you?*'

'I've never been so happy in my life,' Charlotte said.

'I'm glad.'

'Sometimes,' Charlotte said slowly, 'I'm so happy that it almost frightens me. Can you understand that?'

'I think so.'

When Ruth went back to the sitting-room, Ernest and Sean were deep in conversation about Wisconsin. Sean was clearly fascinated by Ernest's glowing account of the life there. Maria sat silently. Since returning from the theatre she had not had a word for the cat. But hers was a happy silence, Ruth thought, noting the colour in her sister's cheeks and the soft light in her eyes. She had no time now to ask her about the theatre visit, but clearly it had been a success.

'It's a sight easier to work at something ye enjoy,' Sean said to Ernest.

Ruth felt yet another pinprick of guilt. Sean's life, she supposed, was so much less satisfying than her own. He worked; he drew his small wages; he drank at Donnelly's. He lived in his wife's establishment, surrounded by his wife's business. But New York had given her the company of people she liked and respected, people who depended on her. It had given her a decent living, independence, a bright future. And it had given her her daughter, whom Sean now no longer wished to share.

When Ernest and Maria had gone to bed – Maria as if still floating on a cloud – Sean said, 'I think we should consider it.'

'Consider what?' But she knew.

'Settling in Wisconsin. We could make a fresh start there, Ruth. Leave all our troubles behind us.'

'You can't be serious,' Ruth said. 'We've discussed all this before. I have no wish to make a fresh start in Wisconsin. We're well enough here.'

'*You* are well enough! And that's all that counts, isn't it?' His voice was sharp with bitterness.

'You can't expect me to throw up a thriving business. . . .'

'Ye said yourself – though I suppose it suits ye to forget it now – ye said "once the loan is paid we can sell the business at a profit." Or don't ye remember that?'

'I remember it,' Ruth agreed. 'I said if we wanted to. Well, I don't want to!'

'*You* again,' he shouted. 'When do we start to consider what *I* want? I want to go to Wisconsin.'

'Then go there!' Ruth retorted. 'And in the meantime keep your voice down. You can be heard all over the house.'

'And that's another thing,' he said. 'I want to live where I can raise my voice in my own home. Is that too much to ask?'

'If the home's to be in Wisconsin, yes it is,' Ruth stormed. 'I will not go! I will not leave Appleby's!'

'Appleby's!' Sean said. 'That's the root of the trouble. It's no longer Barnet that stands between you and me. It's Appleby's!'

It was true. She recognised that in her heart she had known for a long time. She had known it on that day, which now seemed an age ago, when the Carsons, Professor Woodburn, and Joss Barnet had between them decided that she could take over the running of the boarding-house, had decided her future for her. She had known it before she was pregnant.

Dr Cooke, behind his large, leather-covered desk, looked at the woman who sat opposite him. Should he tell her or should he not? Every week of his life he faced this dilemma, and came no nearer to solving it. Whichever way he chose he could never be sure that he was right. This young woman who sat there now, so thin, so grey, so desperately ill and so late in coming to him, what did she want of him in the circumstances? Did she want hope? It might be false, but it might strengthen her for a little while. Or did she want the truth, which would be hard and bitter to bear, but, patients had told him, sometimes brought its own strength. Which should he choose?

She answered for him.

'I want the truth, Doctor. The whole truth. I came to you because my husband wanted me to, and because if there was a chance, I wanted to live for my baby. But I think I knew before I came. So please don't put me off.'

She had the same quiet dignity that so many of his patients showed in similar situations. He marvelled at each one of them.

'The growth is inoperable, Mrs Gaunt. It has grown too big.'

'If I had come earlier?' Her voice – a pleasant English voice – she was a long way from home – was steady.

He shook his head. 'It's impossible to tell. Perhaps it would have made no difference.'

'So what is your advice?'

'Go home, Mrs Gaunt. Spend your time with your husband and children. I shall give you a good supply of pills, which will help with the pain. And when you've finished them, write to me and I will send you more.' But she would never finish them. He was certain of that.

'I see. I'm grateful to you for telling me the truth. There's just one thing. . . .'

'Yes?'

'Don't tell my husband. I'd prefer him to think that the pills were a cure.'

'Are you sure?' He had met the husband in the waiting-room before Mrs Gaunt had come in alone for her examination. He seemed a decent sort, the kind of man who would support and comfort his wife. Now they would face her death – for the husband would guess before long if he hadn't already – as two separate, suffering beings, each of them alone.

'I'm quite sure,' Charlotte said. She had dreaded breaking down, and she had not done so. Nor would she now.

She went into the waiting-room, smiling. 'He's given me some pills,' she told Ernest. 'I feel better already, just for seeing him.'

'Will there be swings?' Aurora asked. Swings were the passion of her life. I must get one fixed up for her in the yard, Ruth thought, though who would have the time to push it was another matter.

'Will there be a Punch and Judy?' She had never seen a Punch and Judy show, though Ruth had described it to her from her own memories of Barnswick Fair.

'I don't know that either. But if you don't stand still long enough for me to brush your hair we shall never get there!'

Her daughter, Ruth thought as she set the pale pink bonnet on the child's dark hair and smoothed down her white foulard dress with its tiny basque trimmed with satin ribbon, looked utterly adorable.

'There!' she said. 'You'll do. Uncle Ernest and Aunt Charlotte are waiting for us. I wonder how long Aunt Maria is going to be?'

'Where is Papa?' Aurora asked.

'He has to work today.'

They waited another ten minutes until Maria came from her room, wearing the blue dress she had worn to the theatre, but with a wisp of cream lace filling in the low neckline. Her bonnet was the same blue as her dress, and both matched her eyes. Ruth, catching sight of herself in the mirror, thought how sombre she looked in comparison, in her brown and cream outfit. Even Charlotte was wearing a new bonnet, which Ernest had bought for her on the way back from the doctor yesterday. Both he and Charlotte had returned from the visit looking more cheerful. He had insisted on the new bonnet to celebrate.

May came into the room.

'The hired carriage is at the door, ma'am. And Mrs Cruse says you're not to worry about a thing. We'll manage.'

'Thank you, May,' Ruth said. 'I shall be back in time to help with the supper.'

As they were about to leave the room Sammy appeared behind May.

'Mr Priestley presents his compliments, missa, and says can you spare him a minute before you leave?'

She had been expecting such a message. Last evening Mr Priestley's mother had arrived in New York and he had asked whether he might bring her next day to see Appleby's.

'It will be a come-down after the Astor House Hotel,' Ruth said. 'But Mrs Priestley will be most welcome.'

He smiled. 'Being my mother she would like to see where I live. And I would like you to meet her.'

'Will you wait in the carriage for me?' Ruth asked the others. 'I shan't be long.'

A moment ago she had thought how smart and fashionable Maria looked. Now, confronted by Mrs Priestley, she saw true elegance. Her gown was of heavy satin in two shades of blue, streaked with silver; the deep basque, the shoulder epaulettes and the bottom of the wide, hooped skirt thickly fringed with cream silk. Her bonnet, the brim lined with stiffened lace, perched on the back of her head to show her hair, red-brown like her son's, but brighter.

But it was not only her attire. Her elegance was also in the way she stood, next to her son, one expensively-gloved hand resting lightly on the sofa table, and in her finely-featured, sensitive face.

'Thank you for looking after my son so well,' Mrs Priestley

said. 'He tells me he is very comfortable here.'

'Mr Priestley is not difficult to please,' Ruth replied.

Mrs Priestley nodded agreement. 'And now that he is to leave you. . . .'

Leave? But of course, he was going home to Williamsburg for the long vacation.

'Yes,' Mrs Priestley smiled. 'It is the dearest hope of all of us that his marriage to Miss Bond – so unfortunately delayed by her ill-health – will take place in the fall. We are all praying for it. And my dear boy has been so patient!'

'I did not realise it was to be so soon,' Ruth said. 'But I am glad to hear of Miss Bond's recovery.'

So he would not be coming back to New York. She knew that the couple planned to live in Williamsburg so that his wife would not be too far away from her family. A few days more and she would not see him again.

'Ah!' Mrs Priestley said. 'I can see by your face that he has neglected to tell you! Francis, that was thoughtless of you. Mrs O'Farrell will need to re-let your rooms – so if she faces any loss of money you must be sure to compensate her.'

How could I have thought that she looked sensitive, Ruth asked herself.

'It doesn't signify,' she replied. 'And now if you will excuse me, my family is waiting.'

Although she had seen the outside of the Crystal Palace building, and that of the Latting Tower which stood next to it, Ruth was overcome by its magnificence. It was a miracle of glass and metal, built in the shape of a Greek cross, with a high, graceful dome rising from the centre. It seemed, as they looked at it, as though the July sun was caught and reflected in every one of the thousands of panes of glass; sparkling, gleaming, transforming the whole area in which it stood to a magical wonderland.

Maria, forgetting for a moment her worldly airs, was as transported as a small child who sets eyes on fairyland.

'Oh Ruth, it's just too stupendous for words!' She

screamed in ecstasy, but since several hundred sightseers, dwarfed by its size and looking like so many brightly-coloured insects, were behaving in a similar fashion, it did not matter.

Inside the buildings the broad aisles, the great arched naves, the galleries, were bathed in light and sunshine which gave added colour and glow to the goods with which they were crammed: Sèvres china, Gobelin tapestries, armour from the Tower of London, musical instruments, great sculptures, jewellery.

Ruth gasped. 'There's so much to see! We shall never get around everything!'

'You're right,' Ernest agreed. 'And as I want to look at farm machinery and I know Charlotte wants to see a new way of preserving food, from France, it'd make sense if we split up.' That way, he thought, Charlotte could also take her time, sit down for a rest whenever she wanted to.

So it was agreed. They chose a time and place for meeting up again, after which Ruth and Maria, Aurora held firmly by both hands between them, set off down the main aisle.

'*I* want to see all the silks,' Maria said. 'It said in the paper that they were all the way from Turkey, Kashmir, India, as well as from France. What do you want to see, Ruth?'

'The porcelain, I think. And the glass and the silver. All the things I can't afford to buy.'

'Aurora wants to go on a swing,' the child announced.

'Only notice the fashions, Ruth,' Maria said reverently as they strolled along. 'See how wide the skirts are! And the materials so rich. And such trimmings! Braid, lace, fringing. I declare I'm full of ideas for improving my wardrobe!'

'If the skirts were not so wide we should have more room to move,' Ruth replied. 'I never saw such crowds.'

'And every man in a top hat!' Maria cried estatically. 'What a sight! And all the chatter. Do you hear all the different languages. Ruth? Do you suppose people have come from all over the world?'

'I suspect most of them are immigrants,' Ruth said. 'They say there's every nationality living in New York now.'

'But don't they learn to speak English? How can they manage otherwise?'

'The ones who learn English progress most, I daresay. The others stay inside their own families or mix only with their own race.'

'Oh do look at this beautiful silverware!' Maria interrupted. 'And from England, too!'

It was exquisite: elegant candlesticks, cruets, snuff boxes, vases. Ruth had never seen the like. While she was still immersed in its beauty she felt Maria tugging fiercely at her sleeve.

'Ruth, it's him! It's Clive Masterson, Ruth, he's walking towards us! Oh Ruth, I could *die*!'

As Ruth looked up, Clive Masterson and his companion reached the two women. Maria's face was a burst of sunshine as she greeted the actor, but Ruth turned white as a sheet as she saw the man with him. The companion was Joss Barnet.

He looked at Ruth long and steadily, not smiling, simply looking at her. It was his eyes which betrayed him, as she knew hers must be betraying her. As they looked at each other, the sounds and movements of the scores of people who milled around them blotted out. There was no-one except the two of them in the whole wide world. It was as if the long interval of almost four years was wiped out in a moment's meeting.

# 24

Clive Masterson and Maria spoke simultaneously.

'Why, Mr Masterson, I didn't expect . . .!'

'Miss Appleby!'

They were delighted with each other, both expressing the greatest surprise at the encounter. But he has come on purpose today, Maria thought happily. I knew he would because I told him I would be here.

She was right. Masterson had, with some difficulty because these days Joss Barnet could seldom be dragged away from his work, persuaded his friend to visit the Fair with him. It was only when he'd said, 'I want to introduce you to the prettiest girl in New York, a Miss Maria Appleby,' that Barnet had agreed. If it had occurred either to Clive or Maria that among the thousands who were attending the Fair they might, just possibly, not meet, they had both dismissed the thought at once. In their case, Fate would never be so unkind.

In those first few seconds of rapturous greeting neither had time to notice that Ruth and Joss Barnet were staring at each other in thunderstruck silence.

She is as lovely as ever, Joss Barnet thought. After all this time he still burned with desire at the sight of her and he was well aware that his feelings must show in his face, as hers so clearly did in hers. But he could not dissemble, not yet. It had been so long, he had missed her so much.

Ruth recognised the truth as he looked at her, the truth of his feelings as well as her own. It was all there – the longing, the desire, the frustrations of almost four years – and she knew that the message in his eyes, in those seconds before they spoke, was reflected in her own.

It took Maria to break the spell.

'Why, it's Mr Barnet!' she cried. 'Please forgive me. I had not recognised you, but then we have only met once, briefly, and that some years ago.'

He bowed. 'I could not forget you,' he said gallantly. 'When my friend Mr Masterson waxed lyrical about a certain Miss Appleby he had met, I knew it could only be you!'

Maria gurgled with pleasure. 'But I am forgetting my manners,' she said. 'Ruth dear, allow me to introduce Mr Clive Masterson. My sister, Mrs Sean O'Farrell.'

'I am delighted to make your acquaintance, ma'am,' Clive Masterson said.

Ruth stood silently by while the light-hearted conversation continued. She was glad of the brief respite, for she must try to recover herself. In no way could she allow herself to indulge the feelings which had filled her at the sight of Joss Barnet. They must be suppressed at once, wiped out. There was no room in her life, now, for him. Yet her weakness was such, she thought, that at this moment he would only have to lift his little finger and she would follow wherever he led. He was looking at her again with that intensity which hynotised her. She could not turn away.

'I trust you are well?' he asked.

'Quite well, thank you.'

Words were no good. They could not express what was flowing between them. Then the awkward pause in their conversation, when they each struggled not to say what was in their hearts, was broken by Aurora tugging at her mother's skirt. Ruth had completely forgotten her daughter. For what seemed an age, yet was in reality no more than a minute or two she had felt no presence except Joss Barnet's.

'Mama!' Aurora implored. 'Where are the swings?'

Ruth pulled herself together. 'This is my daughter, Aurora,' she said. 'Our daughter' she wanted to say. 'She was three years old in June. Aurora, say how-do-ye-do to Mr Barnet.'

Two pairs of dark eyes surveyed each other as Aurora greeted Joss Barnet. They are so alike, Ruth thought. Surely Maria must notice? And there was little wonder that Sean had taken against the child. The miracle was that he had not done so earlier. But perhaps when the child was younger the likeness had not been so apparent. It was as her daughter developed, left babyhood behind and became more of a person, that every day she grew more and more like her real father.

'Aurora,' Joss Barnet said. 'That's a pretty name.' She was flesh of his flesh and he could not take his eyes off her. He was drawn to her like a magnet. Though he had never grieved for his wife when she had left him, he missed his children sorely and scarcely ever saw them. How could he ensure that he did not lose this little creature, with the face so like the reflection he saw in his shaving mirror every morning? He longed to pick her up, hug her close to him. All he could do now was to hold out his hand and take her small one in it.

That was all he would ever be able to do. Though his blood was in her, she was not his. She belonged to her mother and to Sean O'Farrell, and there was no way he would ever be allowed to come near her.

'I want to go to the swings,' Aurora persisted.

'We must leave you,' Ruth said. 'There is so much to see and, as you can hear, my daughter has her priorities!'

'Then, Mrs O'Farrell, I hope I may be permitted to call upon you in Spring Street,' Clive Masterson smiled.

'Certainly,' Ruth replied.

It tore at her heart to leave Joss Barnet. It would have been better not to have met him. She must do everything in her power to forget him, to forget what she had seen in his eyes.

'How do you like him? What do you think of him?' Maria gushed hardly before they were out of earshot of the men. 'Don't you think he is quite devastatingly handsome?'

It took Ruth a second to realise that her sister was talking about the actor, who in the circumstances she had scarcely noticed.

'Why yes,' she said. 'He seems agreeable enough.'

'Agreeable?' Maria cried. 'Oh Ruth, he is *so* much more than agreeable! I do believe he is the most charming, good-looking man I have ever met in my life. I can't wait to have him call on us!'

'I doubt that he'll wait long, either,' Ruth said.

She made an effort, walking around the Fair, to show interest in all the exciting and wonderful things on show, but her mind strayed constantly to Joss Barnet. In the few minutes she had been with him she had felt blinded to everything except his presence, almost as if he was touching her, holding her, while the world around them stood still. Now her thoughts were released, but though they ranged here and there, they came back all the time to him. He was thinner. He looked older, as if the past four years had not treated him kindly. She wondered about his marriage, asked herself, fearfully, if there was another woman in his life.

Then her thoughts went to Sean. Her husband needed her now as perhaps he had never done before. Poor Sean! He was so unsure of himself, so full of doubts. She would not let him down. She would do everything she could to make their marriage work. Everything, her conscience whispered, except go to Wisconsin.

'Maria?'

'Yes? Oh Ruth, do look at this brocade!' Maria's head was full of Clive Masterson yet, in contrast to her sister, the thought of him only enhanced the pleasure she took in everything she saw around her.

'I would be grateful if you would not mention to Sean that we met Mr Barnet.'

'If you say so.' Maria glanced at her sister with curiosity. She seemed in such a strange, faraway mood.

'The only reason is that to Sean, Mr Barnet's name acts as a red rag to a bull. They quarrelled when Mr Barnet was his employer and Sean cannot forget or forgive.'

'What did they quarrel about?' Maria asked.

'I don't remember,' Ruth said.

She was glad when the time came to meet up with Ernest

and Charlotte. They had walked what felt like miles without, in the whole of the Fair, finding a swing for Aurora. But there was a puppet show, and that had sufficed.

'Here is the tea pavilion. We can have tea and cream puffs and listen to the band while we rest. Oh my poor feet!'

'What about you, Charlotte? Are you not tired?' Ruth asked.

'I am a little,' Charlotte admitted. 'But we have rested several times. And it's all so exciting that I didn't feel as tired as I expected.'

After tea they left the Fair, but Ernest and Ruth wanted to go up the great tower which had been designed by Mr Waring Latting and erected nearby, as one of the great attractions of the Fair.

'There are seats here; I would rather wait for you,' Charlotte said.

'Me too,' Maria agreed. 'We'll sit on a bench and watch the world go by.'

Afterwards, the visit to the Latting Tower was clearer in Ruth's mind than any of the wonders she had seen in the Fair. Meeting up with her family had brought her thoughts back to reality and she could at last appreciate what was going on around her.

Not that she appreciated the ride in the new steam lift up the tower. She was afraid that at any minute the steam might give out and they would all be marooned in mid-air.

'What would happen to us then?' she asked Ernest nervously. Most of the women were asking the same question and all the men had the answer.

'We men would be able to climb down the iron framework,' a man standing next to her assured Ruth. 'You ladies would be hampered by your skirts – though come to think of it they might act as parachutes!' He laughed uproariously at the thought. 'But you need have no fear, ma'am. You would be rescued by the Fire Department, who would use ropes.'

Ruth shuddered. It sounded terrible. But the lift made its slow, jerky way to the second level, where they got out to climb a winding iron stairway to the top platform. 'Three hundred and fifty feet to the ground!' Ernest said. 'It doesn't seem possible.'

Standing on a cloud must be like this, Ruth thought. All New York was spread out before her. She felt like God: separate, remote, all-seeing.

Looking south she could see the city solid with buildings as far up as Twenty-Third Street, and far higher than that the long straight avenues were already laid and paved, but by no means built up. She tried to pick out Appleby's, taking her bearings from the clearly visible Washington Square and the university – but too many buildings got in the way.

She walked around the platform and joined Ernest, who was standing on the north side. 'There's plenty of open country this way,' he said. 'They'll never build on all that.'

'I suppose not,' Ruth agreed. 'See! That's where the new Central Park is to be!' It had been discussed for years, and now a site had been chosen.

Together they walked around to the east platform, where Ruth was lucky enough to get a turn on the telescope, which so far had been monopolised by youths. She looked due east, seeking First Avenue and Dutch Hill, about which Sean had told her, though he would never let her go there, saying it was quite unsuitable.

'Sean says the people there are almost wild,' she told Ernest. 'Some live in shanties, but a lot live in the open, among the rocks like wild animals. They work in the quarries when there's work to be had.'

Ruth wondered what these people – they were said to be mostly German – had expected when they had left their own country and made that terrible voyage across the ocean. Surely not this? She thought about the bustling, prosperous crowds on Broadway, the shops filled with goods, the fashionable men and women passing through the doors of the hotels, visiting the theatres, walking in the squares. It was true what Sean said. In New York there were two worlds.

Deep in thought, she didn't realise until someone nudged her in the back that a line of people had formed behind her, waiting to use the telescope. Surely the platform was more crowded now? Supposing the structure gave way? Who knew how many it would hold – and where was Ernest? He was nowhere to be seen. In a panic, she called his name.

'Ernest! Ernest!'

Of course he would never hear her. Her voice would be carried away on the wind. She called again, louder, and then she felt his hand on her shoulder.

'I think we should go,' she said quickly. 'There are too many people. Something awful might happen.'

He laughed. 'Nowt's going to happen. But we should go. Charlotte and Maria'll think we've vanished into the sky!'

But Charlotte and Maria, when they rejoined them, showed no signs of anxiety. They were sharing a bench with a woman and two small boys.

'The time passed quickly,' Maria said. 'We have been talking with this lady while Aurora played with her children.'

'I think we must take the omnibus back,' Ruth suggested. 'It won't be easy to hire a carriage.' She did not often take Aurora on the omnibus for fear of infection, but today she would make an exception.

As the omnibus made its way up Forty-Second Street, across to Fourth Avenue and then down to Union Square Ernest held his wife's hand. 'Home tomorrow, lass,' he whispered. She gave his hand an answering squeeze. It was where she wanted to be; home with her children, home with Benjamin.

Maria thought of Clive Masterson. When would he call? What should she wear? Should they offer him tea, or would it be more fashionable to proffer a glass of Madeira wine?

Ruth forgot everything about the day except that she had seen Joss Barnet. In the incongruous atmosphere of the omnibus, pressed in on all sides by sweating bodies, her daughter heavy on her lap, she longed to be in his bed and in his arms. It was a long time since she had made love with anyone.

'Would you like to help me serve the parlour tea, Maria?' Ruth asked that same evening. 'Unless you wish to, Sean?'

'I do not,' he said emphatically.

So Ruth poured the tea and Maria handed it around. She was prettily flushed, and had the air of excitement she had worn all day. Handing Mrs Seaford's tea she whispered to her, 'He was there! Clive Masterson was at the World's Fair!'

'I shall be going away in a day or two,' Miss Fontwell said to Ruth. 'I have received an invitation to stay with my brothers in Buffalo for the summer vacation. First one and then the other.' Ruth was touched to see the pleasure with which Miss Fontwell imparted this information. She wondered if she had never before been invited.

Appleby's would soon be quite depleted. Professor Woodburn had already left for a walking holiday in the Vermont hills and would not return until early September. Mr and Mrs Wellbake had gone to stay with relatives in Concord, Massachusetts. And I wish the relatives the joy of Martin, Ruth thought.

'And I have been invited to stay with my friend, Miss Cassell, at her parents' home on Staten Island,' Miss Potter announced. 'Where thank heaven there will be no small children!'

'Dear me! My husband and I will be quite bereft, everyone going off like this,' Mrs Seaford said. She was truly thankful that Maria was no longer tied to Stewart's. They would be able to arrange several little trips to help pass the time. Then there was the affair of Clive Masterson, which promised a little excitement. The days were so long here, with no household responsibilities to discharge.

When Ruth returned with Maria to her own sitting-room she was aware, as soon as she stepped through the doorway, that there was an atmosphere. Ernest and Sean were talking, but broke off abruptly. In the silence which followed

Ruth looked to Sean for an explanation. He met her look defiantly as though she had already criticised him.

'We've been discussing Wisconsin,' he said quickly. 'I want us to go. It'll be better for us there. New York isn't healthy.'

Ruth bit back the angry retort which rose to her lips. At all costs she must keep calm.

'New York is perfectly healthy, Sean,' she replied. 'Maria, would you help me to serve our supper? I'm sure everyone must be hungry.'

There was an uncomfortable silence while they took their places at the table, broken only by Maria who said, '*I* think New York is the best place in the world!' No-one took any notice of her.

'It's no use avoiding the subject,' Sean declared as Ruth served the food. 'It won't go away.'

'Nevertheless I think it better not to discuss it just now,' Ruth stated firmly.

'You mean not in front of Ernest and Charlotte,' Sean said. 'But that's where you're wrong. They're concerned. You know they've always wanted us to go, and I for one am in favour.'

'And I am not,' Ruth retorted.

'Well, goodness knows I don't want to come between man and wife,' Ernest said. 'But I don't think you're giving it enough consideration, Ruth. You were always the same when you got an idea into your head; wouldn't budge for no-one. It's a grand life there. I know you'd do well and be happy.'

'I'm doing well enough here,' Ruth pointed out.

'But are ye really happy here?' Sean persisted. 'Tell the truth!'

She didn't answer. It was a question she felt he had no right to ask in front of other people, even those as close as Ernest and Charlotte. She had known moments of pure happiness and times of deep distress in New York – and most of the time something in between. Life wasn't one level plain of contentment. But she wasn't prepared to argue this at the supper table.

Sean thumped the table so that the dishes rattled. 'Well, I tell ye here and now, Ruth. I'm going to Wisconsin. My mind's made up. I won't ask ye to come and rough it with me. I'll work hard and build a home for us, and then I'll come and fetch ye both.'

Charlotte, listening uncomfortably, felt a wave of her old resentment. Why should Ruth have her way smoothed for her? Why shouldn't she rough it like everyone else? But the resentment passed quickly. She wanted Ruth to come. Ruth would give strength and comfort to Ernest in the future.

'And what sort of life do you think it would be for Aurora?' Ruth demanded.

'Here, steady on . . .!' Ernest broke in. '*We've* got children, you know!'

'I'm sorry, Ernest. I'm sure it's a good life if it's what you want for your family. People just want different things, that's all.'

'I don't want to leave New York,' Maria cried. She couldn't bear it now, to have to leave Clive Masterson.

'It's a healthy normal life there,' Sean said. 'What's so marvellous about being brought up in a New York boarding-house? Where does a child fit into that?'

'She fits in with me,' Ruth snapped. 'My daughter fits with me!'

She knew at once that she had said the wrong thing. It didn't need the wounded look on Sean's face to tell her that. At a time when he was deeply feeling the distance between himself and Aurora, Ruth had, by her hurtful words, pushed him further away than ever. She could have bitten out her tongue.

'We'd best be getting to bed,' Ernest said. 'You look tired, Charlotte love.'

When they, and Maria, had gone, Sean returned to the subject. He had quietened down now, but inside himself he felt more than ever determined. He must somehow make Ruth see that there was no happiness for the two of them here, and never would be. Here they had separate goals; sometimes he felt they lived separate lives. Everything, just about everything, came between them. In the country everything would right itself. In no time at all they would probably have children.

'I've got to talk to ye, Ruth,' he said.

'What more is there to be said?'

She was tired. The events of the day, the meeting with Joss Barnet, had drained her emotions. Since arriving home she had tried hard to keep Joss out of her mind, and because there had been plenty to do she had almost succeeded. But now she felt worn out. She wanted to close her eyes against everything.

'Just to repeat what I told ye earlier, Ruth. I'm going. And when the time's right I shall fetch ye. You're my wife and I'll expect ye to come.'

'And I repeat – I shan't. Now or ever. If you come back it must be because you want to be here with me.'

'But don't ye see, Ruth,' Sean pleaded, 'I've never belonged here. It's not my place!'

Hearing those words, she thought she did understand. It was why she had left Yorkshire – because there had been no place for her. Now, though she was not totally sure she had found her final place, she felt that it was near, waiting to be discovered. But for Sean, she thought, there might still be a long search.

Two days later Ruth went to the railroad station to see her cousins off – and Sean with them. She had announced to the boarders that Sean's health had been giving some concern and that he was to have a lengthy visit to her cousins to build him up again. She couldn't tell whether they believed her or not, but if not, they put up a convincing pretence, and that was all she required from them. Mrs Seaford, Ruth was sure, did not believe a word of it. Sooner or later she would worm the truth out of Maria.

They were early for the train. The waiting on the platform, in the July heat, seemed interminable; and between Sean and Ruth, at any rate, there were no words left to be said.

At last it was time to board. Ruth embraced her cousins, wondering, as she held Charlotte's thin body against her own, whether she would ever see her again. She watched Sean lift Aurora into his arms and hold her close for a second. When he put her down again she started to cry. 'Aurora wants to go with you, Papa! Take Aurora with you!'

Maria took her niece by the hand and tried to comfort her, while Ernest and Charlotte boarded the train and Ruth and Sean made their farewells.

'I bear ye no ill will, Ruth,' Sean said.

'Nor I you, Sean.'

He hesitated, as if he didn't know what to say next, or how to move away.

'Do ye remember the picnic by the Hudson River, Ruth? Do ye remember that day?'

'I do,' she said. 'It was a happy one.'

'And our wedding day?'

'That was happy too, Sean. I owe you more than I can ever repay. I don't forget.'

He kissed her with cold lips. There were tears in his eyes, and in hers. Then he turned away and boarded the train only seconds before it began to move. Maria, Aurora and Ruth stood on the platform, waving until the train was out of sight.

When they reached home, May and Mrs Cruse were all sombre excitement, which had nothing to do with Sean's departure.

'Mr Priestley had one of those new telegraph wire things,' May said. 'Only it was a piece of paper. I don't see how. . . .'

'What did it say?' Ruth asked impatiently.

'Oh, I don't know that,' May said. 'I took it straight to Mr Priestley. He left straight away. He looked ever so upset.'

'May, stop blethering and give Mrs O'Farrell the note,' Mrs Cruse ordered. 'He left a note for you.'

'To be given to you as soon as you came in – and here it

is!' May produced it triumphantly from her apron pocket.

Ruth tore it open.

'Dear Mrs O'Farrell (she read) I have just received the sad news that my fiancée is very ill and I must go to her. I cannot say when I shall be back in New York but as soon as I have news I shall let you know.

My thoughts were with you on your sad errand today as I hope yours might be with me in my present distress.

Sincerely

Francis Priestley.'

'As I thought,' Ruth said. 'His fiancée is very ill. Poor Mr Priestley. They were to have been married in the fall.'

'Let's hope they still will be,' Mrs Cruse sighed.

'He could marry her on her death-bed,' May said lugubriously. 'It would be ever so romantic!'

Suddenly, Ruth felt utterly spent. She turned to Maria who had just come into the kitchen. 'Maria, will you look after Aurora for a little while? I have a blinding headache and I must lie down.'

She went to her bedroom and lay down on the bed, where from now on she must sleep alone. Then she buried her face in the pillow and wept, though whether for herself, for Joss Barnet, for Sean – or even for Francis Priestley's sorrow – she was not sure. Everything came together in a torrent of grief.

After a while she got up again. She bathed her face in cold water, smoothed her hair, and went down to the kitchen to make a start on the cooking.

Three days had passed since the visit to the World's Fair and Clive Masterson had not called. 'Why?' Maria asked her puzzled reflection in the mirror. 'Why, why, why? Can he already have forgotten me? Has he met someone else?' She didn't doubt that the world of the theatre was full of beautiful women, and who would they have their eyes on except Clive Masterson? It stood to reason, and the thought drove her to the edge of despair. Yet there was nothing, absolutely nothing she could do about it. She had stayed in the house every single moment for the last three days so as not to miss him. But where was he? Please God, only let him call and I'll be good forever, she prayed. If Providence would arrange the first visit she felt confident that she could do the rest.

The reflection she saw in the mirror was pretty enough. In spite of her worries she looked blooming, and the anxiety in her blue eyes only made them more appealing. If only he would come!

She went downstairs and sat with her sewing. Perhaps by the time she had reached the end of this seam. . . .

'Could you go down to Canal Street for me?' Ruth asked. 'I need some fresh marjoram.'

'Oh Ruth, I don't feel like going out,' Maria said.

Ruth looked anxiously at her sister. Maria was besotted. 'You can't stay in the house forever, Maria. For your own sake. If he calls while you are out I will somehow make certain that he comes again.'

'I can't go out now,' Maria said firmly. She felt certain that he must come today.

An hour later her feelings were triumphantly justified as Clive Masterson was shown into the room.

'Why, what a surprise! I had not expected to see you so soon!' Maria said demurely.

He bowed over her hand. As his lips brushed her fingers she tingled from top to toe.

'It would have been sooner,' he replied, 'had I not been visited by an indisposition. Something I ate at the Fair, I daresay.'

'Oh dear! Then you have been out of the play?'

'In truth I should have been. But I could not disappoint my public,' he said bravely.

'Oh I do understand,' Maria told him fervently. 'You are speaking to one who recognises these things, don't forget. The show must go on!'

'What a breadth of understanding you have,' he said. 'I have thought that from the first!'

Maria went pink with pleasure. Ruth felt touched by her

sister's transparent happiness. She was like someone lit up from within.

'Will you take a glass of Madeira wine, Mr Masterson?' she asked.

'We usually take one at this time of day,' Maria broke in. We do no such thing, Ruth thought.

'Then in that case it will be my pleasure to join you,' Clive Masterson said.

Ruth longed to ask him how it was that he knew Joss Barnet, but even more than that, how Joss Barnet fared. Where he lived; what he was doing – and with whom? She wanted to hear everything about him, but she could not ask. As if he had read her thoughts, Clive Masterson spoke.

'What a coincidence it was that you knew my friend, Mr Josiah Barnet!'

'I had not seen him for some time,' Ruth said. 'Almost four years.' Had Joss spoken of her afterwards, she wondered? What had he said?

'Ah, then you are an older friend than I,' Masterson acknowledged. 'I met him only last year when he visited Richmond, and then renewed that friendship when we came to play in New York this season. Mr Barnet is fond of the theatre.'

'I didn't know that.' How little she really knew about him. Their times together had been brief, and always for the same purpose. She had no part in the rest of his life, though she had never wanted to shut him out of hers.

'Is he well? And his family?' she ventured.

'He is well enough. He spends most of his time working. As for his family, I have not met them and I think he does not see them often. His children live with his wife from whom, as I'm sure you know, he is divorced.'

'I had heard. And he does not. . . .' She faltered. 'He does not think of marrying again?'

Clive Masterson smiled. 'Who can say what he thinks of? He is the most enigmatic of men. But I have observed that he is a great favourite with the ladies!'

'I daresay *you* are that,' Maria said. She really thought

that Ruth had talked to Mr Masterson quite long enough. After all, he had come to see *her*.

'But there is no special one?' Ruth persisted.

'Oh, that I cannot tell you,' Clive Masterson said. 'I am not to that extent in his confidence.' But this conversation had gone on long enough. He had not come here to talk about Barnet. Though Mrs O'Farrell was quite charming, he had come to pay court to the delectable Maria.

'You flatter me!' he said, turning to her. 'But you of all people know what it is like in the profession. We are gods!' He took a thoughtful sip of his Madeira and turned his head so that his profile was etched against the light from the window. An actor must always be aware of the lighting.

Never had Maria been so conscious of the swift passage of time. It seemed they had only been chatting a few minutes when the clock on the mantelpiece chimed and she realised that a whole hour had passed. And not for one minute had Ruth left them! Not once had she excused herself to see to some household task. It was really too bad of her and Maria was sure that Clive Masterson must be equally disappointed. Were they never to see each other alone?

The visitor rose to his feet, reached for his hat and gloves.

'I must detain you no longer, ladies. I am sure you have many duties.'

'I was just about to walk down to Canal Street when you arrived,' Maria said quickly. 'In fact you were fortunate - and so was I - that you found me in. But I suppose I really must put on my bonnet and go now. Ruth is quite desperate for some fresh herbs and I cannot disappoint her, no matter how great the heat in Broadway.'

Ruth opened her mouth to protest, but Clive Masterson was too quick for her.

'Why, Miss Appleby, I am going down Broadway myself! Allow me the pleasure of accompanying you!'

We shall be alone at last, Maria thought ecstatically! Never mind that there would be a thousand people milling around Broadway. They did not count.

* * *

Three days later Maria and Ruth sat at the breakfast table.

'You should try to eat more,' Maria said. 'Once again you've eaten no breakfast. How can you do a morning's work on no more than a cup of coffee?'

'I'm not hungry,' Ruth replied. 'It's the heat. It takes one's appetite.'

'Not mine!' Maria said. She smothered her third corn-cake in maple syrup and poured herself another cup of coffee.

'And what tremendous task are you stoking yourself up for this morning?' Ruth asked.

'Didn't I tell you? I'm going with Doris Seaford to Arnold and Constable's on Canal Street. They say it's quite the best place for fabrics and she's going to help me make a new dress. Clive has seen me three times now in the same dress.'

'So it's "Clive", is it?' Ruth teased. But underneath her teasing she was anxious. There was no doubt in her mind that Maria fancied herself in love with Clive Masterson, and while he was personable and charming, well-mannered and generous – what did they really know about him? As an actor he would be here today and gone tomorrow. He might – perish the thought – even have a wife tucked away in Richmond, Virginia.

Maria blushed. They had been 'Clive' and 'Maria' to each other since they had walked down Broadway together a couple of days ago, but she had not told Ruth. Nor had she told Ruth that Clive was coming to take her for a walk tomorrow when he did not have a matinee.

'Oh Ruth, you do like him, don't you? Please say you do?'

'Of course I do. I like him very much. But I hope you're not too serious about him, Maria. We don't really know him, do we?'

'I do,' Maria said. 'Which is what really matters. I know he has a mother and two sisters who live in Richmond, Virginia. They are quite well off. He will go back there when the season here is finished.'

Six weeks only, she thought desperately. What would she do when he was gone? How would she live without him? At twenty, surprisingly late, she knew for the first time what it was like to be deeply in love. Ruth could not possibly understand. Between Ruth and Sean she was sure there was nothing like this. Indeed, she wondered if anyone had ever loved as she did. And she was sure Clive cared for her, therefore Fate could not be so cruel as to part them. She refused to believe that such a thing could happen.

Mrs Seaford came in. 'Are you ready, Maria?' she asked.

In the week since Sean's departure the friendship between Maria and Mrs Seaford had blossomed. They would have their heads together over the *Home Journal* to which Mrs Seaford subscribed, or be reading aloud to each other from the Society columns of the newspaper, or be endlessly discussing fashion. Except that they were too often in her sitting-room when she would have liked it to herself, Ruth did not mind. Indeed, she hoped that Mrs Seaford's ploys would divert Maria a little from Clive Masterson. She herself did not greatly care for Mrs Seaford, but no doubt she was harmless, and meant well.

'We'll take Aurora with us if you like,' Mrs Seaford offered. 'The fresh air will do her good.'

'There's not much freshness about it,' Ruth replied. 'Everywhere is stifling. But I'm sure she'd like to go.'

It was an added bonus of Mrs Seaford's friendship with Maria that both women were unusually fond of Aurora, and willing to have her with them whatever the occasion.

'I can't decide what colour for my new dress,' Maria said thoughtfully. 'Perhaps pale green. Pale green is so cool and elegant. But is it right for my colouring? Would a rich, rose-pink be better?' If only she knew Clive Masterson's favourite colour.

'I'm sure you'll look well in either,' Ruth told her. 'Please see that Aurora keeps in the shade as much as possible. The left-hand side of Broadway is shadier in the morning.'

'Oh Ruth, don't fuss!' Maria said. 'Of course we'll be sensible with her.'

'Well, I know what the summer heat of New York can do,' Ruth sighed. 'It certainly takes the life out of me.'

But she knew it was not only the heat which was affecting her. She had a listlessness of the spirit which was nothing to do with the weather. In some ways she had been relieved to see Sean go. It meant freedom from quarrels, from his drinking, from embarrassment in front of her staff and boarders and from the frustration and irritation which, lately, his presence had so often aroused in her. But in another way the fact that he was no longer there was a clear pointer to her failure. She felt lonely – and lonelier still since the brief meeting with Joss Barnet.

When she had first known Sean he had been the kindest, the most generous of men. She owed him so much. Yet she had not been able to make him happy. During the last three years she had become so used to thinking of herself as successful, as being able to achieve anything she set out to do, that she had hardly noticed how far she fell short in some – and in the more human – ways. But a week of nights in which she had lain awake thinking about these things had taught her a great deal.

'I must say you look rather pale,' Mrs Seaford said. 'I don't doubt you're missing Mr O'Farrell.'

'I daresay. Anyway, I must set to work. I intend to make some profiteroles this morning and they're fiddly things. Also, since no-one is interested in food in this hot weather, I thought I would do something in aspic for supper.'

'You spoil us,' Mrs Seaford said.

Ruth thought she was probably right. But as usual when she was not happy with her own behaviour, she sought some justification in trying to please her boarders. Penance in aspic!

Soon after Maria and Mrs Seaford had left with Aurora the postman called with a letter from Francis Priestley.

'Dear Mrs O'Farrell (he wrote) It is with a heavy heart that I write to inform you that my dear fiancée, Miss Helen Bond, died a few days ago and was buried yesterday.

My only consolation is that I was able to be with her at the end.

I shall be returning to New York sometime in the fall. I am by this same post acquainting Professor Woodburn of my sad loss.'

She passed on the news to May and Mrs Cruse. May shed a ready tear. Mrs Cruse, more closely acquainted with real life, took it philosophically.

'A blessing in disguise,' she said. 'An ailing wife is a burden to a man. Likewise a husband of course. I was thankful Cruse was taken sudden.'

When Aurora returned with Maria and Mrs Seaford she complained that her head hurt.

'Whereabouts, my love?' Ruth asked. 'Show Mama.'

'All over,' Aurora told her.

'I expect it's the heat of the day,' Ruth said. 'Come here and Mama will wash your hands and face in nice, cool water. Then you shall have a drink of lemonade.'

The hands Ruth took in hers were dry and burning, and minutes after she had washed the child's face it was flushed again and hot to the touch.

'Really Maria, you have let her be in the sun too long!' Ruth complained. 'How could you be so careless?'

'I have done no such thing!' Maria retorted. 'When we had finished shopping we went on the omnibus to Union Square and sat in the shade of a tree, watching the fountains. Aurora sat quite quietly beside me.'

'I'm sorry,' Ruth apologised. 'Only she is unusually hot. Oh, how I hate this weather!'

'I think you should lie down, and Aunt Maria will make a cool, wet pad to lie on your forehead,' Maria said to Aurora. 'That will send the nasty pain away.'

But before anyone could move, Aurora was sick on the floor, and began to whimper in a frightened little voice.

'Never mind, Aurora. Mama will soon make you better,' Ruth comforted.

The child refused to be soothed, continuing to whimper,

turning her head from side to side.

'Aurora's throat hurts,' she said.

'I'm not blaming you, Maria,' Ruth said. 'But I think that in spite of your care, she *has* got a touch of the sun. Bed, with the curtains drawn and as many cold drinks as she will take will be the best thing.'

'Then I'll look after her while you do the suppers,' Maria promised.

Between them they put Aurora to bed. 'Go to sleep, my love,' Ruth said gently. 'When you waken in the morning you'll be better.'

But she was not.

# 25

When Ruth looked in on Aurora, immediately the boarders' supper was over, her daughter was sound asleep. She looked flushed, but Ruth put that down to the heat. She herself was particularly tired and decided to have an early night, leaving the door to Aurora's room open in case she should call out. In spite of her weariness, Ruth lay awake for hours. It was almost morning before she fell into a sleep, from which she was wakened by the sound of Aurora being sick.

Ruth jumped to her feet and ran into her daughter's room. The child was burning with fever, her limbs were hot to the touch and the eyes which she turned piteously to her mother were glassily bright. When Ruth took off Aurora's nightshift to clean her up she saw a fine, bright red rash across her chest. What could it be? When Willie was small she had nursed him through childish coughs and colds, even bronchitis, but never anything like this. And then there had been neighbours to turn to, now there was no-one. She longed for Mrs Cruse, but she would not be here for some hours yet. While she was thinking, worrying, she sponged Aurora down, put a clean shift on her and gave her a drink of water.

'Poor little Aurora,' she said. 'Can you tell Mama where it hurts now?' She spoke soothingly, not wishing to let the child see her anxiety.

'Aurora hurts all over.' It was such a pathetic voice, so unlike her usual demanding tones, that Ruth found it difficult not to add her tears to those of her daughter.

'I'm going to give you another drink,' she said. 'Then you shall go to sleep again. Later on the doctor will come and he'll give you some nice medicine to make you better.'

The child clearly had difficulty in swallowing the water. Ruth wondered if she was doing the right thing, or if more liquid would make her sick again. She simply did not know what to do and she was appalled at her own ignorance.

Within a few minutes Aurora had quietened down. Ruth went up to Maria's room and wakened her.

'Will you fetch the doctor?' she asked. 'I really do think it's necessary. His name is Dr Burdell and he's in Bond Street, number fifty-one. It's only four blocks away. He knows Appleby's. You remember he attended Mr Gossop? Please hurry, Maria!'

'Very well,' Maria mumbled. She was so sleepy.

'*Please*, Maria! I'm worried.'

Maria sat up. 'I'll come and look at Aurora, and then I'll go at once,' she said. She was wide awake now.

When the sisters went to Aurora's bedroom the child was sleeping, but now the rash was beginning to show on her face, as bright as a poppy.

'Poor lamb!' Maria whispered. 'I won't be long, Ruth.' As she left the house she remembered that this was the day Clive would call to take her out for a walk.

Ruth supposed that, in reality, Maria was back quite quickly, but waiting for her seemed an age. Aurora had wakened again, wailing in a feverish manner as if she didn't quite know where she was. Ruth heard May go into the kitchen, and then Mrs Cruse arrive. She rang the bell for the latter.

'Mrs Cruse, I'm afraid Aurora is ill. Maria has just gone to fetch Dr Burdell. In the meantime could you start the breakfasts? I'll be with you just as soon as I can.'

'Of course I will,' Mrs Cruse agreed. 'Don't you worry about a thing. Shall I just take a look at the little love?'

'Better not,' Ruth said. 'She has a rash. It might be something she ate, or it might be infectious. You have your own family to think of.'

'Very well,' Mrs Cruse said. 'Though my lot's as healthy as oak trees and don't take much harm. Except Alfred. He's not strong, being the last of six.'

Maria burst in, breathless.

'I ran all the way' she panted. 'Four blocks is longer than you'd think. Dr Burdell says he'll come the minute he's had his breakfast, and in the meantime you're to do nothing except to keep her warm.'

'Keep her cool would be more to the point,' Ruth said. 'She's as hot as fire.'

It took Dr Burdell no more than two minutes to make his diagnosis. He looked at Aurora's chest, at her tongue which was now a brilliant red, and held his fingers against the back of her neck.

'Always judge a fever by the back of the neck, ma'am,' he said. 'The forehead is deceptive, but the back of the neck tells the truth. Your little girl has scarlet fever!'

'*Scarlet fever?*'

'For certain. A pretty sharp dose. The fever is very high. Has she been playing with other children in the last week or two?'

'No. None at all,' Ruth said.

'Well she's picked it up somewhere. And she'll need careful nursing and strict isolation. I don't see how you can manage that with a boarding-house to run, Mrs O'Farrell. She'd better go to the isolation hospital.'

'Isolation hospital!' Ruth gasped. 'Never! Never! She could pick up anything there. Typhoid. Yellow fever! I couldn't think of it. Besides, she needs me.'

He shrugged.

'You have your boarding-house to think of,' he said. 'It won't do you any good if word gets around – which it will. Of course scarlet fever isn't a thing grown people often catch, but it's possible, and people are always afraid. Are there any children in the house?'

'None. The only one left a week ago. He hadn't been near my daughter.'

'Well, that's all to the good,' Dr Burdell said. 'But I must warn you, Mrs O'Farrell, your little daughter is very ill and will be worse before she's better. She must have constant, careful nursing – and you won't get a professional nurse at this time of the year. Besides, they don't care for infectious illnesses. It spoils their chances with other patients.'

'*I* could nurse her,' Maria broke in. 'If you would tell me what to do.'

The doctor regarded Maria thoughtfully.

'Well, it's true there's nothing complicated about it,' he said. 'Because there's not a great deal that can be done. Just constant attention, day and night, and everything you can to reduce the fever. Sponging down. Drinks. While the fever stays high there's a risk to the heart and the kidneys. I can't deny that. And of course her hair must be cut off.'

'Her hair cut off?' Ruth cried.

'Yes indeed. It is essential. It must be cut as close to the scalp as possible.'

'Her lovely hair!' Ruth protested.

'This is no time for vanity, Mrs. O'Farrell,' he said sharply. 'You mothers are all alike. You worry about the inessentials.'

'Doctor, tell me truthfully,' Maria asked. 'I have no experience. Shall I be able to look after her well enough?'

He looked at her again.

'Do you love the child?'

'With all my heart.'

'Then you can do it. The best nursing is common sense combined with loving care. The cure is in God's hands, if he wills it.'

'Will you let me, Ruth?' Maria said quietly. 'Will you trust me?'

With all her heart Ruth wanted to say 'I will do it myself'. But from somewhere came the confidence that Maria, in spite of her lighthearted ways, would nurse Aurora as well as *she* would; and that the best thing for everyone was to let Maria do it while she herself concentrated on the house. That Maria, not I, nurses Aurora will be my loss only, Ruth thought. And in no way must she put Aurora in the position where she would have to be sent to the isolation hospital.

'Of course I'll let you, Maria. I trust you completely and I thank God that you are here with me.'

'Then I suggest Miss Appleby isolates herself in these rooms with the little girl. Is it possible for you to move elsewhere?' the doctor asked.

'Yes. I can take my sister's room. She can be quite cut off from the rest of the house here.'

Isolated. The word struck Maria like a blow. Clive was coming. He was coming that very morning. How could she isolate herself from him? How could she bear not to see him? Supposing, just supposing, that Aurora was ill for weeks and weeks and he went back to Richmond and she never saw him again! It was impossible! She couldn't do it!

She became aware that the doctor was speaking to her.

'Now here are my instructions, and I want you to follow them exactly. Remember that scarlet fever is a most serious and highly infectious illness. Burn the clothes which the child wore yesterday. Strip all the covers and hangings from the sickroom and see to it that everything is made scrupulously clean – scrubbed where possible. Hang bunches of aromatic herbs in the room, and if you can get them, burn juniper and cedarwood in the grate. Eucalyptus oil, if sprinkled freely, helps to combat the infection. Tie up your hair and wear a clean apron whenever you enter the sickroom. Allow no visitors. Even the child's mother, if she is to mix with the rest of the household, must not go near the little girl until I give permission. Is all that clearly understood?'

'Yes,' Maria said. But she could not go through with it.

'Very well. If you will send someone to my dispensary in an hour's time, Mrs O'Farrell, I will make up a draught which might help. I shall call again this evening. Good day to you both.'

As he was about to leave the house Ruth put her hand on his arm and detained him.

'She is going to be all right isn't she, Doctor?'

'We shall have to see,' he said quietly. 'We shall have to wait and see. I will provide the medical care – not that there's much I can do, for the illness will take its course – and your sister will provide the nursing.'

'Is there *nothing* I can do?' Ruth pleaded.

'You can provide the prayers, Mrs O'Farrell,' he said.

She had seen him to the door. When she closed it on him and turned around, Mrs Seaford was descending the stairs.

'Didn't I just see Dr Burdell leaving?' she asked. 'Is someone ill?'

'Aurora.'

'Oh, the poor little bairn!'

The concern in Mrs Seaford's voice was too much for Ruth. She burst into tears and rushed back to the sitting-room, Mrs Seaford following. She was in the room before Ruth could prevent it.

'I'm sorry,' Ruth said. 'You shouldn't be here. Aurora has scarlet fever. You must go at once.'

'Leave? Rubbish! If Aurora's ill I'm here to help.'

Ruth turned to Maria. 'Please explain . . .' she began – and then she noticed that Maria also was in copious tears.

'Oh Maria,' Ruth cried, 'I'm sure it's going to be all right! And I can never, ever thank you enough for saying you'll nurse Aurora!'

Maria wept even harder at Ruth's words. What could she do? She couldn't desert her sister and her little niece – but neither could she desert Clive.

'I'm sorry,' she sobbed. 'But you don't understand. I want to nurse Aurora, I *will* do so – but Clive is coming this morning to take me out! Oh Ruth, I can't bear not to see him! I must see him this once. I must explain everything to him.'

'That's all right,' Mrs Seaford said briskly. 'You can keep out of the sickroom until after you've seen Mr Masterson. I'll take over. Of course you'll have to explain that you can't go on seeing him, not until Aurora's better.'

'Oh if I can only see him this once!' Maria cried. 'I can explain everything – and after that we can write to each other.'

'He can write to you,' Mrs Seaford said. 'You can't send letters to him. Nothing carries infection more than paper. Mrs O'Farrell, you realise we'll have to burn any books you or Aurora may have? Now tell me exactly what the doctor said.'

Ruth and Maria between them repeated all Dr Burdell's instructions.

'Then if you'll allow me, I shall move in with Maria,' Mrs Seaford said. She had a new firmness in her voice. 'There's plenty of work for two pairs of hands, and I'll be company for Maria. Besides. . . .' She blinked rapidly and looked away. '. . . Everyone knows how fond I am of Aurora. I was here when she was born, remember? There isn't anything I wouldn't do for her.'

'But Mr Seaford?' Ruth asked doubtfully. 'He won't let you do such a thing.'

'Oh yes he will,' Mrs Seaford said. 'I'll just go and have a word with him before he leaves. Then I'll gather a few things together and I'll be back in no time. Maria, while you're seeing Mr Masterson I'll be taking down the curtains and removing the covers, and I'll make a start on the scrubbing.'

'Oh Doris, you are an angel! But leave it all for me. I'll do anything once I've seen Clive!'

Ruth was beyond protesting. In any case she was sure that Mrs Seaford would take no notice.

'She'll be company for me,' Maria said when Mrs Seaford had gone off in search of her husband. 'Most of all, she'll help Aurora – which is what she really wants to do. Oh Ruth, thank you for understanding about Clive. I just *have* to see him!'

Ruth knew she had done nothing about that. Mrs Seaford had decided everything. Nevertheless, she knew how her sister felt. She remembered, all too vividly, the times when she would have deserted anything and anybody for the sake of one hour with Joss Barnet. Did men have this terrible compulsion, she wondered?

She managed to see Mr Seaford before he left for work.

'It's Mrs Seaford's own idea, not mine,' she explained. 'I should never forgive myself if your wife caught the infection.'

'Don't think about it,' he said. 'You have enough to worry about. And there's no stopping Doris when she's made up her mind. Besides, she's a good nurse.'

'It's unbelievably kind of her; and of you to allow it.'

'Well, you know how fond she is of Aurora. Also. . . .' he paused.

'Yes?'

'Nothing. I forget what I was going to say!'

He was all of a sudden brusque, quite unlike his genial self. 'Good day, Mrs O'Farrell,' he said. 'I must be off. Mr Stewart doesn't countenance lateness in his employees.'

When Clive Masterson called at Appleby's he was surprised to be left waiting in the entrance hall while Sammy went in search of Maria. He had thought his standing with the two sisters was now such that he would have been shown straight in. But Maria did not keep him waiting for long. In less than two minutes she was with him, bonnet and gloves on, ready to leave the house. He had thought he might meet Ruth again, be offered a glass of Madeira. He wanted to make a good impression on Ruth, though only because of Maria.

'Good morning, Maria!'

'Good morning, Clive!' It was clear from her face that something was wrong. The little dear was pale, her lips trembled, she had obviously been crying. Indeed, tears still threatened the large blue eyes which looked so unhappily into his.

'Why Maria, my love!'

Her heart leapt at the endearment, though she must pretend not to hear it since in no way had he declared himself, nor she permitted such familiarity.

'Why Maria, you looked distressed. Is something wrong?'

'I will inform you as we walk,' she said. 'It's all too terrible!'

While they walked towards Washington Square she told him about Aurora. 'My niece is very, very ill,' she said. 'We are all beside ourselves with worry. There will be a great deal of nursing to do, of which I must take the lion's share because my sister cannot.'

'That is a noble sentiment, with which I entirely agree,' Clive replied. 'But you must not wear yourself out, Maria. I shall call on you every day that I do not have a matinee, and we will take a short walk together to refresh you.'

His kind words were too much for Maria. The tears spilled over and Clive knew the embarrassment of escorting a weeping woman through the streets.

'My dear Maria,' he said. 'Please do not cry! Passers-by will think I am ill-treating you!'

'Oh Clive, as if you ever could! But you don't understand the position.'

They had reached Washington Square. He led her to the nearest bench and they sat down. She looked so forlorn. It did seem to him, though, that such grief over her little niece was perhaps excessive and premature. He longed to take her in his arms, to comfort her. He moved a little closer.

'No! No, do not come so near me!' Maria cried in alarm. 'In fact it would be best if you were to sit at one end of the bench and I at the other.'

'But why?' he asked, perplexed.

'Because of Aurora. Because the doctor has said she must be isolated - and the moment I start to nurse Aurora properly *I* shall be also. Oh Clive, I shall not see you! As long as Aurora's illness lasts we may not meet together! I shall be a prisoner!'

'Oh my dear Maria! Then you are even nobler than I gave you credit for. That you would make this sacrifice so that I should not catch the illness touches me deeply. But you are right. It is my duty to keep well at all times, for the sake of my public.'

Maria had not until now seen the situation in that light. Selfishly, she had thought only of her own loss in not seeing him - but now that he had spoken she felt comforted. In a way, she thought, she was giving him to all those people. All the same. . . .

'But you will write to me, will you not?' she asked.

'Every day,' he assured her. 'Every single day!'

'Even though I shall not be able to reply?'

'Even so,' he promised. 'You are doing it for my sake.'

'Then I shall be brave. I shall try not to cry again.' She took out a small lace-edged handkerchief and dried her eyes.

She really was the most adorable creature he had ever known. So pretty, so sensitive. He was really and truly in love with her – and of course she was quite devoted to him. Since he was not to see her for goodness knew how long, he determined to declare himself. He took a good deep breath, as he always did before delivering himself of an important line.

'Maria!'

'Yes, Clive?' What a beautiful resonant voice he had. 'What is it?'

'Maria, we have known each other but a short time, yet in that time we have grown so close. . . .'

'Oh Clive, we have!' He scarcely heard her interruption.

'You must realise that I admire you above all other women. I adore you! Maria. . . .' He slid off the seat and bent one immaculately trousered knee to the hard dusty ground. 'Maria, will you do me the honour of becoming my wife?'

'Oh Clive!' She thought she must surely swoon with joy.

'Say you will, Maria! Tell me quickly!' He had the uncomfortable feeling that if he were to remain kneeling much longer a crowd might gather.

'Oh, I will! I will, Clive!' She was in esctasy.

He rose from his knees, dusted down his trousers and, sitting beside her, made as if to take her in his arms. She recoiled in horror.

'Oh no, my love! You must not embrace me! Even now I might be infectious. And no harm must come to you. You are more precious to me than ever now!'

She was right. What a fount of womanly wisdom she was. He moved to the far end of the bench.

'Oh Clive, when shall we be married . . .?' she asked.

'Quite soon,' he said. 'As soon as your little niece recovers, and before I return to Richmond. I want to take you there as my wife.'

'Oh Clive!'

'I cannot leave my precious one alone in New York while I am in Virginia. I will speak to your sister as soon as possible. As you have no parents she will wish to ascertain my prospects – which I have to admit, my dear, are entirely vested in my talents!'

'But such talents! And you are so masterful, Clive. But now I must be firm and say that I have to go home.'

'So soon?' he begged. 'Must you?'

'You would not wish me to shirk my duties, I know. No Clive, I shall not take your arm. The risk is too great. Indeed, we must walk as far apart as possible.'

They set off. Returning through the streets he kept to the edge of the sidewalk while Maria walked as close as she could to the buildings, each of them smiling happily at the other across the space in between.

Ruth stood in the doorway of Aurora's room. Her daughter lay on the bed, her head tossing from side to side, her lips dark and cracked with fever.

'Mama!' she called in a thin voice. 'Mama! Papa!' Then came a stream of jumbled words which Ruth could not follow.

'You mustn't go in to her,' Maria warned. 'Not one step further. In fact you must really go away now, Ruth. Leave me and Mrs Seaford to get on with things.'

She felt immense confidence in herself now. Though she had not yet broken the news to Ruth, and if she could possibly help it did not intend to until Aurora took a turn for the better, was she not now a woman engaged to be married to the most marvellous of men? A woman of position.

'Try not to fret, Ruth,' Mrs Seaford said kindly. 'We'll look after Aurora every minute of the night and day.'

'I know you will,' Ruth whispered. 'I don't know how to thank you.'

'Save it for later. And in the meantime get Sammy to bring some buckets of hot water and leave them outside the door. And plenty of soda and a couple of scrubbing brushes. And we'll need a good supply of bed linen.'

'You shall have everything you need,' Ruth promised. 'Everything.'

She gathered together her toilet things and a few changes of clothing, and took them up to Maria's room. In a daze, she washed herself from top to toe, put on clean clothes and went down to the kitchen.

'I'm afraid there'll be a lot of extra work,' she told Mrs Cruse. 'Trays to Mrs Seaford and Maria, and all to be kept separate. And we must make lots of fresh lemonade for Aurora.' But she would be glad of the extra work. At least she would feel she was doing something to help.

'Work's nothing,' Mrs Cruse said. 'We shall manage all right.'

'And next week you are due to start your week's holiday,' Ruth reminded her. While so many of the boarders were away she had arranged a few days off for each member of her staff in turn.

'Lord bless you, I wouldn't hear of it! Not until Aurora's completely better,' Mrs Cruse declared. 'Besides, I've never been used to holidays from work, let alone paid for.'

Ruth took Mrs Cruse's thin, hard hand in her own. 'Dear Mrs Cruse, you are such a comfort to me.'

She found herself in need of comfort often in the days which followed, and she did not know where to turn for it. She felt herself shut out from the loving care which surrounded Aurora, helpless to do anything for the person she loved most in the world.

At the end of each day, when she had done everything needful for her boarders, she enveloped herself in an apron and tied up her hair, and was allowed to stand outside the door of her daughter's room with the door opened an inch or two for her to peer in.

There was no comfort there. Though Aurora's fever-bright eyes occasionally looked in her mother's direction, there was no recognition in them. Her dark head, surprisingly small and rounded now that the hair had been cut close to the scalp, tossed and turned on the pillow. There was no peace in her delirium and Ruth wondered what troubled dreams could invade the mind of so small a child.

'She's no better, is she?' she asked. 'This is the fourth day now.'

'We can't get the fever down,' Mrs Seaford admitted. 'No matter what we do.'

She looked drawn and anxious, as did Maria, though in her sister there was a strength Ruth had not suspected. In theory Mrs Seaford and Maria rested in turn in Ruth's bed, but she doubted if either of them had slept much.

'Did you do as Mrs Cruse suggested and sponge her down with vinegar and water?' Ruth asked.

'We did that. We're doing everything we can think of.'

'I think you should go now, Ruth,' Maria said gently. 'I promise to call you if there's any change.'

With that Ruth had to be content. In bed she lay awake, thinking, trying deliberately to turn her thoughts in all directions so as to tire her mind and, hopefully, send her to sleep. She thought a great deal about Sean. Ought she to let him know about Aurora? But how long would a letter take?

She thought about her boarders. Those who were still in the house had been wonderfully understanding. She had spoken to them directly about the precautions she was taking and there had been no word of reproach or any suggestion that she should send Aurora away. But there was no-one she could talk to, no-one close with whom she could share the terrible fears which haunted her every working moment. She sorely missed Professor Woodburn.

She thought, too, about Joss Barnet. She thought a great deal about Joss Barnet. He had been so taken by Aurora when they had met at the World's Fair, couldn't take his eyes off her. He was the child's father; ought she to let him know what was happening to his daughter?

None of her thoughts brought sleep and she tossed and turned until morning.

Very early next day she dressed, and left the house. The street was quiet, but already the night's coolness had been absorbed by the heat of the new day. On leaving the house she had made no conscious decision about where she was going, but now, as she turned into Broadway and walked northwards, she knew that her steps were taking her in the direction of Grace church.

She went inside and sat in a pew at the back. A black-cassocked figure moved quietly about in the sanctuary but she could not tell whether or not it was the Reverend Taylor. She knelt down and covered her face with her hands.

After a while she heard the man walk in the direction of the vestry, and then there was silence. She looked up again. The sun was well risen now, casting pools of colour on the pews and on the floor. A shaft caught her clasped hands and turned them crimson. She knelt there a minute or two longer, and then rose to her feet and left. She had found nothing to say to God except her daughter's name, over and over again. Aurora, Aurora. She had not the slightest feeling that he had heard her.

When she got back to the house there had been no overnight change in Aurora. After breakfast Ruth said, 'I'm going out to do some marketing. I might be just a little longer than usual.'

She had decided to visit Joss Barnet at the bank. He was, after all, Aurora's father, she reminded herself again. If Aurora were to. . . . She couldn't bring herself to utter the word, even in her thoughts. But she wanted him to know.

She had no difficulty this time in getting to Joss. There was a different doorman, but the secretary was the same. He looked at her with interest. Though the name was different she was the same woman who had visited her employer four years ago, the one who had left behind a shopping basket which still rested in a cupboard, despite his suggestion, from time to time, that it might be disposed of.

When Ruth entered Joss Barnet's office this time he was not sitting behind his desk, but standing in front of it, waiting to greet her. There was no barrier between them and, as the secretary left the room, Joss stepped towards Ruth and took both her hands in his. Vibrant life and warmth flowed from his hands to hers, suffusing her body. Though she trembled at his touch, she felt a strength in her that she had not known for days.

'My dearest Ruth,' he said. 'Whatever brings you here I am grateful, glad of it.'

Having to break the news of their child's illness brought her back to earth.

'You will not be when I tell you why I came. Aurora is very ill. Oh Joss, I'm afraid she might die! I'm so terribly afraid!' It was the first time, even to herself, that she had admitted fears, and now that she did so she was engulfed by them. She broke into sobs which racked her body – and then she was in Joss Barnet's arms. He was holding her close, stroking her hair, whispering her name.

'Ruth, my darling Ruth!'

His loving gentleness, a quality she had never expected to find in him, made her weep all the more. The grief of her sleepless nights, of her separation from her daughter, poured out of her.

'Oh Joss, what shall I do? Is God punishing me for my wickedness? I've tried hard to be good. I've tried so hard! But I couldn't help thinking about you sometimes, wanting you. Is that so very wicked?'

'If it is, then I've been wicked too,' he said. 'But I don't believe so, any more than I believe God would punish Aurora for your behaviour and mine.'

It was the truth that he had thought of her, long and often. In the last year or two of his loneliness it was not of the wife who had left him that he thought; it was of Ruth. And of his children whom he seldom saw, and missed badly. There had been other women, but they were transient and never touched his heart. Only Ruth had ever done that and he didn't know why. There was a magic about her that was indefinable. So why then, when she had needed him most, had he treated her so badly? He would give a year of his life to undo the harm, but it was too late. And now, through their child, she was suffering again and he could do nothing to help her.

'What can I do?' he asked. 'I'll do anything. Only tell me.'

'Nothing,' she replied. 'Only pray. I have prayed but God doesn't hear me.'

'I would like to see my daughter,' Joss said. 'But I know I can't come to the house. Your husband. . . .'

'Sean has left us. He's gone to Wisconsin with my cousins. But you still can't come to the house. There is my sister and the boarders. Perhaps when Professor Woodburn returns from his vacation. . . .'

She had been quietly thrilled to hear him say 'My daughter' but there was nothing he could do, except that he had given her a little more strength to face whatever might come. As for the rest, she knew that she loved him as much as ever, and believed now that he loved her too. She knew also, with a terrible finality, that nothing could come of it. She felt, though she knew it was illogical, that her daughter's life was at stake against her own behaviour. Give me back Aurora, dear God, and I'll be good, she prayed.

When she arrived home there was a letter from Sean.

> 'I already have a job' he wrote, 'looking after horses on a nearby farm, and other small jobs in between. It's a small beginning but I will do better. I have sworn off the drink and look forward to when you and Aurora join me in this grand life.'

Charlotte, he added, showed no improvement.

More than a week had passed from the onset of Aurora's illness and still the fever raged in her. Maria and Mrs Seaford never left her side, and though they tried to appear cheerful, Ruth could see the fear in their eyes. But I must not lose hope, she told herself. For Aurora's sake I must never lose hope.

When she went to bed that night, full of foreboding, she fell surprisingly quickly into a shallow sleep, and then soon afterwards wakened. She knew on the instant, and without any doubt at all, that she must go at once to her daughter. She would take no more precautions. No matter what the consequences she must hold Aurora in her arms. Nothing and no-one could prevent her. She jumped out of bed and ran downstairs.

Maria, fully clothed, was asleep on the bed. Ruth walked through to Aurora's bedroom. The door was open. Mrs Seaford was sitting by the bedside, but it was towards her daughter that Ruth looked, dreading what she might see.

Aurora lay peacefully sleeping, her breath coming evenly and untroubled. Beneath the rash on her face the skin was no longer flushed. Her short hair lay damply against her head and there was a film of sweat on her forehead.

Ruth turned to Mrs Seaford. The woman was looking at her with a radiant smile on her tired face and tears rolling down her cheeks.

'Don't come too close, love,' she whispered. 'You've been very good. Don't spoil it now.'

'She's going to be all right, isn't she? She *is?*'

Mrs Seaford nodded.

'Should I waken Maria and tell her the crisis is passed?' She wanted to tell the whole world. She wanted everyone to rejoice with her.

'Let her sleep,' Mrs Seaford said. 'And you go back to bed. Aurora will have a good, long sleep now.'

It was true. Aurora slept for twelve unbroken hours, and when she wakened her convalescence began. When Ruth gave Mr Seaford the news he told her what he had been about to say on that first morning.

'We had a little girl of our own. She died when she was three years old. Doris nursed her night and day, but to no avail. I couldn't tell you that before, could I?'

It was why they had left their home in England. Mrs Seaford, her husband said, knew she could never have another child. 'I thought she'd die herself, from grief,' he said. 'I had to get her away.'

Ruth never told Mrs Seaford what she knew, but whenever she thought of that brave woman who was prepared to re-live her own terrible experience out of devotion to another woman's child, she felt ashamed that she had ever found her tedious and tiresome. She wished she could say she would never do so again, but it would not be true.

On the day after Aurora's turn for the better, Ruth sent a note to Joss Barnet at his bank. She could not trust herself to face him in person. The feelings between them were too strong. If she was ever to see him again it must not be by her own contrivance, only if Fate ruled. But she was already in debt to Fate, or to some other power, for the life of her daughter. She could not tempt it any further.

A few days later Clive Masterson called, requesting to take Maria for a walk.

'Oh Ruth, can you spare me?' she asked. 'I do so want to go!'

'Of course. It will do you good to get out in the fresh air for an hour - put some roses in your cheeks.' She would never, as long as she lived, forget Maria's devotion to Aurora through all those dreadful days and nights. She had not thought that her flibberty-gibbet sister had it in her to be so caring.

When Clive and Maria returned from their walk they came into the sitting-room hand in hand. Ruth looked from one to the other in surprise. Maria's eyes, though dark-ringed from lack of sleep, were like stars in her pale face. Clive Masterson's handsome face glowed with pleasure. The warmth emanating from the two of them was almost tangible.

'We're engaged to be married!' Maria announced. 'Oh Ruth, I'm so happy! I'm so deliriously happy! We got engaged on the day Aurora was taken ill but I kept it a secret until she was better.'

'We didn't want to worry you further,' Clive said. 'Not that our betrothal would worry you . . . but losing a sister. . . .'

When I might also have lost a daughter, Ruth thought. How considerate they had been.

'You were *engaged* all the the time you were nursing Aurora?' she asked. 'You kept it a secret?'

'It wasn't easy,' Maria admitted. 'Oh Ruth, we got engaged in Washington Square. Clive went down on his knees in the dust and got his trousers dirty!' She gurgled happily. 'Oh how glad I am that it's not a secret any longer. Say that you give us your blessing, Ruth. You do give us your blessing, don't you?'

'Of course,' Ruth said. 'I'm very happy for you both.' But she was worried. What did they know of Clive Masterson? Maria had met him for the very first time only a few weeks ago and she had seen him only four times before today. Ruth herself had hardly spoken two words to him. It was quite impossible that she should entrust her sister to this man, charming though he seemed to be, until they had had time to get to know him better.

'There is nothing at all against you being engaged to marry,' she told them. 'But naturally, Clive, as you will readily understand, my sister cannot marry you until she has known you longer. A year would not be unreasonable, I think.'

'A year!' Maria gave a cry of anguish. 'We can't possibly wait a year! We have plans. Everything is arranged between us. Oh I couldn't! I just couldn't! Tell her, Clive!'

'Mr Masterson – Clive – is a man of the world,' Ruth said. 'I am sure he understands perfectly that I can't consent to my sister's marriage until we know him better. I feel sure he will prove a worthy suitor, but we must give it time.'

Clive Masterson opened his mouth to speak, but Maria rushed in before him.

'I don't need your permission, Ruth! You are not my parent.'

'I am your elder sister. I stand in place of a parent,' Ruth said.

'You're only a year older,' Maria stormed. 'When you were my age you were married and had a child. Have you forgotten that?'

I have not forgotten, which is why I want to guard you, Ruth thought. But she could not say it. And Maria had always seemed so much younger than her years.

'The situation is, Mrs O'Farrell, that I must leave New York in October, when our season ends, and return to Richmond. I want to marry Maria before then, and to take her with me. Your sister has expressed a strong desire to join the company and I think that can be arranged.'

'We shall be on tour together!' Maria said blissfully. 'One day, I haven't the slightest doubt, we shall be a famous husband and wife team!' She blushed at her use of the word 'husband'. 'Oh Ruth, can't you see how wonderful it will be?'

'And when we are not touring we shall make our home with my mother and sisters in Richmond,' Clive went on. 'I know how delighted they will be to welcome my new wife.'

It was all quite plausible. And in nursing Aurora Maria had, Ruth admitted, shown a maturity beyond her years. But she must not let her gratitude to her sister cloud her judgement.

'I understand how you feel,' she said.

How could she possibly understand, Maria thought fretfully. Dear down-to-earth Ruth, always so sensible. How could she know how it felt to be so deeply, so ecstatically in love?

'Allow me to give it a little more thought then,' Ruth said.

Clive bowed. 'As you wish. But not too long I hope. I will take my leave now. May I call upon you both tomorrow?'

'As often as you wish,' Ruth told him. 'And now I will leave Maria to make her farewells. I know I'm wanted in the kitchen.'

When she returned a little later he was gone. Maria turned on her as soon as she came in at the door.

'I want to marry him,' she said. 'I mean to marry him and to go to Richmond before the end of October. *Nothing* you can do or say will stop me!'

# 26

Charlotte stood by the side of Benjamin's crib, looking down at him as he slept. He slept so peacefully; small pink mouth pursed, closed eyelids faintly blue-tinged, with long dark lashes splayed against his skin, which was always shades paler in sleep than when awake; his breathing scarcely moving his body. He was a good baby, had been from the first, as if he knew how little strength his mother had left, and wanted to spare her. Rightly or wrongly, and she was past feeling guilty, she had a stronger bond with Benjamin than with any of her other children, though she loved them all. At this moment she wanted to pick him up, to snatch him out of his crib and hold him close. She wanted never to let him go. But she contented herself with touching his rounded cheek with the tip of her finger.

'He's a good little mite,' Emily Watson said, standing behind Charlotte. Charlotte did not answer. She wanted Benjamin entirely to herself, didn't want anyone else even to look at him. She would have liked the two of them to be together all the time. In the six weeks since they had returned from New York she had felt herself gradually drawing away from the rest of her family, even from Ernest. Perhaps most of all from Ernest because of what was unspoken between them. Within the distance between herself and everyone else she was able to bear what was happening to her body. But she could not distance herself from Benjamin.

Emily – young, strong, willing – saw to everything: washing, ironing, cleaning the house, looking after the menfolk and the four older children, all with unbounded energy and good humour. Over the last six weeks Charlotte had, in her heart as well as physically, relinquished all those things. All she wanted, all she was determined to keep, was Benjamin. He would be hers to the end.

'I'm just off to take the coffee down to the menfolk,' Emily said. 'I'll take the children with me. You get some rest.'

The three men – Sean had finished his stint on the neighbouring farm and was now working with Ernest and Matthew – were at work a distance from the house, cutting down trees, clearing more land for the plough. When the winter frosts came they would break up the soil ready for planting in the spring. While the men were so busy, making the most of what fine weather was left, Emily took food and hot coffee down to them in the middle of each day, Enoch and Jane helping to carry the baskets. They would all picnic together. It did the children good, Emily thought, to escape from the sadness of the house for a while.

Sean, straightening up, axe in hand, saw them approaching and waved.

'Here comes Emily with the children,' he said. He felt a warm pleasure at the sight of her. In spite of being only nineteen, she held the household together, not only because she looked after them physically but because she was cheerful and good-natured. Attractive, too. Her coal-black hair and lively blue eyes, her small features and tilted nose, reminded him of the colleens in Ireland. Though she laughingly denied it, he felt sure there was Irish blood in her somewhere.

When Emily unpacked the baskets everyone sat on the ground to eat the fresh bread and corned beef pasties. There was ginger cake and milk for the children.

'I left Mrs Gaunt resting. Benjamin was asleep,' Emily said, answering the question in Ernest's eyes. Everyone spoke as though the mistress of the house was a little, and only temporarily, unwell; as though next week, next month, she would be fit again, ready to take up the duties she now no longer attempted. But Emily knew by the haunted expression in their eyes – the master's, the old father's, even sometimes Sean O'Farrell's, that none of them believed this. There was no expression at all in the mistress's eyes, except when she looked at the baby with such hungry love.

'Good!' Ernest said. 'She must get all the rest she can.' Though he pretended, he was not deceived. He had seen her in the night, many nights now, wracked with pain, greedily reaching out for Dr Cooke's pills. He could do nothing for her; she always told him to go back to sleep. At these times the pain was her companion, there was no room for anyone else, not even for Benjamin, until the worst of it passed. But in spite of the fact that they did not deceive themselves, they chose to deceive each other. 'Plenty of rest and you'll be better by Christmas,' he told her cheerfully. 'You're quite right,' she said.

When they had all eaten Emily gathered up the remains and repacked the baskets.

'That's it then. We'll be getting back.'

'We'll not be late,' Ernest said.

When the men returned to the house in the early evening Emily had a nourishing stew ready for them. While they sat around the table and ate, Charlotte remained by the stove, a shawl around her shoulders, nursing Benjamin. She was not hungry but she was always cold, though now that they were well into September the stove was lit all day.

When the meal was over Matthew cleared the table and set about washing the dishes. He did this every day now, though it was not man's work and he was more tired than he liked to admit when evening came. The work was hard and he felt himself getting old. He was contented enough, and his son was good to him, his daughter-in-law made him welcome; but he missed his Sarah, more so as time went on. Sometimes he missed the Yorkshire farm where he had been born and brought up, but it was his wife he longed for at the end of each day. He saw what was happening to Charlotte – though nobody said – and sometimes he wished that it could be him instead of her. But you couldn't change these things.

'I'll give you a hand putting the children to bed,' Sean said to Emily. That way, with the old man busy at the sink, Ernest could spend time with Charlotte. Not that they seemed to have much to say to each other, and this evening, as on most evenings, as soon as Charlotte had kissed the clean-bathed children goodnight, she went to bed. Matthew, when he had put away the last of the dishes, followed suit, to the room he shared with Enoch.

'I'll be going too,' Ernest said.

Emily brought out the workbox and sorted through a pile of socks which needed darning.

'Shall I be keeping you from your bed if I do some mending?' she asked Sean. 'It mounts up so.' She asked him because he slept here in the living-room.

'Not a bit of it. I'm going to work on the chair for a while yet and I'll be glad of your company.'

He was making the second of a set of chairs intended for the family, so that everyone could sit to the table instead of as now, the children either sitting on a grown-up's lap or standing on a box to the table. He brought out the wood and his tools, and set to work.

She made a pretty picture, he thought, with the lamp shining on her hair, her hands moving deftly as she guided the needle and pulled the wool through the socks. She had a fine figure too; slender waist, long, slender column of a neck merging in a high, full bosom. In a way she reminded him of Ruth, except that Ruth, this last summer, had been thinner. As Emily bent over the workbox, searching for the right-coloured wool, he observed the shadowy cleft between her breasts and was suddenly filled with urgent desire. It came upon him so swiftly, so unexpectedly, that the chisel in his hand slipped, nicking his skin and drawing blood.

'Damn!'

Emily looked up quickly and saw, not the graze on his hand which had caused him to cry out, but the need in his eyes. And for the first time she felt the same, elemental, answering need in her own body, so that her breasts tingled and a strange feeling of excitement made her catch her breath. Though she was not conscious of taking her eyes off Sean, she was somehow aware that his hand was bleeding, and that a drop of blood splashed on the wooden floor – but also that he was ignoring it, looking fixedly at her.

'Your hand is bleeding,' she whispered.

She could not bear the way he was looking at her. It tore into her body, invaded her. Yet although she could not bear it, all the time she wanted it.

'I'll bathe it for you,' she said.

She fetched a basin of water and started to swab the wound. It was not deep, no more really than a surface scratch. As she held his hand she noticed the fine, red hairs on the backs of his fingers and his hands, growing more thickly where his shirt cuffs met his wrists. She had never noticed them before and she wanted to stroke his hand. At that moment one of the children cried, the thin, frightened cry of a child in a nightmare. She jumped to her feet.

'It's Meg! Another bad dream.'

She was turning away when he caught her hand, pulled her back.

'Don't go, Emily. She'll quieten down. Please stay!' But the child continued to whimper.

'She'll wake the household,' Emily said. 'We don't want that. Besides. . . .'

'What?'

'I think I'd better go to bed now. Goodnight, Mr O'Farrell.'

He was trembling when she left him. He knew that if she had stayed, if the child had not cried, he would have taken her there and then. He was quite sure, also, that he would have been able to do so.

His hand had stopped bleeding now. He tidied away, banked up the stove for the night, then lay down on the sofa under a blanket. But there was no sleep in him. His body was too alert, too on edge to let him rest. He thought of Ruth, and of Aurora, as he did every night, but this time only briefly. His mind and thoughts were filled with Emily Watson.

It came as no surprise to him, rather as something which was inevitable, when in the middle of the night he heard the creak of her bedroom door and, in the light from the September moon which was streaming in through a partly-opened shutter, saw her coming towards him. He held back the blanket and without a word from either of them she came into his arms.

The moon had set and it was almost morning, though they were both still awake, satisfied in each other's arms, when the cry came from Ernest's and Charlotte's bedroom. It was a long cry of pain, and it came not from Charlotte but from Ernest, and was then repeated.

Sean was in the bedroom first, Emily close behind him, as she might have come from her own room. Ernest was kneeling on the bed, cradling Charlotte in his arms, crying her name. Her left arm, escaping from his embrace, hung lifelessly down. The baby, beginning to cry now, lay on top of the bedclothes where it had fallen from Charlotte's arms at the moment of her death.

Emily picked up the baby, and Sean, after a minute, gently prised Charlotte away from Ernest and laid her almost weightless body back against the pillows. Her eyes were closed. A stray lock of red hair fell over a face which was serenely free from pain.

Sean turned to Emily. 'Do you know what to do? For Charlotte, I mean?'

'No. But I'll try.'

'I'll ride into Mazomanie,' he said. 'I'll fetch Meg Atkinson.'

Aurora was completely fit again, though the doctor said that she must take care and not get overtired for some weeks to come. One by one the boarders had returned, seemingly refreshed after their summer vacations; but Captain Forsyth, apparently not able to stand the influx, had taken himself off to a boarding-house in Washington, from which he had written requesting that all his belongings be sent on to him since he intended remaining there. Also, Francis

Priestley had not returned. The others had been back at least a week before Ruth heard from him. 'Expect me within a day or two' his message said.

On the day he was due back she went up to his room to see that all was in order for him. There was nothing left to do; Mrs Cruse had seen to everything. Ruth walked slowly around the room, touching this and that. She hesitated before a photograph of his fiancée, wondered whether she should put it away in a drawer. But it was not her business to do so.

She was staring out of the window, at the trees which must soon turn scarlet and crimson and yellow again, and at first she did not hear him enter. When he spoke she turned quickly, uncomfortable at being found there. But the expression on his face was one of welcome, almost of contentment, she thought, at being back. What a shame it was that he was not to be married after all. He would be a wonderful husband for some fortunate woman. Now if Maria had set her sights on Francis Priestley instead of Clive Masterson, I would have no worries, Ruth thought. But of course that was nonsense. He would never look in Maria's direction anyway, pretty though she was. He would only marry a lady. One had only to think of his mother to realise that.

'Welcome back,' Ruth said. 'I was just checking to see that everything was all right in your room. I hope you are well.'

'Very well, thank you. And you? How are things going with you?'

'Quite well, thank you.' Except, she thought, that her husband had left her, her daughter was only just recovered, and she was at loggerheads with Maria and Clive Masterson.

She had confessed to Professor Woodburn her worries about Maria and Clive. 'It isn't that I don't like him,' she said. 'That's far from the case. He's a most personable young man and I quite understand why Maria is in love with him. But we know nothing at all about him except what he has told Maria himself. Of course she believes every word of it, but I would be happier with some corroboration.'

'And you have no mutual acquaintances?' he queried.

She could not think why it had never entered her head before! Of course, there was Joss Barnet! When she had first met Clive Masterson at the World's Fair he had been in Joss Barnet's company. How could she have forgotten?

'There is Mr Barnet,' she replied. 'I had almost overlooked that I'd met them together.'

'Well then,' Professor Woodburn said. 'I'm sure Mr Barnet is an adequate judge of character. He will either set your mind at rest or confirm your fears.'

Could she face going to see him again at the bank? Their last meeting had been so painful and she was far from sure that she could trust herself in his presence again. She felt bruised from all that the summer had done to her. She wanted nothing else which would arouse her emotions. All she desired was to stay tucked inside Appleby's, get on with her life there. But she had a clear duty towards Maria.

'You are right, Professor,' she agreed hesitantly. 'Though I am not sure. . . .'

'Would you like me to contact Mr Barnet for you?' he asked.

'I would be extremely grateful.'

'Then I shall do so at once.'

She waited until next day to inform Maria of what she had arranged. Maria was furious.

'How dare you mistrust what Clive says!' she exclaimed indignantly. 'He is the soul of honour!'

'It's quite likely that you are right,' Ruth said. 'But we don't *know*. I am your elder sister and it's up to me to look after you. If you won't go into these matters for yourself then I must do so.'

'You need do nothing of the kind!' Maria cried. 'I don't require *you* to look after me. Clive will do that. I trust him absolutely.'

'Then in that case, if you have no doubts, you won't mind

Mr Barnet being consulted. You can expect him to confirm all you say. And after all, he is Clive's friend. He will *prefer* to speak up for him if he can do so.'

'Whether he does or not, I shan't change my mind,' Maria said. 'Clive has asked me to marry him and I shall do so.'

'I've only asked you to wait a little while,' Ruth pointed out. 'Even if Mr Barnet speaks well of Clive, I hope you will wait until you are twenty-one. It's only six months.'

'Seven and a half months,' Maria corrected her. And every day now felt like a week, every week like a month. They were so much in love. 'Besides, we want to be together for the beginning of the new season. We want to travel together, work together. I am to be his new leading lady! Just think – "Clive and Maria Masterson". How well it sounds!'

'Maria, don't be so foolish!' Really, her sister was exasperating. 'How can you possibly be his leading lady? How can he promise you that? You know, that in spite of what you lead people to believe, you have never acted before. How do you know you have the talent?'

Tears of rage filled Maria's eyes. Oh, how cruel Ruth was! Of course she had talent! By now she had made several more visits to the theatre, had watched Georgina de Monclare, Clive's leading lady, closely. She was convinced that she could act equally well, if not better. After all, Clive would inspire her. They would inspire each other. And though he had not *quite* promised that she could take Miss de Monclare's place, she was certain he had it in mind. He had as good as said so.

'Clive believes in me, even if you do not,' she sobbed. 'I don't believe you want me to be happy. I believe you are jealous!'

'Nonsense!' Ruth said. 'I want your happiness with all my heart. But I want you to be happy for the rest of your life, not for a few weeks or months.'

'I *shall* be!' Maria cried. 'If I marry Clive – *when* I marry Clive – I shall be happy forever. If I were not to marry him I should die! You would have my death on your conscience!' She was in a paroxysm of angry grief, sobbing hysterically, drumming her clenched fists on the table top. Ruth put an arm around her sister's shoulder and bent down to hold her, but Maria flung her away.

'Don't pretend you care about me! You care about no-one except yourself and getting your own way. You don't know what love is. You sent Sean away because you didn't care, but you shan't drive Clive away. I won't let you!'

Ruth felt as though she had received a stinging slap in the face. She was deeply shocked by her sister's words. Was it true what Maria said? Was that how other people saw her? Cold, selfish? But it was emphatically not true. She denied it utterly. She cared deeply for a number of people, including Sean. She was as capable of love as was Maria, perhaps more so. It was the pain of caring which had bedevilled her life. Her grandfather, father, Aunt Sarah – it was because she had loved them all so much that she had felt pain, though she was sure their deaths had not touched Maria. Sean she cared for deeply in her own way, though it was not his. And the pain of loving Joss Barnet would be with her for the rest of her life. How could anyone say, because she was outwardly calm, that she did not love?

Maria, unnerved by her sister's silence, looked up. Ruth saw her tear-stained, woebegone face, and hardened her heart against it. What about me, she thought rebelliously? *I* am hurt, *I* am wounded. Who is there to comfort me?

She turned her back on Maria, and was leaving the room when May came in and handed her a letter. She read it in silence and then spoke quietly to Maria.

'Charlotte is dead. She died peacefully, in her sleep. The funeral has already taken place.'

Maria stared. 'Oh no!' she whispered. 'No, I don't believe it! She was getting better.'

'Thirty-four years old,' Ruth said. 'Poor Charlotte! Poor Ernest. What will he do now?'

A dreadful thought struck Maria. But Ruth couldn't do that, could she?

'Ruth, you shan't send me to Wisconsin! I won't go, do you hear me?'

'Of course I can't send you,' Ruth replied coldly. 'You know that. But I think it would mean a great deal to Ernest and the children if you were to visit for a few months.'

'This is your way of preventing me marrying Clive,' Maria said. 'You know perfectly well that he's soon to leave New York. But I won't do it, Ruth. You shan't persuade me. I'm sorry about Charlotte's death, but it won't change my mind. Moreover, I shall tell Clive that you are setting your friend Mr Barnet to inform on him. But he is Clive's friend too. Don't forget that!'

She flounced out of the room. Ruth re-read Ernest's letter. She wondered how Sean was faring. There was no mention of him.

In the late afternoon – Maria had gone out alone, Ruth suspected to meet with Clive – Joss Barnet called on Professor Woodburn. When he had been in the house a little while, May brought Ruth a message that Mr Barnet would like to see her.

'Will you ask him if he will be kind enough to come to my sitting-room?' Ruth asked.

As he stood in the doorway of her room, filling it with his height and breadth, Ruth vividly recalled the first time she had seen him, standing in the kitchen at Millfield. She had thought then that he was the most handsome man she had ever seen in her life. She still thought him so. The sight of him still moved her unbearably; she, who Maria said didn't know how to love! Yet shouldn't the fact of her feelings for Joss give her more understanding of Maria?

'Please sit down. Aurora, move your doll from the chair.' She had forgotten, in the scene with Maria, that Aurora was there, quietly taking it all in. Now she was surprised at the steadiness of her voice. It gave away nothing of the tumult inside her.

'Professor Woodburn has told you of my concern for my sister,' she said. 'Is there anything you can say about Mr Masterson which could have any bearing on Maria's wish to marry him – in fact her determination to do so? We know nothing at all about him except what he himself has told us, and that's very little.'

'I can't add much,' Joss replied. 'I don't know him at all well. I was introduced to him in Richmond when I was there on business. I was invited to a theatrical party there. But of one thing I can assure you – he gave no appearance of being already married and I am fairly sure he is not.'

'Thank heaven for that!' Ruth said. 'It is what I feared most.'

'Naturally. Also, he has a mother and two sisters, all of whom I have met.'

'Is his mother an agreeable person?' Ruth asked. 'Will she welcome Maria?'

He smiled. 'I have met your sister only two or three times, Ruth. She struck me as a lively young lady, able to hold her own even against a mother-in-law. But it is Clive Masterson she will be marrying, not his mother. And as the young couple expect to travel, they and Mrs Masterson senior won't be living in each other's pockets.'

'You are being quite tactful,' Ruth said. 'I think you mean that Mrs Masterson is a dragon. But it will be up to Maria to get along with her in-laws. So you have nothing else to say about Clive Masterson?'

Joss Barnet hesitated.

'I can see that you have,' Ruth prompted.

'Perhaps I would say, if I were to be pressed. . . .'

'I am pressing you.'

'I would say that he is no good at handling money. He is totally honest – I have no doubt of that – but money slips through his fingers.'

'Is he in debt?'

'I think not now.' But he has been, Ruth thought quickly. And you have bailed him out.

'But I'm sure of one thing,' Joss went on. 'He truly loves your sister.'

'And she is head-over-heels in love with him.'

'I envy them,' Joss said quietly. 'Everything else can be

solved where there is enough love.'

You are wrong, Ruth thought. I love you with all my heart, yet it solves nothing. It only makes life more difficult.

She could not look at him. She fixed her attention on Aurora, who was sitting on the hearthrug, playing with her doll. 'Don't you think Aurora looks well?' she asked.

'Very well. And very pretty. I have brought a small gift for her. May I give it to her?'

'If it is not too valuable.' She wanted to protest, but it would be cruel. She had seen the look in his eyes as he watched Aurora. Just once, she would let him give his daughter a present.

From his pocket he pulled a glove puppet in the shape of a clown. He slipped it over his hand and, using the puppet, beckoned Aurora over to him. She came at once, and when he invited her, through the puppet, to sit on his knee, she did so with alacrity. She was fascinated by the clown, by the fact that it spoke to her, took her hand. Ruth, watching the child who in face and features was so like the man on whose lap she sat, swallowed the lump which came into her throat.

Presently, and with obvious reluctance, Joss put Aurora gently down. 'I must leave. I have an appointment at the bank.'

'It was good of you to come,' Ruth said. 'Thank you.'

'Ruth. . . .'

'Yes?'

'Couldn't I see you from time to time? As a friend?'

Now Sean was no longer here, he meant. But for Ruth Sean's presence was still between them, and must remain so. In any case, there was no way they could simply be friends. It could not stop at that.

'I'm sorry.' She couldn't bear that he should go out of her life again, and yet he must.

'Then if you ever need me?' he said unhappily.

'I will come to you,' Ruth promised. She needed him all the time. She would always need him. But it was impossible.

* * *

In Wisconsin Ernest was surprised at the speed with which the household settled down to normality after Charlotte's death. He was ashamed of the relief he felt that he no longer had to see his wife's ravaged body, her grey face, or hear the gasps of pain which she had not always managed to conceal. For weeks before her death he had been afraid to touch her for fear it should start the pain. Sometimes, in the night, he would have liked to have held her in his arms to comfort her; but she did not want it. Long before her actual death she had left him.

They had buried Charlotte in the small graveyard which held the emigrants, some of whom should never have come here due to sickness or old age, in the first place, others who had not been able to withstand the harshness of the life, and the babies who had not survived long enough to know it. From the moment they had returned from the funeral there had been an orderliness in the home. It became good to come back to the cabin at the end of the day. The children were clean and cared for, the food was ready for the table. Surprisingly quickly, there was laughter again.

Ernest knew that it was due to Emily Watson. He knew it and thanked God for it every day. He couldn't have survived without her, none of them could. Now, though he was grateful for the years he had had with Charlotte, and would never forget her, he felt he could begin to look forward to the future.

Sean's feelings were not so good. Emily, who had been in his arms at the moment of Charlotte's death, had refused to have anything more to do with him. She was polite. She tended to his needs – made his meals, washed his shirts, mended his socks – but not even a look, let alone words, of intimacy passed between them. In the end he tackled her about it.

'I'm sorry,' she said firmly. 'It wouldn't be fitting. It was wrong, what we did, and I'm ashamed of it.' Inside herself she still felt disturbed that at the moment she had given herself up to illicit ecstasy, perhaps at the very instant, Charlotte had given up her life. Sometimes she felt drenched in guilt, which she tried to work off with an extra burst of scrubbing and cleaning. She would come through it in time, and she knew without a doubt that the way to do so was to devote herself to Ernest Gaunt and his children. There must be no more Sean O'Farrell.

'There's no call for ye to be ashamed,' Sean protested. 'It was a natural and loving thing.'

'If I was married to you,' she replied. 'But I'm not. And you're married to someone else.'

'If you can call it a marriage,' Sean said, quietly. He felt in his bones that he would not see Ruth again.

'You should go away,' Emily told him. 'Go back to your wife.'

He would never do that. But perhaps he should go away. There was nothing for him here.

A few days later, after supper, he said, 'I'm moving on. I'm not settled here.'

Ernest didn't argue the point. He knew that Sean didn't fit in. 'Where will you go?' he asked.

Sean shrugged. 'Anywhere.'

'There are jobs in the lead mines in Iowa County, in the south-west of Wisconsin, over towards the Mississippi,' Ernest said.

'Then I might go there. Earn some money, then join a wagon train west to California. That's the place to go.'

'Have you told Ruth?'

'I'll write to her tonight,' Sean said. He would tell her he was going out of her life; for good.

The next morning he left. He promised to send money for the horse he rode as soon as he made some. Ernest and his father, Emily and the children, stood outside the house and watched him go. When he was almost out of sight along the trail, he turned and waved.

Maria had been unusually subdued for days now, Ruth thought. Nothing was right between them, though the quarrelling had stopped. During the day Maria spent much of her time out of the house, presumably with Clive Masterson, but sometimes, when he had matinees, with Mrs Seaford. Mealtimes were silent, and after supper Ruth sat with her menus or household books, or in rarer moments with the newspaper, while Maria sat stitching, as now, at a new blouse.

Suddenly Maria broke the silence.

'Very well then. If it's what you want I'll go to Wisconsin. But only for a visit, mind!'

Ruth stared at her in amazement.

'Maria, I never asked you to go! I can't go myself and I wouldn't ask you to do so.'

'Nevertheless, you can't deny it's what you'd like me to do.'

'I think Ernest would be delighted to have you there,' Ruth agreed. 'We know he has Emily Watson, but it can't be the same. I should miss you very much, but my loss would be his gain.'

'You really don't care about my loss, or Clive's, do you?' Maria said bitterly.

Ruth had not told her sister the whole outcome of her meeting with Joss Barnet, only that he had confirmed that Clive Masterson was of a decent Virginian family and had no encumbrances. Of his attitude to money she had not spoken. She had remained adamant, however, that Maria ought to wait until she was twenty-one to marry. This was still the bone of contention between them.

'Of course I care,' Ruth objected. 'I simply want you to have a little time to get to know each other better.'

'And how will we do that if I am in Wisconsin, or New York, and Clive is in Virginia?' Maria demanded.

'So why then have you decided to go to Wisconsin?' Ruth asked.

'I don't know. But I shall go soon. Before I change my mind. The day after tomorrow.'

'So soon? Is that the day Clive leaves?'

'You know it is,' Maria replied sharply. 'I refuse to stay in New York a minute after he's gone!'

'Very well. Then tomorrow I shall help you pack,' Ruth said.

'There is no need. I can do my own packing.'

Ruth sighed. At least she would have liked to part friends with Maria, but it seemed impossible.

Maria spent most of the next day in her room, presumably packing, except for an hour when she went out to see Clive. She returned from that visit pale, and even more subdued. Ruth's heart ached for her.

On the morning of Maria's departure Ruth said, 'It is almost time for the carriage. Just give me a minute to put on my cloak and bonnet.'

'You are not to see me to the railroad station,' Maria said. 'If you come, I shan't go!'

'Then who will help you with all this luggage?' Ruth asked. 'I can't think why you need to take so much.'

'Clive will see me off, of course. He would not dream of doing otherwise.'

'Very well then,' Ruth said.

When the last minute came and Maria was getting into the carriage she turned and flung her arms around Ruth, standing there on the sidewalk.

'Oh Ruth, I'm sorry if I've been horrid!' she cried. 'Please forgive me!'

'Why, there's nothing to forgive,' Ruth said. 'And believe me, I do understand.'

She understood even better next afternoon, when the telegram came from Washington.

'Married here yesterday. Leaving for Richmond tomorrow. Forgive us and wish us happiness. Maria and Clive.'

Ruth ran upstairs to Mrs Seaford's room and hammered on the door, then burst in before Mrs Seaford had time to answer.

'Did you know about this?' she cried. 'Were you in the plot to deceive me?' She flung the telegram at Mrs Seaford. She had no need of an answer. The dark flush which swept over Mrs Seaford's face, even before she read the telegram, said everything.

'I didn't want to deceive you,' Mrs Seaford said. 'If I had I'd have agreed to Maria's request to hide all her luggage in my room, and help her to smuggle it to the station when you were out. I refused to be party to that under your roof, which was why she invented the story about Wisconsin. You should have guessed she would never have gone there.'

'You could have told me,' Ruth said angrily.

'It would have done no good. She would have gone with Clive Masterson whatever you said. She'd made up her mind about that and you couldn't have stopped her. Her deception was designed just to get her out of the house without fuss. And if you'd quarrelled even worse with Maria you'd have lost her forever.'

'I have lost her,' Ruth cried 'When shall I ever see her again? What will become of her?'

It was a day for loss. She was glad that Mrs Seaford could not know the contents of the letter at present in her pocket. It had arrived from Sean, not long before Maria's telegram. It was equally to the point.

> 'I'm not much good at writing, nor at anything else. I'm striking out west, maybe California – who knows? I don't regret anything we had together but this is good-bye, Ruth. Give Aurora a kiss for me.'

What was she, Ruth thought, leaving Mrs Seaford's room – what was she that people left her like this? That she had deserved what Sean was doing to her made it no less painful.

When she was halfway down the stair the doorbell rang. Not waiting for Sammy, she answered it herself, and saw Joss Barnet standing there. He followed her through to her sitting-room.

'I can see by your face that you've heard!' he said.

'And you? How do you know?' He could surely not have known of the plot? *He* could not have deceived her so. It would be more than she could bear.

'Masterson sent me a telegram from Washington. Try not to worry, Ruth. You can do nothing now except leave Maria to get on with her own life. It could turn out better than we expect. She might surprise us all.'

'She never ceases to do that,' Ruth said quietly. 'And I had this today, also. It hasn't been the best of days for me.' She took Sean's letter out of her pocket and handed it to him. He read it with an expressionless face and handed it back to her.

'Oh Joss, what have I done?' she cried. His face was blurred by the tears which filled her eyes. 'Oh Joss, everyone is going out of my life!'

He looked at her steadily, then held out his hands to her.

'I will never do so, Ruth. I will never go out of your life.'

'You are the one I must *send* away!' Ruth cried.

'But I shan't go.'

# *Part Four*

# 27

'Do hurry, Aurora!' Ruth pleaded. 'You'll be late for school again. And fasten up your collar. There's a nip in the air this morning.'

Aurora pulled a face. 'I hate school. Why do I have to go to school?'

'Because you have to be educated,' Ruth said patiently.

'I *am* educated,' Aurora retorted. 'I can read and write, and I'm the best in the class at painting. Who wants to do stupid history and geography?'

'Get your things together and stop arguing,' Ruth commanded. 'And don't forget your new apron. Such a lovely tartan apron – you'll be the best-dressed girl in the class.'

'I shall not,' Aurora contradicted. 'Violet Pleasant is the best dressed. Also she has a white porcelain slate. She's the only girl in the school who has one. No wonder her sums look better than anyone else's! I long for one with all my heart.'

Violet Pleasant was a new girl. Ruth had not yet set eye on her but she was the most important person in Aurora's life. It seemed she had the longest hair, the prettiest dresses, the richest parents and the largest number of enviable possessions of any girl in the world.

'Well, no school tomorrow,' Ruth said. 'Tomorrow is a holiday for the Prince of Wales!'

'Violet is to watch him from a *balcony*,' Aurora announced. '*Her* mother has a friend who has a house with a balcony right on Broadway. Violet will have a splendid view.'

'Good for her,' Ruth said. 'Though I daresay you won't do so badly. Since Uncle Clive and Aunt Maria are visiting I expect between us we'll be able to lift you up high enough to see everything. And now here is May to take you to school.'

Over the last six years May had gradually moved out of the kitchen. She helped in other parts of the house, but spent much of her time keeping an eye on Aurora when Ruth was busy. That was frequently the case these days, since Appleby's was now greatly increased in size. A year ago the house next door had become empty and Ruth, though with trepidation which sometimes kept her awake in the middle of the night, had immediately rented it, with permission to make some structural alterations. A door opened up here, a wall knocked down there, rooms divided or extended and the kitchens reorganised had transferred her modest boarding-house into a small hotel, though she had not, and never would have, changed the name.

Before this happened, Appleby's had already become known as a first-class, comfortable place to live, a true home from home, and she had a waiting list of people who had expressed a wish to board with her should the opportunity arise. Consequently - she would have hesitated to undertake it otherwise - she was able to fill most of the rooms in the new extension the moment they were ready. She was making quite a nice profit, thank you, even with the extra staff she had had to take on.

'I don't need May to take me to school!' Aurora protested. 'I'm nine years old. I'm not a baby!'

Ruth frowned, shook her head. 'But you have to cross Broadway - and the traffic gets worse and worse. I couldn't possibly let you go alone.'

Watching the two of them leave, Aurora still arguing the toss, Ruth sighed. Her daughter was not an easy child. Ruth was quietly aware that she spoilt her a little, was over-protective, but she could never forget that once she had almost died of scarlet fever. She had never felt totally secure about her since. Also, she tried always to compensate for the fact that she was the child's only parent, tried to be both mother and father to her. The absence of her father never seemed to worry Aurora. She never spoke of Sean and Ruth was almost sure she had forgotten him.

When May and Aurora had left, and she had watched them for a little way along the street, Ruth hurried to the dining-room. She had hoped to catch Mr Pierce before he quitted the house.

'I'm afraid you're too late,' Mrs Seaford said. 'He left ten minutes ago.'

She and Miss Fontwell were the only boarders left at breakfast, the latter because it was her late-starting morning, Mrs Seaford because she had nothing better to do. Miss Fontwell, Ruth thought, is the least changed of any of us. It was as if she was frozen in time, like the historical characters who made up her life.

'Miss Fontwell, I wanted to see you too,' Ruth said. 'Shall you be taking the day off tomorrow for the Prince of Wales?'

'Certainly not!' Miss Fontwell replied tartly. She had no sense of history in the making, only for that past and gone, the longer ago the better.

'I was just thinking about meals,' Ruth explained. 'People coming and going at unusual times. I was hoping to ask Mr Pierce if Lord and Taylor's would be closing. Do you happen to know, Mrs Seaford?'

Mr Pierce had moved to Lord and Taylor's a year ago when they had opened their splendid new store at the corner of Broadway and Grand. It was five storeys high, built of white marble, with a great glass chandelier made by Tiffany's hanging in splendour over the staircase. 'More like an Italian palace than a place for the sale of broadcloth,' Mr Seaford had said at the time. 'And is the chandelier really *safe*, one wonders?' Stewart's (and therefore Mr Seaford) had also moved, to a magnificent new building near to Grace church. Even so, there was constant rivalry between the two men.

'I think not,' Mrs Seaford said. 'Mr Pierce thought they

might close at the moment the procession passed, so as to let the staff watch. I only hope that both stores do the same thing, whatever it is, or those two men will come to blows!'

Ruth laughed. 'They might have done so long ago were they not both such amiable gentlemen.'

'I hoped Maria might have been down to breakfast this morning,' Mrs Seaford said. 'I wanted to persuade her to come shopping with me.'

'Well, you know what theatricals are,' Ruth replied. 'Up until all hours at night and spend most of the morning in bed, even when they're "resting".'

Clive and Maria had been 'resting' in Virginia most of the summer, which, Ruth suspected, was what had driven them northwards to New York for a visit which had lasted several weeks. It was the first time they had returned to the city in six years though the sisters had long ago made up their quarrel, and wrote to each other from time to time. Though she told herself that one day she would do so, Ruth had not yet visited Richmond. It was impossible for her to leave Appleby's.

Mrs Seaford sighed. 'I suppose they'll be going back to Richmond soon?'

'In just a few days.'

'A pity!'

Ruth went into the kitchen.

'I'm just going to make a start on the bedrooms with Leila,' Mrs Cruse said. 'Agnes is doing the dishes, Mrs Traill is sorting the laundry and Morris is cleaning the silver – so everything's in hand.'

Agnes, Mrs Traill and Leila were new additions to the staff since the enlargement of Appleby's. Morris, a youth of eighteen, not very bright but as strong as an ox, had replaced Sammy, though he did not act as a page-boy. Ruth had never liked having a page-boy.

'Do you ever hear what happened to Sammy?' she asked Mrs Cruse. He had left Appleby's three years ago, hoping to find a job working on the development of Central Park, which would pay him more. The City had set aside a sum of money for this, mainly to create jobs for the unemployed. Also, since Sammy's family had moved to the north of Manhattan, where the black population was beginning to settle, Spring Street was too far away for him.

'Not a word,' Mrs Cruse replied. 'I guess he chose a bad time to leave. Forty thousand men out of work in the city, begging in the streets and standing in line for a bowl of free soup. But you can't tell the young anything.'

'Well, I hope he's all right,' Ruth said. 'And now I must get on with my marketing. I'm sure many of the shops will be closed tomorrow, so I must buy for two days.'

As Ruth was leaving the kitchen Mrs Cruse called out to her, 'We could do with more pumice powder; if you're going near Dent's perhaps you could put some on the order.'

What would Mrs Cruse think if she knew exactly where I was going, Ruth asked herself? Did Mrs Cruse, or anyone else in the house, suspect that on some of her excursions she not only did the shopping, she went to meet her lover? She thought it unlikely. They had been discreet.

Looking critically at herself in the mirror, Ruth tied her bonnet strings carefully in a bow under her chin. Bonnet ribbons were much wider now and she was not good at tying a bow which would stay in place. This afternoon she would wear the blue shawl which Joss had given her for a birthday present in the spring, but before long she must bring out her cloak. The weather, though continuing bright, was cool for October.

In Broadway she boarded the omnibus. Sitting there, as it jerked its way northwards, she thought back over the years since she and Joss had become lovers again. From the moment Sean had left her, Joss had begged her to come to him. He had made every opportunity to see her. Sometimes his visits to Spring Street were ostensibly to see Professor Woodburn, but increasingly he gave no excuse at all.

'My wife has left me; your husband has deserted you,' he pleaded. 'Why shouldn't we take the happiness we know can be ours?'

'When Aurora was so ill,' Ruth told him, 'I promised God that if he let her live, I would be good. She *did* live.'

'But God isn't like that!' Joss protested. 'Not as far as I understand these things. He doesn't exact promises under duress. You don't need to drive bargains with God. I'm not a religious man, but some who are might say that God it is who puts love into our hearts; yours for me, mine for you. Why should we deny that love?'

For three years she had held out against him: years in which it seemed that Sean was gone forever, years in which her heart and body longed for Joss. There were times when she feared that he would wait no longer, would leave her forever, though he himself never threatened that. In the end his persistence, and their mutual need, overcame every other feeling.

'But I can't visit you in Gramercy Park,' she said. 'That belongs to another part of your life.' And never again could she countenance an establishment like that in Broome Street. They had come too far for that.

'I understand,' Joss told her. 'I don't want you to do so.'

He took a spacious apartment in a new, custom-built service block at Twenty-Second Street and Fourth Avenue, the first of its kind to be built in the city.

'This is for you and me, Ruth,' he'd said. 'A place where you and I can be alone together, no-one to intrude. A place where we can forget the rest of the world.'

That was how it had been ever since. She had never regretted her decision, so hardly taken. And though it had happened many times now, she would never forget the first time they had made love there. There had been a sense of freedom – perhaps because they were the very first occupants of the apartment, there were no spirits there to haunt them, it had been created just for them – which they had never known before in their relationship. In total liberty and without constraint they had abandoned themselves to each other, keeping back nothing; discovering an ecstasy which seemed, at its peak, to belong to another world. It was a world in which their whole beings – physical, mental, spiritual – came together in one tremendous explosion.

Alighting from the bus, walking along Fourth Avenue, Ruth thought of how many times in the last two years she had trodden this sidewalk. She had done so when it was deep in frozen snow; on rainy days when the passing traffic had soaked her skirts with dirty water from the gutter; on hot, steamy July days when there was no escape from the sun. And always she had felt the same sharp tingle of excitement, the same warm anticipation. On this October morning, with the breeze ruffling her hair and stripping the leaves from the trees in Union Square to swirl them about her feet, she felt it again. Familiarity never diminished it.

Apart from what it meant to the two of them, this way of living suited Joss well. He needed no servants since the resident supervisor and his wife, and the uniformed doorman, between them looked after most of his needs. In addition there was a first-class meals service from a nearby restaurant. It was the new way of living in New York, especially for single people and couples without children, and he liked it. Ruth was free to come and go as she pleased, to let herself in with her own key as she did now.

Joss had heard her key in the lock, and as she stepped into the apartment he took her at once in his arms, holding her close as if he would never let her go.

'Ruth, my dearest, it's been so long!' His voice came muffled as he buried his face in her hair.

'Ten days. But. . . .'

He stopped her words with a long, hard kiss. Then at last he let her go, holding her at arm's length, looking at her from top to toe.

'Well, if you will go to Millfield,' Ruth said.

'I know. But for once Naomi agreed to let the children visit with me there.'

'Did she bring them?' Ruth asked quickly. The thought depressed her. There were still so many areas of his life she could not enter. Millfield, which he still visited regularly, which she longed to see again, was one of them. His work was another. Three years ago, in that terrible financial panic when many of New York's bankers and speculators had lost fortunes, she knew that he had not gone unscathed, though he himself never talked about it. The fact that well before the crash, he had diversified into shipping, was what had saved him. Now he had ships which took goods from New York down to the South, and picked up cotton from the Southern States to carry to Liverpool.

'Naomi didn't bring them,' he said. 'They are old enough now to travel without her. But it wasn't a successful visit and won't be repeated. I think they are closer to their stepfather than to me.'

'I'm truly sorry,' Ruth said.

He shrugged, and turned away, and Ruth knew that the subject was closed. His former marriage was another subject he never discussed, though Ruth believed he had been as surprised and shocked as the rest of New York society when Naomi had left him for another man. Whether the affair had touched his heart as well as his pride was another matter. Ruth's only assurance about this was the love he so clearly had for herself.

Within seconds he turned back to her.

'Let me look at you,' he said. 'Let me see if you've changed in the last ten days!'

But in his eyes she never changed, unless it was to grow lovelier. She was still the same eager-spirited girl he had met ten years ago, still as attractive to him as she had been then. At Millfield recently he had walked to the hilltop where he had first taken her in his arms. Would it have been better for her, he'd thought as he stood there, if on that occasion he'd ridden past her, not stopped to dismount?

'Well, have I changed?' Ruth asked.

'Yes. You're prettier.'

Ruth saw little change in Joss Barnet in the time she had known him. A few lines around his eyes, a little grey beginning to show in his dark hair, only made him more handsome. At thirty-eight he was in the prime of his life and his looks.

'I can't stay long,' she said.

'Why not?'

'Such a mundane reason. I have two days marketing to do and the shops are at sixes and sevens with the Prince's visit. I'm afraid of them selling out before I get there. But I had to come here first. I couldn't wait to see you.'

'Come and sit beside me,' he said, suddenly serious. 'I have something important to say to you, Ruth.'

She knew what it would be. He had said it many times – and still she couldn't give him the answer he wanted.

'When are you going to marry me, Ruth?' he demanded.

She sighed. 'It's all been said before, Joss. I'm already married. . . .'

'. . . To a man you've neither seen nor heard from in six years. A man who might not even be alive.'

'But Joss, we've been over this again and again. You know I believe he's still alive somewhere. While we don't know, how can I marry you? It isn't as if. . . .'

'It isn't as if we're not lovers,' he said. 'I know. And I'm grateful. But it's not the same, is it?'

'Of course it's not the same. Oh Joss, do you believe I don't feel it too? Do you think it doesn't hurt that I can't meet you openly, can't be seen with you in public? You know that I want to be with you all the time. Do you think I don't waken in the middle of the night and want to turn to you and be in your arms?'

There had been nothing from Sean since the letter she had received at the time of Maria's elopement, nor had Ernest heard a word. At first she had wanted to hear from him, to be assured that he was all right, but those feelings had long ago left her. Her sense told her that he might well be dead, might not have survived the hazards of that perilous trek to California – but how could she ever be sure?

'You could divorce him,' Joss said. 'After six years . . . I can't wait forever, Ruth!'

She shivered at his words. How could she bear to lose him again? And if she did, this time she knew it would be for good. And yet . . . even to herself she could not explain her deep reluctance to do as Joss wanted, although with all her heart she wanted it herself.

'Oh Joss, please let's not talk about it now,' she begged. 'Let's be happy as we are!'

'We can't go on shelving it,' he said. 'In time we shall both grow tired of this hole-and-corner relationship.'

'Never! Never, Joss!'

'It's inevitable. And it's not necessary. Ruth, I'm making an ultimatum. Listen to me. I want your promise, here and now, that if you haven't heard from Sean O'Farrell by the end of another year, then you'll take steps to have your marriage dissolved on the grounds that he's missing, presumed dead. It will be seven years then, and I'm not prepared to wait a day longer. I want you for my wife.'

'Joss, I promise I'll think about it!'

He shook his head. 'No Ruth, that won't do. I want your promise now, that in a year's time you'll marry me.'

His eyes were suddenly hard. There was no compromise in him. In this mood she was almost afraid of him.

'But if Sean. . . .'

He jumped up from the sofa where they had been sitting together, and began to pace the floor in long, angry strides.

'There are times when I could kill Sean O'Farrell!' he cried angrily.

'I don't believe you could kill anyone,' Ruth said. She had experienced his tenderness towards herself, seen his love for Aurora, discovered a side to him which he had kept hidden from the world, which saw him as the inflexible, supremely successful businessman. It was a side of him which she had not even guessed at in the early days of their affair, and one which bound them close. It was so different from his present demeanour.

He stood still, and faced her.

'You're wrong,' he said. 'There are some things for which a man – almost any man – would kill. For the woman he loves; for his child; in defence of his country.'

She was shaken by the passion in his voice.

'You would kill for those reasons?'

'Definitely!'

'Then thank heaven they are causes which won't arise,'

Ruth said, shivering a little.

'You haven't answered my question,' Joss persisted. 'Will you promise to marry me in a year's time? I love you, Ruth.'

He held her by the shoulders, looked deep into her eyes. She was everything to him, this English girl who had been no more than a servant with whom he had elected to spend a little time, and who ever since had held him by the heart strings. But he had waited long enough.

'Promise!' he repeated.

The silence between them seemed to go on forever. In the end it was Ruth who could hold out no longer.

'Very well. I promise,' she said quietly.

At the very moment she uttered the words her spirits soared. Joy swept through her like a tide. Why, oh why, had she ever had the slightest doubt? She ran to him and was in his arms.

'Oh Joss, you know I love you!' she cried. 'I long to marry you!'

He held her against him and his lips sought hers. His hands caressed her body, stroking her back, her throat, her breasts. She pressed herself against him and caressed him with an ardour equal to his.

'Come to bed, Ruth,' he whispered.

She drew away from him. 'I can't! There isn't time.'

'Time?'

'But you know how much I want to.'

He let her go. 'Appleby's calls,' he said, 'what a dutiful girl you are. Very well – but another time you won't get away so easily. And in a year from now you'll belong to me always. You will have all the time in the world.'

'I truly long for it,' Ruth replied.

Before she left she said, 'Don't forget you're having supper with us tomorrow evening, after the procession. Your friendship with Clive at least gives us another excuse to meet.'

She walked all the way back to Spring Street, did her shopping on the way.

'The streets are choc-a-bloc,' she told May. 'And Broadway is impossible.'

'But how pretty it looks with all the decorations! I never saw so much bunting nor so many flags,' May said. 'Oh, how I'm looking forward to seeing the Prince! They say he's ever so handsome, and half the ladies in Europe are in love with him. Imagine marrying a prince!'

Ruth had long ago formed the opinion that the reason why May was not married was because the kind of man she aspired to was only to be found in the pages of a novel and did not exist in real life. But perhaps she was as happy in her dreaming as those who chose reality.

Three hundred thousand people jammed the streets and occupied the rooftops all the way from the Battery to the Fifth Avenue Hotel at Twenty-Third Street where the Prince of Wales was staying, just to see him go by in his carriage. Ruth found the dense crowd unnerving, and only the fact that everyone was in such good spirits made it bearable. She caught the merest glimpse of the Prince, a pleasant-looking young man with dark hair and whiskers, but Maria had a better view and Clive hoisted Aurora on to his shoulders so that she could see everything. Nevertheless, the child was bitterly disappointed.

'He's only a man!' she complained.

'But such a charming, handsome man,' Maria said. 'And our very own prince!'

'Then why isn't he wearing a crown?' Aurora demanded. 'And a velvet cloak with fur? He's just like Mr Pierce!'

Maria laughed. 'You must tell Mr Pierce that. He will be delighted.' What a poppet Aurora was, though quite wilful, usually wanting her own way. She had been sad for a little while when she and Clive did not have a child, but now she was resigned to it. Almost. No doubt it would have been inconvenient when they were travelling around. She might even have to stay behind with her mother-in-law, and heaven knew she had had enough of that. Besides, she would always have her dear Clive to look after.

At that evening's meal, which they took late, after the boarders had been fed and Aurora settled down, it was inevitable that the conversation should turn to the day's events.

'So what did *you* think of your prince?' Joss smiled at Ruth as he asked the question. It was so good to be with her here in this relaxed, domestic situation. With all his heart he looked forward to the time when he could always be openly with her, though naturally it would not be in Appleby's. When she was his wife she need never earn her living again. 'Did the sight of him make you homesick? Do you still miss Yorkshire?'

'I suppose I do,' Ruth said thoughtfully. 'But I think of it less often than I did. And when I do it's the high hills and the solitude which come to mind. But the people I love are no longer there – except Willie, who I daresay has forgotten me.'

Mentioning her family brought Ernest to mind. She had not seen him since Charlotte died, though from time to time they wrote to each other. He had married Emily Watson within a few months of Charlotte's death and now they had three children of their own to add to his and Charlotte's five. Enoch would be thirteen next month. Uncle Matthew, in his sixties, was still going strong.

She was roused from her reverie by Clive speaking to Maria.

'One day, my love, when we do our tour of the theatres of England you shall take me to your famous Ilkley moors and Yorkshire dales. I long to see them!'

'Well, I don't!' Maria answered firmly. 'I'm more than happy to be in New York and I only wish we could stay here longer.' There was really nothing to send them back to Richmond, and her in-laws. They had no work at present. Clive had not had a part for several months now, and *she* had scarcely ever had a part, not what you could call a part, not anything more than walking on and delivering one line.

Her dreams of being Clive's leading lady had been shattered almost at once. Georgina de Monclare would not hear of it; George Potter, the manager, wouldn't countenance it. The partnership of the popular Miss de Monclare and the handsome Mr Clive Masterson, he pointed out, was what got them their engagements. Also, it would never do for Clive's public to know that he was married. So Mr Potter had given her, as a consolation prize, the job of wardrobe mistress, which meant that she spent her time making, mending, even laundering, the costumes of the cast. Into Miss de Monclare's garments she sewed dislike and frustration with every stitch.

But engagements of any kind had been thin over the last year or two, even when they had condescended to appear at second-rate theatres. The company's repertoire was too small and most of Virginia had already seen it. All summer they had been resting. Mrs Masterson senior had never approved of her son going into acting. He should have been a lawyer like his dear, late father. But if acting was bad, 'resting' was a thousand times worse. Only grudgingly, and for reasons of family respectability, did she give them hospitality – which they were obliged to take because they had no money for board and lodgings elsewhere.

'Couldn't we stay on here a little longer?' Maria persisted. Quite apart from the attractions of New York, Appleby's was a good place to stay. Ruth was generous and denied them nothing.

'We have discussed this before, my love,' Clive said gently. He was unfailingly courteous, even when denying his wife what she wanted. 'We must return soon. I must be available when the call comes from my public!' He never had any doubt at all that it *would* come; he was not forgotten. And when it did, it would be from his native Virginia, not from New York. He had always suspected that he wouldn't quite make it in New York. The engagement six years ago had been a fluke – or perhaps the hand of Fate so that he should meet his darling Maria.

When the meal was over they left the table and sat in comfortable armchairs, drinking coffee. If Mrs Gutermann were to come back now, Ruth thought, she wouldn't know where she was. Over the years she had completely changed the appearance of the room. The dark, heavy hangings had gone. Everything was fresh and light, in clear, delicate colours, even though such was not the fashion.

Nor were the walls modishly covered with ornately-framed pictures. She had one or two water-colours and she had the painting of New York harbour which had been her wedding present from the boarders. There was a photograph taken by Mr Matthew Brady – not of herself, she had still not achieved that – of Aurora in a white organdie dress, with a bow in her hair. But pride of place was given to her most precious possession, her Grandmother Appleby's sampler.

'You may both wish by this time next year that you had never left Yorkshire,' Joss said suddenly.

The three of them looked at him. Was he jesting? But when Ruth saw his face she knew that he was not.

'Well, I won't for one,' Maria retorted emphatically. 'I was glad to leave and I never want to return.'

'What do you mean, Joss?' Ruth asked. He of all people knew that she would never wish that. She could never leave him now.

'I mean I think there will be a war.'

His words, spoken with quiet conviction, sent a wave of cold shock through Ruth. She saw Clive's troubled face and realised at once, and to her surprise, that the idea was not new to him. Only Maria was able to brush it aside.

'War? How could that happen?' she asked. 'New York is so prosperous. There is nowhere as lively and prosperous as New York!'

'My dear Maria, New York is not the whole of America,' Joss replied. 'There are things happening in the rest of America which, if not dealt with, must lead to war.'

'You are referring to the slave trade,' Clive said quietly. 'Isn't that so? And you know that Virginia is a slave state – but I assure you that we are not the least ashamed of it. We treat our slaves well. It's simply that in the North you don't understand us.'

'Perhaps it's the lack of understanding, you of us, we of

you, that's at the root of the trouble,' Joss suggested.

'But there are no slaves in New York,' Maria said. 'Why should a war affect New York?'

Clive smiled at her. 'You are a little ignoramus, my darling. And if it comforts you, you must stay one.'

'It's partly a matter of trade,' Joss said. 'A great deal of New York's trade depends on doing business with the South. My own ships, for instance, would be at a standstill if they didn't take manufactured goods of all kinds from the North to the South, and pick up cargoes of cotton from the South to take to Liverpool. The South depends on such ships too. She has very few of her own. So war would badly affect New York's trade.'

'And take her men,' Ruth spoke quietly. No-one seemed to hear her.

'It's perhaps not slavery in itself which will cause the war,' Joss continued. 'With respect to you, Clive, I believe slavery to be wrong, but I also believe that it would die out of its own accord within a few years. Slowly but surely, slaves are being freed in many places.'

'Then what . . .?' Ruth began.

'There are those in the North who won't wait, and those in the South who think everything may happen too soon. Seward, New York State's own senator, has said that in the Union all States must be free or all must be slave-owning. This pronouncement frightens both North and South.'

'But your Mr Seward is not now going to be President,' Clive said.

'That's true. But he has influenced others and the fear is spreading. It's not slavery in itself, but its use as a weapon which will bring war.'

'But surely you're not saying that war is *inevitable?*' Ruth pleaded. She was suddenly living in a nightmare. How had this day, so pleasant for all of them, come to this awful ending?

'Perhaps not yet, but it soon will be,' Joss said. 'There's a point in most affairs when things can be put right by common sense and goodwill, but when that point is passed, there's no going back. And there are those on both sides right now who are stoking the fire.'

'Well, I *hate* all this talk about war!' Maria objected. 'Of course it won't happen! No-one could be so stupid!'

'I would also prefer to talk about something else,' Ruth said. She was suddenly and quite terrifyingly afraid. She wanted Joss to take her in his arms and comfort her, tell her that none of it was true. He met her look and was instantly contrite.

'I'm sorry,' he said. 'It was wrong of me to talk so.'

But you meant it, Ruth thought. You meant every word of it.

'It's midnight,' Maria announced. 'They'll be starting the firework display for the Prince. We simply must watch it!'

When Ruth drew back the curtains they saw that the display had indeed begun. 'We shall see more if we go outside,' she said.

The four of them went outside, and were joined by some of the boarders. The air was filled with the sight and sound and smell of fireworks. As they stood watching, Maria clapped her hands like a small child.

'It's wonderful!' she cried. 'I just adore it!'

Ruth watched a rocket rise into the air, make an arc of flame against the dark sky, finish with an explosion and a shower of sparks which fell to earth and expired. She was enveloped in fear.

'You're shivering, Ruth,' Joss said. 'You must go indoors.' Then he lowered his voice so that the others would not hear.

'When will you come?'

'Tomorrow.' She wanted to be with him all the time.

Long after everyone in the house had gone to bed, she lay awake. The fireworks went on into the early hours. Sometimes she saw them momentarily light up the sky, frequently she heard their noise. When sleep came closer she was not always sure whether she heard fireworks, or the sound of distant gunfire.

# 28

They did not have long to wait for the real gunfire. Only a few months after that October day when Joss had shadowed the evening with his talk of war, the first shots were fired. In the intervening time there were pointers which many people, Ruth among them, would have preferred to ignore, but which others, like Joss Barnet, could not.

No sooner had Lincoln been elected President than half a dozen states left the Union, and by February 1861 the South had set up its own government, with Jefferson Davis as Provisional President.

'But does it matter?' Ruth asked Joss. They were walking in Union Square, as they sometimes did when time permitted. It was a place where they were not so likely to meet anyone they knew.

Joss looked at her in astonishment. 'Of course it matters!'

'Why? Surely they can go their own way, and we ours. It seems simple to me.'

'Well, you're not the only one who thinks so,' he admitted. 'Mayor Wood would like to set up New York as a free, neutral city. Have it run its own affairs, with no responsibility to anyone.'

'And why not?' Ruth asked.

'Because it wouldn't work. The strength of America is in the different parts which go to make up the whole. If we each had our own frontiers, laws, armies, there'd be more risk than ever of war.'

'Why?' she persisted.

'What a question, Ruth! Because it's in the nature of man, that's why.'

'But not of woman. There'd be no wars if women ruled!'

'So women always say. Anyway, to change the subject, how is my little Aurora? What outrageous thing has she said today?'

'Never mind Aurora,' Ruth said firmly. 'I don't want to change the subject. I'm trying to be serious, to learn from you. So you insist, do you, that war must come?'

She knew her own foolishness in asking the question, and she dreaded the answer. She would have preferred to have dismissed all thoughts of war, but the subject nagged at her like a hollow tooth which she must everlastingly probe with her tongue, in spite of the ensuing pain. What she wanted to know, what tore at her all the time, was what Joss would do if there was a war. He never said, always shying away from the subject, and she couldn't bring herself to ask him outright.

'My darling, I don't *insist* there'll be war. I fear there will,' he said.

Joss was not the only worry. There was Maria. She was back in Richmond now, living with her in-laws. And Virginia had not yet left the Union . . . but if she did. . . .

'Anyone who looks can see the signs in New York,' Joss went on.

'Well I've never understood New York politics,' Ruth confessed. 'They eddy and swirl about like waves in the sea.'

'But you read the newspapers,' Joss said. 'You know how much trade has been affected over the last few months. And trade is what New York lives by.'

That evening when she was serving tea to the boarders, the subject came up again. Her boarders didn't often discuss the subject of war, perhaps because they had fewer personal stakes than most, but trade was another matter.

'The trouble is,' Mr Pierce declared, 'that this city has so many of its best customers in the South. I myself know a number of producers of textiles who make exclusively for the South – and now the South has stopped buying and men are losing their jobs.'

'It's not only textiles,' Mr Seaford said. 'Manufactured goods are also affected. They say that thousands of New York tailors will soon be out of jobs. And harness-makers!'

'*Harness-makers?*' Miss Fontwell queried.

'But of course. The best harness-makers are right here in the city and they work largely for the South because that's where the horses are.'

'Well, let's hope none of it will affect the retail trade,' Mrs Seaford said comfortably. 'I daresay Lord and Taylors, and Stewart's, will be all right. What do you say, Mrs Munster?'

Lavinia Munster and her husband Karl were new boarders since Ruth had enlarged her premises. Karl was an engineer, earnestly dedicated to the building of bridges, and to his pretty, frivolous wife, who reminded Ruth so much of Maria.

'It would be too, too awful if they were not,' Lavinia replied gravely.

'Well, dear ladies, in a trade recession sooner or later everyone suffers,' Mr Seaford said in a kindly manner. 'Fashion is part of trade. I don't want to depress you, but it could be that one day you will go into Stewart's and not find the exact shade of ribbon you require!'

'I happen to know,' Mr Pierce told them confidentially, 'that the hooped skirt industry depended so much on the South that it has gone out of business overnight. Only a little while and there will be no more hooped skirts!'

'Thank heaven for that,' Miss Fontwell said. 'It will give us all more room to move!'

'And of course,' Mr Seaford continued, 'it isn't only that the South isn't placing orders. They're refusing to pay for the goods they've already had.' He sighed, and passed his cup to be refilled.

Ruth seldom joined in the boarders' conversation, unless invited, but for once she couldn't keep silent.

'Well I'm thankful it's trade we're talking about and not

war,' she said. 'I daresay we can all make do with a little less, so long as we're left in peace.'

Outwardly, things didn't seem so bad. One read that there were more unemployed, but the long lines of men waiting for free soup were not seen, as in some previous winters. Ruth noticed that her marketing cost more, but by careful management (and slightly lower profits) she could cope with that. And then on a freakishly warm February day, the kind of day that only New York could throw up in the middle of a cold winter, Abraham Lincoln visited the city and the whole of New York went wild with excitement, everyone suddenly exuberant and lighthearted.

'I shall take you to see the procession,' Ruth said to Aurora. 'After all, Lincoln is your President.'

They took up places on the sidewalk opposite to Astor House, where Lincoln was staying. At their banks was Barnum's museum, and since Barnum had decided to display some of his menagerie on the sidewalk, Aurora was much more interested in that.

'I want to go inside Barnum's and see the Aztec children and the seahorses,' she protested. 'They'll be much better than a silly old president!'

'The President first,' Ruth said firmly.

It was all over so quickly. The band played. A company of men marched in front of the carriage in which Lincoln stood bowing to the crowds, looking a little surprised to see them there. Ruth thought how white and tired he looked, how little the new whiskers he was growing suited his long face. Then a minute later a group of people rushed out of Astor House to greet him, and he was gone. It was the last time he would come to New York alive, though the crowds would be even greater for his funeral.

Ruth made an excuse not to take Aurora into Barnum's. It reminded her too much of her wedding day with Sean. Last October, to please Joss, she had written to Ernest to enquire if he knew anything more of Sean's whereabouts, but he did not. She had shown his reply to Joss.

'It is the greatest pity (Ernest wrote) that you could not

see your way clear to joining Sean here. It would have been best for both of you.'

'It's quite clear Ernest blames me,' she said to Joss. 'Perhaps he's right.'

'Nonsense!' Joss was indignant. 'He is *not* right. Apart altogether from you and me, it would have been folly for you to have gone to Wisconsin, or anywhere else, with Sean O'Farrell.'

Right or wrong, she knew she could not have done it. The greatest wrong she had ever done to Sean was to marry him at all.

Mrs Seaford and her new friend, Lavinia Munster, followed every detail of President Lincoln's three-day visit with avid interest. They regaled the other boarders and Ruth with accounts of the meals he had eaten, the visits he had made, the words he had uttered (though these seemed few) until one would have thought that they had been at his left and right hands instead of merely reading the Society columns of the newspapers.

'I have heard that not quite everyone welcomed the President,' Mr Pierce remarked when he could get a word in edgeways. 'There have been effigies of him hanging from the masts of ships in the harbour. Some blame him bitterly for the loss of trade with the South.'

'Well, I don't know about that sort of thing,' Lavinia said. 'I thought him a most attractive man – in a brooding sort of way.'

Lavinia Munster, Ruth thought, took nothing seriously. She was the happiest of creatures and her husband thought her the most perfect thing that ever was.

After Lincoln's visit winter immediately returned to the city, and was still with it in April. When Ruth wakened on the morning of Saturday the thirteenth of April – a date she was never to forget – she felt the room chilly and went to close the window before taking off her nightshift to wash herself. The water in the ewer was icy and she shivered as it stung her skin. If she waited a while, Agnes would bring her a can of hot water, but Saturday was a busy day and she liked to be up and doing early.

She peeped in at Aurora. She was fast asleep, her dark curls spread over the pillow, her face rosy. Ruth closed the door gently. The child could sleep for another hour or two yet.

It was just before she left her room to go to the kitchen that she heard the newsboy shouting in the street.

'Extra, extra! Fort Sumter fired on! Extra!'

She ran out of the house, bought a paper, then hurried back, reading as she went. She knew nothing of Fort Sumter, didn't even know where it was, but a chill went through her to the marrow of her bones as she read, and she knew that whether she understood it or not, this was the beginning of something terrible.

As she went back into the house she met Francis Priestley coming out. He looked tired and drawn, as if he had not slept.

'I heard the newsboy . . .' he began.

She handed him the newspaper and stood beside him in the street as he read.

'So it's started,' he said quietly. 'I must go home at once.'

'Leave New York?'

'I'm a Virginian,' he replied. 'My place is there. Though there are reasons why I would never want to leave New York.' And you are the chief of them, he thought, looking at her standing there, shivering in the cold street. He could never have her. She was a married woman, though for a long time now without a husband. But while he lived he would never want anyone else.

'But Virginia is not involved!' She hated the thought of Francis Priestley leaving. He had been so kind to her. She thought of him as always being there whenever she needed to turn to him. And he was the last man for war; too sensitive and gentle.

'She hasn't joined the Confederate States yet,' he agreed. 'But she will. It's a matter of only a short time. But you are shivering. We must go indoors at once.'

And Virginia will be the battlefield, he thought as he went

into the house. In his mind's eye he saw the State where he had been born and bred, its mountains, forests, rivers, the little white towns and villages, in scenes of carnage, consumed by flames, her ground soaked with spilled blood.

'I shall try to get a train today,' he said.

As for me, Ruth thought, I must see to the breakfasts. She felt she would never face food again, but she had her boarders to think of and so far she had found no event which could diminish their appetites.

More than anything, as the morning went on, she longed to see Joss. She resolved that, as soon as she was able, she would go to the apartment on the offchance of finding him there, though it was unlikely she would. On such an occasion he would no doubt have urgent business in the city. Then, just before midday, he arrived at Appleby's.

He looked less than his usual immaculate self, as if he had dressed in a hurry, not had time to shave properly. His mouth was set straight and grim, his eyes clouded.

'I would have come sooner,' he said. 'I had to go to the city. You've heard, of course?'

'I've read the newspaper. I'm not sure what it means.'

'It's horribly simple. And final. You know the States which left the Union seized all the forts and arsenals in their States, with the exception of three in Florida and one, Fort Sumter, in Charleston Harbour.'

'I don't remember,' Ruth admitted.

'Fort Sumter was surrounded and the garrison left inside with very little in the way of supplies and ammunition. They're desperately short of food. Now the Confederate forces have attacked. The story is confused and the news sparse, but it seems unlikely that the men can hold out.'

'And what will happen if Fort Sumter falls?'

'What happens in every war?' Joss said. 'The North will retaliate, the South will fight back; the North will fight again and the South will retaliate. And so it will go on.'

'How long?' The questions came automatically. She couldn't bear to think.

'Who knows? Perhaps it will be short and sharp. With

luck it could be over by the end of the summer.'

Her heart lightened as she clutched at the hope. If the war was to be short perhaps he wouldn't be needed. There were younger men. . . .

'And what do we do in the meantime?' she asked.

'I think you should telegraph Maria, suggest she and Clive come to New York right away. I have a feeling they'll be safer here than in Richmond.'

Ruth felt instantly ashamed that with her mind full of Joss Barnet she had given not a second's thought to Maria.

'Of course I will,' she agreed quickly. 'I'll telegraph them at once.'

But *you*, she wanted to say. What will *you* do? He answered her question before she nerved herself to ask it.

'I think the peacetime army won't be enough,' he said. 'There are fewer than seventeen thousand men, most of them scattered around the Western frontier, and most of the Fleet is in far waters. President Lincoln is sure to call for volunteers.'

'And if he does?' She could hardly utter the words. But she had to know.

He guided her to the sofa, then sat down beside her, pulling her around so that she had to face him.

'Look at me, Ruth,' he commanded.

When she did so it was to see all her own sadness, fears and longings reflected in his face, but with an added resolution which she herself could not feel.

'I told you once, Ruth, that there were things a man would fight for: his children, the woman he loves, his country. I shall fight, Ruth.'

She could not hold back her loud cry.

'Oh no, Joss, no! Not you! I can't bear it!'

He took her in his arms and held her close. 'I must, my darling. And you will bear it as you have borne everything else in your life.'

On Sunday morning they learnt that Fort Sumter had fallen. General Beauregard, the Confederate soldier to whom Major Anderson had surrendered, was his friend. Years earlier, at the United States Military Academy, Anderson had taught Beauregard the arts of artillery.

'The wonder is they held out as long as they did,' Mr Pierce said. 'Half starved they were, with forces of ten to one against them. But they marched out bravely, the band playing Yankee Doodle! Heroes, every mother's son of 'em!'

It was strange, Ruth thought, how news of what was so clearly a defeat for the Union Army seemed to have cheered and stimulated everyone. Or almost everyone. She glanced at Professor Woodburn, sitting alone at his small table in the corner, and at the same moment he raised his head and looked at her. There was nothing but sorrow in his face. He is grieving for Francis Priestley, she thought, already on his way to Williamsburg. She, too, grieved for him.

'We must fight back now,' Mr Pierce said firmly. 'Nothing is clearer than that! We must fight to the finish, settle this matter once and for all!' He straightened his back, squared his shoulders, his eyes glinting, his mouth determined.

But you will not have to fight, Ruth thought rebelliously. Not one of you here will have to fight. It is others who will fight to the finish.

In the kitchen Mrs Cruse went about her work in rare silence. Of her four sons, three were of fighting age. Ruth put her arm around Mrs Cruse's shoulders as she stood at the table and the older woman reached up and touched her hand.

'Well, thank the Lord they can't touch my little Alfred,' she said. 'He'd never stand it.'

'How old is he now?' Ruth asked. 'I lose count.'

'Fourteen. Just gone. He'll be company for me when the others go – which they will. And now that the girls are married and have troubles of their own.'

Broadway, as Ruth walked up to Tenth Street, was crowded. She was amazed by the obvious high spirits of the people around her. It did not occur to her that after the weeks and months of apprehension a clear road ahead, however difficult, came as a relief to many. It was no relief to her.

Grace church was packed to the doors. With people like me, she told herself guiltily, who only seek God's house when they're in trouble. After the litany the vicar read the prayer to be used in times of war and tumult.

'. . . Save and deliver us we humbly beseech Thee, from the hands of our enemies; abate their pride, assuage their malice and confound their devices. . . .'

She wondered in how many churches in the South the same prayer was being said with equal confidence. She wondered, also, how quickly she would hear from Maria.

In Richmond, Virginia, Maria sat on the porch of her mother-in-law's house rocking gently in the big chair, looking at the view. Ahead she saw the James River, and if she turned a little to the left she could see the great, white colonnaded house which had been placed at the disposal of Mr Jefferson, the Provisional President of the Confederate States, and his wife, Varina. Not visible from where she sat, but not too far away, were the wide streets of the town: Main Street, Broad Street, Grace Street and the rest, with their tree-shaded sidewalks and elegant dwellings. And dotted around the town, on every spare piece of land, were the white tents of the army who, though it was not yet the end of April, had been drafted into the town for instruction in artillery and infantry warfare.

Richmond was a pretty place, and now that it was the Confederate capital, and the streets were full of soldiers in their smart new uniforms, a most fashionable and lively town. If she could not live in New York, Maria thought, then Richmond was as good as anywhere, though of course in her present condition she couldn't take full advantage of it. Oh, if only she and Clive could have their own little house, or even lodgings in a place not unlike Appleby's, she would have been quite contented. But to have to live with her mother-in-law and Clive's two sisters was another matter altogether. It was every day more insupportable and she could not fathom how Clive could not see that for himself.

She picked up Ruth's telegram and read it yet again, then spoke to Clive who sat opposite her, reading the *Richmond Dispatch*.

'I have to say, my love, that I'm quite tempted. Why don't we do as Ruth suggests and go back to New York?'

He leaned over and took the telgram from her, smiling as he did so.

'My dear little kitten, we've already discussed this. You are six months pregnant. Dr Beadle has advised you to take every precaution, which does not include travelling three hundred and fifty miles in the middle of a war!'

Though they had steadfastly denied, even to each other, that they were at all disappointed by the childlessness in her first six years of their marriage, both had been delighted by Maria's discovery, soon after their return from New York, that she was at last pregnant. 'It was undoubtedly something in the New York air,' Maria declared. 'So exhilarating! I daresay if we'd lived there from the beginning of our marriage we'd have had quite a little family by now!'

'Well, I know I must take care, and I mean to,' she answered now. 'And I'm not nearly as worried about the war as you seem to be. Now that General Lee has set up the committee to discuss the defence of the city, really, I feel the war might never touch us here!'

'Which is precisely why I want us to stay, my love,' Clive said reasonably.

Mrs Masterson senior, had come on to the porch as Maria was speaking.

'You deceive yourselves, both of you, if you think the war will go away,' she said. 'All the men in the South are rallying to the flag. All the men who *are* men, that is.' The dig was meant for Clive, as both he and Maria well knew.

'We were discussing my sister's invitation to stay in New York,' Maria replied. 'I should like to go.'

Mrs Masterson looked at her coldly. Why had Clive chosen this flibberty-gibbet from New York, even though she was English, when he could have had his pick of any number of wholesome Virginian girls?

'That is quite impossible,' she said. 'Clive will naturally wish to do his duty by Virginia and by his country. One hopes that he will enlist sooner rather than later.'

Clive sighed. 'That is not my reason for not wishing to go to New York, Mother. I have already explained to you that I shall not enlist while Maria is pregnant.'

Mrs Masterson sniffed. 'There are men all over the South leaving pregnant wives behind. You'd be surprised how the population manages to increase itself even under the most adverse conditions. In any case, Maria will have myself *and* Flora and Beth, to look after her. Men are not needed at such times.'

I hate her, Maria thought. How can she be so cruel? As for Flora and Beth, they were everlastingly pushing Clive into being a soldier. It seemed to her that all the women in Richmond were doing it to all the men. They were unbelievably and sickeningly patriotic. If Clive left her to be a soldier she thought she would die!

'Surely, Clive, you will wish to do your duty?' Mrs Masterson demanded. 'It would be most unnatural not to do so.'

'I do so wish,' Clive said. 'But I see my first duty, at present, as being towards my wife.'

Mrs Masterson pursed her lips, went back into the house. There was no point in pursuing the subject at the moment. Clive could be quite obstinate. But she would return to it later. There was no way he was going to be allowed to disgrace the family.

'I will telegraph Ruth to tell her you cannot come because of the baby,' Clive said to Maria. 'She'll wonder why you haven't told her sooner.'

'I should have,' Maria agreed. 'It's just that I feel so superstitious about the child. So apprehensive. Promise you won't leave me, Clive!'

He took her hand in his. 'I promise I'll be with you until the baby is born.'

'And afterwards?'

His face clouded. He had no stomach for fighting, but his mother was not altogether wrong when she said he would want to do his duty. The Mastersons had been in Virginia as long as anyone could remember. A lot of loyal, albeit reluctant, blood ran in his veins.

'I daresay the war will be over soon.' He sounded more cheerful than he felt.

'You are so comforting,' Maria said. 'Once you've sent the telegram I shall write to Ruth, tell her that all is well here and there's no cause for her to worry.'

'I will go down to the post office at once,' Clive said.

Within minutes of his departure, Maria fell into a doze. She was always tired now, not sleeping much at night because she could not get comfortable. She was still asleep when he returned, and was roughly awakened by his sharp, urgent command.

'Into the house at once! Quickly!' He was white-faced, shaken.

'Whatever is the matter? What is happening?' She felt confused, not sure whether she was still asleep and dreaming.

'Quickly, my love!' He pulled her to her feet and rushed her into the house. 'I must bar the doors, close the shutters. In the meantime, stay in the parlour with my mother and the girls. You will be safer there.'

'But what is *happening?*' Maria persisted. 'You must tell us at once. Why are you so alarmed?'

'The tocsin was sounded when I was in the post office. Everyone is running about the town in a panic, and dispatches have been posted. . . .'

'But what do they *say?*' Flora demanded.

'If they're true, you'll know soon enough,' Clive said grimly. 'It's reported that the U.S. warship, the *Pawnee*, has been sighted, sailing up the James River with the intention of shelling Richmond.'

'Oh no!' Cold terror swept through Maria. 'What will happen to us?'

'The soldiers, thousands of them, are marching down to

Rocketts and forming a line of battle on the high ground commanding the approaches. . . .'

'We can be sure our brave men will defend us,' Mrs Masterson said. 'We must keep calm.'

'The howitzers are already in position,' Clive went on. 'And two long French guns were already passing through Main Street as I was there, though one of them broke down and had to be abandoned outside the post office. But my mother is right, Maria my love. There is nothing we can do except to stay indoors and sit it out.'

Mrs Masterson kept silent, though the look she gave her son said everything. You should be out there with the soldiers, you should be manning a gun, her hard eyes flashed the message. She picked up the army socks she was knitting, and signalled her daughters to do likewise. Clive, when he had closed all the shutters, so that the lamps had to be lit, stood by Maria's chair, his arm around her trembling shoulders.

'I will try to be brave,' Maria said.

For what seemed like a day or a night, but was in reality no more than four hours, they sat in the parlour. Conversation quickly died. The only sounds were the clicking of knitting needles, punctuated by deep sighs from Beth, who was, with great difficulty, turning a heel. In the end Clive said, 'I am sure not a shot has been fired. We should have heard it here. I propose to go and find out what is happening.'

'Oh no!' Maria cried. 'You can't!'

'He can and he should,' Mrs Masterson said firmly. 'Are we to stay holed up like rats forever, then?'

He was gone for an hour – a long, silent hour. Maria felt she would almost rather have braved the danger with him than endured to wait in the gloomy parlour. When he came back she rushed into his arms and he held her close, stroking her hair.

'It's all right! Everything's all right! A false alarm – though the feeling is that it was deliberately done by the enemy to deflect us from any idea we might have had of attacking Washington!'

Maria ran outside, on to the porch; took great breaths of

fresh air. If ever Clive leaves me, she vowed, if ever he enlists, either before or after I have the baby, I shall somehow get to Ruth. I cannot stay here. It will not always be a false alarm.

Everywhere, events had been moving quickly. With the firing of the first shot at Fort Sumter the cold war had ended and the real war began. The very next day Lincoln had called on the North for volunteers and they came running in their thousands. It was because she refused to see her sons fight against the South that Virginia joined the Confederacy. The North had most of the men, three-quarters of the railroads and factories, all the fighting ships and most of the money. The Southerner's armour was his deep love of the verdant land for which he must now fight. His strength was in his determination to defend it.

At a factory in Massachusetts craftsmen worked overtime to turn out drums by the thousand for the Union Army; drums which smooth-cheeked boys, too young to shave, rushed for the honour of carrying at the head of long columns of soldiers. They speedily learnt how to sound the rally to battle, how to quicken the tired men on long marches over the rough roads; how to keep the gentler time when the soldiers sang songs of home. And from every state in the Union men heard the beat of the drum, and followed.

At Appleby's a flushed and sparkling Lavinia Munster, followed by her husband, burst in on Ruth.

'Oh, Mrs O'Farrell, I'm so excited! Karl is to enlist! He is to go to the recruiting office first thing in the morning! I am so proud of him. He will look so handsome in his uniform!'

She was beside herself. Ruth felt Lavinia's attitude so contrary to her own that she could hardly believe they were living in the same world. She turned to Karl for a saner view.

'Tell me your wife is exaggerating. You cannot be doing this so soon?'

'Oh but I am,' he assured her. 'It would be dishonourable not to defend what I believe in.'

'But so quickly!' Ruth protested. 'Surely one should wait and see?'

'There is no time for that, Mrs O'Farrell. Besides, I want to make sure of serving in the Engineers Company. Bridges will be needed, as they are in all wars.'

'*I* want him to join the Zouaves,' Lavinia burbled. 'Their uniform is *so* distinguished. There's nothing like it. Red pantaloons tucked into white gaiters; a great, broad, red sash, and the most wonderful headdress – a turban with a tassel!'

Karl put his arm around her.

'My little wife believes that even a soldier can be fashionable,' he said fondly. 'I think she's rather cross with me that I won't go for the smartest uniform.'

'Not cross, dearest. Just a little disappointed. You would look so splendid. But no matter. As an Engineer you will have *yellow* cord on your collars and cuffs.'

Karl turned to Ruth.

'And you will look after my wife while I'm away, Mrs O'Farrell? You promise?' His tone was light, but Ruth saw fear in the eyes which met hers.

'I promise,' she said. 'She will be safe with me until you return.'

Next day he joined the Engineers Company of the 12th New York Infantry.

On Monday evening Ruth went to see Joss in his apartment. She had an almost overwhelming desire to be with him all the time now. Events were moving too fast. New York was in the grip of war fervour and no-one, it seemed, could speak of anything else. She had hoped in Joss to find an escape from it, but it was a vain hope.

'We can't pretend it isn't happening,' Joss said. 'However much we both hate the thought, I shall soon be leaving you, my dear, and there are matters we must discuss.'

She tried hard to quell the awful tumult inside her, to speak calmly, rationally. Moreover she intended to do everything she could to make him change his mind.

'What about your business?' she asked.

'I'm leaving it in good hands. I doubt my ships will be

sailing much. The President is sure to call for a blockade of the Southern ports. There will be no more of taking cargoes there from New York, or loading cotton in the South for shipment to England. All that will cease and I shall not try to run the blockade. I have therefore placed my ships at the service of the Union, should they be needed – perhaps to help to maintain the blockade.'

'Joss, please don't go!' Ruth begged desperately. 'Please change your mind. Leave the fighting to younger men. There's no end of good a man like you can do for the war, right here in New York.'

But she had only to look at him to know that he was implacable. His reply, though it seemed to her like a death sentence, came as no surprise.

'You know I won't change my mind, Ruth.' His voice was gentle, yet so stern. 'Nor could I now. I have to tell you that today I took a commission in the 16th New York Infantry.'

She ran into his arms. 'I can't bear it!' she cried. 'I can't bear it! How shall I live without you, Joss?' She beat her fists against his chest until he held her by the wrists and stopped her.

'You will live bravely,' he said. 'As always. And you will write to me often. You will tell me all about the little things: what Aurora has said, what the boarders are up to; what's happening in New York. Promise me you'll be brave, Ruth.'

She had to search for her voice. When it came, it sounded like a stranger's.

'Very well, I'll try. I don't know how I'll manage it but I'll try. And promise you'll write to me whenever you can? Even if it's only a few lines to tell me you're alive and well.'

'Whenever I can,' he promised. 'And when the war is over I shall come back and we'll be married. Nothing will keep us apart then.'

Suddenly there was no bravery left in her. She broke into bitter sobs which tore at her body. Joss folded his arms around her and tried to comfort her, though, God knew, he needed comfort himself. He had no stomach for what lay before him. At twenty it would all have been an adventure: in his late thirties it was something to be dreaded. And his heart was like a heavy stone at the thought of leaving Ruth. Then as he held her close and she clung to him, the urgent needs of both their bodies came to their aid, and all their doubts and fears were laid aside as they made love.

The next day Ruth stood on Broadway while the Seventh Regiment – that darling of New Yorkers, which she had watched drill in Washington Square in her first summer here – marched past on their way to Jersey City Ferry, there to embark for their journey to Washington. In their sky-blue overcoats with white leather belts, their shako hats all worn at precisely the same angle, they looked smart enough to be going to a party, and as pleased as if they were. The sun shone brightly. The dense crowd, pushing and jostling to get a better view, waved their flags and cheered so loudly that the music of the regimental band was drowned out. Ruth wished them well, but she had no voice for cheering.

They were the first of so many men to march down Broadway. She saw Colonel Elmer Ellsworth's Zouaves Brigade, made up of men from the Fire Department and escorted to the ferry by the fire brigade itself. She watched the New York 39th, with their Italian-style plumed hats which earned them the nickname of 'Garibaldi Guards'. And tens of thousands of others, less flamboyantly dressed. Sometimes it seemed to her, as day after day the marching went on, that all the troops in North America were marching to the war by way of Broadway, New York City. But wherever they came from – Maine, Massachusetts, Vermont, New Hampshire – the citizens of New York sent them off to the sound of cheering.

Karl Munster's regiment left within three days. Ruth went with Lavinia and Mrs Seaford to watch him go. They saw him clearly as his Company passed. A strangely assorted group of men they were, in their dark-blue coats and sky-blue trousers, uniforms to which they were not accustomed and which sat strangely on them. Lavinia was, for once, still and silent, standing with her head held high. Ruth took her hand and squeezed it.

When the regiment had passed Lavinia said, 'He was out of step, my poor darling! Did you see that he was out of step?' There were tears in her bright eyes, but she did not allow herself to shed them. Shall I be as brave tomorrow, when Joss marches away, Ruth asked herself fearfully?

Joss asked the same question when she went to him later that evening.

'I'll try,' she promised.

'And you will watch us march past, my love? It will mean so much to me to know that you're there, even though I might not see you.'

'Of course I shall. You know that,' Ruth said.

That evening they made love more passionately than ever before, and when it was over they clung to each other as if neither could bear ever to let go.

'Let me stay with you!' Ruth begged. 'I want to stay all night.'

Joss shook his head.

'No, my darling. I want to see you safely home to Appleby's, where you belong until I return. Besides, I have to report to my Company at five-thirty in the morning. But I shan't ever forget this evening, nor all the others. Your sweet memory will lighten whatever I have to face.'

They walked back to Appleby's together, through streets which, though dark, were still thronged. It was as if New York, in the grip of war fever, never slept. In Union Square, where only a few days earlier Washington's statue had been draped in the tattered flag from Fort Sumter and a hundred thousand people had given Major Anderson a hero's welcome, they stood for a moment.

'I will come here every day,' Ruth said suddenly. 'Every day until you return!'

'Then I shall think of you here,' Joss replied. But he would think of her in so many places: at Millfield, in the house in Broome Street, in his office and in his apartment.

'No matter where you are?' Ruth asked.

'No matter where.'

They went towards Broadway and walked arm in arm to Spring Street. Lights blazed in the hotels and a group of revellers was leaving Niblo's. At the corner of Spring Street Ruth stopped.

'This is where I shall stand tomorrow,' she said. 'On this exact spot.'

He kissed her, and finally she broke away from him and walked the few yards to Appleby's. Before opening her own front door she turned, and saw him standing there, and as she watched he raised his hand in a salute. He was in uniform. His light-coloured straw hat, that incongruous headgear worn by the men of the Sixteenth Regiment which was to make them so dangerously conspicuous on the battlefield, gleamed in the light from the gas lamp.

Next day, after a night in which she had not slept at all, Ruth was at the corner of the street early, so as to be in front of the crowd when Joss passed by. When the moment came she saw him clearly. How handsome he was in his uniform. She was reminded of the first time she had seen him, standing arrogantly in the kitchen at Millfield. But now he was infinitely dearer to her. If he did not return – she forced herself to face the thought – if he did not come back to her she would not wish to live. Life was so long. She couldn't face it without him.

If he saw her in the seconds it took his rank to pass Spring Street, he gave no sign. When it was over, when for the time being the last soldier had disappeared from view and Broadway was once again a seething mass of traffic and people, she turned and walked quietly northwards in the direction of Union Square. She could not face Appleby's yet, not while the tears rained unchecked down her face and sobs constricted her throat.

When, finally, more than an hour later, she did return home, May was in the lobby to meet her.

'I've been watching for you,' she said quickly. 'I thought you'd never come!'

'I went for a walk,' Ruth told her. Then she looked at May's face, white as a sheet, and knew at once that something was wrong.

'Aurora!' she cried. 'Something has happened to Aurora!'

She pushed past May and ran to her sitting-room. As she entered, Sean O'Farrell rose from his chair to greet her.

# 29

Ruth's first thought was to turn and run, as fast and as far as she could. But, as if in a nightmare, her legs refused to move. She could only stand there, trembling from head to foot, staring at him in silent horror. It wasn't true, it couldn't be happening!

And then before she realised his intention he was beside her, she was in his embrace. It was not until she felt his arms around her – she had forgotten how strong he was – that she came to. She twisted violently, and freed herself, backing away from him as far as she could.

'No! No, it isn't true!'

At the revulsion in her voice it was Sean's turn to look incredulous.

'Ruth, you're looking at me as if I was a ghost, no less! I'm real! It's me – your own husband. I've come back to ye. Say something, Ruth. At least tell me I'm welcome!'

'I . . . thought . . . you were dead!' She forced the words out.

'Well I'm not, as ye can see for yourself! I'm very much alive, I'm pleased to say. I've come home, Ruth. It's been a long time and a weary journey.'

She continued to stand there, stupidly staring.

'I could do with a drink,' he said. 'And since you're not offering me one I'll help meself. And one for you at the same time. Ye look as if ye could do with it.'

He crossed the room and with total familiarity took the whisky decanter and glasses from the cupboard. He poured himself a generous measure and handed a smaller one to

Ruth. Her hands were still trembling and as she took the glass from him the whisky splashed over her shirtwaist.

'Get it down!' he ordered. ' 'Twill help ye get over the shock – though I wish ye could look as though it was a pleasant one.'

She had never tasted neat whisky before. She coughed and spluttered as the strength of it hit her throat, but as its fire spread through her body she began, in spite of herself, to relax.

'That's better,' Sean said. 'Have a drop more.'

'No. No thank you.' She heard her voice, formally polite, as if it belonged to someone else. Sean poured himself another drink and set the whisky on a handy table before sitting down where he had always sat, in the large armchair.

'If ye won't come over here,' he said, 'at least sit where I can see ye.'

She took a chair as far away from him as she could get in the room which seemed suddenly too small. Sean eyed her keenly.

'Except to tell me ye thought I was dead, ye've not spoken to me,' he pointed out. 'Am I to take it that your husband is not welcome?'

She found her voice.

'Where have you been? It's nearly seven years!'

He looked more than seven years older, she thought. Now she saw in him something of the man she had first seen on the *Flamingo*. His face, though tanned, as if he had lived a great deal out of doors, was drawn and hollowed, with deep lines running from his nose to the corners of his mouth. His blue eyes were duller, the whites yellowed. He looked like a man ten years his senior.

He was thinner, too. His jacket, roughly patched as if by himself, hung loosely on him. His hair was dirty, falling in an untidy mess almost to his shoulders, and he needed a shave. Had Ruth's revulsion not been so strong, the sight of him might have aroused her pity.

'It's been a long seven years!' He spoke defensively, seeing her look. 'I've been everywhere. I set off for California once, got as far as Denver but it didn't work out. I've been in Illinois the last two years. There are good farms in Illinois.'

He reached out and helped himself to more whisky. Ruth put up a hand, leaned forward in her chair, then sat back again.

'You needn't be alarmed,' he said. 'One thing I've learned is how to hold my liquor. Yes, I've seen a lot of the world since I was last with you, Ruth! Illinois I liked best.'

'Then if Illinois was so good, what brings you back to New York?' She hardly dared to ask, dreading the answer.

His blue eyes looked directly into hers. There was an intensity about him which made her uncomfortable, apprehensive.

'*You* do, Ruth, And the war. I'm going off to the war. And the place a man wants to be before he goes off to fight is at home with his loved ones.'

She recoiled at the tone of his voice and the maudlin look on his face. In spite of his boast about holding his liquor, she thought he was half drunk already.

'And it's not the drink speaking,' he said. ' 'Tis the truth in me. Oh, I can still read your beautiful face, Ruth. The same disapproval if a man takes a drink or two. But I mean what I say. I wanted to be back with you and Aurora. I've done with wandering. When the war is over - and please God it will not last long - I mean to settle down. I'll be a good husband to ye then, Ruth - have no fear!'

She heard him with a horror she couldn't disguise.

'But you can't! It's not possible! You can't stay away for seven years and then expect everything to be the same!'

He gave her a sharp look, all sentimentality gone.

'You're still my wife. Ye'd not be forgetting that? Ye wouldn't . . .' his face grew cunning '. . . ye wouldn't be telling me ye took someone else, thinking I was dead. Hoping I was, maybe?'

She knew at once, and without a doubt, that he must never learn about Joss, and though the thought of her last sight of him, marching down Broadway such a short time ago, filled her heart, she must not show it. She must think and speak with great care.

'Seven years is a long time. I've made my own life. There's no place in it for you, Sean.'

'Then there *is* someone else?'

She looked at him straight in the face.

'No,' she lied. She could not have borne to have uttered Joss's name in Sean's presence. 'But I repeat, there's no longer a place for you. You left it.'

'But I'm your husband, Ruth,' he protested. 'I love you. It's you I'm going to fight for.'

'I'm sorry, Sean. Don't fight for me. Fight for the Union, or whatever else you believe in, but don't fight for me.'

'A man fights for the woman he loves,' Sean said stubbornly. 'You're the kind of woman a man would want to fight for.'

He could not know how these words stabbed at her. They were the very words Joss had used, but without Sean's histrionics. She felt as though Sean was debasing them. Yet – she checked her thoughts – wasn't she judging him too harshly?

'Perhaps in your own way you do love me,' she acknowledged. 'Though I think if you did you would not have left me, nor stayed away all these years without a word. But I don't love you. I've never pretended to. You know that, Sean.'

His face turned dusky with anger. She saw his knuckles whiten as he gripped the whisky glass, and wondered that it didn't break in his strong fingers.

'You were fine and ready to take my name!'

She flinched at the bitter truth of his words.

'I know. And I was grateful, and will always be so. I did you a great wrong, Sean. But am I to go on paying forever?'

'I don't ask for much . . .' he began.

His face and voice had changed again. Now he was sentimental, pleading. In this mood she was no longer afraid of him, but she disliked it above all others. Her reply was brusque.

'You ask more than I can give. I cannot have you as my husband, either now or when the war is over. Do you understand?'

'I hear what you're saying. You'll not stop me trying.'

'I mean what I say, Sean.'

'I'll make ye change your mind!'

It was useless to argue further.

'Have you already enlisted?' Ruth asked.

'With the Sixty-Ninth, The Fighting Irish – under General Corcoran. Who else would I fight with?'

'Who else indeed? You don't forget your origins, do you?'

'Nor never shall,' he said. 'Any more than you can. Don't tell me you no longer think of your beloved Yorkshire. I'd not believe ye.'

It would be spring there, she thought. Spring came late on the high moor. The larks would be nesting in the tussocky grass. And in Nordale the fells would be bright green after the winter and the valley meadows would be dappled white with ewes and their lambs. And there would be no war. She doubted if war had touched Nordale since its men had gone off to fight the Scots at Flodden Field.

'When do you leave?' she asked.

'In three days time. We have to have our uniforms, and be kitted out. And do a spot of drill, for what good that'll do us.'

It was the grossest, maddest folly, Ruth thought desperately. Company after Company of men; marching, marching, marching South. Untrained; knowing next to nothing of the weapons they must use, totally unprepared for living in the open, for going short of food. And on the other side, like men in the same position marching to meet them. Joss marching towards Francis Priestley, so that they could get near enough to shoot at each other. And what of Clive, who was a convincing soldier on the stage but would be hopeless in real life?

'You may stay here until you leave,' she said suddenly. 'I take it you have nowhere else to go in New York?'

'Where would I go except my own home?'

'Very well. You may have the small room Maria used to occupy. She is married now and lives in Richmond.'

He looked startled at that.

'Then you must get her out, and quickly! We shall march on Richmond. The Union Army will take Richmond in no time at all.'

'I've sent her a telegraph,' Ruth said. 'She's not yet replied.'

'Then send her another while there's still time,' Sean urged. '*If* there is. Any day now there'll be no more communication with the South, except between soldier and soldier.'

He was exaggerating, Ruth thought. Matters would not move so quickly, not for ordinary people like herself and Maria. But because of the grim note in Sean's voice, and just in case, she resolved to telegraph again before the day was out.

'While you are here we'll try to behave as reasonable people,' she said. 'But there is nothing more to it than that, Sean. And I would be grateful if you didn't drink too much. I don't wish Aurora to see it.'

A smile spread over his face. He looked suddenly younger.

'My little Aurora! Where is she? I can't wait to see her!'

In the kitchen Ruth spoke to the staff. 'Mr O'Farrell is here, as I expect May has told you. He will be staying for three days, until his regiment leaves. Mrs Cruse, will you see that my sister's old room is prepared for him, please?'

Her voice was calm, as if it was an everyday matter for a husband to turn up after a seven-year absence and then be denied his wife's bedroom. But when Mrs Cruse's eyes met hers there was sympathy in them and Ruth wondered if the older woman guessed, knew even, a little of what was in her employer's heart.

Soon aftrwards, when Sean had gone to his regiment's headquarters in Essex Street to be issued with his uniform,

Ruth visited the post office to send another telegraph to Maria, and then took the horse omnibus to Union Square. She was more than ever determined that this time should be set aside for Joss, that she would put all other thoughts out of her mind and be only with him. Where was he now, she wondered? When he reached Washington for regrouping and dispersal, perhaps he would find a minute in which to write to her.

She walked around Union Square – for how long? perhaps half an hour – willing herself to dismiss the present, to recall the happy times with Joss. Then, on an impulse as she left the square, and because her longing for him was so great, instead of crossing to Broadway she turned and walked down Fourth Avenue. She still had the key to his apartment.

She let herself in. Everything in the room spoke to her of Joss: the pictures on the wall, the leather-bound books, the smell of cigars which still hung in the air, as if he had only slipped out and might return any minute.

She went through to the bedroom and looked at the white-counterpaned bed. When, if ever, would they share it again?

She lay on the bed, on her side, her arm flung across the empty space where her lover should be. 'Oh Joss,' she cried. 'Oh Joss, why did you have to leave me?'

It seemed that Sean, in the few days which remained, had decided to behave himself. Ruth refused to repeat the conversation of the first day, or to talk about either the past or the future. She intended, while he was there, to live only in the present and to take each day as it came. And when he saw that she was determined, he took her at her word.

Just once he slipped up. He said: 'When I come out of the army I shall ask William Tweed to give me my old job back.'

'Aside from the fact that you left him without a word,' Ruth replied, 'you'll not get your job back because Tweed Brothers, Chairmakers, have gone out of business.'

'Gone out of business? I don't believe it!'

'It's true enough. William Tweed has filed for bankruptcy, though he still seems prominent enough in City affairs. They say it was too little time spent on his business and too much on politics which caused the failure.'

'Oh well, I'll find something,' he said.

Ruth closed her mind to his threat. She couldn't face it now.

Aurora was delighted with Sean. His presence, it seemed, stirred no early memories. She took what was offered – an indulgent father appearing out of the blue, and in uniform at that – and accepted it wholeheartedly. And, of course, she twisted him around her little finger.

Ruth was on tenterhooks. Supposing Aurora mentioned Joss? Normally she didn't talk about him much; she took him for granted as just another family friend. And now she was living in the present, concentrating on Sean. But the danger was there, so that Ruth didn't dare to leave her daughter alone with Sean. If an innocent remark was made, she had to be there to pick it up. So when Sean said, 'I'd like to take Aurora somewhere special in the short time that's left,' Ruth quickly replied, 'Why not take both of us?' – and felt horribly guilty at the look of pleasure on Sean's face.

'Of course! Where would you like to go?'

'I'd like to go to Barnum's museum,' Aurora said promptly. 'We saw the seahorses and the Aztec children outside when President Lincoln came, but I want to go inside and see everything.'

'So you shall,' Sean promised. 'This very afternoon.'

Aurora loved every minute of the outing and Ruth took pleasure in her daughter's happiness. To her great relief no mention was made of Joss. He might not have existed – indeed for Aurora, right now, he probably didn't.

Ruth had informed her boarders that her husband was home for a few days before going off to the war, and when Sean, in his uniform, appeared among them for a few minutes they treated him with as little surprise as if he had been away no more than a month. After Aurora was in bed that evening Ruth went and knocked on Professor Woodburn's door.

'Come in,' he called.

He remained standing until she had seated herself. Seeing him every day, she had not noticed until now how the last few years had aged him. Now she observed it with a pang of fear. His hair was quite white, his skin had the parchment pallor of age. There were brown blotches on the loose skin of his finely-shaped hands. But his eyes were as alert as ever and he gave her the same kind smile as always.

'Let me pour you a glass of Madeira,' he said. 'What a long time it is since you and I had a drink together.'

'I need to talk to you,' Ruth told him. 'Though you must think I only seek you out when I'm in trouble.'

'I am always delighted to see you,' he said courteously, 'but especially glad that you turn to me on such occasions.'

'You know why I've come?'

'I can guess. Now drink this, Ruth. It will do you good.'

She took a sip of the wine, then put the glass down on the table.

'What am I to do? I don't mean temporarily, during Sean's visit. Whether you judge me right or wrong, I've made up my mind about that.'

'*I* don't judge you,' he said. 'It is right to offer your husband hospitality. Beyond that - well, I'm sure you are following your conscience.'

How strange, Ruth thought, that she should be consulting this elderly bachelor, this most unworldly of men, about affairs of the heart and body which were almost certainly outside his experience.

'Sean says he will come back here when the war ends. He wishes to live here again, to be my husband. Oh Professor Woodburn, I believe you know how I feel. What am I to do?'

He picked up her glass and handed it to her.

'Finish this,' he said. 'You ask what you are to do, and I say that you should do nothing. The time has not come to do anything. All that is in the future, and the future has a way of solving its own problems.'

'But not always in the way we want.'

'You have a loving heart, Ruth,' he said. 'Keep your heart open and you will know what to do at every stage as it comes.'

He had offered her no solution, yet she felt strengthened and comforted.

On his last night in New York Sean drank too much. Ruth found it excusable when he came in late, worse for wear. He was surely only one of many men who did so in the last few hours before going off to war. He was unsteady on his feet and, what she really disliked, his manner was a mixture of mawkishness and belligerence.

'Our last night together, Ruth,' he muttered thickly.

There was a longing in his eyes which both nauseated and frightened her. A tingle of fear ran at the back of her neck. She knew she must get out of the room – but he stood between her and the door.

'I'll make some coffee,' she said steadily. 'It will do you good.'

'I thought you had servants to do that,' he said. 'I thought my wife was a grand lady now, with servants to wait on her.'

'It's late. They're in bed. Though of course they'd come at once if I called,' she amended hastily.

'I don't want coffee,' Sean said petulantly. 'I'd rather have a drop of whisky. That's what puts life into a man. You want me with a bit of life in me, don't you?'

'I haven't any whisky. You drank the last this morning. I don't buy whisky for myself.' She wished she had replaced it so that he could have drunk himself senseless.

'Then who do you buy it for? Tell me that!'

'I expect I bought it for Clive, Maria's husband. He likes a drink occasionally.'

'Maria's a lovely girl,' Sean said tipsily. 'A lovely girl, but not as lovely as her sister. Not as womanly. A good enough figure, but not like my wife's!'

Ruth saw his eyes linger on her breasts, and then move

slowly down her body. She knew in his mind he was undressing her. She felt sick.

'Why don't you and me go to bed,' he said. 'Our last night together, Ruth! You wouldn't deny me on our last night?'

'Don't be foolish, Sean.' She tried to keep her voice steady.

'Foolish, is it? Foolish to want to go to bed with my own wife? You *are* my wife, Ruth, and don't you forget it. I have my rights.'

He lurched towards her. He had always been aggressive when in drink and she knew that physically she was no match for him. In the next second he had her in his arms and he was carrying her through to the bedroom. He threw her on to the bed and was on top of her, kissing her hungrily, lasciviously, bruising her lips under his. She fought him with all her might, beating her fists against him, but he was too strong for her. He fumbled at the neck of her dress and then his hand went to her breast. Later, when it was all over, he was suddenly, for a moment, stone-cold sober. He looked at her with eyes full of pain.

'I didn't mean it to be like that, Ruth!'

When he had gone to his own room she began to tremble, and then to cry. Deep sobs tore at her shaking body, and she called out her lover's name. 'Joss, forgive me! Oh Joss, forgive me!'

Sean left the house early next morning. Ruth did not see him go.

In the end, it was the time Sean had spent in New York, his behaviour, especially on that last night, which brought the reality of the war home to Ruth. She had somehow glimpsed in him all the emotions of the soldier: the faith in the cause, the patriotism, the glory – and side by side the doubt and fear, fear that he would not measure up, fear that he might not survive. It was in the light of the understanding which came to her that she was able to forgive him that night.

Eventually she had a letter from Joss, written in

Washington. She forbore to open it until later in the day, when she was in Union Square. (She had not been to his apartment again, nor would she; it was too painful.)

He was well, he said. Washington was hot and humid, worse than New York, and was filled with soldiers, all of them training hard.

> '. . . Every bit of ground as far as the eye can see is dotted with white tents. Fatigue parties building forts; soldiers drilling, or at artillery practice, or in their spare time writing home. Every soldier carries writing materials in his knapsack. . . .'

They would soon be moved on, he thought, though he didn't know where, and in any case couldn't tell her.

She read his letter a score of times, and the loving messages with which it ended a hundred times more, until she knew it all by heart. '. . . I miss you every moment of the day and night, my dearest one, and I pray for a quick end to the war. When that day comes we shall marry. We have already waited too long.'

But would she ever marry Joss, or would she be tied to Sean forever?

She now had an army post office address to which she could reply, though if he was already on the march it was possible that he would not receive the letters she regularly sent. She had decided that her letters should not mention Sean. It was a burden she would not share with Joss. 'Do nothing' Professor Woodburn had said. He was right.

And then, as if on command from on high (but more likely because of the exhortations in the newspapers) all the women in New York started making comforts for the troops. If the energies of the women in *her* house were anything to go by, Ruth thought, there would be more comforts than troops to use them.

'The women of Appleby's have rallied to the cause!' Lavinia Munster declared.

With Ruth's doubtful agreement she had invited all the women to a meeting, one evening, in the parlour.

'I'm sure there isn't one amongst us who doesn't wish to

do all she can for our gallant men who are so bravely defending us,' she said earnestly.

She made it sound as though at this very minute enemy troops were assembled on the New Jersey shore, ready to cross the Hudson River and attack New York. In fact, there had been no news of any battle since Fort Sumter, and when one did take place it was likely to be many miles away. But for all her lightness, Lavinia judged people well.

'Hear, hear!' Mrs Seaford exclaimed.

'I am prepared to do all I can,' Miss Fontwell said. 'I am not good with a needle, but if our boys can learn to fight, then I can learn to knit and sew!' There were round patches of colour in her cheeks, and her eyes shone. Ruth had never seen her like this before.

'I'm sure we all feel the same,' Mrs Carstairs agreed.

After Miss Fontwell, Mrs Carstairs was the last person in the world to involve herself in anything. She and her husband had been at Appleby's for two years now, and though they were pleasant enough, they kept themselves to themselves.

'Havelocks are the thing!' Miss Fontwell said suddenly. 'All our soldiers will need havelocks!'

'Havelocks?' Ruth queried. 'I've never heard of them.'

'That's because you came from England, where the weather is so cold they're never needed. Havelocks cover the military cap and hang down the back to protect the neck from the sun. They are a most essential item to soldiers on the march. I shall write to all the newspapers and suggest this.' Which she did, thus being initially responsible for the tide of havelocks which, gathering momentum, eventually threatened to swamp the Union armies in every theatre of war.

'What are they made of?' Mrs Seaford enquired.

'White linen,' Mrs Carstairs replied. 'And Miss Fontwell is quite right. Havelocks will certainly be needed.'

'Well then,' Lavinia said, 'there is a very good line of white linen at Haughwort's. I noticed it only yesterday when I thought of making a collar. It is good quality, which we must have, but at a reasonable price. Mrs Seaford and I could go down tomorrow.'

'As long as it is on the ground floor and I don't have to go in that Otis elevator,' Mrs Seaford stipulated firmly. 'I don't mind admitting, it frightens the life out of me.'

Haughwort's, at Broome Street and Broadway, was the first store in America to instal a passenger elevator, serving its five floors. There were ladies who loved it and others who were terrified of it. Children, including Aurora, were taken for a ride in the Otis elevator as a special treat.

'You can always use the stairs, Doris,' Lavinia said. 'For my part I could ride the elevator all day!'

'But what about the money for the linen?' Mrs Carstairs asked. 'Where is it to come from?'

'That's a very practical question,' Ruth said.

She thought none of her boarders was well off, and aside from Miss Fontwell and herself, the women depended on their husbands.

Then, with unerring timing, May came into the room with a note from Mr Pierce. The men had been asked to remain in the dining-room while the women met.

'Ladies, let me read this to you,' Lavinia Munster said. 'Mr Pierce writes "Do not worry about the cost of any scheme you may have in mind for the well-being of our soldiers. The men of Appleby's are determined to bear it!" '

Miss Fontwell clapped her hands. 'Good old Pierce!'

'Then Mrs Seaford and I will go to Haughwort's tomorrow,' Lavinia said.

'Unless Stewart's or Lord and Taylor's can offer us a better bargain,' Mrs Seaford interrupted. 'We must get the very best price we can.'

'There is just one thing,' Miss Fontwell said hesitantly. 'Though I know havelocks were my suggestion, is it essential that we should all make them, or might some of us be permitted to knit socks? I am not good at knitting but I am far worse at sewing.'

'That goes for me too,' Ruth concurred. 'It's likely that any havelock I make will be liberally marked with my life's blood, I prick myself all the time.'

'But what could be better as a mark of sacrifice?' Lavinia said ecstatically. She almost envied Ruth her clumsiness.

'Nevertheless, like Miss Fontwell I would rather knit,' Ruth stated. 'I'll get some yarn for both of us.'

'Oh, I shall be so pleased to have something real to do,' Mrs Seaford said. 'Time hangs so heavily for me. *You* have plenty to do, Ruth!'

But not enough, Ruth thought, to prevent myself longing for Joss every moment of the day. And from worrying about Sean.

The next evening, with Mrs Seaford instructing her in the few minutes she could spare from cutting out havelocks on the table in Ruth's sitting-room, Ruth started to knit. What had made her think that she could knit better than she could sew, she couldn't now imagine. And to knit socks, which meant manoeuvring needles with points at both ends, was torture.

'I *cannot* get the hang of it,' she complained. 'While I'm busy watching the stitches at the front of the needle, they slip off at the back! Perhaps I should knit a scarf?'

'Scarves will not be needed in the summer,' Lavinia pointed out. 'Not until the cold weather comes.'

'It would be Christmas at least before I finished a scarf,' Ruth said. 'And I doubt if I shall finish these socks before the end of the war, whenever that is.'

'You must concentrate,' Mrs Seaford said kindly. 'It will come to you in the end. Did Lavinia tell you that we bought our linen from Stewart's? Mr Stewart allowed my husband a discount as it was for the war effort.'

There was white linen all over Ruth's sitting-room and she resigned herself to it being so for the duration of the war. She learned later that hers was only one of many New York parlours buried under such an avalanche. The men of the Union army, their womenfolk determined, should not want for havelocks. If havelocks could win the war. . . .

Was Maria stitching havelocks for the Confederate army, Ruth wondered suddenly? If only she could know what was happening to her sister! There had been no reply to either of her letters or to her two telegraphs. Perhaps they had never reached their destination? The thought of Maria was a constant weight on Ruth's mind, though she tried to tell herself that peace would be restored long before the Union army reached Richmond.

And what of Francis Priestley, that gentle, scholarly man? Was he already wearing the Confederate grey, and what did his proud mother feel? His room in Appleby's was exactly as he had left it. Under no circumstances would she re-let it. Under no circumstances except. . . . She pushed the thought out of her mind.

Yet another dropped stitch brought her back to the present reality with a cry of anguish.

'I think the socks I am knitting should be sent to the enemy,' she said. 'They will truly be weapons of sabotage.'

'Mine are not much better,' Miss Fontwell confessed. 'I suppose it's a mercy we both knit so slowly. Given a fair turn of speed and sufficient yarn we could ruin the feet of half the Union army!'

Maria never received Ruth's second telegraph, and only the first of her letters, in which she informed them that Joss had enlisted. Clive paled when he heard the news.

'It's unthinkable!' he protested. 'Suppose I were to meet him on the field of battle? What should I do? He is my friend, one of the few I have.'

'It *is* unthinkable,' Maria agreed. 'Yet it is happening all the time. They say General Robert E. Lee himself has had to break with his sister in Baltimore, to whom he was very close, because she's a Unionist. He resigned his commission in the Union army rather than fight against his native Virginia.'

'And now he's in command in Virginia, he'll have to fight against his Northern friends,' Clive said.

Maria, in her heart, was determined that Clive should not fight at all. He was simply not cut out for it. She had his promise that he would not enlist until after the baby was born and after that she was determined to find other ways to keep him at her side. She tried to talk of the war as little as possible. Sometimes, she had found, if one ignored things they were not too bad. But it was not easy with her mother-in-law and Flora and Beth so patriotic.

The Masterson's friends were all the same. The house seemed always to be filled with committees for fund-raising, or working parties of eager women, sewing, knitting, gossiping. And when they were not at their sewing circles the young women of Richmond were all too often at the new diversion, the 'danceable teas' which were held in the town. There the afternoon's sewing was followed by dancing, by way of a reward – though by now, she had heard, dancing often took up the whole afternoon and sewing was put off for another occasion. It would not have been so bad if she could have attended. She longed to dance, but her pregnancy precluded all public appearances, more was the pity. Ah well! Only a month to go now. She was so tired of her swollen body, so weary in the Virginian heat.

And now everything, but especially food, was getting more and more expensive because of the sea and river blockade. And not only expensive, but scarce.

'The only thing in favour of the blockade,' Maria said, 'is that we have all these delicious strawberries! While the ships can't take them out of the James River and up to the Northern ports, we have to eat them all ourselves!' She spoke through a mouthful of ripe red fruit.

'And you're doing your best to help!' Clive teased.

'Mmmm! Delicious! Yes, I'm showing allegiance to your native State, my dear – though your mother says that if I don't stop eating so many my baby will have a strawberry birthmark.' She paused with a berry halfway to her lips. 'You don't believe that, do you?'

'Not really, beloved,' Clive said.

She finished the berry in her hand, then pushed the dish away. Perhaps she'd better not take any more chances, now that the time was close.

'Since there's going to be another sewing meeting here

this afternoon, I shall go for a walk,' Clive told her. He did not wish to stay in the house, to meet the frigid, barely civil greetings of his sisters' and mother's friends. He knew what they thought of him, though they were too polite to say it in his own home. They considered him a coward. But he had made his promise to Maria and he would keep it until the baby was born.

Not long now, he thought, leaving the house, taking a narrow path down the hill where with luck he wouldn't meet anyone. He would be glad when it happened. He would, he admitted it to himself, be happy to get away. Though he had no stomach for being a soldier, he had less for being what he had begun to think of as a deserter.

He took a long walk, so that by the time he returned to the house the sewing party had dispersed. He went into the dining-room with Maria, and his mother and sisters. They were about to sit down to the meal when a servant brought in a parcel, addressed to himself. A bulky parcel.

'Oh how exciting!' Maria cried. 'Oh, how I do love a parcel! Whatever can it be? Do open it quickly, Clive!'

He broke the seals, carefully untied the knots in the string.

'Oh you are an old slowcoach!' Maria protested. His mother and sisters stood by, not speaking.

He turned back the layers of paper. Inside the parcel was a crinoline dress, a woman's chemise, petticoat, stockings. Lying on top of the clothes was a note which he picked up and unfolded.

'Why not wear these clothes (he read). They are more suited to you than the men's clothes you now wear.'

There was no signature.

He swept the clothes to the floor and ran out of the house. Maria turned on the other women.

'You bitches! You unfeeling, cruel bitches! You're at the bottom of this, I'm sure of that?'

'As a matter of fact we are not,' Mrs Masterson said coolly. 'Though the fact that it has happened doesn't surprise me in the least. As for being cruel, it is you who are that. You are holding my son here against his wishes. Surely you can see that?'

As fast as she was able, Maria ran after Clive and found him on the hill path.

'Is it true?' she demanded. 'Don't lie to me, Clive. Is it true what your mother says, that you want to go?'

'It is true,' he replied slowly. 'I can't deny it. But I won't break my promise to you.'

Maria held out her arms to him. 'You needn't do so,' she said. 'I release you from your promise. I shall be all right, my love, never fear.' Her eyes were bright, too bright, as she smiled at him.

On the following morning he joined one of the two artillery companies of the First Regiment of the Virginia Volunteers. Two days later he was uniformed, and in training, in camp in Richmond.

'Who knows, I might still be close enough to visit you when the baby is born,' he said to Maria. 'But if I am not, please promise me something.'

'What is it, Clive?'

'Promise me that as soon after the birth as you are able, you will try to get to New York, to Ruth. I don't know how, but there must be a way. Promise me you will find it and take it. I will come to you there when the war is over.'

'Oh my dearest, I promise,' Maria said.

# 30

'Good morning, Mrs Cruse!' Ruth said. 'You're bright and early, as usual.'

She spoke mechanically, not really looking at Mrs Cruse, whose face was in any case hidden as she bent to refuel the stove. Why isn't Morris doing that, Ruth wondered. There was no sign of him. May and Agnes were not in the kitchen either, but then they had chores in other parts of the house.

Before starting the day's work she had read Joss's last letter yet again, as she did every morning. He had left Washington now, but she had no idea where he might be. Of one thing she was more than ever sure, that she had been right not to tell him of Sean's reappearance. However heavily it weighed on her – and it was seldom far from her mind – it would be time enough for Joss to know it when he had to.

'Good morning, ma'am.'

Ruth looked up quickly. This didn't sound like her Mrs Cruse; always cheerful, ever ready with a quip, or a sharp retort for the younger servants when she thought they needed it. Her voice was now a dull, flat whisper.

'Mrs Cruse, what's wrong? Turn around and let me look at you!' Some accident must have befallen her on the way to Appleby's.

When she reluctantly turned, Ruth saw a face pale and puffy, eyes red-rimmed and so swollen that she could scarcely see out of them. She realised it was tears which had choked the woman's voice.

'Why, whatever is it, Mrs Cruse? Whatever is the

matter? Come and sit down at once and tell me.'

Gently, she coaxed Mrs Cruse to a chair by the table. Mrs Cruse seated herself, and buried her face in her hands.

'I've cried till I can't cry no more,' she said in a muffled voice. 'All night long, ever since I heard.'

'But what have you heard, Mrs Cruse?'

It must be one of her sons. What else could put her in this state? They had all, except young Alfred, gone into the army at once, even before Joss or Karl Munster. Ruth felt suddenly and horribly guilty that she had been so wrapped up in her own affairs that she had given precious little thought to this woman who had parted with three loved ones. It *must* be one of them. Her mind raced over what could have happened. As far as she knew there had been little fighting. But perhaps – her whole body turned cold at the thought – perhaps the war had flared up again in earnest? Was this how people like Mrs Cruse and herself would learn of it? In a telegraphic message from Washington? '. . . We regret to inform you. . . .'

'Please tell me, Mrs Cruse! Is it one of your sons?'

'No,' Mrs Cruse said. 'I mean yes. But it's not one of *them*. It's little Alfred. He's gone!'

'Gone? Gone where?'

'He's enlisted! Gone to be a drummer boy!'

'But he's only fourteen!'

'He lied about his age. Said he was sixteen. But they're not fussy, you know. I've heard there's drummer boys as young as nine years old.'

'I don't believe it!'

'It's true. He didn't tell me nothing, knowing I'd stop him if I knew. He must have hidden his uniform or kept it at the barracks. When I got home there was a note. . . .' She faltered, then took a deep breath and went on again, her voice shaking.

' "By the time you get this," he said, "I shall be marching in front of my Company." To think, ma'am, he must have marched down Broadway yesterday and no-one to see him off! I would have seen him off, no matter what!'

Her tears came in a flood now. She searched her apron pockets for a handkerchief and found none. Ruth handed over her own.

'I should have known,' Mrs Cruse sobbed. 'I should have seen it coming. He couldn't bear it when his brothers left. On all the time about the war lasting long enough for him to join up.'

Ruth tried desperately to think of something to say.

'They won't let him fight,' she ventured. 'He'll beat the drum for them to march to, but they won't let him go into battle. I daresay he'll be a sort of mascot and they'll treat him especially well.'

But what if the enemy charges, overruns them, a voice inside her said? What if his Company is scattered on the battlefield – what will happen to the drummer boy then? It was too much to hope that Mrs Cruse wasn't asking herself the same questions.

The two of them sat there silently for several minutes, Ruth holding Mrs Cruse's hand. May and Agnes came into the kitchen and Ruth motioned them to keep quiet and get on with the breakfasts. Presently Mrs Cruse dried her eyes and sat stiffly upright.

'Well, crying won't win the war!' she said. 'I'd best get on with the work, especially seeing that Morris hasn't turned up.'

She rose, and moved towards the stove, then she turned around again. She was trying to smile now, and the sight brought tears to Ruth's own eyes.

'The best of it is, ma'am – my Alfred can't keep time! He could never keep a beat, not for love nor money! It's going to be the funniest marching Company in the whole of the army!'

'Does anyone know where Morris is?' Ruth asked presently.

'It's my belief he's gone to enlist,' May said. 'He's been on about it for days.'

She was right. He called, nonchalantly, that afternoon to collect the wages due to him. Ruth wished him luck but she wasn't sorry to see him leave Appleby's. He'd never been good at the job, always finding ways of pushing his chores on to the others.

'He doesn't really want to go for a soldier,' May said when he'd gone. 'It's the bounty he's after. Money from New York as well as three hundred dollars from the government. It's more than he's ever seen in his life!'

It was common knowledge that many unemployed men had enlisted to get money for their families, and who could blame them, Ruth thought – though Morris had no dependants.

'He'll go through it like a hot knife through butter,' May prophesied. 'Wine, women and song!'

Ruth was back in her own room when Lavinia Munster burst in, her eyes shining with excitement.

'It's come!' she cried. 'It's arrived! A letter from Karl!'

'There you are!' Ruth said. 'I told you it would. Is he well?'

'Very well. I'll read it to you. Well . . .' she blushed, '. . . I'll read you some of it.

' "My own dearest" . . . well, I'll skip the next bit. Yes, here we are:

' "One soldier has a fiddle which he plays in the evening and the men dance. They also sing a lot. The favourite songs are 'Listen to the mocking bird' and 'The girl I left behind me'. Do you know the words of that, dearest . . .?" '

She broke off, looked up at Ruth.

'I do,' Ruth said. ' "How swift the hours might pass away with the girl I left behind me." What else does he say?'

'He says, "we have seen no sign of the Paymaster and some say it could be weeks before he comes. I have no money to send you but I hope you can manage . . ." '

She looked at Ruth anxiously. 'I'm afraid. . . .'

'Don't worry about that,' Ruth comforted her. 'You needn't think about paying me until the money comes through, no matter how long it takes.'

'Oh Mrs O'Farrell – Ruth – you are so kind. You're

like a sister to me. I do appreciate it. And so will my Karl.'

Standing there, a tremulous smile on her face, she looked so like Maria. If only I could just know that Maria is all right, Ruth thought.

That evening the ladies of Appleby's met together as usual for their war work, Ruth struggling with her knitting.

'It's impossible!' she grumbled. 'I swear I have only to glance away for a second and the stitches hurl themselves off the needle.'

Lavinia Munster giggled. She was in high spirits, hemming her umpteenth havelock, her small hands plying the needles through the linen like two butterflies dancing over a flower.

'You really are funny, Mrs O'Farrell! And what we shall all suffer when you come to turning the heel I dread to think!'

'I'm sure there are other ways I could help the war effort,' Ruth said. 'Anyway, tomorrow I'm going to the Cooper Union rooms to see if they can give me something more suitable.'

A number of society women in New York – Mrs William Rice, Miss Schuyler, Mrs d'Oremieulx and several others – had banded together to organise the women of New York in relief work for the war. Ruth regularly passed the premises they had taken on Broadway on her way to Union Square. The next day, instead of passing, she went in.

She was attended to by a soft-spoken woman wearing a plain dress of heavy blue silk, the skirt cut fuller and wider than anything Ruth had ever possessed. Her dark hair was neatly braided around her head. Ruth learned later that she was Miss Schuyler.

'I wondered if I could help,' Ruth said. 'I'm willing to do anything, so long as it's not havelocks, or knitting socks.'

Miss Schuyler broke into a peal of laughter and Ruth wondered what she had said to amuse her.

'I can promise you it won't be havelocks,' Miss Schuyler told her. 'By now the whole country must be awash with them. I have a vision of the banks of the Potomac River white with havelocks. But it would be helpful if you could knit.'

'I'm sorry,' Ruth said firmly.

'Well, never mind. We'll find something else for you. Our object is to obtain supplies for the comfort of our troops when they come to need them. When the heavy fighting starts, as it must, they will especially need medical supplies. Could you make a start by rolling bandages?'

'I'm sure I could,' Ruth said.

'Good! And when the supplies mount up we shall need people to pack boxes and label them for despatch. Is it possible that you could come here to do that – perhaps one day a week?'

'I have a boarding-house to run,' Ruth explained. 'But I'm sure I can do something. If not a whole day, then perhaps one or two afternoons.'

'Good! And of course we're saying to all volunteers that if they can collect any money to *buy* supplies, it will be most warmly received. Perhaps you could do that in your boarding-house?'

'I'll think about it,' Ruth promised.

'Do you have a husband in the war?' Miss Schuyler asked.

'Yes.'

'I hope he's well.'

'Thank you. Yes, I believe so.'

But she thought, not of Sean, but of Joss, whose name, if she heard it, Miss Schuyler would almost certainly know. Though she wished him well, hoped that he was safe, she was in a way relieved not to have heard from Sean and she prayed that as time went on he would forget her.

Miss Schuyler showed Ruth how she wanted the bandages rolled and gave her a large parcel of materials to take home, to be delivered back as soon as possible.

Ruth didn't tell Lavinia and the others what Miss Schuyler had said about havelocks. As far as she could judge, they had almost reached the end of their material and Ruth doubted if any draper in New York would have an inch of white linen left in stock. She did tell them, though diffidently, what had been said about collecting money and they decided at once that they would each manage to put a dollar a week in a special box.

'And I'm sure if we ask them the men will be pleased to do the same,' Lavinia said. Even Mrs Cruse, when she heard about it, asked to be allowed to contribute her dollar, though Ruth was sure she couldn't afford to.

'Look at it this way,' Mrs Cruse told her. 'Who stands to get most out of it if not me, with four of 'em at the front?'

Several evenings a week Ruth rolled bandages, praying, though she knew it was selfish, that they might never be used for anyone she loved. She read the same thought in Lavinia's eyes when, her sewing completed, she started to help.

Each day Ruth read the newspapers avidly, searching out every word about the progress of the war. The news was sparse. The Union troops had crossed the Potomac River and there were frequent skirmishes in Virginia, with first one side and then the other routed. Everything seemed inconclusive. No great losses were reported and the big battle, the thought of which kept taut the nerves of those who waited at home, did not come. Nowhere did Ruth find any mention of the Sixteenth Regiment, and Richmond, therefore Maria, seemed to be so far inviolate, in spite of the exhortation of the Northern newspapers, 'On to Richmond!' There was no further word from Joss, and Ruth tried to tell herself that no news was good news.

'Do you think it might all fizzle out?' Lavinia Munster asked hopefully. 'Then my Karl could come home and build his bridges. After all, no-one seems to be doing much.'

'Thank God for that,' Ruth said. 'The less action the better.'

But a few days later there was action which reminded a largely complacent New York, engaged in its usual social whirl, that the war was still on. Colonel Elmer Ellsworth hauling down a Confederate flag from a tavern, was killed, the first officer of the war to die.

'I remember Colonel Ellsworth,' Ruth said. 'He rode at the head of the Fire Department Zouaves down Broadway when they went to war.'

She recalled him vividly: a dark-haired young man, proud and handsome, vigorous and full of life, with his men in their strange exotic uniforms marching behind him.

'He was a brave man,' Lavinia said.

'I'm sure he was.' Ruth spoke bitterly. 'For myself I'd rather the tavern had flown its stupid flag and he'd remained alive. He was only twenty-four.'

It seemed as though the young colonel's death goaded the North into action. Less than two months later the real war began.

Joss Barnet sat, for a few idle moments, in the shade of an oak. They had ended the day's march on the bank of a stream and already some of the men had plunged into the cool water, hardly stopping to take off their uniforms. Later they would wash their shirts and socks, spreading them on the ground to dry. And if they were not dry by the morning, too bad! Either they'd have to go on damp, or else be tied to a musket so that they could dry in the air as the owner marched along.

It was the third day of marching, and because yesterday his horse had gone lame, today he had had to lead it. Everything was so disorganised that there were no spare horses. He had had to walk like the men. All day the sun had been cruelly hot, far hotter than in New York. He had been grateful for his wide-brimmed straw hat. His uniform was close and uncomfortable. The sweat ran in rivulets down his body. The clanking of his bayonet, as he walked, irritated him.

It was worse for the men. They carried bayonet, haversack, cross belt, canteen, rolled blanket, and goodness knew what else beside, all on their person. Sometimes they could hardly keep their balance. Their shoes were ill-fitting and badly made, so that most of them already had blistered feet. A few had discarded their shoes and walked barefoot, and in the end, as their feet hardened, they might be the better for it.

But they were mostly younger than he, he reflected. He was twice as old as some of them.

They were an undisciplined lot, which was why it had taken so long to get little more than twenty miles from Washington: a long straggling column of thirty-five thousand soldiers snaking their way along under the command of General McDowell, who all but despaired of them. They thought nothing of breaking ranks to pick and eat blackberries by the wayside.

The trouble was that most of them were volunteers who had signed on for ninety days, and their time was nearly up. They'd seen no fighting – all the time drilling and training – and they were bored. There'd been too many soldiers and too few amenities and amusements in Washington to go round. And now they were marching towards Manassas Junction, where the railroad which could have taken the Union troops straight into Richmond was blocked by the Confederates. It shouldn't be difficult, though, to deal with that. A few more miles tomorrow – though it being a Sunday, would they rest? – and they'd be there. If there was a bit of a skirmish, so much the better. About time, and they were ready for it.

What they did not know was that a little more than three miles to the south-west, on the far side of a meandering stream called Bull Run, General Beauregard waited with thirty-two thousand Confederate soldiers. They were weary too. Some of them had come, partly by rail but a great deal of the way on foot, from the Shenandoah valley. Others – including one, Clive Masterson of the Second Artillery Company of the Virginia Volunteers, who ached in every bone and muscle in his body from the unaccustomed exercise, and only kept himself sane by going through, in his head, the lines of all his favourite stage roles – had marched from Richmond.

Joss debated whether he would strip off his uniform and plunge into the river – it was an attractive idea – or whether he would first write a letter to Ruth. He wondered whether she ever received the numerous letters he sent. He had had only two from her. But writing to her brought her nearer. He missed her so much.

He decided to write the letter. It was possible there would be no time to do so tomorrow. He could bathe later, by the light of the moon.

On that Sunday morning in July, Aurora pestered Ruth to take her down to Battery Park.

'It's ages since we've been there,' she complained.

'Very well,' Ruth said. 'I'll take you this afternoon – if it isn't too hot.'

Strolling by the harbour, the air coming off the water was just a fraction cooler. It was such a lovely place, with crowds of happy, smiling people all dressed in their best. If it hadn't been for the sprinkling of uniforms among the crowd you wouldn't have known there was a war on. Even the uniforms were clean and unsullied, not yet having seen battle.

'Oh look!' Aurora cried. 'That man looks just like Papa!'

Aurora was pointing to a soldier with a young woman on his arm, and, yes, he did have a look of Sean.

'Where is Papa now?' Aurora asked.

'He's gone to the war, as you know.'

'Whereabouts is the war?'

'In a great many different places. I don't know just where at the moment.'

How could she know that on the banks of that pretty stream, Bull Run, men were already lying dead? And that others, terrified by their first experience of war, were running, running anywhere to get away from the blood and the noise and the smell: hiding in the woods, sheltering in the treetops; frightened out of their wits by the sound of cannon and the sight of the dead and wounded? There were men who deserted on that July Sunday who never went back to war again, but stayed in hiding.

But of this Ruth and Aurora, enjoying the spectacle of the

fashionably-dressed ladies, the elegant men, the boats on the sparkling water, knew nothing.

When Joss Barnet wakened at first light on the morning of Sunday the twenty-first of July, the day was already warm. Rolled in his blanket, his haversack serving as a pillow, he had slept only fitfully. All the men, and some of the officers – himself included – had slept in the open, while the most senior officers had found hospitality in nearby Centreville, where they had set up a temporary base.

He blamed his disturbed night not on the hard, uneven ground, or the snores of his fellow soldiers, but on last night's supper of salt pork and hard tack. His stomach wouldn't take it.

With grunts and groans, curses and swearing, or snatches of song – it was all according to their early-morning temperaments – the men were getting up now, preparing for a new day. They were dressing – those who had bothered to undress – breakfasting, shaving, washing in the stream, checking weapons. It was all done in an easy manner. It wouldn't be a hard day.

'Straight for Manassas Junction,' a fellow officer said. 'Take that, as of course we shall, and we're all set for Richmond.'

'I suppose so,' Joss replied. The sooner they took Richmond, the sooner the war would be over.

When the soldiers had breakfasted – it was hard tack again, this time dipped in coffee – they rolled their blankets, packed their haversacks and filled their water containers. It was just about this time that the people of Washington were getting up. Something, they remembered sleepily, was to happen today.

Ah yes! Today was the day General McDowell was going to thrash his old classmate, General Beauregard. Yesterday they had watched the troops march off, and in no time at all the news had been all around the city. Of course one couldn't have a bet on the outcome. It was too sure. But what fun! How marvellous it would be to watch such a spectacle! And come to think of it, why not? Centreville wasn't all that far from Washington.

Afterwards no-one seemed to know where that idea had started; whether it had occurred simultaneously to several people, or started with one person and spread as rapidly as the plague. Whatever it was, the men got out the gigs, wagons, carriages, while the women prettified themselves for this unusual but exciting event in the social round.

Senators and their ladies were thick on the ground, but there were humbler folks too. In fact almost anyone who could provide or beg transport joined in the fun, not forgetting to take flags and banners to cheer on the brave soldiers. The dirt road from Washington to Centreville was choc-a-bloc with vehicles. But at Centreville disappointment awaited them.

Captain Joss Barnet was one of those who meted it out, dampening this holiday mood. Mounted on his horse, he wove in and out through the crowded streets and in the open fields around the little town, issuing instructions. He hated the job, and was annoyed that he had been detailed to stay back at the base and do it. He had not joined the army to keep a horde of unruly sightseers in order. But the sightseers liked him. He was so handsome, sitting so upright on his coal-black horse.

'The battle has moved six miles to the south. You can't go any further than this. Only military personnel allowed.' He said it for the twentieth time, trying hard to be polite.

A man standing near spoke up, jutting out his chin in defiance.

'Perhaps you don't know that I'm a senator? This lady is my wife. We've come specially to see what our soldiers are doing.'

'Sorry, Senator. Those are my orders. No civilian beyond Centreville.' Joss didn't even try to keep the contempt out of his voice.

The senator turned to his disappointed wife.

'Never mind, my dear. The day isn't over yet. Something might still happen.'

'At least you can hear the cannon, and if you listen carefully, the gunfire. Unfortunately you are just too far away to see the flashes!' Joss's voice was heavy with sarcasm, which was totally lost on the lady, though the senator flushed angrily.

'Thank you, Officer,' she said graciously. She turned to her husband. 'He is quite right, Senator. I can hear it distinctly. Shall we have our picnic?'

Joss moved on through the crowd, repeating his instructions, noting the expressions of disappointment, followed by resignation, and then a degree of pleasure as chicken pies, joints of beef, new bread, pickles and preserves, lemonade and cordials were unpacked and spread out. He was disgusted and nauseated, and though he was more than once offered a tasty morsel by a smiling young lady, he felt it would have choked him to eat. He would be glad when it was time for him to be relieved and he could join his Company at the front.

It was more than two hours before that happened. During that time soldiers rode to and from the front at great speed, bringing news of the battle to the base camp. Everything was going well! Couldn't be better! The Federal troops were certainly winning! Whenever the good news was relayed to the crowd they cheered loudly, and waved their flags. It was not as spectacular as they had hoped, but nevertheless they were enjoying themselves. When his time came, Joss rode away with great thankfulness. For a few seconds after his horse, and his dark uniform, had melted into the landscape, his pale straw hat was still visible, and then he was gone to join the battle.

It was no picnic there, along the six-mile front where the North and South had fought since morning. The quiet backwaters of the Bull Run, a pretty, placid stream when left to itself, were tinted with blood. Union or Confederate, in the water it was all the same. Joss rode along the bank until, with some difficulty, he found his Company on the right flank.

Away to the left, Clive Masterson had been in the thick of

it for three hours. It was worse, far worse, than anything he could ever have imagined. He was soaking wet from a fall he'd had when crossing the stream, and he had lost a shoe in the water. He was terrified when the gunfire came, which was most of the time. His bowels turned to water where he stood, and shamed him. He stank. Men on either side of him and all around him, companions, had fallen dead or wounded, but there was no time to attend to them. He couldn't think why he had been spared, but it couldn't be for long now. They were lost. He was destined not to survive his first engagement. The Union forces would march into Richmond – and then, oh God! What would happen to his little Maria?

But Clive was wrong. It was not over yet. Through his glass General Bee stared at the hill where Jackson's brigade still stood, resolute and defiant as ever against the Union army. 'There stands Jackson like a stone wall!' Bee shouted. 'Rally on the Virginians!'

How was that possible, Clive thought wearily. Those who were left were half-dead with exhaustion and they had almost no ammunition. He had just three cartridges.

It was then that the roar started. Afterwards, those who had heard it never forgot it. It started as an ear-splitting shout of triumph from a Confederate Company which, after a long struggle, had at last captured an enemy battery. The racket was instantly taken up by troops on either side, until it spread across the whole battle line, every Confederate soldier there shouting his heart out. It was tremendous, incredible, unearthly.

It was said afterwards, by some, that it was the 'rebel yell' which finally put the whole of the Union forces to rout. Clive fired his last three cartridges and continued to surge forward with the rest, shouting with all his strength. His voice was now his only weapon but he knew how to use it better than a gun. Had he not been trained to do so in that civilian life which seemed a million miles away?

The sightseers from Washington were not disappointed after all – or should not have been. In the late afternoon the

Yankees came right where they were; running, running, running, with the Confederates in hot pursuit. They ran like madmen towards Washington; mingling with the picnickers, getting in the way of careering carriages, supply wagons, fashionable ladies and gentlemen. And now – a not uncommon end to a picnic – the rain pelted down on what was left of an army of staggering, exhausted men.

They didn't know that the Confederates had dropped back, were returning to Richmond. In Washington Lincoln stayed up all night, waiting for the Rebel army. They never came. But there were those who didn't get back to Washington or to Richmond. In the evening, and all through the night by the light of lanterns, people, mostly women, came from Manassas, from Centreville, from the countryside round about, searching for the wounded. Even one or two women from the Washington crowd had stayed behind to do this. They searched over the fields and on the banks of the stream, among the wounded and the dead, looking for a face familiar to them.

A woman with a lantern called out into the night. 'Henry! Henry! I'm looking for you, my son!'

She was the one who came across a soldier whom she thought at first *was* her son. But he was not. He was in the Yankee uniform; she sought the Confederate grey. The soldier was badly wounded, she reckoned by his grey pallor that he wouldn't last until morning. He was unconscious, but in a moment of pity she moistened his cracked, blackened lips with some of the water she'd brought to give to her own son when she found him. He opened his eyes for a second, and spoke, so quietly that she had to bend her head close to his mouth to hear him.

'What did you say?'

'Ruth. . . .' But he had closed his eyes and was unconscious again. Poor young man, she thought. Perhaps he had come from a long way off. There would be no-one to search for him.

When Monday dawned the wagons were already arriving to collect the wounded – Union or Confederate, it didn't matter. There was nothing they could do about the dead. The living had to be seen to.

At the moment when the Rebel yell went up from the Confederate soldiers, Maria gave her final yell of agony, and then release, as her son was born. He was fine and healthy and, she thought as she studied his red, screwed-up face, the image of Clive.

'What is the newsboy shouting?' Ruth asked May. 'Listen! Something about a battle. Run quickly and get a newspaper!'

It was all there in the paper, though what was truth and what was conjecture she had no way of knowing. She read through quickly, searching for details of the regiments. There was no mention of the Sixteenth. Oh Joss, oh Joss please be safe, she prayed.

Lavinia Munster came into the room while Ruth was still reading. 'Does it list all the regiments?' she asked anxiously.

'I don't think so,' Ruth said. 'But how are we to know? It says "Men from New York and New England, including Burnside's Rhode Island Brigade, the Seventy-first, the Thirteenth, and the Sixty-ninth, the Fighting Irish under General Corcoran who was himself wounded and taken prisoner." '

Sean's regiment! She wondered how he had fared. Would she be informed if anything had happened to him?

'May I look at the paper?' Lavinia asked. 'The Twelfth *could* have been there.'

'It won't do to think like that,' Ruth said. 'They could just as easily have been a hundred miles away.' But her words were braver than her thoughts.

# 31

When Maria wakened, late on Monday morning, it was to see the nurse standing by the bed. For a moment she wondered why, and then with a wave of pure delight she remembered her baby. She turned her head towards the crib at the side of her bed, but there was no movement, no sound; she was instantly alarmed.

'Nurse! Is he all right? Tell me at once!'

The nurse smiled.

'Of course he's all right. He's perfect. And any minute now he's going to waken and want feeding. He's had a good sleep, like you. The birth is just as difficult for the baby as it is for the mother. Some people forget that.'

It had been difficult all right, Maria recalled. All through Saturday and on and on until Sunday afternoon. But strangely enough, though her body was sore and uncomfortable, the agony of the pain had already faded.

But not her longing for Clive. She had wanted him all the time. There had been more than one moment when she'd bitterly regretted letting him off his promise to stay until after the birth. Where was he now? All she knew was that his Company had left Richmond three or four days ago. Would anyone be able to get a message to him to tell him that they had the son they had both wanted so much?

'I'd like to hold my baby. May I have him?' she asked.

'Well, for a minute or two only. And then when I've made the pair of you clean and tidy I'll give him to you to feed. I'm sure the milk will have come in by now.'

Maria, holding the baby in her arms, gazed at him with

awe and wonder. He was so tiny, so fragile, that she thought if she held him close she must damage him. He was exquisite – though all she could see of him inside his long, voluminous garments was his face, with its deep blue eyes and button mouth, and two small, perfect hands which he waved in the air, for all the world as if he was conducting an orchestra. Perhaps he would grow up to be a famous musician? Why not? She touched his hand and he grasped her finger, clinging tightly. It was the most wonderful moment of her life.

'I once said I didn't like babies!' she told the nurse.

'Ah! Different when they're your own!'

'And you must admit, he is particularly, extra-specially beautiful,' Maria said seriously.

'Naturally, madam. Of course!'

'Has my mother-in-law seen him this morning?' Maria asked.

'No. I was to tell you that Mrs Masterson senior, and Miss Flora and Miss Beth, have gone into the town. They'll be back as soon as they can.'

'Gone into town? So early on a Monday morning? And all three of them?' Surely with a new baby in the house – Clive's baby – one of her in-laws might have stayed behind? Were they entirely without feeling?

Then she caught the expression on the nurse's face: troubled, worried.

'Is there something wrong? I do believe you know some special reason why they've gone, don't you? Is it to do with my husband?'

The nurse shook her head. 'Nothing to do with your husband. Not directly; I daresay not even indirectly. But . . . well, you'll have to know, it can't be kept from you. There's been a battle.'

Maria's eyes grew round with horror. 'A battle?'

'At Manassas Junction. They're bringing the wounded into Richmond.'

'Oh my God! It's Clive! He's been wounded! He has, hasn't he? They've sent for his mother and sisters! That's what you're trying to tell me, isn't it?' She sat upright, clutching the baby. As her voice rose to a scream the child began to cry.

'Now, now, Mrs Masterson, it's not like that at all! You must calm yourself or you'll sour the baby's milk, and what will he do then, poor little mite? Here, give him to me.'

She took the baby in her arms, rocking him gently until his crying stopped.

'The ladies have gone into town because there's to be a citizens' meeting, at which everyone will decide what to do, how to look after the men when they come. It might all be a deal better than we expect, but you know how public-spirited Mrs Masterson and her daughters are.' Even so, she reckoned, one of them could have stayed behind with the new mother. It wasn't her job to break this kind of news to her patients.

'And nothing at all was said about Mr Masterson? You're quite sure?'

'Nothing,' the nurse assured her. 'And in this case I'd say no news is good news.' She didn't quite believe that. The rumour was that it had been a terrible battle, thousands killed on both sides, but the happiness and welfare of her mothers and new babies came first. It was too late now, but perhaps she shouldn't have mentioned the battle at all.

'Now,' she said cheerily. 'We'll give the little fellow his very first feed. Let me have a look at you, Mrs Masterson.' She unbound Maria's swollen breasts and with expert fingers squeezed the nipple to express the first nourishing drops. 'Splendid!' She nodded with approval, picked up the baby and held him to the breast. Now, would he take to it or wouldn't he?

'He's sucking!' Maria cried. 'Nurse, he's sucking! Oh isn't he just wonderful!'

'Absolutely,' the nurse agreed.

In Richmond all was chaos. Mothers, fathers, sisters – who had sons and brothers in the army – were fleeing from the city to the battlefield to search for their men. Doctors and nurses, who had left while the battle was still raging, were expected back any minute with the first wounded. Every train which came into or left the Richmond, Fredericksburg and Potomac railroad station on Broad Street was packed to overflowing, and the open space in front of the station was crowded with anxious-faced relatives. By the time Mrs Masterson arrived there with Beth and Flora the crowd was having to make way for the stretchers coming in.

On Main Street the post office was besieged with people wishing to send telegraphic messages, sometimes without any real reason. Capitol Square was thronged with citizens who waited for information, though there was little to be had. Everyone was eager to help, but there was no-one to tell them what to do.

Mrs Masterson sent Flora and Beth off to the army barracks to see what news there was of Clive's Company.

'I will wait here at the railroad station,' she said. 'Come back to me here, and if there is any news of Clive from any quarter, you shall take it back to Maria.' She paused. 'But only if it is good news.' She felt differently towards Maria this morning, just a little. She was, after all, the mother of her first grandchild. Moreover, she had given birth with great courage. It had been a painful labour. Mrs Masterson admired courage.

Another train was drawing in. She pushed her way to a strategic position from which she could view the occupant of every stretcher, scan the face of every battle-stained, wounded soldier who was helped down from the train. When the last soldier had left the train and Clive was not amongst them, she moved away and walked around again, searching the stretchers in case she had missed him.

When Flora and Beth returned an hour later it was without news of Clive.

'Nothing is known yet,' Flora told her mother, 'except that his Company was there at Manassas.'

'And what we did hear, in Capitol Square, is that the citizens' meeting is not to take place until this afternoon,' Beth said. 'Should we not go home in the meantime?'

'You and Flora must return home,' Mrs Masterson agreed. 'I shall wait here. I daresay there will be another train.'

'But Mama, it's so hot for you!' Flora protested.

'From time to time I can search for a patch of shade,' Mrs Masterson said. 'I'm better off than those poor boys lying in the sun. One hopes that they will soon be moved.' But where to, she wondered? There was no way that Richmond's hospitals could take them all.

As her daughters turned to go she called them back.

'Please don't say too much to Maria. It wouldn't be wise.' She sighed. Her daughter-in-law couldn't have chosen a more inconvenient time to give birth. 'And perhaps one of you had better stay in the house this afternoon, in case news comes. Unless it's good news, Maria must not be the first to hear. Flora, you can return and relieve me here so that I can attend the citizens' meeting.'

What happened at the meeting was that anyone and everyone who had any room at all to spare, volunteered to take wounded soldiers into their homes. Some who had large houses took as many as twenty; no-one, including Mrs Masterson, took fewer than two. And a generous Mr Dickinson tendered the entire use of the St Charles Hotel for the housing of the badly wounded who could not be accommodated in the hospitals.

'What about prisoners of war?' someone asked. 'Many of them are wounded.'

It was generally agreed that tobacco warehouses and other similar buildings should be fitted up for the prisoners. Such places would not be ideal – the smell would take some getting used to – but what else was there?

'Though these men must be treated well,' one speaker said. 'Whatever we have, even if it is in short supply, must be shared equally with them. It is a point of honour.' There was no dissent from this. Southern hospitality was at stake.

When the meeting was over Mrs Masterson returned for one last visit to the railroad station. It proved as fruitless as the rest, though more wounded had arrived. Then, weary, hot and dirty, she went home. When she had washed and changed her clothes, she went to see Maria and the baby.

'There is no more news,' she said. 'But information is coming through all the time. I feel sure we shall hear something tomorrow. In the meantime you must try your best not to worry. For the sake of the baby.'

Her own heart was like a stone. There had come a point early in the day when she had faced the fact that Clive might not be among the wounded for the simple reason that he was already dead. She would mention this fear to no-one, though she could hardly hope that the thought wouldn't occur to Maria. Privately she resolved that if there was no word in the next day or two, and if her wounded soldiers allowed it, she would go to Manassas Junction herself to search for her son.

Maria turned away from her mother-in-law, buried her face in the pillow. How could she possibly not worry? She had thought of Clive every moment since the nurse had given her the news of the battle. Of course she loved the baby, but she didn't want it as a substitute for Clive.

The next day two young soldiers were billeted in the Masterson home. They were both infantry officers, in their twenties. Mrs Masterson hoped that her two susceptible daughters would not be swept off their feet at the sight of them, not until she knew a little more about the men. One had a shoulder injury, the other a slight wound in the chest. They seemed not to want to talk about the battle and, having ascertained that they could tell her nothing about Clive's Company, she didn't encourage them to do so. Naturally they didn't see Maria, but as they sat on the porch that first day, passing the time with card games, it comforted them to hear the homely sound of a baby crying.

On Wednesday night when everyone had gone to bed and the house was securely locked and bolted – for one could not be too careful in these troublous times – and Maria had given the baby his last feed until the nurse should bring him in the middle of the night, there was a loud and persistent knocking at the door.

Maria wakened from a sleep into which she had just drifted and sat up in bed, trembling. Mrs Masterson, to whom sleep had not come, got out of bed quickly and put on her wrapper. In the entrance hall she picked up the stout walking-stick which had belonged to her late husband. The knocking still continued. Before she drew back the heavy bolt she called out.

'Who is it? What do you want at this time of night?'

The answering voice was weak and faint, but instantly recognisable. As rapidly as she could, fumbling in her excitement, she opened the door. Clive took two steps into the house before falling in a faint at her feet. In the next second the two soldiers were beside her. (How, she wondered afterwards, did Beth and Flora sleep through the racket?)

'It's all right, gentlemen,' she said. 'This is my son. If you would just help me to lay him on the sofa. . . .' She prided herself on never weeping, so it was strange that the sleeve of her wrapper was damp where she had brushed her eyes.

She revived him with a tot of brandy, instructed a sleepy-eyed servant who had come downstairs to see what the commotion was to build up the fire and then heat up a bowl of soup. In spite of it being July, Clive was shivering. His face was grey, his skin black with gunpowder dust, his eyes bloodshot and red-rimmed. There was a grubby blood-stained bandage around his left arm, which was held in a makeshift sling. He wore no jacket and his shirt was sweat-stained and torn.

'Don't talk,' Mrs Masterson said. 'When you've drunk your soup I'll clean you up and get you to bed. Time enough to talk in the morning.'

'Maria?'

Mrs Masterson smiled.

'She's well. And you have a son!'

He started to rise to his feet but she pushed him back again.

'She mustn't see you like this. And you're not fit to go

near a baby! Wait just a little while until I've dealt with you. Then you shall see them.'

Maria had heard Mrs Masterson go to the door. After that, from her room at the other end of the house, all seemed quiet. Was anything happening? Would anyone think to tell her? Didn't they understand how anxious she was? Even so, when her bedroom door opened she was already drifting into sleep. She was still tired from the birth of the baby.

When she opened her eyes and saw Clive standing there she thought she was dreaming. Or that he was a ghost – he looked as pale as a ghost. But when he took her in his right arm – she cried out with compassion at the sight of his injured left arm – she knew it was her husband, alive, and miraculously restored to her.

The next day, and ever after that, they could get next to nothing out of him as to what had happened. Yes, he confirmed, he had been in the battle. He had been wounded at the last minute by a stray shot which might even have come from one of their own men, so confused was everything. He had walked all the way back, on his own, and because he had been too weak to cover long stretches at a time it had taken him three days. He had no idea what had happened to the rest of his Company.

That was all he would say, and he refused to embellish it or go on repeating it. All he wanted, in the hours he wasn't sleeping, was to be with Maria and the baby.

'You will have to report to your regiment soon,' Mrs Masterson said. 'You owe it to them. They are trying hard to trace everyone.'

'I know,' he replied tersely. 'I know what I have to do, Mother. For now, let it be.'

'I don't care if you never report back,' Maria told him when Mrs Masterson had left the room. 'I'm just so thankful to have you here with me and the baby. Oh Clive, sometimes I thought I'd never see you again!'

'Nor I you, my darling!' he said.

The baby was a week old now but they had not decided on a name. Mrs Masterson wanted 'Beauregard', but neither

Maria nor Clive liked that. On Sunday Mrs Masterson, Flora and Beth and the two soldiers went to the special service of thanksgiving for victory in the battle, held at St Paul's church. Flora and Beth were more than a little pleased to be escorted by two good-looking young men in uniform. They returned home after the service full of chatter.

'Everyone was there!' Flora said. 'President Davis and his wife . . . all the big-wigs. . . .'

'And General Lee,' Beth put in. 'Don't forget General Lee!'

'There's the name for the baby!' Maria cried suddenly. 'We'll call him Robert Lee! What do you say to that, Clive?' She felt an empathy with General Lee. He too had a sister in the North from whom he was separated.

'Robert Lee Masterson! I like it,' Clive said. 'You've made a good choice, Maria.'

'A most suitable choice,' Mrs Masterson conceded.

As the days went by – it was August now – Clive knew that he must report to his regiment. He had never intended not to do so, but the temptation to stay at home with Maria and the baby was so strong. He would never make a soldier. He was an actor, and didn't know how to be anything else. With all his soul he dreaded being sent into battle again. He had not run away at Manassas, he had fought to the end, but it seemed to him that one day, in another battle, he might do so. If that happened he would never be able to live with himself. If he was a coward, how would he face his son?

He and Maria were sitting on the porch, on the shady side of the house, with Robert Lee Masterson in his crib a yard or two away. Clive took Maria's hand in his own and spoke quietly.

'Maria, I have to report back. I'm going to do so tomorrow.'

'Clive, you can't! You mustn't! You mustn't leave us now. Surely you've done your share?' She searched for words to persuade him.

He shook his head.

'I have to do it. I'm a soldier now, Maria. Until the war is over I can't choose what to do.' But he would never let her know how he hated it, how afraid he was. He knew that that, because she loved him, would only add to her burdens.

'There is something I want you to do, Maria,' he said.

'What?'

'We've spoken of it before, but now it's more than ever important. I want you, as soon as I've gone, to leave Richmond, to try to get to New York. It will be safer there both for you and the baby.'

'Do you mean we're not going to be safe here? Why, look how the Confederates drove the Yankees back only a week or two ago!'

'The Yankees will come again,' Clive said. 'It's inevitable. And we might drive them back again – but each time that happens it will be worse. Before long Richmound will be in a stranglehold, a beleaguered city. The greatest aim of the Union is to take Richmond. Why, even President Davis has sent his children away to a safer place. You and our son are no less precious than the Confederate President's family.'

'But how would I do it?' Maria asked. 'I can't just pack my bags and go. I wouldn't be allowed.'

'It won't be easy,' Clive agreed. 'But somehow you must find a way. I have one idea which might be worth following. If it isn't then you must think of something else. The Reverend Moses Drury Hoge is the pastor of the Second Presbyterian Church in Richmond. When I was in the instruction camp in the city he used to come to address the soldiers, two or three times every week. But he didn't just preach, he listened to their troubles. A man like that might help you.'

'But the Reverend Hoge is a loyal Virginian,' Maria said. 'I know of him. Why would a loyal Virginian help me to get away?'

'He's a man of compassion and true religion also,' Clive replied. 'And *you* are not a Virginian. You must tell him that it is something I deeply wanted – for the baby's sake also – and that you will be safer with your sister in New York until the war is over.'

'Then why don't you and I go to see him while you are still here?' Maria suggested.

He shook his head.

'No. I believe it will be better, I believe you will stand more chance of help, as an Englishwoman on your own, with a small baby. Promise me you will try, Maria!'

She knelt on the floor at his feet, buried her face in his lap.

'I'll try, Clive. I really will try. But oh, my darling, you know that if I succeed, if I get to New York, then we can neither see nor hear from each other until the war is over!'

He stroked her hair.

'I know, my love. But the war won't last for ever. As soon as it's over I shall come to you in New York. Then we shall do whatever suits us best.'

That evening Clive spoke to his mother.

'I have Maria's promise that she will take the baby and leave Richmond, try to get to her sister in New York. I want your promise, Mother, that even if you can't or won't actively help her, you won't try to prevent it.'

'Leave Richmond? Take the baby?' She stared at him in disbelief.

'It won't always be safe here. Perhaps not for much longer. I'm sure you're aware of that. I wish I could get you and my sisters away also.'

'I would never leave Richmond,' Mrs Masterson said. 'I was born and raised here. I married here. Your father is buried here. No matter what happens I shall never leave.'

'But you'll not try to prevent Maria,' Clive persisted. 'I want my wife and baby safe. After the war you will see us again.'

There was a long pause. Clive knew it was a promise his mother would find hard to make.

'Very well,' she said in the end. 'I won't try to prevent her. Insofar as it lies in my conscience, I shall try to help her.' After all, it was her grandson she would be sending into safety. Robert Lee Masterson.

* * *

When Ruth went to the Cooper Union on the day after the Battle of Bull Run (which the Confederates called the Battle of Manassas) there was a completely different feel to the place. Everyone was hard at work, no-one sitting around chatting. The war was real enough now.

'I was wondering, Mrs O'Farrell, if you could now spare some time to come in and help us to pack and label boxes,' Miss Schuyler asked her. 'We must despatch them as soon as possible.'

'I can come in two afternoons a week,' Ruth said. 'And I think that at least one of my boarders might do likewise.'

So for the rest of that year she spent every Tuesday and Thursday afternoon at the Cooper Union, packing chests. With each box she packed, Ruth hoped that some of its contents might reach Joss. In the weeks, stretching to months, which had gone by since Bull Run she had heard nothing from him. It weighed heavily, the more so because there was no-one with whom she could share her fears.

Both Mrs Seaford and Lavinia Munster agreed to spend a few hours a week at the Cooper Union, and in the evenings they still worked at Appleby's on the bandages. But there were no more havelocks.

'The Sixty-Ninth received twelve hundred havelocks,' Miss Schuyler said, laughing. 'I've heard they used them for coffee-strainers and dishcloths! Anyway, that kind of waste won't happen again. The new Sanitary Commission finds out what's needed, and where. We learnt a lot about that from your fellow countrywoman.'

'My fellow countrywoman?'

'Miss Florence Nightingale.'

Ruth liked Miss Schuyler. Though she was one of New York's leading socialites, she never condescended, always worked alongside whoever was there.

Though Ruth had not heard from Joss for so long she still wrote to him regularly, care of the army post office. She told him of the little everyday things; what the weather was like, which flowers bloomed, how Aurora had been to the dentist in Bond Street and had hated it. She didn't write about the war and she never mentioned Sean.

And then, in late September, as the leaves were beginning to turn, a letter came. He made no mention of where he was, or if he had been in the fighting, but it was enough for Ruth to know that he was alive. She read and re-read the letter. She could hear his voice in every word.

'. . . Today I received a letter from you. I can't tell you how wonderful it is when the mail comes. The saddest men in the Company are those who don't hear from home. . . . I spoke with a soldier yesterday who had met up with Karl Munster. I don't know where he is and I couldn't tell you if I did, but my informant said he was well. . . . I love you and miss you every minute of my life. . . .'

Lavinia was in raptures at the news, but three days later she had a letter herself. All was sunshine; Karl was fit and well. It seemed at that time as though real life was lived through letters.

'Listen to this!' she said.

'. . . The quality of our uniforms is so abominable that they are already worn out and we are a ragged mob. We try to repair the seats of our trousers by gathering up the holes with straw, as if we were fastening bags of grain . . .!'

'Poor Karl,' Lavinia sighed. 'He does so like to look smart!'

Towards the end of November everyone in Appleby's had a terrible shock. It was the day after Thanksgiving. Ruth felt that, as far as the war allowed, they had had a happy Thanksgiving. Whatever worries she, Lavinia Munster and Mrs Cruse still had, at least they could give thanks that their men, as far as they knew, were still safe. Mrs Cruse was proud of all four of her sons, especially of Alfred, who, to judge by his letters, was enjoying life as a drummer boy.

When Ruth served the parlour tea on the Friday evening she thought the atmosphere particularly pleasant. She stayed longer than usual, drawn into conversation by Mr Pierce.

'I read that our General McLellan's forces have moved into winter quarters,' he said. 'I daresay there'll be no more fighting now until the spring comes.'

'Will the war make any difference to the Christmas trade in New York?' Ruth asked.

'I don't think so at all,' Mr Seaford chipped in. 'People are spending money like water – of course there's a lot being made by some. I think we're going to be very busy and I shall be ready for my day off when Christmas Day comes!'

But for Mr Seaford, Christmas did not come. He went to bed that night and fell asleep quickly, and when Mrs Seaford wakened early next morning he was already stiff and cold beside her. He had died of a heart attack – as unobtrusively as he had lived, disturbing no-one.

Ruth remembered how she and Professor Woodburn had debated whether the Seafords, being in trade, were suitable for Gutermann's, as it then was.

'We made the right choice, Ruth,' the professor said after the funeral on a cold December day. 'We did indeed. And now what is to become of that poor widow?'

Ruth's heart ached for Mrs Seaford. She and her husband had been everything to each other.

'I don't know how I shall live without him,' she said. 'It's as simple as that.'

She grew thinner, lost interest in everything, and then one day she knocked on Ruth's sitting-room door.

'Come in and sit down,' Ruth invited. 'I'll get some tea.'

'No,' Mrs Seaford said. 'I'd rather come straight to the point. I shall have to leave here.'

'Leave? What do you mean? Are you going back to England?'

It had never occurred to Ruth that Mrs Seaford would not stay. By now most of her boarders were so much part of her family that she could never envisage them going.

'No. I shan't do that. There's no point in going back to

England. I've no-one left there except an elderly great-aunt. But I can't stay here.'

'Why ever not?'

'I can't afford it,' Mrs Seaford said. 'I shall have to find somewhere cheaper. My husband had no income apart from his salary and he has left very little capital. Not enough to keep me for long at Appleby's. And though I wish it were not so, since I am only forty-seven I might have many more years to live.'

'Have you thought where else you might go?' Ruth asked. This was terrible. There must be something she could do.

'Not really. But I know there must be cheaper places, though not nearly as nice, if I were to go further downtown – or perhaps on the Lower East side.'

Cheap and horrible, Ruth thought. And how Mrs Seaford, with her love of pleasant things, would hate them.

'Please don't decide in a hurry,' she said. 'Tell me frankly what is the most you can afford to pay for board and lodgings and I'll see if I can arrive at a solution. No-one would want you to leave Appleby's. We would all be most upset.'

At that Mrs Seaford broke down and wept, but, oddly enough, with the first vestige of happiness she had shown since her husband's death.

'That's the nicest thing anyone has ever said to me,' she said, drying her eyes. 'I shall never forget it, no matter what happens.'

'I have an idea in mind,' Ruth told her. 'I'd like to think about it and I'll put it to you tomorrow.'

When she came to see Ruth next day Mrs Seaford already looked more cheerful, though still apprehensive. She mentioned a sum she could just afford to pay. 'I'm sorry it's not more,' she said.

'Well, I think everything will be all right,' Ruth replied. 'There is a way in which you can make up the rest if you're willing to do so. Would you care to assist me by taking over the care and repair of all the linen, and also Aurora's sewing? It would be a great help to me, and would certainly make up the difference between what you have paid in the past and what you can afford now.'

'I'd like it more than anything in the world,' Mrs Seaford said quietly. 'I'd do almost anything to stay on at Appleby's. Mr Seaford and I were so happy here. We often said it was like home to us. And you know how much I enjoy sewing. I shall be glad to do it.'

So it was arranged. She wept again, but in a healing way. It was the beginning of her recovery.

Some problems, Ruth thought, watching her go, are more easily solved than others. Since Joss's last letter she had thought a great deal about Sean. How would it all work out?

# 32

Maria removed the baby from her breast and fastened up her bodice. These days, suckling Robert Lee was the activity she enjoyed most. Nothing else brought her such a measure of tranquillity. When she looked down at him, sucking greedily, noisily, as if he might be smacking his lips at the sweet-tasting substance which she was able to provide in such abundance, she could forget for a few minutes all that was going on in the world outside. And he thrived on her milk. At three months old he already weighed eleven pounds, possessed a clear, rosy skin, and blue eyes which grew brighter and took in more every day. He was a good baby too, crying little and sleeping well at night. If only Clive could see him.

She had no idea where Clive was now. What was left of his Company had quickly been reformed and had left Richmond only a few days after he had reported back. There had been no further fighting close to Richmond, but in other parts of the South the war went on. Reports said that Missouri was largely in the hands of the North. St Louis had fallen, and the battle of Wilson's Creek had been furious. Could Clive have been there? It was a thought which was with her all through the daytime and which kept her awake at night.

She held the baby over her shoulder, patting his back to get up the wind. The nurse had left some weeks ago. Though in peacetime she might have been kept on, now there was a great call for nurses. Even a midwife had some skills which could be used to help the wounded who still crowded Richmond's hospitals.

Mrs Masterson came into the room. She would always be a

cool, austere woman, Maria thought, but since the birth of the baby she had softened a little, especially towards her grandson. The corners of her lips curved into a smile as she saw him now, in Maria's arms.

'May I hold him?' she asked.

'Of course. He's just been fed. He should fall asleep quite soon.'

Mrs Masterson sat on the low rocking-chair, looking down at the child.

'I have been in the town, trying to get some supplies,' she told Maria. 'But mostly in vain. There is so little in the shops. Food is shorter than ever, and with so many people in Richmond to be fed. . . . As for medicines, they are almost unobtainable, even if one could afford them. Quinine, what little there is, has doubled in price over the last few weeks. How are our sick soldiers to be treated if there is no quinine?'

The sea blockade, tighter than ever now, had done its work. Four thousand miles of coastline, from the north of Virginia round the gulf of Mexico to Texas, was in the hands of the Federal troops. Only rarely did a Confederate ship run the blockade to bring in desperately-needed supplies, or a British ship sneak through with arms. And, in the case of poor Richmond, there were the enemy ships at the mouth of the James River to contend with. Ironically, the best source of food and medicines in recent months had been those abandoned in a hurry when the Union troops fled from Manassas, though these had largely been used for the benefit of the soldiers in Richmond.

'It will get worse,' Mrs Masterson said quietly. 'So far we have not actually gone hungry – those of us who have a little money – but soon we shall. Money will have no value when we can't buy flour to make bread or butter to spread on it.'

She sounded despondent, and that was unlike her, Maria thought. Were things *really* so serious?

'I think it is time you took note of Clive's wishes,' Mrs Masterson continued, after a pause. 'You've told me that in his last two letters he has urged you to leave Richmond, and in his letter to me he asks me to press you. I don't know for certain, but I believe you've done nothing about it?'

'Not so far,' Maria confessed. 'I was waiting until the baby was a little older. He's so small.' But it was not only the baby. She admitted to herself that she was hesitant about undertaking a journey which could be hazardous, if not downright dangerous.

'You promised Clive,' Mrs Masterson said firmly. 'And, all things considered, it will be better for you to go while the child is so young. As long as you are feeding him yourself he won't go hungry. Later, who knows?' She traced his round, chubby cheek with her fingers. What was she saying? How could she bear to part with him?

'Do you think I *want* him to go?' she asked sharply. 'I'm trying to think what is best for him, as you should. And best for you too,' she added hastily. 'It's my belief you should go and see the Reverend Hoge as soon as possible. Every day, every week, it will be more difficult to get away.'

Her mother-in-law was right, Maria acknowledged. On his last day at home she had made her solemn promise to Clive, and so far she had done nothing to fulfil it. She had had two letters from him since he had left Richmond, and in both of them he had exhorted her, if she was still there, to go soon.

'Very well,' she said. 'Though I'm not so sure that I believe that conditions in Richmond will be as bad as you say. . . .'

'They will be worse,' Mrs Masterson interrupted.

'. . . But I did promise Clive, so tomorrow I will call on the Reverend Hoge. Whether he will help me is quite another matter!'

Richmond, when Maria went next day, was chaotic. And the air, as always, reeked of tobacco. Here in the town one smelled it, breathed it, absorbed it in one's clothes. She felt sorry for the prisoners of war who were confined in the tobacco warehouses. One could more or less get used to the smell in the streets, though she never became accustomed to the fact that the men – even gentlemen – chewed the stuff, and used the streets as a spittoon.

Putting off the moment when she must face the Reverend Hoge, she went first to the market on the corner of Main and Seventeenth streets. There were hundreds of people milling around, but nothing to buy. Everywhere the streets were crowded. There were those coming and going because Richmond was the Confederate capital; there was its own indigenous population; there were the soldiers from the training camps parading the streets, their uniforms still clean and smart, unsullied by battle.

Most of all it was the wounded she noticed: men minus legs, men with empty sleeves, with bandaged heads; some on crutches, some in wheelchairs or in invalid carriages. *Their* uniforms were stained and dirty, their faces grey. And in every one of them she saw Clive.

Outside the Old Dominion hospital a funeral passed: a soldier's funeral, the coffin draped in the Confederate flag. She stood on the sidewalk, watching until it was out of sight. It was a common enough sight these days, but supposing, just supposing . . . and if she was not here when the news came? She tightened her fingers around Clive's letter in her pocket, his reminder of her promise to him. 'For my sake' he had written.

Though she had no appointment, the Reverend Hoge agreed to see her.

'I am on my way to Camp Lee,' he told her. 'But I can spare you a few minutes.'

'My husband spoke of your visits to the camp when he was there,' Maria said. 'He greatly appreciated them.'

'Your husband is in the army?'

She nodded. 'He was at the Battle of Manassas. I don't know where he is now.'

'Well, my dear lady, I can't help you there. If I knew where he was I couldn't tell you.'

'That isn't why I've come.' Now that she was here she felt dreadfully nervous. 'The truth is . . . my husband wanted me, still wants me, to leave Richmond, to go to my sister in New York.'

He frowned. 'Why should you do that?'

'He wants it because we have a new baby – our first. He thinks Richmond will not be a safe place for women and children.'

'I'm sure he's right,' the Reverend Hoge said. 'Yet there are many who will remain.'

'I know,' Maria answered. 'I would do so myself. Believe me, I would not be here at this minute were my husband's wishes not so strong. Perhaps you would be good enough to glance at his last letter?'

She took the well-thumbed paper out of her pocket and handed it to him, watching anxiously while he read it.

'His wishes are certainly clear,' he said. 'And of course you are English, and the English aren't too popular in Virginia just now. But you realise that *if* you were to go – and I say "if" because I don't know whether it would be possible, or how you would accomplish it – then you would have no further communication with your husband until the war was over?'

'That is my reason for not wishing to go,' Maria replied. 'But I made a solemn promise to my husband. I just live in the hope that the war won't last long.'

The Reverend Hoge shook his head. 'I doubt that, my dear. The war front is wide and there are many battles to be fought. As long as Richmond holds out – and you can be sure she'll do that to the last breath – then the war will go on. I don't say this to depress you, only to make you understand that if you take this step, then it might be a very long time before you hear anything of your husband. Anything.'

'I understand,' Maria whispered. 'I understand everything you say.' Good or bad, he meant.

'Very well then. I shall write you a note at once, which you can take to the Consul, who deals with such matters. That is the most I can do for you.'

She waited while he wrote. When he handed her the note he said, 'God go with you, my dear Mrs Masterson. And with your baby and your brave husband.'

She went at once to the Consul's office, which was temporarily housed in the Mechanics' Institute. One glance into the waiting-room told her that she couldn't possibly stop to see him. It was crowded to the doors and a babel of English, Scotch and Irish voices assailed her. She would be here for hours and it was already well past Robert Lee's feed time. Aside from the fact that her breasts were painful, he would soon be crying for food.

She fared no better the following day. Though she was at the Institute early, twenty or thirty people were there before her. From the talk going on around her, it seemed as though most of them were seeking permits to go North. But they were not, as she had thought yesterday, all British. There was a fair sprinkling of Americans from the North, a family of rich-looking Jews from Europe, as well as English, Irish and Scottish, either from the Northern States or from Europe. Men, women, and just a few children – and what they had in common was that they had been caught in Richmond when the war started, and now they wanted to leave.

'But what's more than six months ago,' Maria said to the person next to her, a young Englishwoman. 'Please don't tell me it takes so long to get a permit!'

'Oh no, I'm sure it doesn't,' the woman replied. 'And perhaps some of these people are here to see the Consul for other reasons. Let's hope so. At first, you see, I didn't intend to leave. I have a job here as a governess. But the English are no longer as welcome here as they once were. I prefer not to stay anywhere where I'm not welcome. Though as a matter of fact I don't feel English any longer. I settled in Vermont with my parents when I was a child, and that's my home now.'

'But why don't they like the English?' Maria asked. 'I thought a great many Virginians were of English descent.'

The woman shrugged. 'So they are. But who knows what crazy things people think in wartime? They see the English as wanting to abolish all slavery. And of course Queen Victoria's attitude hasn't helped.'

'Queen Victoria?' How ignorant I am, Maria thought.

'She declared Great Britain neutral, but at the same time

condemned the South as belligerent. Napoleon the Third, in France, then did the same. So you can see why they don't like Europeans here.'

'But British ships try to run the blockade,' Maria objected. 'Surely that's a friendly act?'

The woman smiled. 'You are *naive*, my dear. Any ship-owner who runs the blockade does so entirely for profit. And a jolly fat profit he gets for every ounce of cargo he brings!'

Maria found the conversation disturbing. She had not encountered hostility – but then she was a member, by marriage, of a respectable Virginian family.

She waited almost three hours. A few people, at long intervals, were shown by officials to another room, but the crowd of people waiting hardly seemed to thin at all. At the end of three hours a clerk came and spoke to them collectively.

'The Consul is sorry, he can't see anyone else today. Please come back tomorrow.'

Each day, for four more days, Maria spent several hours on the hard benches of the consular waiting-room. After that first time she never saw the Englishwoman from Vermont again, though some of the others were there as regularly as she was herself. The chief topic of conversation was by what route they would leave if ever, as a result of all this waiting, they were fortunate enough to obtain a pass. Some favoured trying the railroad which, with several changes, might get them to Baltimore.

'That's no use,' someone else said. 'I know a gentleman who tried that, and was turned back, sent back all the way to Richmond. I shall try coach or wagon myself and get there by stages.'

A young man on his own proposed going by horseback all the way. But he would never make it, the others advised him. The roads were terrible and there were mountains to cross – and soldiers everywhere.

By the time Maria had listened to all the tales of horror she wondered if she would ever dare to set out, especially with a baby.

In the end, on the fourth day of waiting and just as she was about to go home, a clerk called her.

'The Consul is too busy to see you but his deputy, Mr Thornton, will do so.'

Mr Thornton motioned her to a seat in front of his large desk, but otherwise took no notice of her whatever, continuing to scratch away with his pen, concentrating on a pile of papers in front of him. In the end, by which time Maria was so angry that she thought of getting up and flouncing out of his office, he raised his head and spoke.

'What is it you want?'

'I want a pass, if you please, so that my baby and I can leave Richmond to join my sister in New York. I understand I can get nowhere without such a pass.'

He grunted. 'That's true. But I assure you we don't give out passes like penny buns. They're only for special cases.'

'I think I am a special case,' Maria said levelly. At all costs she must keep her temper. 'I have a letter here from the Reverend Moses Drury Hoge which explains my circumstances.'

He skimmed through the letter and handed it back to her.

'I can't help you here. You should apply to go under the flag of truce. Secretary of War's office. Room seventeen. I'll give you a note for him. And you're too late today. Better come back tomorrow.'

Tomorrow, and the day after, and the day after that, were as fruitless as ever. Three days she sat in ante-rooms waiting to see some representative of the Secretary of War. Then on the fourth day she saw an assistant, a stiff, dry man who clearly had little sympathy for anyone who wanted to leave Richmond. With a gloomy face he listened to her story, and read both the notes she gave him.

'We're cutting down on passes,' he said. 'Too many people are applying to go under the flag of truce. However, I'll put you on the list. You'll have to wait, of course.'

'How long?' Maria asked.

'Who can say?'

You can, Maria thought angrily. You can tell me whether

it's days, weeks, months, or the rest of my life! You are the rudest man I have ever met, she wanted to say. She wanted to shout at him, to call him what he was, a jumped-up jack-in-office. But she daren't show her anger. With an effort she controlled herself. He could so easily refuse to put her name on the list.

'What shall I do in the meantime?' she asked.

'How should I know? Wait until you get a letter.' He waved her away.

She had seldom felt so angry in her life, but there was nothing, just nothing, she could do about it. Nevertheless, the man's attitude achieved in her something that all reasoning had failed to do. As she left his office she felt herself filled with a determination as strong as steel. She *would* get away. No-one should stop her. By some means or other, no matter whom she had to pester and however long it took, she and her baby would go to New York.

'I must *do* something,' she said to Mrs Masterson when she arrived home. 'I've seen enough of these officials now to realise that if I just sit back and wait they'll forget all about me. But what *can* I do?'

Mrs Masterson shook her head. 'I don't know. Though there is just one faint possibility. I don't know if it would work. . . .'

'Whatever it is, let me try it!' Maria said eagerly. 'I'll do anything.'

'There is a Mr Bartlett. He has a senior post in the office of the Secretary of War. I don't know him – I met him once at a social event – but Mrs Bartlett is a fellow member on the Orphanage Committee. If I were to presume on this . . . give you a note . . . though it might not do any good. . . .' She was hesitant.

'Please do!' Maria cried. 'Surely it can do no harm? If you just ask that he would see me, let me put my case.'

'Very well then. You should go to him tomorrow. Every day lost will make matters more difficult. And there is one more thing. . . .'

'Yes?'

'It is my experience,' Mrs Masterson said smoothly, 'that most men cannot bear to see a woman cry. It unnerves them. Not having the gift of easy tears myself, I have often thought how unfair it was that my sisters who had it could so often get their own way. And then again, if a weeping woman is also carrying a small, defenceless baby. . . .' She broke off.

'You need say no more,' Maria told her. 'I understand you perfectly. And if by chance the baby were also to cry . . .?'

'It would would take a man of iron. . . . On the occasion when I met Mr Bartlett he did not strike me as a hard man.'

The next morning, as soon as she had fed him, Maria walked to the town carrying Robert Lee. By the time she had waited an hour and a half to see Mr Bartlett she did not need to pretend to be tired and weary; she was. The baby, though he had slept soundly all the time, was a weight in her arms.

When she was shown, at last, into Mr Bartlett's office he was clearly startled at the sight of the child.

'Please sit down,' he said courteously. He seemed a nice man. She felt ashamed of what she might find it necessary to do in the next few minutes.

He read Mrs Masterson's note of introduction, also Clive's letter and the note from the Reverend Hoge.

'I understand the circumstances,' he said. 'But it is not so easy. At the present time there are so many people. . . .' He went on and on, in a kindly manner. She realised she was getting nowhere.

It was not difficult to burst into a torrent of tears. She had only to think of Clive, to recall the humiliations of all those hours of waiting in the past weeks, to want her sister, and to think of Clive again. Tears coursed down her cheeks and her shoulders shook with sobs.

'My dear young lady!' Mr Bartlett was filled with consternation. 'My dear young lady!'

Robert Lee opened his blue eyes and gazed at his mother. Cry, my little one, she willed him! Oh please do cry! I need your help!

But in spite of her noisy sobs he lay impassive in her arms. Very well, she thought – and you must forgive me because it's for your sake too. With reluctant firmness she pinched him: hard, on his buttocks.

His outraged yell almost drowned her own crying. The cacophony of their combined protests filled the office. Mr Bartlett looked plainly terrified, helpless.

'My dear Mrs Masterson . . . pray don't distress yourself so . . . and your baby!'

'He is crying to be fed,' Maria said between sobs. 'My poor little mite is hungry. We have waited so long. I suppose . . . I suppose there is nowhere I could feed him?' Her fingers strayed, ever so tentatively, to the top button of her bodice. She managed to blush, but not nearly as deeply as did Mr Bartlett.

'My dear young lady . . . we are not equipped. . . .' He searched for words. 'But I will give you your pass, and my assistant shall find you a hackney cab so that you can take the little fellow home as quickly as possible.'

It took him less than five minutes to make out the pass, during which time Maria dried her eyes but Robert Lee continued to yell. As Mr Bartlett handed over the pass the baby became quiet.

Maria waited until she was in the cab before reading the pass. It said: –

> 'By Order of the Secretary of War
> Allow Mrs Maria Masterson, an Englishwoman, and her baby, Robert Lee Masterson, to pass beyond the lines by flag of truce. This pass is subject to the control of the Commanding General.
>
> (Signed)
>
> Horatio Bartlett'

She raised the piece of paper to her lips and kissed it. Then she kissed the baby. 'I'm sorry, little fellow,' she said. 'But it was absolutely necessary!'

What did it mean, 'Subject to the control of the Commanding General'? And how was she to go? No-one seemed to know that.

Over the next few days she asked everyone, and received shoals of conflicting advice. 'Have a carriage,' one said. 'The last thing you can do is hire a carriage,' another told her. 'They are not to be had for love nor money. Besides, it wouldn't take you far enough.'

'Go by Fredericksburg', 'Go to Harrison's Landing', 'Go by way of Petersburg', various people said – while an equal number of people advised against all these routes.

'I'm totally confused,' Maria said to her mother-in-law. 'What *shall* I do?'

'Well, it does seem that most people advise Petersburg,' Mrs Masterson replied. 'I believe you should plump for that. Also I know of an hotel there, in case you should have to wait around. But you must go soon. Winter is beginning and it will be more difficult for you to travel with Rober Lee as the weather gets colder.'

A week later Maria, with Robert Lee tucked warmly into a basket, left Richmond by the three o'clock train on a cold morning. She had made her farewells to the few people she knew in Richmond, and now there was only her mother-in-law. Mrs Masterson, poker-faced, insisted on seeing Maria to the railroad station. In the end, and much to her surprise, Maria found herself sad to be leaving her. In Clive's absence she had been a true friend. At the last minute, when the train was almost ready to leave, she flung her arms around Mrs Masterson and held her close.

'We shall all meet again when the war is over,' she said. 'I promise you that.'

'Promise me also,' Mrs Masterson asked in a voice quite unlike her own, 'that you will tell Robert Lee about his grandmother in Virginia. He cannot remember me, but I should like him to know that I exist.'

'Oh I will, I will!' Maria cried.

'And now you must board the train or it will leave without you.'

The train journey was horrid. The carriage was crowded, dark, odorous, with the windows tightly closed against the night air. When daybreak came it was relief to open a window and breathe in the cool, fresh air – though that didn't last long because the other passengers complained of a draught. There was, fortunately, a poky little ladies' room where she was able to feed and change the baby, and he was as good as ever.

In Petersburg a cab from the station quickly took her to the hotel Mrs Masterson had recommended. Within minutes of arriving she sought the advice of the proprietor's wife – a pleasant, homely woman who cooed and clucked over Robert Lee.

'I am to go under the flag of truce,' Maria said. 'Can you advise me when, and from where it goes?'

'The flag of truce train goes from the railroad station here, to City Point, where you board a boat. But it doesn't go every day. It depends.'

'On what?' Maria asked anxiously.

'On whether there's a boat available and how many people are to go. It's not regular.'

Maria heard the news with dismay. She didn't possess a great deal of money and Pitersburg was only the beginning of her journey.

'There's another thing,' the woman said. 'You should have a pass from the Provost Marshal here in Petersburg. If I were you I'd go and get that today. I'll look after the baby for you.'

There was no difficulty in getting the pass; just a tedious wait in the dingy, dirty waiting-room of the Provost Marshal's department. But the official, when she reached him, was efficient and polite.

'Can you tell me when another flag of truce train is leaving?' Maria asked.

'Perhaps in two days, maybe three. I will let you know at your hotel.'

He kept his word. Three days later, by which time there were half a dozen people in the hotel eagerly awaiting it, a message came to say that the flag of turce train would leave at noon on the following day.

The flag of truce train consisted of only one carriage into which about twenty passengers were crowded. Their luggage had been taken from them and put into a separate tender. Maria wondered if they would ever see it again. She had brought the minimum amount, hardly anything for herself, but essential clothes for the baby, and what few medicines Mrs Masterson had been able to get together, in case of sickness on the journey, were in the trunk.

Some of the people in the carriage were lighthearted and talkative, others were pale, and obviously nervous.

'I hope the flag will be quite clearly visible,' an elderly woman said. 'It wouldn't be the first time Federal troops had fired on this train!'

There was a shocked silence. Surely, Maria thought desperately, surely we haven't come so far only to be fired on?

'We shall be all right, madame,' a man said. 'You need have no fear. The train conductor has been appointed to see us through. He knows exactly what to do.'

City Point, where they left the train, was the port of Petersburg, on the James River. The train drew up beside a large wooden pier. All around there were warehouses, stores, shabby buildings, as well as the railway depot. It looked drab and uninteresting. The passengers herded themselves together in a tight group, afraid to stray far from each other, waiting for the train conductor, who had temporarily left them, to return and tell them what to do. There were boats drawn up in the river. One of them, Maria supposed, must be for them. They all looked far too small.

After a time the conductor returned.

'You are to present yourselves to the Federal Officer commanding, and answer his questions. Don't be afraid. Just answer truthfully.'

Because she had the baby, Maria was one of the first to be called. Trembling from head to foot, she stood in front of the officer, trying to tell herself that he was only a man, doing his duty. He was a man, like her husband. Perhaps he was a father. His only difference was in the colour of his uniform. But nothing that she told herself stopped the trembling.

'Where do you wish to go?' he asked.

'To New York.'

'I see you are an Englishwoman. Why do you wish to go

to New York?' He was quite civil, though stern. Maria began to breathe more easily.

'My sister has lived there for several years. I wish to join her, with my baby.'

'I see. You realise that your luggage may be searched. If it contains any contraband you will not be allowed to proceed.'

What was contraband? Were the medicines contraband? She had no idea. 'My luggage contains only personal belongings,' she replied. 'Mostly for my baby. I have no objection in the world to having it searched.' Whatever doubts she had, better to put a bold face on it now.

'Very well. You may proceed,' he said. 'Wait over there until an officer is ready to show you on board.'

While she waited for the others, Maria saw the trunks being put aboard. In a surprisingly short time the enquiries were over. They were all handed aboard and ushered into the stern of the boat where, to her dismay, they were closely guarded by armed soldiers. What in the world do they think we can do, Maria asked herself? Women, a few elderly men, and a baby? But it was not a question to ask out loud.

The winter afternoon, as they sailed down the James River, was heartrendingly beautiful; the sun, low in the sky, lighting the masts of the ships at anchor, making red-gold paths across the water. Boats large and small plied the river, though they all seemed threatened by the gunboats which were at anchor. The land beyond the river, too, was bathed in the sun's light. Maria felt a terrible sadness at the thought of leaving Virginia.

The inquisition was not over. More questions had to be asked on board before a Federal passport, without which not one of them could proceed, would be issued. The questions, fired at her now by several men grouped around a long table, were much as before. There were just more of them.

'When were you born?'

'Where?'

'When did you come to America?'

'How long did you live in Richmond?'

'Have you any relatives in the North?'

And so on. Maria felt the sweat trickling down her back as she stood there under interrogation. She was telling the truth, yet somehow she was made to feel that she was lying. In the end, when she felt that she must faint from standing and all the voices were beginning to merge into one, she heard a single, clear voice saying 'Very well. You may have your Federal passport.'

She took it away with her, an insignificant-looking scrap of paper which was her key to freedom, and read it avidly.

> 'Know ye that the bearer, Mrs Maria Masterson, has permission to pass with her son, Robert Lee Masterson, from this landing to Baltimore.'

Not everyone was given a passport. Some who had come all the way to this point were sent back.

It was midnight when those with passports were taken by ferry boat to a large passenger ship which awaited them at the mouth of the river. Maria was icy cold and wearied to death after twelve hours of anxious travel, especially by the changes from boat to boat, up and down steps and companionways, carrying the baby in his basket. But now, when she was shown to her cabin, it all seemed worthwhile. The cabin was tolerably roomy, decently furnished and warm. And in a very short time her luggage was delivered to her intact.

A stewardess brought her warm water to bathe the baby. She changed him into clean clothes and then, with great pleasure, and to her comfort and his, she fed him. When he was satisfied she laid him in his basket, after which she washed herself from top to toe, then lay under the blanket on her bunk. She never knew, so sound asleep was she, when the ship sailed.

When, after a blessedly uneventful voyage she left the ship in Baltimore, she took a cab at once to the post office and telegraphed Ruth.

'Arriving shortly New York with my baby. Maria.'

The winter of 1862 was immeasurably brightened for Ruth by Maria's arrival, and the sight of Robert Lee lightened all their spirits. And as if this was not enough, letters began to arrive regularly from Joss. As Mr Seaford had foreseen, the fighting had died down over the winter, which was perhaps the reason why the mail came through.

On a bright day in March, a day when she had heard from Joss, Ruth walked in Union Square and rejoiced at the first signs of spring. The buds on the trees were beginning to swell and the birds sang loud, contentious songs as they claimed their territorial rights. She wondered if the same kind of birds sang for Joss, wherever he was.

All the way back down Broadway her spirits soared because of the spring. Something good must come of it. Everything would somehow work out. She called in at the Relief Centre to pick up some more work. As a change from rolling bandages they were now padding splints.

'A lovely day,' she said. Miss Schuyler was not on duty. It was a woman Ruth didn't know.

'Beautiful,' she agreed. 'But fine weather is fighting weather!'

Immediately, Ruth wished she had not spoken, had not called in at the Centre; anything so that this stupid woman could not have clouded her day. Sure enough, when she went out again into Broadway, a sneaking north wind had risen, stabbing at her back as she walked home.

But it was when she entered the house, walked into her room, that the sky really darkened. And from that afternoon, from the moment she opened the letter which awaited her, she wondered if she would ever see the sun in the sky again.

The letter was from the matron of a military hospital in Washington. It was brief and to the point.

> 'I write to inform you that your husband, Corporal Sean O'Farrell, will shortly be transferred from this hospital to the temporary military hospital at Fourth Avenue/Forty-first Street, New York City. It is regretted that your husband's papers gave no information as to his next of kin and, though he has been with us several months, the nature of his injuries did not permit us to obtain this information from him until now. All further enquiries should be made to the New York hospital.'

# 33

Maria came into the room carrying Robert Lee on her hip. At eight months old he was quite a weight, and far too active to be left for long in his crib.

'Ruth, do you think I could. . . .'

She stopped short, seeing the expression on her sister's face, the letter in her hand.

'Ruth, what is it? It's Clive, isn't it? Something has happened to Clive!' She was never free of her fear for Clive, never would be.

'How could it be? Who would write to *me* about Clive?' Ruth spoke in a whisper, her voice flat, not quite steady. As she looked up at Maria her face was chalk-white.

'Of course! How stupid anxiety makes me! But something is wrong. What *has* happened, Ruth?'

Ruth handed over the letter. Maria read it, then put the baby down on the rug and went towards her. She wanted to take her sister in her arms, to comfort her, but there was a tight look on Ruth's face which warned her that she must not. Ruth, the strong one, the comforter, was suddenly unapproachable, as if she had retreated into some remote place where no-one was welcome.

Maria struggled for something to say. She felt helpless.

'What does it mean? It says "injuries", but we understood there'd been no fighting through the winter – though I expect we've been misinformed about that as about so much else,' she added bitterly. Whenver she thought about fighting she saw Clive in the middle of it. She was grateful to be with her sister, felt that she and the baby were now safe, but Clive seemed a million miles away. All her loving thoughts did not bring him any nearer.

'It's eight months since Bull Run. But it does say he's been in hospital several months.' Ruth spoke without emotion, as if she had no feeling left. Maria found her stillness frightening. Her sister looked stricken.

'Poor Sean!' she said. 'And poor you.'

Ruth turned away. With her back to Maria, she started rearranging everything on the mantelpiece. 'I shall go to the hospital in the morning,' she stated. 'I doubt he'll be there yet.'

'Well until then, Ruth dear, try hard to put it out of your mind,' Maria said.

How stupid Maria was, Ruth thought. Well-meaning, but quite stupid. It was impossible that the situation would ever be out of her mind again, even for a second.

In the next few hours, dry-eyed, quiet-voiced, she went through all the ordinary jobs of her ordinary existence: organising, cooking, speaking with boarders and staff, attending to Aurora (who must not yet be told anything), all with automatic efficiency. And every minute of the time thoughts of Sean, and inevitably of Joss, whirled around in her head; never settling, never forming a coherent pattern.

Repeatedly, without needing to look at them, for one reading had seared them into her mind, she considered the words of the letter, interpreting them in half a dozen different ways. Was Sean convalescent, being returned to New York for his final recovery? Was it that the hospital beds in Washington – so much nearer to the war front – were needed? Perhaps all convalescent men were being moved out. Would he go back into the army or was he so badly injured that he was coming home to die? When her mind turned in that direction she was afraid of the wickedness of her thoughts and shied away from them, trying to close a shutter in the darkest part of her being.

After breakfast next morning – she had lain awake all night, willing the day to come quickly, yet dreading it – she took the omnibus up Broadway and walked through to

Fourth Avenue. She had not known there was a hospital here, and indeed when she found it, it proved to be some assembly rooms, hastily and badly converted to their new use.

In the lobby utter confusion reigned. There were stretchers, mercifully empty now but bearing signs of recent occupation, around the floor, crutches leaning against the walls. Boxes of the kind she had spent so many hours filling with medical supplies were piled on top of each other, some of them open and the contents spilling out. While she stood there wondering where to go next, women enveloped in white aprons, their hair tied up in kerchiefs – they were volunteers who had never seriously expected to be called upon – crossed and recrossed the lobby, disappearing through the door or up the stairs. No-one took the slightest notice of her until, in the end, Ruth stood in the path of a nurse in uniform who looked more official than the rest, and barred her way.

'I'd like to see the matron please. I have a letter here. . . .'

'I'm sorry,' the nurse said quickly. 'Matron's impossibly busy. We had our first big intake last night. . . .'

'Of whom one is almost certainly my husband.' Ruth interrupted. 'Please read the letter and find someone who will deal with me!' She spoke with such force that the nurse was startled into compliance. When she had read the letter she said, 'If you'll wait here, Mrs O'Farrell, I'll try to find someone.'

She returned ten minutes later.

'I'll take you to Matron,' she said.

'Good morning, Mrs O'Farrell,' Matron said briskly. 'You were not expected quite so soon. Your husband arrived late last night and he has not yet had time to settle in.'

'He's arrived? I didn't know that. This letter is the only information I've had.' Ruth spoke as sharply as had the matron, annoyed by the woman's attitude.

The two women studied each other like adversaries

preparing for a fight. But how stupid, Ruth thought; and perhaps Matron thought the same, for when she spoke again her voice was gentler.

'Please sit down, Mrs O'Farrell. I'm afraid what I have to tell you may come as a shock.'

Ruth seated herself on the very edge of a chair. She was trembling. She hoped she would not make a fool of herself by fainting.

'Your husband has been badly injured,' Matron said. 'He was injured at Bull Run, as were many brave men in his regiment. I have his papers here but it is strange that he had no note of you as his next of kin. Otherwise we would have informed you earlier.' She looked at Ruth keenly, awaiting an explanation. Ruth gave none.

'How was he injured?' she asked.

'I'm coming to that, Mrs O'Farrell. He was shot in the left hand and I'm afraid has lost two fingers. According to this report - and I can confirm it, having seen him - his hand has healed well.'

'Then that is clearly not the reason he has been in hospital so many months,' Ruth broke in. 'What are his other injuries? Please tell me.'

'Head wounds,' Matron said abruptly. 'Severe ones. And there has been some infection. But he recovered enough to be moved from Washington. We are woefully short of beds there and I'm afraid we shall need every one of them when the spring offensive starts.'

'And he will recover further, now that he is here?'

Matron paused before answering. The pause was no more than a second or two but to Ruth it seemed to go on forever. It was almost impossible to bear what was in her mind. Her head was throbbing now and with every beat she felt that she was committing murder.

Why doesn't the woman speak, she asked herself? Why doesn't she stop my wicked thoughts?

'We do indeed hope so,' Matron said quietly. 'We do indeed hope so. It seems that he has been making a visible, though slow, recovery - which was why one day he was able to give your name. But it must be very slow, and there will be relapses.'

'He won't. . . ?' She couldn't say the word.

'No, Mrs O'Farrell. He won't die. You will have your husband. But when he leaves hospital, and that might not be for some months yet, he will need a great deal of looking after. I'm afraid that you must be prepared for that, and for the fact that he may never be quite fit enough to work again, though he may seem physically strong.'

Ruth said nothing. There was nothing to say. She had been delivered from her murderous thoughts, but there was no comfort in it. Matron, watching her, wondered why Mrs O'Farrell did not look happier at the promise of her husband's recovery. But shock took people in different ways. She must really *feel* happier. Her husband could so easily have died.

'And now, if you wish, you may see him for a few minutes,' she said. 'He is not expecting you, and if he should recognise you. . . .'

'What do you mean – recognise me?'

'As I said, there are relapses. He is in such a period now and I don't think he will know you. But if he does it will be a great shock to him. You must not stay too long, though you may come every day, in the afternoon.'

She rang a bell on her desk and the nurse came and led Ruth away.

'You look very pale, Mrs O'Farrell,' the nurse said. 'Shall I get you a glass of water?'

'If you please. And if I might sit in the corridor for a minute. . . .'

She could not go in to see him! She could not. If she went in to Sean now, she would be saying goodbye to Joss. There would be no turning back. She could not do it . . . yet she knew she must.

She fumbled in her purse and took out Joss's letter, unfolded it. It didn't matter that her eyes wouldn't focus on the words. She knew them by heart '. . . I am kept going by the thought of you, the thought that when this is over, Ruth, we shall be together. . . .'

But there was no real choice. She put the letter away, took a final sip of water, and called to the nurse.

'I'm ready now.'

Ruth followed the nurse through double doors into a large room she had glimpsed on her way in. Without thinking what she was doing, she immediately covered her nose and mouth with her hand. Though the hospital was newly-opened, the sweetish smell of decaying flesh – there is no stench in the world like gangrene – had already seeped into the air. She felt physically sick and took a deep breath to steady herself. Then she saw the nurse watching her.

'I'm sorry,' Ruth apologised.

'I don't think one ever gets used to it,' the nurse said. 'But we try not to let it show. Are you all right?'

'Yes thank you.'

Halfway down the ward the nurse stopped by a bed.

'Mr O'Farrell!' She spoke in a high, bright voice. 'A lovely surprise for you! Here's your wife to see you!'

'Only five minutes,' she cautioned Ruth.

Left to herself, Ruth would have walked straight past the bed without recognising the man in it, sitting motionless, propped against pillows. His face, curiously shrunken, deeply lined by pain, was as white as the bandages which swathed his head. His eyes, still intensely blue, stared from deep hollows. There was no expression in them. His mouth, those curving red lips which had been one of the first things Ruth had noticed about Sean when she had met him at Millfield, hung slackly open.

His arms lay straight out in front of him, symmetrically, on the tight white coverlet. It was as if they had been placed that way to look as neat as possible and he had not dared to move them.

'Hello, Sean,' Ruth said.

He gave no sign that he had either seen or heard her. She made herself look at his injured hand, at the gap where two small stumps took the place of his middle fingers. Then, holding her breath, she stretched out her hand and touched his. His flesh was icy cold.

She was not sure why she thought he knew what she had done. There was not the slightest answering movement, not the faintest flicker in his eyes: nevertheless she did think so.

'I hope you're feeling better, Sean,' she said.

It sounded so inadequate, so inane. She had no idea what to say. She wanted to weep at the pitiful sight of him, for she remembered him now not as the obstinate, heavy-drinking man who had so revolted her in those last few days before he had gone to the war, but as the young man she had known at Millfield: laughing, handsome, full of lively talk; driving his master's horses too fast through the countryside.

'Aurora is well,' she said, clearly. 'She is at school today. And Maria is with us. She has a little son.'

He remained totally inert. Ruth saw the nurse motioning to her and realised that her time was up.

'I have to go,' she told Sean. 'I'll come again tomorrow.'

On the way out the nurse said, 'What do you think of him?'

A great tide of anger surged in Ruth, and overflowed.

'I think he would have been better off if the bullet had gone clean through his brain!' Her anger was not for herself, for her own loss, nor was it for Joss. It was all for Sean.

The nurse looked shocked. Ruth supposed she had the professional instinct which counted as a victory every patient who was kept alive.

'I understand,' the nurse said. 'And I daresay today is not one of his good days. The journey from Washington has upset most of our patients. But according to his chart he does have better days.'

He must have, Ruth thought, or he would never have been able to tell them about me. There must have been a lucid interval when he was able to remember.

She walked all the way back to Spring Street. She wanted to walk and walk, forever, never to reach her journey's end. In that long tramp through New York's busy streets, oblivious to the bustle, the noise, the traffic, the people, to everything which was happening there, she saw her whole world changing, and knew that she did not want to live in the future which lay ahead of her. When Joss came home from the war it could no longer be to her. She could never divorce a man who was an invalid. It was not in her, though the realisation was bitter. And however far Sean recovered it seemed as though he would always be dependent on her. She would have to bear it. One went on living, whether one wanted to or not.

There was only one other decision to be made. Should she now tell Joss the truth, or should she allow him to go through the rest of the war in ignorance, and therefore in false hope? The question of right or wrong didn't enter her mind; only what would be best for him. But if she didn't tell him, how would she bear his loving, optimistic letters, so full of plans for the future?

It did not occur to her that she might not be called upon to bear them; that after the letter she had received only yesterday, before the world had changed, there would be a long silence.

She had no recollection of walking down Broadway, or of turning the corner into Spring Street. When she walked into Appleby's Maria cried out at the sight of her.

'Ruth! Where have you been? You're soaking wet!'

'Is it raining?'

Maria stared at her. 'It's been raining heavily for the last half-hour.' She put her arm through Ruth's and took her through to the sitting-room.

'I've been thinking,' Maria said later that afternoon. 'Do you know you've been running Appleby's for more than ten years now?'

She had made Ruth change into dry clothes, then sit and rest, her feet on a footstool, all afternoon. Ruth had not protested.

'I suppose I have,' she replied. 'I hadn't realised it was so long.'

'And in all that time you haven't had a break, except for a few days when Aurora was born?'

'I haven't needed one,' Ruth said. 'I didn't know it when I came to New York – I didn't know what I wanted then – but Appleby's was the right thing for me. It turned out well.' Though nothing else had, she thought, and now never could.

'Well, it's time you had a break,' Maria told her. 'Oh, I'm well aware you can't go away, with the war on, and Sean as he is. But I do believe you could take a rest from Appleby's. I'm sure Doris Seaford and I could run things for you for a few weeks – and Lavinia Munster would help. It needn't be for long. I don't doubt you'll soon be your old self again.'

I shall never be my old self, Ruth thought. That self is gone. And where would she get the strength for the new person she would have to be?

'I don't say we'd do everything as well as you,' Maria continued. 'But you'd be there to turn to if we needed you.'

It was not an idea which would ever have occurred to Ruth, though now that Maria had put it forward it was undeniably tempting. She was so tired. Suddenly she wanted to be rid of every responsibility she had ever known.

'You could also give up the Relief Centre for a little while,' Maria suggested.

'I wouldn't do that,' Ruth said quickly. All along she had had this superstitious feeling that the boxes she packed were some sort of insurance against Joss's safety; that if she neglected to do her bit for other soldiers, God would cease to watch over Joss.

'But I must admit,' she told Maria, 'that a few weeks respite from the house would be welcome, especially as it seems that I shall need to visit Sean every day.'

So it was settled. Mrs Seaford welcomed the opportunity and Lavinia Munster was more than willing to help. 'It will keep me from brooding about Karl,' she said.

That evening Ruth told her boarders about Sean, and that she intended shedding her responsibilities towards them for a little while.

'But not for long,' she assured them. 'And I shall be here if I'm needed.'

'However much we miss you, we shall try not to need

you,' Mr Pierce said. 'You must concentrate on your husband now. I'm sure I speak for all of us.'

After that she visited Sean every day, sitting by his bedside, bringing herself to hold his mutilated hand in hers, watching for the flicker of interest which never came. She stayed longer with him now, sometimes for the whole afternoon. One day Matron called her into her office.

'Don't give up hope, Mrs O'Farrell,' she said. 'I'm sure your visits do nothing but good. One day he'll look up and recognise you and then his cure will begin. It might be that he does already. We can't know what goes on in his mind.'

And it's as well, Ruth thought, that you can't know what goes on in mine.

Though her heart was filled with pity for Sean, she could not give him love. Nor, however hard she tried, could she cease to love Joss, or prevent herself thinking about him for a single hour. Perversely, she never thought about Joss more than when she sat at Sean's bedside.

She explained about Sean to Miss Schuyler. 'I shall have to adjust my hours here to fit in with hospital visits,' she said.

'I'm so sorry that you have this terrible burden,' Miss Schuyler sympathised. 'I should tell you that in May Mrs Valentine Mott is to open a hospital for sick and wounded soldiers on Lexington Avenue. The conditions there will be very good, much better than where your husband is now.'

'They do their best,' Ruth said.

'I'm sure they do. But those assembly rooms have never been properly adapted and the soldiers can't be as comfortable. Mrs Mott is a personal friend of mine, I could speak to her about Mr O'Farrell if you wished.'

'It seems that it would benefit my husband, therefore I'd be most grateful,' Ruth replied.

So in May Sean was moved to the Lexington Avenue hospital. There were more doctors in attendance and a larger ratio of nursing staff to patients. Also the wards were brighter, and a little smaller. But it was strange, Ruth thought, how quickly the smell of sickness and death came to pervade the building.

Also in May, in the small, quiet town of Williamsburg, Virginia, the smell of sickness and death pervaded the Baptist chapel, which had been turned into a hospital for those Confederates who had been wounded in the recent battle there.

It had been a short, sharp, fierce battle; noisy too, with the terrified inhabitants of Williamsburg trying to cover their ears against the sound of guns and the whistle of bullets. It had been a battle fought, from first to last, in a deluge of rain which turned the whole battleground into a quagmire, so that soldiers on both sides fought knee-deep in mud. When General Johnston withdrew his defeated rebel forces they could retreat at no more than a mile an hour. It didn't matter. The same mud impeded the Union army in pursuit.

Wading into it, the Union troops soon took possession of the town. One of the first things they did, all along Duke of Gloucester Street, was to hang their Union flags so that they draped over the sidewalk where the people of Williamsburg had to walk beneath them.

Not so Mrs Priestley. On her way to take comforts to the Confederate soldiers who had been crowded into the Baptist chapel, she walked defiantly down the middle of the road. There had been no rain since the battle, but the ruts were still full of mud and she had to hold her skirts above her ankles. She didn't like doing this, aware that the Union soldiers were watching her, laughing at her.

'You shouldn't be walking in the road,' a soldier called. 'You'll get in the way of the horses!'

'I refuse to walk beneath the Union flag!' She shouted it out, wanting to be heard.

'Be careful what you say, old lady!' the soldier replied.

The sun was strong on her head, too. But she would rather suffer sunstroke than be shaded by the enemy flag.

She visited the chapel every day now, doing what she

could. A week after the battle, wounded were still being brought in. As she worked, she hoped that someone, somewhere, would look after Francis if he needed it. Each day she looked for him here among the wounded. Other local men had unexpectedly been brought in, so one never knew. It was a pity that the Union troops wouldn't allow them to be moved so that they could be nursed in their own homes.

Moving between the crowded beds - not really beds, but straw-filled mattresses on the ground - carrying a pitcher of cool lemonade which she had made that morning - she found Francis. He was lying on a mattress in the far corner of the chapel, among half a dozen others who had been brought in during the night. He lay on a grey blanket, but he had no pillow and there were no covers over him, not even a sheet.

At first she didn't recognise him. Under a layer of grime, for no-one had had time to wash him, his face was a sickly-greenish hue. The collar and the front of his tunic was stiff with a mass of dried, congealed blood. She needed no second glance to tell her that her son would not live. But die in this state, he would not. She would not let him! She went at once to speak to the nurse in charge.

'I have found my son,' she said. 'He will not live long, but I wish him to die with some comfort and dignity. I would like a messenger to go to my house and bring back clean sheets and pillows.'

'I'm afraid there's no-one available,' the nurse replied. 'Is it not possible for you to go?'

'There is no time,' Mrs Priestley said. 'I beg of you to let someone do this. I will work for you night and day afterwards, to repay you.'

'Very well, Mrs Priestley,' the nurse agreed.

While she waited for the sheets and pillows Mrs Priestley fetched warm water and a sponge and gently washed Francis. Under the grime there wasn't a scratch on his face, though he had several days' growth of beard which, in other circumstances, she knew he would have hated, for he was a fastidious man. There was nothing she could do about the tunic, short of cutting it off, and this she dare not do.

When the messenger returned with the clean bedding she carefully placed a pillow under her son's head and a crisp white linen sheet over him, hiding his stained uniform. One could almost believe now, except for his terrible colour, that he was simply asleep. As she smoothed out the last crease from the sheet Francis opened his eyes. He, too, knew he was dying. She could read it in his face. He spoke, and she bent her head to hear what he said.

'Tell Ruth,' he whispered. 'Tell her I loved her. I would have come back for her.'

After that it was all over quite quickly. She drew the sheet over her son's face, said a prayer, rose to her feet. She would ask the Federal Commander if she might have her son's body to bury in the family grave. Surely he would not refuse her that?

When the war was over she would give Francis's message to Mrs O'Farrell. She would do it, even though her heart burned with a fierce hatred of all Northerners.

In Northern Virginia the winter had been bitter: snow, ice, rain, wind. The troops had been under canvas, or in rough wooden huts, and food had been none too plentiful, though apparently, or so they were told, the Rebels were in a worse state than the Yanks. So that was something to be thankful for. Or was it, Joss thought? What did it profit anyone?

He had vowed never to tell Ruth about the privations they endured, about the awful conditions, and he had kept that vow. Whenever he put pen to paper he steeled himself to write with cheerful optimism.

It hadn't been easy. Sticking out the worst winter in memory, waiting for the weather to let up, had been almost worse than being in battle. After Bull Run his Company had never moved far from Centreville, and sometimes he wondered if they ever would. President Lincoln, so rumour said, had requested that all Union troops should surge forward on every front on the twenty-second of February,

Washington's birthday; but on the Potomac General McClellan was infuriatingly cautious.

Then in spring the rain came, unbelievably heavy, as it was throughout Virginia. The roads along which Joss and his men had now begun to move were churned up into swamps by marching men, horses, mules, supply wagons, gun carriages. Half the time the horses couldn't move and the wagons were bogged down axle-deep. They were supposedly on their way to Richmond, but at this rate it would take them all the summer to get there. And in the meantime, wouldn't the Confederates be moving to defend their capital?

But let's get there, Joss thought impatiently. Let's take Richmond no matter what the cost, and then we can finish this foul, bloody, stinking war. That there would be bitter fighting he had no doubt.

He dismounted from his horse because in the mud it could not manage his weight. Picking his way carefully, he tried to lead it on to firmer ground. Stepping calf-deep into yet another bog, he longed for New York, for hot water, clean clothes, a good meal - and for Ruth. Above everything, and all the time, for Ruth.

So the spring passed and the summer came. New York was as bright, as gay, as electric as ever; the social round with its balls and picnics, parties and horse-racing, every bit as hectic as in peacetime. Some said it was more so. Others asked, wasn't it their *duty* to enjoy life? Wasn't it culture and liberty and the good things of life which our brave soldiers were fighting for, out there in Tennessee, in Missouri, Illinois, Kentucky, Texas, and all along the Potomac? Of course it was, and the New Yorkers would support them with every penny they could raise.

The ladies' dresses, that summer, were prettier than ever. The sun shone. Every day in Central Park bright new carriages with bright new occupants appeared. There was money to be made in the war, and a man was a fool, and unfair to his family, who didn't seize the opportunity.

Unpatriotic too, for didn't our boys need guns, and new uniforms to replace the ones which were falling off their backs? Besides, money was the passport to society, no matter what the Old Guard like the Astors might say.

Prices rose. Mrs Seaford and Maria returned from every shopping expedition with complaints, not now of ribbons and silks, but of the price of butter, milk, sugar.

'As for tea and coffee!' Mrs Seaford said. 'They're prohibitive! We shall simply have to serve it weaker. And the gentlemen aren't being let off. Plug tobacco and cigars are going up by leaps and bounds.'

So the poor, especially those whose men were at the war, had to tighten their belts. But thankfully the rich were quite generous and gave freely whenever a collection was made.

Throughout May, Ruth sat by Sean's bed, waiting for him to know her. She had a lot of time to think. She thought about Polly Beard, the lady's maid she'd met at Millfield, and wondered what might be happening to her in her beloved Virginia. She thought about Francis Priestley. She thought about Ernest and Uncle Matthew who, if their infrequent letters were anything to go by, seemed undisturbed by the war.

In June, when General McClellan's men were no more than nine miles from Richmond, Sean opened his eyes and looked around. For some reason not clear to him, he had expected to see Ruth, but she wasn't there.

# 34

'Another hot day,' Ruth said, passing a nurse in the corridor on her way to see Sean.

'It's blistering in the ward,' the nurse replied.

She did not exaggerate, Ruth thought a moment later. The heat and the smell struck her like a blow in the face as she entered. Though the blinds had been drawn as a shield from the sun, nothing could keep out the heat. It burned its way through every open door and window. But closed doors in the ward were not to be borne; there the men lay covered by one thin cotton sheet each, with which, for decency's sake, Sister would not allow them to dispense.

By now Ruth had made the acquaintance of some of the men in the ward. Visiting every day, sitting silently by Sean's bed, she was the object of friendly curiosity. And as the men got used to her she was able to do small errands, post letters and the like, or in the nurse's absence shake up an uncomfortable pillow. Most valuable of all to them, she was a creature from the world outside, the world for which they all longed.

The man in the next bed to Sean, Thomas Morton, had lost a leg at Bull Run and the amputation was taking a long time to heal, but now at least he could get around on crutches and he had appointed himself Sean's guardian. He watched longer at Sean's bedside even than Ruth. As she came into the ward this afternoon he greeted her with great excitement.

'He was crying in the night!' he said. 'I heard him!'

'Crying? Did the nurse hear? She didn't say anything to me.'

'It was the night nurse,' Thomas said. 'I told her when she did the round, but he'd stopped then.'

To Ruth's eyes Sean appeared exactly the same as always: completely devoid of any emotion. Over the weeks in which she had been visiting he had made a physical improvement – there was more flesh on his bones and his face had lost its awful pallor. He seemed, as far as anyone could tell, not to suffer; but then he seemed to experience no feelings, neither pain nor pleasure, interest or aversion. He simply lay there, inhabiting some remote country from which it seemed his spirit was loth to return.

'You're sure you weren't dreaming, Thomas,' Ruth suggested gently.

'I wasn't dreaming, ma'am. I went across and had a good look at him. I can get out of bed now,' he added proudly. 'Soon be leaving here, I daresay.'

'Yes, I know.' They had this particular bit of conversation every day. 'You're doing very well. Very well indeed. Was Sean dreaming then?'

Thomas shrugged. 'Can't say for that. He could have been. But there were tears on his face. I wiped them away with the sheet.'

On either side of the bed they studied Sean, weighing up the possibilities. To Ruth he seemed unchanged, totally inert.

'He doesn't look any different now,' Thomas admitted. 'But I *know* he was crying, even if it was only his dream. Quietly, it was – but I heard him. I don't sleep much anyhow.'

'I see. Well, will you look after Sean for a minute while I speak to Sister?' Thomas liked to be left in charge of Sean whenever Ruth left the ward.

' 'Course I will. He'll be all right with me.'

'I know nothing of the episode,' Sister said. 'The night staff was on duty, of course; but Mr O'Farrell wasn't mentioned in the report, therefore I don't think anything unusual could have occurred.'

'It would have been unusual, would it not, for my husband to have wept?' Ruth asked.

'Yes. And an improvement. For him to show any emotion would be a great step forward. It's what we're waiting for. But I think perhaps Mr Morton was dreaming. Or exaggerating. Sometimes our patients lie to manufacture their own little bit of drama, to relieve the monotony. Night nurse may have judged it as that.'

'I see.'

Ruth walked back to the bed. Though not the slightest signs of animation now showed in Sean, knowing Thomas she believed that he was telling the truth. And she did not think he had been dreaming.

'Thank you, Thomas,' she said. 'I'm going to sit here a little longer now.'

Reluctantly he shuffled off down the ward to visit another patient.

Ruth took Sean's hand – she had long ago ceased to have any qualms about touching it – and held it. She felt sure that it was less cold than usual.

Sitting there, wondering what was happening behind that impassive face, she made a decision – and realised with a stab of guilt that she should have made it weeks ago. While she sat with Sean, she determined, she would try to concentrate her thoughts on him, and on him alone. It was not enough for her to sit there passively, letting her thoughts wander where they would. She would stop dreaming about herself, about everything that had ever happened to *her*, all the people she had ever known. She would even try, for this period each day, not to think about Joss, though she knew that that might prove impossible.

'Hello, Sean,' she said quietly. 'It's Ruth. Don't you know me? Don't you remember Ruth?'

She kept on talking; slowly, with pauses, as if she waited for her words to reach some distant place where they might be received and understood.

'Do you remember the boat on the river?' she asked. 'All

those people waving at us? And Polly Beard drinking too much rum?'

And after a pause. 'Do you remember when we went to Barnum's museum? The cherry-coloured cat?'

She tried to remember all the pleasant happenings of the past, and was saddened to realise how sparse her memories were of happy times shared with Sean. But she concentrated on him, first talking, then pausing, then talking again; repeating the process over and over.

It was while she was saying, 'I saw Mr Tweed in the distance yesterday,' that Sean moved his eyes; slowly, then rapidly, but without direction, and then at last focusing on her.

'Sean, it's me!' She tried to hold his eyes with hers, hardly daring to breathe.

His eyes remained steadily on her face. Without looking away she raised her arm high in the air and beckoned to Thomas Morton, who was coming towards her down the ward. Seeing her signal he increased his clumsy progress. She prayed that his crutch would not slip on the polished floor.

'Fetch Sister, Thomas! Go as quickly as you can, but be careful.'

While she waited what seemed an eternity but was probably less than a minute, she continued to hold Sean's gaze, willing him with all her strength to stay with her.

'I'm holding your hand, Sean,' she said. 'Can you feel me holding your hand?'

There was the slightest, the very slightest, pressure of his hand in hers. But so slight that she wondered afterwards whether she had imagined it.

When Sister arrived Sean was still looking at her. Two seconds later his eyes were dead again.

'But you *saw* him, Sister? You did *see* him?' Ruth cried.

'Yes I saw him, Mrs O'Farrell. It's true enough. It's what we've hoped for all this time.'

'Then I shall stay longer and see if it happens again,' Ruth said.

'I think you should go now,' Sister advised. 'He's fallen asleep already. I'm quite sure he shouldn't be rushed. But you will be here tomorrow, won't you?'

'Of course. I'll come earlier.'

'I'll tell you if he cries in the night again,' Thomas offered.

Sister looked at him thoughtfully.

'Perhaps you were right,' she conceded.

To the east of Richmond, no more than eight or nine miles from the city, Joss Barnet waited with his Company. They had waited several days now, in this mosquito-ridden swamp, and it was not clear why. Some said that McClellan had asked for reinforcements and, cautious as ever, would not begin the attack until they arrived. Whatever the reason, the delay was a godsend to Robert E. Lee, waiting there in Richmond. While McClellan's men sweated in the heat, irritated by the whine of mosquitos, Lee set his soldiers to digging trenches all around the city. Toiling in the hot June sun, every so often the Southern men stopped to lean on their shovels and say what they thought of him. 'King of Spades' they called him – and then went back to their digging.

That wasn't all Robert E. Lee did. One hot, humid afternoon – Joss was writing to Ruth, his men were idling around, playing cards, singing, sleeping, anything to pass the time – they heard the thunder of horses' hooves, and through the trees, unbelievably close, saw the grey Confederate uniforms and the flash of the sun on metal as a troop of Rebel soldiers galloped across the adjoining field.

'To horse!' Joss commanded. 'Catch them!'

They mounted as quickly as they could, and gave chase, but without the slightest success. The Rebels easily outdistanced them, disappearing into the distance before a shot was fired.

'So what was all that about?' Joss asked a fellow officer as they rode back.

The man shrugged. 'Who knows? But who can understand anything about this war?'

Robert E. Lee could have told them that he had boldly sent

a troop of cavalrymen all around the perimeter of the Federal troops, looking for gaps, and on McClellan's right flank, where the Sixteenth waited, they had found one. Lee at once sent for Stonewall Jackson and his men, who had been busy in the Shenandoah Valley, to fill that gap.

The waiting ended. Late in June the people of Richmond clearly heard the cacophony of war: the muskets, the guns. They were not quite near enough to hear the cries of the wounded, but they would do so later, when so many casualties were brought into the town that sometimes stretchers had to be laid in the streets. Mrs Masterson looked all the time for Clive, but never found him.

The battle lasted seven days. When it ended, McClellan's men had been driven back eighteen miles from Richmond's gates. Though Joss's Company was one of those which retreated, disbanded and in confusion, to the Union base at Harrison's Landing, he didn't make it with them.

On the afternoon of the sixth day the shivering and burning which swept every inch of his body, the terrible fever which had been with him for two days now, conquered him. He recognised that he had a severe bout of malaria and knew that there was no quinine left in his saddlebag. Also there was a deep wound in his arm from which he was losing blood. He half slid, half fell from his horse's back and crawled into a ditch where there was a patch of shade from an oak tree. His body shook so severely that it seemed as though the ground moved. It was only a matter of time, he thought, before the Rebels found him.

He had thwacked his horse and set it off, so that its presence shouldn't give him away. But how long ago was that? He was confused about the time and thought he must have lost consciousness for a while.

It was in this confused state that he heard the Rebel yell. But did he really hear it, or was he remembering Manassas where it had frightened the lives out of them? Also, it was growing dark, though it wasn't night. How could that be?

When the Confederates came, soon afterwards, he no longer heard or saw anything.

In New York confused despatches came from Mechanicsville, White Oak Swamp, Savage Station, Gaines Mill, with reports of nearly sixteen thousand Union losses and two and a half thousand Union soldiers left behind to the mercy of the Confederates, at Savage Station field hospital.

The news filled the New York papers, causing a momentary halt in the city's round of pleasure. But it was the time of the year for packing up to get away from the heat - and thank goodness there were still places, conveniently situated, which the war had not touched, where one could be sure of a breath of country air and a restorative vacation.

There was one particular edition of the newspaper which Maria tried, without success, to keep from Ruth. Ruth read, with fear clawing at her heart, how in the Seven Days Campaign the New York Sixteenth had been made conspicuous by their light-coloured straw hats and had, as a consequence, suffered many losses.

'It's not to say that Joss is among them,' Maria said. 'He is just as likely to be safe and well!' It was what she tried to tell herself about Clive, but with even less conviction.

Over the next few weeks Sean improved a little each day. His times of 'knowing' became longer and more frequent though they were never, it seemed, in his control. Sometimes Ruth sat by his bedside for two hours or more, talking to him, stroking his hand, but with no visible effect whatsoever. What she did notice was that his arms were not always as tidily outstretched as they had been, but lay at different angles on the sheet, the fingers often relaxed and curled. Also, his mouth was more often closed in its own firm line than hanging open. But he did not speak.

Each day when she was with him she concentrated her mind as well as ever she could; talking to him, repeating the same phrase again and again. Sometimes, if she thought they were of any especial interest to him, she brought him snippets of news from the world outside the hospital.

'It was a day for Ireland yesterday,' she said. 'General Corcoran, who was taken prisoner, has been released by the Confederates and returned to New York. *Your* General Corcoran, Sean. The fighting Irish! He was given a hero's welcome, Sean. I wish you could have seen him.'

Privately she thought it would have been a nice gesture if the general had visited some of the men of his regiment who still lay in hospital after Bull Run.

But that was one of the days when Sean remembered nothing and all her efforts seemed worthless. Nor was it easy to concentrate on him. Her inside churned with worry about Joss. She felt disaster in her bones.

It was no surprise, therefore, when she received a telegraph message later that day from Washington.

'Regret inform you Captain Josiah Barnet missing believed killed after Seven Days Campaign.'

Ruth sat down quickly, crumpling the telegram into a ball in her hand. They put it so bluntly. But what other way was there? Death was the bluntest of facts.

'Oh Ruth, how terrible!' Maria cried. But she was puzzled. 'Why have they informed *you*?'

'He gave me as his next of kin.'

'His next of kin?'

'We love each other. We always have. We planned to marry. I thought Sean had gone for ever. Oh, don't worry,' Ruth added, seeing Maria's startled face. 'I shan't desert Sean. I should never have married him but I shan't desert him now. Well, I shan't need to, shall I? Without Joss what will it matter?'

Maria stepped quickly to her sister, folded her in her arms. 'Oh Ruth, I'm so sorry! But it doesn't actually say he's dead.'

'Missing, believed killed. But I know what I feel.'

Ruth did not weep, either then or in the months which followed the telegram. She was too dead in her heart for the tears to come. It was as if everyone else around her went on living, their lives touching hers at various points, while she, in the centre of all the activity, was dead. But at least being dead she didn't feel. Except that there was always a moment, when the day's work was done and she went to bed, totally alone – in the long interval before sleep came – when she came alive. It was in these moments, though she still didn't cry, that all the fears, terrors, agonies, pains of living, pricked, wounded and assaulted her.

Perhaps it would have been better if Maria and Mrs Seaford had not continued to run Appleby's. Ruth might have found in her boarders her quickest source of healing. But Maria thought otherwise, and Ruth acquiesced.

'You've done too much for too long,' Maria said. 'You've left yourself no reserves of body or spirit. And you have Sean to think of.'

Lavinia Munster, incredibly, still received letters regularly from Karl.

'You wouldn't think to read them that he was in the middle of a war,' she said. 'He writes about such ordinary things, like finding wild figs and eating them. Or. . . .'

She broke off, embarrassed. Though she was far from clear about Ruth's situation, Maria had cautioned her about speaking too much of the war in front of Ruth.

'Please don't be afraid to mention Karl,' Ruth said. 'I want to hear about him.'

Strangely, it no longer upset her to hear about the war. What was taking place now was all a long way off and somehow did not concern her. Her war was over.

Sean had improved out of all recognition, by coincidence from the very day Ruth had had news of Joss. On her visit the next day, though she had felt in the pit of despair, he had smiled at her. A few days later he spoke her name.

'Ruth'. And then again, 'Ruth'. His voice was surprisingly strong.

On Ruth's next visit to the hospital Sister asked her to step into her office.

'I want to talk to you about Mr O'Farrell,' she said. 'He's making the most remarkable recovery, and I don't need to tell you how delighted we are. But more than ever now, *you* are the one who will help him most. Of course you have done so ever since he came here, but now you must redouble your efforts.'

'In what way?' Ruth asked.

'There is still a great deal to be done. By far the most important thing is that you should encourage and strengthen his will to get better, the will to live. Encourage him all the time to look forward with hope to the future.'

Stop! Be quiet! With the greatest difficulty Ruth choked back the protest which rose to her lips. How could she? How could she do what this cool, starched woman asked? She had no hope to give to anyone.

'Talk to him in a positive manner,' Sister went on. 'Discuss the time when he will be back with you in his own home. Make him look forward to leaving this place.'

'When will that be?'

'The doctor thinks not long. It's September now; let's think in terms of him being home for Thanksgiving, if all goes well. That would be a true thanksgiving for both of you, would it not?'

Ruth had given no thought to Sean's homecoming. When she first saw him in hospital, in spite of the matron's assurances she had not believed that he would live; or if he did, she'd thought, it would always be in hospital. Joss's homecoming had been the one she had envisaged then. Since his death – she made herself use the word, even in her thoughts – she had not looked ahead even as far as the next day. She dared not, because of the long, slow passage of time which stretched before her.

'The strange thing is,' Ruth said to Maria, 'that I don't resent the idea of Sean coming back here. I shall find no difficulty in looking after him.'

'Ruth, that's not like you!' Maria protested. 'Oh, I don't mean that you shouldn't have Sean back, or anything like that. But this resignation! It's not you. I've always thought of you as someone who fights.'

'Not really. I railed against fate, perhaps; and occasionally kicked at life when it didn't go my way. Nothing more.'

'Well, I wish you'd take a kick or two now,' Maria said. 'Just to show you're the same person.'

'But I'm not,' Ruth replied. 'I shall never be the same person again.'

Early in September General Lee crossed the Potomac River and pushed north to Sharpsburg, in Maryland. For the time being there were no Union troops left in Virginia. And then, on a Wednesday in mid-September, back and forth, back and forth across a cornfield, Union and Confederate soldiers massacred each other in the Battle of Antietam, the bloodiest one-day battle of them all. Maria felt sure, as the reports came through, that Clive was in this battle; that his was one of the hundreds of dead bodies defacing the golden stubble of the cornfield. What made it worse to bear, what made it worse all the time, was that there was no way she could get news, either good or bad.

Though Ruth tried, her own experience wasn't one to comfort Maria. It took Mrs Seaford to do that, which she did unintentionally by going down with a sharp attack of lumbago, so that extra work, as well as the care of Robert Lee who at fourteen months was walking, and into everything, fell on Maria.

'Don't worry, Mrs Seaford,' Ruth said. 'I can do extra until you're well again.'

'Please don't, Ruth,' Mrs Seaford replied. 'It's better for Maria to be busy.'

Early in October the wounded from Antietam began to fill the New York hospitals and Ruth was asked if she would nurse Sean at home.

'Now that your husband is getting up every day,' Sister said, 'there's nothing we can do that you can't. And we're desperate for beds.'

'Very well,' Ruth agreed. She felt no emotion of any kind at the prospect. 'May I come back to you for advice if I need it?'

'By all means. And of course you must put Mr O'Farrell in the care of your own doctor. And now I think you should be the one to give him the news.'

In the ward, Sean was sitting on a chair beside his bed. Though Ruth knew he had been out of bed every day for a week now, she had not seen him up. She was struck by how much more normal he looked than when lying against his pillows.

'Hello, Sean,' she said. For the first time since she had seen him in hospital she didn't take his hand. It had seemed a natural thing to do when he was ill and helpless; now that he looked more of a man she didn't want to do it. But he held out his hand to her and she couldn't deny him.

'Can you stand some good news?' she asked.

'Try me!' His voice was getting stronger too, his Irish accent more pronounced.

'How would you like to leave here? To come home?'

It was as if she had offered him the sun, moon and stars. She had seen his face light up like this just once before – on the day she had agreed to marry him. But in the next moment his face clouded over with suspicion.

'Ye'd not be having me on?'

'Having you on?' She was shocked at the thought. 'Why would I do that? The doctor says you can leave. You'll have to give me a day or two to get things ready for you. And when you do come back you'll have to take things easy for a while, do as you're told.'

'Whatever you say, Ruth! Always, whatever you say!' He was beside himself with joy.

'Then the end of the week, say?'

'Where will he be sleeping?' Maria asked hesitantly when Ruth gave her the news.

'In the small room he had before he went into the Army. But of course during the day he'll be sharing the sitting-room with us. He won't trouble you, Maria. You'll find him quite different.'

'He never did trouble me,' Maria said. 'I was thinking of you.'

Ruth knew it was impossible that she should ever again share her bed with Sean. She had faced that problem squarely. He should have everything else she could give him, but not that. No-one, ever again, should have what she had given so freely, so lovingly, to Joss. She had no desire for anyone else and knew she never would have

So three days later, to a warm welcome from Maria, the boarders, the staff, and a delighted reception from Aurora, Sean came home. Robert Lee took to him at once. When Maria saw them playing so happily together she ran out of the room in tears. Ruth followed her.

'Oh Ruth, I don't want to be mean! I just can't help thinking. . . .'

'That you want it to be Clive, playing with Robert Lee. I understand. And one day I'm sure he will!'

Sometimes, and this was one of the times, Maria wondered if she had been wrong to leave Richmond. At least there she would have had a chance of *knowing*. But, she reminded herself, she had done what Clive wanted her to do.

It was clear from the first day that Aurora would be the one to help Sean settle. He came alive in her presence.

'My, but you're a fine, tall girl!' he remarked. 'You'll be taller than your mother in no time at all.'

'I'm the tallest girl in the class,' Aurora said complacently. 'Though some of the girls are twelve and I'm only eleven years and four months.'

If Sean remembered how tall and broad Aurora's father was he gave no sign. From the day of his homecoming he behaved always as though he was her natural father, and to her, and to everyone else except Ruth, he was. Ruth dreaded that one day Aurora would mention Joss, but it never happened. Aurora had the great gift of living only in the present.

There was to be another surprise before that eventful year was over. On the afternoon before Thanksgiving the front door of Appleby's opened and in walked Karl Munster, his arm in a sling, his face white and strained, his uniform filthy.

May, crossing the lobby, was the first one to see him. The

shriek she gave brought Maria, Lavinia, Ruth and a couple of boarders to investigate the calamity. For the first time since she had had the news of Joss, Ruth felt tears in her eyes. They were partly tears of joy at the loving greeting which sprang between Lavinia and her husband, oblivious to everyone around them.

He had been at Antietam, but he refused to speak of it, either that night or for a long time to come. All he would say was that he had been wounded in the arm and shoulder - nothing serious - and that he had leave to remain at home until he was recovered. *That* he owed to the fact that the hospitals were full with the more seriously wounded.

Next day they sat down to Thanksgiving dinner, Mrs Seaford with Ruth and her family, since that was where she now seemed to fit more naturally. Ruth had also invited Karl and Lavinia Munster. Sean had rested most of the day, to conserve his strength. Aurora had been allowed to stay up late.

For some around the table it was an occasion of thanksgiving, but not for all. Ruth saw the sadness in Mrs Seaford's eyes and guessed that she was thinking of this evening a year ago. Then she watched her square her shoulders and smile again. Ruth's own heart ached with longing for Joss, but she was able to keep her feelings in check until they had all parted for the night; Mrs Seaford and Maria to their single beds, Sean to his own room, Aurora to the room next to Ruth's, where she still slept; Karl and Lavinia to their rediscovered bliss.

Ruth lay awake a long time that night. Once she got up and looked out of the window. Although it was late November, it wasn't cold. Bright stars shone in a dark sky. She wondered under what stars Joss had died, or whether it was possible, just possible, that he was lying at this moment in some far-off Confederate hospital, or in a prisoner-of-war camp? When the war was over, even though she thought him dead, she would go and search for him.

Then she remembered that she could not do so. She had Sean to look after.

# 35

Only a few days after that Thanksgiving dinner saw the start of a long, dreary winter. It began inauspiciously for the North with the Union defeat at Fredericksburg in the middle of December. But in spite of the slaughter of brave men on both sides the war was no nearer its end.

'There'll be many a sad Christmas in this city,' Mrs Seaford remarked. She was sewing sheets sides to middle while Ruth sat at her desk, struggling with accounts. 'There were a lot of New York regiments at Fredericksburg.'

'I fear so,' Ruth replied. 'Which puts what I'm doing right now in perspective.' She put down her pen and pushed the ledger away from her. She was tired of trying to balance the books. Almost certainly she would have to increase her rates to the boarders. Not that this would surprise them. Rents were going up all over the city and money went nowhere.

'They say that's why President Lincoln wanted to keep the news of Fredericksburg quiet until after Christmas,' she said. 'So as not to depress everyone.'

'Rubbish!' Mrs Seaford drove her needle into the cloth as if she was stabbing the President himself. 'How can anybody keep something like that secret? The man's stupid, even if he is the President!'

'I suppose he meant well.'

'Meant well?' Mrs Seaford was indignant. 'It's not enough to mean well. It's time he stopped the war. If he's the President why can't he do that?'

The same question was being asked everywhere; on the

streets, in the shops, wherever people met. It was asked by women whose sons were still fighting for a cause which seemed already won. It was asked by more important people, who were politically motivated. Everywhere there was a strong feeling of resentment, and when, early in 1863, a rumour went around that far from the war ending, men were to be conscripted into the army, the resentment grew a thousandfold.

Mrs Cruse had something to say about that.

'The New Yorkers won't stand for the Draft,' she declared. 'They'll resist *that* all right – just you wait and see. I'm a New Yorker and I *know!* My lads were proud and happy to volunteer, but they wouldn't have stood being drafted, I can tell you!'

Her sons, including young Alfred, were still all miraculously alive, though they had been in the thick of the fighting. Ruth knew she lived in daily fear that this could not last.

'What I don't understand,' Maria said, 'is why the Draft is needed, with all those men who volunteered at the beginning.'

'It's simple,' Sean told her. 'Many of them only volunteered for three months. They were back almost before the fighting started. And of those who signed on for longer, it's well known that scores deserted when they found out what war was like. 'Tis certain sure there are hundreds of deserters in New York City right now. And then there's some like meself,' he added, his voice taking on a plaintive tone, 'who've had their fight, and now will be no use to anybody, any more.'

'And there will be those who will never return,' Ruth said quietly.

Maria gave her sister a sharp look. Joss Barnet was never mentioned now. It couldn't have been otherwise in Sean's presence, but Maria thought Ruth's hurt would have healed more cleanly if she had been able to speak of him.

Early in the year when the winter weather put a temporary stop to the fighting, Confederate and Union troops on either bank of the narrow Rappahannock River one day serenaded each other with their own songs of home. At the end, when all the other songs had been sung, Yankee and Rebel voices alike joined in singing 'Home Sweet Home' until the cold air rang with the sweet sound. It was all any of them ever longed for in this bitter winter, when most of them slept in holes dug in the ground, with branches woven over to form a roof. Some of them would freeze to death. Those who survived would, when the better weather came and the blood began to course more strongly in their veins, raise their guns and shoot at each other again.

In Richmond Mrs Masterson searched every day for groceries: a morsel of butter, a screw of sugar, some acorn coffee or a precious bar of soap. Anything. Food was so scarce that, so rumour said, the rats came out of their holes to beg for it. General Lee was quite fortunate. He shared his tent with a hen which obligingly laid him an egg most days. Mrs Masterson gave thanks to God that her grandson was not in Richmond, and beseeched Him to keep Clive safe. Meanwhile, Flora and Beth fashioned tolerable shoes from bits of old carpet. They were quite the thing: no-one could get real shoes any longer.

In New York Karl Munster was pronounced fit and called to rejoin his regiment.

'But you're not strong enough yet!' Lavinia protested.

'Of course I am,' he said. 'Anyway, I don't suppose the war will last much longer and then we shall be together for the rest of our lives.'

So the inhabitants of Appleby's returned to their everyday tasks, and the winter, through rain and sleet and biting cold, dragged on towards the spring.

Ruth's main preoccupation now was with Sean. She had a strong compulsion to cure him completely. Whether it arose from guilt or compassion, or just the need to immerse herself in some task, she didn't know; but it was easy to convince herself that every hour she spent with him, however difficult for her, would aid his recovery. For this reason she had given up the Relief Centre.

'I think you're wrong,' Maria said. 'At least the Relief Centre would give you a change of scene and different company. You spend too much time in the house. Doris and I are quite capable of looking after Sean for a couple of afternoons a week. It would make a change for him too.'

'What do you mean by that?'

'Well you have to admit that sometimes you get on each other's nerves,' Maria said.

It was true. Ruth felt driven to screaming pitch. She wanted to shout, to throw things, physically to shake this man out of his whinging invalid state. But because *he* was surely the victim, she felt she could not relieve herself as Sean did, by morning-to-night small grumbles, railings against fate, bouts of self-pity. And, from time to time, by outbursts of uncontrollable temper. She told herself she must keep calm, though sometimes she felt she would burst from the pressure inside her.

'As soon as the better weather comes,' she told Maria, 'I shall take Sean out. That will be good for him.'

'In the meantime you can't tell me you're not needed at the Relief Centre. There must be a great demand for medical supplies.'

'All right. You've made your point,' Ruth said. 'If they need me I'll start again.' She felt an immediate relief at having made the decision.

Miss Schuyler gave her a warm welcome. 'We really do need you here,' she said. 'It's a bit like the army. So many people volunteer in the beginning, all full of enthusiasm, then they lose the incentive. How is your husband?'

'He's improving. He's not in any pain. But he doesn't find life easy.'

She set to work on her boxes and for most of that afternoon Miss Schuyler worked with her.

'Do you think there *will* be conscription?' Ruth asked.

'I feel certain of it. I don't see how President Lincoln can manage without it.'

The President confirmed that with his Conscription Act, and in April announced that three hundred thousand men would be needed. The date set for the Draft to start in New York City was Saturday the eleventh of July.

'But the war could be over by then,' Maria said.

'Let's hope it will be over, or there'll be trouble of another sort,' Ruth replied.

'If I had my health and strength I'd be back in the army this very day,' Sean declared. 'But only as a volunteer, mind. I'd never stand being drafted.'

'Does it make much difference in the end?' Ruth asked.

'Of course it does! It's a matter of freedom, is it not? Freedom's what we're fighting for!'

'And the Irish like a fight!' Ruth was teasing him, but he couldn't see it. He turned on her in a fury.

'Sure! And where would *this* city be if it wasn't for the Micks? Who are the poor sods who are going to get caught in the Draft? Answer me that?'

'Sean . . . please don't. . . .'

'I'll tell ye for nothing. The poor bloody Irish, that's who! There's precious few of *them* will have three hundred dollars to buy themselves out when their name is picked out of the drum!'

The biggest bone of contention about the Draft was that if a man's name was drawn he could at once buy himself out by paying three hundred dollars – the amount it would cost to pay for a substitute.

'You know I agree with you about that,' Ruth said. 'It's iniquitous.'

'Rich man's money, poor man's blood,' Sean said hotly. It was a phrase on many lips and before long it would be chanted everywhere.

'Please try to keep calm,' Ruth begged. 'You do yourself no good by getting upset.'

It was the wrong thing to say.

'Try to keep calm? Try to keep calm?' he shouted. 'How the devil am I supposed to keep calm?'

But the very next minute he *was* calm; as tranquil as if the stormy scene had never taken place. And Ruth knew he would stay so until the next sudden flare-up, which might be over an important issue like war or, equally, over the fact that his coffee was too hot. Once, when he had considered it *was* too hot, he had flung it at her, cup and all. If his aim had been better she would have been scalded.

'I think we should start to go out a little,' Ruth suggested. 'If you wrap up well you should come to no harm.'

He was by this time quite capable of going for a walk and she thought it might get rid of some of his energy. In fact he was capable of doing much more than he did. She had tried to interest him in some of the jobs in the house which Sammy, and then Morris, used to do, and now had to be carried out by whoever had the time. But he resisted that.

'You want me for a slavey,' he said. 'That's it, isn't it? Well, let me tell ye, I'll be no woman's slavey. Oh I know I can't pull me weight and be a proper man, but I'll not be a servant.'

'No-one wants to make you one, Sean,' Ruth told him. 'I'm not asking you to do anything I wouldn't do – have done at times. And we could do with your help.'

She didn't remind him that he had been a servant, and a good one at that. She spoke to him patiently, trying to understand his feelings, though she was sure that it would be good for him to be physically occupied. He was not as helpless as he made out, but the habit of dependence had grown on him during his months in hospital and he couldn't or wouldn't shake it off.

It was a full fortnight after she first suggested it that Sean at last agreed to come out for a walk with her.

'But not too far,' he said nervously. 'I don't think I can walk far!'

'No farther than you want to,' Ruth promised. 'We'll walk along Spring Street and down Broadway, and we can turn back the moment you wish. The sun will do us both good.'

It was April sunshine, pale and with little warmth, but everyone in Broadway looked the brighter for it and there was an epidemic of new spring bonnets. Another week or two, Ruth thought, and people would start painting the outsides of their houses, and by May everything would be fresh again.

With something of a shcok she realised, as she walked down Broadway with Sean clinging to her arm, that for the very first time in almost nine months she had looked forward not only to the next day, but more than a week ahead.

'Are you enjoying this?' she asked. 'Doesn't it make you feel better to be out amongst people?'

'It's a bit frightening, but yes! Sure I'm enjoying it. Why wouldn't I be with you and the sunshine and all?'

He was at his most rational on that day. Ruth thought how much easier life would be when – if ever – he got over his violent swings of mood. The doctor would not commit himself as to when this might be.

'I enjoyed that,' Sean said when they were back at the house. 'It did me good.'

'I'm glad. We'll go a little further each day. If you like, I'll hire a carriage and we'll have a drive around. We could go to Battery Park and have a whiff of sea air.'

'I'd like that fine,' Sean agreed.

So in the following week, which was a little warmer, that was what they did. At Battery Park they dismissed the carriage and strolled along the waterfront. The harbour, as always, was crowded with shipping, though now there were warships amongst the other craft.

'Once when I was here,' Ruth said, 'I saw the *Monitor*. It was strange to see a warship made of iron. I daresay you'd have enjoyed that.'

When Ruth judged they had walked enough she hired another carriage to take them home. She sat back, prepared to enjoy being driven up Broadway, but after a few minutes she noticed that Sean seemed perturbed. He was clasping and unclasping his hands, blinking rapidly. She wondered if he was about to erupt in one of his strange passions.

'Did I say something wrong, Sean?' she asked.

'All these negroes!' he said testily. 'All these blacks – what are they doing here?'

'Blacks? I see no more than usual. We've always known negroes in New York, just as we've always known Irish and German and English.'

'Don't you compare the niggers with the Irish!' he said fiercely. 'I won't have that!'

'I'm not comparing anyone with anyone. I'm just saying we've always known negroes here. New York is a free city. They can come and go as they please. Isn't that what you fought for?'

'I didn't fight for any niggers,' he said. 'They're trash. They take our jobs. They work for less money. If we don't keep 'em down they'll swamp us!'

He was shaking now, disturbingly agitated. The driver turned around and stared at him. Until that moment Ruth had not even noticed that the driver was black.

'I'm sorry,' she said quietly. 'My husband isn't well. He was badly wounded. . . .'

The driver turned away again, flicked his horse and concentrated on finding a way through Broadway's heavy traffic.

'Let's discuss it when we get home, Sean,' Ruth said. 'Let's enjoy the fresh air while we can. What do you say if Aurora comes with us for a walk tomorrow?'

It was strange how quickly the thought of Aurora diverted him. He chatted happily about her until they were back at Appleby's. Ruth felt deeply ashamed before the driver and gave him an extra large tip. Then she felt worse that she had assumed that money would compensate for Sean's outburst. But she could say nothing more for fear of arousing Sean, who was now as happy as a songbird and gave not the slightest sign that he had ever been upset.

'Your outing's done you good,' Mrs Seaford told Sean. 'You ought to go out more often.'

'We intend to,' Ruth said. 'From now on we shall take the air every fine day. Though not always in a carriage. That was a special treat.'

'You have a kind and thoughtful wife, Mr O'Farrell,' Mrs Seaford said.

'Don't I know it. The best in the world!' Sean gave Ruth a broad smile.

Though it was sincerely meant, Ruth wished that neither

of them had paid the compliment. Only she knew with what little real love she did what she did for Sean. She had resolved that she would do her duty by him to her dying day; but duty it was, and could never be more, though she tried desperately not to show that, to act always as though she loved.

A week or two later at the Relief Centre Miss Schuyler asked, 'Did you know there was an Invalid Corps in New York? It might interest your husband.'

'I didn't,' Ruth said. 'Who are they? What do they do?'

'They're mostly ex-soldiers who've been wounded and aren't fit for active service in the field. Or reasonably fit convalescents. And of course a few malingerers, as you'd expect. As for what they do - well, mostly guard duties I think. Arsenals and suchlike. One doesn't quite know what they'd be like in a real emergency, but at least the Corps gives them something to do. They feel they're still useful; not left out of things.'

'It sounds a good idea,' Ruth said. 'I'll mention it to my husband.' That same evening Ruth mentioned the idea to Sean. She spoke of it idly, aware of his obstinacy if he thought anyone was trying to push him. She needn't have worried. He latched on to the idea at once.

'A *man's* job!' he said. 'And I'll get paid for it too. It'd suit me to be more independent.'

'You mustn't do it for that reason,' Ruth told him. 'You know that whatever I have is yours.'

So he applied, and with his doctor's recommendation, was accepted.

'I'm to start guard duties three times a week at the Armoury, Second Avenue and Twenty-first Street,' he said jubilantly. 'I'll be back in uniform!'

Ruth found the hours when Sean was out of the house a tremendous relief to her. To be on her own, not to have someone constantly watching her, wanting to be talked to, fussed over, was heaven. Sometimes she went for a walk - usually to Washington Square; never, now, to Union

Square. And in the warmth of the June sun, soothed by the sight of the fresh green of the trees in the square, she began to return to life.

But she discovered that to return to life was to return to pain. In the months since the news of Joss's presumed death she had tried to push every thought of her lover away from her, back into the past where he belonged. So adept had she become at this that sometimes she could almost think of him as someone she had once known, a long time ago. Now, in this summer when she began to feel again, all the pain of loss which she had so resolutely pushed away rushed towards her.

She tried to hide it, and she thought she succeeded, except from Maria, who was too sharp.

'What is it, Ruth?' she asked. 'Please tell me!'

'It's Joss,' Ruth said slowly. 'I can't stop thinking about him. I haven't thought about him like this since he was killed.'

'Why do you say "killed"?' Maria demanded. 'Why do you assume the worst? It's never been confirmed that he was dead.'

'Or that he's alive,' Ruth said.

Maria gave her a long, steady look.

'All I know is that if Clive was reported missing I'd go on expecting him for the rest of my life. I'd never give up hope!'

'I'm married to Sean,' Ruth said.

'That's not what we're talking about. Is that a reason for letting Joss die in your heart?'

'I've found out he won't die,' Ruth said. 'For his sake if not for mine, I want him to be alive. Even if I might never see him again.'

In the days which followed it came to Ruth that she had not so resolutely closed her mind to Joss's return; in that she had allowed him to enter, she must have believed in her heart that he was still alive. That somewhere, somehow, she was in his heart as he was in hers. it came as no great shock when she received the telegraph from Washington at the end of June.

'Captain Josiah Barnet reported alive and well in Confederate prisoner-of-war camp. Letter follows.'

She crossed the lobby and went into her room. She was

aware that Miss Fontwell passed her and made some remark, to which she didn't reply. In the sitting-room Maria's head was bent over the menu book. Ruth thanked God that Sean was on duty and wouldn't be back for several hours.

'Do you think that chicken would be a nice change for Sunday?' Maria asked, not looking up. 'Or should we stick to beef?'

Ruth heard the question clearly, and wondered how anyone could be concerned with chickens when the world had just caught fire. Maria looked up.

'Ruth!' she gasped. 'Whatever is it? You look as though you've seen a ghost!'

Ruth handed her the telegraph. Maria leapt to her feet with a scream of delight, and her arms went around Ruth and they were both crying.

'Ruth, oh Ruth. I told you so! Didn't I tell you so?'

'You did. And I should have known. But now I do. Oh Maria, I'm so happy!'

And to prove it she burst into another paroxysm of tears.

'You must have a sip of brandy,' Maria said. 'It will calm you down.'

She unlocked the cupboard with a key from the bunch at her waist, and poured out a small measure.

'You too,' Ruth said. 'You're trembling as much as I.'

'Oh Ruth, if only. . . .'

'I know. If only it could be Clive also. But it will be one day, Maria. You have so much faith I just know it will.'

'I must continue to believe so,' Maria said quietly.

For a while they both fell silent, then Maria asked, 'What will you do, Ruth?'

Ruth knew what she meant. What will you do about Sean?

'Nothing. Except that I must tell Professor Woodburn. He can then tell whom he pleases.'

'And Sean?'

'I don't ever want to talk about Joss in front of Sean.'

'But when Joss comes back? What will you do then?'

'It's too soon to know.' But she couldn't leave Sean in his present state, she knew that, even if it broke her heart to stay with him. He depended on her, as in another crisis, which now seemed a lifetime ago, she had on him.

'I'm going out,' she said to Maria. 'I'd like to be on my own, to walk.'

'Of course,' Maria replied. 'Stay out as long as it suits you. Oh Ruth, I do so want you to be happy!'

'And I you, Maria,' Ruth said.

She made straight for Union Square. In spite of the heat she moved quickly through the crowds on Broadway, as if she had a rendezvous for which she was already late, which in a way she was, as she had not been to the square since before Sean had left hospital.

There was an empty seat in the shade of a tree. She had sat there with Joss so many times, and often at this hour of the day. Now she felt reunited with him. And in the next hour the pain of the two years since he had left her, and all her anxiety for the future, were wiped out by her remembrances of the loving experiences they had enjoyed over their years together. She remembered everything.

Sean was already home when she returned, playing a game of Ludo with Aurora. They looked up briefly when Ruth entered, and then resumed their game.

'It is hot,' Ruth said. 'And such crowds shopping on Broadway! Some people certainly have money to spend.'

'Sure,' Sean replied. 'While others go hungry. Now if you were to take a walk around Five Points you'd find a different story. No fashionable ladies and fat-bellied men there!'

'I know,' Ruth said. 'That's one of the things I *don't* like about New York. Such contrasts!'

'Ah well, they'll not lie down under it forever,' Sean prophesied. 'You'll see.'

'What do you mean?'

'Isn't the Draft in less than two weeks' time? Isn't the day coming when the rich toss in their money and the poor go off and fight? And no-one gives a twopenny damn about what happens to their families. Well, they'll not stand for it. I'm telling you, they'll not stand for it!'

'But what will they do?' Ruth asked. 'How can they stop the law?'

'Ways and means,' Sean said. 'Ways and means. You'll see what they'll do. When that bloody day comes you'll see what they'll do.'

'Papa, it's your turn to play,' Aurora complained. 'Please shake the dice!'

On the sixth of July, a Monday, the letter came. Ruth had been watching for it ever since the arrival of the telegraph, and now she held it in her hand. She went at once to Maria's room.

'May I read it here?' she asked.

'Of course. I was just going down to the kitchen.'

'Wait, and I'll tell you what it says . . .'

' "Captain Josiah Barnet (she read) is presently held in prisoner-of-war camp in Virginia. Our information is that he is well, but has had pneumonia and needs to regain his strength. There is some possibility of an exchange of prisoners. Should Captain Barnet prove to be included we will communicate with you further." '

'They go on to say I may write to him at this address. Oh Maria, I can't believe it! But I wonder how ill my poor darling has been, and if he's really recovering?'

'You must *trust* that he is,' Maria said. Poor Maria, Ruth thought, who had to take so much on trust.

'Of course he can't be *fighting* fit or they wouldn't contemplate an exchange. I daresay he needs careful nursing and good food. They say the Confederates are dreadfully short of food.' Ruth could have bitten out her tongue the moment she had said the words.

'Oh Ruth, what if my poor Clive is ill, and starving!'

Ruth put her arms around Maria. 'All I meant was that the Confederates might let some prisoners like Joss come home so that they'll have more food for their own men.'

'I know,' Maria said. 'And I'm truly pleased for you. But what will you do when Joss *does* come home?'

'I don't know,' Ruth admitted. 'Nothing is going to be easy. Real life doesn't end up like a fairy tale. But I'm just so grateful to know that he's alive.'

There had been talk for a week or two of Sean moving permanently into barracks with the Invalid Corps, but Ruth didn't consider him fit enough for that. Physically he was. He seemed as strong as an ox now and he could walk long distances without tiring. But mental fatigue overtook him more quickly than physical and he still had violent swings of mood. Ruth thought he needed the security of a home for a little longer.

'I'm sure it's more comfortable for you here,' she said.

'Comfort's not everything,' Sean replied.

'What do you mean? What is it you want?'

Really, she *knew*. He desired a more stimulating atmosphere than Appleby's. He wanted men's company. He wanted to be able to play poker, faro, dice; to be able to join in singing and telling jokes. And, she suspected, to drink whenever he felt like it.

She could well understand all that. What she couldn't understand was her own reluctance to let him go. She didn't enjoy his company and they had few interests in common. Yet she had developed, against all her inclinations, this protective feeling for him, so that she was anxious whenever he left the house. She knew if Sean were to become, in time, truly independent, it would simplify her own future, but she didn't believe it possible. Perversely, since she had learned that Joss was alive, though she loved him and longed for him as much as ever, she reminded herself even more often that her obligations were to Sean.

'Will you be on duty at the weekend?' she asked. 'I thought we might take Aurora and picnic in Central Park. It should be a little cooler there.'

'Sure I'll be on duty, all through the weekend. You can't have forgotten that they start drawing the names for the

Draft on Saturday. Every man in the Corps is on duty.'

'Why?'

'Because they're expecting trouble, isn't that why? And don't they know no man's going to take this lot lying down, and small blame to him I say. Every man who resists the Draft has my sympathy, that's for sure.'

'But you're a soldier,' Ruth said. 'You have a duty to be on the side of law and order.'

'Oh I understand my duty all right,' Sean replied. 'I'll do my duty, don't you worry. But as for picnics in the park, you'd be wise not to stir out of the house this weekend. And I forbid Aurora to do so.'

'I'm sure you exaggerate,' Ruth said. 'We're not living in the middle of the battlefield!'

# 36

At the Relief Centre, all the talk was of the Draft.

'Mr Seymour says that in his opinion the Act is unconstitutional and can't be enforced,' Miss Schuyler said. (Mr Seymour was the Governor of New York State.) 'If people will only wait, he says, he'd be more than willing to take some cases to tribunal.'

'But will they wait?' Ruth asked. 'I'm sure what angers most people is the substitution clause. To a rich man three hundred dollars is nothing; to a poor man it's impossible, therefore he's asked to give his life.'

'Oh, I agree with you,' Miss Schuyler said. 'But then so do many young men who *can* afford to pay. I have several friends who will choose to fight.'

'Do you believe there'll be trouble?' Ruth asked.

'I hope not – though I fear so. New York at the moment is almost without soldiers. They're all at Gettysburg. I do know that for this very reason Major Opdyke has asked for the Draft to be postponed.'

'Then why isn't it?'

'Because Governor Seymour thinks the police – together with the Invalid Corps – will be able to deal with the situation. It looks as though your husband and his friends will really be needed, Mrs O'Farrell.'

Ruth would have been happier if Sean's sympathies had not so openly lain with those who were prepared to resist the Draft. Her own lay in the same direction, but she was not a soldier, not under command to keep down those with whom she most identified. She was afraid that the mental strain might prove more than Sean could bear.

But when Saturday came it seemed as though everyone's fears might prove groundless.

The drawing of the names for the Draft was to start in premises at Forty-Sixth Street and Third Avenue, and Sean was in a contingent of the Invalid Corps which had been ordered there in case of trouble.

'Now remember,' he told Ruth, 'we're not to go anywhere near that neighbourhood. I'd prefer that ye didn't go out at all. But if ye must – then don't take Aurora.'

'I promise not to take Aurora,' Ruth said. 'I can't promise not to go out myself. I have some errands to do.'

Though not for the world would she have told him so, Ruth had every intention of going to the scene of the Draft. She had an irrational idea that she must be on hand.

She was delayed in the house and the draw had already started when she reached Forty-Sixth Street and Third. There was a large crowd outside the building where the drum, supervised by the Provost-Marshal, Colonel Nugent, was being spun. There were policemen at the door of the building, but not a soldier to be seen.

Ruth stayed on the edge of the crowd and kept her eyes open watching for trouble. None came. There was some muttering in the crowd, but no action. When it was announced that a thousand names had been drawn, and that no more names would be drawn until Monday, the crowd gradually dispersed.

'I don't understand it at all,' Ruth said to Maria that evening. 'Though of course I'm relieved.'

'You were mad to go near,' Maria told her. 'You don't know what might have happened.'

In the newspapers next morning there were lists of men whose names had been drawn, and when Mr Pierce returned from church he said that similar lists were posted on church and chapel doors.

Ruth had started the habit, when supplies had been easier, of serving her boarders with a glass of Madeira before Sunday luncheon, for which they gathered in the parlour. It wasn't easy now to continue the habit, but she did so whenever possible, and this Sunday she thought it a good idea.

'Everyone's studying the lists,' Mr Pierce said. 'I understand they're posted up in hotels and beer halls too. There are a lot of people wandering around the streets in a manner I don't like. I can't put a finger on it, but there's an odd feeling in the air.'

'According to the Sunday papers,' Mr Carstairs said, 'several well-known citizens have already paid their three hundred dollars substitution money. *That* can't help matters.'

'Well, I think you ladies would be well advised to stay indoors today,' Mr Pierce told them. 'Or if you must go out, choose very carefully where you will go. I don't like the atmosphere. I don't like it at all.'

As far as Ruth knew, everyone took his advice except Maria and herself. In the afternoon Ruth said:

'It's no use, Maria, I must have some fresh air. Will you come out with me if Mrs Seaford sees to Aurora? We won't go far. Perhaps just to Washington Square.'

Broadway was busy, but then it always was. In Washington Square people sat beneath the trees, or promenaded around, much as on any other Sunday, except that outside one large house on the north side of the square a group of rough-looking people chanted 'Rich man's money, poor man's blood'. They chanted the words over and over again, their voices getting louder and louder, until two policemen came and moved them on.

'I think that's where Mr Jamieson Howarth lives,' Maria said. 'He was named in the paper today as having paid substitution money.'

When they arrived back at Appleby's Sean was home. He had been on guard duty since early morning and his face was chalk-white with fatigue.

'You look all in,' Ruth told him. 'I'm going to pour you a stiff whisky!'

He raised an eyebrow at her unusual gesture and at the

generosity of the measure she handed him.

'Get that down you,' she said. 'And now I'm going into the kitchen to make you a meal, something light. Then I think you should get some sleep. Are you on duty again in the morning?'

'Yes. Ruth, I do beg of ye not to go out tomorrow! I know I was wrong about Saturday – but there'll be nothing good tomorrow. All the signs are against it.'

She didn't answer. Nor did she tell him where she had been on the previous day.

On Monday morning Ruth saw Sean off early. 'Be careful,' she warned him. 'Don't take any foolish risks.'

He seemed almost excited as he left the house, with an inner liveliness Ruth had not seen in him for a long time. She wondered if he might actually be looking forward to the day's dangers.

Ruth also had her plans.

'Will you between you look after Aurora?' she asked Maria.

'Of course we will,' Maria agreed. 'She'll be all right. It's you I'm worrying about. Please don't go to Third Avenue, Ruth!'

'I promise that wherever I go I'll be careful,' Ruth said. 'It's just that I'm worried about Sean.'

'But you can't do him any good by being there!' Maria cried. 'You don't even know where he'll be. And if there's a crowd – which there will be – you won't see him anyway.'

'I know. Everything you say is reasonable. But it's this feeling I have. I must go.'

She left the house and walked up Broadway. In Union Square she turned east, towards Third Avenue. Joss was in her mind as she crossed the square; but then he always was. Nothing drove him out entirely.

How long before she would see him again? And how short a time after that must they part? But for now, she thought, she must put him completely out of her mind. She must concentrate on Sean.

It was a long walk on that hot, humid Monday morning.

It would have been more sensible to have taken the streetcar. But she was in the mood to walk.

So, it seemed, as she turned into Third Avenue, was half the population of New York. Coming towards her, up the centre of the avenue, was a crowd of what must have been thousands, reeling and swaying forwards like a great, writhing snake. But they were not silent like a snake. Everyone in the never-ending column was shouting and chanting. Most of the people in the crowd carried crude banners, saying 'No Draft', or brandished sticks. Those who had neither banners nor sticks waved their fists in the air. As the column drew near, the clamour resolved itself into words. 'Rich man's money, poor man's blood! No draft, no draft, no draft!' The words were shouted in precise, rhythmic time, like the beat of a drum.

It had not been Ruth's intention to join the crowd. She had meant to stand apart, watching for Sean. How could she have thought that such a thing would be possible?

They were almost on her now. In spite of anything she could do, whichever way she turned she was caught up. They filled the avenue, pushing and jostling, sweeping her along with them against her will. She found herself marching between a workman and his wife, both about the same age as herself.

'I say let the rich fight the war,' the woman declared. 'What's in it for the likes of us, except starvation if my man goes? What do I care about negro slaves?'

'Too many niggers in New York as it is,' her husband chimed in. 'If we free the rest of 'em they'll all be up here, taking our jobs. What'll we live on then? It's bad enough now.'

Ruth was shocked by the bitterness in their voices. In her own small world of Appleby's it was an attitude she'd not met with. And then she remembered Sean's outburst on the day they had visited Battery Park. Was that how most of New York thought?

'The crowd seems to be getting thicker,' she said nervously. 'Where is everyone coming from?'

'They're leaving their jobs, that's what,' the man told her. 'Same as me. We've all walked out this morning to show this lot we won't stand for it. They'll get what's coming to them before the day's out!'

By the time they reached Fortieth Street the avenue was almost totally blocked. Nothing could move in any direction. Yet in spite of that a carriage, drawn by two horses, attempted to cut a slow way through. It was hopeless from the start, but when a corner of the carriage hit against a man in the procession, and he cried out with a stream of abuse, a dozen people who were nearby closed in on the carriage and began to rock it. The occupants, a middle-aged man and woman, shouted and screamed in terror.

'Stop it! Have mercy! Let us out!'

They had no chance to say more. In the next minute the carriage was on its side and its occupants were thrown out screaming. As the horses reared in terror, and tried to cut loose, Ruth rushed forward to where the woman lay moaning on the ground. She was stopped by a man who grabbed her arm.

'Where do you think you're going?' he demanded.

'She's hurt!' Ruth cried angrily. 'Can't you see?'

'Now lady, remember what you're here for,' he said. 'You didn't come on this march to help carriage folk!'

'But she'll be trampled underfoot!' Ruth struggled to escape but the man held her firmly in his strong grip.

'Very fitting too,' he said roughly. 'I've been trampled underfoot all my life. No-one put out a hand to save *me!*'

That was the mood of the crowd. No mercy shown, no quarter given. Ruth was pulled along by the man until they had left the carriage well behind. Then he let her go, and she ran forward away from him.

Now she was marching beside a young woman with a child in her arms.

'Where's your husband, then?' the woman asked.

'He's. . . .'

Ruth stopped herself in time. Sean, in his present position, would be the sworn enemy of this mob. And yet she knew that in his heart he was akin with them. What would he do if a confrontation came? And where *was* the Invalid Corps? There was no sign of them.

'He's nearer the front. We got separated,' she lied. 'I must try to make my way through and find him again.'

Inch by inch she squeezed and shoved her way through. Whenever a barrier of bodies blocked her she screamed, 'Let me through! I've got to find my husband!' Each time a way was made, so that eventually she was at the head of the crowd, standing in front of the Draft Office at Forty-Sixth Street. This time more policemen surrounded the entrance, but there were no soldiers to be seen.

'Where's the army?' she asked a man standing next to her.

'At Gettysburg,' he said. 'Where do you think?'

'No. I mean the Invalid Corps. I thought they'd be on guard here.'

He laughed. 'Fat lot of good they'd be! Have you ever seen 'em, lady? Lot of poor bloody cripples. God knows where they are, but who needs 'em?'

He was still speaking when they heard the shot fired at the back of the crowd. It was the signal for a barrage of rocks and stones to be hurled through the air, high over the heads of the crowd towards the Draft Office. It took no more than a minute for every window in the building to be shattered, but the stones still came, and those outside could hear the cries of the people within as the missiles found their mark.

Then, with a roar which chilled the blood in Ruth's veins, a roar like that of a ravening beast, and a concerted movement as if there was one controlling mind, the mob surged forward, broke into the building, found its prey.

There was a nightmare moment when Ruth was quite sure that she must be trampled to death, that this was to be the ignominious ending of Ruth Appleby. She screamed and screamed at the top of her lungs. 'Help! Save me!' No-one heard her cries. Then by some miracle she was flung violently sideways, and towards the building. With a great effort she managed to twist her body around and hold her back against the wall, wedging herself so that she wouldn't sink to the ground.

She was facing the mob now. The stones were still being hurled, but with less precision. Before she could dodge it, one caught her sharply on the forehead. The blood gushed out, streaming down her face and into her eyes. No-one took the slightest notice of her. She held her arm up to the cut, trying to staunch the blood with her sleeve.

At that moment those of the crowd who had entered the building came out again, triumphantly bearing the Draft records in their hands, holding them aloft for the crowd to see. Then, to the accompaniment of frenzied cheering, they tore them into shreds, flung them into the air like confetti.

'We've broken the bloody machine!' a man by the doorway cried. 'We've smashed it to pieces. There'll be no damned Draft here!'

But it wasn't enough to satisfy them. They needed more, much more. Someone in the crowd bawled 'Burn the place down!' The cry was taken up by hundreds of voices. Ruth listened in horror as again they chanted in unison. 'Burn, burn, burn! Burn, burn, burn!' It was like some dreadful incantation, the working of a spell.

A man – he seemed to come from nowhere – dashed past her carrying a bucket of liquid which looked like water. As he passed he spilled some on her skirt and the smell came up to her strongly. It was not water.

'Stop him!' she shrieked. 'Stop that man! It's turpentine!'

It was too late. He was already in the building. He poured the contents of the bucket on the floor, set light to it, tried to run back from the fire, but a tongue of flame caught his face.

Smoke and flames poured from the doorway, and then quite quickly from the glassless windows. The whole of the front of the building was alight. She could feel the heat where she stood. Heedless of the fact that she was faint and dizzy from the cut on her head, she began to run. But the only way she could run was headlong into the crowd.

Hemmed in now, unable to move in any direction, she

stood and watched the building burn, and listened to the continuing howl from the mob. 'Burn, burn, burn! Burn, burn, burn!' The fire engines came, but they were barred from using the hydrant until the whole block, from Forty-Fifth to Forty-Sixth Street, was alight. It was too late then.

By this time, frightened by the heat and the falling debris, the crowd had moved back a little and Ruth was able to escape. She turned down the nearest side street and knocked on the door of the first house she came to. She knocked and knocked, but no-one came. As she was about to turn away the door was opened a narrow crack. The woman in the doorway looked terrified, and would have closed the door again, seeing Ruth's state except that Ruth wedged her foot in the opening.

'Please help me! I'm injured. A stone caught me. Could you let me come in, please? Let me bandage my head, give me a drink of water?'

'I'm letting no-one in,' the woman said. 'It's not safe.'

'But you can see for yourself that I haven't got a weapon,' Ruth pleaded. 'You can see I'm empty-handed. I only want a bandage for my head. I can't stop the bleeding.'

'Wait there then.'

The woman reappeared a moment or two later. Through the smallest possible opening she handed Ruth a cup of water and a square of white towelling.

'It's all I can find. Now please go away.'

Ruth drank the water greedily. When she handed back the cup the woman slammed the door to, and locked it.

Ruth leaned against the wall. She felt sick and faint and knew she should make her way home, but she was more than ever desperate to find Sean. He couldn't be far away, and she felt, it was irrational she knew, that without her he would come to harm.

And then she heard a woman say, 'They've sent for the soldiers. They'll only be the poor old Invalid Corps, but they've got guns. We've only got our bare hands!'

'Then we must arm ourselves as best we can!' The reply came from a great big giant of a man. Without more ado he bent down and began to tear up the streetcar tracks, his strong hands pulling the metal apart as if it was cardboard. Ruth could hardly believe her eyes.

What he started, since he had the strength to loosen the tracks, all the men near him were able to continue; and soon everyone around, men, women and a few children, was armed with a weapon of some sort. A man thrust a piece of heavy, shining metal into Ruth's hands.

'Here you are, missus! See you put it to good use!'

She took it, not daring to refuse in case he turned awkward.

The crowd was thinning out now, though it was no less savage. Newly-armed, sections of it were breaking away to search for other areas of conflict. It seemed as though the Invalid Corps might never show up.

'Who'll follow me to Broadway?' a man shouted. 'The Draft Office in Broadway. Follow me, friends, and we'll burn that down!'

A portion of the crowd went with him and the rest now move a little faster along Third Avenue, brandishing their weapons. Ruth stayed with them, sure in her own mind that sooner or later they must meet with the Invalid Corps. She had no idea what she would do then. It happened as they reached Forty-First Street.

'Here come the soldiers! What a sorry sight!' someone shouted. 'If that's the best they can do we'll soon deal with them!'

They looked pathetic: as if someone had ordered the inmates of a hospital ward out of bed and dressed them in any old uniforms they could find, before sending them out on the streets, hobbling, limping, grey-faced.

She was close to the front of the crowd now, which was why she saw Sean so quickly. He was marching in the second rank. He marched better than most, but the high colour in his cheeks, against the whiteness of his skin, was not natural to him. He looked almost as if he had a fever. He didn't see Ruth coming towards him, a strip of metal in her hand.

'Let's be at 'em!' a man at the front of the crowd yelled. He had a strong Irish accent, exactly like Sean's.

'Don't forget they have guns!' a woman screamed.

'Then we'll take their bloody guns from them!' the Irishman shouted.

That was when the police appeared, as if from nowhere. Ruth was moving as fast as the crowd would allow her towards Sean, the only thought in her mind to reach him. The cut on her forehead was a nuisance. It had started bleeding again and the blood ran into her eye. The piece of towelling was useless now, blood-soaked.

The police moved in among the crowd, indiscriminately wielding their heavy wooden clubs, and the people fought back with their metal bars. Then the Corps officer gave the order for the soldiers to fire into the crowd. Afterwards, some said that this first round was only blank shots, but it sounded real enough at the time. If it was intended to subdue the crowd, it failed. It incited them still further, and they rushed towards the soldiers, who broke rank and scattered.

'Sean!' Ruth screamed at the top of her voice. 'Sean, I'm here!' Her voice was totally lost in the tumult.

She kept him in her sight, all the time trying to get nearer to him, so that when the incident took place she was no more than a few yards away. She saw everything.

There was a woman not far from Sean. She held a twisted piece of metal aloft in her hand as if she was ready to strike. A fresh-faced young policeman, forestalling her, raised his club and struck her to the ground. She fell without a sound. Ruth rushed towards her but then she saw what Sean was about to do and instead she dashed forward to stop him.

She was too late. Before she could reach him, Sean raised his gun and fired at the policeman. So quickly did the one action follow the other that when the policeman dropped to the ground he fell on top of the woman he had clubbed. There was no doubt that he was dead.

Ruth thought it was the result of having two fingers missing which made Sean clumsy, so that when he had fired the gun he immediately and inadvertently dropped it. It clattered to the ground and skidded a yard or two. Instantly a man rushed forward to pick it up. Ruth recognised the Irishman.

It was likely that he had not seen Sean's action. He saw only a soldier, a soldier who had come to put down the Draft resisters and would use his gun to do so. He raised the gun and fired. Ruth reached Sean as he hit the ground.

She knew at once that it was no good. She knelt down and held Sean's head on her lap. He was not yet dead, but death was on his face. His eyes were closed and she didn't expect to see them open again – but they did, and he looked up at her. From some great depths he found the strength to speak.

'And what would you be doing here?'

Ruth smiled at him. 'I came to fetch you home.'

Afterwards she was never quite sure how long she had sat on the ground on Third Avenue, cradling her dead husband. It has been several hours, and all the while the sun beating down on her head.

But though the day was hot, long before anyone came to rescue them Sean's body had grown cold. In the end it was a sort of ambulance-like conveyance which took him to the mortuary.

'Could I accompany my husband?' Ruth asked.

The driver looked embarrassed.

'I'm sorry, there won't be room, ma'am. You see. . . .'

She gathered that he was collecting dead bodies from the street as one might collect rubbish.

'I'm afraid you'll have to make your own way home,' he apologised. 'And the sooner the better. You don't look too good to me and it's dangerous in the streets.'

As she watched him out of sight she thought how suitable it was that the conveyance was drawn by two coal-black horses.

So she walked home. Later she didn't remember too much about the journey, or about the night which followed, except that Maria had never left her.

The riots lasted three days, and then took another three

days to die down. Armouries were raided, shops looted, houses of war profiteers razed to the ground. The Coloured Orphan Asylum was smashed up and then set on fire. A negro was hanged from a lamp-post. Mr Pierce saw that with his own eyes and was never to forget it to his dying day. There were families who fled north from the city, to White Plains and Yonkers, never to return.

When the worst was over, though parts of the city were still smoking, soldiers brought from Gettysburg moved in.

# 37

In the months which followed Sean's death Ruth heard nothing from, or about, Joss. She sent letters regularly, but she never had a reply. Most likely he didn't receive them. There was no order in this war. Nothing had been done about the exchange of prisoners and it seemed as though the idea must have fallen through.

'He's going to spend the rest of this slow, dragging war in prison camp,' she said to Maria. 'We've all heard how terrible the conditions are there.'

'At least he's safe from the enemy,' Maria replied sharply. 'I worry about Clive night and day. And I daresay the Yanks are every bit as bad captors as the Rebels.'

Ruth was immediately contrite.

'I'm sorry, Maria. And I do wish with all my heart that something nice could happen for you.'

Maria sighed. 'Well at least I've got you, and Robert Lee. That's some comfort. I wonder how poor Mrs Masterson is faring?'

Reports said that conditions in Richmond were terrible. The city had been under martial law for more than a year now and the enemy never far away, a constant threat. Maria's heart ached for the mother-in-law she had once disliked.

But Joss is living *with* the enemy, Ruth thought. How were they treating him? Were they cruel, revengeful? Was he ill again? Was he starving ? It was said that there was very little food left in the South and everyone knew that before the Confederates surrendered at Vicksburg they had been reduced to eating rats. She tried to keep such thoughts out of her head but it was impossible.

Nor had she been able to throw off the depression into which Sean's death and her own experiences during the Draft riots had plunged her. Physically she was well enough, but her spirits were low. Night after night she lay awake, reliving every terrible moment. She tried to explain her feelings to Maria.

'It's not only Sean's death, though I genuinely mourn such a waste of a life. It's the manner of it. There was no nobility in his death, no purpose. It has freed me, but I don't feel free. I feel full of guilt. As if Sean has paid for my freedom.'

'But Ruth, that's nonsense,' Maria protested. 'How can you possibly be guilty? You did everything you could for Sean, from the moment he was brought back to New York to the day he died – when you risked your own life. Oh yes you did!'

Ruth shook her head.

'It was never enough.' Only she knew what feelings she had withheld from Sean.

'Well I know it's a trite thing to say, Ruth, but we must both look forward to the future. It's all we can do, and it's all that keeps me going.' She picked up Robert Lee and held him close in her arms. 'If only I knew there *was* a future for us,' she added quietly.

'I'm sorry again,' Ruth said. 'Your troubles are far worse than mine, and here I am, moaning!'

'I suppose we can be thankful that the winter will stop the fighting,' Maria said. 'Surely, Ruth, the war will be over by the spring?'

That evening Ruth wrote again to Joss. Even if the letter never reached him, to write in the hope that it would was balm to her spirit. For so long, when she had believed he was dead, she had been denied the solace of sending her thoughts to him. And now she decided that the time had come to tell him about Sean.

It was long past midnight when she laid down her pen.

She went to bed and slept like a child, and wakened next morning to a world which seemed new, and she a new person in it.

'You look chirpy,' Mrs Cruse said. 'Best I've seen you look for a long time.'

'I'm feeling better today,' Ruth admitted. 'How are things with you? Have you heard from your sons lately?'

Two of Mrs Cruse's sons had been wounded at Gettysburg, though not seriously.

'Benny got the nurse to write me a letter, on account of his hand,' Mrs Cruse said. 'He's all right. So are the others, though I think they'll be glad to get back to home comforts.'

Christmas came and went. Ruth made it as happy a time as she could, especially for Aurora and her boarders. For that one day they ate and drank and gave each other presents as if there were no shortages and everything was not prohibitively expensive.

On New year's Eve, when Ruth was serving the parlour tea, Lavinia Munster said, 'Eighteen sixty-four tomorrow! This is the year I've been waiting for. In April, Karl's three years will be up. He can come out of the army then if he wishes to.'

Joss too, Ruth thought – though he would need to be home first. When would he be home?

'What shall you do when Joss comes home?' Maria asked Ruth when they were on their own, later that evening.

'We shall marry,' Ruth replied. 'Joss has waited ten years now to marry me, and I seem to have waited for him half a lifetime. I was eighteen when I first saw him. I shall be thirty-two in a few weeks' time.'

'And I thirty-one soon after,' Maria said. 'Oh Ruth, we're getting *old*. And I want to have lots more children yet. Will there be time is what I ask myself?'

'Of course there will be, silly goose!' Ruth laughed 'Time for another half-dozen.'

'I shall go back to Richmond,' Maria said. 'But not just for Clive's sake. I daresay I shall quite enjoy it. But what will you do about Appleby's? Joss won't want to live here.'

It was a question Ruth had asked herself a hundred times. Appleby's was immeasurably dear to her. It was more than a house, more than a collection of dear, pleasant people of whom she had grown so fond over the years. It was infinitely more than a profitable business. Appleby's was a place she had made for herself in a world once so hostile that it had seemed there was no room for her. It had given her a life worth living. How could she ever desert it?

'I have an idea,' Maria said.

'About Appleby's?'

'Yes. Lavinia Munster, though she doesn't know about your affairs, or that you'll be getting married, has often said how much she would like to run a place like this. She would do it well, and care for everyone. Will you talk to her, Ruth?'

Ruth saw Lavinia next day. When it was put to her Lavinia trembled with excitement at the prospect.

'But how would Karl feel about it?' Ruth asked.

'He'd be agreeable. It's something we've discussed – not Appleby's of course, but something like it. And I have some capital of my own, left to me by my father.'

'Forgive me if I intrude,' Ruth said. 'But when you and Karl have children. . . . You see, I've sometimes felt that it wasn't the best life for Aurora. . . .'

'It's unlikely I'll ever have a child.' Ruth looked up sharply at the tremor in Lavinia's voice.

'Of course you will. When Karl comes home and you settle down. . . .'

'I shall not,' Lavinia interrupted. 'I know I shall not. I went to see a doctor when Karl was last home. We wondered why I hadn't conceived. It seems I never can.'

'Doctors can be wrong.' Ruth didn't know what to say.

'In this case I think not. So you see, I would have plenty of time to look after Appleby's. And I know that Mrs Seaford would want to be involved. I would like to employ her.'

'Well, you must let me think about it,' Ruth said. 'It wouldn't be for some time yet. In the meantime, I'd prefer you didn't discuss it with anyone. Anyone at all except Karl.'

'I promise I won't,' Lavinia agreed. 'When do you think you might know?'

Ruth smiled at Lavinia's eagerness. 'It's an important decision. But I'll try not to keep you waiting too long.'

Ruth intended to consult Professor Woodburn. She had to be sure that the boarders, who accepted them readily in the short term, would be happy with Lavinia and Mrs Seaford permanently, especially as Maria would also be leaving. Professor Woodburn would tell her the truth. She would see him tomorrow. There was no time now since she was due at the Relief Centre.

All the talk at the Centre was, and had been throughout the winter, of the Metropolitan Fair which was to be held in New York in April. Its sole purpose would be to raise money for more supplies and comforts for the troops. Chicago had had such a fair, so had Cincinnati; Boston was to have one any day now and Brooklyn had pulled a fast one on New York City and was to open its fair on the twenty-second of February. But though New York's would not be the first, it would be far and away the biggest, the best, the most spectacular, the most successful. No-one doubted that for a moment, least of all New Yorkers.

Miss Schuyler gave Ruth a brisk welcome when she walked in that morning.

'You're off boxes,' she said. 'No more boxes for you from now on. You've got a new job!'

'New job?'

'Don't look so startled. You'll enjoy it. We want you to work at the Receiving Depot in Great Jones Street. The gifts for the fair are coming in so quickly that we really can't cope.'

The idea behind the New York fair was that it should be one great market, selling absolutely everything, both of American origin and from countries overseas, and that every item on sale should have been donated. The idea received vast publicity, far beyond the city, far beyond America. Committees were set up in London, Paris, Hamburg, Geneva – and several other cities – and all had their groups of workers collecting goods for New York's Fair.

'You'll find the strangest assortment of things,' Miss Schuyler said. 'One can hardly move in the place, though there are two months to go yet and most of the overseas stuff is still to come. However, Dr Bellows did say that nothing would be refused, however large or however trivial.'

So for two mornings every week Ruth went to Great Jones Street and every day the citizens of New York came with their gifts: books, flower vases, penholders, chairs, musical instruments, kitchenware, blotters, jewellery, lamps, clothing. Carriers brought cartons and parcels from all over the Union, and from the ships which arrived in New York harbour.

'The carriers won't charge a penny for their services,' Miss Schuyler said. 'Isn't that wonderful?'

Rome sent paintings; royalty and important people in England and in other countries sent autographs. Newcastle, England – though privately Ruth thought this an imaginative rather than a practical gift – sent a few tons of coal.

In spite of the magnificence of so many of the gifts, Ruth was most impressed by those which were brought by poor people. An old woman brought a flowered plate, handing it over carefully. Four ragged children came with a pan their mother had sent, and a small boy brought a tin whistle. One morning a little girl handed Ruth a doll. Its garments were clean and pressed and its hair tied with a pink ribbon.

'Her name's Lucy,' the little girl said.

'Are you sure you want to part with her?' Ruth asked gently.

'She's for the soldiers. My daddy's a soldier.' There were tears in the child's eyes as she turned away without her doll. Ruth took out her handkerchief and gave her own nose a good blow.

* * *

After her first morning at Great Jones Street Ruth had knocked on the door of Professor Woodburn's room.

'Can you spare me a few minutes?' she asked.

'At any time,' he said. 'Come and sit down and tell me what you've been doing today.'

Ruth told him about the depot.

'I must find a contribution for you,' he said. 'And now I think there is something else?'

'Yes. It will perhaps not come as a surprise to you. When Mr Barnet comes home, he and I plan to marry.'

'It doesn't surprise me,' he said calmly. 'And you couldn't stay at Appleby's. Is that what you are trying to tell me?'

'Yes.'

'Well, that is reasonable. One would not expect you to.'

'But there is another possibility.'

She told him about her conversation with Lavinia Munster.

'I am willing,' Ruth said. 'But only if you think that Mrs Munster and Mrs Seaford will be totally acceptable to you all.'

'I'm sure they will be,' he replied. 'They are well liked, and they do the job competently. But no-one will ever take your place, my dear Ruth, either with me or with any of the boarders. You are a very special lady.'

He reached out and took her hand. She kept a tight hold on herself so as not to cry.

'You are special too,' she said. 'All my boarders are special people, but you most of all. Hardly anything of importance I have done here would have been possible without you. But that isn't why you are special. May I tell you why?'

He shook his head, and raised his hand as if to stop her, but she refused to be silenced.

'You are special,' Ruth continued, 'because from the first moment I came here you treated me as if I mattered. Though I was a servant, you called me "Miss Appleby". You would stand aside to let me pass, rise to your feet when I entered a room. No-one had acted towards me like that before. If I'm a special lady it's because you treated me like one. Why, you once offered to show me around the university!'

'You never came,' he said, smiling. 'And now, if I am not being impertinent, there is the matter of the sale of Appleby's. You mustn't let it go for a song, you know. You have built it into a thriving business.'

'I don't intend to,' Ruth assured him. 'The money is to be for Aurora when she's older. But I was helped when I needed it and if, for instance, Mrs Seaford should require help to buy herself a partnership. . . .'

'That seems reasonable.'

'There is one other thing,' Ruth said hesitantly. 'And if you would rather not. . . . But now that it is all so long ago, could you not tell me who my benefactor was? I would so much like to thank him before I hand over Appleby's.'

He considered her question for a moment, then said:

'I think you *should* know. But it is "her", not "him". It was Miss Fontwell who advanced the money. It was a large part of her savings. She wanted to do it for you because you were a woman, and women do not find it easy to get a start in life.'

Ruth stared at him. 'I can't believe it!'

'It is quite true.'

'Then I must thank her at once. I hardly know what to say.'

He shook his head. 'Say nothing, my dear. She would much rather not be thanked. I know that.'

'But I can't. . . .'

'I'll tell her of your gratitude,' he said. 'That will be enough.'

That evening Ruth asked Mrs Seaford and Lavinia Munster to her sitting-room. Maria was already there.

'I wanted to tell you that I am to be married again,' Ruth announced. 'When he comes home from the war I am to marry Mr Josiah Barnet.' (But when will he come, she asked herself again?) 'When that happens I must leave Appleby's. I know that Lavinia would like to take it over, and having thought about it carefully, I am agreeable to that, providing you, Doris, would run it with her.'

There was no doubt that Lavinia had kept her secret. Mrs Seaford's mouth dropped open in astonishment; and then she smiled, a smile of radiant happiness. She turned from Ruth to Lavinia, and back again, not knowing what to say.

'Unless you have other plans?' Ruth asked.

'Other plans! What else could I possibly want to do that would be half as good! Oh Ruth! Oh Lavinia - are you sure you want me?'

'I couldn't manage without you,' Lavinia declared.

'Then it's settled,' Ruth said. 'But I would rather no-one knew about our plans until Mr Barnet came home - except for Karl, of course. So please keep my secret for just a little longer.'

'You need have no fear,' Mrs Seaford replied. 'I shan't tell a soul. I'm so happy I could shout it from the rooftop, but I won't. You've always been good to me and I'll never forget it.'

Her voice trembled. Ruth thought there would be tears.

'Nonsense!' she said briskly. 'You're an easy person to please, Doris. Now let's seal our bargain with a glass of sherry wine. I have a little left over from Christmas.'

She poured the wine, and was about to raise her glass when Mrs Seaford put out a hand and stopped her.

'No! First of all, Ruth, I'd like to drink to you and Mr Barnet, to your future. I hope you'll both be as happy as Mr Seaford and I were. I couldn't wish you better than that.'

Every day now, Ruth looked for a letter which would tell her that Joss was on his way home. None came. She had been to his apartment in Fourth Avenue, told the supervisor that one day soon Captain Barnet might come home, and that when he did, everything must be ready for him.

It was February now, the winter at its worst, but, Ruth, though anxious for news, was no longer depressed. On the surface, it seemed that no-one in the North was depressed. In Washington builders were hard at it erecting the Capitol, while the social life of the city went on there as vigorously as ever. In New York there were parties, balls, plays, soirées; something happening all the time. After all, the North was winning the war, wasn't it?

Even in poor beleaguered Richmond everyone made a tremendous effort to keep up appearances. Citizens tightened their belts a little further over empty stomachs, and went to the theatre, visited friends, danced the polka or made music. But in both the North and the South, the bereaved wept; and the wounded were seen in the streets, the anxious waited for news.

Ruth was working one morning alongside Miss Schuyler, sorting out the hundreds of paintings and drawings which had come in from all over the world. She was stacking the pictures against the wall, according to size and type. She straightened up for a minute to ease her back, and saw Maria enter the long room at the far end, and walk quickly towards her. It wasn't so much that she was here – sometimes she dropped in when she was out shopping – but there was something in her manner which alarmed Ruth. As she drew nearer she was almost running, and she was as flushed and breathless as if she had run the four blocks from Spring Street.

'Ruth, you must come. . . .' She could hardly get the words out.

'What is it? What has happened? Tell me at once!'

Maria had taken Ruth's cloak and bonnet from the peg and was handing them to her.

'Quick! Put them on!'

'Maria, stop babbling! Tell me at once what's wrong!'

Maria stared.

'Nothing is wrong! Didn't I say? Joss is home!'

Ruth went into him alone, where he waited for her in the sitting-room. For a moment she was afraid, but when she saw him standing there, saw the love in his eyes, her fear vanished. It was the crowning point of her life and she knew that however long she lived no moment of joy would ever exceed this. She didn't know how she would bear it, but it was Joss who showed her how. He held out his arms and she was in them, and he was holding her as if he would never let her go.

Eventually he released her and held her at arm's length.

'Let me look at you, Ruth! I've hungered for the sight of you. Yes, you are as beautiful as I remembered you; more beautiful.'

'Let me look at *you*,' Ruth said. 'Sometimes I thought I might forget your dear face.'

He smiled. The smile was so familiar, as if he had never been away. It was in his eyes before it reached his mouth and, as always, there was something sardonic in it, as if he was secretly amused.

'If you must,' he said. 'I can never have looked worse in my life.'

He was shockingly emaciated, deep hollows in his face and neck and by his wristbones, the skin tight over his jaw. His hands were fined down almost to transparency. His dark hair, greyer now, was dull and matted, and he was badly in need of a shave. What was left of his tattered, dirty uniform hung on him as if it had been made for a much larger man.

'You are the most beautiful sight I have ever seen,' Ruth told him.

When she was in his arms again she felt the thinness of his body under her hands. What had they done to him? But it didn't matter. He was here. She would build him up, make him better, look after him for the rest of his life.

'How did you get here?' she asked. 'I had no further word about an exchange of prisoners.'

'I escaped. Walked out. I had your letter – the only one I had from you – about Sean O'Farrell's death. The moment I finished reading it I decided I would escape, no matter what. You'd gone through so much, Ruth. I had to be with you.'

'How . . .?'

'I didn't plan anything,' Joss said. 'The very next day I

was working in the field and I chose a moment when I heard the guards quarrelling among themselves – it was a badly-run camp and they were always at loggerheads – and I walked out. As far as I know, no-one tried to trace me. I was one less mouth to feed.'

He had walked, he told her, or hitched lifts on carts. Once he had jumped a train. He had begged for food and people had given him what they could.

'No-one, Northerners or Confederates, seemed to care that I was an escaping prisoner,' he said. 'They just helped me on my way as best they could.'

The weather had been bitter. At one point, if a farmer and his wife had not given him shelter and food for three days, he thought he might have died.

'But I didn't,' he said. 'They cared for me so well. Bathed my sores, saw to my feet, even de-loused me. We were all full of lice and sores in the camp. And now here I am, my darling Ruth. Nothing else matters.'

He took her in his arms again. When he looked at her she felt her colour rise at the longing in his eyes, and knew that he would see the same longing in hers.

'You know what I want, Ruth?'

'Yes. And I too, my darling.'

'Soon. Very soon.'

'Yes,' she said. 'Yes! But I want you to myself. I want nothing to spoil it, nothing to come between us. So not here in Appleby's, Joss.'

'Then where, and when?' He spoke fiercely. 'Don't keep me waiting, Ruth!'

'Do you think I want to wait,' she said gently. Couldn't he tell that her body was tingling, burning with impatient longing?

'The apartment is ready for you,' she told him. 'I've kept it ready for a long time now, always hoping. I'll come to you there tomorrow afternoon, and when that time comes there'll be no-one in the world except the two of us.'

She thought with yearning of the apartment, of the wide bed she wanted to share with him again. She could hardly bear to face the desire in his eyes, so sharply did it increase her own. But soon she would be there with him. She would be in his arms and in his bed and they would be lovers again – and for always.

'I'll try to be patient,' Joss said. 'It's a lot to ask and no-one has ever called me a patient man.'

'You can stay here for tonight,' Ruth offered.

He shook his head. 'That I can't do. If I knew you were in the same house, I would break your door down!'

'I have to settle Appleby's,' Ruth said. 'And even more important, there's Aurora to think of. She suffered from Sean's death more than anyone. We must be gentle with her.'

'Will she accept me?' Joss asked. 'Will she love me as I love her?'

'I'm sure she will, given time.'

'Is she never to know that I'm her real father?'

'I can't say,' Ruth told him. 'I would like to tell her the truth, though we must do what's best for her. I'm sure that in time she'll think of you as her father, and perhaps then will be the time to tell her.'

'I will do everything to be a real father to her,' Joss promised. 'To earn her love.'

'I came to a decision when I was in the camp,' he said a little later. 'You see I always knew that one day we would be together again.'

'What decision?'

'That I'm going to take you to Europe for our honeymoon. To England. To your beloved Yorkshire. You'd like that, wouldn't you?'

For a moment Ruth could neither move nor speak. Then she flung her arms around Joss's neck in ecstasy.

'Oh Joss! More than anything in the world!'

'If one of my own ships isn't available we'll sail in one of Mr Cunard's. I planned it all in my mind when I was in the prison camp. We'd sail away the very day after my discharge, I thought. But if you say we must wait until June, then I'll try my best to do that.'

Ruth was in his arms again when she remembered Maria. How could she have been so selfish as to forget her sister? She drew away from Joss.

'Joss, I can't promise when I shall be able to leave New York. Oh, we can marry – which is what counts most. But I can't leave Maria while the war is still being fought and we don't know what's happening to Clive. I couldn't have kept going without Maria these last few years. I can't desert her now.'

The fact that he agreed with her, though he was disappointed, showed the change in him, Ruth thought. She had not thought him capable of unselfishness, but now he was.

'Very well then,' he said. 'But if we must postpone our honeymoon, then we'll start building our house.'

'House? Surely we shall live here?'

'I thought you might like a beautiful new house on Fifth Avenue. Of course if you don't want it . . .!'

'Oh Joss, it would be wonderful! But I would like to live here first, for a little while. We've been so happy here.'

'We shall be happy wherever we are from now on,' Joss said. 'But we'll stay here until the new house is ready for us. There'll be a lot to see to. I want it to be quite perfect for you.'

'But if the war ends soon, and Clive comes home, then we shall leave everything and set sail,' Ruth said. 'And until then we shall see each other every day.'

'We shall see each other every day for the rest of our lives,' Joss smiled.

There was a great deal to do in the weeks which followed. To her mother's relief, Aurora showed nothing but pleasure at the news of the coming marriage. She was to be the chief and only bridesmaid, allowed to choose what she would wear – and when they moved into the new house she was to have her own beautiful room, overlooking Fifth Avenue. It was all excitement. She spent hours discussing it with anyone who would listen. Ruth, meanwhile, in spite of preparing for her wedding, visiting the site and approving the plans for the new house, still went to the Receiving Depot.

'I must give something myself,' she told Miss Schuyler.

'You have already given a great deal to the war,' Miss Schuyler replied. 'You have been one of our most faithful workers, never letting us down, even when life was at its worst for you.'

'Nevertheless I must make a gift,' Ruth said.

She did not say to Miss Schuyler that in those spring days of 1864 her heart was bursting with gratitude for everything that New York had given her in the fourteen years since she had landed from the *Flamingo*, with nothing except a meagre bundle of belongings in her hand and a great need in her heart. Also, that sharing with the city in some of its bad days had made her feel more than ever that she belonged here.

And then one day in her sitting-room she looked up and saw what she must give: her Grandmother Appleby's sampler. It was her most precious possession, and for that reason the most suitable.

As she took down the sampler from the wall she thought of her Aunt Sarah, who had given it to her, and of her grandfather, whose wife had worked it. She thought of Barnswick and the moor, which she would soon see. She was sure that both her aunt and her grandfather would have approved of her giving the sampler.

'But this is *beautiful!*' Miss Schuyler exclaimed next morning. 'It will fetch a lot of money. Are you sure you want to part with it?'

'Quite sure,' Ruth said.

Uncle Matthew and Ernest were much in her mind all that day. In the evening she sat down and wrote to them, inviting them to the wedding. 'As many of you as can come will be most welcome,' she wrote. 'There will be room for you in Appleby's and I can't tell you how I long to see you again.' She hoped they would accept.

In April Lavinia Munster had a letter from Karl.

'He's in hospital! He's coming home!' she gabbled. 'Oh Ruth, I'm so excited!'

'In hospital? Is he wounded?'

'No, no. He has dysentery.' She dismissed dysentery as if it was a cold in the head. 'He's being sent home on convalescent leave. And then I shall persuade him to go back to his bridge-building. I'm sure he'll agree, now that I'm taking over Appleby's. Oh Ruth, isn't life wonderful?'

But Ruth had only to look at Maria's face to know that it was not so for everyone.

The Metropolitan Fair was a great success. To Ruth's delight her grandmother's sampler sold for a gratifying sum. Mrs Seaford was still recalling the Fair as she put the final stitches into Ruth's wedding dress of cream silk.

'Wasn't it just too wonderful?' she enthused. 'Did you ever see anything like that procession in all your life?'

'Never. Is my dress almost finished then?'

'A few stitches to the hem, which I shall put in on the day itself. It's bad luck to finish it beforehand. Oh Ruth you're going to look so beautiful, and I'm so proud to have made your dress!'

Joss had wanted Ruth to have her wedding dress made by New York's finest dressmaker, or even, he said, to order one from Paris, but she had refused.

'After we're married you may buy me lots of beautiful clothes, and I shall enjoy wearing them,' she said. 'But for now I would prefer to wear what Mrs Seaford has made. It's going to be very pretty.'

'Do you think I shall care about that?' Joss teased. 'Do you think I shall even *see* your dress?'

'I had a letter from Ernest today,' she said. 'Listen, I'll read it to you.

' "Emily and me would like to come," he writes, "but it can't be managed. We are very busy on the farm – I have a hundred and fifty acres now and plan to buy more as soon as I can. And Emily is expecting our fifth child next month. But I know you will be pleased to hear that Father and Enoch plan to come to your wedding. Enoch is seventeen now. He hankers after seeing New York and will be able to look after Father on the journey." '

When Enoch arrived, the day before the wedding, Ruth caught her breath at the sight of him. He was the double of

Charlotte, as Ruth had first seen her in her aunt's kitchen. But he was more outgoing than his mother had ever been; excited at the prospect of seeing New York.

'You must both stay as long as you like,' Ruth said.

'A week at the most, our Ruth,' Uncle Matthew replied. 'We're needed on t'farm. Even me at my age!' He looked fit and healthy, proud to be of use, younger, in some ways, than when he had arrived in America.

'Well, I'm glad you've come to my wedding,' Ruth said. 'It will make the day for me. Uncle Matthew, will you do me a great favour, and at such short notice. Will you give me away? Professor Woodburn was to do so but I know he will understand.'

'I'd be proud and honoured,' Uncle Matthew smiled. 'Proud and honoured, lass!'

The wedding day was clear and sunny.

'Not a cloud in the sky,' Mrs Cruse declared. 'I hope it'll always be the same for you.'

'And doesn't Aurora look adorable in her bridesmaid's dress?' Mrs Seaford said. 'She and I have planned some nice little outings for next week.'

Ruth and Joss were to go for a week to Millfield.

After the wedding, which every one of Ruth's boarders, as well as Mrs Cruse, May and the rest of the staff, attended, they returned to Appleby's for the reception which Maria had planned. When everyone had drunk the health of Joss and Ruth, Professor Woodburn called for silence.

'I have a most pleasant duty to perform,' he said. 'And that is to give the happy couple a wedding present. It comes with love and gratitude from everyone here in Appleby's.'

He handed the parcel to Ruth. With difficulty, because her hands were shaking, she untied the ribbons and folded back the paper to reveal the present. It was her Grandmother Appleby's sampler.

'We bought it from the Fair, between all of us,' Maria said. 'We couldn't bear to think of you not having it.'

* * *

It was to be another ten months before the war ended. There were more battles, more men killed and wounded on both sides – and an abortive attempt at a peace treaty. In the end, as had been predicted from the beginning, it was the fall of Richmond which finished the war.

When the city was set on fire, the flames and smoke rising into the sky as if from some great funeral pyre, Mrs Masterson, Flora and Beth took what they could carry – after four years of war there were few valuables left in the house, they had all been sold to buy food – and left. On her own Mrs Masterson thought she would have stayed, but she had a duty to her daughters.

Four days later, when the flames had died down, though smoke, and the smell of charred wood, hung over the city like a pall, they returned. Their own house was intact, though not many were. Richmond was full of Union soldiers – they were everywhere – but they were not unkind. There was no need to be. It was all over.

On Palm Sunday General Robert E. Lee signed the peace agreement and was pleased and thankful that General Grant allowed him to keep his sword. Two days after that Maria received a telegram.

She turned deathly pale as it was put into her hand; then she gave it to Ruth.

'Please open it for me. I'm afraid to.'

Ruth's hands were trembling as she tore it open. Dear God, if it should be bad news now, after so long!

She read it – and cried out.

'It's all right, Maria! It's all right! See for yourself!'

Maria took the telegram and read it.

' "Am coming to fetch you and Robert Lee home. All my love. Clive." '

'Oh Ruth, Ruth!'

The sisters were in each other's arms, crying and smiling at the same time.

'Oh Ruth, sometimes I thought it would never happen!' Maria exclaimed. 'I thought I would never see my dear Clive again! Oh Ruth, I'm so happy!' Her face, framed in its flaxen curls, shone like the sun.

'You deserve happiness,' Ruth said. 'There was never a truer wife. And no-one in the world ever had a better sister than I.'

'Stuff and nonsense!' Maria retorted, though nevertheless she blushed with pleasure.

'It's the honest truth,' Ruth declared. 'I don't know what I would have done without you in the last three years. I couldn't have existed.'

'Nor I without you, dear Ruth,' Maria said softly. 'Where would I have been?'

'Maria!'

'Yes?'

'Let us never lose touch again, even though we'll be miles apart. Promise me!'

'Oh Ruth, I promise. We shall come to New York, Clive and I – and Robert Lee – and you must all come to Richmond. We will never be apart for long. Oh Ruth . . .' she broke off as a sudden thought struck her. 'Ruth, do you think Clive will find me changed? Do I look older?'

'Not a day!' Ruth laughed. 'And you are prettier than ever. Clive will adore you – as always – and be proud of you.'

'Do you really and truly think so?'

'I'm sure.'

Clive arrived at Appleby's ten days later, in the evening when Robert Lee was in bed and asleep. When Maria came face to face with him she caught her breath and stifled the cry of dismay which rose to her lips. This was not her Clive! This hollow-eyed, haggard skeleton of a man was not the handsome young husband who had left her to go to the war. But then she saw the love in his eyes and the longing in his face, and when he held out his arms and she went into them, was folded in his embrace, she knew he was her husband, her true love, and no stranger.

Tears coursed down her cheeks and Clive, burying his face in her shoulder, was shaken by sobs which shuddered through his whole body.

'Oh Clive, my darling Clive, what have they done to you?' She held him close, stroking his hair, until he was calmer.

'Oh Maria, I thought I should never see you again. Yet it was only the hope of doing so which kept me alive.'

No-one would know, he would never tell, not even his dear Maria, the years of fear and agony which a soldier's life had brought him; the temptations to run away, to hide, to desert his companions who were all so much braver than he. But he had kept faith. He had not run. He could face the world.

He lifted his head to look again at Maria. He could never have enough of his darling. She blushed at the intensity of his gaze.

'Oh Clive, do you find me changed? Do I look older?'

'You will never look older,' he assured her.

' "For as you were when first your eye I eyed, Such seems your beauty still!" '

For the first time she laughed. 'Oh my darling, when I hear you quoting your beloved Shakespeare, I know I have my own dear Clive back again!' And his voice was still strong, sweet, resonant – utterly unspoilt by whatever he had gone through.

'And I?' he asked anxiously. 'How do I look?'

'More handsome than ever,' Maria declared. Actually, it was true, she now thought. His lean, ascetic look suited him admirably. How could she ever have thought otherwise? Yet he needed to be looked after, cared for. She would devote herself to him.

'There is so much to talk about,' Clive said. 'But not just now, not yet, not while I can hold you in my arms. Tomorrow is soon enough to talk about the rest of the world.'

They stayed in New York for a week only. Clive, as he gained strength from Maria's love and from his delight in Robert Lee, was full of plans for the future.

'There will be new opportunities in the theatre,' he said. 'After such a war, people will long for it. Why, Maria, I thought we might even start up our own little company in

Richmond or thereabouts! Small to begin with, of course; not too ambitious at the start. . . .'

Maria clapped her hands in delight.

'Oh Clive, what a splendid idea! You are bound to succeed. And who knows, perhaps at long last I can be your leading lady! Oh think of it, Clive!'

He drew her into his arms, kissed her long and hard on the lips. 'You've been my leading lady since I first saw you, with a face swollen with toothache! You always will be.'

Towards the end of May Joss and Ruth, leaving Aurora in the care of a more-than-willing Mrs Seaford, sailed for England on the evening tide. They stood on the deck of one of Joss's own luxurious steamers, arms around each other, watching the city of New York disappear from sight as they sailed out of the harbour. There were happy tears in Ruth's eyes as she turned to look at her husband. She was filled with joyful anticipation at the thought of the long days they would spend together at sea. And after that, her beloved Yorkshire.

She raised her hand in a wave.

'I shall be back, dear city,' she said. 'You are my place now. I belong.'

THE END

**MIDSUMMER MEETING**
by Elvi Rhodes

It was an unexpected legacy which brought Petra to the close village community of Mindon. An imposing stone house in the middle of the village, left to her by an old friend of her mother's, promised a very different way of life from Petra's lonely and unsettled life in Yorkshire, and she was immediately made welcome by the local residents – in particular, by the members of the local Amateur Dramatic Society. Presided over by the formidable Ursula, who liked to run things her way, the ambitious decision had been made (mainly by Ursula herself) to put on *A Midsummer Night's Dream* as the next production. Petra, to her surprise and pleasure, was put in charge of the scenery.

Rivalries, squabbles, love affairs and seething resentments threatened to scupper the production, and all Ursula's management skills were needed to prevent disaster. But Petra had more pressing things on her mind than the set designs. A mystery from the past had begun to haunt her – and the answer to that mystery might solve the puzzle of why she had been left such a beautiful house by a total stranger.

0 552 14715 X

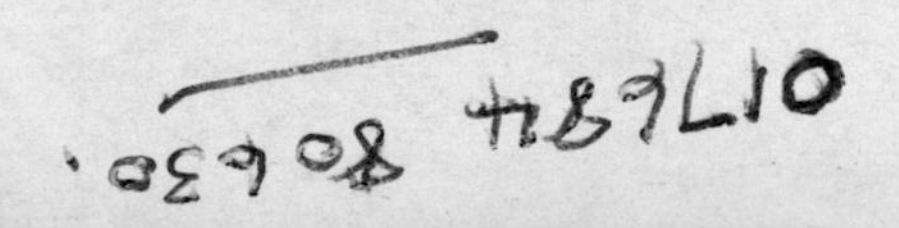